An old friend or two, and a couple of new ones

It can be fascinating to listen to an interview with one of your favorite authors. Not too long ago I caught one with Lee Child on Leonard Lopate's NPR radio show, and it was like hearing the voice of an old friend. In the interview, Child talks about the genesis of his Jack Reacher character back in the '90s and how the name of his hero comes from Child's own above-average height: Whenever he went to the supermarket, people were always asking the lanky author for help getting items off the top shelves, hence the nickname of Reacher. In fact, Child's wife suggested at the time that if his writing career didn't pan out, reaching could be a career alternative for him.

Child also speaks about how he alternates first- and third-person voices in his storytelling; then he casually mentions that sales around the world of Jack Reacher novels are estimated at the rate of one per second. It's worth tracking down the interview at npr.org, but whether you hear the interview or not, you'll still enjoy a visit with Jack Reacher in this volume's *Nothing to Lose.* Throw in another old friend, Sophie Kinsella of *The Undomestic Goddess* and the Shopaholic novels, and two exciting newcomers to Select Editions, David Rosenfelt and Gareth Crocker, and you've got friends both old and new.

Enjoy.

Jim Menick
Executive Editor

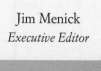

SELECT EDITIONS

U.S. EDITORIAL

Executive Editor: James J. Menick

Senior Editors: Thomas S. Clemmons, Amy M. Reilly

Art Director: Robin Arzt

Production Editor: Lorraine Burton

Production Assistant: Joanna Luppino

INTERNATIONAL EDITIONS

Executive Editor: Gary Q. Arpin

Senior Editor: Bonnie Grande

RIGHTS AND PERMISSIONS

Manager: Carol Weiss Staudter

Rights Associate: Arlene Pasciolla

Rights Administrator: Ann Marie Belluscio

SELECT EDITIONS

Selected and Edited by Reader's Digest

THE READER'S DIGEST ASSOCIATION, INC.

PLEASANTVILLE, NEW YORK • MONTREAL

DON'T TELL A SOUL
David Rosenfelt

Someone is framing Tim Wallace for crimes he's never even heard of, much less committed. Get ready for a fast ride with one twist after another.

AFTERWORDS: *The eccentricities of David Rosenfelt, plus some safe skyscrapers.*

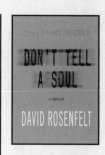

page 320

LEAVING JACK
Gareth Crocker

EXCITING NEW AUTHOR!

G.I. Fletcher Carson and Jack, an amazing yellow Lab army service dog, forge a unique bond in this classic story filled with heart.

AFTERWORDS: *Getting to know Gareth Crocker, and the real dogs of war.*

page 466

page 169

page 317

page 464

page 574

A JACK REACHER
NOVEL

LEE CHILD

NOTHING TO LOSE

1

THE sun was only half as hot as he had known sun to be, but it was hot enough to keep him confused and dizzy. He was very weak. He had not eaten for seventy-two hours or taken water for forty-eight.

Not weak. He was dying, and he knew it.

The images in his mind showed things drifting away. A rowboat caught in a river current, straining against a rotted rope, pulling, tugging, breaking free. His viewpoint was that of a small boy in the boat, sitting low, staring back helplessly at the bank as the dock grew smaller.

Then the images faded, because now words seemed more important than pictures, which was absurd, because he had never been interested in words before. But before he died, he wanted to know which words were his. Which applied to him? Was he a man or a boy? He had been described both ways. *Be a man*, some had said. Others had been insistent: *The boy's not to blame.* He was old enough to vote and kill and die, which made him a man. He was too young to drink, even beer, which made him a boy. He had been called both. He had been called unhinged, disturbed, deranged, unbalanced, all of which he understood, except unhinged. Was he supposed to be hinged? Like a door? He considered the question for a long moment, and then he batted the air in frustration. He was babbling like a teenager in love with weed.

Which is exactly all he had been, a year and a half before.

He fell to his knees. The sand was only half as hot as he had known sand to be, but it was hot enough to ease his chill. He fell facedown, exhausted, finally spent. He knew as certainly as he had ever known anything that if he closed his eyes, he would never open them again.

But he was tired. More tired than a man or a boy had ever been.

He closed his eyes.

THE line between Hope and Despair was exactly that: a line, in the road, formed where one town's blacktop finished and the other's started. Hope's highway department had used thick dark asphalt rolled smooth. Despair had a smaller budget. They had top-dressed a lumpy roadbed with hot tar and dumped gray gravel on it. Where the two surfaces met, there was an inch-wide trench of no-man's-land filled with a black rubbery compound. An expansion joint. Jack Reacher stepped over it mid-stride and kept on walking.

Hope and Despair were both in Colorado. Reacher was in Colorado because two days previously he had been in Kansas, and Colorado was next to Kansas. He was making his way west and south. He had been in Calais, Maine, and had taken it into his head to cross the continent diagonally, all the way to San Diego in California. The Atlantic to the Pacific, cool and damp to hot and dry. He took buses where there were any and hitched rides where there weren't. He had arrived in Hope in a bottle-green Mercury Grand Marquis driven by a retired button salesman. He was on his way out of Hope on foot because that morning there had been no traffic heading west toward Despair.

He remembered that fact later, and wondered why he hadn't wondered why.

In terms of his grand diagonal design, he was slightly off course. He should have been angling directly southwest into New Mexico. But he wasn't a stickler for plans, and the Grand Marquis had been a comfortable car, and the old guy had been fixed on Hope because he had three grandchildren to see there before heading onward to Denver to see four more. And then in Hope he had looked at a map and seen Despair seventeen miles farther west and had been unable to resist the detour. Once or twice in his life, he had made the same trip metaphorically. Now he figured he should make it for real.

The road between the two towns was a straight two-lane. It rose very gently as it headed west. The Rockies were visible up ahead, blue and massive and hazy. They looked very close. Then suddenly they didn't. Reacher breasted a slight rise and stopped dead and understood why one town was called Hope and the other Despair. Settlers struggling west a hundred and fifty years before him would have stopped over in what came to be called Hope and would have seen their last obstacle seemingly within touching distance. Then after a day's or a week's repose, they would have moved on again and breasted the same slight rise and seen that the Rockies' apparent proximity had been nothing more than a cruel trick of topography. From the top of the rise, the great barrier seemed once again remote. Enough to drive the impatient from hope to despair.

Reacher stepped off Despair's gritty road and walked through crusted sandy earth to a table rock the size of a car. He levered himself up and lay down with his hands behind his head and stared up at the sky. It was pale blue and laced with long, high feathery clouds.

Back when he smoked, he might have lit a cigarette to pass the time. But he didn't smoke anymore. Smoking implied carrying at least a pack and a book of matches, and Reacher had long ago quit carrying things he didn't need. There was nothing in his pockets except paper money, an expired passport, an ATM card, and a clip-together toothbrush. There was nothing waiting for him anywhere else, either. No storage unit in a distant city, nothing stashed with friends. He owned the things in his pockets and the clothes on his back, and that was all. Everything he needed, and nothing he didn't.

He got to his feet and stood on tiptoe, high on the rock. Behind him to the east was a shallow bowl, maybe ten miles in diameter, with the town of Hope roughly in its center, eight or nine miles back, maybe ten blocks by six of brick-built buildings and an outlying clutter of houses and barns. Ahead of him to the west were tens of thousands of flat square miles, completely empty except for the town of Despair about eight or nine miles ahead. Despair looked larger than Hope. It was teardrop-shaped, with a conventional plains downtown about twelve blocks square, mostly south of the main drag, and then a wider zone of activity beyond it, maybe industrial in nature. Despair looked less pleasant than Hope. For a brief moment, Reacher considered backtracking, but he dismissed the thought. Reacher hated turning back. Everyone's life needed an organizing principle, and relentless forward motion was Reacher's.

He climbed off the rock and rejoined the road. There was still no oncoming traffic. Reacher raked the hair off his forehead and pulled his shirt loose on his shoulders and kept on walking.

REACHER had seen movies about small-town America in which the sets had been artfully dressed to look more perfect and vibrant than reality. This place was the exact opposite. Despair's Main Street looked like a designer and a whole team of grips had worked hard to make it gloomier than it needed to be. Traffic on the streets was light. Sedans and pickups were moving slow and lazy. None of them was newer than three years old.

Reacher made a random left turn and set about finding a place to get a cup of coffee. He passed a grocery store and a bar and a rooming house and a faded old hotel before he found an eatery. It took up the whole ground floor of a dull brick cube. The ceiling was high, and the windows were floor-to-ceiling plate glass. The place might have been an automobile showroom in the past. The air smelled of boiled vegetables. There was a register station inside the door with a PLEASE WAIT TO BE SEATED sign on a short brass pole with a heavy base. He stood next to the register and waited.

There were eleven customers eating. One waitress. Not an unusual ratio. Reacher had eaten in a thousand similar places, and he knew the rhythm. The lone waitress would soon glance over at him and nod, as if to say, *I'll be right with you.*

But she didn't.

She glanced over, looked at him for a long second, and then carried on with what she was doing. Which wasn't much. She was stopping by tables and asking if everything was all right and refilling coffee cups that were less than an inch down from the rim. Reacher turned and checked his reflection in the door glass to see if he was committing a social outrage with the way he was dressed. He wasn't. He was wearing dark gray pants and a dark gray shirt, both bought two days before in a janitorial surplus store in Kansas. Janitorial supply stores were his latest discovery. Plain, strong, well-made clothing at reasonable prices. His hair was short and tidy. He had shaved.

He turned back to wait.

Customers turned to look at him, appraised him quite openly, and then looked away. The waitress made another slow circuit of the room, looking everywhere except at him. He lost patience. He stepped past the sign and moved into the room and sat down alone at a table for four. The waitress watched him do it, and then she headed for the kitchen.

She didn't come out again.

Reacher sat and waited. The room was silent except for the clash of silverware on plates and the click of cups being lowered into saucers. Nothing happened for close to ten minutes.

Then an old crew-cab pickup truck slid to a stop on the curb outside the door and four guys climbed out. The shortest was probably an inch under six feet, and the lightest was maybe an ounce over two hundred pounds. Two of them had broken noses, and none of them had all their teeth. They all looked pale and vaguely unhealthy. And they all looked like trouble.

They grouped themselves into a tight little formation, paused a beat, and came inside. They headed straight for Reacher's table. Three of them sat down in the empty chairs, and the fourth stood at the head of the table.

"I don't want company," Reacher said. "I prefer to eat alone."

The guy at the head of the table was the biggest of the four, by maybe an inch and ten pounds. He said, "You need to get going."

"Going?"

"Out of here."

"You want to tell me why?"

"We don't like strangers."

"Me, either," Reacher said. "But I need to eat. Otherwise, I'll get all wasted and skinny like you four."

"Funny man."

"Just calling it like it is," Reacher said. He put his forearms on the table. He had thirty pounds and three inches on the big guy, and more than that on the other three. And he was willing to bet he had a little more experience and a little less inhibition than any one of them. But if it came to it, it was going to be his two hundred and fifty pounds against their cumulative nine hundred. Not great odds.

The guy who was standing said, "We don't want you here."

"Why?"

"Just leave now."

"You want me to leave, I'll need to hear it from the owner."

"We can arrange that." The guy headed for the kitchen. A long minute later he came back out with a man in a stained apron. The man walked up to Reacher's table and said, "I want you to leave."

"Why?" Reacher asked.

"I don't need to explain myself."

Reacher said, "I'll leave when I've had a cup of coffee."

"You'll leave now."

"If I get a cup of coffee, I'll walk out of here. If I don't get a cup of coffee, these guys can try to throw me out, and you'll spend the rest of the day shopping for new chairs and tables."

The guy in the apron said nothing.

Reacher said, "Black, no sugar."

The guy in the apron stood still for a long moment and then headed back to the kitchen. A minute later the waitress came out with a single cup balanced on a saucer. She set it down in front of Reacher, hard enough to slop some of the contents out of the cup and into the saucer. "Enjoy," she said.

Reacher lifted the cup and wiped the base on his sleeve. Set the cup down on the table and emptied the saucer into it. Set the cup back on the saucer and squared it in front of him. Then he raised it again and took a sip.

Not bad, he thought. A decent commercial product, better than most diners. The cup was a porcelain monstrosity with a lip about three-eighths of an inch thick. It was cooling the drink too fast. Too wide, too shallow. Reacher was no big fan of fine china, but he believed a receptacle ought to serve its contents.

The four guys were still clustered all around. Reacher drank, slowly at first, and then faster as the coffee grew cold. He drained the cup and set it back on the saucer. Pushed it away, slowly. Then he moved his left arm fast and went for his pocket. The four guys jumped. Reacher came out with a dollar bill and flattened it and trapped it under the saucer.

"So let's go," he said. He scraped his chair back and stood up. He pushed his chair in neatly and headed for the door. He sensed the four guys behind him. Heard their boots on the tile floor.

Reacher pushed the door and stepped outside to the street. The air was cool, but the sun was out. Reacher turned left and took four steps. Then he stopped and turned back. The four guys formed up in front of him. The guy who had stood at the head of the table said, "You need to get out."

Reacher said, "I am out."

"Out of town."

"You want to tell me why?"

"We don't have to tell you why." The guy on the end of the line pushed his cuffs above his elbows and took a step forward.

Reacher said, "You're picking on the wrong man."

"You think?"

Reacher nodded. "I have to warn you. I promised my mother a long time ago. She said I had to give folks a chance to walk away."

"There are four of us. One of you."

Reacher's hands were down by his sides, relaxed, gently curled. His feet were apart, securely planted. He folded the fingers of his left hand flat against his palm. Raised the hand very slowly, brought it level with his shoulder, palm out. The four guys stared at it. The way his fingers were folded made them think he was hiding something. *But what?* He snapped his fingers open. *Nothing there.* In the same split second, he moved sideways and heaved his right fist up like a convulsion and with a colossal uppercut to the jaw, caught the guy who had stepped forward. The massive impact snapped his jaw shut and lifted him up off the ground and dumped him back down in a heap on the sidewalk. Unconscious before he got halfway there.

"Now there are only three of you," Reacher said. "You can still walk away."

The guy who had been doing the talking said, "You got lucky."

Reacher nodded. "Maybe. Maybe one of you will stay on your feet long enough to get me. The question is, Which one will it be?"

Nobody spoke. Stalemate. Reacher rehearsed his next moves. A right-footed kick to the groin of the guy on his left, spin back with an elbow to the head for the guy in the middle, duck under the inevitable roundhouse swing incoming from the guy on the right, let him follow through, put an elbow in his kidney. Main difficulty would be restraints, limiting the damage. It was always wiser to stay on the right side of the line, closer to brawling than homicide.

In the distance beyond the three guys, Reacher could see people going about their business, cars and trucks driving on the streets.

Then he saw one particular car blow straight through a four-way and head in his direction. A Crown Victoria, white and gold, push bars on the front, a light bar on the roof, antennas on the trunk lid. A shield on the door with DPD scrolled across it. *Despair Police Department.* A heavyset cop in a tan jacket visible behind the glass.

The Crown Vic braked hard in the gutter. The door swung open. The driver took a riot gun from a holster between the seats. Climbed out. Pumped the gun and held it diagonally across his chest. He was a big guy. White, maybe forty. Black hair. He surveyed the scene.

The cop said, "Back off now." The three guys stepped backward. The cop stepped forward, moved his gun. Pointed it straight at Reacher's chest.

"You're under arrest," he said.

Reacher stood still and asked, "On what charge?"

The cop said, "I'm sure I'll think of something." He swapped the gun into one hand and used the other to take the handcuffs out of the holder on his belt. One of the guys behind him stepped forward and took them from him and looped around behind Reacher's back.

"Put your arms behind you," the cop said.

"Are these guys deputized?" Reacher asked.

"They're deputized," the cop said.

The guy behind him pulled Reacher's arms back and cuffed his wrists. The guy who had done all the talking opened the cruiser's rear door and stood there holding it like a doorman with a taxicab.

"Get in the car," the cop said.

Reacher stood still and considered his options. Didn't take him long. He was handcuffed. The cop's riot gun was a Mossberg. He didn't recognize the model, but he respected the brand.

"In the car," the cop said.

Reacher moved forward and looped around the open door and jacked himself inside butt-first. The cop got back in the front. The suspension yielded to his weight. He reholstered the Mossberg.

THE police station was in a brick building four blocks west and two blocks south of the restaurant. There was one other car there. Small town, small police department. The cops had the ground floor. The town court was upstairs. Reacher's trip to the booking desk was uneventful. He was uncuffed and gave up the stuff from his pockets and his shoelaces. He was escorted down a winding stair and put in a six-by-eight cell.

"Lawyer?" he asked.

"You know any?" the desk guy asked back.

"The public defender will do."

The cop nodded and locked the gate and walked away. Reacher lay down on the cot and closed his eyes.

Welcome to Despair, he thought.

REACHER dozed for two hours, and then the cop who had arrested him clattered down the stairs and unlocked the cell.

"The judge is ready for you," he said.

Reacher yawned. "I haven't seen a lawyer."

"Take it up with the court," the cop said.

Reacher shrugged to himself and swung his feet to the floor. Walking was awkward without his shoelaces. On the stairs, he had to hook his toes to stop his shoes from falling off altogether. He shuffled past the booking desk and followed the cop up another flight to the courtroom. There was a center aisle and four rows of spectator seating. Then a bullpen rail and a prosecution table and a defense table, a witness stand and a jury box and a judge's dais. All the furniture was pine, lacquered dark and then darkened more by age and polish. There were flags behind the dais, Old Glory and something Reacher guessed was the state flag of Colorado.

The room was empty, and it smelled of dust. The cop pointed Reacher toward the defense table. The cop sat down at the prosecution table. They waited. Then a door in the back wall opened and a man in a cheap suit walked in. The cop jumped up and said, "All rise." Reacher stayed in his seat.

The man in the suit clumped up three steps and slid in behind the dais. He was bulky and somewhere over sixty and had a full head of white hair. He picked up a pen and straightened a legal pad in front of him. He looked at Reacher and said, "Name?"

"I haven't been Mirandized," Reacher said.

"You haven't been charged with a crime," the old guy said. "This is an administrative matter. But I do need to ask you some questions. Name?"

The guy's manner was reasonably courteous, so Reacher said, "Jack Reacher. No middle initial."

The guy wrote it down. "Address?"

Reacher said, "No fixed address."

The guy wrote it down. Asked, "Occupation?"

"None."

"Purpose of your visit to Despair?"

"Tourism."

"How do you propose to support yourself during your visit?"

"I have a bank balance," Reacher said.

"What was your last address?"

"An APO box."

"Army Post Office? How long did you serve?"

"Thirteen years."

"Until?"

"I mustered out ten years ago."

"Unit?"

"Military Police."

"Final rank?"

"Major."

"And you haven't had a permanent address since then?"

"No, I haven't."

The guy made a pronounced check mark on the legal pad. Then he asked, "How long have you been out of work?"

"Ten years," Reacher said.

"You haven't worked since you left the army?"

"Not really."

"Yet you have a bank balance?"

"Savings," Reacher said. "Plus occasional casual labor."

The guy made another check. "Where did you stay last night?"

"In Hope," Reacher said. "In a motel."

"And your bags are still there?"

"I don't have any bags."

The guy made another check mark.

"You walked here?" he asked.

"I couldn't find a ride," Reacher said.

"What had you heard about our little town?"

"Nothing at all."

"Yet you decided to visit?"

"I have to be somewhere. And thanks for the big welcome."

The guy made another big check mark. Then he skipped his pen down his list, slowly and methodically. He said, "I'm sorry, but I find you to be in contravention of Despair's vagrancy ordinance. I'm afraid you'll have to leave."

"I'm not a vagrant," Reacher said.

"Homeless for ten years, jobless for ten years, you beg rides or walk from place to place. What else would you call yourself?"

"Free," Reacher said. "And lucky."

The judge nodded and said, "I'm glad you see a silver lining. But this is a quiet, old-fashioned town, and we err on the side of caution. Itinerants have always been a problem."

Reacher said nothing. The judge said, "The officer will drive you to the town line. Get a job and a home, and we'll welcome you back with open arms. But don't come back until you do."

THE cop took him downstairs again and gave him back his cash and his passport and his ATM card and his toothbrush. Then he handed over his shoelaces and waited while Reacher threaded them through the eyelets in his shoes and tied them off. Reacher walked ahead of him through the lobby and stepped out the street door. It was late in the day, late in the year, and it was getting dark. The cop moved to his cruiser. "In the back," he said.

Reacher heard a plane in the sky, far to the west. A single-engine, climbing hard. A Cessna or a Beech or a Piper, small and lonely in the vastness. He pulled open the car door and slid inside.

The cop got in the front. He took off down the street and headed north. Six blocks to Main Street, Reacher figured. If he turns left, takes me onward, to the west, maybe I'll let it go. But if he turns right, takes me back east to Hope, maybe I won't.

Reacher hated turning back.

Forward motion was his organizing principle.

Six blocks, six stop signs. At each one, the cop braked gently and slowed and then rolled forward. At Main Street, he came to a complete halt. He paused. Then he hit the gas and turned right. East.

Back toward Hope.

2

TWELVE minutes later the car slowed and braked to a stop. The cop climbed out and opened Reacher's door.

"Out," he said.

Reacher slid out and felt Despair's grit under his shoes.

The cop jerked his thumb to the east.

"That way," he said.

Reacher stood still. Then he stepped forward, three paces. Saw the moon rising on the far horizon. Saw the end of Despair's rough gravel and the start of Hope's smooth blacktop. The car was stopped with its push bars directly above the expansion joint. The boundary. Reacher shrugged and stepped over it.

The cop called, "Don't bother us again."

Reacher didn't turn around. He faced east and listened as the car backed up and turned and crunched away across the stones. When the sound was gone, he shrugged again and started walking.

HE HAD walked less than twenty yards when he saw the headlights. A big car, coming straight at him out of the gathering darkness, moving fast. When it was a hundred yards away, he saw it was another cop car, another Crown Vic, painted black and white. It stopped short of him, and a spotlight mounted on the windshield pillar lit up and played its beam up and down him twice. Then it clicked off again and the car crept forward and stopped with the driver's door exactly alongside him. The door had a gold shield painted on it, with HPD scrolled across the middle. Hope Police Department. The window buzzed down, and a dome light came on inside. Reacher saw a woman cop at the wheel, short blond hair backlit by the weak yellow bulb.

"Want a ride?" she asked.

"I'll walk," Reacher said.

"It's five miles to town."

"I walked out here; I can walk back."

Reacher took three steps and heard the car's transmission go into reverse, and then the car came alongside him again, driving backward, keeping pace as he walked. The woman said, "Give yourself a break, Zeno."

Reacher stopped. Said, "You know who Zeno was?"

The car stopped. "Zeno of Citium," the woman said. "Founder of Stoicism. I'm telling you to stop being so long-suffering."

"Stoics have to be long-suffering. Stoicism is about the unquestioning acceptance of destinies. Zeno said so."

"Your destiny is to return to Hope. Doesn't matter to Zeno whether you walk or ride."

"What are you, anyway—a philosopher or a cop or a cabdriver?"

"The Despair PD calls us when they're dumping someone at the line. As a courtesy."

"This happens a lot?"

"More than you'd think."

"Why do they do it?"

"Get in and I'll tell you, Reacher."

"You know my name?"

"Despair PD passed it on. As a courtesy."

Reacher shrugged and put his hand on the rear door handle.

"Up front, you idiot," the woman said. "I'm helping you, not arresting you."

So Reacher looped around the trunk and opened the front passenger door. The seat was all hemmed in with radio consoles and a laptop terminal on a bracket. Up front, the car smelled of oil and coffee and perfume and warm electronics. The laptop screen showed a GPS map. A small arrow was blinking away at the far edge of a pink square labeled HOPE TOWNSHIP. Next to it Despair township was shaped like a blunt wedge. Its eastern border matched Hope's western limit exactly; then it spread wider. Its western line was twice as long as its eastern and bordered gray emptiness. Unincorporated land, Reacher figured. Spurs came off I-70 and I-25 and clipped Despair's northwestern corner.

The woman cop buzzed her window back up and craned her neck and glanced behind her and K-turned across the road. She was slightly built under a crisp tan shirt. Probably less than five feet six, probably less than a hundred and twenty pounds, probably less than thirty-five years old. No jewelry, no wedding band. According to the badge pinned over her left breast, her name was Vaughan, and she was a pretty good cop. She seemed to have won a bunch of awards and commendations. She was good-looking, but different from regular women. She had seen stuff they hadn't.

He asked, "Why did Despair run me out?"

The woman called Vaughan turned out the dome light. "Look at yourself," she said. "What do you see?"

"Just a guy."

"A blue-collar guy in work clothes, fit, strong, and hungry."

"I'm more green-collar than blue," Reacher said. "I was in the army. Military cop."

"When?"

"Ten years ago."

"You working now?"

"No."

"Well, then. You were a threat."

"How?"

"West of downtown is the biggest metal recycling plant in Colorado. There's nothing else in Despair's economy."

"A company town," Reacher said.

Vaughan nodded at the wheel. "The guy who owns the plant owns every brick of every building. Half the population works for him full-time. The other half works for him part-time. The part-timers are insecure. They don't like people showing up, willing to work for less."

"I wasn't willing to work at all."

"You tell them that?"

"They didn't ask."

"They wouldn't have believed you, anyway. Standing around every morning waiting for a nod from the foreman does things to people. It's kind of feudal. The whole place is feudal. The money the owner pays out in wages comes right back at him in rents. Mortgages, too. He owns the bank. No relief on Sundays, either. There's one church, and he's the lay preacher."

"So why don't people move on?"

"Some have. Those who haven't never will."

Vaughan slowed. Hope's first built-up block was ahead in the distance. A mom-and-pop hardware store. That morning, an old guy had been putting stepladders and wheelbarrows out on the sidewalk, building a display. Now the store was all closed up and dark.

He asked, "How big is the Hope PD?"

Vaughan said, "Me and two others and a watch commander."

"You got sworn deputies?"

"Four of them. Why?"

"Are they armed?"

"No. In Colorado, deputies are civilian peace officers."

"How many deputies does the Despair PD have?"

"Four, I think."

"I met them."

"And?"

"Theoretically, what would the Hope PD do if someone got into a dispute with one of your deputies and busted his jaw?"

"We'd throw that someone in jail real quick."

"Why?"

"You know why. Zero tolerance for assaults on peace officers. You'd have felt the same in the MPs. Why do you ask?"

Reacher didn't answer directly. Instead, he said, "I'm not a Stoic, really. Zeno preached the passive acceptance of fate. I'm not like that. I don't like to be told where I can go and where I can't."

Vaughan slowed some more and pulled in at the curb. Put the transmission in park and turned in her seat. "My advice?" she said. "Get over it and move on. Despair isn't worth it."

Reacher said nothing.

"Go get a meal and a room for the night," Vaughan said. "I'm sure you're hungry."

Reacher nodded. "Thanks for the ride," he said. "And it was a pleasure to meet you."

He opened the door and slid out to the sidewalk. He knew there was a diner a block away. He had eaten breakfast there. He set out toward it and heard Vaughan's Crown Vic move away behind him. He heard the civilized purr of its motor and the soft hiss of its tires on the asphalt. Then he turned a corner and didn't hear it anymore.

AN HOUR later Reacher was still in the diner. He had eaten soup, steak, fries, beans, apple pie, and ice cream. Now he was drinking coffee. The diner had a bottomless-cup policy, and Reacher abused it mercilessly. He drank most of a Bunn flask all on his own. It was a better brew than at the restaurant in Despair. The mug was still too thick at the rim, but closer to the ideal.

He was thinking about Despair, and he was wondering why getting him out of town had been more important than busting him for the assault on the deputy.

It was dark when he left the diner. Nine o'clock in the evening. He walked three blocks to a small grocery, where he bought three one-liter bottles of Poland Spring and some chocolate-chip Power-Bars and a roll of black thirteen-gallon garbage bags. The clerk at the register packed them all carefully into a paper sack, and Reacher took his change and carried the sack four blocks to the same motel he had used the night before. He got the same room, at the end of the row. He went inside and put the sack on the nightstand and lay down on the bed. He planned on a short rest. Until midnight. He didn't want to walk seventeen miles twice on the same day.

REACHER got off the bed at midnight and checked the window. No moon. He packed his purchases into one of the black garbage bags and slung it over his shoulder. Then he left the motel and headed west. There was no traffic. No pedestrians. The sidewalk ended twenty feet west of the hardware store. He stepped off the curb onto the asphalt and built up a rhythm. Route-march speed, four miles an hour. Not difficult on the smooth, flat surface.

Five miles later he stepped over the line between Hope and Despair. He got off the road immediately and looped fifty yards into the scrub north of the road. Near enough to retain a sense of direction, far enough to stay out of a driver's peripheral vision. The night was cold. The ground was uneven. No chance of getting close to four miles an hour. No chance at all. He had no flashlight. A light would be worse than climbing up on a rock and yelling, *Here I am.*

A slow mile later the clock in his head told him it was quarter to two in the morning. He heard an aircraft engine, far away to the west. A single-engine plane, coming in to land. A Cessna, or a Beech, or a Piper. Maybe the same one he had heard take off hours before. He listened to it until he imagined it had touched down and taxied. Then he started walking again.

FOUR hours later he was about level with the center of downtown, three hundred yards out in the scrub. The night was still cold. He drank water and ate a PowerBar. Then he studied the town. Darkness and stillness and the hidden glow from occasional lit windows. Farther in the distance, he saw more lights. The residential areas, he guessed. He figured people were getting up for work.

Ten minutes later he saw headlight beams coming north. Two, three sets. Their light funneled through the cross streets, paused at Main Street, and then swept west. More came after them. Soon every cross street was lit up bright by long processions of vehicles.

Sedans and pickups and old-model SUVs. They all drove north to Main Street and paused and jostled and swung west.

A company town. Six o'clock in the morning.

The people of Despair, going to work.

Reacher followed them on foot, four hundred yards to the north. He stumbled on through the crusted scrub, tracking the road. A mile or more ahead, the horizon was lit up with an immense glow. Not dawn. That was going to happen behind him, to the east. The glow was from arc lighting, a huge rectangle of lights on poles surrounding some kind of a massive arena. It looked to be about a mile long. Maybe a half mile wide. *The biggest metal recycling plant in Colorado,* Vaughan had said.

Looks like the biggest in the world, Reacher thought.

In front of the glow, the convoy of vehicles peeled off and parked in neat rows on acres of beaten scrub. Their headlights shut down, one by one. Reacher watched men file inside, shuffling forward in a long line, lunch pails in their hands. The gate was narrow, a personnel entrance. Reacher guessed the vehicle entrance was on the other side of the complex, convenient for the highway spurs.

The last worker filed inside, and the personnel gate closed. Reacher moved on, staying hidden. The sky was lightening, landscape features becoming visible. But the terrain was pitted with enough humps and dips to provide decent concealment.

The recycling plant was ringed by an endless solid wall welded out of metal plates painted white. The wall was topped with a continuous horizontal cylinder six feet in diameter. Impossible to climb. Like a supermax prison. His initial estimate of the size of the place had been conservative. It looked bigger than the town itself. Like a tail that wags a dog.

Work was starting inside. Reacher heard the groan of heavy machinery and the ringing sound of metal on metal. He moved around to the northwest corner, fifteen minutes' fast walk. The vehicle gate was right there. A section of the wall was standing open. A wide road ran from the horizon straight to it.

The road was a problem. If Reacher wanted to continue his

progress, he would have to cross it somewhere. He would be exposed. But to whom, exactly? He guessed the Despair cops would stay in town, east of the plant. And he didn't expect any roving surveillance teams out of the plant itself.

But that was exactly what he got.

Two white Chevy Tahoes came out of the vehicle gate. They drove fifty yards down the road and then plunged off it, one to the left and one to the right, onto beaten tracks of packed scrub created by endless previous excursions. The Tahoes had the word SECURITY stenciled in black across their doors. They drove slowly, maybe twenty miles an hour—one clockwise, one counterclockwise, as if they intended to lap the plant all day long.

Reacher struck out west, staying in the dips and washes as far as possible. Ten minutes later he crouched just east of a table rock and watched for the Tahoes.

They came around much less often than he had predicted. Which was inexplicable but good. What wasn't good was that the road itself was starting to get busy. The largest recycling plant in Colorado clearly needed input, and it clearly produced output. They trucked scrap in and then trucked ingots out. A lot of scrap, and a lot of ingots. Shortly after seven o'clock in the morning, a flatbed semi roared out of the gate and lumbered onto the road. It was laden with bright steel bars. It drove a hundred yards and was passed by another flatbed, heading inward. This one was loaded with crushed cars, dozens of them, layered like thin stripes. A container truck with Canadian plates left the plant and passed the semi. Then the counterclockwise Tahoe showed up and bounced across the roadbed and kept on going. Three minutes later its clockwise partner rotated in the opposite direction. Another semi left the plant, and another headed in. It was like Times Square.

Reacher waited for the Tahoes to pass one more time. Then he got up and just walked across the road. He accepted the risk of being seen. For one thing, he had no real choice. For another, he figured the Tahoes would stick to their own private itineraries.

Safe enough.

He headed south, tracking the long side of the plant. The wall continued. It was maybe fourteen feet high, welded out of what looked like the roofs of old cars. The six-foot cylinder along the top looked to be assembled from the same material, molded to the correct contour, and welded together. Then the whole assembly had been sprayed glossy white.

It took Reacher twenty-six minutes to walk the length of the plant, which made it more than a mile long. At its far southwest corner, he saw why the Tahoes were so slow. There was a second walled compound. Another huge rectangle. Similar size. Tire tracks showed that the Tahoes were lapping it, too, passing and repassing through a fifty-yard bottleneck in a giant distorted figure eight.

The second compound was walled with fieldstone, not metal. It was residential. There was a screen of trees placed to block any view of industrial activity. There was a huge house built out of wood in a chalet style more suitable to Vail than Despair. There were out-buildings, including an oversized barn that was probably an aircraft hangar, because inside the whole length of the far wall was a wide graded strip of dirt that could only be a runway.

Reacher moved on. He looped west again and aimed to circle the residential compound, too, as if both enclosures were one giant obstacle. By noon, he was holed up way to the south, looking back at the recycling plant from the rear. The residential compound was closer and to his left. Far beyond it to the northwest was a small gray smudge in the distance. A group of buildings, maybe five or six miles away. Maybe a gas station or a truck stop or a motel. Reacher couldn't make out any detail.

He turned back to the nearer sights. Nothing much was happening at the house. He saw the Tahoes circling and watched trucks on the distant road, a continuous stream of them. The plant belched smoke and flame and sparks. Its noise was softened by distance, but up close it must have been fearsome. The sun was high, and the day had gotten warm.

Reacher watched and listened, and then he headed east for a look at the far side of town.

IT WAS BRIGHT DAYLIGHT, SO HE stayed cautious and moved slow. There was a long, empty gap between the plant and the town itself. Maybe three miles. He covered them in a straight line, well out in the scrub. By the middle of the afternoon, he was level with where he had been at six o'clock in the morning, but looking at the backs of houses, not the fronts of commercial buildings.

The houses were one-story ranches with shingle siding and asphalt roofs, cheaply but adequately built. Some had garages, some didn't. Most had satellite dishes, tilted up and facing southwest like a regiment of expectant faces. It was a strange little suburb, with empty vastness all around. Reacher suddenly understood that Despair had been built by people who had given up. They had come over the rise and seen the far horizon and had quit. And their descendants were still in town.

REACHER ate his last PowerBar and drained the last of his water. He hacked a hole in the scrub with his heel and buried the wrappers and the empty bottles and his garbage bag. Then he dodged from rock to rock and got a little closer to the houses. The low noise coming from the distant plant was getting quieter. He guessed it was quitting time.

The first cars and pickup trucks straggled back close to twelve hours after they had left. A long day. They scattered toward driveways. Engines stopped. Doors creaked open and slammed shut. Lights were on inside houses. The blue glow of televisions was visible behind windows. The sky was darkening.

Reacher moved closer. Saw men carrying empty lunch pails into kitchens. He saw hopeful boys with balls and mitts looking for a last game of catch. He saw some fathers agree and some refuse.

He saw the big guy who had blocked the end of the restaurant table. The senior deputy. He got out of the old, listing crew-cab pickup truck that Reacher had seen outside the restaurant. He clutched his stomach with both hands. He passed by his kitchen door and stumbled on into his yard. Then he bent from the waist and threw up in the dirt. He stayed doubled up for maybe twenty seconds and then straightened, shaking his head and spitting.

Reacher got within twenty yards, and then the guy bent again and threw up for a second time. Reacher heard him gasp. Not in pain, but in annoyance and resignation.

"You okay?" Reacher called out of the gloom.

The guy straightened up. "Who's there?" he called.

Reacher said, "Me." He moved closer. Stepped into a bar of light coming from a neighbor's kitchen window.

The guy said, "You."

Reacher nodded. "Me."

"We threw you out."

"Didn't take."

The guy shrugged. "I'm going inside. I didn't see you, okay?"

"How's your buddy? With the jaw?"

"You bust him up good."

"Tough," Reacher said.

"I'm going inside," the guy said again. "I'm sick."

"Bad food?"

The guy paused. Then he nodded. "Must have been," he said.

He headed for his house, slow and stumbling. Reacher watched him go, and then he turned and walked back into the shadows.

Way to the west, he heard the aircraft engine again, straining hard, climbing. The small plane, taking off once more. Seven o'clock in the evening.

Reacher loosened the neck of his shirt and set off east, back toward Hope. When the houses fell away, he looped left into the dark toward where he figured the road must be. Eventually he saw a black stripe in the darkness. He lined himself up with it and fixed its direction in his mind and retreated sideways a safe ten yards and then moved on forward. Walking was difficult in the dark. He stumbled into bushes. Twice he tripped on low football-size boulders and fell.

The third time he tripped was not on a rock.

He sprawled forward, and some kind of a primitive instinct made him avoid landing right on top of the thing. He kicked his legs up and tucked his head in and rolled. He ended up on his back, winded, and hurting from having landed on sharp stones. He lay still for a moment and then rolled on his front and pushed himself to his knees. He opened his eyes wide and stared into blackness.

He shuffled forward on both knees and one hand, with the other held low in front of him. A slow yard later it touched something.

Soft.

He spread his fingers. Clamped them loosely. Cloth. Rubbed his fingertips and the ball of his thumb left and right. Squeezed.

A leg. He had his hand on a human leg. The size· and heft of a thigh was unmistakable. The cloth was thin and soft. Probably cotton twill, worn and washed many times. He skipped his hand three feet to the right and slid it up a back to a shoulder blade. Walked his fingers to a neck, and a nape, and an ear.

No pulse.

He shuffled closer on his knees and opened his eyes so wide the muscles in his face hurt.

Too dark to see. Nothing to hear. He wasn't about to try tasting anything. That left smell and touch. Reacher had smelled more than his fair share of deceased organisms. This one wasn't particularly offensive. Stale sweat, ripe hair, the faintest trace of methane from early decomposition. No blood. No real information.

So . . . touch. He started with the hair. Maybe an inch and a half or two inches. Wiry, with a tendency to wave. Caucasian. The forehead was ridged and bony, and the chin and the upper lip were rough with maybe four days of stubble. The cheeks and the throat were smoother. A young man, not much more than a boy.

The cheekbones were pronounced. The eyes were hard and dry, like marbles. The facial skin was firm and shrunken, the mouth dry, inside and out. No fat anywhere.

Starved and dehydrated, Reacher thought.

He found folds of cloth at the hip and the shoulder and rolled the body on its side. It was reasonably heavy. The way his hands were spaced told him it was maybe five eight in height, and the weight was probably close to one-forty.

The pants were loose at the waist. No belt. The shoes were some kind of athletic sneakers.

Reacher wiped his hands on his own pants and then started again from the feet upward, looking for a wound.

He found nothing. No gashes, no gunshot wounds, no contusions, no broken bones.

The hands were small and fairly delicate. No rings on the fingers.

He checked the pants pockets. No wallet, no coins, no keys, no phone. Nothing.

He sat back on his heels and stared up at the sky, willing a cloud to move and let some moonlight through. But the night stayed dark. He had been walking east, had fallen, had turned around. Therefore, he was now facing west. He stood up, made a quarter turn to his right. Now he was facing north. He started walking slowly, concentrating hard on staying straight. Five yards, ten, fifteen, twenty.

He found the road. The packed scrub gave way to the tarred pebbles. He butted three stones together and stacked a fourth on top, like a miniature cairn. Then he glanced up at the sky. Still solid.

Nothing more to be done.

He stood up again and turned left and blundered on through the dark, east toward Hope.

3

THE clock in his head said that it was midnight. Reacher had made good progress. Despair's cheap road crunched loudly under his feet, but the hard-level surface allowed him to speed up. It was still cold, still pitch, dark. But he sensed the new blacktop ahead. He felt it coming. Then his left foot pushed off rough stones, and his right landed on velvet-smooth asphalt.

He was back over the line.

He stood still for a second. Held his arms wide and looked up at the black sky. Then a spotlight clicked on and played over him, head to foot and back again.

A cop car.

Then the beams died as suddenly as they had appeared and a dome light came on inside the car and showed a small figure at the wheel. Tan shirt, fair hair. Half a smile.

Vaughan.

She was parked head-on, just waiting in the dark. Reacher walked toward her. He stepped to the passenger door and put his hand on the handle, opened it, and crammed himself inside. The interior was full of soft radio chatter and the smell of perfume.

He asked, "So are you free for a late dinner?"

She said, "I'm working the graveyard shift. I don't get off until seven. Besides, I don't eat with jerks."

Reacher smiled at her and said nothing.

She asked, "What were you doing?"

"Taking a stroll."

"You're a stubborn man."

Reacher nodded. "I wanted to see Despair, and I did."

"Was it worth it?"

"Not really."

Vaughan started the motor and backed up a little and then turned across the road in a wide arc that took the front wheels off the blacktop. She straightened up and accelerated.

"How did you know I was out here?" Reacher asked.

"I guessed. And our video has night-vision enhancement." She leaned forward and tapped a black box mounted on the dash. "Traffic camera and a hard-disc recorder." She moved her hand again and hit a key on the computer. The screen changed to a ghostly green wide-angle image of the scene ahead.

"I saw you half a mile away," she said. "A little green speck." She tapped another key and spooled back through the time code, and Reacher saw himself, a luminous sliver in the dark, coming closer.

"Very fancy," he said.

"Homeland Security money. Got to spend it on something."

Vaughan drove slow, thirty miles an hour, as though she had more to say. She had one hand on the wheel, the other in her lap.

"You should eat," she said. "The diner will still be open."

"I might go take a nap instead."

"Go eat in the diner first."

"Why?"

"Someone was asking about you."

"Who?"

"Some girl. She was asking if anyone had been thrown out of Despair more recently than her."

"She was thrown out?"

"Four days ago."

"Who is she?"

"Just some kid. I told her about you. I said if you were still in town, you might be eating in the diner tonight. So I think she might come looking for you."

"What does she want?"

"She wouldn't tell me," Vaughan said. "But my impression was her boyfriend is missing."

REACHER got out of Vaughan's cruiser on First Street and walked straight down to Second. The diner was all lit up inside, and three booths were occupied. A guy on his own, a young woman on her own, two guys together.

The sidewalks close to the diner were deserted. No girls hanging around. No girls watching who was going in and coming out. Reacher went in and headed for a booth in the far corner, where he could see the whole room at once. A waitress came over and gave him a napkin and silverware and a glass of ice water. She was young, could have been a college student.

The menu was a laminated card with pictures of the food on it. The waitress came back, and Reacher pointed to a grilled cheese sandwich and said, "And coffee." The waitress wrote it down and walked away, and Reacher settled back and watched the street through the windows. He figured that the girl who was looking for him might pass by once every fifteen or twenty minutes. It was what he would have done. Longer intervals might make her miss his visit. Most diner customers were in and out pretty fast.

But nobody passed by. The waitress came over with his sandwich and a mug of coffee. The coffee was fresh, and the sandwich was okay. The cheese was sticky in his mouth and less flavorful than a Wisconsin product would have been, but it was palatable. Reacher was no kind of a gourmet.

After fifteen minutes, he gave up on the girl. He quit staring out at the sidewalk and started looking at the other customers inside the diner and realized she was already in there waiting for him.

The young woman, sitting three booths away.

Stupid, Reacher, he thought.

She was maybe nineteen, dirty blond hair with streaks, wearing a short denim skirt and a white sweatshirt. Her features didn't add up all the way to beauty, but she had a kind of irresistible glowing good health that he had seen before in American girls. Her skin was perfect, honey-colored.

She was the one he was waiting for. He knew that because as he watched her in his peripheral vision, he could see she was sizing him up and deciding whether to approach. Deciding against, apparently.

Reacher didn't blame her. It was late at night, she was looking at an old guy twice her age, huge, disheveled, somewhat dirty, and surrounded by an electric stay-away aura he had spent years cultivating, like a sign on a fire truck: STAY BACK 200 FEET.

So she was going to sit tight and wait him out. She was looking up, looking down, kneading her fingers, glancing suddenly in his direction as new thoughts came to her, and then glancing away again as she resolved them. Reacher gave it five more minutes and then fished in his pocket for cash.

He left some bills on the table. Got up and headed for the door. At the last minute, he changed direction and stepped over to the young woman's booth and slid in opposite her.

"My name is Reacher. I think you wanted to talk to me."

The girl looked at him and blinked and opened her mouth and closed it again.

"A cop called Vaughan told me you were looking for someone who had been to Despair."

"You're mistaken," the girl said. "It wasn't me."

She wasn't a great liar.

Psychologists have figured out that the memory center is located in the left brain and the imagination engine in the right brain. Therefore, people unconsciously glance to the left when they're remembering things and to the right when they're making stuff up. This girl was glancing right so much she was in danger of getting whiplash.

"Okay," Reacher said. "I apologize for disturbing you." But he didn't move. He stayed where he was, sitting easy. Up close, the girl was prettier than she had looked from a distance. She had a dusting of freckles and a mobile, expressive mouth.

"Who are you?" she asked.

"Just a guy," Reacher said. "In Despair, they called me a vagrant."

She said, "They called me a vagrant, too."

Her accent was unspecific. She wasn't from New York or Minnesota or the Deep South. Maybe somewhere in the Southwest.

"What's your name?" he asked her.

She glanced to her right. "Anne."

Whatever her name was, it wasn't Anne.

The girl who wasn't Anne asked, "Why did you go to Despair?"

"I liked the name. Why did *you* go there?"

She didn't answer.

He said, "Anyway, it wasn't much of a place."

The girl went quiet. Reacher saw her weighing her next question. She put her head on one side and looked beyond him. "Did you see any people?" she asked.

"Lots of people," Reacher said.

"Did you see the airplane?"

"I heard one."

"It belongs to the guy with the big house. Every night, he takes off at seven and comes back at two o'clock in the morning."

Reacher said, "No law against joyriding."

"People don't joyride at night. There's nothing to see."

"Good point."

The girl was quiet for another minute, and then she asked, "When you were there, what people did you see?"

Reacher said, "Why don't you just show me his picture?"

"Whose picture?"

"Your boyfriend's."

"Why would I do that?"

"Your boyfriend is missing. As in, you can't find him. That was Officer Vaughan's impression, anyway."

"You trust cops?"

"Some of them."

She said, "Show me your wallet."

"I don't have a wallet."

"Prove it. Empty your pockets."

Reacher nodded. He understood: The boyfriend is some kind of a fugitive. She needs to know I'm not an investigator. He lifted his butt off the bench and dug out his cash, his old passport, his ATM card, his motel key. His toothbrush was in a plastic glass next to the sink in his room. The girl looked at his stuff and said, "Thanks."

He said, "Now show me his picture."

"He's not my boyfriend. He's my husband."

She hauled a gray messenger bag into her lap and rooted around for a moment and came out with a fat leather wallet. There was a plastic window on the outside with a California driver's license behind it with her picture on it. She opened the billfold and eased a snapshot out.

It showed the girl standing on a street with golden light and palm trees and a row of neat boutiques behind her. She was smiling widely, vibrant with love and happiness. She was in the arms of a guy about her age.

"This is your husband?" Reacher asked.

The girl said, "Yes."

Reacher squared the snapshot on the tabletop in front of him and asked, "How old is this photo?"

"Recent."

"May I see your driver's license?"

"Why?"

"Something I need to check."

"I don't know."

"I already know your name isn't Anne."

The girl said nothing.

Reacher said, "I'm not here to hurt you."

She paused and then slid her wallet across the table. He glanced at her license. Her name was Lucy Anderson.

"Lucy," he said, "I'm pleased to meet you."

"I'm sorry about not telling you the truth."

"Don't worry about it."

Her license said she was coming up to twenty years old. It said her address was an apartment on a street in L.A. Her eyes were listed as blue, which was an understatement, and she was five feet eight inches tall.

Which made her husband at least six feet four. He towered over her. He was huge. He looked to be well over two hundred pounds. His arms were as thick as the palm trunks behind him.

Not the guy in the dark. Not even close. Way too big.

Reacher slid the wallet back across the table.

Lucy Anderson asked, "Did you see him?"

Reacher shook his head.

"No," he said. "I didn't. I'm sorry."

"He has to be there somewhere."

"What's he running from?"

She looked to the right. "Why would he be running?"

"Just a wild guess," Reacher said.

"Who are you?" she asked. "And how did you know my name wasn't Anne?"

"A long time ago I was a cop. In the military. I still know things."

Her skin whitened behind her freckles. She fumbled the photograph back into its slot and fastened the wallet and thrust it deep into her bag.

"You don't like cops, do you?" Reacher asked.

"Not always," she said.

"Doesn't matter," Reacher said. "I didn't see your husband. And I'm not a cop anymore. Haven't been for a long time."

"What would you do now? If you were me?"

"I'd wait right here in town. Your husband looks like a capable guy. He'll probably show up sooner or later. Or get word to you."

"I hope so." Lucy Anderson secured the flap of her bag and slid off the bench and stood up. "Thank you," she said. "Good night."

She walked to the door and pushed out to the street. He watched her huddle into her sweatshirt and step away through the cold.

HE WAS in bed before two o'clock in the morning. He set the alarm in his head for six-thirty. He was tired, but he figured four and a half hours would be enough. He wanted time to shower before heading out for breakfast.

IT WAS a cliché that cops stop in at diners for doughnuts before, during, and after every shift, but clichés were clichés only because they were so often true. Therefore, Reacher slipped into the same back booth at five to seven in the morning and fully expected to see Officer Vaughan enter inside the following ten minutes.

Which she did.

She came in and saw him and paused for a long moment and then changed direction and slid in opposite him.

He asked, "Coffee?"

"I don't drink coffee with jerks."

"I'm not a jerk. I'm a citizen with a problem."

"What kind of problem?"

"The girl found me."

"And had you seen her boyfriend?"

"Her husband, actually. But no. I saw someone else."

"Who?"

"Not saw, actually. It was pitch-dark. I fell over him."

"Who?"

"A dead guy."

"Are you serious?"

"As a heart attack."

"Why didn't you tell me last night?"

"I wanted time to think about it."

"You're yanking my chain. There's a thousand square miles out there, and you just happen to trip over a dead guy in the dark?"

"I figure he was doing the same thing I was doing. Walking east from Despair, staying close enough to the road to be sure of his direction, far enough away to be safe. That put him in a pretty specific channel."

Vaughan said nothing.

"But he didn't make it," Reacher said. "He died. He was Caucasian, by the feel of his hair. Maybe five eight, one-forty. Young. Emaciated and dehydrated. No wounds."

"What, you autopsied this guy? In the dark?"

"I felt around."

"This is unbelievable."

"It happened."

"Where exactly?"

"Maybe four miles out of Despair."

"You should call the Despair PD."

"I wouldn't piss on the Despair PD if it was on fire."

The waitress came over. Reacher ordered coffee and eggs. Vaughan ordered coffee. Reacher took that as a good sign. He waited until the waitress had bustled away and said, "I want to go back and take a look right now, in the daylight. You can drive me."

"It's not my jurisdiction," Vaughan said. "I can't do it."

"Unofficial. Off duty. Like a tourist."

"Would you be able to find the place again?"

"I left a pile of stones on the shoulder."

The waitress came back with the coffee and the eggs, which had a sprig of fresh parsley arrayed across them.

Vaughan said, "I can't drive a Hope police cruiser in Despair."

"So what else have you got?"

She was quiet for a moment. Then she said, "I have a truck."

SHE made him wait on the sidewalk near the hardware store. The store was still closed. The window was full of tools. The aisle behind the door was piled high with the stuff that would be put out on the sidewalk later. Reacher wondered why hardware stores favored sidewalk displays. There was a lot of work involved. But maybe consumer psychology dictated that large utilitarian items sold better outdoors. Or maybe it was just a question of space.

Close to twenty minutes later an old blue Chevy pickup pulled up on the opposite curb, a plain secondhand truck about fifteen years old. It had a wheezy four-cylinder motor. Vaughan was wearing a red Windbreaker and a khaki ball cap. Reacher climbed in next to her. The cab smelled of leaked gasoline and cold exhaust.

They covered Hope's five miles of road in seven minutes. Seven minutes inside enemy territory, Vaughan started to slow.

"Watch the left shoulder," Reacher said. "Four stones, piled up."

There was some trash on the shoulder. Not much, but enough that Reacher's small cairn was not going to stand out like a beacon. There were plastic water bottles, glass beer bottles, soda cans, small, unimportant parts of vehicles. Reacher twisted around in his seat. Nobody behind. Nobody ahead. Vaughan slowed some more.

"There," Reacher said.

His little cairn was thirty yards ahead on the left, a speck in the middle of nowhere.

Vaughan passed the cairn and turned a wide circle. She came back east and stopped exactly level with the stones. She put the transmission in park and left the engine running.

Reacher got out and stepped over the stones. In the dark, the world had shrunk to an arm's length around him. Now it felt huge again. To the south, the land ran all the way to the horizon, flat and essentially featureless. Vaughan stepped alongside him, and he walked south with her—five paces, ten, fifteen. He stopped after twenty paces. He stood on tiptoe and craned his neck and searched.

He saw nothing.

He turned a careful one-eighty and stared back at the road to make sure he hadn't drifted too far west or east. He hadn't.

"Well?" Vaughan called.

"It's gone," he said.

"How accurate could you have been in the dark?"

"That's what I'm wondering."

Reacher walked ten more yards east and started to trace a wide circle. A quarter of the way through it, he stopped.

"Look here." He pointed at the ground.

Vaughan said, "Footprints."

"My footprints," Reacher said. "From last night. Heading home."

They turned west and backtracked. Followed his footprints back toward Despair. Ten yards later they came to the head of a small diamond-shaped clearing. The clearing was empty.

"It's not here," Vaughan said.

"But it was. This is the spot."

The crusted sand was all churned up by multiple disturbances. There were dozens of footprints, facing in all directions. There were scrapes and slides and drag marks. Reacher crouched down and pointed at a depression in the center of the clearing.

"This is where the boy gave it up," he said. Then he pointed to a messed-up stony area four feet to the east. "This is where I landed after I tripped over him. On these stones. I could show you the bruises, if you like."

"Maybe later," Vaughan said. "We need to get going."

Reacher pointed to four sharp impressions in the sand. Each one was a rectangle about two inches by three at the corners of a larger rectangle, about two feet by five.

"Gurney feet," he said. "Folks came by and collected him. Maybe four or five of them, judging by the footprints." He stood up and checked and pointed north and west. "They came in that way and carried him back out in the same direction, back to the road."

"How did they find the body in the first place?"

"Buzzards," Reacher said. "The obvious way on open ground."

"So the proper authorities got him. Problem solved."

Reacher nodded vaguely and gazed due west. "I think there's more to it than that."

VAUGHAN lifted off the gas and slowed as they hit the edge of Hope. The hardware guy now had his door open and was piling his stuff on the sidewalk. He had some kind of a trick stepladder that could be put in about eight different positions. He had set it up like a painter's platform, good for reaching second-story walls. Vaughan made a right on the next block and then a left, past the back of the diner. She pulled in to a marked-off parking space outside a low brick building. The building could have been a suburban post office. But it wasn't. It was the Hope Police Department. It said so in aluminum letters neatly fixed to the brick. Vaughan shut off the engine, and Reacher followed her down a neat brick path to the door. The door was locked. Vaughan used a key from her bunch and said, "The desk guy gets in at nine."

Inside, the place still looked like a post office. Dull, worn, institutional. The watch commander's office was behind a solid door, in the same corner a postmaster's would be.

Reacher asked, "What happens next?"

"Always better to get out in front of a thing like this. You should call in and volunteer information."

"No."

"Why not?"

"I was a soldier. I never volunteer for anything."

"Well, I can't help you. It's out of my hands."

"You could call the state police, find out what they know."

Vaughan stepped past the counter and headed for a desk that was clearly hers. Efficient and organized. There was an old-model computer front and center and a console telephone next to it. She opened a drawer and found a number in a book. Clearly, contact between the Hope PD and the state police was rare. She didn't know the number by heart. She dialed the phone and asked for the duty desk and identified herself and said, "We have a missing-person inquiry. Male, Caucasian, approximately twenty years of age, five eight, one-forty. We don't have a name."

Then there was a pause. She moved the phone a little ways from her ear, and Reacher heard the faint tap of a keyboard in the distant state office. Denver, maybe. Then a voice came back on and Vaughan clamped the phone tight and Reacher didn't hear what it had to say.

Vaughan listened and said, "Thank you." Then she hung up. "Nothing to report," she said. "Apparently, Despair didn't call it in." She shook her head. "They should have. An unexplained death out in open country, that's a matter for the coroner. Which means it would show up on the state police system about a minute later."

"So why didn't they call it in?"

"I don't know. But that's not our problem."

Reacher thought of Lucy Anderson. He looked across at Vaughan and said, "It is our problem, kind of. The kid might have people worried about him."

Vaughan nodded. Went back to her phone. She dialed, and he heard a reply in her ear, "Despair Police Department." She ran through the same faked inquiry—missing person, Caucasian male, five eight, one-forty. There was a pause and then a short reply.

Vaughan hung up. "Nothing to report," she said.

Reacher sat down, and Vaughan moved stuff around on her desk. She put pencils away in drawers and flicked at dust and crumbs with the edge of her palm.

"Maybe the kid was local," Reacher said. "They knew who he was, so he wasn't a candidate for your missing-persons inquiry."

Vaughan shook her head. "Any unexplained death has got to be reported to the coroner. In which case, it would have showed up on the state system. The state police would have said, 'We heard there was a dead guy in Despair this morning; you should check it out.' "

"But they didn't."

"Because nothing has been called in from Despair."

"Maybe they're covering something up. Maybe because they ran him out of town, which might embarrass them."

Vaughan shook her head again. "They didn't run him out of town. We didn't get a call. And they always call us."

"They never dump them to the west?"

"There's nothing there. It's unincorporated land."

Reacher said nothing.

Vaughan said, "Maybe there were no cops involved. Maybe someone else found him."

"Civilians don't carry stretchers in their cars," Reacher said.

Vaughan nodded. "Start over," she said. "Who was this guy?"

"Caucasian male," Reacher said.

"Not Hispanic? Not foreign?"

"I think Hispanics are Caucasians, technically. All I'm going on is his hair. He wasn't black. That's all I know for sure."

"How did his skin feel? Olive skin feels different from pale skin. A little smoother and thicker."

"Really?"

"I think so. Don't you?"

Reacher touched his cheek, under his eye. "Hard to tell," he said.

Vaughan got up and stepped across to Reacher's desk. "Now compare. Try my face."

Reacher paused a beat.

"Purely for research purposes."

He reached up and touched her cheek with the ball of his thumb. "Texture was thicker than either one of us. Smoothness was somewhere between the two of us."

"Okay." She touched her face. Then she leaned down and touched his cheek with her hand. He felt a tiny jolt of voltage.

She said, "So he wasn't necessarily white, but he was younger than you. Less wrinkled and weather-beaten. Less of a mess."

"Thank you."

"You said he was thin—wasted, in fact."

"Noticeably. But he was probably wiry to begin with."

"How long does it take for a wiry person to get wasted?"

"I don't know for sure. If you're moving around out-of-doors, burning energy, maybe two or three days."

"That's a lot of wandering," Vaughan said. "We need to know why the good folks of Despair put in two or three days of sustained effort to keep him out of there."

Reacher shook his head. "Might be more useful to know why he was trying so hard to stay. He must have had a reason."

4

REACHER was quiet for a moment. Then he asked her, "Can I borrow your truck?"

Vaughan said, "No. You'll go back to Despair, you'll get arrested, and I'll be implicated."

"Suppose I don't go back to Despair? I want to see what lies to the west. I'm guessing the dead guy didn't come through Hope. You would have seen him and remembered him. Likewise with the girl's missing husband."

"Good point. But there's not much west of Despair."

"Got to be something."

Vaughan was quiet for a moment. Then she said, "It's a long loop around. You have to go back practically all the way to Kansas."

Reacher said, "I'll pay for the gas."

"Promise me you'll stay out of Despair."

"Where's the line?"

"Five miles west of the metal plant."

"Deal."

Vaughan sighed and put her keys on the desk. "Go," she said.

THE old Chevy's seat didn't go very far back. The runners were short. Reacher ended up driving with his back straight and his knees splayed, like he was at the wheel of a farm tractor. The steering was vague, and the brakes were soft. But it was better than walking. Reacher was done with walking, for a day or two at least.

His first stop was his motel in Hope. His room was at the end of the row, which put Lucy Anderson in a room closer to the office. She couldn't be anywhere else. He hadn't seen any other overnight accommodation in town.

The motel had its main windows all in back. The front of the row had a repeating sequence of doors and lawn chairs and head-high pebbled-glass slits that put daylight into the bathrooms. Reacher walked down the row looking for the white blur of underwear drying over a tub. In his experience, women of Lucy Anderson's station and generation were very particular about personal hygiene.

The twelve rooms yielded two possibilities. One had a larger blur than the other. An older or a larger woman. Reacher knocked at the other door and stepped back and waited. A long moment later Lucy Anderson opened up and stood in the inside shadows, warily.

Reacher said, "Hello."

"What do you want?"

"I want to know why your husband went to Despair and how he got there."

She was wearing sneakers and a pair of cutoff denims. Above the shorts was a sweatshirt, mid-blue.

She said, "I don't want you looking for my husband."

"Why not? You were worried about him yesterday. Today you're not?"

She stepped forward into the light, just a pace, and glanced left and right beyond Reacher's shoulders. The motel's lot was empty. Nothing there except Vaughan's old truck parked at Reacher's door. Lucy Anderson's eyes were full of panic.

"Just leave us alone," she said, and stepped back into her room and closed the door.

REACHER sat a spell in Vaughan's truck with a map from her door pocket. It confirmed what Vaughan had told him. He was going to have to drive east almost all the way back to the Kansas line, then north to I-70, then west again, then south on the same highway spur the metal trucks used. Total distance, close to two hundred miles.

And two hundred miles back, if he obeyed Vaughan's injunction to keep her truck off Despair's roads.

Which he planned to. Probably.

The old truck's battered exhaust was leaking fumes, so he kept the windows cracked down an inch. At a steady sixty, the wind whistled in, a mellifluous high-pitched chord. The truck was a pleasant traveling companion on the state roads. On I-70, it was less pleasant. Passing semis blew it all over the place. Reacher's wrists ached from holding it steady. He stopped once for gas and once for coffee, and both times he was happy to get a break.

The spur off I-70 west of Despair was the same piece of road Reacher had observed leaving the plant at the other end. Same sturdy construction, same width, same coarse blacktop, same sand shoulders. Exactly four hours after leaving Hope, he slowed and coasted and came to a stop with two wheels in the sand. Traffic was light, limited to trucks of all types heading in and out of the recycling plant twenty miles ahead. They were mostly flatbed semis, but with some container trucks and box vans mixed in. Plates were mostly from Colorado and its adjacent states, but there were some from California and Washington and New Jersey and some from Canada. They blew past, and the old truck rocked on its suspension.

Fifteen miles away was the group of low gray buildings Reacher had seen before, a tiny indistinct blur. A gas station, maybe. Or a truck stop. Maybe it was the kind of place where he could get a high-calorie meal.

Maybe it was the kind of place Lucy Anderson's husband and the unidentified dead guy might have gotten a high-calorie meal, on their way into Despair. Maybe someone would remember them.

Reacher bumped his right-hand wheels back onto the road and headed for the horizon. Twelve minutes later he stopped again, just short of a sign that said ENTERING DESPAIR, POP. 2,691. A hundred yards the wrong side of the line was the group of low buildings.

They weren't gray. That had been a trick of light. They were olive green.

THERE WERE SIX LOW BUILDINGS, identical metal prefabrications ringed by a razor-wire fence. The fence continued west to enclose a parking lot. The lot was filled with six up-armored Humvees. Each one had a machine-gun mount on top.

Not a gas station. Not a truck stop.

An army facility.

More specifically, a military police facility. More specifically still, a temporary encampment for a combat MP unit. Reacher recognized the format and the equipment mix.

Four guys were in the guard shack. Two came out. They were dressed in boots and armored vests and helmets, and they were carrying M16 rifles. They formed up side by side, executed a perfect left turn, and jogged toward Reacher's truck, exactly in step, as they had been trained. When they were thirty yards away, they separated. One guy came up on Reacher's right and swapped his rifle into the ready position. The other guy looped around and checked the truck's load bed and then came back and stood off six feet from Reacher's door and called out in a loud clear voice. He said, "Sir, please lower your window. Keep your hands where I can see them."

Reacher put his hands high on the wheel and kept on staring left. The guy he was looking at was a specialist, young but with pronounced squint lines on either side of his eyes. He was wearing glasses with thin black frames. The name tape on the right side of his vest said MORGAN.

"At ease, Corporal," Reacher said. "Nothing to see here."

The guy called Morgan said, "Sir, that's a determination I'll need to make for myself."

Reacher glanced ahead. Morgan's partner was still as a statue, the stock of his M16 tucked tight into his shoulder. He was sighting with his right eye, aiming low at Reacher's front right-hand tire.

Morgan said, "Sir, you appear to me to be surveilling a restricted military installation."

"You're wrong. I'm lost," Reacher said. "I'm looking for Hope."

Morgan took his left hand off his rifle and pointed straight ahead. "That way, sir," he said. "Twenty-two miles to downtown Hope."

Reacher nodded. Morgan was pointing south but hadn't taken his eyes off Reacher's hands. He was a good soldier. Experienced. Well turned out. The eyeglasses added a vulnerable human detail that balanced the alien appearance of the weapons.

Morgan stepped in close to Reacher's fender as a truck blew by. A New Jersey semi loaded with a closed forty-foot shipping container. Like a giant brick, doing sixty miles an hour. Noise, wind, a long tail of swirling dust. Morgan's pants flattened against his legs, but he didn't blink behind his glasses.

He asked, "Sir, do you have registration and insurance?"

"Glove compartment," Reacher said, which was a pretty safe guess. Vaughan was a cop. Cops kept their paperwork straight.

Morgan asked, "Sir, may I see those documents?"

Reacher said, "No."

"Sir, now it seems to me that you're surveilling a restricted military installation in a stolen vehicle."

"Relax, Corporal," Reacher said. "This is Colorado, not Iraq. I'm not looking to blow anything up."

"Sir, I need you to show me those documents. Just wave them at me, if you like. To prove to me you can put your hands on them."

Reacher shrugged and leaned over and opened the glove compartment. Dug through ballpoint pens and packs of tissues and found a plastic wallet. It was the kind of cheap thing found for sale at gas stations alongside air fresheners shaped like pine trees.

Reacher opened the wallet out of Morgan's sight. On the left was an insurance certificate, on the right a current registration.

Both were made out to David Robert Vaughan of Hope, Colorado.

Reacher waved the wallet in Morgan's direction.

Morgan said, "Sir, thank you."

Reacher put the wallet back in the glove compartment and slammed the lid.

Morgan said, "Sir, now it's time to be moving along."

Which gave Reacher another problem. If he moved forward, he would be in Despair. If he U-turned, Morgan would wonder why he had abandoned Hope as a destination and would be tempted to call in Vaughan's plate.

Which was the greater danger?

Morgan, easily. A contest between the Despair PD and a combat MP unit was no kind of a contest at all. So Reacher put the truck in gear and turned the wheel. "Have a great day, Corporal," he said, and hit the gas. A yard later he passed the green sign and temporarily increased Despair's population by one, all the way up to 2,692.

REACHER saw all the same stuff he had seen the day before, but in reverse order. The plant's long end wall, welded metal, bright white paint, the sparks and the smoke coming from the activity inside, the moving cranes.

He saw the clockwise security Tahoe bouncing across the scrub in the distance far to his right. Its counterclockwise partner was coming on slow. It crossed the road right behind Reacher. He saw it slide past, huge in his mirror. He drove on, and then the plant was behind him and downtown Despair was looming up on the right.

A mile ahead a cop car pulled out of a side street. A Crown Vic, white and gold, a light bar on the roof. It nosed out and paused a beat and turned left.

Straight toward Reacher.

Reacher cruised on. The sun was behind him and therefore in the cop's eyes, which was a good thing. Reacher took his left hand off the wheel and put it against his forehead, like he was massaging his temple against a headache. He kept his speed steady and stared straight ahead.

The cop car blew past.

Reacher put his hand back on the wheel and checked his mirror.

The cop was braking hard. Not good.

Now he was pulling through a fast U-turn.

Why? Despair was a company town, but its road had to be a public thoroughfare. Unfamiliar vehicles could not be rarities.

Reacher checked the mirror again. The Crown Vic was accelerating after him. Nose high, tail squatting low.

Maybe the security guy in the counterclockwise Tahoe had called it in. Maybe he had seen Reacher's face and recognized it. Maybe the deputies from the restaurant took turns as the security drivers.

Reacher drove on. He hit the first downtown block.

Ten blocks ahead a second Crown Vic pulled out.

And stopped, dead across the road.

Reacher braked hard and pulled a fast right into the checkerboard of downtown streets. A desperation move. He was the worst guy in the world to win a car chase. He wasn't a great driver.

He hit three four-way stops in succession and turned left, right, left without pausing or thinking. He figured the downtown area was about twelve blocks square, which meant there were about two hundred and eighty-eight distinct lengths of road between opportunities to turn off, which meant that if he kept moving, the chances of direct confrontation were pretty low.

But the chances of ever getting out of the maze were pretty low, too. As long as the second cop was blocking Main Street at its eastern end, then Hope was unavailable as a destination. And presumably the metal plant Tahoes were on duty to the west.

Reacher turned a random left, just to keep moving. The chase car flashed through the intersection, dead ahead, moving right. Reacher turned left on the same street and saw it in his mirror, moving away from him. Now he was heading west. He turned right and headed north to Main Street.

The second Crown Vic was still parked across the road, its light bar flashing red. It was nearly eighteen feet long. One of the last of America's full-sized sedans. A big car, but at one end, it left a gap of about four feet between the front of its hood and the curb.

Vaughan's Chevy was close to six feet wide. Reacher could get past the cop with two wheels up on the curb. But then what? He would be faced with a twelve-mile high-speed chase in a low-speed vehicle. No good.

He turned right again and headed back to the downtown maze. Saw the first Crown Vic flash past again, this time hunting east to west, three blocks away. He turned left and headed away from it.

He saw the police station twice, and the barber shop and the bar and the rooming house and the faded old hotel that he had seen before. He saw a storefront church. Some kind of a strange fringe denomination, something about the end times. The only church in town, Vaughan had said. The town's feudal boss was the preacher.

He drove on, making random turns. He saw the first Crown Vic three more times, twice ahead of him and once behind him in his mirrors. The fourth time he saw it he was paused at a four-way. It came up at the exact same moment and paused in the mouth of the road directly to his right. Reacher and the cop were ten feet apart. The cop was the same guy who had arrested him. He looked over and smiled. Gestured *Go ahead,* like he was yielding.

Reacher was a lousy driver, but he wasn't stupid. No way was he going to let the cop get behind him. He jammed the old Chevy into reverse and backed away. The cop turned, aiming to follow. Reacher waited until the guy was halfway through the maneuver and jammed the stick back into drive and snaked past him, close, flank to flank. Then he hung a left and a right and a left again until he was sure he was clear.

He drove on, endlessly. He passed the church and the old hotel for the third time each. Then the rooming house. Its door opened. From the corner of his eye, he saw a guy step out.

A young guy. Tall and blond and heavy. Blue eyes and a buzz cut and a dark tan.

Reacher stamped on the brake and turned his head. But the guy was gone, moving fast around the corner.

In his mirror, Reacher saw the chase car three blocks west. Turned left, turned right, drove more wide, aimless circles.

He didn't see the young man again. But he saw the cop twice more. The guy was nosing around through distant intersections, like he had all the time in the world. Which he did. The lone road was bottlenecked at both ends of town. He had Reacher trapped, and Reacher knew it.

Time to stand and fight.

REACHER PULLED TO THE CURB outside the restaurant and got out of Vaughan's truck. He took up a position leaning on one of the restaurant's floor-to-ceiling plate-glass windows. He chose to assume that however half-baked the Despair cops might be, they wouldn't risk shooting with bystanders in the line of fire.

Behind him, nine customers were eating late lunches. Collateral damage, waiting to happen.

He unbuttoned his cuffs and folded them up on his forearms. He flexed his hands and rolled his head in small circles to loosen his neck. Then he waited.

Two minutes and forty seconds later the Crown Vic came in from the west. It stopped two intersections away and paused, like the guy was having trouble processing the information right in front of him: The truck, parked. The suspect, just standing there. Then the car leaped forward and came through the four-ways and pulled in tight behind the Chevy. The cop left his engine running and opened his door and slid out into the roadway. He took his Glock off his belt and held it straight out, two-handed.

"Get in the car," he called out.

"Make me."

"I'll shoot."

"You won't."

The guy went blank for a beat and then shifted his focus beyond Reacher's face to the scene inside the restaurant. "Get in the car," he said again.

Reacher said, "I'll take a pass on that."

The cop paused. Then he shuffled back toward the driver's door. He kept his gun tight on Reacher and fumbled one-handed through the car window and grabbed up his microphone. He brought it to his mouth and clicked the button. Said, "Bro, the restaurant, right now." He clicked off again and tossed the microphone back on the seat and put both hands back on the gun.

"Chicken," Reacher called. "A thing like this, you should have been able to handle it on your own."

The cop's lips went tight, and he shuffled forward, tracking with his gun. He stepped up out of the gutter onto the sidewalk.

Now he was five feet away, one cast square of concrete sidewalk.

Reacher kept his back against the glass and moved his right heel against the base of the wall.

The cop stepped closer. The Glock's muzzle was within a foot of Reacher's throat.

Taking a gun from a man ready to use it was not always difficult. Taking one from a man who had already decided not to use it verged on the easy. The cop took his left hand off the gun and braced to grab Reacher by the collar. Reacher slid right, his back hard on the window, and moved inside the cop's aim. He brought his left forearm up and over, fast—one two—and clamped his hand right over the Glock and the cop's hand together. The cop was a big guy with big hands, but Reacher's were bigger. He squeezed hard and forced the gun away in one easy movement. He got it pointing at the ground, and then he looked the cop in the eye and smiled briefly and jerked forward off his planted heel and delivered a colossal head butt direct to the bridge of the cop's nose.

The cop sagged back on rubber legs.

Reacher kept tight hold of the guy's gun hand and kneed him in the groin. The cop went down more or less vertically, but Reacher kept his hand twisted up and back so that the cop's own weight dislocated his elbow as he fell. The guy screamed, and the Glock came free pretty easily after that.

Reacher scrambled around the Crown Vic's hood and hauled the door open. He tossed the Glock inside and slid into the seat, then buckled the seat belt and pulled it snug and tight. Reacher put the transmission in reverse and backed away from the Chevy and spun the wheel and came back level with it, in the wrong lane, facing east. Just waiting.

THE second Crown Vic showed up within thirty seconds. It burst around a distant corner, fishtailed a little, then accelerated down the narrow street toward the restaurant, hard and fast and smooth.

When it was thirty yards away, Reacher stamped on the gas and smashed into it head-on. Sheet metal crumpled, and hoods flew open, and glass burst, and air bags exploded. Reacher was smashed forward against his seat belt. Then the air bag collapsed, and he was tossed back against the headrest. He pulled the Mossberg pump out of its between-the-seats holster and forced the door open against the crumpled fender and climbed out of the car.

The other guy hadn't been wearing his seat belt. He was lying sideways across the front bench with blood coming out of his nose and his ears. Reacher was pretty sure both cars were undrivable but he was no kind of an automotive expert, so he made sure by racking the Mossberg twice and firing two booming shots into the tires. Then he tossed the pump back through the first Crown Vic's window and walked over and climbed into Vaughan's Chevy and backed away from all the wreckage. The waitress and the nine customers were all staring out through the restaurant windows. Two of the customers were fumbling for their cell phones.

Reacher smiled. *Who are you going to call?*

He K-turned the Chevy and headed north for Main Street and made another right and cruised east. He felt the roughness of Despair's road under his tires, but the roar was quieter than before. He was a little deaf from the airbags and the twin Mossberg blasts.

Twelve minutes later he bumped over the expansion joint and cruised into Hope at exactly three o'clock in the afternoon.

REACHER guessed Vaughan had gotten her head on the pillow a little after nine that morning, which was six hours ago. Eight hours' rest would take her to five o'clock. Or maybe she was already up. Some people slept worse in the daytime than the night. He decided to head for the diner. Either she would be there or he could leave her keys with the cashier.

She was there. Alone in the booth they had used before. She had an empty plate and a coffee cup in front of her. She looked tired.

He locked the truck and went in and sat down opposite her.

"I have a confession to make."

"You went to Despair. In my truck. I knew you would."

"I had to."

"Sure."

"There's a military base just inside the town line. Fairly new. Why would that be?"

Vaughan said, "There are military bases all over."

"This was a combat MP unit. Why would they put an MP unit out there?"

Vaughan said, "I don't know why. The Pentagon doesn't explain itself to neighboring police departments."

The waitress brought a cup for Reacher and filled it from a Bunn flask. Vaughan asked, "What does a combat MP unit do exactly?"

Reacher took a sip of coffee and said, "It guards things. Convoys or installations. It maintains security and repels attacks."

"What's to defend in Despair?"

"Exactly," Reacher said.

"And you're saying these MPs made you drive on through?"

"It was safer. They would have checked your plate if I hadn't."

"Did you get through okay?"

"Your truck is fine. Although it's not exactly yours, is it?"

"What do you mean?"

"Who is David Robert Vaughan?"

She looked blank for a second. Then she said, "You looked in the glove compartment. The registration."

"A man with a gun wanted to see it."

"Good reason."

"So who is David Robert?"

Vaughan said, "My husband."

5

REACHER said, "I didn't know you were married." Vaughan turned her attention to her lukewarm coffee and took time to answer.

"That's because I didn't tell you," she said.

They were silent for a long moment.

Then Reacher said, "I think I saw Lucy Anderson's husband."

"In Despair?"

"Coming out of the rooming house."

"That's way off Main Street."

"I was dodging roadblocks," Reacher said. "Long story."

"But?"

"The Despair PD is temporarily understaffed," he explained.

HE LEFT her alone with the truck keys on the table in front of her and walked down to Third Street. He stopped in at a pharmacy and bought shaving gear. Then he bought socks and underwear in an old-fashioned outfitters next to a supermarket. Then he headed up to the hardware store. He picked his way past ladders and wheelbarrows and found a rack of work pants and flannel shirts. He chose dark olive pants and a mud-colored check shirt. Not as cheap as he would have liked, but not outrageous. The clerk folded them up into a brown paper bag, and Reacher carried it back to the motel and shaved and took a long shower and dried off and dressed in the new stuff. He crammed his old clothes into the trash receptacle.

Better than doing laundry.

He stepped out and walked down the row to Lucy Anderson's door. He knocked and waited. A minute later she opened up. She looked just the same. Young and vulnerable. And wary and hostile. She said, "I asked you to leave me alone."

He said, "I'm pretty sure I saw your husband today. In Despair."

Her face softened, just for a second. "Was he okay?"

"He looked fine to me."

"What are you going to do about him?"

"What would you like me to do about him?"

Her face closed up again. "You should leave him alone."

"I am leaving him alone. I told you, I'm not a cop anymore."

"I don't believe you. You're a cop."

The motel clerk stepped out of the office, forty feet to Reacher's left. She was a stout woman of about fifty. She saw Reacher and saw the girl and stopped walking and watched. Reacher figured she was the nosy kind. He stepped back a pace.

Lucy turned her head and saw the clerk's approach, and then she ducked back inside and slammed her door. Reacher turned away but knew he wasn't going to make it in time. The clerk was already within calling distance.

"You leave that girl alone," she said. "If you want to stay here."

"I'm trying to help her."

"You should investigate some real crimes."

Reacher said, "I'm not investigating any crimes. I'm not a cop."

The woman didn't answer.

Reacher asked, "What real crimes?"

"Violations. At the metal plant in Despair."

"I'm not an EPA inspector. I'm not any kind of an inspector."

The woman said, "Then you should ask yourself why that plane flies every night."

REACHER was halfway back to his room when Vaughan's pickup turned in off the street, moving fast. She braked hard and stopped with her radiator grille an inch away from him. She leaned out the window and said, "Get in—now."

Reacher asked, "Do I have a choice?"

"I'm not kidding. I'll use my gun and my cuffs if that's what it takes. Get in the car."

Reacher studied her face through the windshield glass. She was serious about something. And determined. So he climbed in. Vaughan waited until he closed his door behind him and then said, "We got a courtesy call. From Despair. They're coming for you."

"They can't be. They can't even have woken up yet."

"Their deputies are coming. All four of them."

"So I hide in your car? All night?"

"Damn straight."

"You think I need protection?"

"My town needs protection. I don't want fighting in my streets." She pulled a U-turn and headed back the way she had come.

Reacher said, "I could leave town. Temporarily."

"And go where?"

"Despair, obviously. I can't get in trouble there, can I? Their cops are in the hospital, and their deputies will be here all night."

Vaughan stayed quiet for a moment, and then she said, "There's another girl in town today. She came in with the supermarket delivery guy. He drives in from Topeka every few days. He gave her a ride. Like Lucy Anderson, but dark, not blond. She's sitting around staring west now, like she's waiting for word from Despair."

"From a boyfriend or a husband?"

"Possibly."

"Possibly a dead boyfriend or husband, Caucasian, about twenty years old, five eight and one-forty. I should go there."

Vaughan drove past the diner and kept on driving. Motion, just for the sake of it. Small yards, picket fences, mailboxes on poles that had settled to every angle except the truly vertical.

"I should go there," Reacher said again.

"Wait until the deputies get here. You don't want to pass them on the road."

FOR the second time that day, Vaughan gave up her pickup truck and walked home. Reacher drove to a quiet side street and parked in the shadow of a tree and watched the traffic on First Street. Daylight was fading fast. The world was going gray and still.

At six-thirty-two, he saw an old crew-cab pickup truck flash through his field of vision. Moving smartly, from the Despair direction. A driver and three passengers inside. Big men.

Reacher recognized the truck. The Despair deputies.

He paused a beat and started the old Chevy's engine and moved off the curb. He checked his mirror. The old crew-cab was already a hundred yards behind him. The road ahead was empty. He passed the hardware store and hit the gas and forced the old truck up to sixty miles an hour. Five minutes later he thumped over the expansion joint and settled in to a noisy cruise west.

Twelve miles later he turned left into Despair's downtown maze. First port of call was the rooming house. He parked on the curb out front and killed the motor and wound the window down. Heard a single aircraft engine in the far distance, climbing hard. Seven o'clock in the evening.

He climbed out of the truck. The rooming house had a wooden board on the wall next to the door: ROOMS TO RENT. He went up the stone steps and pushed the front door. It was open. Behind it was a hallway with a brown linoleum floor and a steep staircase on the right. Inside, the air smelled of dust and cabbage. There were four interior doors, all dull green, all closed. Two were in back and two were in front, one at the foot of the staircase and the other directly opposite it, across the hallway. In Reacher's experience, the super always chose a ground-floor room at the front to monitor entrances and exits. Tenants had been known to sneak out quietly just before payment of long-overdue rent had been promised.

He opted for the door at the foot of the staircase. Better surveillance potential. He knocked and waited. A long moment later the door opened and revealed a thin man in a white shirt and black tie. The guy was close to seventy years old, and his shirt wasn't clean.

"Help you?" the old guy said.

"I'm looking for a friend of mine," Reacher said. "From California. I heard he was staying here."

No reply from the old man.

"Young guy," Reacher said. "Very big. Tan, with short hair."

"Nobody like that here."

"What about another guy—shorter, about twenty?"

"No guys here at all, big or small."

Reacher said, "Can I see the rooms?"

"You think I'm lying?"

"I'm a suspicious person."

"I should call the police."

"Go right ahead."

The old guy stepped away into the gloom and picked up a phone. Reacher crossed the hallway and tried the opposite door. It was locked. He walked back, and the old guy said, "There was no answer at the police station."

"So it's just you and me," Reacher said. "Better that you lend me your passkey. Save some repair work later, with the door locks."

The old guy bowed to the inevitable. He took a key from his pocket and handed it over. It was a worn brass item with a length of furred string tied through the hole.

THERE were eleven guest rooms. All eleven identical. All empty. Each room had a narrow iron cot against one wall. The cots were like something from an old-fashioned fever hospital or an army barracks. The sheets had been washed so many times they were almost transparent. Near the ends of the beds were pine kitchen tables with two-ring electric burners plugged into outlets with frayed old cords. Basic accommodations, for sure, but they were in good order. The floors were swept shiny. The beds were made tight. A dropped quarter would have bounced two feet off the blankets.

Reacher stood in the doorway of each room before leaving it, smelling the air and listening for echoes of recent hasty departures. He found nothing and sensed nothing, eleven times over. So he headed back downstairs and returned the key and apologized to the old guy. Then he asked, "Is there an ambulance service in town?"

The old guy asked, "Are you injured?"

"Suppose I was. Who would come for me?"

"How bad?"

"Suppose I couldn't walk. Suppose I needed a stretcher."

The old man said, "There's a first-aid station up at the plant. And an infirmary. In case a guy gets hurt on the job. They have a vehicle. They have a stretcher."

"Thanks," Reacher said.

HE DROVE Vaughan's old Chevy on down the street. Paused for a moment in front of the storefront church. It had a painted sign: CONGREGATION OF THE END TIMES. In one window, it had a poster written in the same way that a supermarket would advertise brisket: THE TIME IS AT HAND. A quotation from the book of Revelation. Inside, the place was as dark and gloomy as its exterior messages. Rows of metal chairs, a wood floor, a low stage, a podium. More posters, each one predicting that the clock was ticking. Reacher read them all and then drove on, to the hotel. It was dark when he got there. He remembered the place from earlier sightings as looking dowdy. By night it looked worse, like a prison. Inside it had an empty and unappealing dining room on the left and a deserted bar on the right. Dead ahead was a deserted reception desk.

When searching a hotel, the place to start is the register. Which over the years had become increasingly difficult. With computers, there were all kinds of function keys to hit and passwords to discover. But Despair was behind the times. The register was a large square book bound in old red leather.

According to the handwritten records, the last room had rented seven months previously, to a couple from California, who had stayed two nights. Since then, nothing.

Reacher left the hotel without a single soul having seen him and got back in the Chevy. Next stop was two blocks over.

THE town bar was on the ground floor of yet another dull brick cube. One long, narrow room. Low light. No music. No television. No pool table. No video games. Not exactly happy hour. All the customers were men. They were all tired, all grimy, all sipping beer.

Reacher stepped into the gloom, quietly. Every head turned, and every pair of eyes came to rest on him. *Stranger in the house.*

Reacher stood still and let them take a good look. *A stranger for sure, but not the kind you want to mess with.* Then he sat down on a stool and put his elbows on the bar.

The bartender was a heavy pale man of about forty. He didn't look pleasant. Reacher raised his eyebrows and put a beckoning expression on his face and got no response at all.

A company town.

He swiveled his stool and faced the room. "Listen up, guys," he called. "I'm not a metalworker, and I'm not looking for a job. I'm just a guy passing through, looking for a beer."

Sullen and hostile stares.

Reacher said, "First guy to talk to me, I'll pay his tab."

No response.

"For a week."

No response.

Reacher turned back and looked the bartender in the eye and said, "Sell me a beer or I'll start busting this place up."

The bartender moved. But not toward his draft pumps. He picked up his telephone instead and dialed a long number. Reacher waited. The guy listened to a lot of ring tone and then started to say something but then stopped and put the phone down again.

"Voice mail," he said.

"Nobody home," Reacher said. "So it's just you and me. I'll take a Budweiser, no glass."

The guy glanced beyond Reacher's shoulder, out into the room, to see if any ad hoc coalitions were forming to help him out. They weren't. Reacher was already monitoring the situation in a dull mirror directly in front of him. The bartender decided not to be a hero. He shrugged and pulled a cold bottle out from under the bar. Opened it up and set it down. Foam swelled out of the neck and ran down the side of the bottle. Reacher took a ten from his pocket and folded it lengthways and squared it in front of him.

"I'm looking for a guy," he said. "A young guy. Maybe twenty. Suntan, short hair, as big as me."

"Nobody like that here."

"I saw him this afternoon. In town."

"I can't help you."

"What about another guy? Same age, much smaller. Maybe five eight, one-forty."

"Didn't see him."

Reacher took a long pull on his bottle.

"You ever work up at the plant?"

"Couple of years, way back."

"And then?"

"He moved me here."

"Who did?"

"Mr. Thurman. He owns the plant."

"And this bar, too?"

"He owns everything."

"Is that Mr. Thurman's plane that flies every night?"

"Nobody else here owns a plane."

"Where does he go?"

"I don't ask."

Reacher drank a little more of his beer. The bartender stayed close. Reacher glanced at the mirror. Checked reflections. Nobody was moving. He asked, "What happens to dead people here?"

"What do you mean?"

"You got undertakers in town?"

The bartender shook his head. "Forty miles west. There's a morgue and a funeral home."

Reacher went quiet again, and the bartender said, "So you're just passing through?" A meaningless for-the-sake-of-it conversational gambit, which confirmed what Reacher already knew. Bring it on, he thought. He glanced at the fire exit in back and checked the front door in the mirror. He said, "Yes, I'm just passing through."

I've been working on this beer for six minutes, Reacher thought. Maybe ten more to go. He waited for the bartender to fill the silence, like he had to. Like he had been told to.

The guy said, "A hundred years ago there were only five miles of paved road in the United States."

Reacher said nothing.

The guy said, "Then county roads got built, then state, then the interstates. Towns got passed by. We were on the main road to Denver once. People use I-70 now."

Reacher said, "Hence the closed-down motel."

"Exactly."

"And the general feeling of isolation."

"I guess."

Reacher thought, Eight minutes to go. Unless they're early.

Which they were.

Reacher looked to his right and saw two deputies step in through the fire door. He glanced in a mirror and saw the other two walk in the front.

FOUR deputies heading east to make a surprise arrest would not tip their hand with a courtesy telephone call. Not in the real world. Therefore, the courtesy call was a decoy, designed to flush Reacher westward into safer territory. It was an invitation.

Which Reacher had accepted.

And the bartender had not called the station house. He had dialed too many digits. He had called a deputy's cell and spoken just long enough to let the deputy know who he was and therefore where Reacher was. Whereupon he had turned talkative and friendly to keep Reacher sitting tight. Like he had been told to.

Which is why Reacher had not left the bar.

The big guy who had thrown up the night before was one of the pair that had come in the front. With him was the guy Reacher had smacked outside the restaurant. Neither one looked in great shape. The two who had come in the back looked large and healthy enough, but manageable. Four against one—no cause for concern.

Then the situation changed.

Two guys stood up from the body of the room. They scraped their chairs back and stepped forward. One lined up with the guys in back, and one lined up with the guys in front. They could have been the deputies' brothers. They looked the same and were built the same.

Reacher clamped his jaw, and the beer in his stomach went sour. Six against one. Twelve hundred pounds against two hundred and fifty. Rotten odds.

He took a last sip of Bud and set the bottle back down. Swiveled his stool and faced the room. He saw the other customers sidling backward toward the far wall, hunkering down.

Both sets of three men took long paces forward.

The big guy spoke from six feet inside the front door. He said, "You're in so much trouble you couldn't dig your way out with a steam shovel."

Reacher said, "You talking to me?"

"Damn straight I am."

Reacher stayed on his stool, tensed up and ready, but not visibly. Outwardly he was still calm and relaxed. His brother, Joe, had been two years older, physically very similar, but temperamentally very different. Joe had eased into fights, meeting escalation with escalation, reluctantly, slowly, rationally. Therefore, he had been a frustrating opponent. Therefore, Joe's enemies had turned on Reacher, the younger brother. The first time, confronted with four baiting seven-year-olds, the five-year-old Reacher had felt a jolt of real fear. The fear had sparked wildly and jumped tracks in his brain and emerged as intense aggression. He had exploded into action, and the fight was over. When his four assailants got out of the pediatric ward, they had stayed well away from him, forever. Reacher learned a valuable lesson: Hit early, hit hard. Get your retaliation in first.

He slipped forward off his stool, turned, bent, grasped the stool, spun, and hurled it head-high as hard as he could at the three men at the back of the room. Before it hit, he launched the other way and charged the new guy, next to the guy with the damaged jaw. He led with his elbow and smashed it flat against the bridge of the guy's nose. The guy went down like a tree. Reacher jerked sideways and put the same elbow into the big guy's ear. Then he bounced away from the impact and backed into the guy with the bad jaw and buried the elbow deep in his gut. The guy folded forward. Reacher shoved him away and turned around fast.

The barstool had connected. One of the deputies and the other new guy were sidelined for the moment. They were turned away, bent over, with the stool still rolling noisily at their feet.

The other deputy was untouched. He was launching forward with a wild grimace on his face. Reacher danced two steps and took a left hook on the shoulder and put a straight right into the center of the grimace. The guy stumbled back. Reacher's arms were clamped from behind in a bear hug. The big guy, presumably. Reacher snapped a reverse head butt that made solid contact. Then he accelerated all the way backward and crushed the breath out of the guy against the wall. A mirror smashed, and the arms loosened. Reacher pulled away and met the other deputy in the center of the room. He dodged an incoming right and snapped a right of his own. It rocked the guy enough to open him up for a colossal left to the throat that put him down in a heap.

One guy down for maybe a seven count, four down for maybe an eight count, the big guy still functional.

Time to get serious.

The deputy in the back of the room was rolling around and clutching his throat. Reacher kicked him in the ribs hard enough to break a couple, and then he moved on to the two guys he had hit with the stool. One was crouched down, clutching his forearm. Reacher put the flat of his foot on the guy's backside and drove him headfirst into the wall. The other guy had maybe taken the edge of the seat in the chest. He was having trouble breathing. Reacher kicked his feet out from under him and then kicked him in the head. *So far so good.*

Which puzzled Reacher, deep down. He was winning a six-on-one bar brawl, and he had nothing to show for it except two bruised shoulders. It had gone way better than he could have hoped.

Then it started to go way worse.

The big guy put his hands in his pants pockets and came out with two switchblades. He popped the first blade with a precision click and then paused and popped the second.

Reacher hated knives. Guns can miss. Knives don't miss. If they touch you, they cut you.

The best defense against knives is distance. Reacher clubbed a spectator out of his seat and grabbed the empty chair and held it out in front of him. He jabbed forward like a fencer. The big guy brought his right hand up to shield his face and took the chair on the forearm. Reacher stepped back and jabbed again hard. Got one chair leg in the guy's solar plexus and another in his gut. The guy staggered one short step and then came back hard, arms swinging, the blades hissing through the air.

Reacher backed off. Shoved another spectator out of his seat and threw the empty chair high and hard. The big guy jerked his arms up, and the chair bounced off his elbows. Reacher was ready. He stepped in and jabbed hard and caught the guy below the ribs, two hundred and fifty pounds of weight punched through the blunt end of a chair leg into nothing but soft tissue.

The big guy stopped fighting.

He dropped both knives and clamped his hands low on his stomach and puked on the floor. He fell to his knees and puked again. He braced his spread fingertips and tried to push himself upward. But he didn't make it. He collapsed and curled into a fetal ball.

Game over.

So five for five, plus some kind of a medical explanation for the sixth. The big guy in the fetal position looked very weak and pale. Reacher bent down and checked the pulse in his neck and found it weak and thready. He went through the guy's pockets and found a five-pointed star in the front of the shirt. It was made of pewter, and two lines were engraved in its center: TOWNSHIP OF DESPAIR, POLICE DEPUTY. Reacher put it in his own shirt pocket. He found a bunch of keys and a thin wad of money. He kept the keys and left the cash. Then he looked around until he found the bartender.

"Call the plant," Reacher said. "Get the ambulance down here."

His beer was where he had left it, still upright on its napkin. He drained the last of it and set the bottle back down again and walked out the front door into the night.

6

REACHER thumped back over the expansion joint at nine-thirty in the evening and was outside the diner at nine-thirty-five. He figured Vaughan might swing by there a couple of times during the night. He figured that if he left her truck on the curb, she would see it and be reassured that he was okay. Or at least that her truck was okay.

He went inside to leave her keys at the register and saw Lucy Anderson sitting alone in a booth. She was gazing into space and smiling. The first time he had seen her, he had characterized her as not quite a hundred percent pretty. Now she looked pretty damn good. She looked like a completely different person.

She noticed him and looked over and smiled. It was a curious smile. There was contentment in it, but a little triumph, too. Like she had won a victory at his expense.

He handed Vaughan's keys to the cashier, and the woman asked, "Are you eating with us tonight?" He thought about it. His stomach had settled. The adrenaline had drained away. He was hungry. No sustenance since breakfast, except for some empty calories from the bottle of Bud in the bar. And he had burned plenty of calories in that bar. So he said, "Yes, I guess I'm ready for dinner."

He walked over and slid into Lucy Anderson's booth. She looked across the table at him and smiled the same smile all over again.

"What's changed?" he asked her.

"What do you think?"

"You heard from your husband."

She smiled again. "I sure did," she said.

"He left Despair."

"He sure did. Now you'll never get him."

"I never wanted him."

"Really," she said in the exaggerated and sarcastic way young people used the word. *How big of an idiot do you think I am?*

"What did your husband do?" Reacher asked.

"You already know."

"I'm not a cop, Lucy. I don't know anything."

She smiled again. Happiness, triumph, victory.

Reacher asked, "Where has he gone?"

"Like I'd tell you *that*."

"When are you joining him, wherever he is?"

"In a couple of days."

The waitress came by, and Reacher asked her for coffee and steak. When she had gone away again, he looked across at Lucy Anderson and said, "There are others in the position you were in yesterday. There's a girl in town right now, just waiting."

"I hope there are plenty of us."

"I think maybe she's waiting in vain. I know that a boy died out there a day or two ago."

Lucy Anderson shook her head.

"Not possible," she said. "None of us died. I would have heard."

"Us?"

"People in our position."

The waitress brought his coffee. He took a sip, and then he put the mug down and looked at the girl again and said, "Lucy, I wish you luck, whatever you're doing and wherever you're going."

"That's it? No more questions?"

"I'm just here to eat."

HE ATE alone, because Lucy Anderson left before his steak arrived. He was through by ten-thirty and headed back to the motel. He dropped by the office to pay for another night's stay. He always rented rooms one night at a time, even when he knew he was going to hang out in a place longer. It was a comforting ritual, intended to confirm his absolute freedom to move on. The day clerk was still on duty. The stout woman. The nosy woman. He assembled a collection of small bills and waited for his change.

Then the woman turned away and busied herself with an entry in a book. As he waited, he glanced at the row of hooks behind the clerk's shoulder and saw that four keys were missing. Therefore, four rooms were occupied. His own, Lucy Anderson's, one for the woman with the large underwear, and one for the new girl in town, he guessed. The dark girl, who he hadn't met yet, but who he might meet soon. He suspected that she was going to be in town longer than Lucy Anderson, and he suspected that at the end of her stay, she wasn't going to be skipping away with a smile on her face.

He put his change in his pocket, went back to his room, and showered, but he was too restless to sleep. So as soon as the stink of the bar fight was off him, he dressed again and went out and walked. On a whim, he stopped at a phone booth and pulled the directory and looked up David Robert Vaughan. He was right there in the book. Vaughan, D. R., with an address on Fifth Street.

Two blocks south.

Perhaps he should take a look.

FIFTH Street was a nice place to live, probably. Trees, yards, picket fences, mailboxes, small neat houses resting quietly in the moonlight. Vaughan's house had a mailbox out front, mounted on a wooden post. The box had VAUGHAN written on both sides with stick-on italic letters. They had been carefully applied and were perfectly aligned. Rare, in Reacher's experience. To get seven letters each side level spoke of meticulous planning. The house and the yard had been maintained to a high standard, too. Reacher was no expert, but he could tell the difference between care and neglect.

The house itself was a low one-story ranch, maybe fifty years old. The siding and the roof tiles were not new, but they had been replaced within living memory and had weathered into pleasant maturity. Some drapes were halfway open, and some were all the way open. No light inside except for a tiny green glow in one window. Probably the kitchen, probably a microwave clock.

Once upon a time, Reacher had made his living storming darkened buildings, and more than once it had been a matter of life or death to decide whether they were occupied or not. He had developed a sense, and his sense was that Vaughan's house was empty.

So where was David Robert?

Maybe they both worked nights. Some couples chose to coordinate their schedules that way. Maybe David Robert was a nurse or a doctor or worked night construction on the interstates. Or maybe he was a long-haul trucker or an actor or a musician and was on the road for lengthy spells.

Reacher was no insomniac, but he didn't feel like sleep. Too early. Too many questions. He was no social animal, either, but right then he wanted to see people, and he figured the diner was the only place he was going to find any.

He found three. The waitress, a middle-aged guy alone in a booth with a spread of tractor catalogs in front of him, and a frightened Hispanic girl alone in a booth with nothing.

Dark, not blond, Vaughan had said.

She was tiny, eighteen or nineteen years old. Mid-brown skin and jet-black hair framed a face that had a high forehead and enormous eyes. The eyes were brown and looked like twin pools of terror and tragedy. Reacher guessed she had a pretty smile, but she certainly hadn't used it for weeks. She was wearing a blue San Diego Padres warm-up jacket with a blue T-shirt under it. There was nothing on the table in front of her.

Reacher stepped to the far side of the register, where the waitress was standing. "That girl," he whispered. "Didn't she order?"

"She has no money."

"Ask her what she wants. I'll pay for it." He moved to a different booth, where he could watch the girl without being obvious. He saw the waitress approach her, saw incomprehension on the girl's face, then doubt, then refusal. The waitress stepped to Reacher's booth and whispered, "She says she can't possibly accept."

Reacher said, "Go back and tell her there are no strings attached. I'm not hitting on her. Tell her I've been broke and hungry, too."

The waitress went back. This time the girl relented. She pointed to a couple of items on the menu. Then she turned a little in her seat and inclined her head in a courteous little nod, full of dignity, and turned back and went still again.

The waitress came straight back to Reacher, and he asked for coffee. The waitress whispered, "Her check is going to be nine-fifty. Yours will be a dollar and a half." Reacher peeled a ten and three ones off the roll in his pocket and slid them across the table. The waitress picked them up and thanked him and asked, "So when were you broke and hungry?"

"Never," Reacher said.

"You made that up to make her feel better?"

"Sometimes people need convincing."

"You're a nice guy," the waitress said.

From a distance, Reacher watched the Hispanic girl eat a tuna melt and drink a chocolate shake. Good choices, nutritionally. Protein, fats, carbs, some sugar. If she ate like that every day, she would weigh two hundred pounds, but in dire need, it was wise to load up.

Reacher had seen plenty of people doing what the Hispanic girl was doing, in cafés and diners near bus depots and railroad stations. She was staying warm, saving energy, passing time. She was enduring. He watched her and figured she was a lot closer to Zeno's ideal than he was. *The unquestioning acceptance of destinies.*

Then she moved. She shifted sideways on her vinyl bench and stood up all in one smooth, delicate motion. She faced the door, and then she came to some kind of a decision and stepped toward Reacher's booth. She stood off about a yard and said, "Thank you for my dinner." Her voice was small and delicate, lightly accented.

Reacher asked, "You okay for breakfast tomorrow?"

She was still for a moment while she fought her pride, and then she shook her head.

"You okay at the motel?"

"That's why. I paid for three nights. It took all my money."

Reacher thought, Ten bucks a meal is thirty bucks a day, three days makes ninety, plus ten for contingencies or phone calls makes a hundred. He peeled five ATM-fresh twenties off his roll and fanned them on the table.

The girl said, "I can't take your money. I couldn't pay it back."

"Pay it forward instead. You know what that means?"

"I'm not sure."

"Years from now you'll be in a diner somewhere and you'll see someone who needs a break. So you'll help them out."

The girl nodded. "I could do that." She stepped closer and picked up the bills. "Thank you," she said.

"Don't thank me. Thank whoever helped me way back."

"Have you ever been to Despair?"

"Four times in the last two days."

"Did you see anyone there?"

"I saw lots of people."

She moved closer still and put her slim hips against the end of his table. She hoisted a cheap vinyl purse and rooted around in it for a moment and came out with an envelope. It was stiff and nearly square. She opened the flap and pulled out a photograph.

"Did you see this man?" she asked.

It was a standard six-by-four print. Glossy paper, no border.

In the background was an expanse of grass, and in the foreground was a thin guy of about nineteen or twenty wearing a green T-shirt.

Not thin, exactly. Lean and wiry.

He looked to be about five eight.

He looked to weigh about a hundred and forty pounds.

He was Hispanic, but as much Mayan or Aztec as Spanish. He had shiny black hair and prominent cheekbones.

He hadn't shaved.

His chin and his upper lip were rough with black stubble.

His cheeks and his throat, not so much.

Young. Not much more than a boy.

The girl asked, "Did you see him?"

Reacher asked, "What's your name?"

"*My* name? Maria."

"What's his name?"

"Raphael Ramirez."

"Is he your boyfriend?"

"Yes. Did you see him?"

Reacher looked again at Raphael Ramirez.

"No," he said, "I didn't see him."

THE girl left the diner. Reacher watched her go, and then he roused the waitress from the book she was reading and had her bring him more coffee.

"You'll never sleep," she warned.

"How often does Officer Vaughan swing by during the night?" he asked.

The waitress smiled. "At least once," she said. She took the flask away and headed back to her book and left him with a steaming mug. He dipped his head and inhaled the smell. When he looked up again, he saw Vaughan's cruiser glide by outside. She slowed, as if she was noting that her truck was back. But she didn't stop.

Reacher drank three mugs of coffee. He read a copy of the previous morning's newspaper all the way through and then jammed himself into the corner of his booth and dozed upright for an hour. He left the diner at one o'clock in the morning.

You'll never sleep, the waitress had told him.

But not because of the coffee.

He got up and walked straight to the register and took Vaughan's truck keys off the counter. The waitress looked up but didn't speak.

Five minutes later Reacher thumped over the line and was back in Despair.

MAIN Street was deserted and silent. No cars, nobody on the sidewalks. The police station was dark. The rooming house was dark. The bar was closed up and shuttered. The hotel was just a blank façade, with a closed street door and a dozen dark windows. The church was empty and silent.

Reacher headed on, west. The metal plant was shut down and dark. The wall around it glowed ghostly white in the moonlight. The personnel gate was closed. The acres of parking were deserted. Reacher followed the wall and steered the truck left and right until its weak low beams picked up the Tahoes' tracks. He followed their giant figure eight all the way around the plant and the residential compound. He stopped where the figure eights' two loops met, in the throat between the plant's metal wall and the residential compound's fieldstone wall. He shut off his lights and shut down the engine and rolled down the windows and waited.

HE HEARD the plane at five past two in the morning. A single-engine, far in the distance, feathering and blipping. He craned his neck and saw a light in the sky, way to the south. A small plane, on approach, buffeted by nighttime thermals. He saw it jump left, correct right, line up with the lights. It was coming in from Reacher's left. When it was three hundred yards out, he saw that it was a smallish low-wing monoplane. When it was a hundred yards out, he identified it as a Piper, probably some kind of a Cherokee.

It came in low, left-to-right across his windshield, in a high-speed rush of light and air and sound. It cleared the fieldstone wall by six feet and dropped out of sight. Reacher imagined the plane taxiing like a fat self-important insect, bumping sharply over rough ground. Then he heard it shut down, and silence flooded in his windows, even more intense than before.

He saw and heard nothing more.

He started the truck and drove away on the blind side, with the bulk of the plant between him and the house. He bumped through the acres of empty parking, skirted the short end of the plant, and joined the truck route. Four miles later he figured he'd gone far enough to be safe. He pulled to the shoulder and stopped. He turned his headlights off and got comfortable in his seat.

AT SIX o'clock in the morning, he was back at the metal plant.

The parking lot was filling up fast. Headlights were streaming west out of town, dipping, turning, raking the rough ground, stopping, clicking off. The start of the workday.

Reacher parked neatly between a sagging Chrysler sedan and a battered Ford pickup. He slid out and locked up and put the keys in his pocket and joined a crowd of men shuffling their way toward the personnel gate. An uneasy feeling. Like entering a baseball stadium wearing the colors of the visiting team.

The gate was a double section of the metal wall, folded back on hinges. The path through it was beaten dusty by a million footsteps. There was no jostling, no impatience. The men needed to clock in, but clearly none of them wanted to.

The line shuffled slowly forward, a yard, two, three.

The guy in front of Reacher stepped through the gate.

Reacher stepped through the gate.

Immediately inside there were more metal walls, head-high, like cattle chutes, dividing the crowd left and right. The right-hand chute led to a holding pen where Reacher guessed the part-time workers would wait for the call. It was already a quarter full with men standing quiet. The guys going left didn't look at them.

Reacher went left.

The left-hand chute carried the line of shuffling men past an old-fashioned time clock centered in a giant array of punch cards. Each man pulled his card and offered it up to the machine and then put the card back again. The rhythm was slow and relentless.

Reacher walked straight past the machine. He followed the guy in front for thirty feet and then stepped out into the northeast corner of the arena. It was staggeringly huge. The total enclosed area must have been three hundred acres. Three *hundred* football fields.

Trucks and cranes were moving. Some of the cranes were bigger than anything Reacher had seen in a dockyard. Some of the trucks were as big as earth-moving machines. There were gigantic crushers set on enormous concrete plinths. There were crucibles as big as sailboats and retorts as big as houses. There were piles of wrecked cars ten stories high. The ground was soaked with oil and rainbow puddles of diesel and littered with curled metal swarf. Sharp chemical smells drifted everywhere. Roaring and hammering rolled outward in waves, beat against the metal perimeter, and bounced back in again. Bright flames danced behind open furnace doors.

Like a vision of hell.

Some guys seemed to be heading for preassigned jobs, and others were milling in groups as if waiting for direction. Reacher skirted around behind them and followed the north wall, tiny and insignificant in the chaos. Way ahead of him the vehicle gate was opening. Five semi trailers were waiting to move out. On the road, they would look huge and lumbering. Inside the plant, they looked like toys. The two security Tahoes were parked side by side, tiny white dots in the vastness. Next to them was a stack of forty-foot shipping containers. They were piled five high. Each one looked tiny.

South of the vehicle gate was a long line of prefabricated metal offices. They were jacked up on short legs to make them level. At the left-hand end of the line, two offices were painted white and had red crosses on their doors. The first-aid station. Next to it a white vehicle was parked. The ambulance. Next to the ambulance was a long line of fuel and chemical tanks. Beyond them a sinister platoon of men in black welding masks used cutting torches on a pile of twisted scrap. Blue flames threw hideous shadows. Reacher hugged the north wall and kept on moving. A quarter of the way along the wall, his path was blocked by a giant pyramid of old oil drums. They were painted faded red and stacked ten high, stepped like a staircase. Reacher paused and glanced around and levered himself up to the base of the tier. He climbed halfway up the stack and then turned to get an overview of the whole place.

He hadn't seen the whole place. There was more.

What looked like the south boundary was in fact an interior partition. Same height as the perimeter walls, same construction, with the sheer face and the horizontal cylinder. But it was only an internal division, with a closed gate. Beyond it the outer perimeter enclosed at least another hundred acres. Another hundred football fields. Inside the gate, there were heavy cranes and high stacks of shipping containers piled in chevron shapes. They were placed carefully to block a direct view of ground-level activity from any particular direction.

The internal gate had some kind of a control point in front of it. Reacher could make out two tiny figures stumping around in small circles, bored, their hands in their pockets. He watched them for a minute and then lifted his gaze again beyond the partition. Cranes and screens. Distant sparks. Some kind of activity. Other than that, nothing to see. He waited another minute and watched the plant's internal traffic. Plenty of things were moving, but nothing was heading for the internal gate. It was going to stay closed.

He turned back and got his balance and climbed down the oil-drum staircase. Stepped off to the rough ground. Reacher turned slowly, and then he saw the two men.

One was big, and the other was a giant. The big guy was carrying a two-way radio, and the giant was carrying a two-headed wrench as long as a baseball bat. The guy was easily six six and three hundred and fifty pounds.

The guy with the radio asked, "Who the hell are you?"

Reacher said, "You first. Who are you?"

"I'm the plant foreman. Now, who are you?"

Reacher pulled the pewter star from his pocket and said, "I'm with the PD. The new deputy. I'm familiarizing myself with the community."

"We didn't hear about any new deputies."

"It was sudden."

The guy raised his radio to his face and clicked a button and spoke low and fast. Names, codes, commands. Reacher didn't understand them, but he guessed the general drift. He glanced west and saw the Tahoes turning and getting set to head over.

The foreman said, "Let's go visit the security office."

Reacher stood still.

The foreman said, "A new deputy should want to visit the security office. Establish liaison. If that's what you really are."

Reacher didn't move. He glanced west again and saw the Tahoes halfway through their half mile of approach. He glanced south and saw knots of men walking his way. The crew in the welders' masks was among them. Plenty of others were coming in from other directions, maybe two hundred men. They were close enough that Reacher could see tools in their hands. Hammers, pry bars, cutting torches, foot-long cold chisels.

Not good.

He said, "So let's go. I can give you five minutes."

The foreman said, "You'll give us whatever we want." He waved to the nearer Tahoe, and it turned in close. Reacher heard oily stones and curly fragments of metal crushing under its tires. The giant opened its rear door, and Reacher climbed up into the backseat. The giant climbed in after him and crowded him against the far door panel. The foreman climbed in the front next to the driver and slammed his door, and the vehicle took off, headed for the line of office buildings south of the vehicle gate. It drove through the middle of the approaching crowd, slowly, and Reacher saw faces staring in at him. Gray skin smeared with grease, bad teeth, white eyes wide with fascination.

The Tahoe stopped directly outside the security office at the north end of the array, closest to the vehicle gate. Next to it was a tangled pile of webbing straps, presumably once used to tie down junk on flatbed trailers. Reacher spilled out of the car ahead of the giant and found himself at the bottom of a short set of wooden steps that led up to the office door. He pushed through the door and found himself inside a plain metal prefabricated box that had probably been designed for use on construction sites. Inside, there was carpet, leather armchairs, and a mahogany desk. On the corner of the desk was a Bible.

Behind the desk was a man Reacher assumed was Mr. Thurman. He was wearing a three-piece suit made of wool. He looked to be close to seventy years old. He looked pink and plump and prosperous. He had white hair, worn moderately long and combed and teased into waves. He had a big patient smile on his face. He could have been a game-show host or a televangelist.

The giant waited for a nod, then left. Reacher sat in a leather armchair and said, "I'm Jack Reacher. You've got five minutes."

The guy behind the desk said, "I'm Jerry Thurman. I'm very pleased to meet you."

Reacher said, "Now you've got four minutes, fifty-six seconds."

"Actually, sir, I've got as long as it takes." Thurman's voice was soft and mellifluous. His cheeks quivered as he spoke. Too much fat, not enough muscle tone. "You've been making trouble in my town, and now you're trespassing on my business premises."

"Your fault," Reacher said. "If you hadn't sent those goons to the restaurant, I would have eaten a quick lunch and moved on. No reason to stay. You're not exactly running the Magic Kingdom here."

"I don't aim to. This is an industrial enterprise."

"So I noticed."

"But you knew that days ago. I'm sure the people in Hope were quick to tell you all about us. Why poke around?"

"I'm an inquisitive person."

"Evidently," Thurman said. "Which raised our suspicions a little. We have proprietary processes here, methodologies of our own invention, which might be called industrial secrets."

"I'm not interested in metal recycling."

"We know that now," he said. "We made inquiries. You are exactly what you claim to be. A passerby. A nobody who used to be in the army ten years ago."

"That's me."

"But you're a very persistent nobody. And you took a badge from a deputy in a fight. So we ask ourselves, Why are you so keen to know what happens here?"

"And I ask myself, Why are you so keen to hide it?"

Thurman shook his great white head.

"We're not hiding anything," he said. "And I'll prove it to you. I'm going to give you a tour of the plant. I'll be your personal guide, and you can ask me anything."

THEY went in Thurman's personal vehicle, which was a Chevy Tahoe the same style and vintage as the security vehicles, but painted black, not white. The keys were already in the ignition. Thurman drove himself, and Reacher sat next to him in the front. They headed away from the vehicle gate, moving slow. Thurman described the various office functions, which in order of appearance were operations management, and invoicing, and purchasing. Then he pointed out the first-aid station and described its facilities and capabilities and made a mildly pointed comment about the people Reacher had put in there. Next they moved on to the line of storage tanks, and he described their contents, which were gasoline and diesel and a liquid chemical called trichloroethylene, which was an essential metal degreaser, and oxygen and acetylene for the torches.

Reacher was bored rigid after sixty seconds.

He tuned Thurman out and looked at things for himself. He got the general idea. Old stuff was broken up and melted down, and ingots were sold to factories, where new stuff was made, and eventually the new stuff became old stuff and showed up again.

Not rocket science.

Close to a mile later they arrived at the internal partition. Beyond the wall, no more sparks were flying and no more smoke was rising. Activity seemed to have been abandoned for the day. He asked, "What happens back there?"

Thurman said, "That's our junkyard. Stuff that's too far gone to work with goes in there. But our processes have gotten very developed. Not much defeats us anymore."

"Are you a chemist or a metallurgist or what?"

Thurman said, "I'm a born-again-Christian American and a businessman, in that order of importance. But I hire the best talent I can find. Our research and development is excellent."

Reacher nodded and said nothing.

Thurman asked, "Are you born again?"

Reacher said, "Once was enough for me."

"I'm serious. You should think about it."

"My father used to say, Why be born again when you can just grow up?"

"Is he no longer with us?"

"He's in a hole in the ground in Arlington Cemetery."

"Another veteran?"

"A marine."

"Thank you for his service."

"Don't thank me. I had nothing to do with it."

Thurman said, "You should think about getting your life in order, you know, before it's too late. The book of Revelation says, 'The time is at hand.' There are signs. And the possibility of precipitating events." He said it primly and smugly and with a degree of certainty, as if he had regular access to privileged insider information.

Reacher said nothing in reply.

They arrived at the mouth of the cattle chute leading to the personnel gate. He stopped the truck and jiggled the stick into park and sat back in his seat.

"Seen enough?" he asked.

"More than enough," Reacher said.

"Then I'll bid you goodbye," Thurman said. "I imagine our paths won't cross again." He offered his hand and Reacher shook it. It felt soft and warm and boneless, like a child's balloon filled with water. Then Reacher opened his door and slid out and walked through the chute and back to the acres of parking.

Every window in Vaughan's truck was smashed.

7

REACHER stood for a long moment and ran through his options and then unlocked the truck and swept pebbles of broken glass off the seats and the dash. He raked them out of the driver's footwell. He didn't want the brake pedal to jam halfway through its travel. Or the gas pedal. The truck was slow enough already.

The drive back to Hope was like riding a motorcycle without eye protection. Reacher's face was numb and his eyes were watering by the end of the trip. He passed the diner a little before nine o'clock in the morning. Vaughan's cruiser wasn't there. He drove south and turned left on Fifth. Way ahead of him, he could make out Vaughan's cruiser parked at the curb. He pulled level with the mailbox with the perfectly aligned letters. Then he parked and slid out. He hooked her key ring on his finger and tapped her doorbell briefly, just once. If she was awake, she would hear it. If she was asleep, it wouldn't disturb her.

She was awake.

The door opened, and she looked out of the gloom straight at him. Her hair was wet from the shower and combed back. She was wearing an oversized white T-shirt. Possibly nothing else. She looked younger and smaller than before.

She said, "How did you find me?"

He said, "Phone book."

She saw the truck keys on his finger. He said, "I have a confession to make. Someone broke all the windows."

She pushed past him to face the driveway and studied the damage and said, "Damn." Then it seemed to dawn on her that she was out in the yard in her nightwear, and she pushed back inside.

"Who?" she asked.

"One of a thousand suspects. I stopped by the metal plant."

"You're an idiot."

"I know. I'm sorry. I'll pay for the glass." He slipped the keys off his finger and held them out.

She didn't take them. Instead, she said, "You better come in."

THE kitchen seemed to be the heart of the home. The dishwasher was running, and the sink was empty and the counters were tidy, but there was enough disarray to make the room feel lived in. And there were what Reacher's mother had called "touches." Dried flowers, antique spoons. Reacher's mother had said such things gave a room personality. Vaughan's kitchen had personality.

Her personality, he guessed.

It seemed to him that one mind had chosen everything and one pair of hands had done everything. There was no evidence of compromise or dueling tastes. In fact, there was no evidence of a second person in the house. Not a trace. From his position at the sink Reacher could see into the living room through an arch that was really just a doorway with the door taken out. There was a single armchair in there, and a TV set, and a bunch of moving boxes still taped shut.

Vaughan said, "Want coffee?"

"Always."

Vaughan rinsed her coffeepot and filled her machine with water. The machine was a big steel thing with CUISINART embossed on it in large letters. It looked reliable. She spooned coffee into a gold basket and hit a switch. She said, "Last night the deputies from Despair headed home after an hour."

"They found me in the bar," Reacher said. "They flushed me west with the phone call and then came after me. It was a trap."

"And you fell for it."

"*They* fell for it. I knew what they were doing. I used to deal with worse folks than you'll ever find in Despair."

"What happened to the deputies?"

"They joined their full-time buddies in the infirmary."

"All four of them?"

"All six of them. They added some on-site moral support."

"You're a one-man crime wave."

"That's the point," Reacher said. "They came at me six against one, and I walked away with bruises. They're all weak and sick."

"So what's that about?"

"The clerk at my motel figures they're breaking environmental laws. Maybe there's all kinds of poisons and pollution out there."

"Is that what they're hiding?"

"Possibly," Reacher said. "But it's kind of odd that the victims would help to hide the problem."

"People worry about their jobs," Vaughan said. "Especially in a company town. They don't have any alternatives." She opened a cabinet and took out a mug. It was white, perfectly cylindrical, four inches high, and two and a half inches wide. It was made of fine bone china. She glanced at the living room but placed the mug on the kitchen table instead. Reacher glanced at the boxes and the lone armchair in the living room and said, "Just moved in?"

"A year and a half ago," Vaughan said. "I'm slow unpacking."

"From where?"

"Third Street. We had a little cottage with an upstairs, but we decided we wanted a ranch."

"We?"

"David and I."

Reacher asked, "So where is he?"

"He's not here right now."

"What does he do?"

"Not so much anymore." She sat in one of the chairs without the mug in front of it and tugged the hem of her T-shirt down. Her hair was drying and going wavy again. She was naked under the shirt, and confident about it. Reacher was sure of that. She was looking straight at him, like she knew he knew.

He sat down opposite her.

She asked, "What else?"

"A quarter of the plant is screened off. There's a secret area. I think Thurman's got a Pentagon contract to recycle military scrap, classified stuff. Hence, the MP unit down the road."

"So that's all? Legitimate government business?"

"No," Reacher said, "that's not all." He took the first sip of his coffee. It was perfect. Hot, strong, smooth, and a great mug. "There are at least two other things going on."

"Two?"

He nodded. "There are at least two other factions in play, separate and probably unaware of each other. Like this morning, Thurman had me checked out. He saw that my paper trail went cold ten years ago, and therefore I was no obvious danger to him. So he played nice and gave me a guided tour. But meanwhile, someone was busting your windows. The left hand doesn't know what the right is doing."

"So what are the two other factions?"

"I have no idea. But Lucy Anderson's husband and the dead guy are involved somehow. When was the last time any normal person entered Despair and stayed as long as he wanted? To your certain knowledge?"

"I don't know," Vaughan said.

"There's an entry in the hotel register from seven months ago."

"That sounds about right."

"And I met the new girl last night," Reacher said. "Sweet kid. Her name is Maria. I'm pretty sure the dead guy was her boyfriend. She showed me his picture. His name was Raphael Ramirez."

"Did you tell her?"

"No. She asked if I'd seen him. Truth is, I didn't. It was dark."

"So she's still swinging in the wind."

"I think she knows, deep down."

"What happened to the body?"

"I don't think it ever left Despair. The metal plant has furnaces that could vaporize a corpse in five minutes flat."

Vaughan got up and poured herself a glass of water from a bottle in the refrigerator. She stood with her hips against the counter and stared out the window. The cotton of her T-shirt was slightly translucent. The light was behind her, and she looked spectacular.

She asked, "What else did Maria say?"

Reacher said, "Nothing. The wives and the girlfriends aren't going to tell us anything. Their husbands and their boyfriends aren't just hiding out in Despair. They're aiming to get help there. They're aiming to ride some kind of an underground railroad for fugitives. The women want to keep it secret."

"What kind of fugitives?"

"I don't know what kind. But the Anderson guy was the right kind, and Raphael Ramirez was the wrong kind."

Vaughan took Reacher's mug from him and refilled it from the machine. Then she refilled her glass from the refrigerator and sat down. She took her free hand out of her lap and laid it on the table, her fingers spread. Reacher wondered whether it was a gesture, conscious or subconscious. An appeal for a connection.

No wedding band. *He's not here right now.*

He put his own free hand on the table.

She asked, "How do we know they were fugitives at all? Maybe they were undercover environmental activists, checking on the pollution. That worries me, if they're using poisons over there. We share the same water table."

"Thurman mentioned something called trichloroethylene. I don't know whether it's dangerous or not."

"I'm going to check it out."

"But the Anderson guy wasn't an environmental activist. He was a guest. They gave him a place to stay and protection."

"And Ramirez was left to die."

"So why help one and keep the other out?"

"Because Ramirez was different in some way," she said. "More dangerous to them."

"Maybe I'm wrong," Reacher said. "Maybe they didn't try to keep him out. Maybe they never even knew he was there."

Vaughan took her hand off the table.

"We need to know exactly who he was," she said. "We need to talk to Maria."

"She won't tell us anything."

"We can try. We'll find her in the diner. Meet me there later."

"Later than what?"

"We both need to sleep."

Reacher said, "May I ask you a personal question?"

"Go ahead."

"Is your husband in prison?"

Vaughan paused a beat and then smiled, a little surprised, a little sad. "No," she said, "he isn't."

THE coffee didn't keep Reacher awake at all. He took a long, hot shower and climbed into bed. He was asleep within a minute.

He got out of bed at four o'clock and took another long, hot shower. He knew he was out of step with the Western world in terms of how often he changed his clothes, but he tried to compensate by keeping his body scrupulously clean. The motel soap came in a small, thin paper-wrapped morsel, and he used the whole bar. He rinsed and stood under the water for a moment more and then shut it off and heard someone knocking at his door. He wrapped a towel around his waist and padded across the room and opened up.

Vaughan.

She was in uniform. Her HPD cruiser was parked neatly behind her. She was staring in at him, openly curious. Not an unusual reaction. He was a spectacular mesomorph, built of nothing except large quantities of bone and sinew and muscle. But with his shirt off, most people saw only his scars. He had a dozen minor nicks and cuts, plus a dimpled .38 bullet hole in the left center of his chest, and a wicked spiderweb of white lacerations on the right side of his abdomen, crisscrossed by seventy clumsy stitches done quick and dirty in a mobile army surgical hospital. Souvenirs of childhood mayhem, of a psychopath with a small revolver, and shrapnel from a bomb blast. All survivable. He had been a lucky man, and his luck was written all over his body.

Vaughan's gaze traveled upward to his face.

"Bad news," she said. "I went to the library. Trichloroethylene is called TCE for short. It causes cancer. Breast cancer, prostate cancer, all kinds of cancers. Plus heart disease, liver disease, kidney disease. The EPA says a concentration of five parts per billion is acceptable. Some places have been measured twenty or thirty times worse than that. There was a case in Tennessee."

"That's a long way from here."

"This is serious, Reacher. We drink the groundwater."

She went quiet.

He said, "What else?"

"Maria is missing. She's not here in the motel, she's not in the diner, she's not in the library, and there isn't anywhere else."

THE clerk in the motel office had no useful information. Maria had left her room before seven o'clock that morning on foot. She hadn't come back. That was all she knew. Vaughan asked her to open Maria's room. The clerk handed over her passkey. No fuss about warrants or due process. Small towns, Reacher thought.

Maria's room was identical to Reacher's, with only very slightly more stuff in it. A spare pair of jeans hung in the closet. Above them on the shelf were a spare pair of cotton underpants, one bra, and one clean cotton T-shirt, all folded together. On the floor of the closet was an empty blue suitcase, small, sad, battered.

On the shelf next to the bathroom sink was a vinyl bag. Its contents were laid out next to it. Soaps, shampoos, lotions.

"Day trip," Vaughan said. "She's expecting to return."

"Obviously," Reacher said. "She paid for three nights."

"She went to Despair. To look for Ramirez."

"That would be my guess."

"But how? There's no bus. There's never any traffic."

"Maybe there was," Reacher said. "I came in with an old guy in a car. He was visiting family, and then he was moving on to Denver. And if he was dumb enough to give me a ride, he'd have given Maria a ride for sure."

"If he happened to leave this morning."

"Let's find out."

They returned the passkey and got into Vaughan's cruiser. She fired it up, and they headed west to the hardware store. The sidewalk was piled with ladders, buckets, and wheelbarrows. The owner confirmed that he had been building the display early that morning. He had seen a small dark girl in a blue warm-up jacket. She had been standing on the far sidewalk at the edge of town, half-turned, looking east but clearly aiming to head west. A classic hitchhiker's pose. Then later the store owner had seen a large bottle-green car heading west.

"A Grand Marquis," Reacher said. "Same car. Same guy."

The owner had not seen the car stop, but the inference was clear.

"Is she in danger?" Vaughan asked.

"I don't know," Reacher said. "But she's probably not having the best day of her life."

"We can't go to Despair in this car."

"So what else have you got?"

"Just the truck."

"It's breezy without the windshield."

"Too late. I already had it towed. It's being fixed."

Reacher said, "Maria's domiciled in Hope. Now she's missing. The HPD should be entitled to go there and make inquiries."

"Domiciled? With one change of underwear?"

"What's the worst thing that can happen?"

Vaughan started to say something, then shook her head and sighed.

THEY drove eleven miles into the setting sun with nothing to show for it except eyestrain. The twelfth mile was different. Way ahead in the glare, Reacher saw what looked like a shadow, like a lone cloud blocking the sun and casting a random shape on the ground. He craned his neck and looked. The sky was clear.

Vaughan drove on.

Three-quarters of a mile out the shape grew. The sun blazed behind it and winked around its edges. It looked like a low, wide pile of something dark. The pile looked to be fifty feet wide, maybe twenty deep, maybe six high.

From a half-mile out, it looked to be moving.

From a quarter-mile out, it was identifiable.

It was a crowd of people.

Vaughan slowed. The crowd was two or three hundred strong. Men, women, and children. They were formed up in a rough triangle, facing east. Maybe six people at the front. Behind the six, twenty more. Behind the twenty, sixty more. Behind the sixty, a vast milling pool of people. The whole width of the road was blocked.

Vaughan stopped fifty yards out.

The crowd compressed. People pushed inward. They made a human wedge. A solid mass, but they didn't link arms.

They didn't link arms, because they had weapons in their hands.

Baseball bats, pool cues, axe handles, broom handles, split firewood, carpenters' hammers. Two or three hundred people, moving as one. They were rocking in place from foot to foot and jabbing their weapons up and down in the air. And they were chanting.

Reacher dropped his window an inch and heard the words: *Out! Out! Out!*

Vaughan was pale. "Unbelievable," she said. "What are we going to do?"

Reacher watched and said, "Drive on and see what happens."

"Are you serious?"

"Try it."

Vaughan took her foot off the brake, and the car crept forward. The crowd surged forward to meet it.

Vaughan stopped again, forty yards out.

They were ordinary people dressed in work shirts and faded sundresses and jean jackets, but collectively they looked primitive. Like a weird Stone Age tribe.

Reacher said, "Can you get around them?"

She shook her head. "The Crown Vic is no good on the scrub. We'd bog down and they'd be all over us."

The chanting grew louder: *Out! Out! Out!*

They were close enough now to see clearly. Faces contorted with hate and rage and fear and anger.

Reacher didn't care for crowds. He had been in Somalia and Bosnia and had seen what angry organized crowds could do.

He said quietly, "Put the car in reverse."

Vaughan moved the lever.

"Back up a little."

Vaughan backed up.

The crowd had tracked the move.

Reacher stared ahead through the windshield. He felt a change coming. He sensed it.

Vaughan asked, "What do we do?"

Reacher didn't have time to answer. The change came. The chanting stopped. There was silence for a second. Then the six men at the front of the crowd raised their weapons high, with clamped fists and straight arms. They screamed a command.

And charged.

They bolted forward, weapons still high, screaming. The crowd streamed after them. Two or three hundred people, full speed, yelling, stampeding, eyes wide, mouths open. They filled the windshield, a screaming mass of humanity coming straight at them.

They got within five feet. Then Vaughan stamped on the gas. The car shot backward, the engine screaming, the low gear whining loud, the rear tires howling and making smoke. She got up to thirty miles an hour going backward, and then she flung the car into an emergency one-eighty and smashed the shifter into drive. She accelerated east and didn't stop for miles. She took most of the last mile to coast to a stop. They were still in Despair's territory, but all was quiet behind them. Vaughan slumped in her seat. "We need the state police," she said. "We've got mob rule back there and a missing woman. And whatever exactly Ramirez was to those people, we can't assume they're going to treat his girlfriend kindly."

"We don't know for sure she's there," Reacher said.

"So what do we do?"

"We verify. We call Denver."

"What's in Denver?"

"The green car," Reacher said. "And the guy who was driving it. We'll call him up, ask him if he gave Maria a ride, and if so, where exactly he let her out."

"You know his name?"

"No."

"Number?"

"No."

"Great plan."

"He was visiting three grandchildren in Hope. You need to get back to town and check with families that have three kids. Ask them if Grandpa just came by in his green Mercury. One of them will say yes. Then you'll get a number."

"What are you going to do?"

"I'm going back to Despair."

HE GOT out of the car at five-thirty-five, a little more than eight miles west of Hope, a little more than eight miles east of Despair. Right in the heart of no-man's-land. He watched Vaughan drive away, and then he turned and started walking.

By eight o'clock he was making his first approach. He was expected out of the east; therefore, he was coming in from the southwest. Not a guarantee of safety, but better than a poke in the eye. Reacher figured competent individuals would be distributed all around the town but not equally. In the dark, they would have to spread out, like a human perimeter. But they would stick fairly close together, each group in visual contact with the next. A circle a mile in diameter would barely enclose the town. Cover would be thin.

It won't be a huge problem, Reacher thought.

He paused behind a rock, fifty yards from the back of a long line of workers housing. Low one-story dwellings, well separated laterally. There were guards armed with clubs and bats in the gaps between houses. Together they made a chain that went armed guard, house, armed guard, house, armed guard, house, armed guard.

They thought the houses themselves were defensive elements.

They were wrong.

He could hear dogs barking here and there in the distance. The guy second from the right between the houses had a flashlight. He was clicking it on at predictable intervals, sweeping an arc of ground in front of him and then clicking it off to save the battery.

Reacher moved left.

He lined himself up behind a house that was entirely dark. He dropped to the ground and low-crawled straight for it. He budgeted five minutes. Fast enough to get the job done; slow enough to get it done safely. Generally, the human brain notices speed and discontinuity. A tortoise worries nobody.

He stayed low all the way to the back stoop. Then he stood up and listened for reaction, either outside the house or inside.

Nothing.

He put his hand on the door handle, lifted, and stepped into a dark and silent kitchen. A worn linoleum floor, the smell of fried food. He moved to the hallway. Smelled dirty carpet and worn furniture from a living room on his right. The front door was a plain hollow slab. He turned the handle and lifted. Eased it open, silently.

Ahead of him was a short path and a dark street. More houses on the other side. No guards between them. The guards were all behind him now, and they were all facing the wrong way.

REACHER THREADED BETWEEN houses and stayed off the roads where possible. He saw nobody on foot. Once, he saw a moving vehicle two streets away. A designated supervisor, possibly, on an inspection tour. He ducked low behind a wooden fence and waited until the car was well away from him. Then he moved on. He stayed in the shadows.

The street with the police station on it had one streetlight burning. It cast a weak pool of yellow light. The police station itself was dark and still. The street door was locked. Reacher took out the keys he had taken from the deputy in the bar. He looked at the lock and looked at the keys and selected a long brass item and tried it. The lock turned, and the door swung open.

Like the town's hotel, the Despair PD was still in the pen-and-paper age. Arrest records were on the booking desk in a large black ledger with gold-painted edges. Reacher carried it to a window and tilted it so that it caught what little light was coming through. He flipped through the pages until he found his own entry, dated three days previously: "Reacher, J, male vagrant."

The entry immediately before his own was three days older and said: "Anderson, L, female vagrant."

He flipped backward, looking for Lucy Anderson's husband. He didn't expect to find him, and he didn't. Lucy Anderson's husband had been helped, not hindered. Then he looked for Ramirez. No trace. He had never been picked up. If he had ever been there at all.

He leafed backward, a random three-month sample. Saw six names—Bridge, Churchill, White, King, Whitehouse, Andrews—five male, one female, all vagrants, roughly one every two weeks.

He flipped ahead again, looking for Maria. She wasn't there.

Reacher closed the book and stacked it back on the desk and walked down the stairs to the cell block. All the bulkhead lights were burning. But all the cells were empty.

REACHER'S next stop was out of town, which meant passing through the perimeter again, this time heading in the other direction. Easy to sneak up to the line; hard to walk away with a thousand eyes on his back.

He sorted through the bunch of keys, found the one he wanted. Then he put the keys in his pocket and moved back to the booking desk and started opening drawers. What he wanted was in the third drawer down. A quarter-full pack of Camel cigarettes and three books of matches.

He cleared a space on the floor under the booking desk and put the arrest ledger in its center, standing on its edge with the pages fanned out. He piled every scrap of paper he could find around it. He balled up memos and posters and old newspapers and built a pyramid. He hid two matchbooks in it, with the covers bent back and the matches bent forward at varying angles.

Then he lit a cigarette with a match from the third book. He inhaled gratefully. He liked Turkish tobacco. He smoked a half inch and folded the cigarette into the matchbook in a T shape and used a paper clip to keep it secure. Then he nestled the assembly into the base of his paper pyramid and walked away.

He left the street door open two inches to set up a breeze.

HE HAD seen the big deputy's house from the back the first night, when the guy got home from work and threw up in the yard. It was a five-minute walk that took him ten, due to stealth and caution. The house was another swaybacked old ranch. No yard. The old crew-cab pickup was parked right next to it.

The driver's door was unlocked. Reacher slid in behind the wheel. The seat was sagging, and the upholstery smelled of sweat and grease and oil. Reacher pulled the bunch of keys and found the car key. Plastic head, distinctive shape. He tried it, just to be sure. He put it in the ignition and turned two clicks. The wheel unlocked, and the dials lit up. He turned it back again and climbed over the seats and lay down in the rear of the cab.

It took more than thirty minutes for the townspeople to realize their police station was on fire. By which time it was well ablaze. From his low position in the truck, Reacher saw smoke and sparks and the tentative start of leaping flames well before anyone reacted.

Then there was pandemonium.

The perimeter collapsed inward like a leaking balloon. Reacher lay still, and people streamed past him, few and hesitant at first, then many and fast. They were running, looking at nothing except the bright glow ahead of them. The streets were suddenly crowded, and the flow was all one way.

Reacher smiled. *Like moths to a flame. Literally.*

Then he scrambled over the seat backs and turned the key all the way. The engine turned over once and fired. He drove away slowly, with the lights off, heading a little south of west, through the deserted scrubland. He saw headlights on the roadway to his right. Almost certainly the security Tahoes coming in from the plant, plus maybe some firefighting equipment. He kept on going, slowly, bouncing over washboard undulations and jarring over rocks. It took more than seven minutes before he saw the white gleam of the plant's wall in the darkness.

THE wall was a sheer eight-foot-high vertical plane, topped with a continuous horizontal cylinder six feet in diameter. Like a roll of toilet paper balanced on a thick hardcover book. It was a design derived from prison research. Reacher knew the theory. Stone walls or brick walls could be climbed. Broken glass set in the tops could be cushioned. Barbed wire could be cut. But six-foot cylinders were unbeatable. Their surfaces were slick and offered no grip at all.

So he drove on, through the empty acres of parking, hoping against hope that the personnel gate would be open. But it wasn't, and none of the deputy's keys fit. Because it didn't have a keyhole. It had a gray metal box instead, set into the wall. Inside was a ten-digit keypad laid out like a telephone. A possible 3,628,800 variants. It would take seven months to try them all.

Reacher drove on, tracking the north wall, hoping against hope that the vehicle gate would be open. He was slightly optimistic. The Tahoes had left in a hurry, and people in a hurry didn't always clean up after themselves.

The vehicle gate was open.

Reacher parked the deputy's truck nose-out, blocking the gate's travel. He walked a hundred feet into the plant. He glanced right at the offices and storage tanks. Beyond them, nearly a mile away, was the secret compound. He took half a step in its direction.

Then the lights came on.

There was an audible whoomp as electricity surged through cables, and a split second later the whole place lit brighter than day. Reacher screwed his eyes shut, and when he opened them, he saw Thurman walking toward him. He turned and saw the plant foreman heading in from a different direction. He turned again and saw the giant with the three-foot wrench blocking his path to the gate.

Thurman came close and took up a position alongside him, nearly shoulder to shoulder, as if they were two old buddies standing together, surveying a happy scene.

Thurman said, "I thought our paths were not going to cross again."

Reacher said, "I can't be responsible for what you think."

"Did you set our police station on fire?"

"You've got a human wall all around the town. How could I have gotten through?"

"Why are you here again?"

Reacher paused a beat. Said, "I'm thinking about leaving the state." Which was true. "Before I go, I thought I'd drop by the infirmary and tell my former opponents no hard feelings. Clearing the air is always good for a person's mental well-being."

"I can't permit a visit to the infirmary."

"You can't prevent one."

"There's only Underwood there at the moment. The others are home now on bed rest."

"Which one is Underwood?"

"The senior deputy. You left him in a sorry state."

"He was sick already."

"You need to leave now," Thurman said. "I'm not joking."

"You are," Reacher said. "You're a fat old man telling me to leave. That's pretty funny."

"I'm not alone here."

Reacher turned and checked. The foreman was standing ten feet away. The giant was twenty feet away, holding the wrench.

Reacher said, "You've got an office boy and a broken-down old jock with a big wrench. I'm not impressed."

"They could do you considerable harm."

"I doubt it. The first eight you sent didn't do much."

Thurman said nothing.

Reacher said, "I'm going to the infirmary now. You are, too. Your choice whether you walk there or I carry you in a bucket."

Thurman's shoulders slumped in an all-purpose sigh and shrug, and he raised a palm to his two guys, one after the other, like he was telling a couple of dogs to stay. Then he set off walking toward the line of cabins, Reacher at his side. They passed the security office and three other offices that Reacher had seen before on his tour, the one marked OPERATIONS, the one marked PURCHASING, the last marked INVOICING. Then Thurman heaved himself up the short flight of steps of a white-painted unit and opened the door.

It was a real sick bay. White walls, white linoleum floor, the smell of antiseptic. There were medicine cabinets, blood pressure cuffs, sharps-disposal cans on the walls, and sinks with lever taps. There were four hospital cots. One was occupied by the big deputy.

Only he looked smaller than before. His hair looked thinner. His breathing was shallow and irregular. There was a medical chart clipped to the rail at the foot of his bed. Reacher scanned it. The guy had a whole lot of things wrong with him. Fever, fatigue, weakness, breathlessness, headaches, rashes, blisters, sores, chronic vomiting, diarrhea. Reacher dropped the chart back into position and asked, "You have a doctor working here?"

Thurman said, "A paramedic. We're doing the best we can."

Reacher stepped alongside the bed. "Can you talk?"

The big deputy rolled his head from one side to the other. Tried to speak but got hung up. He breathed hard and started again. "The . . ." And then he paused for breath and started over, apparently with a new thought. He said haltingly, "You did this to me."

"Not entirely," Reacher said.

The guy rolled his head again, away and back, and gasped once and said, "No, the—" And then he stopped again, fighting for breath. Thurman grabbed Reacher's elbow and pulled him back and said, "We need to leave now. We're tiring him."

"Did this guy work with TCE?"

Thurman paused a beat. "What do you know about TCE?"

"A little. It's a poison."

"It's a standard industrial product."

"Whatever. Did this guy work with it?"

"No. And those that do are well protected."

"So what's wrong with him?"

"Like he said, you did this to him."

"You don't get symptoms like these from a fistfight."

"I heard it was more than a fistfight."

Reacher closed his eyes, saw the barroom again, the air thick with dust and the smell of fear. *Two hundred fifty pounds of weight punched through the end of a chair leg into soft tissue.* He opened his eyes again and said, "He needs to be in a proper hospital."

Thurman didn't answer. Reacher took a last look at the guy in the bed and then stepped away and walked out the door, down the steps, back to the blazing arena. The foreman and the guy with the wrench stood where they had been before. Reacher heard Thurman close the infirmary door and clatter down the steps behind him.

Thurman asked, "Are you leaving now, Mr. Reacher?"

"Yes," Reacher said. "I'm done here."

The guy with the wrench was looking at Thurman, waiting for a sign, maybe *hoping* for a sign, slapping the wrench against his palm.

Thurman must have shaken his head, because the guy just paused a beat and then stepped aside.

The sick deputy's truck was where Reacher had left it, with all its windows intact.

8

REACHER looped around Despair to the north, through the scrub. He navigated by the glow of the fire to his right. It looked to be going strong. In his experience, brick buildings always burned well. The floors and the ceilings go first, and then the roof, with the outer walls holding up and forming a tall chimney to enhance the airflow.

He skirted the town on a radius he judged to be about four miles, and then he shadowed the road back east. When the clock in his head hit midnight, he figured he was less than a mile short of the line. He veered right and bounced up onto the tarred pebbles and finished the trip like a normal driver. He thumped over the line, and Hope's thick blacktop made the ride go suddenly quiet.

Vaughan was waiting a hundred yards ahead. She was parked on the shoulder with her lights off. He slowed and held his arm out his window in a reassuring wave. She put her arm out her own window, hand extended, fingers spread, an answering gesture. He coasted and came to a stop with his fingertips touching hers. To him the contact felt one-third like a mission-accomplished high-five, one-third like an expression of relief to be out of the lions' den again, and one-third just plain good. He didn't know what it felt like to her. She gave no indication. But she left her hand there a second longer than she needed to.

"Whose truck?" she asked.

"The senior deputy's. His name is Underwood. He's very sick."

"With what?"

"He said I did it to him. But I didn't give him diarrhea or blisters or sores, and I didn't make his hair fall out."

"So is it TCE?"

"Thurman said not."

Vaughan held up a plastic bottle of water. "This is a sample. Tap water from my kitchen. I called a friend of a friend of David's. He knows a guy who works at the state lab in Colorado Springs. He told me to take this in for testing. And to find out how much TCE Thurman actually uses."

"The tank holds five thousand gallons."

"But how often does it get used up and refilled?"

"I don't know."

"How can we find out?"

"There's a purchasing office, probably full of paperwork."

"Can we get in there?"

"Maybe."

Vaughan said, "Go dump that truck back over the line. I'll drive you to town. We'll take a doughnut break."

So Reacher steered the truck backward into the sand and left it there, keys in. Way behind him, he could see a faint red glow on the horizon. Despair was still on fire. He didn't say anything about it. He just walked forward and crossed the line again and climbed in next to Vaughan.

"You smell of cigarettes," she said.

"I found one," he said. "Smoked a half inch for old times' sake."

"They give you cancer."

She took off east, at a moderate speed, one hand on the wheel and the other in her lap. "I called Denver," she said. "About Maria. The old man picked her up, but he didn't let her out in Despair. She wanted to go to the MP base."

THEY got to the diner at twenty minutes past midnight. They didn't order doughnuts. Reacher ordered coffee, and Vaughan ordered juice, a blend of three exotic fruits.

"You're very healthy," Reacher said.

"I try."

"Is your husband in the hospital? With cancer from smoking?"

She shook her head. "No," she said, "he isn't."

Their drinks arrived, and they sipped them in silence for a moment and then Reacher asked, "Did the old guy know why Maria wanted to go to the MPs?"

"She didn't tell him. But it's a weird destination, isn't it?"

"Very," Reacher said. "It's an active-service operating base. Visitors wouldn't be permitted. Did the old guy see her get in?"

"Sure," Vaughan said. "He waited, like a gentleman."

"Therefore, a better question would be, If they let her in, what did they want from her?" Reacher shook his head. "I can't make it all work. There's a logic problem. Almost mathematical."

"Try me," Vaughan said. "I did four years of college."

Reacher smiled. "There are three things going on over there. The military contract, plus something else, plus something else again."

"Okay," Vaughan said. She put the saltshaker, the pepper shaker, and the sugar shaker in the center of the table. "Three things."

Reacher moved the saltshaker to one side immediately. "The military contract is what it is. Nothing controversial. Nothing to worry about. No reason for the townspeople to get excited."

"But the townspeople are excited about something."

He held up the sugar shaker in his right hand. "That's the bigger of the two unknowns, because everyone is involved in it." Then he held up the pepper shaker in his left hand. "This other thing is smaller. It involves a subset of the population. Everyone knows about the sugar; most *don't* know about the pepper; a few know about both the sugar *and* the pepper."

"So maybe Thurman's doing something and everyone is helping, but a few are also working on something else behind his back?"

Reacher nodded. "And that something the few are working on behind his back involves these young guys. They get through or they don't, depending on who they bump into first—the many sugar people or the few salt people."

"The odds will always be against them."

"Exactly."

"Which was Ramirez's problem."

"Ramirez didn't bump into anyone," Reacher said. "I checked the records. He was neither arrested nor helped."

"Why? What made him different?"

"Great question," Reacher said.

THE clock in Reacher's head hit one in the morning, and the clock on the diner's wall followed it a minute later. Vaughan looked at her watch and said, "I better get back in the saddle."

Reacher said, "Okay."

"Go get some sleep."

"Okay."

"Will you come with me to Colorado Springs? To the lab with the water sample?"

"When?"

"Tomorrow, today, whatever it is now."

"What time?"

"Leave at ten?"

"You still trying to keep me out of trouble?"

"I've given up on keeping you out of trouble, but I'd like your company."

REACHER showered and was in bed by two o'clock in the morning. He slept dreamlessly and woke up at eight. He showered again and walked the length of the town to the hardware store. He went inside and found the racks of pants and shirts and chose a new one of each. Prewashed, and therefore softer. Less durable in the long term, but he wasn't interested in the long term.

He changed in his motel room and left his old stuff folded on the floor next to the trash can. Maybe the maid had a needy male relative his size. He walked to the office. The clerk was on her stool. Behind her shoulder, the hook for Maria's room had no key on it. The clerk saw him looking and said, "She came back this morning." She looked both ways and lowered her voice and said, "In an armored car. With a soldier."

Reacher said, "A Humvee."

The woman nodded. "The soldier didn't stay. Which I'm glad about. I couldn't permit a thing like that."

Reacher paid his bill and walked back down the row. He stopped outside her door and knocked. A minute later she opened the door.

"You okay?" he asked her, which was a dumb question. She didn't look okay. She looked lost and bewildered.

He said, "You went to the MP base asking about Raphael. They couldn't help you."

She didn't answer.

He said, "Maybe I could help you. You want to tell me what it's all about?"

"I can't tell you," she said. "I can't tell anyone."

Simple as that. She couldn't tell anyone.

"Okay." Reacher walked away, to the diner, and had breakfast.

AT FIVE to ten, he was sitting in the plastic lawn chair outside his door. Vaughan showed up at three minutes past the hour in a plain black Crown Vic. An unmarked squad car, like a detective would drive. She stopped close to him and buzzed the window down. He said, "Did you get promoted?"

"It's my watch commander's ride. He took pity on me and loaned it out. Since you got my truck smashed up."

"Maria is back," he said. "The MPs brought her home."

"Is she saying anything?"

"Not a word." He got out of the chair and walked around the hood and slid in beside her.

The car was plain. Lots of black plastic, lots of mouse-fur upholstery of an indeterminate color. The front was full of police gear, but there was plenty of legroom. The water sample was on the rear seat. Vaughan was looking good. She was in old blue jeans and a white oxford-cloth shirt, the neck open two buttons.

She said, "You've changed."

"In what way?"

"Your clothes, you idiot."

"New this morning," he said. "From the hardware store."

"Nicer than the last lot."

"Don't get attached to them. They'll be gone soon."

VAUGHAN AVERAGED NINETY most of the way to Colorado Springs, charging head-on toward the mountains. Reacher knew Colorado Springs a little. Fort Carson was there, which was a major army presence, but it was really more of an air force town. Aside from that, it was a pleasant place. Scenery was pretty, the air was clean, and the view of Pikes Peak was usually spectacular.

The downtown area was neat and compact. The state water lab was in a stone government building. Vaughan handed over her bottle and filled out a form, and a guy wrapped the form around the bottle, secured it with a rubber band, and carried it away. He came back and told Vaughan that she would be notified of the results by phone and to please let the lab know some figures for Despair's total TCE consumption. The state knew the depth of the county's aquifer to the inch, so the only variable would be the exact amount of TCE heading down toward it.

THEY got back in the car. Vaughan was distracted. She was a cop and a conscientious member of her community, but clearly she was worrying about more than a distant chemical threat to her water table. He wasn't sure why she had asked him to travel with her. They hadn't spoken much.

She pulled out and drove a hundred yards on a tree-lined street and stopped at a light at a T-junction. Left was west, and right was east. The light turned green, and she turned left. "Where are we going?" Reacher asked her.

She didn't answer. She drove a mile between green hills and turned left through a grove of pines on a worn gray road that had no center line. There was no wire and no painted sign, but Reacher was sure the land on both sides was owned by the army. He knew there were thousands of spare acres beyond Fort Carson, requisitioned decades ago, and never really used for much. And what he was seeing out the window looked exactly like Department of Defense property. Nature, made uniform. A little sullen, a little half-hearted, somewhat beaten down, neither raw nor developed.

After another mile, Vaughan slowed and made a right into a half-hidden driveway. She passed between two squat yellow brick pillars. Twenty yards farther on was a billboard on thin metal legs. The billboard had OLYMPIC TBI CENTER on it. Twenty yards later another billboard said: AUTHORIZED PERSONNEL ONLY. After that the driveway ran on straight for a hundred yards to a group of low brick buildings. Army buildings, long ago deemed surplus and sold off. Reacher recognized the architecture. Brick and tile, radiused corners built back when chamfered edges had looked like the future. A billboard next to the main entrance repeated OLYMPIC TBI CENTER.

They walked together to the entrance. Three steps up, through the doors, onto the kind of mottled green tile floor Reacher had walked a thousand times before. Mid-fifties U.S. Army, abandoned and run-down. There was an oak hutch on the right, where once a busy sergeant would have sat. Now it was occupied by a sullen civilian in a gray sweatshirt, about forty, unwashed black hair. He said, "Hello, Mrs. Vaughan." Nothing more.

Vaughan nodded but didn't reply. She walked to the back of the hall and turned into a large room. It was dirty and smelled faintly of antiseptic and urine. It was completely empty, except for two men strapped into wheelchairs. Both men were young; both had open mouths and empty gazes.

Both had shaved heads, and misshapen skulls, and wicked scars. Reacher stood still. He looked at the guys in the wheelchairs.

He was in a residential home.

He thought back to the initials on the billboard: TBI.

Traumatic Brain Injury.

Vaughan had moved on, into a corridor. He caught up with her, halfway along its length.

"Your husband had an accident?" he said.

"Not exactly," she said.

"Then what?"

"Figure it out."

An old army building. Both men were young.

"War wounds," he said. "Your husband is military. He went to Iraq."

Vaughan nodded. "National Guard," she said. "His second tour. They extended his deployment. Didn't armor his Humvee. He was blown up by an IED in Ramadi."

She turned into another corridor. Dust balls had collected against the baseboards. Some were peppered with mouse droppings.

Reacher asked, "Is this a VA facility?"

Vaughan shook her head. "Private contractor."

She stopped at a dull green door. No doubt fifty years earlier it had been painted by a private soldier in a color and in a manner specified by the Pentagon. The soldier's workmanship had been inspected by an NCO, and the NCO's approval had been validated by an officer's. Since then, the door had received no further attention. It had a wax pencil scrawl on it: "D. R. Vaughan."

Vaughan turned the handle and opened the door.

DAVID Robert Vaughan's room was a twelve-foot cube painted dark green. It had a small, sooty window. It had a green metal cabinet and a green metal footlocker. The footlocker was open and held a single pair of clean pajamas. The cabinet was stacked with file folders and oversized brown envelopes. The envelopes were old and torn and frayed and held X-ray films.

A narrow hospital cot was set to a forty-five-degree slope. In it, under a sheet, was a compact narrow-shouldered man. He had blond stubble on his chin and cheeks. His blue eyes were open.

Part of his skull was missing.

A saucer-size piece of bone wasn't there. It left a wide hole above his forehead, and his brain was protruding. It was draped with a thin man-made membrane that stuck to the shaved skin around the hole. Like Saran Wrap.

Vaughan said, "Hello, David. I brought a friend to see you."

No response. There never would be, Reacher guessed. The guy in the bed was completely inert. Not asleep, not awake, not anything.

Vaughan bent and kissed her husband.

Then she stepped over to the cabinet and tugged an X-ray envelope out of the pile. She pulled a film out of the envelope and held it up against the light from the window. It was a composite image that showed her husband's head from four different directions.

"Iraq's signature injury," Vaughan said. "Blast damage to the human brain. Compression, decompression, shearing, impact with the wall of the skull. David got it all. His skull was shattered, and they cut the worst of it away. That was supposed to relieve the pressure. Then they give them a plastic plate later, when the swelling goes down. But David's swelling never went down."

She put the film back in the envelope and pulled another one out. It was a chest film. White ribs, gray organs, and small bright pinpoints that looked like drops of liquid.

"That's why I don't wear my wedding band," Vaughan said. "He wanted to take it with him, on a chain around his neck. The heat melted it, and the blast drove it into his lungs."

She put the film back into the envelope.

"He wore it for good luck," she said.

"This was IED versus Humvee?"

She nodded. "An improvised explosive device against a tin can."

"When was this?"

"Almost two years ago."

Reacher asked, "What was his prognosis?"

Vaughan said, "At first it was reasonable, in theory. They thought he would be confused and uncoordinated, you know, and certainly lacking all his basic life and motor skills."

"So you moved," Reacher said. "You thought about a wheelchair. You bought a one-story and took the door off the living room."

She nodded. "But he never woke up. This is all he will ever be. He can't move, and he can't see and can't hear and can't think."

Reacher said nothing.

Vaughan moved to the head of the bed and laid her hand on her husband's cheek gently, tenderly.

Then she said, "You don't shave very often, do you?"

"Sometimes," Reacher said.

"But you know how?"

"I learned at my daddy's knee."

"Will you shave David?"

"Don't the orderlies do that?"

"They should, but they don't. And I like him to look decent. It seems like the least I can do." She took a grocery bag out of the green metal cabinet. It held shaving gel, a half-used pack of disposable razors, soap, a washcloth. Reacher found a bathroom across the hall and stepped back and forth with the wet cloth, soaping the guy's face. He smoothed blue gel over the guy's chin and cheeks and lathered it with his fingertips and then set about using the razor. A completely instinctive sequence of actions when applied to himself became awkward on a third party. Especially on a third party who had a large part of his skull missing.

While he worked with the razor, Vaughan cleaned the room. She had a second grocery bag in the cabinet that held cloths and sprays and a dustpan and brush. She stretched and bent and went through the whole twelve-foot cube thoroughly. Reacher finished up, and Vaughan stopped a minute later and stood back and looked.

"Good work," she said.

"You, too. Although you shouldn't have to do that yourself."

"I know."

They repacked the grocery bags and put them away in the cabinet. Reacher asked, "How long were you married?"

"We're still married."

"I'm sorry. How long?"

"Twelve years. Eight together; then he spent two in Iraq, and the last two have been like this."

"What are you going to do?"

"I don't know. People say I should move on. Accept destiny, like Zeno. But then I panic. I think, First they do this to him, and now I should divorce him? What do you think I should do?"

"I think you should take a walk," Reacher said. "Now. Alone. I'll bring the car and pick you up before you hit the four-lane."

"What are you going to do?"

"I'll find some way to pass the time."

VAUGHAN SAID GOOD-BYE TO her husband, and she and Reacher walked back along the dirty corridors and through the dismal lounge to the entrance hall. The guy in the gray sweatshirt said, "Good-bye, Mrs. Vaughan." They walked out and headed for the car. Vaughan kept on going. Reacher waited until she was small in the distance, and then he headed back to the entrance. He crossed to the hutch and asked, "Who's in charge here?"

The guy in the gray sweatshirt said, "I am, I guess. I'm the shift supervisor."

Reacher asked, "How many patients here?"

"Seventeen," the guy said.

"You run this place according to a manual?"

"Sure. It's a bureaucracy, like everywhere."

"You want to show me the part where it says it's okay to keep the rooms dirty and have mouse droppings in the corridors?"

The guy blinked and swallowed and said, "There's no point *cleaning,* man. They wouldn't *know.* This is the vegetable patch."

"Wrong answer," Reacher said. "This is not the vegetable patch. This is a veterans clinic. And David Vaughan is my brother."

"Really?"

"All veterans are my brothers."

"He's brain dead, man."

"Are you?"

"No."

"Then listen up. And listen very carefully. A person less fortunate than yourself deserves the best you can give. Because of duty, and honor, and service. You understand those words? You should do your job right, and you should do it well, simply because you can, without looking for notice or reward. The people here deserve your best, and their relatives deserve it."

"Who are you, anyway?"

"I'm a concerned citizen," Reacher said. "With a number of options. I could call the newspapers or the TV. I could get you fired. But I don't do stuff like that. I offer personal choices instead. You want to know what your choice is?"

"What?"

"Do what I tell you or become patient number eighteen."

The guy went pale.

Reacher said, "Your patients served their country with honor and distinction. So you're going to organize your people and you're going to get this place cleaned up. Starting right now. I'm going to come back—maybe tomorrow, maybe next month—and if I can't see my face in the floor, I'm going to turn you upside down and use you like a mop. Then I'm going to kick your butt so hard your colon is going to get tangled up in your teeth. Are we clear?"

The guy paused and blinked. Then he said, "Okay."

"That's good," Reacher said. "And every time Mrs. Vaughan comes by, you're going to stand up and welcome her warmly, and her husband's room is going to be sparkling and her husband is going to be shaved. Are we clear?"

"Okay."

"Are we clear?"

"Yes."

"You've got sixty seconds to get started or I'll break your arm."

The guy made a phone call and then used a walkie-talkie, and fifty seconds later there were four guys in the hall. They had buckets and mops, and a minute after that the buckets were full of water.

Reacher left them to it.

He caught up with Vaughan a mile down the road. She slid in next to him, and he drove on, retracing their route through the pines, through the hills.

"You know why I wanted you to come?"

"You wanted someone to understand why you live like you live and do what you do."

"And?"

"You wanted someone to understand why it's okay to do what you're going to do next."

"Which is what?"

"Which is entirely up to you. And either way is good with me."

She said, "I lied to you before."

He said, "I know. You knew about Thurman's military contract. And the MP base. The Pentagon told you all about them. And you didn't want to talk about it, which means that it's not just any old military scrap getting recycled there."

"Isn't it?"

Reacher shook his head. "It's combat wrecks from Iraq. Has to be. Thurman's place is a secret operation, miles from nowhere."

"I'm sorry."

"Don't be. I understand. You didn't want to talk about it."

"There are blown-up Humvees there," she said. "They're like monuments to me. Like shrines. To the people who died. Or nearly died."

They drove on, across the low slopes of the mountains. Reacher said, "It doesn't explain Thurman's taste for secrecy. And it doesn't explain the MPs, either. What's to steal?"

Vaughan said nothing.

Reacher said, "And it doesn't explain the airplane. And nothing explains all these young guys."

"So you're going to stick around?"

He nodded. "For a spell," he said. "Because I think something is about to happen. That crowd impressed me. Would they have that much passion for the beginning of something or the middle of something? I don't think so. I think they were all stirred up because they're heading for the end of something."

9

THEY hit Hope at five in the afternoon.

"Is your watch commander a nice guy?" Reacher asked.

"Why?"

"Because we need to borrow his car again."

"When?"

"Later tonight."

"Later than what?"

"Than whatever—but first we're going shopping."

THEY got to the hardware store just as it was closing. The old guy was clearing his sidewalk display. Reacher went in and bought a flashlight and two batteries and a two-foot wrecking bar from the old guy's wife. Then he went back out and bought a stepladder that opened to eight different positions. It was light, made of aluminum, and it folded into a neat package about four feet long and a foot and a half wide. It fit easily on the Crown Vic's rear bench.

VAUGHAN invited him over for dinner at eight o'clock. She was very formal about it. She said she needed the intervening hours to prepare. Reacher spent the time in his room. He took a nap, and then he shaved and showered and cleaned his teeth. And dressed. His clothes were new, but his underwear was past its prime, so he ditched it. He put on his pants and his shirt and raked his fingers through his hair and checked the result in the mirror and deemed it acceptable. His appearance was what it was. He couldn't change it.

Fifty yards from Vaughan's house, he couldn't see the watch commander's car. Either it was in the driveway or Vaughan had given it back. Then from thirty yards away he saw the car right there on the curb. Dull glass. Black paint. Invisible in the gloom.

Perfect.

He walked through the plantings on her stepping-stone path and touched the bell. Vaughan got there in nine seconds flat. She was in a black knee-length sleeveless A-line dress. She was freshly showered. She looked young and full of energy. She looked stunning.

He said, "Hello."

She said, "Come in."

The kitchen was full of candlelight. The table was set with two chairs and two places and an open bottle of wine and two glasses. Aromas were coming from the stove.

She said, "The main course isn't ready. I screwed up the timing. It's something I haven't made for a while."

"Three years," Reacher said.

"Longer," she said.

"You look great," he said. "The prettiest view in Colorado."

She said, "You look good, too. You clean up well."

"I try my best."

She asked, "Should we be doing this?"

He said, "I think so."

"Is it fair to David?"

"David never came back. He never lived here. He doesn't know."

"I want to see your scar again."

"Because you're wishing David had come back with one. Instead of what he got."

"I guess."

Reacher said, "We were both lucky. I know soldiers. They fear grotesque wounds. That's all. Amputations, mutilations, burns. I'm lucky because I didn't get one, and David is lucky because he doesn't know he did."

Vaughan said nothing.

Reacher said, "And we're both lucky because we both met you."

Vaughan said, "Show me the scar."

Reacher unbuttoned his shirt and slipped it off. Vaughan hesitated a second and then touched the ridged skin very gently. Her fingertips were cool and smooth. They burned him, like electricity.

"What was it?" she asked.

"A truck bomb in Beirut."

"That's awful." She put her hand flat against the scar and then slid her palm around his back. She did the same with her other hand. She hugged his waist, and then she raised her head and he bent down and kissed her. Her eyes were closed. He cradled her head with one hand and put the other low on her back.

A long, long kiss.

She came up for air. "It's okay to do this," she said.

"I think so," he said.

"Because you're moving on," she said.

"Two days," he said. "Three, max."

"No complications," she said. "Not like it might be permanent."

"I can't do permanent," he said.

He bent and kissed her again. Moved his hand and caught the tag of her zipper and pulled it down. She was naked under the dress. Warm, and soft, and lithe, and fragrant. He scooped her up and carried her down the hallway to where he imagined the bedrooms must be. Two rooms. One smelled unused, one smelled like her. He carried her in and put her down, and her dress slipped from her shoulders.

Afterward they ate. Pork cooked with apples and spices and brown sugar and wine. For dessert, they went back to bed. At midnight, they showered together, and at one o'clock, they went out.

VAUGHAN drove. She insisted on it. It was her watch commander's car. Reacher was happy to let her. She was a better driver than him. Much better. Her panic one-eighty had impressed him. He figured if he had been driving, the mob would have caught them and torn them apart.

"Won't they be there again?" Vaughan asked.

"Possible," he said. "But I doubt it. They got all pumped up yesterday and thought they'd gotten rid of us. They don't have the stamina to do it all again."

There were thick clouds in the sky. No moon. No stars. Pitch-black. Perfect. They thumped over the line, and a mile later Reacher said, "It's time to go stealthy. Turn all the lights off."

Vaughan clicked the headlights off, and the world went dark. She braked hard. "I can't see anything," she said.

"Use the video camera. The night vision," he said.

"What?"

"Like a video game," he said. "Watch the computer screen, not the windshield. It's how tank drivers do it."

She tapped keys, and the laptop screen lit up and then stabilized into a pale green picture of the landscape ahead. Green scrub on either side, vivid boulders, a bright ribbon of road spearing into the distance. She took her foot off the brake and crawled forward, staring at the thermal image, not the reality. At first, she drifted left and right and overcorrected.

"It's killing me not to glance ahead," she said. "It's so automatic."

"This is good," Reacher said. "Stay slow." He figured that at twenty or thirty, there would be almost no engine noise. Just a low purr. He leaned left and put his head on her shoulder and watched the screen. The landscape reeled itself in, silent and green and ghostly. A tiny flare of heat on the horizon showed where the embers of the police station were still warm.

Reacher glanced ahead through the windshield a couple of times, but there was nothing to see. Just darkness. Which meant that anyone waiting ahead in the distance wasn't seeing anything, either. He recalled walking back to Hope, stepping over the line, not seeing Vaughan's cruiser. But she had seen him. *I saw you half a mile away,* she had said. *A little green speck.*

He stared at the screen watching for little green specks.

Two miles. Four. Still nothing ahead. Six miles. Eight.

"We must be getting close," she whispered.

He nodded on her shoulder. The screen showed background glow from the downtown blocks. Then there were window-size patches of brighter color, heat leaking from roofs with imperfect insulation. The car rolled onward.

Then two green specks stepped out ahead.

They were maybe a quarter of a mile away, at the west end of Main Street. Two figures, emerging from a cross street. A foot patrol. Vaughan braked gently and came to a stop.

Reacher turned and stared through the window. Saw nothing. He said, "We can't see them; they can't see us. Laws of physics."

They waited two minutes, then three, then five.

The green specks moved from the center of the screen to the left-hand edge. Slow, blurred, a ghost trail of luminescence following behind them. Then they disappeared into a cross street.

"Foot patrol," Reacher said. "Heading downtown. Maybe worried about fires."

"Fires?" Vaughan said.

"Their police station burned down last night."

"Did you have something to do with that?"

"Everything," Reacher said.

"You're a maniac."

"They're messing with the wrong guy."

Vaughan feathered the gas, and the car rolled forward. One block. Two. The screen held steady. Geography and architecture. Nothing more. The tires were quiet on the battered surface. Then they were through the town and in open country on the other side.

Four minutes after that they were approaching the metal plant.

The thermal image showed the sky above the plant to be lurid, with heat coming off the dormant furnaces and crucibles. The metal wall showed up as a continuous horizontal band of green, brighter at the southern end. The secret compound was glowing like crazy.

"Some junkyard," Reacher said.

The acres of parking seemed to be all empty. The personnel gate was closed. Vaughan said, "No sentries?"

Reacher said, "They trust the wall. As they should. It's a great wall."

They drove on, slow and dark and silent, past the lot. The Tahoes' beaten tracks showed up on the screen, almost imperceptibly lighter than the surrounding scrub. Compacted dirt, therefore no ventilation, therefore slightly slower to cool at the end of the day. Reacher pointed, and Vaughan turned the wheel and they were following the ghostly green image of the Tahoes' ruts counterclockwise, all the way around the metal plant to the place where Reacher had decided to break in.

VAUGHAN followed the white metal wall halfway along its northern stretch. Then she pulled a tight left and nosed slowly head-on toward the wall and stopped with her front bumper almost touching it. The base of the windshield was about five feet down and two feet out from the cylinder's maximum bulge.

Reacher got out and dragged the stepladder off the rear bench. He laid it on the ground and unfolded it and adjusted it into an upside-down L shape. Then he estimated by eye and relaxed the angle a little beyond ninety degrees and locked all the joints. He lifted it high. He jammed the feet into the gutter at the base of the Crown Vic's windshield, where the hood's lip overlapped the wipers. He let it fall forward gently and hit the wall with a soft metallic noise. The long leg of the L came to rest almost vertical. The short leg lay on top of the cylinder, almost horizontal.

"Back up about a foot," he whispered.

Vaughan moved the car, and the base of the ladder pulled outward to a kinder angle, and the top fell forward by a corresponding degree and ended up perfectly flat.

"I love hardware stores," Reacher said.

Vaughan said, "We're not over it yet."

She shut the engine down. The laptop screen turned itself off, and they were forced back to the visible spectrum, which didn't contain anything very visible. Just darkness. She carried the flashlight, and Reacher took the wrecking bar from the trunk. He levered himself up onto the hood, stepped forward to the base of the windshield, and started to climb the ladder. He carried the wrecking bar in his left hand and gripped the upper rungs with his right. The aluminum squirmed against the steel and set up a weird harmonic in the hollows of the wall. He crawled along the short horizontal leg of the L on his hands and knees. He shuffled off sideways and lay like a starfish on the cylinder's top surface. The white paint was shiny and slick. He raised his head cautiously and looked around.

He was six feet from where he wanted to be.

The pyramid of old oil drums was barely visible in the dark, two yards to the west. Its top tier was about eight feet south and eighteen inches down from the top of the wall. He swam forward and grabbed the ladder again. It shifted sideways toward him. No resistance. He called down, "Get on the bottom rung."

The ladder straightened under Vaughan's weight. He hauled himself toward it and clambered over it and turned around and lay down again on the other side. Now he was exactly where he wanted to be. He called, "Come on up."

He saw the ladder flex and sway and bounce a little and the strange harmonic keening started up again. Then Vaughan's head came into view. She made it over the angle and climbed off and lay down in the place he had just vacated. He handed her the wrecking bar and hauled the ladder up sideways, crossing and uncrossing his hands until he had the thing approximately balanced on top of the curve. He glanced right, into the arena, and tugged the ladder closer to him and then fed it down on the other side of the wall until the short leg of the L came to rest on an oil drum two tiers down from the top. The long leg came to rest at a gentle slope, like a bridge.

"I love hardware stores," he said again.

"I love solid ground," Vaughan said.

He took the wrecking bar back from her and stretched forward and got both hands on the ladder rails. He jerked downward, hard, to make sure it was seated tight. Then he supported all his weight with his arms, like he was chinning a bar, and let his legs slide off the cylinder. He kicked and struggled until he got his feet on the ladder. Then he climbed down backward. He stepped off onto the oil drum and glanced around. Nothing to see. He held his end of the ladder steady and called up to Vaughan, "Your turn."

She came down the same way he had, backward.

They clambered down the pyramid and stepped off onto the sticky dirt. They covered the quarter mile to the vehicle gate in less than five minutes.

The white Tahoes were parked close together near one end of it, and there was a line of five flatbed semis near the other. Four, facing outward, were loaded with steel bars. Product, ready to go. The fifth was facing inward. It was loaded with a closed shipping container with the words CHINA LINES stenciled on it. Scrap, incoming. Reacher glanced at it and passed it by and headed toward the offices. Vaughan walked with him. Reacher stopped outside the white-painted infirmary unit. "Underwood might talk without Thurman here," he said.

"The door might be locked."

Reacher raised the wrecking bar.

"I have a key," he said.

But the door wasn't locked. And the sick deputy wasn't talking. The sick deputy was dead.

HE HAD taken his last breath some hours previously, and maybe he had taken it alone. He looked untended. His eyes were clouded. His hair was messy, like he had been tossing on the pillow.

"TCE?" Vaughan said.

"Possible," Reacher said.

We're doing the best we can, Thurman had said.

Bastard, Reacher thought.

"This could happen in Hope," Vaughan said. "We need the data for Colorado Springs. For the lab."

"That's why we're here," Reacher said.

They stood by the bedside for a moment longer, and then they backed out. The door to the office marked PURCHASING was secured with a padlock through a hasp. The padlock was strong, and the hasp was strong, but the screws securing the hasp to the jamb yielded to little more than the weight of the wrecking bar alone.

There were three desks inside and three phones and a wall of file cabinets. A hundred and forty cubic feet of purchase orders.

"Where do we start?" Vaughan whispered.

"Try T for TCE."

The T drawers were crammed with papers. But none of the papers referred to trichloroethylene. Everything was filed according to supplier name. Tri-State had renewed a fire insurance policy eight months previously, Thomas had supplied four new cell phones three months previously, and Tomkins had put tires on two front-loaders. Nothing chemical in nature.

"I'll start at A," Vaughan said.

"And I'll start at Z," Reacher said. "I'll see you at M or N, if not before."

Vaughan was faster than Reacher. She had the flashlight. He had to rely on stray beams. At one point, he found something ordered in the thousands of gallons, but on inspection, it was only diesel fuel. He learned that Thurman's oxyacetylene supplier was Utah Gases and his kerosene supplier was Union City Fuels. He was opening the last of the S drawers when Vaughan said, "Got it."

"Kearny Chemical of New Jersey," she said. "TCE purchases going back seven years." She lifted the file out of the drawer and riffled through the papers.

"Take the whole thing," Reacher said.

Vaughan jammed the file under her arm and pushed the drawer shut with her hip. Reacher opened the door, and they stepped out together into the dark. Reacher stopped and used the flashlight and found the fallen screws and pushed them back into their holes with his thumb. They held loosely and made the lock look untouched. Then he followed Vaughan as she retraced their steps, headed out into open space.

He stopped again. Turned around.

"Flashlight," he said.

Vaughan gave up the flashlight, and he switched it on and played the beam across the side of the China Lines container. It was forty feet long, dirty white, with a vertical row of Chinese characters stenciled low in one corner.

Plus a word, handwritten in capitals, in chalk: "CARS."

Reacher stepped closer. The business end of the container had a double door, secured in the usual way, with four foot-long levers that drove four sturdy bolts that ran the whole height of the container and socketed home in the box sections top and bottom. Three of the levers were merely slotted into their brackets, but the fourth was secured with a padlock.

"I want to see what's inside."

"There are cars inside."

He nodded in the dark. "I've seen them come in from neighboring states on open flatbeds. Not locked in closed containers."

Vaughan was quiet for a beat. "You think this is stuff from Iraq?"

"It's possible."

"I don't want to see. It might be Humvees if it's from Iraq."

"I'll be quick," he said. "Don't watch if you don't want to."

He held the flashlight in his teeth and stretched up tall and jammed the tongue of the wrecking bar through the padlock's hoop. He jerked down with all his strength.

No result.

He tried again. *One, two, jerk.*

Nothing.

He thought about finding some chain and hooking a Tahoe up to it. But the chain would break before the padlock. He let the frustration build. Then he jammed the wrecking bar home for a third try. *One. Two.* On three he jerked downward with all the force in his frame. His whole body weight reinforced the blow.

The padlock broke.

He smacked the levers out of their slots and opened the doors. He lit up the flashlight and took a look inside.

Cars.

There were four of them. Strange makes. Dusty, sandblasted pastel colors. They were opened like cans, ripped, peeled, twisted. They had holes through their sheet metal the size of telephone poles. The license plates were covered with neat Arabic numbers.

Reacher turned in the doorway and called into the darkness, "No Humvees." He leaned down and took Vaughan's hand and pulled her up. She followed the flashlight beam as he played it around.

"From Iraq?" she asked.

He nodded. "Civilian vehicles."

"Why bring them here?"

"I don't know."

"What did the damage?"

"Cannon fire, maybe. Some kind of big shells."

"Artillery versus sedans?" Vaughan said. "That's kind of extreme."

"You bet it is," Reacher said. "Exactly what is going on over there?"

THEY closed the container and hiked the quarter mile back to the oil-drum pyramid and scaled the wall in the opposite direction.

Out, not in. It was just as difficult. They stepped off onto the Crown Vic's hood and slid back to solid ground. Reacher folded the ladder and packed it in the rear seat. Vaughan put the captured Kearny Chemical file in the trunk, under the mat.

She asked, "Can we take the long way home? I don't want to go through Despair again."

Reacher said, "We're not going home."

THEY drove west to the truck route. Four miles past the MP base, Reacher told Vaughan to pull over. "We're going to sleep for a while and then watch traffic," he said. "I'm working on a theory."

"What theory?"

"I can't tell you. I might be wrong, and then you wouldn't respect me in the morning."

Vaughan bumped down off the new blacktop and backed up on the shoulder. They cracked their windows to let some air in and reclined their seats and went to sleep. Four hours, Reacher figured, before there would be anything to see.

REACHER woke up when the first rays of the morning sun hit the left-hand corner of the windshield. Vaughan stayed asleep. She was small enough to have turned in her seat. Her knees were up, and her hands were pressed together between them. She looked peaceful.

The first truck to pass them was heading east toward Despair. A flatbed semi with Nevada plates, loaded with a tangle of rusted-out junk. Washing machines, tumble dryers, bicycle frames, bent rebar. Ten minutes later a second flatbed blew by, heaped with wrecked cars. Its tires whined loud, and Vaughan woke up and glanced ahead at it and asked, "How's your theory doing?"

Reacher said, "Nothing to support it yet. But also nothing to disprove it."

"Good morning."

"To you, too."

Next up was a semi coming west, out of Despair. The bed was loaded with steel bars.

"One of the four we saw last night," Vaughan said.

Reacher nodded. The other three were right behind it. The business day had started.

Another incoming truck blew by. A container truck. A blue China Lines container on it. New Jersey plates.

Vaughan said, "Combat wrecks."

Reacher nodded and said nothing. He was turned in his seat, watching the western horizon a mile away. He could see a small shape wobbling in the haze. A box truck, tan-colored.

He said, "Pay attention now."

The truck had no logo on it. No writing of any kind. It had Canadian plates, from Ontario.

"Prediction," Reacher said. "We're going to see that truck heading out again within about ninety minutes."

"Why wouldn't we? It'll unload and go home."

"Unload what?" Reacher said.

"Scrap metal."

"From Ontario? That's a long distance. Especially considering that Canada has steel mills all its own. Why haul it out here?"

"So what was in that truck?" Vaughan asked.

"My guess is nothing at all."

PLENTY more trucks passed by in both directions. Semis loaded with rusted hulks that might have been locomotives or parts of ships. Reacher kept his focus on the eastern horizon. Vaughan got out and brought the captured file from under the mat in the trunk. She took the papers out, squared them on her knee, and started with the oldest page first. It was a purchase order for five thousand gallons of trichloroethylene. The second-oldest page was identical. As was the third. The fourth fell into the following calendar year.

Vaughan said, "Fifteen thousand gallons a year. Is that a lot?"

"I don't know," Reacher said. "We'll have to ask the state lab."

The second year of orders came out the same. Fifteen thousand gallons. Then the third year jumped way up, to twenty-five thousand gallons.

The fourth and fifth years held steady at twenty-five. The sixth year jumped again. Thirty thousand gallons. Iraq was getting worse. A twenty percent increase. And the current year looked set to exceed even that. There were already six orders in, and the year still had a whole quarter to run. Then Vaughan paused and looked at the six pages again. "No," she said, "one of these is different."

Reacher asked, "Different how?"

"One of the orders isn't for trichloroethylene. And it isn't in gallons. It's in tons, for something called Trinitrotoluene. Thurman bought twenty tons of it."

"When?"

"Three months ago. Maybe it's another kind of degreaser."

"It isn't. Trichloroethylene is TCE," Reacher said. "Trinitrotoluene is TNT."

"Thurman bought twenty tons of TNT? Why?"

"I don't know."

Vaughan riffled back through the pages she had already examined. "He never bought any before," she said. "It's something new."

Reacher glanced ahead through the windshield. Saw the tan box truck heading back toward them. He took the red bubble light off the dash and held it in his hand. "Stand by," he said. "We're going to stop that truck."

"We can't," Vaughan said. "We don't have jurisdiction here."

"The driver doesn't know that. He's Canadian."

VAUGHAN waited for the truck to pass and pulled out onto the road. Reacher opened his window and clamped the bubble light on the roof. Vaughan hit a switch, and the light started flashing. She hit another switch, and her siren quacked twice.

Nothing happened for ten long seconds. Then the truck started to slow. The driver put his turn signal on, then braked and aimed for a spot where the shoulder was wide. Vaughan skipped past and tucked in again, and the two vehicles came to a stop, nose to tail.

She said, "A search would be illegal."

Reacher said, "I know. Just tell the guy to sit tight five minutes. We're going to take a photograph."

Vaughan got out and cop-walked to the driver's window. She spoke for a moment, then walked back. Reacher said, "Back up on the other shoulder at right angles. We need to see the whole truck, side-on, with the camera."

Vaughan reversed across the blacktop in a wide curve and came to rest sideways on the opposite shoulder with the front of her car pointed dead center at the side of the truck. She hit laptop keys, and the screen lit up with a picture of the truck.

Reacher said, "We need to see the thermal image."

Vaughan said, "I don't know if it works in the daytime." She hit more keys, and the screen blazed white. Everything was hot.

Reacher said, "Turn down the sensitivity."

She toggled keys until the road surface and the background scrub showed up as a baseline gray. The truck glowed a hundred shades of green. The hood was warm, with a bright center where the engine was. The cab was warm, a generalized green block where the driver was sitting.

The box body was cold at the rear. It suddenly got warmer three quarters of the way forward. A section five feet long directly behind the cab was glowing bright.

Vaughan said, "It reminds me of the wall around the metal plant. Hotter at one end than the other."

Reacher nodded. Stuck his arm out the window, waved the driver onward, and peeled the bubble light off the roof. The truck lurched as the gears caught, and it pulled across the rumble strip and got straight in the traffic lane and lumbered slowly away.

Vaughan asked, "What did we just see?"

"A truck on its way to Canada."

"Is this part of your theory?"

"Pretty much all of it."

"Want to tell me about it?"

"Later. When it's across the border."

"Why then?"

"Because I don't want to put you in a difficult position."

"You're trying to keep *me* out of trouble?"

Reacher said, "I'm trying to keep everybody out of trouble."

THEY turned around and drove west. They bumped down off the new blacktop and kept on going, all the way to the next township. First stop was a coffee shop for a late breakfast. Second stop was a Holiday Inn, where they rented a beige room and showered and made love and went to sleep. They woke up at four and did all the same things in reverse order. At five-thirty, they were on the road again heading east, back toward Despair.

VAUGHAN drove. The setting sun was behind her, bright in her mirror. It put a glowing rectangle of light on her face. The truck route was reasonably busy in both directions. The metal plant ahead was still sucking stuff in and spitting it out again. Reacher watched the license plates. He saw representatives from all of Colorado's neighboring states, plus a container truck from New Jersey, heading outward, presumably empty.

He thought, License plates.

He said, "I was in the Gulf."

Vaughan nodded.

"We spent most of the time in Saudi and Kuwait, of course. But there were a few covert trips into Iraq. I remember their license plates being silver. The ones we saw last night were off-white."

"You think those weren't Iraqi cars?"

"I think Iran uses off-white plates."

"We're fighting in Iran and nobody knows? That's not possible."

"We were fighting in Cambodia in the seventies and nobody knew. But I think it's more likely there's a bunch of Iranians heading west to Iraq to join the fun every day. Like commuting to a job. Maybe we're stopping them at the border crossings. With artillery."

They passed the MP base just before six-fifteen. Neat, quiet, still, six parked Humvees, four guys in the guard shack. All in order.

They slowed for the last five miles and tried to time it right. Traffic had died away to nothing. The plant was closed. The lights were off. Presumably the last stragglers were heading home. Vaughan made the left onto Despair's old road and then found the Tahoes' ruts in the gathering gloom and followed them as she had the night before, through the throat of the figure eight and around to the back of the residential compound. She parked there and went to pull the key, but Reacher put his hand on her wrist and said, "I have to do this part alone."

Vaughan said, "Why?"

"Because you're permanent and I'm not. You're a cop from the next town. You can't go breaking and entering all over the place."

"I already have."

"But nobody knew. Which made it okay. This time it won't be."

He left the ladder and the wrecking bar and the flashlight where they were, in the car. But he took the captured switchblades from the bar fight with him. He put one in each pocket, just in case.

Then he hiked fifty yards through the scrub and easily climbed the fieldstone wall surrounding Thurman's residential compound.

10

IT DIDN'T take Reacher long to locate the Piper's hangar. He could smell the plane. Oil, unburned hydrocarbons from the tanks. The clock in his head showed one minute before seven in the evening. He leaned against the hangar's blind side, away from the house.

He heard footsteps at one minute past.

Long strides, a heavy tread. The big guy from the plant, hustling. Then more footsteps. Slower. A shorter stride. An older man, overweight, battling stiffness.

Reacher took a breath and stepped around the corner of the barn, into the light.

The big guy from the plant was standing behind the Piper's wing, just waiting, like some kind of butler. Thurman was on the path leading from the house. He was dressed in his wool suit. He was wearing a white shirt and a blue tie.

He was carrying a small cardboard carton, two-handed, out in front of his body, reverentially. He stopped dead on the path. Reacher watched him try to find something to say and then watched him give up. So Reacher filled the silence himself. He said, "Good evening, folks."

Thurman said, "You're trespassing."

"Probably."

"You need to leave now."

"I'll leave when I've seen what's in that box. I'm curious about what part of Uncle Sam's property you're smuggling out of here."

The big guy put himself between Reacher and Thurman. He asked his boss, "You want me to throw him out?"

Reacher saw Thurman thinking about his answer. There was debate in his face, some kind of a long-range calculus, like he was playing a game and thinking eight moves ahead.

Thurman said, "No. Let him stay."

Reacher said, "What's in the box?"

Thurman said, "Not Uncle Sam's property. God's property."

He unlaced the crisscrossed flaps of the box, raised them. The box held crumpled newspaper, with a small plastic jar nested in it.

The jar was a quarter full with black powder. Coarser than talc, finer than salt.

Reacher asked, "What is it?"

Thurman said, "Ash."

"From where?"

"Fly with me tonight and find out. I have nothing to hide. And I'm a patient man. I don't mind proving my innocence—over and over and over again if I have to."

THE big guy helped Thurman up onto the wing and watched as he folded himself in through the small door. Then he passed the box up. Thurman took it and laid it on a rear seat. Reacher ducked into the copilot's seat and buckled his harness. Beside him Thurman buckled his and then hit the starter button. The engine caught with a roar and the prop spun and the cabin filled with noise. The plane lurched forward, out of the hangar, down the taxiway. Reacher watched Thurman's hands. He was operating the controls the same way an old guy drives a car, leaning back in his seat, casual, familiar, automatic.

The taxiway led through two clumsy turns to the north end of the runway. The lights were on. Thurman hit the power, and the wheels started thumping faster below. Then the plane went light and the nose lifted. The plane climbed hard for a minute. Reacher looked over at the dash and saw the altimeter reading two thousand feet. Airspeed was a little over a hundred and twenty. The compass reading was southeast. Fuel was more than half full.

Wind howled around the screens and whistled in through cracks. Altogether the little Piper reminded Reacher of the kind of old cars people use as taxis at suburban railroad stations. Sagging, worn out, clunky, but capable of making it through the ride.

He asked, "Where are we going?"

"You'll see."

Reacher watched the compass. It was holding steady on south and east. He consulted his mental maps and figured they were going to exit Colorado just left of the state's bottom right-hand corner. He thought about Vaughan, alone in her car. She would have heard the plane take off. She would be wondering why he hadn't come back over the wall.

Thurman said, "You broke into a container last night. You saw the cars."

Reacher said, "Did I?"

"It's a fair guess."

"Why do they bring them to you?"

"There are some things government feels it politic to conceal."

"What do you do with them?"

"The same thing we do with all wrecks. We recycle them. Peugeots and Toyotas from the Gulf turn into Fords and Chevrolets from Detroit. Or bicycles or refrigerators."

There was nothing but darkness below, relieved occasionally by tiny clusters of yellow light. Hamlets, farms, gas stations.

Reacher asked, "How is Underwood doing? The deputy?"

Thurman paused a moment. Then he said, "He passed on."

"Did you call the coroner?"

"No need. He was old; he got sick; he died."

"He was about forty."

"A good Christian has nothing to fear in death, Mr. Reacher. One door closes, another opens."

Thurman leaned back, his gut between him and the stick, his hands held low. The air got steadily worse. There was no storm outside, just roiling evening thermals coming up off the plains in giant invisible waves.

Thurman started jerking the stick and hammering the rudder. At first, Reacher thought they were seeking smoother air. Then he realized Thurman was deliberately making things worse. He was diving where the downdrafts were and climbing with the updrafts.

Thurman said, "This is why you need to get your life in order. The end could come at any time. Maybe sooner than you expect."

Reacher said nothing.

They flew on, twenty more minutes. The air went still and quiet. Then dead-on an hour and a quarter total elapsed time, Thurman hit a couple of switches, fired up his radio, and clamped a headset over his ears. Then he said, "It's me, on approach." Reacher heard a muffled reply and saw lights come on below. Red and white runway lights. Thurman started a long, slow descent. The twin lines of red and white drew closer. The plane wobbled and stumbled in the air, and then the wheels touched down and bounced once and settled back. Thurman cut the power, and the plane rolled to a stop. Reacher could see the vague outlines of brick buildings in the middle distance and a vehicle approaching, headlights on. A Humvee.

The Humvee parked twenty feet from the Piper, and a guy climbed out. Battledress uniform, woodland pattern.

A soldier.

THURMAN PASSED HIM THE cardboard carton. Reacher took it one-handed and slid down to the tarmac. Thurman climbed down behind him and took the box from him. The soldier stepped forward. He bowed slightly and took the box and turned on his heel and slow-marched back to the Humvee.

He stowed the box in the Humvee's load bed and then climbed in the front. Reacher and Thurman got in the back. They drove toward a building that stood alone on a patch of lawn. The Humvee parked, and the soldier retrieved the box from the load bed and slow-marched it into the building. A minute later he came back out again without it.

Thurman said, "Job done for tonight, at least."

Reacher asked, "What was in the jar?"

"People," Thurman said. "We scrape them off the metal—all that's left of them. Soot, baked onto steel. We put the day's gleanings into jars. It's as close as we can get to a proper burial."

"Where are we?"

"Fort Shaw, Oklahoma. They deal with recovered remains here."

"You come here every night?"

"As often as necessary."

"What happens now?"

"They give me dinner at the Officer's Club, and they gas up my plane. I won't ask you to join me. They'll have set just one place."

Reacher nodded. He knew how to find food on post.

The soldier climbed back into the front seat, and the Humvee turned again and drove a hundred yards to the main cluster of buildings. The soldier parked by a side door that had a sign that said it led to the Officers Club. Thurman climbed out and disappeared through the O Club door.

The grunt in the front of the Humvee craned around. "Sir, chow in the mess until ten if you're interested."

"Thanks, Soldier," Reacher said. He climbed out, and the Humvee drove away. He stood still for a moment in the sharp night air and then set out walking to the standalone building. He went in the front door and found himself in a small hallway with doors on either side. He tried the right-hand door and found a medic with the rank of captain at a desk, with Thurman's jar in front of him. The guy was young for a captain, but medics got promoted fast.

"Help you?" the guy said.

"I flew in with Thurman. I was curious about his jar. Is it what he says it is?"

"Are you authorized to know?"

"I used to be. I was an MP. I did some forensic medicine with Nash Newman, who was probably your boss back when you were a second lieutenant."

The guy nodded. "He's retired now. But I've heard of him."

"So are there human remains in the jar?"

The guy nodded. "Oxides of potassium, sodium, iron, calcium, maybe a little magnesium. Entirely consistent with burned human flesh and bone."

"What do you do with it?"

"Nothing," the guy said. "There's no DNA in it. It's soot, basically. But Thurman's a sentimental old guy. We can't turn him away. So we hold a little ceremony and accept whatever he brings."

REACHER circled the post until he smelled the aroma of fried food coming out of a powerful extraction vent. The mess kitchen. Reacher went inside and got in line and picked up a cheeseburger the size of a softball, plus fries, plus beans, plus a mug of coffee. The burger was excellent, the fries were fair, and the beans were adequate. All in all, probably better than the limp piece of grilled fish the officers were getting.

He took more coffee and sat in a chair and read the army papers. He figured the PFC would come get him when Thurman was ready to leave. He figured this would get them back to Despair by two.

The mess kitchen closed. Reacher finished the papers and dozed. The PFC never showed. At twelve-ten in the morning, Reacher woke up and heard the Piper's engine in the distance, and by the time he made it outside, the little white plane was lifting off. He stood and watched it disappear into the darkness.

THE HUMVEE CAME BACK FROM the flight line, and the PFC got out and nodded to Reacher like nothing was wrong. Reacher said, "I was supposed to be on that plane."

The driver said, "No, sir. Mr. Thurman told us you had a one-way ticket tonight. He told us you were heading south from here on business of your own. He told us you were all done in Colorado."

Reacher shook his head. He was ninety minutes' flying time from where he needed to be, in the middle of the night, in the middle of nowhere. Outwitted by a seventy-year-old preacher.

He glanced at the Humvee and said, "You want to drive me out to a road?"

"Which road?"

"I need to go north. Back to Colorado. Thurman wasn't entirely frank with you."

"Route 287 goes north. All the way up to I-70."

"How far is that?"

"Sir, I believe it's dead-on two hundred miles."

HITCHHIKING had gotten more difficult in the ten years since Reacher left the army. Drivers were less generous, more afraid. Reacher blamed the movies. They made people scared of strangers.

The Humvee from Fort Shaw let him out at twelve-forty-five, and it was a quarter past one in the morning before he saw his first northbound vehicle, a Ford F150 that didn't even slow down. Ten minutes later an old Chevy Blazer did the same thing.

At ten of two, a dark Toyota pickup slowed and took a look before passing by, which was progress of a sort. Then at a quarter past two, an old Suburban heaved into view. Reacher stepped off the shoulder and cocked his thumb.

The Suburban's brights came on. It slowed. The guy behind the wheel wanted a chance to look over his potential passenger.

A decision was made. The truck rolled forward and stopped. The window came down. The driver was a fat red-faced man. He was clinging to the wheel like he would fall out of his chair if he didn't. He said, "Where are you headed?" His voice was slurred.

Reacher said, "I'm trying to get to Hope, Colorado."

"Never heard of it. Are you a good driver?"

"Not really."

"Are you drunk?"

Reacher said, "Not even a little bit."

The guy said, "Well, I am. A lot. So you drive to wherever, let me sleep it off, and then point me toward Denver, okay?"

Reacher said, "Deal."

The guy heaved himself over into the passenger seat and collapsed its back and went straight to sleep. According to the smell of his breath, he had been drinking bourbon all evening. A lot of bourbon, probably with bourbon chasers.

The Suburban was old and worn and grimy. Its elapsed mileage was a lot of figures, starting with a two. The motor had a lot of weight to haul, and it didn't want to go much faster than sixty miles an hour. There was a cell phone on the center console. Reacher switched it on. It wouldn't spark up. No charge in the battery. There was a charger plugged into the cigarette lighter. Reacher steered with his knees and traced the free end of the wire and shoved it into a hole on the bottom of the phone.

It showed no service. The middle of nowhere.

After a while, Reacher came up behind a U-Haul truck; it was cruising at about fifty-five. He pulled out and tried to pass, but the Suburban bogged down. So he eased off and tucked in behind the truck. Its back panel was like a rolling billboard. An advertisement with a picture of three trucks: small, medium, and large. Each had U-HAUL painted on its front. Each promised a gentle ride, air-conditioning, and cloth seats.

U-Haul.

You haul. We don't. Independence, self-reliance, initiative.

In general, Reacher didn't care for the corruption of written language. *U* for *you, EZ* for *easy.* He had spent many years in school learning to read and spell, and he wanted to feel that there had been some point to it. But he couldn't get too worked up about *U-Haul.* What was the alternative? *Self-Drive Trucks?* Too clunky. Not a catchy business name. He followed behind the rolling billboard, and the triple U-Haul logos blurred together and filled his field of view.

U *for* you.

Then he thought: You *for* U.

You did this to me.

He checked the phone again.

No signal. They were in the middle of the Comanche National Grassland. The drunk guy slept on noisily, and Reacher followed the wallowing U-Haul truck for sixty solid minutes. A small town loomed up ahead. Low, dark buildings, a tall water tower, a lit-up gas station. The U-Haul pulled off for fuel. Reacher checked the Suburban's gauge. Half full. But a thirsty motor and many miles to go. He followed the U-Haul to the pumps. Unplugged the phone and put it in his shirt pocket.

The guy from the U-Haul was youngish, well-built, with long hair. He was wearing a tight black short-sleeve shirt with a clerical collar. Some kind of a minister. Probably played the guitar. He poked a credit card into a slot on the pump and pulled it out again. Reacher used his ATM card and did the same thing. The pump started up, and Reacher selected regular and watched in horror as the numbers flicked around. Gas was expensive. That was for sure. The last time he had filled a car, the price had been a dollar.

REACHER got out of the gas station ahead of the U-Haul and headed north as fast as the old Suburban would go. The drunk guy was leaking alcohol through his pores. Reacher cracked a window. The night air kept him awake, and the whistle masked the snoring. It was four-thirty in the morning. ETA in Hope, around dawn.

Then the Suburban's engine blew.

The motor lost power, and a hot, wet smell came in through the vents. There was a muffled thump under the hood, and strings of tan emulsion blew out of the ventilation slots in front of the windshield and spattered all over the glass. The motor died altogether, and the Suburban slowed hard. Reacher steered to the shoulder and coasted to a stop.

Blown head gaskets. A week in the shop. Not good, he thought. The drunk guy slept on.

Half a mile south Reacher could see the U-Haul's lights coming his way. He leaned over the sleeping guy and found a pen and an old service invoice in the glove compartment. He turned the invoice over and wrote: "You need to buy a new car. I borrowed your cell phone. Will mail it back." He took the Suburban's registration for the guy's address and folded it into his pocket. Then he stepped into the traffic lane and waved his arms above his head. The truck slowed and came to rest a yard in front of Reacher. The window came down, and the guy in the dog collar stuck his head out.

"Need help?" he said. Then he smiled, wide and wholesome. "Dumb question, I guess."

"I need a ride," Reacher said. "The engine blew."

"Want me to take a look?"

Reacher said, "No point, believe me. I'll have to send a tow truck." He didn't want the minister to see the drunk guy. From a distance, he was out of sight on the reclined seat.

"I'm headed north to Yuma. You're welcome to join me."

Reacher nodded. Called up the map in his head. The Yuma road crossed the Hope road about two hours ahead. He would need a third ride, for the final western leg. His ETA was now about ten in the morning, with luck. He said, "Thanks."

THE U-Haul smelled of warm exhaust fumes and hot oil and plastic. But the seat was cloth, as advertised, and reasonably comfortable. Reacher had to fight to stay awake. He wanted to be good company. He asked, "What are you hauling?"

The guy in the collar said, "Used furniture. Donations. Our church runs a mission in Yuma."

"What kind of a church?"

"We're Anglicans, plain vanilla, middle of the road."

"Do you play the guitar?"

The guy smiled again. "We try to be inclusive."

"Where I'm going, there's an End Times Church. What do you know about them?"

"Have you read the book of Revelation?"

Reacher said, "I've heard of it."

The minister said, "Its correct title is The Revelation to Saint John the Divine. It was written either in ancient Hebrew or Aramaic and then translated into Koine Greek and then into Latin and then into Elizabethan English, with opportunities for error and confusion at every single stage. Now it reads like a bad acid trip."

"What does it say?"

"Broadly, the righteous ascend to heaven, and the unholy are left on Earth and are visited by various colorful plagues and disasters."

"Is that the same as the Rapture?"

"The Rapture is the ascending part."

"When is all this supposed to happen?"

"It's perpetually imminent, apparently."

Reacher thought back to Thurman's smug little speech in the metal plant. *There are signs,* he had said. *And the possibility of precipitating events.*

Reacher asked, "What would be the trigger?"

The minister shrugged. "There's something about a red calf being born in the Holy Land. End Times enthusiasts comb through ranches, looking for cattle a little more auburn than usual. They ship pairs to Israel, hoping they'll breed a perfect redhead. They want to get things started. They can't wait."

"That's it? Red calves?"

"Most enthusiasts believe that a major war in the Middle East is necessary, which is why they've been so unhappy about Iraq. Apparently, what's happening there isn't bad enough for them."

There was no more conversation after that, either theological or secular. The Hope road arrived two hours into the trip, a lumpy two-lane crossing their path at an exact right angle. Reacher got out and waved the truck away, and then he walked into the dark, empty vastness. Predawn was happening way to the east, over Kansas. Colorado was still pitch-black. There was no cell phone signal.

No traffic, either.

Not for the first twenty minutes. Then a lone car came north, but it didn't turn off. An SUV came south and slowed, but it turned east, away from Hope.

It was cold. There was a wind coming out of the east, and it was moving rain clouds into the sky. Reacher turned his collar up and crossed his arms over his chest and trapped his hands under his biceps for warmth. Cloudy diffused streaks of pink and purple lit up the far horizon. A new day. Maybe a good day. Maybe a bad day. Maybe the last day. *The end is near,* Thurman's church had promised. Maybe a meteorite the size of a moon was hurtling closer.

Or maybe not.

Reacher saw headlights in the east. A large vehicle, possibly a semi trailer. When the truck was a hundred yards away, he saw that it was a big rigid panel van with a refrigerator unit mounted on top. Fresh-food delivery. Food drivers usually didn't like to stop. They had schedules to keep.

Reacher raised his hand high, thumb extended. *I need a ride.* Then he raised both arms and waved. The distress semaphore. *I really need a ride.*

The driver looked down. Then the truck slowed. The air brakes hissed loud, and the springs squealed, and the truck came to a stop forty feet west of the junction. The window came down, and the driver peered out, a short, wiry man incongruously small in the huge cab. He said, "It's going to rain."

Reacher said, "That's the least of my problems. I'm headed for Hope, and my car broke down."

The guy at the wheel said, "My first stop is Hope."

Reacher said, "You're the supermarket guy. From Topeka."

"I left there at four this morning. Climb aboard."

DAWN chased the truck west and overtook it inside thirty minutes. The world lit up cloudy and pale gold, and the supermarket guy killed his headlights and sat back and relaxed. Reacher asked him if he often carried passengers, and he said that about one morning in five he found someone looking for a ride. Reacher said he had met a couple of women who might have ridden with him.

"Tourists," the guy said.

"More than that," Reacher said.

"You think?"

"I know."

"How?"

"I figured it out."

The guy nodded at the wheel. "Wives and girlfriends," he said. "Looking to be close by while their husbands and boyfriends pass through the state."

"Understandable," Reacher said. "It's a tense time for them."

"And?"

"And nothing. Not my business."

Then he checked his borrowed cell phone again. No signal. There was nothing on the radio, either. The supermarket guy hit a button that scanned the whole AM spectrum from end to end, and he came up with nothing. Just static.

REACHER made it to Hope just before ten in the morning. He got out on First Street and stood for a moment. His cell phone showed good signal. But he didn't dial. He walked down to Fifth and turned east. From fifty yards away, he saw that the old blue Chevy pickup was in Vaughan's driveway. It had glass in its windows again. The glass was still labeled with paper bar codes, and it was crisp and clear. It looked very new against the faded old paint. He walked to the door and rang the bell. He stood on the step for thirty long seconds and then the door opened.

Vaughan looked out at him and said, "Hello."

She was dressed in the same black clothes she had worn the night before. She looked still and calm. The kitchen looked just the same as before. Neat, clean, decorated, three chairs at the table. There was a glass of water on the counter and coffee in the machine.

Reacher said, "I'm sorry I didn't get right back."

"Don't apologize." She took a fine china mug from a cupboard, filled it, and handed it to Reacher. She asked, "What was in Thurman's little box?"

"You saw the box?"

"I was over the wall ten seconds after you. Did you really think I was going to wait in the car?"

"I didn't see you."

"But I saw you. I saw the whole thing. *Fly with me tonight and find out.* He ditched you somewhere, didn't he?"

Reacher nodded. "Oklahoma. An army base."

"What was in the box?"

"Soot," Reacher said. "People after a fire. They scrape it off the metal."

Vaughan sat down at her table. Reacher sat opposite her. "But you can breathe easy," he said. "There are no wrecked Humvees at the plant. Humvees don't burn like that. Tanks do. No way out of a burning tank. Soot is all that's left."

"I see." Vaughan got up and walked over to her counter and picked up her glass of water. Took a sip.

"I got a call this morning," she said. "From the state lab. My tap-water sample was very close to five parts per billion TCE. Border-line acceptable, but it's going to get a lot worse if Thurman keeps on using as much of the stuff as he uses now."

"He might stop," Reacher said.

"Why would he?"

"What does Thurman do with the wrecked tanks?"

"He recycles the steel."

"Why would the Pentagon deploy MPs to guard recycled steel?"

"I don't know."

"The MPs are there to guard something else."

"Like what?"

"Only one possibility. A battle tank's armor includes a thick layer of depleted uranium. It's a by-product from enriching natural uranium for nuclear reactors. It's toxic and radioactive. It's the kind of thing you want to keep track of. Terrorists could steal it and pack it into an explosive device. It would make a perfect dirty bomb."

Vaughan sipped her water and said, "They're cutting it up at the plant. That must make dust. No wonder everyone looks sick."

Reacher nodded.

"The deputy died from it," he said. "He told me so. From his deathbed, he said 'The,' and then he stopped, and then he said, 'You did this to me.' I thought he was accusing me, but he was pausing for breath. He was saying, 'The U did this to me.' He was using the chemical symbol for uranium. He was saying, 'The uranium did this to me.' "

Vaughan said, "The air at the plant must be thick with it. And we were right there."

Reacher said, "Remember the way the wall glowed? On the infrared camera? It wasn't hot. It was radioactive."

Vaughan sipped her water and stared into space. She asked, "Why do you say there are no Humvees there?"

Reacher said, "Because Humvees go somewhere else. Somewhere cheaper. Because they're easy. They're just cars."

"But they send cars to Despair, too," Vaughan said. "We saw them. In the container."

Reacher nodded. "Depleted uranium isn't just for armor. They make shells out of it, too. Those cars were hit with depleted uranium. They're tainted, so they have to be processed appropriately."

Vaughan raised her glass halfway and stopped. She looked at it like she was having second thoughts about ingesting anything. "Tell me what you know about dirty bombs."

"They're the same as clean bombs," Reacher said. "Except a dirty bomb uses contaminated metal, usually radioactive waste, for extra shrapnel inside the casing around the explosive charge."

"How much uranium would they need to steal?"

"The more the merrier."

Vaughan said, "I think they're already stealing it. That truck we photographed? The front of the load compartment was glowing just like the wall."

Reacher shook his head. "No," he said. "That was something else entirely."

Vaughan asked, "What, exactly?"

"All those young guys," Reacher said. "What did they have in common?"

"I don't know."

"They were from California."

"So?"

Reacher said, "When I talked to Lucy Anderson, she was cautious and a little wary, but basically we were getting along. Then when I said I had been a cop, she panicked. I put two and two together and figured her husband was a fugitive."

"Figures."

"Then I checked the rooming house where he was staying. It was empty, but it was very clean."

"Is that important?"

"Crucial," Reacher said. "Because I didn't tell Lucy Anderson that I had been a cop. I told her I had been a *military* cop. That's why she panicked. And that's why the rooming house was so clean. It was like a barracks ready for inspection. The people passing through it were all soldiers. Lucy thought I was tracking them."

"Deserters," Vaughan said. "The truck was from Canada, and they're offering asylum up there."

Reacher nodded. "Like a taxi service. The glow on the camera wasn't stolen uranium. It was a guy in a hidden compartment. Body heat. The shade of green was the same."

Vaughan sat still and quiet for a long time.

Reacher said, "Some kind of an antiwar group must be running an escape line. Maybe California service families are involved. They send guys up here with legitimate metal deliveries, and then their Canadian friends take them north over the border. There was a couple at the Despair hotel seven months ago. A buck gets ten they were the organizers, recruiting sympathizers. And the sympathizers busted your truck's windows. They thought I was getting too nosy."

Vaughan pushed her glass out of the way. "A small subgroup," she said. "The few left-hand people, working behind Thurman's back. Helping deserters."

Reacher said nothing.

Vaughan asked, "Do you know who they are?"

"No idea."

"You knew about this," she said. "You waited until that truck was over the border before you told me. Why?"

"I didn't want you to have it stopped."

"For God's sake, Reacher, you were a military cop. You hunted deserters. And now you've gone over to the dark side?"

Reacher said nothing.

"They had a duty," Vaughan said. "David *did* his duty. They should do theirs, and you should do yours."

"Duty is a transaction, Vaughan. It's a two-way street. We owe them; they owe us. And what they owe us is a solemn promise to risk our lives and limbs if and only if there's a good reason."

"You served thirteen years and you support deserters?"

"I understand their decision. Precisely *because* I served those thirteen years. I loved the army. And I hate what happened to it."

"I hate you."

"No, you don't," Reacher said. "You hate that David didn't go AWOL after his first tour."

Vaughan closed her eyes. She sat like that for a long time, pale, a small tremble in her lower lip. Then she spoke. Just a whisper. She said, "I asked him to. I begged him. I said we could start again anywhere he wanted, anywhere in the world. But he wouldn't agree. Stupid, stupid man."

Reacher held her tight while she cried. She crushed her face into his chest. She cried for her shattered life, her broken dreams, the telephone call two years before, the chaplain's visit to her door, the X-rays and the filthy hospitals.

Afterward they went for a walk together, aimlessly, just to be moving. The sky was gray, and the air smelled like rain. They ended up outside the police station, and Reacher saw her gaze trace the line of twenty aluminum letters fixed to the brick: HOPE POLICE DEPARTMENT. She said, "Why didn't Raphael Ramirez make it?"

Reacher said, "Ramirez was different. One phone call from your desk will explain it, and we might as well go ahead and make it. Maria has waited long enough."

Vaughan said, "One call to who?"

"The MPs west of Despair. Ask them to fax Ramirez's file. They'll say, 'Who?' You'll tell them you know Maria was just there, so you know they know who he is."

"What are we going to find?"

"My guess is, Ramirez was in prison two weeks ago."

ELEVEN minutes after Vaughan finished her call, the Hope Police Department's fax machine sucked a blank page out of the feeder tray and fed it back out with writing on it.

Not much writing. It was a bare-bones summary.

Raphael Ramirez had been a private in the Marine Corps. At the age of eighteen, he had been deployed to Iraq. At the age of nineteen, he had served a second deployment. At the age of twenty, he had gone AWOL ahead of a third deployment. He had gone on the run but had been arrested five days later in Los Angeles and locked up awaiting court martial back at Pendleton.

Date of arrest, three weeks previously.

Reacher said, "Let's go find Maria."

THEY found her in her motel room. They led her outside and sat her in the plastic lawn chair outside her room. Reacher took room 9's chair, and Vaughan took room 7's.

Reacher said, "Raphael was a marine."

Maria nodded. Said nothing.

Reacher said, "He had been to Iraq twice. He didn't want to go back a third time. So nearly four weeks ago he went on the run. Did he call you?"

"He called most days."

"But then he didn't call for two or three days. Right?"

"He lost his cell phone. Then he got a new phone, and he called to say he had found some people. They were going to get him to

Canada through Despair. He said I should come here and wait for his call."

"Did he call from Despair?"

"No."

"Why did you go to the MPs?" ·

"To ask if they had found him and arrested him. I was worried. But they said they had never heard of him."

"And so you came back here to wait some more."

Maria nodded.

Reacher said, "It wasn't exactly like that. Raphael was arrested in L.A. The marines caught up with him. He didn't lose his phone. He was in jail for two or three days."

"He didn't tell me that."

"He wasn't allowed to. My guess is, he made a deal. The Marine Corps offered him a choice. Five years in Leavenworth or go undercover to bust the escape line to Canada. Names, addresses, routes, all that stuff. He agreed, and they turned him loose. The MPs found out what was going on and were told to stonewall you."

"So where is Raphael now? Why doesn't he call?"

Reacher said, "Marines have a code. Did Raphael tell you?"

Maria said, "Unit, corps, God, country."

Reacher nodded. "Raphael's primary loyalty was to his unit, a handful of guys just like him."

"I don't understand."

"I think he agreed to the deal but couldn't carry it through. He couldn't betray guys just like him. I think he rode up to Despair but didn't call in to the marines. I think he stayed out of sight. He hung around on the edge of town, not wanting to know who was involved, because he was afraid he might have to give them away later. He hung out for days, agonizing. He got thirsty and hungry. He started hallucinating and decided to walk over to Hope and find you and get out some other way."

"So where is he?"

"He didn't make it, Maria. He collapsed halfway. He died."

For the second time in an hour, Reacher watched a woman cry.

Vaughan held her, and Reacher said, "He was a good man, Maria. He was just a kid who couldn't take any more. And in the end, he didn't betray what he believed in." He said those things over and over again, in different orders and with different emphases, but they didn't help.

11

REACHER and Vaughan walked to the diner, where Reacher ate for the first time since the burger he had scored in Fort Shaw the night before. He topped up his caffeine level with four mugs of coffee, and when he finished, he said, "There's one more thing on my mind. We need to go see those MPs. Now that you've established contact, we might get away with a face-to-face meeting."

Vaughan said, "We're going to drive through Despair again?"

Reacher shook his head. "Let's take your truck and go cross-country."

THEY peeled the paper bar codes off the new glass, and Vaughan took the wheel. Three miles before Despair, they slowed and bumped down off the road and started a long loop to the north. It was slow going across the open land. Occasionally they found dry washes and followed them through looping meanders at a higher speed. Then it was back to picking their way around table rocks bigger than the Chevy itself.

Vaughan asked, "What exactly is on your mind?"

"I like to be able to explain things to myself," Reacher said.

"What can't you explain?"

"The way they were so desperate to keep people out. The way they found Ramirez's body and dealt with it so efficiently. It was no surprise to them. It's like they set themselves up to be constantly vigilant for intruders. To expect them, even. Everyone in town is involved. The first day I showed up, even the waitress in the restaurant knew what to do. Why would they go to those lengths?"

"They're playing ball with the Pentagon."

"The Pentagon wouldn't ask for that. They trust walls and distance and geography, not people."

"Maybe Thurman asked the people himself."

"I'm sure he did. But why?"

Two miles west of the plant, they bumped up onto the blacktop. Three minutes after that, they arrived at the MP base. Two guys came out of the guard shack immediately. One was Morgan, the bespectacled specialist with the squint lines. Vaughan introduced herself by name and as an officer with the Hope PD. Morgan saluted her in a way that Reacher knew meant the MPs had run her plate the first time around. They had found out what her husband had been and what he was now.

Five minutes later they were face-to-face across a desk with a onestriper called Connor. He was a small, lean man, maybe twenty-six years old. He had been to Iraq. His BDUs were beat up and sandblasted, and his cheekbones were burned shiny. He looked competent and probably was. He was still alive. He asked, "Is this an official visit from the Hope PD?"

Vaughan said, "Yes. Mr. Reacher is a civilian adviser."

"So how can I help?"

Reacher said, "Long story short, we know about the DU salvage at Thurman's plant."

Connor said, "That bothers me a little."

Reacher said, "It bothers us a little, too. Homeland Security rules require us to maintain a register of chemically sensitive sites within twenty miles." He said it as if it was true, which it might have been.

"It's classified," Connor said. "You can't put it in a register."

Reacher nodded. "We understand that. But we should have been made aware of it privately."

"Sounds like you are aware of it."

"But now we want to verify some details. We think we're entitled to know when and how the scrap DU gets transported out and what route is used."

"Worried about it rolling down First Street?"

"You bet."

"Well, it doesn't. The state of Colorado's pretty uptight. They want to close the interstate and use an armed convoy. Which they can't contemplate on a regular basis. Once every five years is what they're thinking."

"How long ago did the first convoy leave?"

"It didn't. The first convoy will happen two years from now."

Reacher said, "So now they're stockpiling the stuff at the plant?"

Connor nodded. "The steel moves out; the DU stays."

REACHER and Vaughan got back in the truck, and Vaughan asked, "Why does it matter that Thurman is stockpiling depleted uranium?"

Reacher said, "I don't like the combination. He's got twenty tons of radioactive waste and twenty tons of TNT. He's an End Times enthusiast. I spoke to a minister last night. He said that End Times people can't wait to get things started. Thurman himself said there might be precipitating events on the way. And the whole town seems to be waiting for something to happen."

"Thurman can't start Armageddon."

"These people seem to think they can nudge things along. They're trying to breed red cows in Israel."

"How would that help?"

"Don't ask me. Another requirement seems to be a major war in the Middle East."

"We've already got one."

"Not major enough."

"How could it be worse?"

"Suppose another country joined in. Suppose a dirty bomb went off in Manhattan. Suppose the guys in the hazmat suits found fragments of Iranian license plates."

Vaughan was quiet for a moment. "Iran is working with uranium. They're boasting about it."

"There you go," Reacher said. "What would happen next?"

"We'd attack Iran, Iran would attack Israel, Israel would retaliate, and everyone would be fighting."

"Precipitating events," Reacher said.

"That's insane."

"We have an End Times nutcase with twenty tons of TNT and twenty tons of DU and four Iranian cars."

Vaughan said, "No judge in America would sign off on a search warrant. Not with what we've got. It's just a crazy theory."

Reacher said, "I'm not looking for a search warrant. I'm waiting for dark."

RAIN came with the darkness. A steady, hard downpour. The roads were running with water, like rivers. Within minutes of leaving the MP station, their old Chevy was the only car on the road.

"This is good," Reacher said.

"You think?"

"Everyone will be indoors. We'll have the place to ourselves."

They drove on. Up ahead, they saw a horizontal sliver of blue light. The plant, lit up. Much smaller than before. But as they got closer, they saw that the glow was smaller because only the farthest quarter was illuminated. The secret compound.

The personnel gate and the main vehicle gate were both closed. The bulk of the plant was dark. Nearly a mile beyond it the secret compound was bright and distant and tempting.

"Okay," Reacher said. "Same place as before."

The Tahoes' beaten ruts were soft and full of water. The Chevy spun its wheels and fishtailed and clawed its way forward. Vaughan found the right place. Reacher said, "Back it in." Vaughan stopped the truck with its tailgate well under the curve of the metal cylinder.

Reacher was soaked to the skin even before he got his stuff out of the load-bed. He knelt in the mud beside the truck and adjusted the ladder to the L-shape that had worked before. He put the flashlight in one pocket and hooked the crook of the wrecking bar in the other. Then he lifted the ladder vertically into the back of the pickup and jammed its feet into the right angle between the load bed floor and the back wall of the cab. He let it fall forward, and the short leg of the L came down flat on top of the cylinder, aluminum against steel, a harmonic clonk that sounded twice, once immediately and then once again whole seconds later, as if the impact had raced around the miles of hollow wall and come back stronger.

Reacher got into the load bed and started climbing. He made it over the angle of the L and stopped. The cylinder was covered in shiny paint, and the paint was slick with running water. Maneuvering had been hard before. Now it was going to be very difficult.

He picked a spot where half the water was sluicing one way and half the other. The geometric dead-center of the cylinder. The continental divide. He lined up with it and eased off the ladder and sat down. An uneasy feeling. Wet cotton on wet paint. No friction. He needed to twist from the waist and lift the ladder and reverse it. But he couldn't move. The slightest turn would unstick him. If he twisted his upper body to the left, the torque would spin his lower body to the right, and he would slide right off the cylinder.

Fourteen feet to the ground. He could survive a controlled fall, but without the ladder on the inside, it wasn't clear how he would ever get out again.

Perhaps he could improvise a ladder out of scrap metal. Perhaps he could learn to weld and build one.

Or perhaps not.

He thought, I'll worry about all that later.

He nudged himself forward and rolled over onto his stomach as he slid. The wrecking bar thumped and banged, and then ninety degrees past top dead-center he was free-falling through empty air.

He hit the ground a whole lot later than he thought he would. His knees were bent, and he went down in a heap and rolled one way, and the wrecking bar went the other. But there was no physical damage beyond mud and grease all over his clothes. He got to his feet and wiped his hands on his pants. Found the wrecking bar and set off walking south and west. Dark shapes loomed up at him. Cranes, gantries, crushers. Beyond them the distant inner compound was still lit up. Its gate was open.

An invitation. A trap, almost certainly. Reacher looked at it for a long moment and then slogged onward. Within ten paces, his shoes were carrying pounds of sticky mud. His hair was plastered to his head, and water was running into his eyes.

Ahead he could see the white security Tahoes parked side by side to the left of the main vehicle gate. When he got there, he turned right and checked the gate. No luck. On the inside, it had the same gray box as on the outside. The same keypad. The same three-million-plus combinations. He walked past the security office and stopped outside purchasing. Scraped his shoes and climbed the steps and used his fingernails to pull the screws out of the padlock hasp. The door sagged open. He went inside.

He headed straight for the row of file cabinets. The T drawer. Pulled the Thomas file. The cell phone supplier. Clipped to the back of the original purchase order were the contracts, the fees, the rebates, the makes, the models. And the numbers. He tore off the sheet with the numbers and folded it into his pants pocket. Then he headed back out to the rain.

Forty minutes later he was approaching the inner gate.

IT WAS still open. Light spilled out in a solid bar the width of the opening and spread and widened like a lighthouse beam that reached a hundred yards.

Reacher hugged the wall and approached from the right. He stopped in the last foot of shadow and listened hard. Heard nothing over the pelting rain. He waited one slow minute and then stepped into the light. No reaction.

He walked in, fast and casual. No alternative. He was as lit up and vulnerable as a stripper on a stage. He was up to his ankles in water. Ahead on the left was a pile of shipping containers stacked in an open V, point outward. To their right and thirty feet farther away was a second V. He aimed for the gap between them. Stepped through and found himself alone in an arena within an arena within an arena. Altogether there were eight stacks of shipping containers arranged in a giant circle. They hid an area of maybe thirty acres.

Apart from cranes and gantries and crushers, backhoes and bull-dozers, and carts and dollies and trailers, all loaded with smaller pieces of equipment, there were two items of interest.

The first was a mountain of wrecked main battle tanks.

It looked like an elephants' graveyard. Bent gun barrels reared up like giant tusks or ribs. Turret assemblies were dumped and stacked haphazardly, peeled open like cans. Side skirts were everywhere, some of them ripped like foil. There were traces of desert camouflage paint, but most of the metal was scorched dull black. Reacher felt he could hear men still screaming under it.

He turned away.

The second item of interest was a hundred yards east.

An eighteen-wheel semi truck. Ready to roll. The Peterbilt tractor was impressive. A fine paint job, an air filter the size of an oil drum, twin smokestacks, a forest of antennas. The container looked shabby in comparison. Dull paint, faded lettering. It was clamped tight to the trailer. It had a double door, secured with the same four foot-long levers he had seen before, all in the closed position.

Reacher pulled himself up on the container's bottom ledge. Got his free hand on the nearest lever and pushed it up.

It wouldn't move.

It was welded to its bracket. An inch-long worm of metal had been melted into the gap. The three others were the same. And the doors had been welded to each other. Reacher jammed the wrecking bar into the space between two welds and pushed hard.

Impossible. Like trying to lift a car with a nail file.

He climbed down and looked again at the trailer clamps. They were turned tight. And welded.

He dropped the wrecking bar and walked back toward the inner gates. They were two hundred yards away.

And they were closing.

THEY were moving slowly but smoothly. A consistent speed. Motorized. Too smooth and too consistent for manual operation.

Reacher started forward involuntarily and then stopped.

Four figures walked in through the closing gap. On the right was Thurman. On the left was the giant with the wrench. In the middle was the plant foreman. He was pushing Vaughan in front of him. She was soaked to the skin, and she was stumbling, as if every few paces she was getting a shove in the back.

Reacher started walking again.

The gates closed with a metallic clang.

The four figures kept on coming.

They met in the center of the hidden space. Vaughan made it to Reacher's side and turned around, put a hand on his arm.

Thurman called, "What are you doing here?"

Reacher said, "I'm looking around."

Thurman said, "I'm losing patience."

Reacher said, "What's in the truck?"

Thurman breathed in, breathed out. He said, "Gifts."

"What kind?"

"Clothes, blankets, medical supplies, prosthetic limbs, dried and powdered foodstuffs, purified water, antibiotics, vitamins."

"Where from?"

"They were bought with tithes from the people of Despair."

"Who are they for?"

"Afghanistan. For refugees and displaced persons. Jesus said whatever you wish that men would do to you, do so to them. Love your enemies and pray for those who persecute you."

Reacher said, "Where are the cars from Iran?"

"The what?"

"The cars from Iran."

Thurman said, "Melted down and shipped out."

"Where is the TNT?"

"The what?"

"You bought twenty tons of TNT from Kearny Chemical."

Thurman smiled. "Oh, that," he said. "It was a mistake. A coding error. A new girl in the office was one number off on Kearny's order form. We got TNT instead of TCE. We sent it back."

"Where is the uranium?"

"The what?"

"You pulled twenty tons of depleted uranium out of these tanks."

"You're standing on it," Thurman said. "It's buried. I keep it in the ground."

Reacher said nothing. He glanced right, at the eighteen-wheeler. Left, at the backhoe. Down, at the ground.

"Satisfied?" Thurman asked.

Reacher said, "I might be. After I've made a phone call."

"What phone call?"

"I think you know."

Thurman said, "This is not the time for phone calls."

Reacher said, "Not the place, either. I'll wait until I get back to Hope. Or Kansas."

Thurman glanced at the gate. "Turn out your pockets," he said.

"Worried about those numbers? Maybe I memorized them."

"Turn out your pockets."

"Make me."

Thurman went still. His eyes narrowed, and debate crossed his face. He spent a second or two on it and then stepped back and raised his right arm. He waved his two employees forward.

The big guy slapped the wrench in and out of his palm. Both guys smiled and moved a step closer. The foreman was on Reacher's right, and the big guy was on his left. Both of them close but not within touching distance.

Reacher said, "You know we don't have to do this. We could walk out of here friends."

The foreman said, "I don't think so."

"Then you won't walk out of here at all."

"Brave talk."

Reacher said nothing. *Get your retaliation in first.*

He feinted left, toward the giant. The big guy rocked back, surprised. Reacher planted his heel very carefully in the mud and jerked the other way. He smashed the foreman in the stomach with his elbow. A five-hundred-pound collision.

The foreman fell face-first into a foot-wide rut filled with water.

Reacher kicked him in the side to roll him out of it. He didn't want the guy to drown. Thurman had backed off. Vaughan was rooted to the spot. The big guy was crouched eight feet away, holding his wrench like a clean-up hitter waiting on a high fastball.

Reacher backed off a pace. The big guy followed. Reacher stopped. The big guy swung. The huge wrench slashed horizontal, at shoulder height. Reacher stepped back a pace, and the wrench missed, and its wild momentum carried the big guy through a complete circle. Reacher stepped back.

Thirty acres. Reacher wasn't fast, and he wasn't nimble, but he had natural stamina. The big guy was breathing hard, and every missed swing was jacking his fury. Reacher kept on moving and stopping and dodging. Eventually the big guy learned. With his fifth swing, he aimed for a spot three feet behind Reacher's back. Reacher saw it coming and dodged the other way. Forward. The wrench hissed through empty air, and Reacher rolled around the guy's spinning back and bent his knees and smashed his elbow up into the guy's kidney. Then he stepped away. The big guy turned. He charged and swung and missed, and Reacher dodged away.

Like a bullfight. Except the big guy's IQ was marginally higher than a bull's. After a dozen fruitless swings, he recognized that his tactics were futile. He sent the wrench spinning away into the marshy ground and got ready to charge. Reacher smiled. Because by then the damage was done. The guy was going to lose. He didn't know it, but Reacher knew it.

And Thurman knew it.

Thurman was hurrying back toward the gate. Hurrying, but slowly. An old man. Reacher called, "Vaughan, don't let him leave. He has to stay here." He saw her move from the corner of his eye.

The giant launched himself. A crazed lunge, across fifteen feet of distance. Three hundred and fifty pounds, coming on like a train. His boots churned in the liquid mud. No traction. Reacher feinted left and stepped right and tripped him. The guy splashed down in the water and slid a full yard. He struggled to get up, his hands and knees scrabbling in the mud.

Fifty feet north Vaughan had hold of Thurman's collar. He was struggling to get free.

Reacher lined up and kicked the scrabbling giant in the head, like he was punting a football, instep against ear. The impact pinwheeled the guy's body two feet and dropped him back in the mud.

The giant lay still. Game over.

Reacher stood still and got his breathing under control and glanced north, through the light. Thurman had broken free of Vaughan's grasp and was heading for the gate again. Reacher set off in their direction. Paused to collect the giant wrench from where it had fallen. He hefted it up and carried it on his shoulder like an ax. He caught Vaughan ten yards from the gate, passed her, and clamped a hand on Thurman's shoulder and pressed downward. The old guy folded up and went down on his knees. Reacher moved onward, to the gate. He found the little gray box. Saw the keypad. Swung the wrench and smashed it to splinters. Hit it again. And again. Wires tore and ruptured.

Thurman was still on his knees. He said, "What are you doing? Now we can't get out of here."

"Wrong," Reacher said. "You can't, but we can."

"How?"

"Wait and see."

Reacher trudged through the mud and rolled Thurman's men into what medics called the recovery position. On their sides, necks at a natural angle, one leg straight and the other knee drawn up. No danger of choking. A slight danger of drowning if the puddles didn't stop filling.

Thurman poked and prodded at the shattered box where the keypad had been. No result. The gates stayed closed. He gave up and slipped and slid back to the center of the hidden area.

Reacher and Vaughan fought their way across to the eighteen-wheeler. It was just standing there, silent and oblivious.

Vaughan said, "You really think this is a bomb?"

Reacher said, "Don't you?"

"What if you're wrong?"

"What if I'm right?"

"How much damage could it do?"

"If they built it right, I wouldn't want to be within three miles of it when it goes off. It won't be pretty."

"How do we get out of here?"

"Where's your truck?"

"Where we left it. They ambushed me. Opened the outer gate and drove me through the plant in Thurman's SUV. It's parked on the other side of the inner gate. Which you just made sure will never open again."

"No big deal."

"You can't climb the wall."

"But you can," Reacher said.

THEY talked for five fast minutes about what to do and how to do it. Knives, welds the average size and thickness of a car's roof panel, canvas straps, Tahoes. Thurman was pacing aimlessly a hundred yards away. They left him there and headed through the mud to the wall. They picked a spot ten feet left of the gate. Reacher took the two switchblades out of his pocket and handed them to Vaughan. Then he stood with his back to the wall, directly underneath the maximum radius of the horizontal cylinder above. Rain sheeted off it and soaked his head and shoulders. He bent down and curled his left palm and made a stirrup. Facing him, Vaughan put her right foot in the stirrup. He took her weight, and she balanced with her wrists on his shoulders and straightened her leg and boosted herself up. He cupped his right hand under her left foot. She stood upright in his palms.

Reacher lifted. Like starting a bicep curl with a free-weights bar loaded with a hundred and twenty pounds. Easy, except that his hands were turned in at an unnatural angle. And his footing was insecure, and Vaughan wasn't a free-weights bar. She was wobbling and struggling to balance.

"Ready?" he called.

"Wait one," she said.

He felt her weight shifting, equalizing.

"Now go," she said.

He boosted her sharply upward, used her momentary weightlessness to shift his hands flat under her shoes, stepped forward half a pace, and locked his arms straight.

She fell forward and met the bulge of the cylinder with the flats of her forearms. "I'm there," she said.

He felt her reach up and straighten her arms. He heard the first switchblade pop open. He heard her stab downward with the knife. The wall clanged and boomed.

"Won't go through," she called.

"Harder," he called back.

She stabbed again. No boom. Just a little metallic clatter.

"The blade broke," she called. "The metal is too thick."

"It's not. It's from an old Buick, probably. It's aluminum foil. And that's a good Japanese blade. Hit it hard. Who do you hate?"

"The guy that pulled the trigger on David."

"He's inside the wall. His heart is the other side of the metal."

He heard the second switchblade open. Then a convulsive jerk through her legs and another dull boom through the metal.

A different boom.

"It's in," she called. "All the way."

He felt her take her weight on the wooden handle.

"It's slicing through," she called.

"It'll stop when it hits a weld."

He felt it stabilize a second later. Called, "Ready?"

"On three," she called. "One, two, *three.*"

She jerked herself upward, and he helped as much as he could, fingertips and tiptoes, and then her weight was gone. He walked away to get a better angle and saw her lying longitudinally on top of the cylinder, legs spread, both hands wrapped tight around the knife handle. She rested like that for a second and then shifted her weight and slid down the far side of the bulge, still holding tight to the knife handle. Her weight started pulling the blade through the metal. It would jam again at the next weld, which he figured was maybe five feet down, allowing for the size of a typical car's roof panel. She would be hanging off the wall at full stretch with about four feet of clear air under the soles of her shoes.

A survivable fall.

He waited what seemed like a long time, and then he heard two hard thumps on the outside of the wall. He closed his eyes and smiled. Their agreed signal. Out, on her feet, no broken bones.

"Impressive," Thurman said from ten yards away.

Reacher turned. The old guy was hatless. His blow-dried waves were ruined.

"But your lady friend can't open the gate, you know. She doesn't have the combination."

"Have faith, Mr. Thurman."

Reacher took up station six feet from the wall and a yard left of where Vaughan had gone over. Thurman backed off and watched.

Three minutes passed. Then four. Then, without warning, a long canvas strap snaked up and over the wall, and the free end landed four feet to Reacher's right. The kind of thing used for tying down scrap cars to a flatbed trailer. Vaughan had driven Thurman's Tahoe up to the security office and had found a strap of the right length in the pile near the door and had weighted its end by tying it around a scrap of pipe. He pictured her after the drive back, twenty feet away through the metal, swinging the strap like a cowgirl with a rope, building momentum, letting it go, watching it sail over.

Reacher grabbed the strap and freed the pipe and retied the end into a two-foot loop. He wrapped the canvas around his right hand and walked toward the wall. Kicked it twice and backed off a step and put his foot in the loop and waited. He pictured Vaughan securing the other end to the trailer hitch on Thurman's Tahoe, climbing into the driver's seat, selecting four-wheel-drive for maximum traction across the mud, selecting the low-range transfer case for delicate throttle control. He had been insistent about that. He didn't want his arms torn off at the shoulders when she hit the gas.

He waited. Then the strap went tight above him and started to

quiver. The canvas around his hand wrapped tight, stretched a little. Then he felt serious pressure under his foot, and he lifted slowly,
smoothly into the air.

"Good-bye, Thurman," he said. "Looks like it's you that's getting
left behind this time."

When his hips hit the maximum curve of the cylinder, he un-
wrapped his hand and hung on. He let the loop around his foot pull
his legs up sideways, and then he kicked free of the loop and came
to rest spread-eagled on his stomach along the top of the wall. He
jerked his hips and sent his legs down the far side and pushed off
and fell, two long split seconds. He hit the ground on his back and
knocked the wind out of himself. He rolled over and forced some
air into his lungs and got to his feet. He unhooked the strap from
the Tahoe's trailer hitch. Then he climbed into the passenger seat
and slammed the door.

"Thanks," he said.

"Where to now?" she asked.

"The hotel in Despair. The first phone call is one that you get to
make."

12

THEY abandoned Thurman's Tahoe next to where Vaughan's old
Chevy was waiting. They transferred between vehicles, and three
miles later they were in downtown Despair. It was still raining. They
threaded through the cross streets and pulled up outside the hotel.
The door was not locked. Inside, the place looked the same. The
empty dining room, the deserted bar, the register on the desk. The
large leather book, easy to swivel around, easy to read. Reacher put
his fingertip under the last registered guests, the couple from California, from seven months previously. He tilted the book so that
Vaughan had a clear view of their names and addresses.

"Call them in," he said. "And if they're helping the deserters, do whatever your conscience tells you to."

"If?"

"I think they might be into something else."

Vaughan made the call from her cell, and they waited for the call back. She said, "Gifts are a perfectly plausible explanation. Churches send foreign aid all the time. Volunteers, too. They're usually good people."

"No argument from me," Reacher said. "But my whole life has been about the people that aren't usual. The exceptions."

"Why are you so convinced?"

"The container was welded to the trailer. And that's not how containers get shipped. They get lifted off and put on boats. The welding suggests they don't want that container to leave the country."

Vaughan's phone rang. A three-minute wait. Agencies talked; computers were linked. She answered and listened, four long minutes. Then she thanked her caller and clicked off.

"Can't rule out the AWOL involvement," she said. "They're listed as activists. And activists can be into all kinds of things."

"What kind of activists?"

"They run a thing called the Church of the Apocalypse in L.A."

"The Apocalypse is a part of the End Times story," Reacher said. "Maybe they came here to recruit Thurman. Maybe they recognized his special potential."

Vaughan said nothing.

"Four more calls," Reacher said. "That's all it's going to take."

THEY drove west and parked on a curb at the edge of town. Three miles away they could see the plant's lights, faint and blue, blurred by the rain on the windshield, a sepulchral glow in the middle of nowhere. Reacher took the cell phone he had borrowed out of his pocket. Then he took out the sheet of paper from the purchasing office. The new cell phone numbers. The paper was wet and soggy, and he had to peel apart the folds very carefully.

"Ready?" he asked.

Vaughan said, "I don't understand."

He dialed the third number on the list. Heard ring tone in his ear, twice, four times, six times, eight. Then the call was answered.

The big guy from the plant.

Reacher said, "How are you? Been awake long?"

The guy said, "Go to hell."

Reacher clicked off and dialed the second number on the list. It rang eight times, and the plant foreman answered.

Reacher said, "Sorry, wrong number."

He clicked off.

Vaughan asked, "What exactly are you doing?"

"How did the insurgents hurt David?"

"With a roadside bomb."

"Detonated how?"

"Remotely, I assume."

Reacher nodded. "Probably by radio, from the nearest ridge line. But if Thurman *has* built a bomb, he'll probably want a lot more distance than that. Which would take a very powerful radio. My guess is, he'll use one built by Verizon or T-Mobile."

"A cell phone?"

Reacher nodded again. "The phone companies are proud of the fact that you can call anywhere from anywhere."

"And the number is on that list?"

"It would make sense," Reacher said. "Three months ago Thurman ordered twenty tons of TNT and four new cell phones. My guess is, he kept one phone for himself and gave two to his inner circle so they could have secure communications. The fourth phone is buried in the heart of that container, with the ringer wired to a primer circuit."

"And you're going to call that number?"

Reacher said, "Soon."

He dialed the first number on the list. It rang, and Thurman answered fast and impatient, like he had been waiting for the call.

Reacher asked, "You guys over the wall yet?"

Thurman said, "We're still here. Why are you calling us?"

"You starting to see a pattern?"

"The last phone was Underwood's. He's dead, so he won't answer. There's no point calling it."

Reacher said, "Okay."

"How long are you going to keep us here?"

"Just a minute more," Reacher said. He clicked off and laid the phone on the Chevy's dash. Stared out through the windshield.

Vaughan said, "You can't do this. You could be completely wrong about him."

"Then there's no problem. Gifts don't explode. We've got nothing to lose."

"But you might be right."

"In which case, Thurman's no better than whoever blew up David's Humvee. Worse, even. David was a combatant. Thurman is going to have that thing driven to a city somewhere. With children and old people all around. Thousands of them."

Vaughan said nothing.

Reacher entered the final number into his phone. Held the phone flat out to Vaughan.

"Your choice," he said. "Green button to make the call, red button to cancel it."

Vaughan didn't move for a moment. Then she took her hand off the wheel. Held her index finger out straight. She held it still, close to the phone's LED window.

She pressed the green button.

NOTHING happened. Not at first. Reacher wasn't surprised. He had read an article in a trade publication abandoned on an airplane. Press the green button and the phone in your hand sends a request by radio to the nearest cell tower, called a base transceiver station. The phone says: *Hey, I want to make a call.* The base transceiver station forwards the plea to the nearest base station. The base-station controller bundles the near-simultaneous requests and moves them on to the closest mobile switching center.

Maybe at this point a ring tone starts up in your earpiece. But it means nothing. It's there to reassure you. You're not even close to connected.

The mobile switching center identifies the destination phone, checks if it's switched on. If all is well, a channel clicks in from your local mobile switching center to its distant opposite number. Then the distant mobile switching center hits up its closest base-station controller, which hits up its closest base transceiver station, which emits a radio blast to the phone you're looking for. A nanosecond later the tone in your ear morphs from phony to real.

Total time lag: an average of seven whole seconds.

VAUGHAN took her finger back and stared forward out the windshield. The Chevy's engine was still running.

Two seconds.

"Nothing," she said.

Reacher said, "Wait."

Four seconds. Five.

They stared into the distance. The blue arena lights hung and shimmered in the wet air, pale and misty.

Six seconds. Seven.

Then: The silent horizon lit up with an immense white flash that filled the windshield and bloomed higher and wider. The rain all around turned to steam as the air superheated and jets of white vapor speared up and out in every direction, like a hundred thousand rockets had launched simultaneously. The vapor was followed by black soot, a raging black hemisphere a mile high and a mile wide. It rolled and tore and folded back on itself as white-hot shrapnel flung through it at more than fifteen thousand miles an hour.

The sound arrived three seconds after the light. First a crisp deafening *crump* and then a banshee screaming from the shrapnel in the air and an otherworldly pelting sound as a million blasted fragments fell to earth from three miles up.

After ten long seconds, there was just the patient rain on the Chevy's roof.

VAUGHAN CALLED OUT THE whole of the Hope PD for crowd control. All four deputies, her brother officer, her watch commander, and the desk guy all lined up on the western edge of Despair's last block. Nobody was allowed through. The state cops showed up next. They confirmed that the MPs had the road blocked to the west. They were already stopping incoming trucks.

Dawn came, and the rain finally stopped, and the sky turned hard blue, and the air turned crystal clear. Every detail was visible. The mountains, their rocky outcrops, their pine forests, their snow channels. Reacher borrowed a pair of binoculars from Vaughan's watch commander and climbed to the third floor of the last building to the west. He struggled with a jammed window and crouched and put his elbows on the sill and focused into the distance.

Not much to see.

The white metal wall was gone. The plant itself was mostly a black smoking pit, with cranes and gantries knocked over, crushers toppled. Thurman's residential compound had been obliterated.

Immense damage.

Better here than somewhere else, Reacher thought.

He came downstairs to a changed situation. Federal agencies had arrived. Gossip was flowing. Air force radar in Colorado Springs had detected metal fifteen thousand feet up. The rain was seen as a mercy. DU dust was believed to be strongly hygroscopic. Nothing bad would drift. Every contractor within a hundred miles had been contacted. A hurricane fence nineteen miles long was needed. The site was going to be fenced off forever, on a three-mile radius. The fence was going to be hung with biohazard signs every six feet.

No hard information was volunteered by the townsfolk. The word on everyone's lips was *accident. An accident at the plant.* It was second nature, a part of the hardscrabble culture. An accident at the mill, an accident at the mine. Consistent with history.

State officials arrived with contingency plans. Food and water were trucked in. Special welfare would be provided for the first six months. Transitional help of every kind would be afforded.

By the middle of the afternoon, Reacher and Vaughan had nothing more to do. They went to Vaughan's house, showered, and dressed again.

Reacher took the borrowed phone out of his pocket and dropped it on the bed. Followed it with the registration from the old Suburban's glove compartment. Asked Vaughan to mail both things back, with no return address on the package. She said, "That sounds like the start of a farewell speech."

"It is," Reacher said. "And the middle and the end."

They hugged, a little formally, like two strangers who shared many secrets. Then Reacher left. He walked down her winding path and walked four blocks north to First Street. He got a ride easily. A stream of vehicles was heading east—emergency workers, journalists, men in suits in plain sedans. Reacher rode with a post-hole digger from Kansas who had signed up to dig some of the sixteen thousand holes necessary for the new fence. The guy was cheerful. He was looking at months of steady work.

Reacher got out in Sharon Springs, where there was a good road south. He figured San Diego was about a thousand miles away, or more, if he followed some detours.

Living the Good Life with
Lee Child

LIFE, as the saying goes, is good—especially when you're Lee Child. The author is at the top of his profession, respected by critics and beloved by readers, and he makes a very, very good living at something he loves to do. Now, after writing twelve top-selling Jack Reacher novels (*Nothing to Lose* quickly hit number one on eight bestseller lists, including the *New York Times* and London's *Sunday Times*), Child owns two apartments in Manhattan—one for living and one for writing—and two houses in St. Tropez—one for living and one for writing. "London is next on the shopping list," he says frankly.

Many of Child's fans are familiar with his basic biography—his studies at law school, his part-time work in the theater, and his eighteen-year stint as a presentation director at Granada Tele-

Vital Stats

BORN: Coventry, England, 1954
REAL NAME: Jim Grant
REASONS FOR PSEUDONYM: "Lee Child" is more memorable and occurs earlier in the alphabet
ORIGINAL TITLE OF *NOTHING TO LOSE*: *Play Dirty*
NUMBER OF TIMES ASKED TO WRITE A JAMES BOND SEQUEL: Two
CHARITY SUPPORTED: Autism Speaks
WEBSITE: www.LeeChild.com

vision, which produced such popular shows as *Brideshead Revisited* and *Prime Suspect*. Then, at the age of forty, Child was fired as a result of corporate restructuring. Seeing opportunity where others might have seen a crisis (and needing to support his wife and teenage daughter), he bought six dollars' worth of paper and pencils and started writing "with a fury that was a perfect balance of creativity and financial necessity," he recalls. The result was his first novel, *Killing Floor*—an instant hit.

These days, Child communicates frequently with his readers, chatting with them at personal appearances, in blogs, and through interviews. One of the most popular topics is Jack Reacher, Child's rootless antihero, whom the author describes as "post-everything. He's post–politically correct, post-feminist, post-macho. He's whatever the opposite of metrosexual is. He wouldn't recognize a gym if you showed him one."

The British scholar Andy Martin describes Reacher similarly: "He's a moody, modern outsider . . . he's anticapitalism, antimaterialism . . . an intellectual with machismo and arms the size of Popeye's."

In Child's next book, Reacher will have his hands full. The plot involves a mysterious and controversial photograph showing Osama bin Laden with an American—a photo that has the potential to be very embarrassing to Osama. The author says he hasn't yet decided what the embarrassing thing will be. But one thing's for sure: Fans will be eager to find out.

Child is often asked why, given his British origins, so many of his books are set in the United

All in the Family

Many Lee Child fans won't be surprised to learn that the author (whose real name is Jim Grant) has a younger brother who is also a writer. His name is Andrew Grant, and his first novel, called *Even,* is coming out in 2009. In an interview, Child described *Even* as a modern-day James Bond adventure. According to Grant's agent, the protagonist of the story—a Bond-like figure named David Trevellyan—could be Jack Reacher's younger brother, if Reacher had joined the British navy instead of the American army. Says Child, "It's a good book. It will be fun to have someone else on the scene."

Reacher on the Silver Screen?

In a recent interview, Lee Child let us in on a little secret—his vision of the ideal person to play series hero Jack Reacher in a movie. Although many readers might expect a famous actor, Child envisions someone a little different—someone who looks like Lawrence Dallaglio.

Lawrence who? you might ask. Dallaglio, 36 years old, is a retired English rugby player and former captain of the English national team. He and Reacher are similar in stature—Dallaglio is 6'3" and Reacher is 6'5"—and they both weigh close to 250 pounds. And both men are well-traveled (Reacher with the army and Dallaglio with his team) and compassionate: Reacher is known as a champion of the underdog, and Dallaglio is active in many charitable causes.

Tom Cruise's production company has bought movie rights to Child's previous Reacher thriller, *One Shot,* so stay tuned.

States. "British crime stories tend to be internal, psychological, claustrophobic. I wanted to do something that was more wide-ranging," he answers. "The idea of writing against a huge landscape, a vast continent where anything could happen, greatly appealed to me. And," he adds, "I also discovered that the emptier I made Reacher, the more of a mirror he became. The reader has a chance to partly create the character himself."

Over the years, Child has grown philosophical about his craft. "It's all about practicality—making useful things and making them well and with pride," he says. "I want the books to be entertaining, and I want them to be easy reads. It's up to me, not the reader, to do the work. If someone says that my books are well written, I worry a little. I don't want that to be noticed. It should be the invisible undercarriage."

Asked for his advice to aspiring thriller writers, he responds: "Just get it done—finish it. Do not under any circumstances listen to any advice. And write exactly what you want to write, even if you feel everyone will hate it. That's the only way of having a living, breathing manuscript that has a chance of winning." ∎

#1
New York Times
BESTSELLING AUTHOR

SOPHIE KINSELLA

Remember Me?

Prologue

OF ALL the crappy nights I've ever had in the whole of my life . . .

On a scale of one to ten, we're talking . . . a minus six. And it's not as if I even have very high standards.

Rain spatters down my collar as I shift from one blistered foot to another. I just want to find a taxi, get home, and kick off these stupid boots. But there's no sign of a cab.

My toes are *agony*. I'm never buying shoes from

Cut-Price Fashion again. I bought these boots last week in the sale (flat black patent; I only ever wear flats). They were half a size too small, but the girl said they would stretch, and I believed her. I'm the world's biggest sucker.

We're all standing on the corner of some street in southwest London with music pounding faintly from the club below our feet. Carolyn got us discounted entry, so that's why we schlepped here. Only now we have to get home, and I'm the only one even *looking* for a cab.

Fi has commandeered the only nearby doorway with the guy she chatted up earlier on at the bar. A few feet away, Carolyn and Debs are sheltering underneath a newspaper, arm in arm, caterwauling "It's Raining Men." I normally love karaoke, too. But I'm not in a singing mood tonight. I feel all sore inside. If only Loser Dave had turned up like he promised. He works in car telesales and has been my boyfriend since we got together at Carolyn's friend's barbecue last summer. I don't call him Loser Dave to insult him—it's just his nickname, the way I'm Snaggletooth. I've been called that since I was eleven. And sometimes Snagglehair. To be fair, my hair is pretty frizzy. And my teeth are kind of crooked. But I always say they give my face character.

(Actually, that's a lie. It's Fi who says they give my face character. Personally, I'm planning to fix them as soon as I've got the cash.)

A taxi comes into sight, and I stick out my hand—but some people ahead flag it down. Great. I shove my hands in my pockets.

It's not just Loser Dave standing me up; it's the bonuses. Today was the end of the financial year at work. Everyone was given paper slips saying how much they'd got and started jumping about with excitement. Except me, with nada, because to get a bonus, you have to have worked for the company for a year, and I missed by a week. One *week*. It's so penny-pinching. I'm telling you, if they asked me what I thought about it . . . as if Simon Johnson would ever ask the opinion of an associate junior sales manager (Flooring).

"Hey, Lexi." I look up to see that Fi has removed herself from the cute guy. She comes over and gets out a lipstick.

"Hi," I say, blinking rainwater off my lashes. "Where's lover boy gone?"

"To tell the girl he came with that he's leaving."

"Fi!"

"What?" Fi looks unrepentant. "They're not an item. Or much of one." She carefully redoes her mouth in pillar-box red. "I'm getting a whole new load of makeup," she says. "I can afford it now!"

"You should!" I nod, trying to sound enthusiastic.

"Oh. Sorry, Lexi. You should have got a bonus. It's not fair." She puts an arm around my shoulder.

"It's fine." I try to smile. "Next year."

"You okay?" Fi eyes me narrowly. "You want to go for a drink?"

"No, I need to get to bed. I've got an early start in the morning."

Fi bites her lip. "I forgot all about that, too. What with the bonuses and everything . . . Lexi, I'm sorry. This is a really bad time for you."

"It's fine!" I say. "It's . . . I'm trying not to make it a huge deal."

No one likes a whiner. So somehow I make myself smile brightly, just to show I'm fine with being the snaggletoothed, stood-up, no-bonus girl whose dad just died.

"Things'll turn around for you," Fi says. "You just have to believe it. Come on." She squeezes me. "What are you, woman or walrus?" Fi's been using that expression since we were both fifteen, and it makes me smile every time. "And you know what?" she adds. "I think your dad would have *wanted* you to turn up to his funeral hungover."

She met my dad a couple of times. She's probably right.

"Taxi!" I instinctively scream the word, almost before I've registered the distant yellow light. I have to get this cab. I *have* to. I run along the pavement, skidding slightly, yelling till I'm hoarse. The pavement is crowded with people, and I skirt around them and up the steps to some grand municipal building. There's a balustraded platform with steps going right and left. I'll hail the taxi from up here, then run down and jump in. "TAXI! TAAA-XEE!"

Yes! It's pulling up. "Here!" I call out. "Just coming . . ."

To my consternation, I notice a guy on the pavement below heading toward the taxi. "It's ours!" I roar, and start pelting down the opposite steps. "Don't you even dare—Argh! *Aaaaargh!*" My foot skids on the wet step. I've slipped on my stupid, cheap, shiny-soled boots. I'm tumbling right over, down the steps. The ground's coming straight toward me. There's nothing I can do; this is really, *really* going to hurt. . . .

One

How long have I been awake? Five minutes? Half an hour, maybe? Is it morning yet? I feel so rough. What happened last night? God, my head hurts. I feel so woozy. What day is it?

For a moment, I just lie still. My head is pounding. I'm dry-throated and aching all over. My skin feels like sandpaper.

Where was I last night? What's wrong with my brain? It's like a fog has descended over everything. I'm never drinking again. I must have alcohol poisoning or something. I'm trying to remember last night, but all that's coming into my head is images from the past, flashing by in random order.

Sunflowers waving against a blue sky . . .

Amy as a newborn baby, looking like a little pink sausage . . .

The taste of bananas . . . Hang on. I force my brain to hold steady for a moment. Through the fog, another memory is glimmering. . . . Yes. Got it. Banana cocktails. We were drinking cocktails.

I can't even open my eyes. They feel heavy and stuck down. Cautiously, I move a hand up to my chest and hear a rustle of sheets. They don't sound like the ones at home. And I'm wearing some soft cottony T-shirt thing I don't recognize. Where am I? What on earth—

With a huge effort, I wrench my eyes open and incline myself up a few inches. I'm lying in a dim room, in a metal bed. There's a panel of buttons to my right. There's a bunch of flowers on the bed-side cabinet. With an inward gulp, I see a drip in my left arm, at-tached to a bag of fluid.

This is unreal. I'm in the hospital. What *happened?*

I mentally prod my brain. Banana cocktails . . . Yes! I was out with the girls from work. At that dodgy club. I can remember nurs-ing my cocktail, totally miserable.

Why was I so down? What had happened?

Bonuses. Of course. And Loser Dave never showed up. Double whammy. But none of that explains why I'm in the hospital.

This is weird. I'll text Fi and ask her what happened. I reach to-ward the nightstand, then realize there's no phone there.

Where's my phone? Where's all my stuff? Wincing, I swivel my head from side to side—but I can't see any clothes or anything. It occurs to me to press a button on the little panel. I select the one that looks like a person, and a few moments later, the door opens. It worked! A gray-haired nurse in a dark blue uniform enters and smiles at me.

"Hello, Lexi!" she says. "Feeling all right?"

"Um, okay, thanks. Thirsty. And my head hurts."

"I'll fetch you a painkiller." She brings me over a plastic cup of water.

"Thanks," I say after gulping the water. "So . . . I'm guessing I'm in the hospital? Or, like, a really high-tech spa?"

The nurse smiles. "Sorry. Hospital. But you don't remember how you got here?"

"No." I shake my head. "I'm a bit hazy, to be honest."

"That's because you had quite a bump on the head. Do you re-member anything about your accident?"

Accident . . . accident . . . And suddenly, in a rush, it all comes back. Of *course.* Running for the taxi, slipping on my stupid cheap boots . . . Jeez Louise. I must have really bashed my head.

"Yeah. I think so." I nod. "Kind of. So . . . what's the time?"

"It's eight o'clock at night."

Eight o'clock? Wow. I've been out of it for a whole *day?*

"I'm Maureen." She takes the cup from me. "You were transferred to this room only a few hours ago. Is there anything else I can get you?"

"I'd love some orange juice, if there is any. And I can't see my phone anywhere, or my bag."

"All your valuables will have been put somewhere safe. I'll check." She heads out, and I look around the silent room. I still don't know which hospital I'm in. . . . Has anyone told my family? And there's something else nagging at me like an undertow. . . .

I was anxious to get home. Yes. That's right. Because—*Oh no!* My dad's funeral. I've missed it. It's not as if I really knew my dad well. He was never around that much; in fact, he felt more like an uncle. The kind of jokey, roguish uncle who brings you sweets at Christmas and smells of drink and cigarettes. He was having a big heart-bypass operation, and everyone knew there was a fifty-fifty risk. But still, I should have been there today, along with Mum and Amy. I mean, Amy's only twelve, and a timid little twelve at that.

I suddenly feel a tear rolling down my face. It's the day of my dad's funeral, and here I am in the hospital, and no one's come to visit me. Where're all my anxious friends and family, sitting around the bed and holding my hand?

The door opens, and Maureen comes in again. She's holding a tray and a tote bag with LEXI SMART written on it in marker.

"Oh dear!" she says as she sees me wiping my eyes. "Are you in pain?" She hands me a tablet and a little cup of water. "This should help."

"Thanks very much." I gulp down the pill. "But it's not that. It's my life." I spread my hands hopelessly. "It's total rubbish, from start to finish. My so-called career is going nowhere, and my boyfriend stood me up last night, and my dad just died."

There's silence. Maureen looks flummoxed. "Well, that does all sound rather . . . tricky," she says at last. She gives me a sympathetic smile and holds out her hand for the cup.

I pass it back—and as I do so, I suddenly notice my nails. Bloody hell. What on earth . . . My nails have always been bitten-down stumps, but these look amazing. All neat and varnished pale pink . . . and long. I blink at them in astonishment, trying to work out what's happened. Did we go for a late-night manicure last night or something and I've forgotten? Did I get acrylics?

"Your handbag's in here, by the way," Maureen adds, putting the tote bag on my bed. "I'll just go and get you some juice."

"Thanks," I say. As Maureen leaves, I reach into the bag—and pull out a smart Louis Vuitton tote with calfskin handles, all glossy and expensive-looking.

Oh *great*. This isn't my bag. They've got me mixed up with someone else. I flop back on my pillows and close my eyes.

I WAKE up to find morning light edging underneath the drawn curtains. Maureen is bustling about in the corner. The drip has magically disappeared out of my arm, and I feel a lot more normal.

"Hi, Maureen," I say, my voice scratchy. "What time is it?"

She turns around, her eyebrows raised. "You remember me?"

"Of course," I say in surprise. "We met last night. We talked."

"Excellent! That shows you've come out of posttraumatic amnesia. Don't look alarmed!" she adds, smiling. "It's a normal stage of confusion after a head injury."

Instinctively, I put my hand up to my head and feel a dressing. Wow. I must really have whacked it on those steps.

There's a knock at the door; then it opens, and a tall, slim woman in her fifties comes in. She has blue eyes, high cheekbones, and wavy graying blond hair. She's wearing a red quilted waistcoat over a long printed dress and an amber necklace, and she's holding a paper bag.

It's Mum. I mean, I'm ninety-nine percent certain it is. I don't know why I'm even hesitating. "The *heating* in this place!" she exclaims in her thin, little-girl voice. Okay, it's definitely Mum. "I feel quite faint!" She fans herself. She glances toward the bed almost as an afterthought and says to Maureen, "How is she?"

Maureen smiles. "Lexi's much better today. Far less confused."

"Thank goodness for that!" Mum lowers her voice a fraction. "It was like talking to a lunatic yesterday."

"Lexi isn't a lunatic," says Maureen evenly, heading to the door. "She can understand everything you say."

The truth is, I'm barely listening. I can't help staring at Mum. What's *wrong* with her? She looks different. Thinner. And . . . older.

"Here you are, darling," she says in overloud, clear tones. "It's me. Your mother." She hands me the paper bag, which contains a bottle of shampoo, and drops a kiss on my cheek.

"Hi, Mum." I reach to hug her—but my arms hit thin air. She's already turned away and is consulting her tiny gold watch.

"I can't stay more than a minute, I'm afraid," she says. "I'm due to see a specialist about Roly."

"Roly?"

"From Smoky's latest litter, darling." Mum shoots me a glance of reproach. "You remember little Roly."

I don't know how Mum expects me to keep track of all her dogs' names. There's at least twenty of them, and they're all whippets.

"I've got a card for you," she says, rooting in her bag. "Where is it, now? From Andrew and Sylvia."

I stare at her, bemused. "Who?"

"Andrew and Sylvia next door!" she says, as though it's obvious.

Our next-door neighbors are Philip and Maggie. "Mum—"

"Anyway, they send their love," she interrupts. "And Andrew wants to ask your advice on skiing."

Skiing? I don't know how to ski. "Mum . . ." I put a hand to my head, forgetting about my injury, and wince. "What are you *talking* about?"

Maureen comes back into the room. "Dr. Harman's just coming along to check you over."

"I must go, darling." Mum gets to her feet. "I'll be back later with Amy and Eric," she says, heading out the door.

Eric? She calls her dogs some really odd names.

My thoughts are interrupted by a knock at the door, and a youngish doctor with dark hair enters.

"Hello there, Lexi," he says in a pleasant, brisk manner. "I'm Dr. Harman, resident neurologist. How are you feeling?"

"Fine! Except my left hand feels a bit weird," I admit. "Like I've been sleeping on it and it isn't working properly?"

"Right." The doctor nods. "We'll take a look at that; you may need some physical therapy. But first I'm going to ask you a few questions. Bear with me if some of them seem blindingly obvious." He flashes a professional smile. "Can you tell me your name?"

"My name's Lexi Smart," I reply promptly. Dr. Harman nods and makes a note in his folder.

"And when were you born?"

"Nineteen seventy-nine."

"Very good." He makes another note. "Now, Lexi, when you crashed your car, you bumped your head against the windshield. There was a small amount of swelling to your brain, but it looks as though you've been very lucky. I still need to do some tests, though."

Doctors don't let you get a word in, do they? "I'm afraid you've mixed me up with someone else. I didn't crash any car."

Dr. Harman frowns and flips back two pages in his folder. "It says the patient was involved in a road traffic accident."

"Well, they must have written it down wrong," I say firmly. "I was running for a taxi and I fell."

Dr. Harman and Maureen are exchanging puzzled looks.

"It was definitely a road traffic accident," murmurs Maureen. "Two vehicles, side-on. I saw her come in."

"I couldn't have been in a car crash." I try to keep my patience. "For a start, I don't have a car. I don't even know how to drive!"

"You haven't got a . . ." Dr. Harman flips over a page and squints at the writing. "A Mercedes convertible?"

"A *Mercedes?*" I snort with laughter. "I'll tell you how much twenty-five-year-old sales associates at Deller Carpets earn, okay? And you tell me if I can afford a Mercedes convertible."

Now Dr. Harman is gazing at me with a grave expression. My stomach starts flip-flopping.

"Is something really wrong with me?" I say almost aggressively.

"Lexi, I want to ask you another question." Dr. Harman's voice is gentler. "Can you tell me what year it is?"

"What *year* it is?" I stare back, thrown.

"Don't be alarmed," he says reassuringly. "It's a standard check."

I look from face to face. "It's 2004," I say at last.

There's a weird stillness in the room, as if no one wants to breathe.

"Okay." Dr. Harman sits down on the bed. "Lexi, today is May the sixth, 2007." His face is serious.

"But . . . that's the *future,*" I say.

"Lexi, this is bound to be a shock," says Maureen, putting a kindly hand on my shoulder. "But it's true. It's May 2007."

"It can't be 2007," I say, trying not to give away how rattled I am. "It's 2004. I'm not *stupid*—"

"Don't get upset," says Dr. Harman. "Let's take this slowly. Why don't you tell us what you last remember?"

"Okay, well . . ." I rub my face. "The last thing I remember is going out with some friends from work. We were trying to get a taxi in the rain, and I slipped on the steps and fell. That was February twenty, 2004." My voice is trembling. "I know the date exactly, because it was my dad's funeral the next day!"

"Lexi, that happened more than three years ago," Maureen says.

Panic is rising inside me as I look at their faces.

"Is your memory foggy at all?" asks Dr. Harman.

"A bit," I admit reluctantly. "So I've been lying here in a coma"—I swallow—"for three years?" I can't believe it.

But Dr. Harman is shaking his head. "No, that's not it. Lexi, you were only admitted five days ago."

What? "I don't understand! Have I gone crazy?"

"No!" says Dr. Harman. "Lexi, I think you're suffering from what we call retrograde amnesia. It's a condition that normally arises following head injuries. You've forgotten a chunk of your life, Lexi. That's all."

I want to cry. My head's whirling with confusion—

And then suddenly I freeze. I've just spotted a small, distinctive V-shaped scar near my elbow. A scar I've never seen before. A scar I don't recognize. It's not new, either. It must be months old.

"Lexi, are you all right?" asks Dr. Harman.

Heart thumping, I slowly move my gaze down to my hands. These nails aren't acrylics. These are my real nails. And there's no way they could have grown this long in five days.

"You're saying I've lost three years of my memory."

"That's what it looks like at the moment." Dr. Harman nods.

It really is the year 2007. Which means I must be . . . Oh my God. I'm twenty-eight. I'm *old*.

THEY'VE made me a nice strong cup of tea. Because that cures amnesia, doesn't it, a cup of tea?

Maureen has gone off duty, and a blond nurse, Nicole, is in the room, scribbling on my chart.

"When people get amnesia," I venture, "do the missing memories ever come back?"

"Usually." She gives a reassuring nod. "Would you like a magazine?" She hands me a copy of *Hello!* I run my eyes down the headlines—and feel a jolt of shock.

" 'Jennifer Aniston and Her New Man,' " I read aloud. "What new man?"

"Oh yes. You know she split up from Brad Pitt?"

"Jennifer and Brad *split?*" I stare up at her, aghast.

"They're divorced now. He went off with Angelina Jolie."

Jennifer and Brad are divorced. The world is a different place.

"Everyone's pretty much got used to it." Nicole pats my shoulder soothingly. "I'll get you some breakfast. Would you like full English, continental, or fruit basket? Or all three?"

"Um . . . continental, please." I open the magazine, then put it down again. "Hang on. Fruit basket? Did the National Health Service suddenly get a load of money or something?"

"This isn't NHS." She smiles. "You're in the private wing."

Private? "I can't afford all this," I say in an embarrassed rush. "I'm sorry, I don't know why I'm in this posh room. I should have been taken to an NHS hospital. I'm happy to move. . . ."

"It's all covered by your private health insurance," she says.

"Oh," I say, taken aback. "Oh, right." I took out private health insurance? Well, of course I did. I'm twenty-eight now. I'm sensible. I'm a different person. I'm not me anymore.

I mean, obviously I'm still *me*. But I'm twenty-eight-year-old me. Someone who can afford private health insurance, obviously, and gets a really good manicure, and . . . Wait a minute. Slowly I turn my head and focus again on the glossy Louis Vuitton.

"Nicole? D'you think . . . Is that bag . . . *mine?*"

"Should be." Nicole nods. "I'll just check for you. . . ." She opens the bag, pulls out a matching Louis Vuitton wallet, and snaps it open. "Yes, it's yours." She turns the wallet around to display a platinum Amex card with LEXI SMART printed across it.

My head is short-circuiting as I stare at the embossed letters. That's my platinum credit card. This is my bag. Where did I *get* it? Am I earning loads of money or something?

"So, I was really in a car crash?" I suddenly want to know everything about myself, all at once. "I was really driving? A *Mercedes?*"

"Apparently." She takes in my expression of disbelief. "Didn't you have a Mercedes in 2004, then?"

"Are you joking? I can't even drive!"

"Look in your bag," suggests Nicole. "Maybe the things inside will jog your memory."

"Good idea." I reach in, and the first thing I pull out is a tiny, gold-plated Estée Lauder compact. I flip it open to have a look.

"You've had some cuts to the face, Lexi," puts in Nicole quickly. "Don't be alarmed; they'll heal."

As I meet my own eye in the tiny mirror, I feel a sudden relief. It's still me, even if there's a huge graze on my eyelid. I move the mirror about, trying to get a good view, flinching as I see the bandage on my head. I tilt it farther down: There are my lips, looking weirdly full and pink, and—

Oh my God. Those aren't my teeth. They're all white. They're all gleamy. I'm looking at a stranger's mouth.

"Are you okay?" Nicole interrupts my daze. "Lexi?"

"I'd like a proper mirror, please," I manage at last.

"There's one in the bathroom." She comes forward. "In fact, it's a good idea for you to get moving. I'll help you."

I manage to totter into the adjoining bathroom. Nicole swings the door shut, to reveal a full-length mirror on the back of it.

Is that . . . *me?* I can't speak. My legs have turned to jelly.

I close my eyes and visualize my old self, just to make sure I'm not going crazy. Mouse-colored frizzy hair, blue eyes, slightly fatter than I'd like to be. Niceish face but nothing special. Black eyeliner and bright-pink lipstick. The standard Lexi Smart look.

Then I open my eyes again. A different girl is staring back at me. Some of my hair has been messed up by the crash, but the rest is a bright, unfamiliar shade of chestnut, all straight and sleek with not one bit of frizz. My toenails are perfectly pink and polished. My legs are tanned golden-brown, and thinner than before. And more muscly.

"I look all . . . sheeny. My hair, my legs, my *teeth* . . ." I can't take my eyes off those immaculate pearly whites.

"They're nice!" Nicole nods politely.

"No. No, no." I'm shaking my head. "You don't understand. I have the worst teeth in the world. My nickname is Snaggletooth."

"Shouldn't think it is anymore." Nicole raises an amused eyebrow.

"And I've lost loads of weight . . . and my face is different." My lips seem fuller somehow. I peer more closely in suspicion. Have I turned into someone *who has work done?*

I tear myself away from the mirror, my head spinning. I grab the Louis Vuitton bag and start yanking things out of it. A Tiffany key fob, a pair of Prada sunglasses, a Lancôme lip gloss. And here's a small, pale green diary. I open it, and a small pile of business cards falls out. I pick one up, glance down at the name—and freeze.

It's a card from the company I work at, Deller Carpets—although it's been given a new trendy logo. And the name is printed in clear charcoal gray: LEXI SMART, DIRECTOR, FLOORING.

I feel as though the ground has fallen away from me.

"Lexi?" Nicole regards me in concern. "You've gone very pale."

"Look at this." I hold the card out. " 'Director.' That's like, boss of the whole department. How could I possibly be the boss? I've only been at the company a year."

Hands trembling, I reach into the bag again. I have to find my phone, call my friends, my family, *someone* who knows what's going on. . . .

Got it. It's a sleek new model that I don't recognize but still pretty simple to work out. I haven't got any voice messages, although there's a new unread text. I select it and peer at the tiny screen: RUNNING LATE, I'LL CALL WHEN I CAN. E

Who's E? I can't think of a single person I know whose name begins with *E*. Someone new at work? I go to my stored texts—and the first one is from E, too: I DON'T THINK SO. E

Is E my new best friend or something?

I'll trawl through my messages later. Right now, I have to talk to someone who knows me, who can tell me exactly what's been going on in my life these last three years. . . . I speed-dial Fi's number.

"Hi, you've reached Fiona Roper; please leave a message."

"Hey, Fi," I say as soon as the bleep sounds. "It's me, Lexi! Listen, I know this'll sound weird, but I'm in the hospital, and I just . . . I need to talk to you. It's quite important. Can you give me a call? Bye!" As I close the phone, Nicole puts a reproving hand on it.

"You're not supposed to use these in here," she says. "You can use a land line, though. I'll set you up with a receiver."

"Okay." I nod. "Thanks." I'm about to start scrolling through all my old texts when there's a knock on the door, and another nurse comes in.

"I've got your clothes here." She puts a bag down on my bed. I reach in, pull out a pair of dark jeans, and stare at them. What are these? The waist is too high, and they're *way* too narrow, almost like tights. How are you supposed to get a pair of boots on under those?

"And here's your jewelry," adds the nurse, holding out a transparent plastic bag. "It had to come off for the scans."

Still stunned by the jeans, I take the bag. There's an expensive-looking bracelet made of hammered gold, a matching necklace, and a watch. "Wow. This is nice." Caught up among the knotted strands of gold is a ring, and after a bit of careful unweaving, I manage to untangle it. There's a general intake of breath.

I'm holding a huge, shiny, diamond solitaire ring.

"Hey!" Nicole suddenly exclaims. "There's something else. Hold out your hand, Lexi." She tips up the bag and taps the corner—then out onto my palm falls a plain gold band.

There's a kind of rushing in my ears as I stare down at it.

"You must be married!" says Nicole brightly.

No. No way. Surely I'd *know* if I was married?

"She is." The second nurse nods. "Don't you remember?"

I shake my head dumbly. "I didn't marry Loser Dave, did I?"

"Look, the ring's engraved!" exclaims Nicole, taking it from me. " 'A.S. and E.G., June 3, 2005.' " She hands it back. "Is that you?"

I'm breathing fast. It's true. It's carved here in solid gold. "I'm A.S.," I say at last. "*A* for Alexia. But I have no idea who E.G. is."

The E from my phone, I suddenly realize. My husband.

I'm twenty-eight, I have perfect white teeth, a Louis Vuitton bag, a card saying "Director," and a husband.

How did all *that* happen?

EDWARD. Ethan. Errol.

It's an hour later, and I'm still in a state of shock. I keep looking in disbelief at my wedding ring, resting on the bedside cabinet.

Elliott. Eamonn. Egbert.

Please God, not Egbert.

I've ransacked the Louis Vuitton bag. I've looked all the way through the diary. I've skimmed through all my stored mobile numbers. But I still haven't found out what *E* stands for.

When the door opens, I stiffen, almost expecting it to be him. But it's Mum again, looking pink and harassed. "Those traffic wardens have no *hearts*. I was only twenty minutes—"

"Mum, I've got amnesia." I cut her off in a rush. "I've lost my memory. I'm really . . . freaked out."

"Oh. Yes, the nurse mentioned it." Now she's sitting down and peeling off her waistcoat. "I know *exactly* how you feel," she begins. "My memory gets worse every day."

"Mum . . ." I inhale deeply, trying to stay calm. "You don't know how I feel. I've lost three years of my life! I don't look the same, none of my things are the same, and . . . am I really *married?*"

"Of course you're married!" Mum appears surprised that I need to ask. "Eric will be here any minute. I told you that earlier."

"Eric's my husband?" I stare at her. "I thought Eric was a dog."

"A *dog?* Goodness, darling! You did get a bump on the head!"

Eric. I'm rolling the name experimentally around my head. *My husband, Eric.* It means nothing to me.

"He had a very important meeting this morning. But otherwise, he's been here with you night and day."

"Right." I digest this. "So . . . so what's he like?"

"He's *very* nice," says Mum, as though she's talking about a sponge cake.

"Is he . . ." I stop. I can't ask if he's good-looking. That would be really shallow. And what if she avoids the question and says he has a wonderful sense of humor?

We lapse into silence. We've never been into cozy mother-daughter chats.

"Did you manage to order those sofa covers for me, Lexi? Off the Internet," she adds at my blank look. "You were going to do it last week."

"Mum, I don't know," I say slowly and clearly. "I don't remember anything about the last three years."

"Sorry, darling." Mum is nodding. "The thing is, I don't remember the name of the website. So if you *do* happen to recall—"

"I'll let you know, okay?" I can't help snapping. "If my memory returns, the first thing I'll do is call you about your sofa covers."

Okay. So in 2007, Mum still officially drives me up the wall. Surely I'm supposed to have grown out of being irritated by my mother?

"So, what does Eric do?" I return to the subject of my so-called husband. I still can't believe he's real.

"He sells property," says Mum. "He's rather good at it, actually."

"Do we live in my flat?"

Mum looks bemused. "Darling, you have a marital home now!"

I feel a pang. I love my flat. It's tiny but cozy, with blue-painted window frames that I did myself, and a lovely squashy sofa, and piles of colorful cushions everywhere, and fairy lights around the mirror. But now I live in a marital home. With my marital husband.

For the millionth time, I look at the wedding ring and diamond solitaire. Then I shoot an automatic glance at Mum's hand. She still wears Dad's ring, despite the way he's behaved toward her—

Dad. Dad's funeral.

"Mum," I venture cautiously. "I'm really sorry I missed Dad's funeral."

"You didn't miss it, darling." She peers at me as though I'm crazy.

"Oh." I stare at her, confused. "Right. Of course." Heaving a massive sigh, I lean back on my pillows. "So, how was it?"

"Oh, it all went off as well as these things ever do . . ." Mum's looking twitchy, the way she always is when the subject of Dad arises. She gets up, as though to remove herself from my questioning. "Have you had any lunch? I'll go and find something for us both. And make sure you eat properly, Lexi," she adds. "None of this no-carbs obsession. A potato won't kill you."

No carbs? Is that how I got this shape? I glance down at my legs. It has to be said, they look as if they don't know what a potato *is*.

"I won't be long." Mum picks up her embroidered shoulder bag. "And Amy should be here any moment."

"Amy's here?" My spirits lift as I visualize my little sister, in her pink fleecy jerkin and flower-embroidered jeans.

"She was just buying some chocolate downstairs." Mum opens the door. "She loves those mint Kit Kats."

The door closes behind her, and I stare at it. They've invented mint *Kit Kats?* It really is a different world in 2007.

AMY'S my full sister—not my half sister like most people presume—but there's twelve years between us, and our mum and dad had split up before she was born. Maybe "split up" is too strong. I'm not sure what went on exactly—all I know is, my dad was never around much when I was growing up. The official reason was that his business was based abroad. The first time he left home, I was seven. Mum said he'd gone on a business trip to America, so when Melanie at school said she'd seen him in the co-op with a woman in red jeans, I told her she was a fat liar.

A couple of years later, he disappeared again, for a few months this time. Then he started up a property business in Spain that went bust. Then he got involved in some dodgy pyramid scheme. Somewhere along the line, he became an alcoholic . . . then he moved in for a bit with some Spanish woman . . . but Mum kept taking him back. Then at last, about three years ago, he moved to Portugal for good, apparently to get away from the tax man. Mum had various other "gentlemen friends" over the years, but she and Dad never divorced. And evidently, on one of his jovial Christmas visits back, she and he must have . . . Well, we got Amy; that's the point. And she's the most adorable little thing.

There's a knocking at the door, and I look up. "Hello? Come in!"

"Hi, Lexi?" A girl of about sixteen has edged into the room. She's tall and skinny, with jeans falling off her midriff, a pierced navel, and spiky blue-streaked hair. I have no idea who she is.

I make an apologetic face. "Look, I'm really sorry, but I'm having problems with my memory. I mean, I'm sure we have met—"

"Lexi?" She sounds incredulous, almost hurt. "It's me! It's *Amy*."

I'm speechless. I'm beyond speechless. This cannot be my baby sister. Amy's turned into a tall, sassy teenager. Practically an adult. I'm mesmerized by the height of her. The *confidence* of her.

She sits down in a chair and swings her long legs over the arm. "So you don't remember anything? That's so cool."

"It's not cool," I retort. "It's horrible. I remember up to the day before Dad's funeral ∴. . and then it just goes fuzzy. All I remember is you being twelve. With your ponytail and braces."

"Don't remind me." Amy mimes puking. "So . . . let me get this straight. The whole of the last three years is a total blank."

"Like a big black hole. And even before that it's a bit foggy. Apparently I'm *married?*" I laugh nervously. "I had no idea!"

"Yeah," she says distractedly. "Hey, Lexi, I don't want to bring this up when you're feeling so ill and everything, but . . ." She twists a strand of hair, looking awkward.

"What?" I look at her in surprise. "Tell me."

"Well, it's just that you owe me seventy quid." She shrugs apologetically. "You borrowed it last week, and you said you'd pay me back. I don't suppose you'll remember . . ."

"Oh," I say, taken aback. "Of course. Just help yourself." I gesture at the Louis Vuitton bag. "I don't know if there's any cash in there."

"There will be," says Amy, swiftly unzipping it with a tiny smile. "Thanks!" She pockets the notes and then looks up.

"So." I try to sound casual. "What's my husband like? Mum said he was nice?" I try to hide my apprehension.

"He is lovely." She nods seriously. "He has a real sense of humor. And they're going to operate on his hump."

"Yeah. Nice try, Amy." I roll my eyes.

"Okay." She appears to relent. "You met him on a TV show."

"Try again." I lift my eyes to heaven.

"It's true! You were on that reality show *Ambition*. Where people want to get to the top in business. He was one of the judges, and you were a contestant. You didn't get very far on the show, but you met Eric, and you hit it off."

"I was on a reality show?" I say skeptically.

"Yeah. It was really cool. You should have won!"

I eye her closely, but her face is totally serious. Is she telling the truth? "Why on earth did I go on a show like that?"

"To be the boss?" Amy shrugs. "To get ahead. That's when you had your teeth and hair done, too, to look good on TV."

"But I'm not ambitious. I mean, I'm not *that* ambitious. . . ."

"Are you kidding?" Amy opens her eyes wide. "You're like, the most ambitious person in the world! As soon as your boss resigned, you went for his job. All the bigwigs at your company had seen you on TV, and they were really impressed. So they gave it to you."

My mind flashes back to those business cards in my diary.

"You're the youngest director they've ever had in the company," Amy adds. "You don't remember *any* of this?"

"No! Nothing!"

The door opens, and Mum appears, holding a tray bearing a covered plate, a pot of chocolate mousse, and a glass of water.

"Here we are," she says. "I've brought you some lasagna. And guess what? Eric's here! He's on his way up right now to see you."

"Here?" The blood drains from my face. "Mum, I'm not sure I can do this," I say in a panic. "I mean . . . I don't feel up to meeting him yet. Maybe I should see him tomorrow."

"Lexi, darling!" remonstrates Mum. "You can't turn your husband away. He's rushed here especially to see you!"

"But I don't know him! I won't know what to say or what to do."

"He might trigger your memory," chimes in Amy, who has helped herself to the chocolate mousse pot and is ripping the top off. "You might see him and go 'Eric! My love! It all comes back to me!' "

"Shut up," I snap. "And that's *my* chocolate mousse."

"You don't eat carbs," she retorts. "Have you forgotten that, too?"

"Nice try, Amy," I say, rolling my eyes. "There's no way I would ever have given up chocolate."

"You *never* eat chocolate anymore. Does she, Mum?"

I'm about to tell her to hand over the mousse, when there's a knock at the door.

"Oh my God." I look wildly from face to face. "Is that him? Already?" My stomach is churning in dread. "Mum. Please. It's too soon. Tell him to come back later."

"Don't be silly, darling!" Mum laughs. How can she *laugh?*

As Mum heads toward the door, I'm gripping the sheets so hard the blood is squashed out of my fingertips. "What if I hate him?"

"Really, Lexi," says Mum, "there's nothing to worry about. He's nice."

"As long as you don't mention his toupee," puts in Amy.

"Amy!" Mum clicks her tongue. "Eric! Come in."

There's an unbearably long pause—then the door opens. And into the room, carrying an enormous bouquet of flowers, walks the most drop-dead gorgeous man I've ever seen.

Two

I CAN'T speak. All I can do is gaze up at him, a bubble of disbelief rising inside me. This man is seriously, achingly good-looking. Like, Armani-model good-looking. He has medium-brown curly hair, cropped short. He has blue eyes, broad shoulders, and an expensive-looking suit. He has a square jaw, impeccably shaved. How did I land this guy? *How?*

"Hi," he says. His voice is all deep and rounded like an actor's.

"Hi!" I manage breathlessly.

"My darling." He strides to the bed in a rustle of expensive flowers. "You look so much better than yesterday. And this room is nicer than the one before. How are you feeling?"

"I feel fine. Um . . . thanks very much." I take the bouquet from him, the most amazing, trendy, designer-looking bouquet I've ever seen. "So you're Eric?" I add, just to be one hundred percent sure.

I can see the shock reverberate through his face, but he manages a smile. "Yes. That's right. I'm Eric. You still don't know me?"

"Not really. In fact . . . not at all."

"I told you," chips in Mum, shaking her head. "I'm *so* sorry, Eric. But I'm sure she'll remember soon, if she makes a real effort."

"I'm *trying* to remember, okay?" I say indignantly.

"We'll take it slowly," says Eric. He sits down on the bed. "Let's see if we can trigger some memories. May I?" He nods at my hand.

"Um . . . yes. Okay." I nod, and he takes it in his.

"Lexi, it's me," he says in firm, resonant tones. "It's Eric. Your husband. We've been married for nearly two years."

I'm too mesmerized to reply. He's even better-looking up close. I wonder what he's like in bed. Surreptitiously, I run my eyes over his body. Well, I married him. He must be pretty good, surely. . . .

"We met nearly three years ago," Eric continues, "at a reception at Pyramid TV. They make *Ambition,* the reality show we were both involved in. We were attracted instantly. We were married the following June and honeymooned in Paris. We had a suite at the George V. It was wonderful . . ." He breaks off. "Do you recall any of this?"

"Not really," I say, feeling guilty. "Sorry." To my slight relief, there's a knock at the door, and I call out, "Come in!"

Nicole enters, holding a clipboard. "Just need to do a quick blood-pressure check—" she begins, then breaks off as she sees Eric holding my hand. "Oh, I'm sorry. I didn't mean to interrupt."

"Don't worry!" I say. "This is Nicole, one of the nurses who's looking after me." I gesture around the room. "This is my mum and sister . . . and my husband, who's called"—I meet her eyes significantly—"Eric."

"Eric!" Nicole's eyes light up. "Very nice to meet you, Eric."

"It's a pleasure. I'm eternally grateful to you for looking after my wife."

"My pleasure." Nicole gives him a professional smile. "Lexi's a great patient." She wraps the blood-pressure cuff around my arm and turns to face me. "I'll just pump this up. . . ." *He's gorgeous!* she mouths, and I can't help beaming back. "Lexi, that all looks fine." Nicole writes something on my notes. "I'm going to ask everyone not to stay *too* much longer." She turns to Mum and Amy. "Lexi's still fragile. She needs to take it easy."

Mum and Amy start to gather their things—but Eric stays put. "I'd like a few moments, just the two of us. If that's okay, Lexi?"

"Oh," I say with a dart of apprehension. "Er . . . fine!"

Then the door closes behind Mum and Amy, and I'm left alone with Eric in still, strange silence.

"So," says Eric at last. "Have the doctors said whether you'll ever retrieve your memories?"

"They think I will. But they don't know when."

Eric gets up and strides to the window. "So it's a waiting game," he says at last. "Is there anything I can do to speed the process?"

"I don't know," I say helplessly. "Maybe you could tell me some more about us and our relationship? Where do we live?"

"We live in Kensington in a loft-style apartment." He proclaims the words as though they're capitalized. "That's my business. Loft-style living." As he says the phrase "loft-style living," he makes a parallel-hands gesture, as though he's moving bricks along a conveyor belt.

"What sort of things do we do together?" I say.

"We eat fine food; we watch movies. We went to see the ballet last week. Had dinner at the Ivy afterward."

Why can't I remember any of this? I shut my eyes tightly, trying to mentally kick-start my brain into action. But . . . nothing.

I open my eyes again, feeling a bit dizzy, to see Eric has noticed the rings on the cabinet. "That's your wedding ring, isn't it?"

"They took it off for the scans," I explain.

"Shall I?" He picks up the ring and takes hold of my left hand.

"I . . . um . . . no . . ." Before I can stop myself, I yank my hand away, and Eric flinches. "I'm sorry," I say after an awkward pause. "I'm really sorry. I just . . . you're a stranger."

"Of course." Eric has turned away. "Of course. Stupid of me."

"I'm sorry, Eric." I bite my lip. "You must be a wonderful person, or I wouldn't have married you. And you look really good," I add encouragingly. "I wasn't expecting anyone nearly so handsome. I mean, my last boyfriend wasn't a *patch* on you."

I look up to see Eric staring at me.

"It's strange," he says at last. "You're not yourself. The doctors warned me, but I didn't realize it would be so extreme." For a moment, he looks almost overcome; then his shoulders straighten. "Anyway. We'll get you right again." He takes my hand. "And just so you know, Lexi . . . I love you."

"*Really?* I mean . . . fab. Thanks very much!"

"Eat your lunch and take a rest." He pats my shoulder. "I'll leave you in peace." He lets himself out quietly. I sit still in the silence for a moment. It's all too much. Amy has blue hair, and Brad Pitt's with Angelina Jolie, and I have a gorgeous husband. I'm half expecting to wake up back in 2004 to find this was all a dream.

BUT I wake up the next morning, and it's still 2007. I'm just eating my third piece of toast when the door opens and Nicole appears, wheeling a trolley laden with flowers. I gape at it.

"So is one of these mine?" I can't help asking.

"All of them. They were left in your old room. You're a popular girl! We've run out of vases!" She hands me a stack of little cards. "Here are your messages."

"Wow." I take the first card and read it.

Lexi—darling girl. Look after yourself, get well, see you very soon, all my love, Rosalie.

Rosalie? I don't know anyone named Rosalie.

Lexi, get well soon! You'll soon be back to three hundred reps! From all your friends at the gym.

Three hundred reps? Me?

Well, I guess that would account for the muscly legs. I reach for the next card—and at last, it's from people I actually know.

Get well soon, Lexi. All best wishes from Fi, Debs, Carolyn, and everyone in Flooring.

As I read the familiar names, I feel a warm glow inside. It's stupid, but I almost thought my friends had forgotten all about me.

"So your husband's quite a stunner!" Nicole interrupts my thoughts.

"D'you think so?" I try to appear nonchalant.

"He's amazing! And you know, he came around the ward yesterday, thanking us all again for looking after you. Not many people do that."

There's a knock on the door, and in come Mum and Amy, lugging between them about six tote bags stuffed with photograph albums and envelopes.

"Lexi, darling, we've brought some pictures to show you. Maybe they'll trigger your memory."

I eye the bag of photos, suddenly excited. These pictures will tell my missing story. They'll show me my transformation from Snaggle-tooth to . . . whoever I am now. "Fire away!" I put down all the flower messages and sit up. "Show me my life!"

"All right." Mum advances toward the bed, holding an unframed print. "I'll hold it up, Lexi. See if the image jogs anything. Ready?" Mum turns the print around. It's a picture of a dog dressed up as Santa Claus.

I try to control my frustration. "Why are you showing me a dog?"

"Darling, it's Tosca!" Mum appears wounded. "And here's Raphael with Amy last week, both looking lovely. . . ."

"I look *hideous*." Amy snatches the picture and rips it up.

"Don't rip up the pictures!" I yell. "Mum, did you bring photographs of anything else? Like, people?"

"Hey, Lexi, do you remember this?" Amy comes forward, hold-ing up a distinctive necklace with a rose made out of jade. I squint at it, trying desperately to dredge some memory up.

"No," I say at last. "It doesn't jog anything at all."

"Cool. Can I have it, then?"

"Amy!" says Mum. She riffles through the pictures in her hand in dissatisfaction. "Maybe we should just wait for Eric to come with the wedding DVD."

The wedding DVD. My wedding.

"He seems nice," I say. "Eric, I mean."

"He's super." Mum nods absently, still leafing through pictures of dogs. "He does a lot for charity, you know. Or the company does, I should say. But it's his own company, so it's all the same."

"He has his own company? I thought he was a real-estate agent."

"It's a company that *sells properties,* darling. Big loft develop-ments all over London. They sold off a large part of it last year, but he still retains a controlling interest."

"He made ten million quid," says Amy.

"He *what?*" I stare at her.

"He's stinking rich." She looks up. "Don't say you hadn't guessed that?"

I'm feeling a bit faint. Ten million quid?

There's a knock at the door. "Lexi? May I come in?"

The door swings open—and there he is, manhandling two tote bags, another bunch of flowers, and a gift basket full of fruit.

"Hi, darling." He kisses me on the cheek. "How are you doing?"

"Much better, thanks." I smile up at him.

"But she still doesn't know who you are," puts in Amy.

Eric doesn't look fazed. "Well, we're going to tackle that today." He hefts up the bags, sounding energized. "I've brought along photos, DVDs, souvenirs. . . . Let's reintroduce you to your life. Barbara, why don't you put on the wedding DVD?" He hands a shiny disc to Mum. "And to get you started, our wedding album." He heaves an expensive-looking album onto the bed.

I open it, and I'm staring at a black-and-white photograph of me as a bride. I'm wearing a long white sheath dress, my hair's in a sleek knot, and I'm holding a minimalist bouquet of lilies. Soundlessly, I turn to the next page. There's Eric standing next to me, dressed in black tie. We look so *glossy*.

From the TV screen suddenly comes the mingled sound of people laughing and chattering. I look up and feel a fresh shock. Up there on the TV, Eric and I are posing in our wedding outfits. We're standing next to a huge white cake, holding a knife together, laughing at someone off the screen. I can't take my eyes off myself.

The camera swings around, catching the faces of people I don't recognize. I spot Mum, in a navy suit, and Amy, wearing a purple strappy dress. We're in some huge, modern-looking space with glass walls and trendy chairs and floral arrangements everywhere.

"Where's this place?" I ask.

"Sweetheart." Eric gives a laugh. "This is our home."

"Our *home*? But it's massive! It's like a football field. And who's that?" I point at a pretty girl in a strapless dress.

"That's Rosalie. Your best friend."

My *best friend?* I've never seen this woman before in my life. She's skinny and tanned, with huge blue eyes, a massive bracelet on her wrist, and sunglasses pushed up on her blond, California-girl hair. She sent me flowers, I suddenly remember. *Darling girl. All my love, Rosalie.*

"Now, this is us on holiday in Mauritius last year. . . ." Eric has fast-forwarded the DVD, and I stare disbelievingly at the screen. Is that girl walking along the sand *me?* My hair's braided, and I'm tanned and thin and wearing a red string bikini.

"And this is us at a charity ball." Eric's fast-forwarded and there we are again. I'm wearing a slinky blue evening dress, dancing with Eric.

"Eric is a *very* generous benefactor," says Mum, but I don't respond. I can't remember walking along a beach in Mauritius. I can't remember dancing with my husband at some grand ball. Hello, brain?

"It's still early days." Eric smiles as he closes the album.

"What if I never remember?" I look around the room. "What if all those memories are lost for good, and I can never get them back? *Ever?*"

THAT afternoon I see a neuropsychologist. He's a friendly guy in jeans named Neil, and I sit at a table with him, doing tests.

"You're functioning extremely well, Lexi," says Neil after he fills in the last check box. "Your executive skills are there; your short-term memory is pretty good, considering; you have no major cognitive problems . . . but you're suffering from a severe focal retrograde amnesia."

"But *why?*"

"Well, it's all to do with the way you hit your head. When you hit the windshield, your brain was thrown around in your skull, and a small area of your brain was, shall we say, tweaked. It could be you've done damage to your warehouse of memories, or it could be that you've done damage to your *ability* to retrieve memories."

"Can't you hit me over the head or something?"

"I'm afraid not. Contrary to popular belief, hitting an amnesiac over the head is not going to bring their memory back." He pushes his chair out. "Let me walk you to your room."

We arrive back at my room to find Mum and Amy still watching the DVD while Eric talks on his mobile phone. Immediately he finishes and claps his phone shut. "How did you get on?"

"What did you remember, darling?" chimes in Mum.

"Nothing," I admit.

"Once Lexi gets back to familiar surroundings, she'll probably find her memory returns quite naturally," says Neil reassuringly. "Although it may take time."

"Right." Eric nods earnestly. "So what next?"

"Well." Neil flips through his notes. "You're in good shape physically, Lexi. I would say you'll be discharged tomorrow. I'll make an appointment for you in a month's time as an outpatient. Until then, the best place for you is home." He looks at Eric and Mum. "You can help by giving Lexi as much information as possible about her life. Write things down. Take her back to places she's been. Any problems, just call me."

The door closes behind Neil. Mum and Eric exchange looks.

"Sweetheart, your mother and I were talking earlier about how we would"—Eric hesitates—"tackle your release. Obviously, I would love it if you wanted to come home and resume your life again. But I appreciate you may find that uncomfortable."

"I said to Eric, you're very welcome to come and stay with me for a bit," puts in Mum. "It will be a *little* disruptive, and you'll have to share with Jake and Florian, but they're good dogs."

"That room smells," says Amy.

"It does not *smell*, Amy." Mum seems affronted. "That builder chap said it was simply a question of dry something or other."

"Rot," says Amy. "And it does smell."

Meanwhile, Eric has come over, his face concerned. "Lexi, please don't think I'll be offended. I'm a stranger to you. Why on earth would you want to come home with me?"

I know it's my cue to answer—but I've suddenly been distracted by an image on the TV screen of me and Eric on a speedboat. We look totally glamorous, like something out of a James Bond movie.

I want this life, rushes through my brain. *It belongs to me. I earned it. I'm not going to let it slip through my fingers.*

Okay. Let's just get my options absolutely clear here:

1. A rotting room in Kent that I have to share with two whippets.

2. A palatial loft in Kensington with Eric my good-looking husband who can drive a speedboat.

"You know what, Eric?" I say carefully, measuring out my words. "I think I *should* come and live with you."

"Are you serious?" His face lights up. "But you don't know me."

"I'll get to know you again!" I say with growing enthusiasm. "Surely the best chance I have of remembering my life is to live it. You can tell me about yourself, and me, and our marriage. I can learn it all again!"

"It would be wonderful to have you back." Eric still looks troubled. "Obviously you won't . . . I mean . . . I'll take the guest suite."

"I would appreciate that," I say. "Thank you, Eric."

"Well, if you're sure about this . . ." His whole face has brightened. "Let's do this properly, shall we?" He glances questioningly at the rings, still lying on the cabinet, and I follow his gaze.

"Yes, let's!" I nod, suddenly excited.

He picks up the rings, and self-consciously I hold out my left hand. I watch, transfixed, as Eric slips the rings onto my finger. There's a hush in the room as I gaze down at my beringed hand.

Damn, that diamond's huge.

IT HAS to be karma. I must have been amazingly noble in a previous existence: rescued children from a burning building or given up my life to help lepers. It's the only explanation I can think of for how I've landed the dream life. Here I am, zooming along with my handsome husband, *in his open-top Mercedes.*

I keep glancing down at myself in wonder. I'm wearing a pair of cropped jeans, *two sizes* smaller than I used to wear. And a top by Miu Miu, which is one of those names I only used to know about from magazines. On the backseat are all the bouquets and presents from my hospital room, including a massive basket of tropical fruit from Deller Carpets. There was a letter attached from someone named Clare, who said she would send me the minutes of the latest board meeting, signed, "Clare Abrahams, Assistant to Lexi Smart."

Assistant to Lexi Smart. I have my own personal assistant. Me!

My cuts and bruises are a lot better, and the plastic staple has been taken out of my head. My hair is freshly washed and glossy, and my teeth are as movie-star perfect as ever. I'm Cinderella. No, I'm *better* than Cinderella, because she only got the prince, didn't she? I'm Cinderella with fab teeth and a red-hot job.

Eric signals left. "Well, here we are." He pulls off the road into a grand pillared entrance, past a porter in a glass box, into a car space, and turns off the engine. "Come and see your home."

My new home is way better than I imagined. As I walk around, I'm awestruck. It's massive. It's light. It has views over the river. There's a vast, L-shaped cream sofa and the coolest black-granite cocktail bar.

"Do you remember any of this?" Eric is watching me intently.

"No. But it's absolutely stunning!"

We must have some cool parties here. I can just see Fi, Carolyn, and Debs perched at the cocktail bar, tequila shooters going, music blaring over the sound system. I pause by the sofa and run my hand along the plushy fabric. "This is an amazing sofa!" I look up at Eric. "It must have cost a packet."

"Ten thousand pounds." Eric nods.

How can a sofa cost that much? What's it stuffed with, *caviar?* I edge away, thanking God I didn't sit down on it.

"I really love this . . . er . . . light fitting." I gesture to a free-standing, undulating piece of metal.

"That's a radiator." Eric smiles.

"Oh," I say, confused. "I thought *that* was a radiator." I point to an old-fashioned iron radiator fitted halfway up the opposite wall.

"That's a piece of art," Eric corrects me. "It's by Hector James-John. *Disintegration Falls.*"

Disintegration Falls. Black radiator. Nope, no idea.

I turn away from the radiator-art thing and focus on a giant screen, which almost fills the opposite wall. There's a second screen across the room, too, by the dining table, and I noticed one in the bedroom. Eric clearly likes TV.

"What would you like?" He notices me looking. "Try this." He picks up a remote control and flicks it at the screen. The next minute I'm looking at a massive blazing, crackling fire.

"Wow!" I stare at it in surprise.

"Or this." The picture changes to brightly colored tropical fish weaving through fronds of seaweed. "It's the latest in home-screen-system technology," he says proudly. "It's art, it's entertainment, it's communication. You can e-mail on these things; you can listen to music, read books. You can even have a virtual pet."

"A pet?" I'm still gazing at the screen, dazzled.

"We each have one." Eric smiles. "This is mine, Titan." He flicks his control, and an image appears of a massive stripy spider.

"Oh my *God!*" I back away, feeling sick. I've never been great with spiders. "Could you possibly switch that off, please?"

"What's wrong?" Eric looks surprised. "I showed Titan to you on your first visit here. You said you thought he was adorable."

Great. It was our first date; I said I liked the spider to be polite, and now I'm stuck with it. "So I have a pet, too?" I say quickly.

"Here you go." He zaps at the screen. "Here's Arthur." A fluffy white kitten appears on the screen, and I cry out in delight.

"He's so *cute!*" I watch him playing with a ball of string, batting it and tumbling over. "Does he grow up into a cat?"

"No." Eric smiles. "He stays as a kitten indefinitely. They have a life capacity of one hundred thousand years."

"Oh, right," I say after a pause. Actually, that's freakish.

Eric's phone beeps. "Sweetheart, my driver's here. I'm going to have to go out briefly to the office. But Rosalie is on her way to keep you company. Until then, if anything bothers you, just call me at once—or you can e-mail me through the system." He hands me a rectangular white gadget with a screen. "Here's your remote control. It controls heating, ventilation, lighting . . . Everything here is intelligent. But you shouldn't need it. All the settings are in place."

"We have a remote-control *house?*" I want to laugh.

"It's all part of loft-style living!" He makes the parallel-hands gesture again, and I nod, trying not to give away how overwhelmed I am.

"So . . . how exactly does Rosalie fit in?"

"She's the wife of my partner, Clive."

"Does she hang out with me and the other girls from the office?" I ask. "Like Fi and Carolyn? Do we all go out together?"

"Who?" Eric looks blank. Maybe he's one of those guys who doesn't keep up with his wife's social life.

"Never mind," I say quickly. "I'll work it all out."

"Gianna will be back later, too. Our housekeeper. Any problems, she'll help you." He comes over, hesitates, then takes my hand. His skin is smooth and immaculate. "Welcome back, darling," he says, a little gruffly. Then he disengages his hand and heads toward the door.

I'm alone. Alone in my marital home. As I look around the huge space again, I realize I can't see that many signs of *me*. There are no brightly colored pottery jugs or fairy lights or piles of paperbacks. Well, Eric and I probably wanted to start again, choosing things together. I pull out my phone and start texting Fi. I *have* to talk to her about all of this: HI! BACK HOME—GIVE ME A CALL! CAN'T WAIT TO C U!!! LXXXX

I send the same text to Carolyn and Debs. Then I put my phone away and swivel around on the shiny wooden floor. A sudden laugh bubbles to my lips. I mean, it's crazy. Me. In this place! I swivel again on the floor, then start twirling, my arms out, laughing madly. I, Lexi Smart, live here in this state-of-the-art, remote-controlled palace!

Sorry, Lexi Gardiner.

Crash. The sound of breaking glass interrupts my thoughts. I stop twirling in horror. Somehow I accidentally caught my hand on a glass leopard that was leaping through the air on a display shelf. Now it's lying on the floor in two pieces. *Damn.* I'm hot with panic. What am I going to do? What if it was worth ten thousand quid like the sofa? What if it's some family heirloom of Eric's?

Gingerly, I pick up the first piece, and then the second—

An electronic bleep interrupts me, and my head jerks up. The giant screen opposite has turned bright blue, with a message in green capitals. "HI LEXI—HOW ARE YOU DOING?"

Damn! He's watching me. It's Big Brother! In terror, I shove the two pieces of glass under a cushion on the sofa.

"Hi," I say to the blue screen, my heart pounding. "I didn't mean to do that; it was an accident. . . ." Silence. The screen isn't reacting.

"Eric?" I try again. There's no reply.

Okay, maybe he can't see me after all. He must be typing this from the car. Cautiously, I venture over to the screen and notice a wall-mounted keyboard plus a tiny silver mouse, discreetly tucked away to the side. I click on REPLY and slowly type "FINE THANKS!"

I could leave it there. I could find a way to fix the leopard. . . . No. Come on. Own up. "HAVE BROKEN GLASS LEOPARD BY MISTAKE," I type in. "REALLY SORRY. HOPE IT'S NOT IRREPLACEABLE?"

I press SEND and pace about as I wait for the reply, telling myself not to worry. I mean, I don't know for certain that it's a priceless ornament, do I? Maybe we won it in a raffle. Maybe it's mine and Eric's always hated it. How am I supposed to know?

There's a bleep from the screen. I catch my breath and look up. "OF COURSE IT'S NOT IRREPLACEABLE! DON'T WORRY."

I feel a huge whoosh of relief. It's all right.

"THANKS!" I type in. "WON'T BREAK ANYTHING ELSE, PROMISE!"

I can't believe I overreacted like that. I can't believe I hid the pieces. What am I, five years old? I lift up the cushion to retrieve the pieces—and freeze. The bloody glass has ripped the bloody sofa. The ten-thousand-pound sofa. I can't tell Eric I've ruined the sofa, too. I *can't.*

Flustered, I rearrange the cushions so the rip isn't visible. There. I grab the bits of glass leopard and head into the kitchen, which is all glossy gray-lacquer cupboards and rubber floor. I manage to track down the bin behind a door and chuck the bits in.

A buzzer sounds through the apartment, and I look up, my spirits lifting. This must be Rosalie, my new best friend.

Rosalie turns out to be even skinnier than she looked on the wedding DVD. She's dressed in black capri pants and a pink cashmere V-neck. As I open the door, she gives a small shriek and drops the Jo Malone gift bag she's holding. "*Oh* my God, Lexi. Look at your poor face."

"It's fine!" I say reassuringly. "Honestly, you should have seen me six days ago. I had a plastic staple in my head."

"You poor thing. What a *night*mare." She retrieves her gift bag, then kisses me on each cheek. "I would have come around earlier, only you *know* how long I waited to get that slot at Cheriton Spa."

"Come in." I gesture to the kitchen. "Would you like a cup of coffee?"

"Sweetie . . ." She looks puzzled. "I don't drink coffee. Dr. André banned me. You know that."

I pause. "The thing is . . . I don't remember. I have amnesia."

"*Oh* my God." Rosalie's hand goes to her mouth. "Eric kept saying things about amnesia. I thought he was joking!"

I want to giggle at her horrified expression. "No, he wasn't joking. To me you're . . . a stranger."

There's a short silence during which I can see Rosalie processing this information. Her eyes widen, and her cheeks puff out, and she chews her lip. "*Oh* my God," she says at last. "*Night*mare."

"I don't know this place." I spread my arms around. "I don't know what my life is like. If you could tell me a few things . . ."

"Absolutely! Let's sit down." She leads the way into the kitchen area. She dumps the Jo Malone bag on the counter and sits down at the trendy steel breakfast table—and I follow suit. "What do you want to know?" She leans forward expectantly.

"Well . . ." I think for a moment. "How did we two meet?"

"It was about two years ago." Rosalie nods firmly. "At a drinks party at Trudy Swinson's. You know, who used to be an airline hostess, but she met Adrian on a flight to New York, and everyone says she zeroed in on him as soon as she spotted his black Amex . . ." She trails off, as if the enormity of the situation is hitting her for the first time. "So you don't remember any *gossip?*"

"Well . . . no."

"*Oh* my God." She blows out sharply. "I have so much to fill you in on. Where shall I start? Okay, so there's me." She pulls a pen out of her bag and starts writing. "And my husband, Clive, and his evil-bitch ex—"

"Do we ever hang out with my friends from work?" I interrupt. "Like Fi and Carolyn? Or Debs? Do you know them?"

Rosalie looks blank. "I've never heard you mention them. As far as I know, you never socialize with colleagues from work."

"What? But we go clubbing and have cocktails."

Rosalie laughs. "Lexi, I've never even *seen* you with a cocktail! You and Eric are both so serious about wine."

Wine?

"You look confused," says Rosalie anxiously. "I'm bombarding you with too much information. What would you like to do?"

"Maybe we could just do whatever we normally do together?"

"Absolutely! We should go to the gym."

"The gym," I echo. "Of course. So, I go to the gym a lot?"

"Sweetie, you're addicted! You run for an hour every other morning."

Running? I never run. I once did a mile-long fun run with Fi and Carolyn, and I nearly died. Although at least I was better than Fi, who walked, smoking a cigarette, and was banned from any future Cancer Research fund-raisers.

"But don't worry, we'll do something lovely and restful today," says Rosalie reassuringly. "A massage, or a nice gentle stretch class. Just grab your exercise clothes and we'll go!"

"Okay!" I hesitate. "Actually, this is a bit embarrassing, but I don't know where my clothes are."

Rosalie looks utterly poleaxed. "You don't know where your *clothes* are?" Tears suddenly spring to her huge blue eyes, and she fans her face. "I'm sorry," she gulps. "But it's just come home to me how horrific and scary this must be for you. To have forgotten your entire wardrobe. Come with me, sweetie. I'll show you."

My clothes are not in a closet; they're in a whole other room, behind a concealed door that looks like a mirror. And the reason they need a whole other room is because there's *so bloody many of them*. Crisp white shirts, tailored black trousers, suits in shades of mushroom and taupe. Chiffony evening wear. Tights rolled up in their own special drawer. Folded silky knickers with La Perla labels. I can't see anything that doesn't look brand-new and immaculate. There are no baggy jeans, no sloppy sweaters, no comfy old pj's.

I leaf through a row of jackets, all pretty much identical apart from the buttons. I can't believe I've spent so much money on beige clothes.

"What do you think?" Rosalie's eyes are sparkling.

"Amazing!"

"Ann has a great eye." She nods sagely. "Ann, your personal shopper."

"I have a personal shopper?"

"Just for the main pieces each season." Rosalie pulls out a dark blue dress with spaghetti straps and the tiniest ruffle around the hem. "Look, this is the dress you wore when we first met. Don't you remember?"

"Not really."

"What about this Catherine Walker? You *must* remember that . . . or your Roland Mouret . . ." Rosalie is whipping out dress after dress, none of which looks remotely familiar. Then her face lights up. "Try the shoes. You *have* to remember your shoes." She heads to the other side of the room and flings open a cupboard door. And I stare in disbelief. I've never seen so many shoes. All in neat rows, most of them high-heeled.

"This is unbelievable." I turn to Rosalie. "I can't even *walk* in heels. I fall over."

"Sweetie." Rosalie's eyes are wide. "You *live* in heels. You were wearing these last time we had lunch." She pulls out a pair of black pumps with four-inch, skinny stiletto heels. "Put them on!"

Cautiously, I slip off my loafers and step into the pointy heels. Almost at once, I topple over and grab on to Rosalie. "You see? I can't balance."

"Lexi, you can walk in these," says Rosalie firmly. "I've seen you do it."

I try another step, but my ankle bends like plasticine. "It's no good." I exhale in frustration. "I wasn't meant to do this."

"Yes, you were. Try again! Find the zone!" Rosalie sounds like she's coaching me for the Olympics. "You can do it, Lexi."

I totter to the other side of the room and cling on to the curtain. "I'll never crack this," I say despairingly.

"Of course you will. Just don't think about it."

Reluctantly, I take a step forward. Then another. Then another. Oh my God. I'm doing it. I'm walking in high heels!

"You see?" crows Rosalie in triumph. "I told you! You *are* a heels girl." She opens a drawer, scoops up some gym clothes, and pops them into an oversized tote. "Come on, let's go."

WE DRIVE to the gym in Rosalie's car. It's a sumptuous Range Rover with designer carrier bags strewn all over the backseat.

"So, what do you do?" I say.

"I do a lot of volunteer work." She nods earnestly.

"Wow." Rosalie didn't strike me as the volunteer-work type, which shows how prejudiced I am. "What kind?"

"Event planning, mainly."

"For a particular charity?"

"No, mostly for friends. You know, if they need a helping hand with the flowers or party favors or whatever. I do the odd bits for the company, too," she adds. "Eric's such a sweetie; he always gets me involved in launches, that kind of thing."

"So you like Eric?" I'm dying to hear what she thinks of him.

"Oh, he's the perfect husband. Absolutely perfect. Mine's a monster. Mind you, I'm a monster, too. Here we are!" She drives into a tiny car park, pulls up next to a Porsche, and turns off the engine.

"Now, don't worry," she says as she pushes her way into a smart reception area. "I'll do all the talking . . . Hi there!"

"Hi, ladies." The receptionist's face falls as she sees me. "Lexi! You poor thing! We heard about the accident. Are you all right?"

"I'm fine, thanks." I venture a smile. "Thanks for the flowers."

"Poor Lexi has amnesia," says Rosalie impressively. "She doesn't remember this place. She doesn't remember *anything*."

"Goodness!"

"Come on!" Rosalie takes hold of my arm firmly. "We'll get changed."

The changing rooms are the most palatial ones I've ever seen. I disappear into a cubicle and pull on a pair of leggings. Then I pull on the leotard bit. It's got a thong, I realize to my horror. Reluctantly I pull it on, then edge out of the cubicle and force myself to take a peek in the mirror.

Actually, I don't look too bad. I look all long and lean and . . . different. Experimentally I flex my arm—and a biceps muscle I've never seen before pops up. I stare at it in astonishment.

Rosalie ushers me into a large, airy exercise studio, where rows of well-groomed women are already in position on yoga mats.

"Sorry we're late," she says momentously. "But Lexi has got amnesia. She doesn't remember *any*thing. About *any* of you."

I get the feeling Rosalie is enjoying this. "Hi." I do a shy wave.

"I heard about your accident, Lexi." The exercise teacher is coming over with a sympathetic smile. "Please take it easy today."

"Okay. Thanks."

"We're trying to trigger her memory," Rosalie chimes in. "So everyone just *act normal*."

I nervously take a mat and sit down. Gym has never exactly been my strong point. I stretch my legs out in front of me and reach for my toes, although there's no way I'll ever be able to—

Bloody hell. I can touch my toes. What's *happened* to me?

In disbelief, I follow the next maneuver—and I can do that one, too! Cautiously, I start tugging on my ankle—and it obeys me! I'm pulling my leg right above my head! I feel like yelling, "Look at me, everyone!"

"Don't overdo it, Lexi." The teacher looks alarmed. "Maybe take it easy now. I'd leave out the splits this week."

No way. I can do the *splits?*

Afterward, in the changing room, I'm exhilarated. "I can't get over it," I keep saying to Rosalie. "I was always so crap at exercise!"

"Sweetie, you're a natural!"

I survey my reflection. For the millionth time, my gaze is drawn to my gleaming white teeth—and my full pink lips.

"Rosalie." I lower my voice. "Did I ever have anything done? Like Botox? Or"—I lower my voice still further—*"surgery?"*

"Sweetie! Sssh! Of course we haven't had anything done!" She winks.

What does that wink mean?

"Rosalie, you *have* to tell me what I've had done . . ." I trail off suddenly, distracted by my reflection in the mirror. Without noticing what I've been doing, I've been taking hairpins from the pot in front of me and putting my hair up on autopilot. In about thirty seconds, I've constructed the most perfect chignon. *How did I do that?*

"What is it?" Rosalie catches my gaze.

"I just put my hair up. I've never done that before in my life."

"Yes, you have. You wear it like that for work."

"But I don't *remember*. It's like . . . it's like Superwoman's taken over my body or something. It's not *me*."

"Sweetie, it *is* you." Rosalie squeezes my arm. "Get used to it!"

We have lunch in the juice bar, and then Rosalie drives me home. As we travel up in the lift, I'm suddenly exhausted. "I feel pretty wiped out," I say. "Do you mind if I go and have a rest?"

"Of course not!" She pats my arm. "I'll wait out here for you."

"Don't be silly." I smile. "I'll be fine until Eric comes home, really. And thanks, Rosalie. You've been so kind."

"Darling girl." She gives me a hug. "I'll give you a call." She's halfway out the door when something occurs to me.

"Rosalie!" I call. "What should I make Eric for dinner tonight?"

She turns and blinks several times. "Sweetie, *you* don't make the dinner. Gianna makes the dinner. Your housekeeper?"

"Oh, right. Of course!"

Rosalie blows me a kiss and closes the door behind her, and I head into the bedroom, which is all cream and luxurious dark wood. Eric has insisted I take the main bedroom, which is very noble of him. I kick off my heels, climb under the duvet, and feel myself instantly relax. I'll just close my eyes and have a tiny nap. . . .

I wake to a dim light and the sound of chinking crockery.

"Darling?" comes a voice from outside the door. "Are you awake?" The door opens and in comes Eric, holding a tray and a shopping bag. "You've been asleep for hours. I've brought you some supper." He switches on the bedside light. "It's Thai chicken soup."

"I love Thai chicken soup!" I say in delight. "Thanks!"

Eric smiles and hands me a spoon. "Rosalie told me you two girls went to the gym today?"

"Yes. It was great." I take a spoonful of soup, and it's absolutely delicious. God, I'm ravenous. "Eric, you couldn't get me a piece of bread, could you?" I raise my head. "Just to mop this up?"

"Bread?" Eric frowns, looking puzzled. "Darling, we don't keep bread in the house. We're both low-carb."

Oh, right. I'd forgotten about the low-carb thing.

"Which brings me to my little gift," says Eric. "Or, in fact, two gifts. This is the first one. . . ." He reaches into the bag and produces a laminated ring-bound booklet, which he hands to me with a flourish. The cover reads *Eric and Lexi Gardiner: Marriage Manual.*

"You remember the doctor suggested writing down all the details of our life together?" Eric looks proud. "Well, I've compiled this booklet for you. Any question you have about our marriage and life together, the answer should be in there."

I flip through the booklet. I can see sections on holidays, family, laundry, weekends . . .

"I've organized the entries in alphabetical order," Eric explains. "And indexed them. It should be fairly simple to use."

I flip to the index and run my eyes down the page at random.

Tomatoes—pp. 5, 23
Tongs—see "Barbecue"
Tongues—p. 24

Tongues? Immediately I start flipping to page 24.

"Don't try and read it now. You need to eat and sleep."

I'll look up "Tongues" later. When he's gone.

I finish the rest of the soup and lean back with a contented sigh. "Thank you so much, Eric. That was perfect."

"It's no trouble, my darling." Eric removes the tray and puts it on the dressing table. As he does so, he notices my shoes on the floor. "Lexi." He flashes me a smile. "Shoes go in your dressing room."

"Oh," I say. "Sorry."

"No problem. There's a lot to learn." Eric comes back over to the bed and reaches into his pocket. "And this is my other gift." He produces a little jewelry box. "I'd like you to have something you actually *remember* me giving you," he says with a rueful smile.

I prize it open—and find a single diamond strung on a gold chain.

"It's . . . it's amazing!" I stammer. "I love it!"

Eric strokes my hair. "It's good to have you home."

"It's good to *be* home," I reply with fervor.

Which is almost true. I can't honestly say this place feels like home yet. But it feels like a really swish five-star hotel, which is even *better*.

"Eric," I say a bit shyly. "When we two first met, what did you see in me? Why did you fall in love with me?"

A reminiscent smile flickers across his face. "I fell in love with you, Lexi," he says, "because you're dynamic. You're hungry for success, like me. People call us hard, but we're not. We're just intensely competitive."

"Right," I say after a slight pause.

"And I fell in love with your beautiful mouth." Eric touches my top lip gently. "And your long legs. And the way you swing your briefcase."

He called me beautiful.

"I'll leave you now. Sleep well. See you in the morning."

Three

It's breakfast time, and we're both sitting in the kitchen. I've been flicking through the marriage manual ever since I woke up this morning, and—oh my God. He has written three paragraphs on foreplay! I splutter into my coffee, and Eric looks up.

"All right, darling?" He smiles. "Is the manual helpful?"

"Yes!" I flick to another section, feeling like a kid looking up rude words in the dictionary. "Just finding out what I have for breakfast."

"Gianna's left some scrambled egg and bacon. And you usually have some green juice." Eric gestures at a jug of what looks like sludgy marsh water on the counter. "It's a vitamin drink."

I suppress a shudder. "I think I'll give that a miss today." I take some egg and bacon and try to quell my longing for toast.

"Your new car should be delivered later on. Although I'm guessing you won't want to drive in a hurry." He wipes his mouth with a linen napkin and gets up. "There's another thing, Lexi. If you don't mind, I'd like to schedule in a small dinner party for next week. Just a few old friends."

"A dinner party?" I echo, apprehensive.

"Gianna will do the catering, but if you're not up to it . . ."

"Of course I'm up to it!" I say quickly. "I'm tired of everyone treating me like I'm an invalid. I feel great!"

"Well, that brings me to another subject. Work." Eric is shrugging on his jacket. "Obviously you're not up to returning full-time just yet, but Simon was wondering if you'd like to go into the office for a visit. Do you remember Simon Johnson?"

"Simon Johnson? The managing director?"

Eric nods. "He called here last night. We had a good chat."

"I didn't think he'd even *heard* of me!" I say in disbelief.

"Lexi, you're an important member of the senior-management team," says Eric. "Of course he's heard of you. We agreed it would be helpful for you to visit the office. It might help bring back your memory—as well as giving reassurance to your department."

"I think it's a great idea," I say with enthusiasm. "I could get to know my new job, see all the girls; we could have lunch."

"Your deputy is standing in for you at the moment," says Eric. "Byron Foster. Just till you return, obviously."

"Byron's my deputy?" I say incredulously. "Byron used to be my boss!"

Eric taps something into his BlackBerry, then puts it away and picks up his briefcase. "Have a good day, darling."

"You, too . . . er . . . darling!" I stand up as he turns to face me—and there's a sudden frisson between us. "Would I normally kiss you good-bye at this point?"

"You normally would, yes." Eric sounds stiff.

"Right." I nod. "So . . . um . . ." I reach out for his waist, trying to appear natural. "Like this?"

"Probably just one hand," says Eric after a moment's thought.

"Okay!" I shift one hand up to his shoulder.

Eric leans forward, and his mouth brushes briefly against mine, and I feel . . . nothing. I was hoping our first kiss would trigger all sorts of sensations, but as he draws away, I feel totally, one hundred percent blank. I can see the anticipation in Eric's face and quickly search for something encouraging to say. "That was lovely! Very . . ." I trail off, unable to think of a single word other than *quick,* which I'm not sure hits the right note.

"It didn't bring back any memories?" Eric is studying my face.

"Well . . . no," I say apologetically. "But, I mean, that doesn't mean it wasn't really . . . I mean it was . . . I feel quite turned on!"

"Really?" Eric lights up, and he puts his briefcase down.

"Not *that* turned on," I amend hastily. "I mean, just enough to know . . . obviously we have a great . . . when it comes to . . . um . . ." *Stop. Talking. Lexi. Now.* "Have a great day."

"You, too." Eric touches my cheek gently, then turns and strides off. That was a bit close. I reach for the marriage manual. This could take me a while.

TWO hours and three cups of coffee later, I've read the manual cover to cover. I've learned that Eric and I often spend weekends away at "luxury boutique hotels." We enjoy watching business documentaries and *The West Wing*. Eric and I share a love of wine from the Bordeaux region. I'm "driven" and "focused" and "work 24-7 to get the job done." I "don't suffer fools gladly," "despise time-wasters," and am "someone who appreciates the finer things in life." Which is kind of news to me.

The more I learn about twenty-eight-year-old Lexi, the more I feel like she's a different person from me. She doesn't just look different. She *is* different. She's a boss. She wears designer clothes. She knows about wine. She never eats bread. She's a grown-up.

How on earth did I get from me . . . to her?

On sudden impulse, I get up and head into the clothes room. There have to be some clues somewhere. I sit down at my minimalist dressing table and regard it. I mean, look at this, for a start. My old dressing table was painted pink and a total mess—all scarves, necklaces, and pots of makeup everywhere. But this is immaculate. Silver pots in rows, a single dish containing one pair of earrings.

I open a drawer at random and find a pile of neatly folded scarves, on top of which is a shiny DVD marked *Ambition: EP1*. It's that program Amy was talking about. This is me on TV! I *have* to see this. I hurry into the living room, eventually manage to locate the DVD player behind a translucent panel, and slot it in. I fast-forward until my face appears on-screen—then press PLAY.

I'm all prepared to cringe with embarrassment, but actually, I don't look that bad! My teeth have already been capped—although my mouth looks much thinner than it does now. (I have *definitely* had collagen injections.) I'm wearing a black suit and an aquamarine shirt, and I look totally businesslike.

"I need to win this," I'm saying to an off-camera interviewer.

Blimey. I look so *serious*. I don't understand it. Why did I suddenly want to win a reality business show?

"Good morning, Lexi!" A voice makes me jump out of my skin. I jab at STOP on the remote and turn around to see a woman in a flowery overall holding a plastic bucket full of cleaning things. "You're up!" she says. "How you feeling? Any better today?"

"Are you Gianna?" I say cautiously.

"Oh my Lord in heaven. Eric warned me. You're not right in the head, poor girl. Well, I am Gianna." She hits her chest.

"Great! Er, thanks." I move aside as Gianna starts flicking over the surface of the coffee table with a duster. How can I just *stand* here watching another woman clean my house?

"What would you like me to cook for dinner tonight?" she says.

"Oh," I say, looking up in horror. "Nothing! Really!" I can't ask someone else to cook my supper. It's obscene.

"Nothing?" She pauses. "Are you going out?"

"No! I just thought . . . I'd do the cooking myself tonight."

"Oh, I see," she says, her face set. "Well, it's up to you."

I've offended her. "Actually, on second thought, maybe you could make a little something. Whatever *you* enjoy cooking!"

How am I ever going to get used to all this?

"Aiee! The sofa has been damaged! Ripped!" Gianna looks at me defensively. "Yesterday I left it in good condition, no rips . . ."

"That . . . that was me," I stammer. "It was a mistake. Please don't tell Eric. I put the cushion over the rip. To hide it."

Gianna stares at me for a few disbelieving moments; then her severe face creases into a laugh. She pats me on the arm. "I'll sew it. Little tiny stitches. He'll never know."

"Really?" I feel a wash of relief. "I'd be so grateful."

Gianna is surveying me with a perplexed frown, her broad arms folded across her chest. "You're sure nothing happened when you bumped your head?" she says. "Like . . . personality transplant?"

"What?" I give an uncertain laugh. "I don't think so." The door buzzer goes. "Oh. I'd better get this." I lift the entry phone. "Hello?"

"Hello?" comes a guttural voice. "Car delivery for Gardiner."

"SIGN here . . . and here . . ." The car-delivery man is holding out a clipboard. I scribble on the paper. "Here's your keys and all your paperwork. Cheers, love." The guy heads out of the gates, leaving me alone with a silver Mercedes convertible. Maybe I'll just check it over inside. In an instinctive gesture, I hold out the key fob and press the little button—then jump as the car bleeps and all the lights flash on.

Well, I've obviously done that before. I open the door and slide into the driver's seat. Wow. Now, *this* is a car. It has the most wonderful scent of new leather. The seats are wide and comfortable. Cautiously I place my hands on the steering wheel. The thing is . . . I *can* drive. At some stage, I must have passed my test.

Experimentally, I push the key into the slot beside the steering wheel—and it fits! I rotate it forward cautiously, a few lights pop on around the dashboard, and there's a kind of rumbling. Right. Collect yourself, Lexi. Hand brake. I know what that is. And the gear stick. Cautiously I release both—and at once the car moves forward. Hastily I press my foot down on one of the pedals, to stop it, and the car bucks, with an ominous grinding noise. I release my foot—and the car creeps forward again. I'm not sure I want it doing that. Trying to stay calm, I press my foot down again, hard. But this time it doesn't even stop; it just keeps going inexorably forward, heading toward an expensive-looking sports car parked opposite. In desperation, I thrust both feet down again, hitting two pedals at once with a shrieking engine-breaking sound. Oh God . . .

Suddenly I notice a dark-haired man in jeans coming through the gates. He sees me gliding forward toward the sports car, and his whole face jolts. "Stop!" he yells faintly through the window.

"I can't stop!" I yell back desperately.

"Steer!" He mimes turning the steering wheel.

The *steering wheel.* Of course. I'm a moron. I wrench it around to the right, and now I'm heading straight toward a brick wall.

"Brake!" The guy is running alongside me. "Brake, Lexi!"

The hand brake, I suddenly remember. Quick. I yank it back with both hands, and the car stops with a judder. My breaths are coming fast and hoarse; I'm never driving again. Never.

"Are you okay?" The guy is at my window. I jab randomly at the buttons on the door until the window winds down. "What *happened?*"

"I . . . panicked. I can't actually drive a car. I thought I'd remember how to, but I've had amnesia, you see. . . ."

I see the guy is just staring at me as if I'm talking a foreign language. He's got a pretty striking face, now that I come to notice it. High cheekbones, dark gray eyes, and slanted eyebrows gathered in a frown, with dark brown untidy hair. He's a bit older than me, maybe early thirties. He also seems totally dumbfounded. Which I guess is not surprising.

"I was in a car crash a few days ago," I explain hurriedly.

"I know you were in a car crash," he says at last. He has a very distinctive voice, dry and kind of intense.

"Wait a minute!" I click my tongue, suddenly realizing. "You called out my name. Do we know each other?"

A jolt passes over the guy's face. "You don't remember me?"

"Um, no," I say with an apologetic shrug. "I'm sorry. I'm not being rude; I don't remember anyone I've met in the last three years. My friends . . . my husband, even." I smile—but the guy doesn't smile back or express sympathy. In fact, his expression almost makes me nervous.

"Do you want me to park that for you?" he says abruptly.

"Oh. Yes, please. This is my brand-new car. If I'd crashed it, I can't even *think* . . ." I wince at the idea. "My husband got it for me to replace the other one. Do you know him? Eric Gardiner?"

"Yes," he says after a pause. "I know him." He signals to me to get out of the way and gets into the car. The next moment he's expertly reversed the car safely back into its parking spot.

"Thanks," I say fervently as he gets out. "I really appreciate it."

"What did they say about the amnesia?" he says suddenly. "Have your memories gone forever?"

"They might come back any time," I explain. "Or they might not. No one knows. I'm just trying to learn about my life again. Eric's being really helpful. He's the most perfect husband!" I smile again. "So where do you fit into the picture?"

There's no response from the dark-haired guy. He's shoved his hands in his pockets, and his face is all screwed up, as though he's in pain. "I have to go," he says. "Bye, Lexi." He turns on his heel.

"Bye . . ." What a weird guy. He never even told me his name.

I'M GOING into work today. I stare at myself in the huge mirror in my dressing room. I'm wearing a black suit with a pencil skirt and a nipped-in waist. My hair is blow-dried and twisted up into my signature chignon. I look like an illustration from a child's picture book. Boss Lady.

Eric comes into the room. "All set?"

"I guess!" I pick up my black Bottega Veneta tote bag.

I tried asking Eric about Fi yesterday, but he barely seemed to know who she was, even though she's my oldest friend—we met at the age of six. It's so weird that she hasn't been in touch. Anyway, I'll see her today, and there'll be some explanation. I expect we'll all go out for a drink at lunchtime and have a catch-up.

DELLER Carpets became a household name back in the eighties. The company tried to change its name a few years ago, to just Deller. There was a new logo and mission statement and everything. But nobody takes any notice of that. You say you work at Deller and people frown, and then say, "You mean, Deller Carpets?"

It's even more ironic because carpets is only a fraction of the company these days. They expanded into all sorts of cleaning products and gadgets, and now the mail-order business is huge. So are soft furnishings and fabrics. But poor old carpets have fallen by the wayside. Trouble is, they're not cool these days, carpets. It's all slate and laminate wood flooring. We do sell laminate flooring—but hardly anyone realizes we do, because they think we're still called Deller Carpets. It's like one big vicious circle that always leads back to shag.

I know carpets aren't cool. And I know patterned carpets are even less cool. But secretly, I really love them. Especially all the old retro designs from the seventies. I've got an old pattern book on my desk, and once I found a whole box of old samples at the warehouse. No one wanted them, so I took them back to the office and pinned them up on the wall next to my desk.

That's to say, my old desk. I guess I've been upgraded now. As I head toward the familiar building, I feel a fizz of anticipation in my stomach. I push open the glass doors to reception—and stop in surprise. The foyer is different. It looks really cool!

"Lexi!" A plump woman in a pink shirt and tapered black trousers is bustling toward me. I know her . . . head of human resources . . .

"Dana." I gasp the name in relief. "Hi."

"Lexi." She holds out a hand to shake mine. "Welcome back! You poor thing! Come this way. I thought we could have a short chat in my office, pop in on the budget meeting, and then see your department!"

"Great! Good idea." *My department.* I used to just have a desk.

We travel up in the lift and get out at the second floor, and Dana ushers me into her office. "Take a seat." She pulls out a plushy chair and sits down at her desk. "So, now, obviously, we need to talk about your . . . *condition.*" She lowers her voice discreetly. "Is this amnesia permanent or temporary?"

"The doctors said I might start remembering things at any time."

"Marvelous!" Her face brightens. "Obviously, from *our* point of view, it would be great if you could remember everything by the twenty-first—that's when our sales conference is," she adds, giving me an expectant look.

"Right," I say after a pause. "I'll do my best."

"You can't do better than that!" She trills with laughter and pushes back her chair. "Now, let's go and say hello to Simon and the others. You remember Simon Johnson, the MD?"

"Of course!" How could I not remember the boss of the whole company? Trying to conceal my nerves, I follow Dana up in the lift again to the eighth floor. She leads me briskly to the boardroom, knocks on the heavy door, and pushes it open.

"Sorry to interrupt! Only Lexi's popped in for a visit."

"Lexi! Our superstar!" Simon Johnson comes over, clasps my hand as if we're old friends, and kisses my cheek. "How are you feeling?" The MD of the whole company just *kissed* me.

"Er . . . fine thanks!" I try to keep my composure. "Much better."

I glance around the room, taking in a whole bunch of other high-powered company people in suits. Byron, who used to be my direct boss, is sitting on the other side of the conference table. He's pale and lanky with dark hair. He gives me a pinched smile, and I grin back, relieved to recognize someone.

"You had quite a knock to the head, we understand," Simon Johnson is saying in his mellifluous, public-school voice.

"That's right."

"Well, hurry back!" he exclaims with mock urgency. "Byron here is standing in for you very well." He gestures at Byron. "But whether you trust him to safeguard your departmental budget . . ."

"I don't know." I raise my eyebrows. "*Should* I be worried?"

There's an appreciative laugh around the table, and I notice Byron shooting me daggers. Honestly. I was only making a joke.

"Seriously, though, Lexi. I need to talk to you about our recent . . . discussions." Simon Johnson gives me a meaningful nod. "We'll have lunch when you get back properly."

"Absolutely." I have no idea what he's talking about.

"Simon." Dana steps forward discreetly. "Lexi may have some problems with memory. . . ."

"Lexi, I have every confidence in you," says Simon Johnson firmly. He turns to a red-haired guy sitting nearby. "Daniel, you two haven't met yet, have you? Daniel is our new finance controller. Daniel, this young woman has had the most meteoric rise through this company. From junior sales associate to director of her department within eighteen months. She's a natural leader. She's inspirational. She has some exciting strategic visions for the future. This is a very, *very* talented member of the company." As he finishes, Simon is beaming at me.

I'm in a state of total shock. My face is puce; my legs are wobbling. No one's ever spoken about me like that, in my whole life.

"Well . . . thanks!" I stutter at last.

"Can we tempt you to stay for the budget meeting?"

"Er . . ." I glance at Dana for help.

"She's not staying long today, Simon," says Dana. "We're popping down to Flooring now."

"Of course." Simon Johnson nods. "Well, you're missing a treat. Everyone loves a budget meeting." His eyes crinkle with humor.

"Don't you realize I did this to avoid the budget meeting?" I gesture at the last remaining graze on my head, and there's another huge laugh.

As Dana and I leave the boardroom, I'm light-headed with exhilaration. I bantered with Simon Johnson. I have strategic visions for the future!

I just hope I wrote them down somewhere.

"So, you remember where the Flooring department is?" Dana says as we descend again in the lift. "I know everyone's eager to see you." Her phone gives a little chirrup. "Oh dear!" she says as she glances at it. "I should take this. Do you want to pop along to your office and I'll see you in there?"

"Absolutely!" I stride down the corridor. The Flooring department is just along to the left. And to the right is Gavin's office. I mean, *my* office. As I reach for the door handle, I see a girl of about twenty darting out of the main office. Her hands go to her mouth.

"Oh!" she says. "Lexi! You're back!"

"Yes." I peer uncertainly at her. "You'll have to forgive me. I've had this accident; my memory's gone. . . ."

"Yeah, they said." She looks nervous. "I'm Clare. Your assistant?"

"Oh hi! Nice to meet you! So I'm in here?" I jerk my head toward Gavin's door.

"That's right. Can I bring you a cup of coffee?"

"Yes, please!" I try to hide my delight. "That would be great."

I have an assistant who brings me cups of coffee. I have really, really made it. I step into the office. *Wow.* I'd forgotten how big this room was. It has a sweeping desk and a plant and a sofa . . . and everything. I'm the boss! I can't help laughing in euphoria as I swing around—then stop abruptly as there's a knocking on the door.

Catching my breath, I hurry over to the desk. "Come in!"

"Lexi!" Dana bustles in. She still looks anxious. "Now, let's go through to the department, reacquaint yourself with everybody."

We head out—and I suddenly see Fi coming out of the Flooring office. She looks different from the way I remember her, with a new red streak in her hair and a thinner face somehow. But it's her.

"Fi!" I exclaim in excitement. "Oh my God! Hi! I'm back!"

Fi visibly starts. She turns, and for a few seconds just gapes at me as if I'm a lunatic. I suppose I did sound a bit overexcited.

"Hi, Lexi," she says at last. "How're you doing?"

"I'm fine!" I say, my words tumbling out eagerly. "How are you? You look great! I love your new hair!"

Everyone's staring at me now.

"Anyway." I force myself to sound more composed. "Maybe we can catch up properly later? With the others?"

"Uh—yeah." Fi nods without looking me in the eye.

Why is she being so off? What's wrong? Maybe we've had some huge row and I just don't remember.

"After you, Lexi!" Dana ushers me into the main open-plan office. I can see Carolyn, and Debs, and Melanie, and several others I know. They all look familiar, but three years on. Their hair and clothes all look different. Debs has super-toned arms and is tanned, as though she's just got back from some exotic holiday; Carolyn's wearing new rimless glasses, and her hair's cropped even shorter than before.

"You all know that Lexi has been ill following her accident," Dana is announcing to the room. "We're delighted that she's back with us today for a visit. She's suffered a few side effects from her in-

juries, in particular amnesia. But I'm sure you'll all help her to remember her way around and give her a big welcome back." She
turns to me. "Lexi, do you want to say a few words to the department?" Her phone chirrups again. "I'm sorry. Excuse me!" She hur-
ries out to the corridor, and I'm left alone, facing my department.

Come on. Simon Johnson says I'm a natural leader. I can do this.

"Hi, everyone!" I give a small wave around the office, which no
one returns. "I just wanted to say that I'll be back soon, and . . ." I
flounder for something motivational. "Who's the best department
in the company? We are!" I give the air a little punch, like a cheer-
leader. "F! L! O! R!—"

"It should be another O," interrupts a girl I don't recognize.

"Sorry?" I stop, breathless.

"There's a double O in *Flooring*." She rolls her eyes. Two girls
next to her are giggling, while Carolyn and Debs are gaping at me.

"Right," I say, flustered. "Anyway . . . well done, everybody . . ."

"So are you back now, Lexi?" demands a girl in red. "I need my
expenses form signed urgently."

"Have you spoken to Simon about our targets?" Melanie is coming forward, frowning. "They're totally unworkable as they are—"

"Have we sorted the Thorne Group order?"

Suddenly everyone in the room seems to be swarming toward me,
asking questions. "I don't know!" I'm saying. "I'm sorry, I can't remember. I'll see you later!" Breathing hard, I back out across the
corridor and into my own office and slam the door.

Blimey. What was all that about?

There's a knock at the door. "Hello?" I call out.

"Hi!" says Clare, coming in under a vast pile of letters and documents. "While you're here, could you just have a quick run-
through of these? You need to get back to Tony Dukes and
authorize the payment to Sixpack, and some guy named Jeremy
Northpool has rung several times, says he hopes you can resume
discussions."

"I can't authorize anything," I say in a panic. "I've never heard of
Tony Dukes. I don't remember any of this stuff!"

"Oh. Well . . . who's going to run the department?"

"I don't know. I mean . . . me. Look, leave all that with me." I try to pull myself together. "I'll have a read-through. Maybe it'll come back to me."

"Okay," says Clare, clearly relieved. "I'll just bring your coffee."

My head spinning, I sit down at the desk and pick up the first letter. It's about some complaint. The next document is a monthly budget forecast for all the departments in the company. There are six graphs and a Post-it on which someone has scribbled, "Could I get your views, Lexi?"

"Your coffee." Clare taps on the door.

"Ah, yes," I say. "Thank you, Clare."

The minute she's gone, I drop my head down on the desk in despair. How on earth do I do it? How do I know what to say and what decisions to make? There's another knocking at the door, and I hastily sit up.

"Everything all right, Lexi?" It's Byron, holding a bottle of water and a sheaf of papers. Truth be told, I never got on with Byron.

"Fine! Great! I thought you were in the budget meeting."

"We've broken for lunch." His eye is running over the pile of papers on my desk. "Have you decided what to do about Tony Dukes? Because Accounts were onto me yesterday."

"Well." I hesitate. "Actually, I don't quite . . . I'm not . . ."

Byron's face suddenly snaps in comprehension. "You don't know who Tony Dukes *is*, do you?" he says.

Tony Dukes. I rack my brain frantically—but nothing.

"I . . . um . . . well . . . no. But if you could just remind me?"

Byron ignores me. He comes farther into the room. "Let me get this straight," he says slowly. "You remember absolutely nothing?"

All my instincts are prickling. He's like a cat prodding a mouse, working out exactly how weak its prey is. *He wants my job.*

"I don't remember *nothing!*" I exclaim quickly, as if the very idea's ridiculous. "Just the last three years is a bit of a blank."

"The last three years?" Byron laughs incredulously. "I'm sorry, Lexi, but in this business three years is a lifetime!"

"Well, I'll soon pick it all up again," I say, trying to sound robust. "The doctors said I might remember everything at any time."

"Or presumably you might not." He adopts a concerned, sympathetic expression. "That must be a great worry for you, Lexi. That your head will be blank forever."

I meet his gaze with as much steel as I can muster. *Nice try.* "I'm sure I'll be back to normal very soon," I say briskly.

"So what do you want to do about Tony Dukes?"

Damn. He's outmaneuvered me. I shuffle the papers on my desk. "Maybe you could make a decision on that?" I say at last.

"I'd be happy to." He gives me a patronizing smile. "I'll take care of everything. You just look after yourself. Don't worry about a thing!"

"So!" Dana appears at the door. "Are you two having a nice chat? Super!" She glances at her watch. "Now, Lexi, I have to shoot off to lunch, but I can see you out if we leave now."

"Don't worry, Dana," I say quickly. "I'll stay on and read through some paperwork." I'm not leaving this building without talking to Fi.

"Okey-doke." She beams. "Well, lovely to see you, Lexi, and let's talk on the phone about when you want to return properly."

The two of them walk away, and I hear Byron saying, "Dana, with the greatest respect to Lexi, she's *clearly* not fit to lead this department. . . ."

Bastard. He didn't even bother waiting until he was out of earshot. I lift a paper at random from the heap in front of me and stare at it. It's something about insurance premiums. How do I *know* all this stuff, anyway? When did I learn it?

Heaving a huge sigh, I put the sheet down. I need to talk to someone. Fi. I lift the phone receiver and dial 352, which is her extension, unless they've changed the system.

"Flooring department, Fiona Roper speaking."

"Fi, it's me!" I say. "Lexi. Listen, can we talk?"

"Of course," says Fi in formal tones. "Do you want me to come in now?" She sounds so remote.

"I just meant we could have a chat! Unless you're busy . . ."

"Actually, I was about to go to lunch."

"Well, I'll come, too!" I say eagerly. "Like old times!"

"Lexi . . ."

"Fi, I really need to talk to you, okay? I don't remember anything. And it's freaking me out. Just hang on, I'll be out in a moment. . . ."

I thrust down the receiver and grab a piece of paper. I scrawl, "Please action all these, Byron. Many thanks, Lexi." I know I'm playing into his hands. But right now all I care about is seeing my friends. I hurry out of my office and into the main Flooring department.

"Hi, Lexi," says a nearby girl. "Did you want something?"

"No, it's okay, thanks. I'm just meeting Fi for lunch . . ." I trail off. I can't see Fi anywhere in the office. Or Carolyn. Or Debs.

The girl looks surprised. "I think they've already gone to lunch."

"Oh, right." I try to hide my discomposure. "Thanks. I expect they meant to meet in the lobby." I swivel on my heel, then walk as fast as I can in my spiky shoes along the corridor—just in time to see Debs disappearing into a lift. "Wait!" I cry out, breaking into a run. "I'm here! Debs!" But the doors are already closing.

She heard me. I know she did.

Thoughts are spinning wildly as I shove open the door to the stairs and clatter down. Are they avoiding me? What the hell has gone on these last three years?

I arrive at the ground floor and almost tumble into the foyer. I see Carolyn and Debs heading out of the main glass doors, with Fi just in front of them. "Wait!" I pelt toward the glass doors and at last catch up with them on the front steps of the building. "I thought we were going to have lunch together!" I say, panting.

There's silence. No one is meeting my eyes.

"What's going on? Fi, why didn't you return any of my messages?" None of them speaks. "You guys." I attempt a smile. "Please. You have to help me out. I've had amnesia. Last I remember, we were best mates! Going out on a Friday night. We had banana cocktails, Loser Dave stood me up, we did karaoke . . . remember?"

"Look." Fi sighs. "That was a *long* time ago. Let's just leave it. You've had this accident; you're ill. We don't want to upset you."

"Don't *patronize* me!" My voice is sharper than I meant. "I need you to tell me the truth." I look around the group in desperation. "What's wrong? What happened?"

"Lexi, nothing happened." Fi sounds awkward. "It's just . . . we don't really hang out with you anymore. We're not mates."

"But why not? Is this because I'm the boss now?"

"It's not because you're the *boss*—" Fi breaks off. "If I'm honest, it's because you're a bit of a . . . snotty cow."

"Total bitch-boss-from-hell, more like," mutters Carolyn.

Bitch-boss-from-hell? Me?

"I . . . I don't understand," I stammer. "Aren't I a good boss?"

"Oh, you're great." Carolyn's voice drips with sarcasm. "You penalize us if we're late. You time our lunch hours. You do spot checks on our expenses. Oh, it's a bundle of fun in Flooring!"

My cheeks are throbbing as though she's hit me. "I can't be a bitch," I manage at last, my voice trembling. "I can't be. I'm your friend! We have fun together; we go out dancing together." Tears are pricking my eyes. "I'm me! Lexi. Snaggletooth. Remember *me?*"

Fi and Carolyn exchange looks. "Lexi," says Fi, almost gently. "You're our boss. We do what you say. But we don't have lunch. And we don't go out." She sighs again. "Look, come along today if you want to. . . ."

"No," I say, stung. "It's okay, thanks." And I turn and walk away.

I'M NUMB with shock.

All the way home from the office, I sat in my taxi in a kind of trance. Somehow I managed to talk to Gianna about the dinner-party arrangements, and now it's early evening and I'm in the bath. But all the time my thoughts have been circulating, round and round. *I'm a bitch-boss-from-hell. My friends all hate me.* Have I really turned into a bitch over the last three years? But how? *Why?*

I wrap a towel around myself and pad into the dressing room. I pick out a little black dress and some black satin shoes. As I trail back into the bedroom, I let my towel drop onto the floor.

"Hi, Lexi!"

"Aargh!" I jump in fright. The big screen at the base of the bed has lit up with a huge image of Eric's face. I clap my hands over my chest. "Eric, can you see me?" I say in a high-pitched voice.

"Not right now." He laughs. "Put the setting to 'Camera.'"

"Oh! Okay!" I say in relief. "Just give me a sec."

I sling on a dressing gown, then quickly start gathering the clothes I've dropped about the room. Something I've learned pretty quickly is Eric doesn't like things lying around. I shove them all under the duvet.

"Ready!" I head to the screen and swivel the dial to CAMERA.

"Move back," instructs Eric. "Now I can see you! Is everything set up for dinner?"

"I think so!"

"Excellent." His huge pixilated mouth spreads in a jerky beam. "And how was work?"

"It was great!" Somehow I manage a cheerful tone. "I saw Simon Johnson and all my department and my friends . . ." I trail off. Can I even describe them as friends anymore?

"Marvelous. I'll see you later, darling."

"Wait," I say on impulse. This is my husband. I may barely know him—but he knows me. If anyone can reassure me, it's him. "Today, Fi said . . ." I can hardly bring myself to say the words. "She said I was a bitch. Is that true?"

"Of course you're not a bitch."

"Really?" Eric sounds so sure, I relax in relief.

"I'd say you were . . . tough. You're focused. You're driven. You drive your department hard." He smiles. "Now, I must go."

The screen goes dark, and I stare at it, more alarmed than ever. Isn't "tough" just another way of saying "bitch-boss-from-hell"?

IT'S an hour later, and my spirits have risen a little. I've put on my new diamond necklace, and I've had a sneaky little glass of wine. So maybe I've fallen out with my friends; maybe Byron is after my job; maybe I don't have a clue who Tony Dukes is. But I can put it all right. And I'm still the luckiest girl in the world. I have a gorgeous husband, a wonderful marriage, and a stunning apartment. Tonight the place looks even more jaw-dropping than ever. There are arrangements of lilies and roses everywhere. The dining table has been extended and laid for dinner with gleaming silverware and crystal and a centerpiece like at weddings.

I carefully apply my Lancôme lipstick and blot it. When I've finished, I step back, and automatically the lights change from the mirror spotlight to more of an ambient glow. The "intelligent lighting" in this room is like magic: It figures out where you are from heat sensors and then adjusts accordingly.

"Darling!" I jump, and turn to see Eric standing at the door, in his business suit. "You look wonderful," he declares.

"Thanks!" I glow with pleasure and pat my hair.

"One tiny thing. Briefcase in the hall. Good idea?" His smile doesn't waver, but I can hear the annoyance in his voice.

"I'll move it," I say hastily. "Sorry."

"Good." He nods. "But first, taste this." He hands me a glass of wine. "It's the Château Branaire-Ducru. I'd like your opinion."

"Right." I try to sound confident. "Absolutely."

Cautiously, I take a mouthful, racking my brain for all the wine-buff words I can think of. Okay, I'll say it's a divinely full-bodied vintage with hints of strawberries. I swallow the mouthful and nod knowledgeably at Eric.

"You know, I think this is a div—"

"It's shocking, isn't it?" Eric cuts me off. "Corked. Totally off."

Off? "Oh! Er . . . yes! Urggh." I make a face.

That was a close shave. I put the glass down on a side table, and the intelligent lighting adjusts again.

"Eric," I say, trying not to give away my exasperation. "Can we have a lighting mix that just stays the same all night? I don't know if that's possible—"

"*Anything* is possible." Eric sounds a bit offended. "We have infinite choice. That's what loft-style living is all about." He passes me a remote control. "Here. Pick a mood."

I head into the sitting room, find LIGHTING on the remote, and start experimenting with moods. "Daylight" is too bright. "Cinema" is too dark. I scroll much farther down. "Disco" . . . Hey. We have disco lights? I press the remote—and the room is suddenly filled with pulsating, multicolored light beams. Now let's try "Strobe." A moment later, the room is flashing black and white, and I gleefully start robotic dancing around the coffee table. This is like a club!

"Lexi, what are you *doing!*" Eric's voice pierces the flashing room. "You put the whole apartment on strobe light!"

Guiltily I jab the remote until we're back on "Disco." "You never told me we had disco and strobe lights! This is fantastic!"

"We never use them." Eric's face is a multicolored whirl. "Now find something sensible, for God's sake." He turns and disappears.

How can we have disco lights and never use them? What a waste! I *have* to have Fi and the others around for a party. And then I remember. That won't be happening anytime soon.

MY PLAN for the dinner party was to memorize each guest's face and name using visualization techniques. But this scheme disintegrates almost at once when three golfing buddies of Eric's arrive together in identical suits, with identical faces and even more identical wives. I sip my drink and smile a lot, and ten more guests arrive at once, and I have no idea who anyone is except Rosalie.

After a bit, my ears are ringing and I feel dizzy. Gianna is serving drinks, and her niece is handing out canapés, and everything seems under control. So I murmur an excuse and head out to the terrace.

I take a few lungfuls of clean air, my head still spinning.

"Darling! There you are!" I turn to see Eric pushing the sliding doors open. "Let me introduce Jon, my architect." Eric ushers out a dark-haired man in black jeans and a charcoal linen jacket.

"Hey!" I exclaim. "You're the guy from the car."

An odd expression flickers across the man's face. Almost like disappointment. "That's right. I'm the guy from the car."

"Jon's our creative spirit," says Eric, slapping him on the back. "He's the talent. I may have the financial sense, but this is the man who *brings* the world"—he pauses momentously—"loft-style living." As he says the words, he does the parallel-hands-sweeping-bricks gesture again.

"Great!" I try to sound enthused. I know it's Eric's business and everything, but that phrase "loft-style living" is really starting to bug me.

Jon takes a sip of his drink. "So, you still don't remember anything?"

"Nothing." I shake my head.

"That must be strange for you."

"It is, but I'm getting used to it. And Eric's really helpful. He's made this book to help me remember. It's like a marriage manual."

"A manual?" echoes Jon, and his nose starts twitching. "You're serious?"

"Ah, there's Graham." Eric isn't even listening to the conversation. "I must just have a word. Excuse me . . ." Eric heads off inside, leaving me and Jon the architect guy alone.

"What's wrong with a marriage manual?" I hear myself demanding.

"Nothing." He shakes his head gravely. "It's very sensible. Otherwise you might not know when you were supposed to kiss each other."

"Exactly! Eric's put in a whole section on—" I break off. Jon's mouth is crinkled up as if he's trying not to laugh. Does he think this is *funny?* "The manual covers all sorts of areas," I say rather stonily. "And it's been very helpful for both of us. You know, it's difficult for Eric, too, having a wife who doesn't remember the first thing about him! Or perhaps you hadn't appreciated that?"

There's silence. All the humor has melted out of his face. "Believe me," he says at last, "I appreciate it."

Then the sliding doors open, and Rosalie comes tottering over. "Eric says dinner's about to begin."

"Oh, we'd better go in. D'you two know each other?"

"Jon and I are *old* friends," says Rosalie sweetly. "Aren't we, darling?"

"See you." Jon disappears through the glass doors.

"Awful man." Rosalie makes a face at his departing back.

"Awful?" I echo in surprise. "Eric seems to like him."

"Oh, Eric likes him," she says disdainfully. "And Clive thinks he's the bee's knees. He's visionary and wins prizes, blah blah blah." She tosses her head. "But he's the rudest man I ever met. When I asked him to donate to my charity last year, he refused. In fact, he laughed."

"He *laughed?*" I say. "That's terrible! What was the charity?"

"It was called An Apple a Day," she says proudly. "I thought the whole idea up myself. Once a year, we'd give an apple to every schoolchild in an inner-city borough. Full of lovely nutrients!"

"Er . . . great idea," I say cautiously. "So, did it work out?"

"Well, it started off well," Rosalie says. "We gave out *thousands* of apples, and we had a van with an apple logo to drive about in. It was such fun! Until the council started sending us stupid letters about fruit being abandoned in the street and causing vermin."

"Oh dear." I bite my lip. The truth is, now *I* want to laugh.

We've come back inside, and as I find my place at the long glass dining table, nodding and smiling as people greet me, I feel like I'm in some weird dream. These people all know me. And I've never even *seen* them before.

Gianna and her niece serve dinner, and I talk to someone named Ralph about his divorce settlement. And then the plates are cleared, and Gianna is taking coffee orders.

"I'll make the coffee," I say, jumping up. I've grown increasingly uncomfortable seeing her scurrying around the table with heavy plates. No one even looked at her as they took their food.

"Lexi!" says Eric with a laugh. "That's hardly necessary."

"I want to," I say stubbornly. "Gianna, sit down."

Gianna looks perplexed. "I'll go and turn down your bed," she says.

I smile around the table. "Now, who would like coffee? Hands up . . ." I start counting the hands. "And anyone for mint tea?"

"I'll help," says Jon the architect, pushing his chair back.

"Oh," I say, taken aback. "Well . . . okay. Thanks."

I head into the kitchen, fill the kettle, and switch it on. Then I start looking in cupboards for cups. Meanwhile, Jon is just pacing around the kitchen in some distant daydream, not helping at all.

"Are you okay?" I say at last, with a flash of irritation.

Jon stops pacing and regards me, an even stranger expression on his face. "You really don't remember? This isn't some kind of game you're playing with me?"

"Remember *what?*" I say, totally bewildered.

"Okay. Here's the thing. I love you."

"What?" I look at him in confusion.

"And you love me," he continues. "We're lovers."

There's silence between us, the most prickling silence I've ever known.

"I . . . don't understand," I say, trying to summon some composure. "You're trying to tell me we've been having an *affair?*"

"We've been seeing each other for eight months." His dark gaze is fixed on mine. "You're planning to leave Eric for me. We'd made plans—then you had the accident." His face is deadly serious.

"But that's ludicrous! I'm not the unfaithful type. Plus, I have a great marriage, a fantastic husband. I'm happy—"

"You're not happy with Eric," Jon interrupts me. "Believe me."

"Of course I'm happy with Eric! I have the dream life!"

"The dream life? That's what you think?"

"Of course!" I swing my arms around the kitchen. "Look at this place! At Eric! It's all fantastic! Why would I throw it away—"

I break off abruptly as the kitchen door swings open.

"Sweetheart." Eric beams at me from the doorway. "How are those coffees going?"

"They're on their way," I say, flustered. I turn away to hide the blood pumping through my cheeks and start spooning coffee messily into the cafetière. I just want this man to *leave.*

"Eric, I'm afraid I have to go," says Jon behind me, as though reading my mind. "Thanks for a great evening. Good-bye, Lexi. Nice to make your acquaintance again."

"Good-bye, Jon." Somehow I force myself to turn and present a hostessy smile. He bends forward and kisses me lightly on the cheek.

"You don't know anything about your life," he murmurs in my ear, then strides out of the kitchen without looking back.

Four

IT CAN'T be true.

Morning light is creeping in around the blinds, and I've been awake for a while, but I haven't got out of bed. I thought I was getting to grips with this new life of mine, but now it's like everything is slipping away. Fi says I'm a bitch-boss-from-hell. Some guy says I'm his secret lover. What next? I discover I'm an FBI agent?

This Jon guy is probably a psycho. There's no evidence we're having an affair. None. I haven't seen any mention of him, no scribbled notes, no photos, no mementos.

But then . . . I'd hardly leave them around for Eric to find, would I? says a tiny voice at the back of my brain.

I lie perfectly still for a moment, letting my thoughts swill around. Then inspiration hits me. Underwear drawer. If I was going to hide anything, it would be there. I get up and head into my clothes room. I open the wardrobe and pull open my knicker drawer. I reach down among the La Perla—but I can't feel anything. Nor in my bra drawer . . .

"Looking for something?" Eric's voice makes me jump. I turn my head to see him standing at the door, watching me search.

"Hi, Eric! I just thought I'd look for . . . some bras!"

Okay, this is the main reason why I can't be having an affair. I'm the most crap liar in the world. Why would I need "some bras"? Do I suddenly have six boobs?

"Actually, I was wondering," I continue hastily. "Is there any more of my stuff anywhere? Letters, diaries, that kind of thing?"

"There's your desk in the apartment office. That's where you keep all your files."

"Of course." I thought the office was more Eric's domain than mine.

"It was a marvelous evening last night, I thought." Eric comes into the room. "Bravo, darling. You weren't too overwhelmed?"

"A little." I shoot him a smile. "There's still so much to learn."

"Well, you know you can ask me anything about your life. That's what I'm here for." Eric spreads his hands. "Is anything on your mind?"

I stare back at him speechlessly for a moment. "Well." I clear my throat. "Since you ask, I was just wondering. We are happy together, aren't we? We do have a happy . . . faithful . . . marriage?" I'm thinking I dropped in "faithful" quite subtly there, but Eric's keen ears pick it up straightaway.

"Faithful?" He frowns. "Lexi, I would never *think* of being unfaithful to you." He looks quite shocked. "Has someone been saying otherwise?"

"No! I just thought I'd ask. Just out of interest."

I shut the bra drawer and open another at random. I should move away from this subject area. But I can't help it; I have to probe.

"So, um, that guy." I wrinkle my brow artificially. "The architect. He seems like a pretty good guy." I try to appear casual.

"Jon? Oh, one of the best," says Eric firmly. "He's been a massive part of our success. That guy has more imagination than anyone I know."

"Imagination?" I seize on this. "Like a bit of a fantasist?"

"No." Eric seems puzzled. "Not at all. You'd trust Jon with your life."

To my relief, the phone gives a shrill ring before he can ask why I'm so interested in Jon. He disappears into the bedroom to answer, and I shut the drawer.

A few moments later, Eric heads out and I hear the front door bang. Mum's coming over to visit at eleven, but I have nothing to do till then. On impulse, I head into the office. There's my desk, all spick-and-span with the chair pushed under tidily. I sit down and open the first drawer. It's full of letters, tidily clipped together in plastic files. The second is full of bank statements, threaded onto a piece of blue office string.

Jeez Louise. Since when did I become so *anal?*

I pull out the bank statements and flick through them, my eyes widening as I clock my monthly salary. Most of my money seems to be going out of my single account into the joint account I hold with Eric, except one big sum every month, going to something called "Unito Acc." I'll have to find out what that is.

I put the bank statements away and reach into the bottom drawer. It's empty apart from two scraps of paper. One is covered in my own handwriting but is so abbreviated I can't make anything out. It's almost in code. The other has three words in pencil scrawled across it: *I just wish*

I stare at it, riveted. What? What did I wish?

MUM has brought three of the dogs along with her. Three huge, energetic whippets. To an immaculate apartment full of immaculate things.

"The poor things looked so lonely as I was leaving." She embraces one of them. "Agnes is feeling *vulnerable* at the moment."

"Right," I say, trying to sound sympathetic. "Poor old Agnes. Could she maybe go in the car?"

"I can't just abandon her!"

To my horror, I notice one of the dogs is on the sofa grabbing a cushion in its jaws. "Mum, could you get that dog off the sofa?"

"Raphael won't do any harm!" says Mum, looking hurt. She lets go of Agnes, who bounces over to join Raphael and whatever the other one is called. There are now three whippets romping joyfully on Eric's sofa.

"Have you got any Diet Coke?" Amy has sauntered in behind Mum.

"In the kitchen I think," I say distractedly. "Here, dogs! Off the sofa!"

All three dogs ignore me.

"Come here, darlings!" Mum produces some dog biscuits out of her cardigan pockets, and the dogs magically stop chewing the upholstery. One sits at her feet, and the other two snuggle up beside her, resting their heads on her faded skirt. "There," says Mum. "No harm done."

I look at the mangled cushion. It's not worth saying anything.

"There's no Diet Coke." Amy reappears from the kitchen.

I look at her, suddenly distracted. "Shouldn't you be at school?"

"I've been suspended." With a swagger, Amy heads over to a chair, sits down, and puts her feet up on the coffee table.

"*Suspended?* Why?" I look from her to Mum.

"I'm afraid Amy's been up to her old tricks again," says Mum.

"Old tricks? What did you do, Ame?"

"It was nothing! They so *totally* overreacted." Amy sighs with exaggerated patience. "All I did was bring this psychic into school. I charged ten quid each, and she told all the girls they'd meet a boy tomorrow. Everyone was happy. Until some teacher found out."

"Ten quid? No wonder you got in trouble!"

"I'm on my final warning," she says proudly.

"Why? Amy, what else have you done?"

"Nothing much! Just in the holidays I collected money for this math teacher, Mrs. Winters, who was in the hospital." Amy shrugs. "I said she was on the way out, and everyone gave loads. It was so cool!"

"Darling, it's extorting money under false pretenses," says Mum.

I'm trying to find something to say, but I'm too gobsmacked. How did my sister turn from cute, innocent little Amy into . . . *this?*

"I need some lip salve," Amy adds, swinging her legs down off the sofa. "Can I get some off your dressing table?"

"Um, sure." As soon as she's out of the room, I turn to Mum. "What's going on? How long has Amy been getting into trouble?"

"Oh . . . for the last couple of years." Mum doesn't look at me but addresses the dog on her lap. "She's a good, sweet girl really, *isn't* she, Agnes? She just gets led astray. Some older girls encouraged her into the stealing; that really wasn't her fault."

"Stealing?" I echo in horror.

"Yes. Well. She took a jacket from a fellow pupil and sewed her own name-tape into the back. But she really was very repentant."

"But . . . *why?*"

"Darling, nobody knows. She took her father's death quite badly. That reminds me. I've got something for you." Mum reaches into her bag and produces a DVD. "This is the last message from your father. He did a farewell recording before the operation, just in case. It was played at the funeral. If you don't remember it, you should probably see it."

I take the DVD and stare at it. "It'll be like seeing him again. How amazing that he did a recording."

"Well. You know your father. Always had to be the center of attention."

"It's fair enough to be the center of attention at your own *funeral.*"

Mum appears not to have heard. That's always her trick whenever anyone starts talking about a topic she doesn't like. She just blanks and changes the subject. Sure enough, a moment later, she says, "Maybe *you* could help Amy, darling. You were going to find her a work-experience placement at your office."

"Work experience?" I frown doubtfully. "I'm not sure about that." My work situation is complicated enough right now without Amy flouncing around the place.

"Just for a week or two. You've done so well in your career."

"Mum, I was wondering about that," I say. "Why did I go on that TV show? Why did I become all hard and ambitious overnight? I don't get it."

"I have no idea." She seems preoccupied. "Natural career advancement."

"But it *wasn't* natural." I lean forward, trying to get her attention. "I was never a high-powered career woman; you know I wasn't. Why would I suddenly change?"

"Darling, it was all so long ago. I really can't remember."

I look up to see Amy approaching us.

"Amy, Lexi was just talking about you doing some work experience at her office!" says Mum brightly. "Would you like that?"

"Maybe," I put in quickly. "There'd have to be some ground rules. You can't rip off my colleagues. Or steal from them."

"I don't steal!" Amy looks stung. "It was one jacket."

"Sweetheart, it wasn't just the jacket, was it?" says Mum.

"Everyone thinks the worst of me. Every time anything goes missing, I'm the scapegoat." Amy's eyes are glittering in her pale face. Suddenly I feel bad. I've judged her without even knowing the facts.

"I'm sorry," I say awkwardly. "I'm sure you don't steal. Come here." I hold my arms out for a hug.

"Leave me alone," she says almost savagely, and backs away.

"But you're my little sister!" I lean forward and give her a tight hug—then draw back almost immediately, rubbing my ribs. "Ow! What the hell—you're all lumpy!"

"Not again." Mum shuts her eyes. "Amy, what have you taken?"

"Give me a break! I haven't taken anything!" Amy yells. She throws her hand up in a defensive motion, and two Chanel lipsticks fly out of the sleeve of her jacket. We all stare at them.

"Oh, Amy," says Mum sorrowfully. "Turn out your pockets."

Shooting Mum a murderous glance, Amy starts unpacking her pockets. Two unopened moisturizers. A Jo Malone candle. A load of makeup. I watch her in silence, goggling at her haul.

"Now take off your T-shirt," orders Mum.

"This is *so* unfair," mutters Amy. She struggles out of the T-shirt, and my jaw drops. Underneath, she's wearing an Armani slip dress that I recognize from my wardrobe, all scrunched up under her jeans, and about five La Perla bras around her middle.

"You took a *dress*?" I suppress a giggle. "And *bras*?"

"It's not *my* fault. Mum won't give me any money for clothes."

"Amy, that's nonsense!" exclaims Mum. "You have plenty of clothes!"

"They're all out of date!" she yells instantly back.

I'm flummoxed by all of this. "Amy, maybe we should have a little talk. Mum, why don't you go and make some coffee or something?"

When she's gone, I sit down on the floor, across from where Amy has plonked herself. "Amy, listen," I say in my best understanding-grown-up-sister-but-still-pretty-cool voice. "You can't steal, okay? You can't extort money from people. You'll get chucked out of school!"

"Screw," says Amy conversationally. "Off."

"Look!" I say, trying to keep my patience. "If you've ever got any problems, I'm here for you. Just call me, or text me, anytime. We could go out for a . . ."

Amy's texting with one hand. With the other she has slowly moved her thumb and index finger into the "Loser" sign.

"Oh, screw off yourself!" I exclaim furiously, hugging my knees.

We sit there in grouchy silence for a bit. Then I reach for the DVD of Dad's funeral message and plug it into the machine. The huge screen opposite lights up, and after a few moments, my father's face appears. Dad's sitting in an armchair, wearing a red plushy dressing gown. His face is gaunt, the way I remember it after he got ill. But his green eyes are twinkling, and there's a cigar in his hand.

"Hello," he says, his voice hoarse. "We all know this operation has a fifty-fifty chance. My own fault for buggering up my body. So I thought I'd do a little message to you, my family, just in case."

He pauses. Suddenly there's a hard lump in my throat. I glance over at Amy. She's watching, too, transfixed.

"Live a good life," Dad is saying to the camera. "Be kind to one another. Barbara, stop living your life through those dogs. They're never going to love you or go to bed with you."

I clap my hand over my mouth. "He *didn't* say that!"

"He did." Amy gives a little snort of laughter.

"You only get one life, loves. Don't waste it. I know I've screwed up here and there. I haven't been the best family man. But I did my best. Cheers, m'dears. See you on the other side." He raises a glass to the camera and drinks. Then the screen goes blank.

As I gaze at the blank screen, I feel even more marooned than before. "That was a really nice message," I say. "Dad came good."

"Yeah." Amy nods. "He did."

THERE'S no evidence. If I was really having an affair, I would have left a trail. A note, or a photo, or a diary, or something. And the point is, I'm happily married to Eric.

It's much later that evening. Mum and Amy left a while ago, and now I'm zipping along in the car with Eric. He's having a meeting with Ava, his interior designer, and suggested I come along and see the show flat of his latest development, "Blue 42." All Eric's buildings are called "Blue" and some number. It's the company's brand.

"Hey, Eric," I say as we drive along. "I was looking at my bank statement today. I seem to pay all this regular money to something called Unito. I rang up the bank, and they said it's an offshore account. Do you know anything about it?"

"No." He shrugs. "Not a bad idea, though, putting some of your money offshore." Eric signals and turns through a pair of electric gates that has opened for us. "Here we are." I can hear the pride crackling in his voice.

I stare up, totally overcome. In front of us is a brand-new white building. It has curved balconies and black granite steps up to a pair of grand silver-framed doors. A uniformed porter opens the door for us. The foyer is all palest marble and white pillars. This place is a *palace*. "It's amazing. It's so glamorous!"

"The penthouse has its own lift." With a nod to the porter, Eric ushers me to the rear of the lobby and into a beautiful marquetry-lined lift. "There's a pool in the basement, a gym, and a residents' cinema. Although, of course, most apartments have their own private gyms and cinemas as well," he adds.

I look up sharply to see if he's joking—but I don't think he is.

"And here we are."

I'm looking at the most massive room. No, *space*. It has floor-to-ceiling windows, a walk-in fireplace on one wall, and on another, a gigantic steel sheet down which are cascading endless streams of water.

"Is that real water?" I say stupidly. "Inside a house?"

"Our customers like a statement. It's fun, huh? Ava?" He raises his voice, and a moment later, a skinny blond-haired woman in rimless glasses, gray trousers, and a white shirt appears.

"Hi there!" she says in a mid-Atlantic accent. "Lexi! You're up and about!" She grasps my hand with both of hers. "You poor thing."

"I'm fine." I smile. "This place is amazing! All that water . . ."

"Water is the theme of the show apartment," says Eric. "We've followed feng shui principles pretty closely, haven't we, Ava? Very important for some of our ultra-high net worths."

"Ultra-what?" I say, confused.

"The very rich," Eric translates. "Our target market. Feng shui is vital for ultra-highs."

Ava nods earnestly. "Eric, I've just taken delivery of the fish for the master suite. They're stunning! Each fish is worth three hundred pounds," she adds to me. "We hired them."

Ultra-high whatevers. Fish for hire. It's a different world.

"Here you are." Ava hands me an intricate scale model made out of paper and wooden sticks. "This is the building. You'll notice I've mirrored the curved balconies in the scalloped edges of the scatter pillows."

"Er . . . excellent! So, how did you think of it all?" I gesture at the water feature, which is now bathed in orange light.

"Oh, that wasn't me." Ava shakes her head. "My area is soft furnishings, sensual details. The big concept stuff was all Jon."

I feel a tiny lurch inside. "Jon?"

"Jon Blythe," Eric prompts helpfully. "The architect."

"Jon, there you are!" Ava calls out. "We were just talking about you!"

He's *here?* My hands clench involuntarily around the model. I don't want to see him. I don't want him to see me. I have to leave—

But too late. "Hi, Eric, Lexi." He nods politely as he approaches—then stares at my hands. I look down and feel a jerk of dismay. The model's totally crushed.

"Lexi!" Eric has just noticed it. "How on earth did that happen?"

"Jon." Ava's brow crumples in distress. "Your model!"

"I'm really sorry!" I say, flustered. "I don't know how it happened."

"Don't worry." Jon shrugs. "It only took me a month to make."

"A *month?*" I echo, aghast. I'm patting at the roof, desperately trying to prod it back into shape.

"Maybe not quite a month," Jon says, watching me. "Maybe a couple of hours."

"Oh." I stop patting. "Well, anyway, I'm sorry."

Jon shoots me a brief glance. "You can make it up to me."

Make it up to him? What does that mean? "The apartment's very impressive, Jon." I adopt a bland, corporate-wife-type manner, sweeping an arm around the space. "Congratulations."

"Thank you, I'm pleased with it," he replies in equally bland tones. "How's the memory doing?"

"Pretty much the same as before."

"You haven't remembered anything new?"

"No. Nothing."

I'm trying to stay natural—but there's an electric atmosphere growing between us as we face each other. I glance up at Eric. Can't he feel it? Can't he *see* it?

"Eric, we need to talk about the Bayswater project," says Ava.

"Lexi, why don't you look around the apartment while Ava and I talk? Jon will show you. It's a great opportunity for you to find out about the company's vision."

"Come this way, and I'll explain the initial concept." Jon gestures at the other side of the room.

Fine. If he wants to talk, I'll talk. I follow Jon across the room, and we pause next to the tumbling streams of the waterfall. How could anyone live with water thundering down the wall like this?

"So," I say politely. "How do you think of all these ideas?"

Jon frowns thoughtfully, and my heart sinks. I hope he's not going to come up with a load of pretentious stuff about his artistic genius.

"I just ask myself, what would a pretentious twit like?" he says at last.

I half laugh with shock. "Well, if I were a pretentious twit, I'd love this."

"There you go." He takes a step nearer and lowers his voice beneath the sound of the water. "So you really haven't remembered anything?"

"No. Nothing at all."

"Okay." He exhales sharply. "We have to meet. We have to talk."

"Are you crazy?" I hiss, glancing over to make sure Eric can't hear. "I'm not meeting you! I haven't found a single piece of evidence that you and I are having an affair. Not one."

"Lexi. It was a secret affair. *An affair that you keep secret.*"

"So you have no proof. I knew it." I turn on my heel and stride away toward the fireplace, Jon following closely behind.

"You want proof?" I can hear him muttering in low, incredulous tones. "Like you have a strawberry mark on your left buttock?"

"I *don't*—" I swivel around in triumph, then stop abruptly as Eric glances across the room at us. I wave at Eric, who waves back.

"I *know* you don't have a birthmark on your buttock." Jon rolls his eyes. "You don't have any birthmarks at all. Just a mole on your arm."

I'm briefly silenced. He's right. But so what?

"That could be a lucky guess." I fold my arms.

"I know. But it's not. Lexi, I'm not making it up. We're having an affair. We love each other. Deeply and passionately."

"Look." I thrust my hands through my hair. "This is just mad! I wouldn't have an affair. Not with you or anyone. I've never been unfaithful to anybody in my life." I wheel around and stride away toward the far end of the space, where a trendy Lucite staircase rises to a mezzanine level.

"Let's take a look at the wet-room complex," Jon says loudly as he follows me up. "I think you'll like it. . . ."

We both reach the top of the staircase, and I turn to face Jon. He *is* kind of sexy. "What do you want?"

"What do I want? I want you to tell your husband you don't love him and come home with me so we can start a new life together."

"You're a total psycho." I shake my head.

"I'm not a psycho," he says patiently. "I love you. You love me. Really. You have to take my word for that."

"I don't have to take your word for anything!" I suddenly resent his confidence. "I'm *married,* okay? I have a husband whom I love."

"You love him? Right deep down here?" Jon thumps his chest.

I want to snap, "Yes, I'm desperately in love with Eric" and shut him up for good. But for some reason, I can't quite bring myself to lie. "Eric's a fantastic guy; everything's wonderful between us," I say.

"Uh-huh." Jon nods politely. "You haven't had sex since the accident, have you?" To my surprise, he reaches for one of my hands. Then, very slowly, he starts tracing over the skin with his thumb. My skin is fizzing; his thumb is leaving a trail of delicious sensation wherever it goes.

"So what do you think?" Eric's booming voice heralds from below, and I jump a mile, whipping my hand away.

"It's great, darling!" I trill back over the balustrade. I draw back, out of sight of the floor below. "Look, I've had enough," I say in a swift undertone. "Leave me alone. I don't know you. I don't love you. I just want to get on with my life, with my husband. Okay?"

"No! Not okay!" Jon grabs hold of my arm. "Lexi, you don't know the whole picture. You're unhappy with Eric. He doesn't *understand* you—you can't throw us away." He's scanning my face desperately. "It's in there. It's all in there somewhere. I know it is."

"You're wrong!" I wrench my arm out of his grasp. "It's not!" I clatter down the stairs without looking back, straight into Eric's arms.

IN THE days since we got back from the show apartment, I've done nothing but immerse myself in the last three years. I've looked through photo albums, watched movies, listened to songs ... But nothing's worked.

Yesterday I went to see that neuropsychologist, Neil. He said maybe it would help to write out a timeline, and I could go see a therapist if I liked. But I don't need therapy. I need my *memory*.

"Lexi? I'm off." Eric comes into the bedroom holding a DVD, out of its box. "Darling, you left this on the rug. Sensible location for a DVD?"

"I'm sorry, Eric." I take the disc from him. It's the *Ambition* DVD.

"Your taxi will be here at ten," says Eric. "I'm off now."

I'm going back into work today, full-time. Not to take over the department—obviously I'm not ready to do that. But to start relearning my job, catching up on what I've missed. I head into the sitting room and slot the DVD into the player. I never did watch the rest of this. Maybe it'll help me get back into office mode.

". . . Lexi and her teammates won't be taking it easy tonight," a male voice-over is saying. The camera focuses in on me.

"We're going to win this task!" I'm saying in a sharp voice to the guys. "If we have to work around the clock, we're going to win. No excuses."

My jaw drops slightly. I've never spoken like that in my *life*.

"As ever, Lexi is taking her team to task," says the voice-over. "But has the Cobra gone too far this time?"

I don't understand what he's talking about. What cobra?

The picture now flashes to one of the guys. "She isn't human," he's muttering. "There's only so many bloody hours in the day. We're all doing our best, you know, but does she bloody care?"

Now the picture cuts to a full, stand-up row between me and the same guy. He's trying to defend himself, but I'm not letting him get a word in. "You're sacked!" I snap at last, my voice so scathing that I wince. "You're sacked from my team!"

"And the Cobra has struck!" the jaunty voice-over adds. "Let's see that moment again!"

Hang on a minute. Is he saying—*I'm* the Cobra?

To menacing music, a slow-motion replay has begun on-screen, zooming right into my face. "You're sssssacked!" I'm hissing.

I stare, light-headed with horror. What have they done? They've manipulated my voice. It sounds like I'm a snake.

"Lexi's in top venomous form this week!" says the voice-over.

A different group of people in suits appears on the screen and starts arguing about a price negotiation. But I'm too shell-shocked to move. Why didn't anyone tell me? Why didn't anyone *warn* me about this?

I'm a snake. No wonder everyone hates me.

As MY taxi wends its way toward the office, I sit rigid on the backseat, clutching three glossy gift bags—I've bought presents for Fi, Debs, and Carolyn—and giving myself a pep talk. Everyone knows the TV skews things. No one really thinks I'm a snake. Everyone's probably forgotten about that TV show.

The taxi deposits me outside the building, and I make my way up to the third floor. As I step out of the lift, the first thing I see is Fi, Carolyn, and Debs, standing by the coffee machine.

"Hi, you guys!" I smile. "I'm back again!"

"Hi, Lexi." There's a general muted reply.

"You look really nice, Fi! That top's great." I gesture at her cream shirt and she follows my gaze in surprise. "And Debs, you look fab, too. And Carolyn! Your hair looks so cool, all cropped like that, and . . . and those boots are fantastic."

I'm gabbling with nerves. No wonder they all seem nonplussed.

"So, anyway." I force myself to slow down a bit. "I got you all a little something. Fi, this is for you, and Debs . . ."

"What's this for?" says Debs blankly.

"Well, you know! Just to . . ." I falter slightly. "Go on. Open them!"

Giving one another uncertain looks, all three start ripping at their wrapping paper.

"Gucci?" Fi says in disbelief as she pulls out a green jewelry box. "Lexi, I can't accept—"

"Yes, you can! Please. Just open it, you'll see."

Silently, Fi snaps it open to reveal a gold bangle watch.

"D'you remember?" I say eagerly. "We always used to look at them in the shop windows. And now you've actually got one!"

"Actually . . ." Fi sighs. "Lexi, I got it two years ago." She lifts up her sleeve, and she's wearing exactly the same watch.

"Oh," I say, my heart sinking. "Well, I can exchange it."

"Lexi, I can't use this," Carolyn chimes in, and hands back the perfume gift set I bought her. "That smell makes me gag."

"But it's your favorite," I say in bewilderment.

"*Was,*" she corrects me. "Before I fell pregnant."

"You're *pregnant?*" I stare at her, overwhelmed. "Carolyn, I'm *so* happy for you. Matt will be the best dad ever—"

"It's not Matt's baby." She cuts me off flat.

"It's not?" I say stupidly. "But what . . . Did you two break *up?*"

They can't have broken up. It's impossible. Everyone assumed Carolyn and Matt would be together forever.

"I don't want to talk about it, okay?" Carolyn says, almost in a whisper. To my horror, I see her eyes have turned pink behind her glasses, and she's breathing hard. "See you." She turns and strides off.

"Great, Lexi," says Fi sarcastically. "Just when we thought she'd finally got over Matt."

"I didn't know!" I say, aghast. "I had no idea. I'm so sorry." I rub my face, feeling hot and flustered. "Debs, open your present." I've bought Debs a cross studded with tiny diamonds. She *has* to love it.

In silence, Debs pulls off the wrapping. "This is a cross!" Debs thrusts the box back at me. "I can't wear this! I'm Jewish."

"You're *Jewish?*" My mouth hangs open. "Since when?"

"Since I've been engaged to Jacob," she says. "I've converted."

"Wow!" I say joyfully. "You're *engaged?*" And of course now I can't miss the diamond ring on her left hand. Debs wears so many rings, I hadn't noticed it. "When's the wedding?" My words spill out in excitement.

"Next month." She looks away.

"Next *month!* Oh my God, Debs! But I haven't got—" I break off abruptly into a thudding silence. I was about to say, "But I haven't got an invitation." I haven't got an invitation because I haven't been invited. "I mean . . . um . . . congratulations!" Somehow I keep a bright smile plastered on my face. "I hope it all goes brilliantly. And don't worry, I can easily return the cross . . . and the watch . . . and the perfume . . ."

"Yeah," says Fi in an awkward voice. "Well, see you, Lexi."

They both walk off, and I watch them go, my chin stiff from wanting to cry. Great work, Lexi. You didn't win your friends back; you just screwed up everything even more.

"A present for me?" Byron's sarcastic voice hits the back of my head, and I turn to see him loping along the corridor, coffee in hand.

God, he gives me the creeps. *He's* the snake.

"Hi, Byron," I say as briskly as I can. "Good to see you."

"It's very brave of you to come back, Lexi," Byron says. "Any questions, you know where I am. Although today I'll be with James Garrison most of the day. You remember James Garrison?"

Bloody bloody bloody. *Why* does he pick the people I've never heard of? "Remind me," I say reluctantly.

"He's head of our distributor, Southeys? They distribute stock around the country? They drive it around in trucks?"

"I remember Southeys," I say cuttingly. "Why are you seeing them?"

"Well," says Byron. "They've lost their way. If they can't improve their systems, we're going to have to look elsewhere."

"Right." I nod in as bosslike a way as I can. "Well, keep me posted." We've reached my office, and I open the door. "See you later, Byron."

I close the door, dump my gift bags on the sofa, open the filing cabinet, and take out an entire drawer's worth of files. Trying not to feel daunted, I sit down at the desk and open the first one.

Twenty minutes later, my brain is already aching. I've started a sheet of paper: *Questions to ask,* and already I'm onto the second side.

"How are you doing?" The door has opened silently, and Byron is looking in. Doesn't he *knock?*

"Fine," I say. "I just have a couple of tiny questions."

"Fire away." He leans against the doorjamb.

"Okay. First, what's QAS?"

"Our accounting system software. Everyone's been trained in it."

"Well, I can get trained, too," I say briskly. "And who's Services.com?"

"Our online customer-service provider."

"But what about the customer-services department?"

"All made redundant years ago," says Byron, sounding bored. "The company was restructured; loads of departments were contracted out."

"Right." I nod. "So what about BD Brooks? What's that?"

"They're our ad agency," says Byron with exaggerated patience. "Really, Lexi, you're never going to pick all this up again." He is surveying me pityingly. "Lexi, face it. You're mentally ill. You shouldn't be putting your head under this kind of strain—"

"I'm not *mentally ill!*" I exclaim furiously, and get to my feet. I push roughly past Byron out of the door, and Clare looks up in alarm, snapping her mobile phone shut.

"Hi, Lexi. Did you want something? A cup of coffee?"

She looks terrified, as if I'm about to bite her head off. Okay, now is my chance to show her I'm not a bitch-boss-from-hell. I'm *me*.

"Hi, Clare!" I say in my most friendly, warm manner. "I just wondered if you'd like me to get you a coffee?"

"You?" She stares as though suspecting a trick. "Get *me* a coffee?"

"Yes! Why not?" I beam, and she flinches.

"It's . . . it's okay." She slides out of her chair, her eyes fixed on me as though she thinks I really *am* a cobra. "I'll get one."

"Wait!" I say, almost desperately. "You know, Clare, I'd like to get to know you better. Maybe one day we could have lunch."

Clare looks even more poleaxed than before.

"Um . . . yeah. Okay, Lexi," she mumbles, and scuttles down the corridor. I turn to see Byron still in the doorway, cracking up.

"What?" I snap.

"You really are a different person, aren't you?"

"Maybe I just want to be friendly with my staff and treat them with respect," I say defiantly. "Anything wrong with that?"

"No!" Byron lifts his hands. "That reminds me. There's one thing I left for you to deal with as director of the department. I thought it only right."

"Oh yes?" I lift my chin. "What?"

"We've had this e-mail from on high about people abusing lunch hours." He reaches into his pocket and produces a piece of paper. "SJ wants all directors to give their teams a bollocking. Today, preferably. Can I leave that one to you?"

I'M PACING about my office, sipping my coffee. I've never told anyone off before. Let alone a whole department.

I look yet again at the printed-out e-mail from Natasha, Simon Johnson's PA.

> Colleagues. It has come to Simon's attention that members of staff are regularly pushing the limit of lunchtime well beyond the standard hour. This is unacceptable. He would be grateful if you could make this plain to your teams asap and enforce a stricter policy of checks.
> Thanks. Natasha

Okay. The point is, it doesn't actually *say* "give your department a bollocking." I don't need to be aggressive or anything. I can make the point while still being pleasant. Maybe I can be all jokey.

Yes. That sounds good. Taking a deep breath, I head out of my office, into the main open-plan Flooring office.

"Hi, everyone!" I say, my face prickling. "How's it going?"

No one replies or even acknowledges that I've spoken. They're all just staring up with the same mute, get-on-with-it expression.

"Anyway! I just wanted to say . . . are your lunch hours long enough?"

The girl at my old desk looks blank. "Are we allowed longer ones?"

"No!" I say hurriedly. "I mean . . . they're *too* long."

"I think they're fine." She shrugs. "An hour's just right."

"Yeah," agrees another girl. "You can just make it to the King's Road and back."

Okay, I am really not getting my point across here. "Listen, everyone! I have to tell you something. About lunch hours. Some people in the company . . . I mean, not necessarily any of *you* . . ."

"Lexi," says Carolyn. "What the hell are you talking about?" Fi and Debs explode with laughter, and my face flames.

"Look, guys." I try to keep my composure. "This is serious."

"Seriousssss," someone echoes.

"Very funny!" I try to smile. "But listen, seriously—"

"Sssseriousssly."

Now almost everyone in the room seems to be hissing or laughing or both. All the faces are alive; everyone's enjoying the joke, except me. In spite of myself, tears spring to my eyes. I turn and stumble out of the office. That was the single most humiliating experience of my life.

AN HOUR later, after three mojitos at the bar at the Bathgate Hotel, around the corner from work, I decide I'm going to have sex with Eric. Maybe that's just what I need! This is my mission.

As I ride home in a taxi, I'm quite excited. As soon as I get back, I'll jump him. The only tiny snag I can think of is I don't have the marriage manual on me. And I can't *totally* remember the order of foreplay. Anyway, it doesn't matter. What I can't remember I'll make up. I mean, it can't be that we do it *exactly the same way* each time, can it?

I let myself into the apartment and call, "Eric!"

There's no answer, so I head toward the office. I am quite drunk, to tell the truth. I arrive at the door of the office and look for a few moments at Eric, who's working at his computer. On the screen, I can see the brochure for Blue 42, his new building. The launch party is in a few days.

Okay, what he should do now is sense the charged sexual vibe in the room and turn around. But he doesn't. "Eric," I say in my most husky, sensual voice, but still he doesn't move. Suddenly I realize he's wearing earphones. "Eric!" I yell, and at last he turns around. "Eric . . . take me." I push a hand through my hair. "Let's do it."

He peers at me. "Sweetheart, have you been drinking?"

"I may have had a couple of cocktails. Or three." I nod, then hold on to the door frame for balance.

Eric raises his eyebrows. "Maybe you should sober up."

What's wrong with him? I was expecting him to leap on me. "Come on." I lift my chin in a challenging way. "I'm your wife."

I can see Eric's mind working as he stares at me. "Well . . . okay!" He shuts down the document, turns off the computer, then walks over, puts his arms around me, and starts kissing me. And it's . . . nice. It is. It's . . . pleasant. His mouth is quite soft. It's a bit weird for a man. I mean, it's not exactly *un*sexy, but—

"Are you comfortable, Lexi?" Eric's breathy voice comes in my ear. "Shall we move to the bedroom?"

"Okay!" I whisper back.

In the bedroom, we resume kissing. Eric seems really into it. Now he's pulling me down onto the bed.

"Are you comfortable with me touching your breasts?" he murmurs.

"I guess so," I murmur back. Why is he squeezing me? It's like he's buying fruit. He's going to give me a bruise in a minute. Ouch.

"I'm sorry," whispers Eric. "Listen, sweetheart, are you comfortable with me touching your abdomen?"

"Er . . . I guess!"

Eric's breath is hot on my neck. I think it's time for me to do something else. I'm about three steps behind on the whole foreplay thing. But Eric doesn't even seem to have noticed.

"Lexi, sweetheart?" he murmurs breathily, right in my ear.

"Yes?" I whisper back, wondering if he's about to say "I love you."

"Are you comfortable with me—"

Before I can stop myself, I push him off me and roll away.

"What's wrong?" Eric sits up in alarm. "Lexi! What happened?

Why weren't you comfortable? Was it some traumatic memory resurfacing?"

"It wasn't because of a traumatic memory," I say, carefully looking past him at the duvet. "It was the way you kept asking me if I was comfortable every two seconds. It made things a bit . . . formal. Don't you think?"

"I'm just trying to be considerate," says Eric stiffly. "This is a pretty strange situation for both of us." Without meeting my eye, he gets up. "I think I'll take a shower."

"Okay." Left alone, I slump back on the pillows. Great. My mission totally failed. Beside the bed, the phone starts ringing. "Hello?"

"Hi," comes a dry, familiar voice. "It's Jon."

"Are you crazy?" I hiss in lowered, furious tones. "What are you ringing here for? It's so risky! What if Eric picked up?"

"I was expecting Eric to pick up." Jon sounds a bit baffled. "I need to speak with him."

"Oh." I halt in sudden realization. I'm so *stupid*. "Oh . . . right."

"But I need to speak with you more. We have to talk. I love you."

"You love the Cobra?" I retort sharply. "The bitch from hell?"

"You're not a bitch from hell. You were unhappy. And you made some pretty big mistakes. But you weren't a bitch."

Beneath my drunken haze, I'm absorbing every word. It's like he's rubbing salve on some raw part of me. I want to hear more. "What . . ." I swallow. "What kind of mistakes?"

"I'll tell you when we meet. Lexi, I've missed you so much."

Suddenly his intimate, familiar tone is making me uneasy. What am I getting into here? "Stop. Just stop!" I cut across him. "I need to think. This is so *frustrating*."

"Tell me about it," says Jon wryly, and I suddenly imagine him standing in his gray T-shirt and jeans, scrunching his face up in that way he does. The image is so vivid that I blink.

"Look, I have to go," I say in a rush. "I'll get Eric for you."

Five

I'VE tried. I really have tried. I've done everything I can think of to show the department that I'm not a bitch.

I've put up a poster asking for ideas for a fun department outing—but no one's filled any in. I've put flowers on the windowsills, but no one's even mentioned them. Today I brought in a massive basket of muffins, together with a sign saying FROM LEXI—HELP YOURSELF!! and not a single one has been taken.

I turn a page in the file I've been reading, then click on the on-screen document. I'm working through paper files and computer files at the same time, trying to cross-reference everything. I'm tired. I mean, I'm *exhausted*. I've been coming in every morning at 7:00 a.m. just to get through some more of this mountain of paper-work. And here I am reading a debate on carpet-fiber cost trends, dating from 2005.

No. Come on. It can't be important. I close the file and open a recent financial report. After a few moments, I lean back. These figures are just confirming what I already know: The department performance is terrible. We're going to be in real trouble if we don't turn things around. I mentioned it to Byron the other day, and he didn't even seem bothered.

Why don't they want my muffins?

They must totally hate me. I mean, you'd have to loathe some-one to refuse a muffin, wouldn't you? On impulse, I leap to my feet and head into the main office.

"So!" I try to sound relaxed. "Nobody wants a muffin?"

"Muffin?" says Fi, her brow wrinkled. "I can't see any muffins." Everyone shrugs, as though equally baffled.

"They do muffins at Starbucks. I could send out if you like," says Debs, barely hiding her giggles.

Ha-ha. Really funny. "Look, I went to a lot of trouble to get these muffins, and now you're pretending you can't even *see* them."

"I'm sorry, Lexi." Fi appears blank and apologetic. "I honestly don't know what you're talking about."

Carolyn snorts with laughter—and something inside me snaps.

"I'm talking about this!" I grab a chocolate-chip muffin. "It's a muffin! If you're not going to eat it, then I will!" I stuff the muffin into my mouth and start chewing it furiously. Huge crumbs are falling all over the floor. "In fact, I'll eat all of them!" I grab an iced blueberry muffin and cram that in my mouth, too. "Mmm, yum!"

"Lexi?" I turn and my insides shrivel up. Simon Johnson and Byron are standing at the door. Byron looks as if he's about to burst with delight. Simon's regarding me as though I'm a crazy gorilla throwing its food around at the zoo.

"Simon!" I splutter muffin crumbs in horror. "Um . . . hi!"

"A quick word, if you're not busy?" Simon raises his eyebrows.

"Of course!" I smooth my hair down, desperately trying to swallow my mouthful. "Come through to my office."

"So, Lexi," says Simon as I close the door. "I just had a good meeting with Byron about June '07. I'm sure he's been filling you in on developments."

"Sure." I nod, but "June '07" means absolutely nothing to me.

"I'm scheduling in a final decision meeting for Monday. I won't say any more just now; obviously discretion is crucial. I know you've had reservations, Lexi. We all have. But really, there are no more options."

"Well, Simon, I'm sure we can work it out," I bluff.

"Good girl, Lexi. Knew you'd come around." He raises his voice again, sounding more cheerful. "Now, I'm seeing James Garrison later on, the new guy at Southeys. What do you make of him?"

Thank God. At last, something I've heard of.

"Ah, yes," I say briskly. "Well, unfortunately, I gather Southeys aren't up to scratch. We'll have to look elsewhere for a distributor."

"I beg to differ, Lexi!" Byron cuts in. "Southeys have just offered us an improved package." He turns to Simon. "I was with them all day last week. James Garrison has turned the place around."

"Lexi, don't you agree with Byron?" Simon asks me in surprise.

I swallow. "I'm . . . I'm sure you're right, Byron." *Bastard*. He has completely shafted me. On purpose. There's a horrible pause. I can see Simon regarding me with puzzled disappointment.

"Right," he says. "Well, I must be off. Good to see you, Lexi."

"Bye, Simon." I usher him out of my office.

"Hey, Lexi," says Byron suddenly, gesturing at my bum. "There's something on your skirt." I grope behind and find myself peeling off a Post-it. Someone's printed, in pink felt-tip, *I fancy Simon Johnson.*

I can't look at Simon Johnson. Byron snorts with laughter. "Just the staff having a bit of . . . fun . . ." I crumple up the Post-it.

Simon doesn't look amused. "Right. Well, I'll see you, Lexi."

He turns on his heel and heads down the corridor with Byron. After a moment, I hear Byron saying, "Simon, *now* do you see . . ."

I stand, watching them go, still quivering in shock. That's it. My career's ruined. I walk back into my office and sink into my chair. I can't do this job. I'm exhausted. Byron's shafted me. No one wants my muffins. I bury my face in my arms, and soon I'm convulsing with sobs.

"Hi."

I raise my head to see Fi standing just inside the doorway. "Oh. Hi." I wipe my eyes roughly.

"Sorry about the Post-it," she says awkwardly. "We never thought Simon would come down. What did he say?"

"He wasn't impressed." I sigh. "But he's not impressed with me, anyway, so what's the difference?" I tear off a bit of chocolate muffin, stuff it in my mouth, and feel better. For about a nanosecond.

Fi is just staring at me. "I thought you didn't eat carbs anymore."

"Yeah, right. Like I could live without chocolate." I take another bite of muffin. "Women need chocolate. It's a scientific fact."

There's silence, and I look up to see Fi still gazing at me uncertainly. "It's so strange," she says. "You sound like the old Lexi."

"I *am* the old Lexi. Fi . . . imagine you woke up tomorrow and it was suddenly 2010. And you had to slot into some new life and be some new person. Well, that's what this is like for me. I don't recognize the new person. I don't know why she is like she is. And it's . . . it's hard."

There's a long silence. "Lexi, I'm sorry." Fi's voice is quiet. "We didn't realize. I mean . . . you don't *look* any different."

"I know." I give her a rueful smile. "I look like a brunette Barbie."

"Look." She's chewing her lip. "Why don't you have lunch with us?"

"That'd be nice." I give her a grateful smile. "But I can't today. I'm seeing Loser Dave for lunch."

"Loser *Dave?* Why? Lexi, you're not thinking of—"

"No! I'm just trying to work out what's happened in my life during the last three years. Fi, do you know how it ended with me and Loser Dave?"

"No idea." Fi shrugs. "You never told us. You shut us all out. It was like all you cared about was your career. So in the end we stopped trying."

"I'm sorry, Fi," I say awkwardly. "I didn't mean to shut you out. At least, I don't *think* I did. I'd better go." I get to my feet. "Fi, really. I'm sorry for whatever I was like—"

"Don't be a sap," Fi cuts me off. "Go and see Loser Dave."

LOSER Dave's done really well for himself, it turns out. I mean, *really* well. He now works for Auto Repair Workshop in some senior sales role. As he emerges from the lift, he's all dapper in a pinstripe suit. I can't help exclaiming, "Loser Dave! Look at *you!*"

Immediately he winces and looks warily around the lobby. "I'm David, okay?" he snaps in a low voice.

"Oh, right. Sorry . . . er . . . David."

His paunch has disappeared, too, I notice. He must be working out properly these days, as opposed to his old routine, which was five heaves of a dumbbell, followed by cracking open a beer and turning on the soccer. I can't believe I put up with him.

We head out of the office toward what Loser Dave calls a "good local eatery," and all the while, he's on his phone, talking loudly about "deals" and "mill," his eyes constantly sliding toward me.

"Wow," I say as he puts his phone away. "You're really senior now."

"Got a company Amex," he says casually. "Use of the corporate ski chalet."

"That's great!" We've reached the restaurant, which is a small Italian place. We sit down, and I lean forward. "David," I begin. "I don't know if you got the message about why I wanted to meet up?"

"My secretary told me you wanted to talk over old times?"

"The thing is, I had this car accident. And I'm trying to piece together my life, work out what happened, talk about our breakup . . ."

Loser Dave sighs. "Sweetheart, is this really a good idea, dredging all that up again? We both had our say at the time."

"But I have no idea what happened! I have amnesia."

Loser Dave stares at me. He shakes his head as a waiter comes over, then goes through the rigmarole of tasting and pouring the wine. "So you don't remember anything?"

"The last thing I remember is the night before my dad's funeral. I was in this nightclub, and I was really pissed off because you didn't turn up, and then I fell down some steps in the rain."

"Yeah." He's nodding thoughtfully. "I remember that night. That's why we split up. You chucked me the next morning, because I never turned up." He takes a gulp of wine, visibly relaxing.

"Really?" I say, astonished. "So, did we have a big row?"

"Not so much a row," says Loser Dave after a moment's consideration. "More like a mature discussion. We agreed it was right to end things. I offered to come along to your dad's funeral, show support, but you turned me down." He takes another gulp of wine. "I didn't bear you a grudge, though. I said, 'Lexi, I will always care for you.' I gave you a single rose and a final kiss. Then I walked away. It was beautiful."

I put my glass down and survey him. His gaze is as open and blameless as it used to be when he conned customers into taking extra premium total-scam insurance on their cars.

"Loser Dave . . . is that *really* what happened?"

"Of course," he says, injured. "And stop calling me Loser Dave."

"Sorry." I sigh. Maybe he's telling the truth. Maybe I did chuck him. "So, did anything else happen back then? Is there anything you can remember? Like, why did I suddenly get so career-oriented?"

"Search me." Loser Dave is perusing the specials menu.

"It's all just so confusing." I rub my brow. "I feel like I've been plonked in the middle of a map, with one of those big arrows pointing, 'You Are Here.' And what I want to know is, how did I *get* here?"

"What you want is a GPS system," Loser Dave says, like the Dalai Lama making a pronouncement on top of a mountain.

"That's it! Exactly!" I nod eagerly. "I feel lost."

Loser Dave is nodding wisely. "I can do you a deal."

"What?" I say, not understanding.

"I can do you a deal on a GPS system." He taps his nose. "We're branching out at Auto Repair."

I don't believe it. Did I actually go out with this guy? "Let's have the garlic bread," I say finally.

WHEN I arrive home later, Eric is looking stressed. "Come on, Lexi. We'll be late."

"For what?"

"For *what?*" echoes Eric. "For the launch!"

Damn. It's the Blue 42 launch party tonight. "Of course," I say hurriedly. "I'll just go and get ready."

In a total fluster, I change into a black silk tailored suit, put on my highest black pumps, and quickly shove my hair up into its chignon. I accessorize with diamonds, then turn to survey myself.

Aargh. I look so boring. Don't I have any brooches anymore? Or any silk flowers or scarves or sparkly hair clips? Anything *fun?* I root around for a bit in my drawers but can't find anything.

"Ready?" Eric strides in. "Let's go." I've never seen him so tense before.

All the way there, he's on the phone, and when he finally puts it away, he just stares out the car window.

"I'm sure it'll go really well," I say encouragingly.

"It has to. This is our big sales push. Lots of ultra-highs. Lots of press. This is where we make Blue 42 into the talk of the city."

As we turn into the entrance gates, I can't help gasping. Burning torches lead the way to the front doors. Lasers sweep the sky. There's a red carpet for guests to walk down and even a couple of photographers. It looks like a film premiere. "Eric, this is amazing." Impulsively, I squeeze his hand. "It's going to be a triumph."

"Let's hope." Eric gives me a quick, tight smile. "Oh, Lexi, before I forget. I've been meaning to give you this." He hands me a piece of paper.

"What's this?" I smile as I unfold it. Then my smile melts away. It's an invoice. *Large Glass Leopard: quantity 1. To pay: £3,200.*

"I ordered a replacement," Eric is saying. "You can settle up any time. Check is fine, or just a transfer into my bank account . . ."

He's *invoicing* me?

"You want me to pay for the leopard?" I force a little laugh.

"Well, you broke it. Is there a problem?"

"No! That's . . . that's fine." I swallow. "I'll write you a check."

It's fine, I tell myself firmly. It's lovely.

I stuff the paper into my bag and follow Eric along the red carpet.

BLOODY hell. This is a real, serious, glitzy party. The whole building is alive with light and thudding music. The penthouse loft looks even more spectacular than before, with flowers everywhere and waiters in cool black outfits holding trays of champagne. Ava and Jon and a few people I don't recognize are gathered by the window, and Eric strides straight over to them.

"People," he says. "Have we done the rundown on the guests? Sarah, you've got the press list? All under control? Let's sell this building."

The next moment, a couple in expensive-looking coats enters, and Eric springs into full-charm offensive, taking them over to see the view. More people are arriving, and soon there's a small crowd, chattering and leafing through the brochure and eyeing up the water feature.

Jon is about ten yards away, to my left, wearing a dark suit. All I'm aware of in this entire roomful of people is him. Where he is, what he's doing, who he's talking to. I dart a glance at him, and he meets my eye. Cheeks flaming, I swivel right away so he's out of my sight line. Eric appears beside me.

"Lexi, darling, come with me." Before I can stop him, he's leading me firmly over to Jon, who's talking to another rich-looking couple. "Let me introduce my wife, Lexi." Eric beams at them. "One of the greatest fans of"—he pauses, and I tense up, waiting for it—"loft-style living!" If I hear that phrase one more time, I'm going to *shoot* myself.

"Hi, Lexi." Jon meets my eye briefly as Eric heads off. "How are you?"

"I'm fine, thanks, Jon." I try to sound calm. "So . . . how do you like the loft?" I turn to the woman.

The couple exchange doubtful glances. "We have one concern," says the man in a European accent I can't quite place. "The space. Whether it is *big* enough."

I'm stumped. This place is like a bloody aircraft hangar.

"You could knock two or even three units together if you need a larger space," says Jon.

"Our other problem is the design," says the man. "At our home, we have touches of gold. Gold paintings. Gold lamps. Gold . . ." He seems to run out of steam.

"Carpets," the woman puts in, rolling the "rrr" heavily.

The man jabs at the brochure. "Here I see a lot of silver. Chrome."

"I see." Jon nods, deadpan. "Well, obviously the loft can be customized. We could, for example, have the fireplace gold-plated."

"A gold-plated fireplace?" says the woman uncertainly. "Would that be . . . too much?"

"Is there such a thing as too much gold?" Jon replies pleasantly. "And Lexi could help you with the gold carpet. Couldn't you, Lexi?"

"Of course." I nod, praying desperately I don't suddenly snort with laughter.

"Yes. Well, we will think about it." The couple moves off.

Jon knocks back his drink. "Not big enough? *Ten* of our units at Ridgeway would fit into this space."

"What's Ridgeway?"

"Our affordable-housing project. We only get planning for a place like this if we put up some affordable units."

"Oh, right," I say in surprise. "Eric's never mentioned it."

"I'd say his heart isn't totally in that aspect of the job," Jon says as Eric steps up onto a small podium in front of the mantelpiece.

"Welcome!" he says, his voice ringing out around the space. "Welcome to Blue 42, the latest in the Blue series of projects, dedicated to . . ."

I hold my breath. Please don't say it, please don't say it . . .

"Loft-style living!" His hands sweep along.

Jon glances at me and takes a step back, away from the crowd. After a moment, I move back, too, my eyes fixed firmly ahead. My whole body is crackling with apprehension. And . . . excitement.

Behind Eric, a massive screen is lighting up with images of lofts from all angles. Punchy music fills the air, and the room becomes even darker. I have to hand it to Eric; this is a fantastic presentation.

"You know, we first met each other at a loft launch like this one." Jon's voice is so low, I can barely hear it above the music. "The minute you spoke, I knew I liked you."

Curiosity prickles at me. "What did I say?" I whisper back.

"You said, 'If I hear that phrase "loft-style living" again, I'm going to shoot myself.' "

"No." I stare at him, then splutter with laughter.

For a few moments, we watch Eric in a hard hat on-screen, striding over a building site.

"You make no sense," I say quietly. "If you think lofts are for rich twits, why do you design them?"

"That's a good question. I should move on. But I like Eric. He gave me my first chance; he runs a great company. . . ."

"You *like* Eric?" I shake my head in disbelief. "Of course you do. That's why you keep telling me to leave him."

"I do. He's a great guy. He's honest; he's loyal. I don't *want* to mess Eric's life up," he says finally. "It wasn't in the plan."

"So why . . ."

"He doesn't understand you." Jon looks directly at me.

"And you do, I suppose?" The lights come up, and applause breaks out around the room. Instinctively, I take a step away from Jon, and we both watch as Eric mounts the podium again.

"So, have you encountered Mont Blanc yet?" says Jon, clapping.

"What's Mont Blanc?" I give him a suspicious glance.

"You'll find out."

"Jon! There you are. Emergency!" Ava appears behind us. "The ornamental rocks for the master bedroom fish tank have only just arrived from Italy. But I've got to see to the kitchen place settings, so can you do it?" She shoves a small sack into Jon's arms. "Just arrange the rocks in the tank before the presentation finishes."

"No problem. Lexi, want to come with me and help?"

I have to say no. "Um . . . yes." I swallow. "Sure."

We head into the main bedroom, and Jon closes the door. "So," he says.

"Look." My voice is sharp with nerves. "I can't carry on like this! All this whispering, creeping around . . . I'm happy with Eric!"

"No." He shakes his head. "You'll try your best; you'll try to mold yourself, but your spirit's too free for him. In the end, you won't be able to stand it anymore."

"Thanks for the warning," I snap. "We should do the rocks." I jerk my head toward the sack, but Jon ignores me. He comes toward me, his eyes intense and questioning.

"All the time we spent together . . . There has to be *something* to trigger your memory. Do sunflowers mean anything to you?"

In spite of myself, I rack my brain. Sunflowers. Didn't I once . . . No, it's gone. "Nothing," I say. "I mean, I *like* sunflowers, but . . ."

He's so close I can feel his gentle breath on my skin. "Does this mean anything to you?" He leans down and brushes a kiss against my neck.

"Stop it," I say feebly, but I can barely get the words out. I want to kiss him. I want to kiss him in a way I didn't want to kiss Eric.

And then his mouth is on mine, and my entire body's telling me this is the right thing to do. He smells right. He tastes right. My eyes are closed. I'm losing myself; this is so right. . . .

"Jon?" Ava's voice comes through the door.

I fly away from Jon, cursing under my breath.

"Sssh!" He looks thrown, too. "Stay cool. Hi, Ava. What's up?"

Rocks. I grab the sack and start chucking rocks into the fish tank.

"Everything okay?" Ava puts her head around the door. "I'm about to lead a party of guests up here for the tour."

"No problem," Jon says reassuringly. "Nearly done."

As soon as Ava disappears, he comes back to me. "Lexi." He grasps my face. "If you only knew, this has been *torture.*"

"Stop it!" I draw away. "I'm married! We can't—" I gasp. "Oh hell!" I'm not looking at Jon anymore. I'm looking at the fish tank.

"What?" Jon follows my gaze. "Oh. Oops."

All the tropical fish are swimming peacefully among the marble rocks. Except one blue stripy one, which is floating on top. "I've killed a fish! I've brained it with one of the rocks."

"So you have," says Jon. "Nice aim."

"What am I going to do? The guests will be here any moment!"

Jon grins. "Okay, I'll go and delay Ava. You flush it away." He holds my hand a moment. "We haven't finished." He heads out of the room, leaving me to reach into the warm water, wincing, and pick up the fish.

I hurry into the high-tech bathroom. I drop the fish in the toilet and look for the flush. There isn't one. This must be an intelligent toilet.

"Flush," I say aloud, waving my arms to set off the sensors.

Nothing happens.

"Flush!" I say with more desperation. "Go on, flush!" But the toilet is totally dead. The fish is floating around, looking even more lurid blue against the white porcelain.

If anything is going to put a customer off a high-end, luxury apartment, it's a dead fish in the toilet. I pull out my phone from my pocket and scroll down the CONTACTS until I find J. That must be him. I press speed dial and a moment later, he answers.

"The fish is in the toilet!" I hiss. "But I can't flush it!"

"The sensors should set it off automatically."

"I know! But they're not. What am I going to do?"

"Go to the panel next to the bed. You can override it and flush it from there. Hey, Eric! How are you doing?" The phone cuts off. I hurry over to the bed and locate a panel in the wall. A scary digital display blinks at me, and I can't help a moan. How can anyone live in a house more complicated than NASA? Why does a house have to be intelligent, anyway? Why can't it be nice and stupid?

My fingers fumbling, I press MENU, then OVERRIDE and OPTIONS. I scan down the list. TEMPERATURE . . . LIGHTING . . . Where's "bathroom"? I start jabbing at random.

A sound draws me up short. It's a wail. A kind of distant siren. The panel is flashing at me in red: PANIC ALERT—SECURE SPACE. I look up to see a metal grille descending steadily over the window.

What the . . . Frantically, I jab again at the panel, but it flashes back at me UNAUTHORIZED, then returns to PANIC ALERT—SECURE SPACE.

Oh my God. I dart to the door of the bedroom and look down to the space below. It's mayhem. The siren is even louder out here. Metal grilles are descending everywhere, over the windows, the paintings, the water feature. All the rich guests are clinging to one another like hostages.

"Is it a robbery?" a woman in a white pantsuit is exclaiming hysterically, wrenching at her hands. "George, swallow my rings!"

"It's coming from the master bedroom!" shouts one of Eric's staff. "Someone's set off the panic alarm. The police are on their way."

I've ruined the party. Eric will kill me; he'll *kill* me. . . .

And then, with no warning, the noise stops. "Ladies and gentlemen." A voice comes from the stairs. It's Jon. He's holding a remote control. "We hope you enjoyed our security demonstration. Rest assured, we are not under attack from robbers."

He pauses, and a few people laugh nervously. Around the room, the grilles have already started retracting.

"However," Jon continues, "as all of you know, in London today, security is of prime consideration. This system is MI5 quality—and it's here for your protection."

He's saved my life. As he continues talking, I totter back into the bedroom suite and find the blue fish still floating in the toilet. I plunge my hand in, grab the fish, and with a shudder, stuff it in my bag. I wash my hands, wait a few minutes, then unobtrusively slip down the stairs. I grab a glass of champagne from a passing waiter and take a deep swig.

"Sweetie!" Rosalie's voice makes me jump. "Wasn't that genius? You know it cost three hundred grand just for the security system!"

Three hundred grand, and the toilet doesn't even flush. "Great!" I say.

"Lexi." Rosalie is giving me a thoughtful look. "Sweetie . . . can I have a little word? About Jon. I saw you talking to him earlier. I know you had your bump on the head and everything. But do you *remember* anything about Jon? From your past?"

"Um . . . not really."

Rosalie pulls me nearer. "Sweetie, I'm going to give you a bit of a shock," she says in a low, breathy voice. "A while ago, you told me something in confidence. Girlfriend to girlfriend."

I'm transfixed. Does Rosalie *know*?

Rosalie hustles closer. "Jon kept pestering you. I just thought I should warn you in case he tried it on again."

Pestering me? "What do you mean?" I stammer.

"What do you think? He's tried it on with all of us." She rolls her eyes. "He told me Clive doesn't understand me. And he went after Margo, too. *Such* nerve. He said he knew her better than her own husband and she deserved more." She clicks her tongue dismissively. "Margo's theory is he targets married women and tells them whatever they want to hear." She peers at me. "Don't you remember any of this?"

"No," I say. "I don't remember any of it. So what did I do?"

"You kept telling him to leave you alone. You were very dignified, sweetie." She suddenly focuses over my shoulder. "Darling, I must dash and have a word with Clive about our dinner arrangements. Are you okay? I just thought I should warn you."

"No." I come to. "I'm glad you did."

Rosalie trips away into the party, but my feet are rooted to the ground. I've never felt so humiliated in my life, so gullible, so *vain*.

I believed it all. I fell for his blarney. *We've been having a secret affair . . . I know you better than Eric does . . .* He took advantage of my memory loss. And all he wanted was to get me into bed like a . . . a trophy. I feel hot with mortification. I *knew* I would never have an affair! I have a decent husband who loves me. And I allowed my head to be swayed. I nearly ruined everything.

Well, not anymore. I take a few deep gulps of champagne. Then I lift my head high and walk forward through the crowd until I find Eric. "Darling, the party's going wonderfully. You're brilliant."

"I think we've pulled it off. Narrow escape with that alarm. Trust Jon to save the day. Hey, there he is! Jon!"

I clutch Eric's arm even more tightly as Jon walks toward us. Eric hands him a glass of champagne from a nearby tray. "Here's to you," he exclaims. "Here's to Jon."

"To Jon," I echo tightly. I'm just going to pretend he doesn't exist.

A bleep from my bag disturbs my thoughts, and I pull out my phone to see a new message. From Jon. I do not *believe* this. He's texting me in front of Eric: OLD CANAL HOUSE IN ISLINGTON, ANY EVENING FROM 6. WE HAVE SO MUCH TO TALK ABOUT. I LOVE YOU. J. PS WHAT DID YOU DO WITH THE FISH??

My face is burning with fury. Rosalie's words ring in my head.

"It's a text from Amy!" I say to Eric, my voice shrill. "I might just quickly reply." Without looking at Jon, I start texting: YEAH. RIGHT. I SUPPOSE YOU THOUGHT IT WAS A LAUGH, TAKING ADVANTAGE OF THE GIRL WHO LOST HER MEMORY. WELL, I KNOW YOUR STUPID GAME. I'M A MARRIED WOMAN. LEAVE ME ALONE.

I send the text and put my phone away. A moment later, Jon frowns at his watch and says, "Is that the right time? I think I'm fast." He takes his mobile phone out and squints at the display as though checking, but I can see him read the message, and his face jerks with shock. "I'm six minutes out," he says, tapping at the phone. "I'll just change the clock." I don't know why he's bothering with an excuse. Eric's not even paying attention.

Three seconds later, my phone beeps again and I pull it out.

"Another text from Amy," I say disparagingly. "She's such a pain." I dart a glance at Jon as I put my finger on DELETE, and his eyes widen with apparent consternation.

"Is that a good idea?" he says quickly. "Deleting a message without even reading it?"

"I'm really not interested." I shoot him a sweet smile, press DELETE, switch off my phone, and drop it into my bag.

"So!" Eric turns back to us, ebullient. "The Clarksons want a repeat viewing tomorrow. I think we have another sale."

"Well done, my darling. I'm so proud of you!" I exclaim, putting an arm around him in an extravagant gesture. "I love you even more now than I did on our wedding day."

I'M STILL a bit shaken the next morning as I go into the kitchen for breakfast. I must have been crazy last night. Why would I kiss some guy in the back bedroom, whatever his story was?

I pour a little green juice into a glass and swirl it around to look like dregs, which is what I do every morning. (I can't drink that pond-weed stuff.) Then I take a boiled egg from the pan. I'm really getting into this low-carb start to the day. I have a boiled egg every morning without fail.

And then sometimes a bagel on the way to work.

As I sit down, the kitchen seems tranquil. But I'm still jittery. I could have wrecked everything. I've only had this marriage for a few weeks, and already I'm risking it. I need to *cherish* it. Like a yucca plant.

"Morning!" Eric breezes into the kitchen. "Sleep well?"

"Great, thanks!"

We're not sharing a bedroom yet, nor have we tried sex again.

But if I'm going to cherish my marriage, maybe we should be getting more physical. I stand up to get the pepper and run my hand down his jawline. Eric's eyes meet mine questioningly, and he puts a hand up to meet mine. I glance quickly at the clock. There isn't time, thank goodness. No. I didn't think that. I need to be *positive*.

I put on my jacket. "Bye, darling."

"Bye, sweetheart." Eric comes over, and we kiss each other good-bye. I am at the door when something hits me.

"Hey, Eric," I say as casually as possible. "What's Mont Blanc?"

"Mont Blanc?" Eric turns, his face searching mine in disbelief. "You're kidding. Do you remember Mont Blanc?"

Okay. I really fell into this one. I can't say, "No, Jon told me." "I don't *remember,* exactly," I improvise. "But the name 'Mont Blanc' came back to me. Does it mean something . . . special?"

"You'll find out, darling." I can see the suppressed pleasure in Eric's face. "I won't say any more for now. This has to be a good sign!"

"Maybe!" I try to match his excitement. "Well, see you later!" *Mont Blanc.* Skiing? Fountain pens? A great big snowy mountain?

I have absolutely no idea.

I GET off the tube, buy a bagel, and nibble it as I walk along. But as I get near work, I have a nasty churning in my stomach. I still don't feel on top of anything.

I head straight up to my office, sit down, and pull my pile of papers toward me, when there's a knock at the door.

"Hi, Lexi." Debs edges her way into the room, holding an envelope. "How are you?" She sounds awkward.

"I'm . . . fine." The door widens to reveal Fi and Carolyn, both looking ill at ease, too. "Hi!" I exclaim. "Is everything okay?"

"I told them what you told me," says Fi.

"We didn't realize," says Debs. "We didn't give you a chance. We just assumed you were still . . ." She casts around for the word.

"A power-crazed nightmare," supplies Carolyn, deadpan.

"We feel bad." Debs bites her lip as she looks at the others.

"Don't we? So, I just wanted to give you this." Debs hands me the envelope. I rip it open and pull out a stiff white engraved card. A wedding invitation.

"Hope you can come." Debs has shoved her hands into her pockets. "You and Eric."

I feel a rush of humiliation. Her body language is obvious. The last thing she wants is us at her wedding. "Look, Debs, you don't have to ask me. It's really kind of you, but you don't really—"

"Yes, I do." She puts her hand on mine, stopping me, and I look up. "You were one of my best friends, Lexi. You should be there."

"Well . . . thanks," I mumble. "I'd love to come." I turn the invitation over, running a finger over the engraving. "How did you get your mother to agree to such a late guest? Did she threaten to stop your allowance?"

"Yes!" exclaims Debs, and we all break into giggles. Debs's mum has been threatening to stop her allowance ever since I've known her—even though she stopped giving Debs an allowance years ago.

"We've bought some muffins, too," says Fi. "To say sorry for yesterday—" She stops as there's a tapping at the door. Simon Johnson is standing in the doorway.

"We'll go," says Fi hurriedly, and hustles the others out. "Thanks for that . . . er . . . information, Lexi. Very useful."

"I won't take up your time," says Simon, shutting the door as they leave. "Just wanted to give you the final rundown for Monday's meeting. Obviously, keep it close to your chest. Within this department, only you and Byron have this information." He holds out a folder.

As I take the folder from him, I see JUNE 07 typed discreetly in the top right-hand corner and feel a twinge of foreboding.

"Looking forward to it!" I pat the folder, hoping I look convincing.

"Good. It's Monday, twelve noon sharp in the boardroom."

The minute Simon has left, I whip open the folder. The first page is entitled "Summary": *June 07 . . . major restructuring . . .*

After a few seconds, I sink down into my chair, feeling overwhelmed. No wonder this is a big secret. The whole company's being changed around. We're acquiring a home technology company; we're amalgamating several departments . . . I flick my eyes farther down. . . . *context of its current sales . . . plans to disband . . .*

What? I read the words again. And again.

With a surge of adrenaline, I leap to my feet, hurtle to the door and out, down the corridor. There's Simon, by the lifts, talking to Byron.

"Simon!" I'm gulping air in my panic. "Could I have a quick word?" I look around, checking there's no one nearby to overhear. "I just wanted to . . . to . . . clarify a couple of things. These plans to disband the Flooring section." I tap the folder. "You can't really mean . . ."

"She's finally twigged." Byron folds his arms, shaking his head with such amusement I want to punch him. He *knew* about this?

Simon sighs. "Lexi, we've been through this many times, as you know. You've done marvels with your sales force; we all appreciate that. But the department is unsustainable."

"But you can't get rid of Flooring! Deller Carpets is all about Flooring!"

"You and Byron will both have new roles in senior management. It's all been worked out." The lift arrives, and he steps into it.

"But, Simon," I say desperately, "you can't just *fire* the whole department." It's too late. The lift doors have closed.

"It's not called firing," Byron's sardonic voice comes from behind me. "It's called making redundant. Get your terms right."

I wheel around, incensed. "How come I didn't know about this?"

"Oh, didn't I tell you?" Byron clicks his tongue in mock self-reproach.

"Where are the files? Why didn't I see this before?"

"I may have borrowed them." He heads toward his office.

"No! Wait!" I push my way in behind him and close the door. "I don't understand. Why are they axing the department?"

"Have you *looked* at our sales recently?" Byron rolls his eyes.

"Lexi, carpet is old news. We've failed to penetrate the other flooring markets. We've only got a couple of contracts to see out. The party's over."

"But those original carpet designs are classics! What about rugs?"

Byron stares at me incredulously for a moment, then bursts into laughter. "You said all this at the first crisis meeting. 'We could make the carpets into rugs!' Give up."

"But they'll all be out of a job! The whole team!"

"Sob, sob," Byron drawls. "You know, you weren't bothered before you had that car crash. You were all for getting rid of Flooring. Once you saw your package. More power for us, more money. What's not to love?"

A coldness creeps over me. "I don't believe you." My voice is jerky. "I would *never* have sold out my friends."

Byron just looks at me pityingly. "Yeah, you would. You're not a saint." He sits at his desk and motions toward the door. "I have work to do."

"You're a *bastard,*" I say, my voice shaking. I stride out of his office.

"Lexi!" My head jerks up, and instinctively I clasp the folder closer to my chest. Fi is standing at the door of the main Flooring office, beckoning me. "Come in! Have a muffin."

I can't refuse. I have to appear normal.

I follow Fi into the main office. A banner has been strung up between two window latches, reading WELCOME BACK, LEXI!!! A plate of fresh muffins is on the filing cabinet, along with an Aveda gift basket.

"We never gave you a proper welcome back," says Fi, her face slightly pink. "And we just wanted to say we're glad you're okay." She addresses the room. "To those of you who didn't know Lexi way back when, I just want to say that I think this accident has changed things. I know she's going to be the most fantastic boss. Here's to you, Lexi." She lifts her coffee mug, and the whole room breaks into applause.

"Thanks, everyone," I manage. "You're . . . all great."

They're all about to lose their jobs. They have no idea. And they've bought me muffins and a gift basket.

Somehow I raise a sick smile. I'm in a bad dream.

I GO down the lift at six thirty with a stuffed briefcase. I'll work all weekend; I'll find the solution; I'll save the department . . .

A beep from my pocket interrupts my thoughts. I pull out my phone and see it's a text from Eric: HOW ARE YOU DOING? WORKING LATE?

As I stare at the words, I'm touched. Eric cares about me: ON MY WAY HOME NOW, I type back. I MISSED YOU TODAY!!

It's not exactly true, but it has the right sound to it.

I MISSED YOU, TOO! comes back instantly.

I knew there was a point to marriage. And this is it. Someone to care about you when everything's crap. The phone beeps once more. FANCY A MONT BLANC?? :) :)

Again the Mont Blanc. What *is* this? A cocktail, maybe? There's only one way I'll find out. GREAT! I text back. CAN'T WAIT!

It only takes about twenty minutes to get home, during which time I stare out of the taxi window, my mind working overtime. I *know* there's still value in the Deller Carpets brand. . . .

"Love?" The taxi driver breaks my reverie. "We're here."

"Oh, right. Thanks." I'm fumbling for my purse when my phone beeps yet again. I'M READY!

Ready? This gets more and more mysterious.

As I let myself into the flat, the lights are dim, on a setting that I recognize as "Seduction."

"Hi!" I call out cautiously, hanging up my coat.

"Hi!" Eric's distant voice seems to be coming from my bedroom. Well, I guess, officially, our bedroom.

I head through to the bedroom and push the door open. And at the sight before me, I nearly scream out loud.

This is Mont Blanc? *This* is Mont Blanc?

Eric is lying on the bed. Totally naked. Except for the most massive mound of whipped cream. "Hi, darling." He raises his eyebrows with a knowing twinkle.

I'm paralyzed with horror as I survey the creamy, whippy mountain. I have to come up with an excuse.

"I feel dizzy!" The words come out of nowhere. I clap a hand to my eyes and back away from the bed. "I'm having a flashback."

"A *flashback?*" Eric sits up, alert.

"Yes! I had a sudden image of . . . the wedding," I improvise.

"Sit down, darling!" Eric is frowning anxiously. "Take it easy. Maybe some more memories will come back."

"I might just go and lie down quietly in the other room, if you don't mind. I'm sorry, Eric."

Before he can say anything, I hurry out and flop down on the big cream sofa. My head is spinning, whether from the Mont Blanc shocker or the whole day . . . I don't know. All I know is, I can't cope with this life of mine. Any of it.

Six

I CAN'T look at Eric without seeing whipped cream. Thankfully we've barely seen each other this weekend. Eric's been doing corporate entertaining, and I've been trying desperately to come up with a plan to save Flooring. I've devised a total relaunch. It'll need a bit of money and faith and cost-trimming—but I'm positive we can kick-start sales. I can't let all my friends lose their jobs.

My stomach heaves yet again with nerves. I'm sitting in the taxi on the way to work, my hair firmly up, my presentation folder in my lap. The meeting is in an hour. All the other directors are expecting to vote to disband Flooring. I'm going to have to argue my socks off.

My phone rings, and I nearly jump off the seat. "Hello?"

"Lexi?" comes a small voice. "It's Amy. I'm in trouble. You have to come. Please."

"What kind of trouble?" I say, alarmed. She sounds desperate.

"Please come." Her voice is quivering. "I'm in Notting Hill, on the corner of Ladbroke Grove and Kensington Park Gardens."

"Amy." I clutch my head. "I can't come now! I have a meeting; it's really important. Can't you phone Mum?"

"Lexi, you said I could ring whenever I wanted, that you were my big sister, that you'd be there for me."

"But I have this presentation . . . Look, any other time . . ."

"Fine. Go to your meeting. Don't worry."

Guilt drenches me. I stare blindly out the window.

"Amy, hold on," I say abruptly. "I'm coming."

AS THE taxi heads up Ladbroke Grove, I'm leaning forward, trying to glimpse Amy. And then suddenly I see a police car. On the corner of Kensington Park Gardens. I'm too late. She's been shot. She's been knifed.

Weak with terror, I thrust some cash at the driver and get out of the cab. There's a throng of people in front of the police car. "Excuse me. It's my sister. Can I get through?" Somehow I manage to push my way in.

And there's Amy sitting on a wall, looking cheery. "Lexi!" Amy turns to the policeman standing next to her. "I told you she'd come."

"What's going on?" I demand, shaky with relief.

"I'm afraid this young lady's in trouble," the policeman says. "She's been exploiting tourists. A lot of angry people here." He gestures at the crowd. "Celebrity tours." He hands me a leaflet. "So-called."

In disbelief, I read the fluorescent yellow leaflet.

Undercover Celebrity Tour of London
Many Hollywood stars have settled in London. See them on
this unique tour. Catch glimpses of:
* Madonna putting out her washing *
* Gwyneth in her garden *
* Elton John relaxing at home *

£10 per person
Important note: If you challenge the stars, they
may deny their identities. Do not be fooled!
This is part of their Undercover Secret!

I look up in a daze. "Is this serious?"

The policeman nods. "Your sister's been leading people around London, telling them they're seeing celebrities. People like her." He gestures across the road, where a thin blond woman is standing on the steps of her big white house, a little girl of about two on her hip.

"I'm not bloody Gwyneth Paltrow!" she's snapping irately at a pair of tourists. "And, no, you can't have an autograph."

Actually, she *does* look rather like Gwyneth Paltrow.

"I'm going to have to reprimand your sister officially." The policeman turns to me. "I can release her into your custody, but only when you've filled in these forms and arranged an appointment at the station."

"Fine," I say, and shoot a murderous look at Amy. "Whatever."

I fill in all the forms as quickly as I can, stamping a furious full stop after my signature. "Can we go now?"

"All right. Try and keep tabs on her," the policeman adds.

"Sure." I give a tight smile. "Come on, Amy." I glance at my watch and feel a spasm of panic. It's already ten to twelve. "We need to find a taxi." I flag one down and bundle Amy into it. "Victoria Palace Road, please. Quick as you can." There's no way I'll make it for the start. But I can still get there and say my piece.

"Sorry," says Amy. "Really, I am."

I sigh. "*Why,* Amy?"

"To make money." She shrugs. "Why not?"

"Because you'll get in serious trouble! If you need money, can't you get a job? Or ask Mum?"

"Ask Mum?" she echoes scornfully. "Mum doesn't have any money. Why d'you think the house is falling down?"

"But that's weird," I say, puzzled. "Didn't Dad leave her anything?"

"Dunno. Not much, anyway."

"Well, whatever, you can't carry on like this. Seriously, you'll end up in jail or something."

"Bring it on." Amy tosses back her blue-streaked hair. "Prison's cool."

"Prison's not *cool!*" I stare at her. "Where d'you get that idea?"

"Well, it's in my genes. Dad was in prison," she declares triumphantly.

"Dad?" I stare at her. The idea's so preposterous I want to laugh.

"He was. I heard some men talking about it at the funeral. So it's like, my fate." She shrugs and takes out a packet of cigarettes.

"Stop it!" I grab the cigarettes. "Dad didn't go to prison. You're not going to prison. And it's not cool." I think for a moment. "Look, come and be an intern at my office. It'll be fun. You can get some experience and earn some money. And maybe I won't tell Mum about this. Deal?"

"Deller Carpets, ladies." The taxi has drawn up in front of the Deller building.

"Oh, right. Thanks." I root in my bag for some money. "Amy, I have to rush. I'm sorry, but this is really, really important." I give her a brief hug, then skitter up the steps. I'm only half an hour late. I hurry to a lift and wait the agonizing seconds it takes to get to the eighth floor.

At last. I burst out, run toward the boardroom—and stop.

Simon Johnson is standing in the corridor outside the board-room, talking cheerfully to three other guys in suits. A man in a blue suit is shrugging on his raincoat.

"What's going on?" I can barely speak.

All the faces turn toward me in surprise.

Simon shoots me a disapproving frown. "We're having a break. We've finished the crucial part of the meeting, and Angus has to leave." He gestures at the guy in the raincoat.

I feel an almighty lurch of horror. "Do you mean—"

"We've voted. In favor of the reorganization."

"But you can't!" I hurry toward him in panic. "I've found a way to save the department! We just have to trim a few costs—"

"Lexi, we've made our decision." Simon cuts me off firmly.

"But it's the *wrong* decision!" I cry desperately. "There's value in the brand. I know there is! Please."

"Lexi, you *cannot* behave like this at directors' meetings." There's steel beneath Simon's pleasant voice; I can tell he's furious. "I know things have been tricky for you since your accident, so what I suggest is you take three months' paid leave. And when you return, we'll find you a more . . . suitable role within the company. All right?"

All the blood drains from my face. He's demoting me.

"If you'd recovered your memory, then things would be different. But Byron's been filling me in. You're not up to a senior position right now."

There's an absolute finality in his voice. "Fine," I manage at last.

"Now, you might want to go down to your department. Since you weren't here"—he pauses meaningfully—"I gave Byron the task of breaking the unfortunate news to them." With a final curt nod, Simon disappears into the boardroom. I run to the lift and head down. I can't let Byron tell them the bad news. I have to do that myself at least. I pelt out of the lift, into my office, and close the door. I'm shaking all over. I've never been so petrified in my life. How am I going to break the news?

And then a voice, outside the door. "Is she in there?"

"Where's Lexi?" chimes in another voice. "Is she *hiding*?"

"I saw her! She's in there! Lexi! Come out here!" Someone bangs on the door. Gingerly I stretch out a hand and open the door.

They know. They're all standing there. All fifteen members of the Flooring department, silent and reproachful. Fi is at the front, her eyes like stone.

"It . . . it wasn't me," I stammer desperately. "Please listen, everyone. It wasn't my decision. I tried to . . ." I trail off. I'm the boss. It was down to me to save the department. And I failed. "I'm sorry," I whisper, tears filling my eyes. "I'm so, so sorry."

There's silence. I think I might melt under the hatred of their gazes. Then they all turn and walk away. I back toward my desk and sink into my chair. How did Byron break it to everybody? What did he *say?*

Then I spot it in my in-box e-mail with the heading: COLLEAGUES—SOME BAD NEWS.

> To all colleagues in Flooring,
> As you may have noticed, the performance of Flooring has been appalling of late. It has been decided by senior management to disband the department. You will all therefore be made redundant in June. In the meantime, Lexi and I would be grateful if you would work with improved efficiency and standards. Remember, we'll be giving your references, so no slacking.
> Yours, Byron and Lexi.

Okay. Now I want to shoot myself.

WHEN I arrive home, Eric is sitting on the terrace in the evening sun. "Good day?" He looks up from the paper.

"To be honest . . . no," I say, my voice quivering. "It was a pretty terrible day. The entire department is being fired." I dissolve into tears. "They're all losing their jobs. And they all hate me. I don't blame them."

"Darling. It's business. These things happen."

"They don't just happen. These are my *friends.*"

"Sweetheart." Eric appears amused. "Do you still have your job?"

"Yes."

"The company's not collapsing, is it?"

"No."

"Well, then. Have a gin and tonic."

How can he respond like that? Isn't he human? "Eric, don't you understand?" I almost shout. "Don't you *get* how terrible this is? These people need their jobs! They're not all ultra-high rich bloody billionaires!"

"You're overreacting," Eric says, and turns a page of his paper.

"Well, you're underreacting! I just don't *understand* you." I want him to look up, to talk about it, but he doesn't. It's as if he didn't even hear me. I wheel around and draw a sharp breath. Jon is standing at the doors to the terrace.

"Hi. Gianna let me in. I'm not intruding?"

"No!" I turn away so he can't see my face. "Of course not."

"Lexi's a little upset," says Eric to Jon in a man-to-man under-tone. "A few people at her work are losing their jobs."

"Not just a few people!" I can't help expostulating. "A whole department! And I didn't do anything to save them. I screwed up."

"Jon." Eric isn't even listening to me. "Let me get you a drink. I've got the Bayswater plans here; there's a lot to talk about." He gets up and steps into the sitting room. "Gianna, are you there?"

"Lexi." Jon comes across the terrace to where I'm standing, his voice low and urgent. He's trying it on again. I don't believe this.

"Leave me *alone!* Didn't you get the message? I'm not interested! And even if I *were,* it's not a good time. My whole department has just crumbled to nothing."

Jon rubs his head as though perplexed. "I don't understand. What happened to your big carpet deal?"

"What carpet deal?" I say aggressively.

"You're not serious. You don't *know* about it?"

"Know about *what?*" I exclaim, at the end of my tether.

"Okay. Lexi, listen to me. You had this massive carpet deal all lined up in secret. You said it was going to change everything. . . . So! You enjoy the view, huh?" He seamlessly switches track as Eric appears at the door, holding a gin and tonic.

Massive carpet deal?

"Eric, darling, I'm sorry about earlier." My words come out fluently. "It's just been a difficult day. Could you possibly get me a glass of wine?"

"No problem, sweetheart." Eric disappears inside again.

"Tell me what you're talking about," I say in low tones. "Quickly."

"If I'd *realized* before that you didn't know . . . You'd been working on this thing for weeks. You had a big blue file. I don't know the exact details, but I know it was using retro carpet designs from some old pattern book. And I know it was going to be huge."

"But why doesn't anyone *know* about it?"

"You were keeping it quiet until the last moment. You said you didn't trust everyone at the office—" He breaks off suddenly as Eric reappears.

"Here you are, Lexi," says Eric cheerfully, handing me a glass of wine. Then he heads to the table, sits down, and gestures at Jon to join him. "So the latest is, I spoke to the planning officer again . . ."

I'm standing perfectly still as they talk, my mind racing. What if it's true? If there's still a chance, even a *tiny* chance . . .

I take a deep swig of wine—then pull out my phone. With fumbling hands, I find Jon's number and type a text: CAN WE MEET? L

A moment later, Jon checks his phone and types back a return text. Eric doesn't even seem to notice.

I casually flip open my phone. SURE. J

WE'VE agreed to meet in a cozy café called Fabian's in Holland Park. As I walk in and look around at the granite bar, the coffee machine, the battered sofa, I have the weirdest feeling, as if I've been here before. Maybe it's wishful thinking.

Jon is already sitting at a table in the corner. "Hi." I join him at the table, where he's drinking coffee. "So. Let's talk about this deal. Is there anything more you can tell me?"

"Lexi, what happened at the party?"

"I don't know what you mean." I pick up the menu.

"Come on." Jon pulls the menu down. "What happened?"

"If you must know," I say tightly, "I spoke to Rosalie at the party, and she told me about your . . . predilections. I know you tried it on her and Margo." An edge of bitterness has crept into my voice. "You just tell married women what they want to hear."

Jon's expression doesn't flicker. "I did try it on with Rosalie and Margo. But you and I agreed I should. That was our cover. We cooked up a story that would fool everyone, so if ever we were spotted together, that could be the explanation. Rosalie fell for it."

"You *wanted* to be portrayed as a womanizer?" I retort.

"Of course not!" There's a sudden heat to his voice. "This hasn't all been pretty." He reaches a hand toward mine. "But you have to trust me, Lexi. Please. You have to let me explain everything."

"Stop it!" I whip my hands away. "We're not here to talk about that, anyway." A waitress approaches and I look up. "A cappuccino, please. So, this deal," I say briskly as soon as the waitress moves away. "It doesn't exist. I've looked everywhere, in the office and at home. The only thing I've found is this." I reach into the briefcase and produce the piece of paper with the coded scribbles on it. "It's my handwriting, but I don't know what it means!" In frustration, I throw the paper down. "Why on earth didn't I keep my notes on the computer?"

"There's a guy at work, Byron? You thought he'd try and screw things up for you. So you were going to present the whole thing to the board when it was already done. I do remember your contact was Jeremy Northam. Northwick. Something like that."

"Jeremy Northpool?" I can remember Clare thrusting a Post-it at me with his name on it. "I think he called while I was in the hospital."

"Well." Jon raises his eyebrows. "Maybe you should call him back."

"But I can't." I drop my hands on the table in despair. "I don't know enough! Where's all the information?"

"You must have moved the file. Hidden it somewhere." Jon is stirring his cappuccino. "You went down to Kent to your mother's house just before the accident. Maybe you took the file with you."

"To my mum's house?" I say skeptically.

"It's worth a chance." He shrugs. "Call her up and ask her."

I stir my coffee moodily. Ringing Mum is bad for my health.

"Come on, Lexi, you can do it." Jon's mouth twitches with amusement at my expression. "What are you, woman or walrus?"

I raise my head, stunned. For a moment, I wonder whether I heard that right. "That's what Fi says," I say at last.

"I know. You told me about Fi."

"What did I tell you about Fi?" I say suspiciously.

"You told me you met in Mrs. Brady's class. You had your first and last cigarette with her. Losing her friendship has been really traumatic." He nods at my phone. "Which is why you should make the call."

This is so *spooky*. What else does he know? Sliding him wary glances, I take the phone out of my bag and key in Mum's number.

"Hello?" Mum's voice on the line tears me away from Jon.

"Oh, Mum! It's me, Lexi. Listen, did I bring some papers down any time recently? Or like . . . a folder?"

"That big blue folder?"

I feel an almighty thrust of hope. "That's right." I try to stay calm. "Do you have it? Is it still there?"

"It's in your room, exactly where you left it." Mum sounds defensive. "One corner may be *slightly* damp. . . ."

I don't believe it. A dog's peed on it. "But it's still legible?"

"Of course!"

"Great!" I clutch the phone tighter. "I'll come and get it today." I flip my phone shut and turn to Jon. "You were right! Okay, I have to get to Victoria; there's bound to be a train. . . ."

"Lexi, calm down." Jon drains his coffee. "I'll drive you, if you like. It'll have to be in your car, though. I'm between cars at the moment."

IT'S a sunny day, and as Jon reverses the car out of its parking space, he retracts the roof. Then he reaches in his pocket and hands me a black hair elastic. "You'll need this. It's windy."

I take the hair elastic in surprise. "How come you have this?"

"I have them everywhere. You *shed* them."

Silently, I put my hair up into a ponytail. Jon turns onto the road. "It's in Kent," I say. "You have to head out of London on the—"

"I know where it is."

"You know where my mother's house is?"

"I've been there."

He's been to Mum's house. He knows about Fi. He has my hair elastic in his pocket. He was right about the blue folder. "So, hypothetically, if we were lovers . . ."

"Hypothetically." Jon nods without turning his head.

"What exactly happened? How did we . . ."

"Like I told you, we met at a launch party. We kept bumping into each other through the company. We'd chat, hang out on the terrace. It was innocuous." He pauses, negotiating a tricky lane change. "Then Eric went away one weekend. And I came over. And after that . . . it wasn't so innocuous."

I'm starting to believe. "So what else happened?" I say. "What did we say? What did we do? Just tell me stuff."

Jon shakes his head, his eyes crinkled in amusement. "That's what you always said to me. 'Tell me stuff.' Okay. Everywhere we've been together, we've ended up buying you socks. You rip off your shoes to be barefoot on the sand or the grass or whatever, and then you get cold, and we need to find you socks. What else? One weekend it rained. Eric was away playing golf, and we watched every single episode of *Doctor Who,* back-to-back." He glances at me. "Should I keep going?"

Everything he's saying is resonating. My brain is tuning up. I don't remember what he's talking about, but I'm feeling stirrings of recognition. It feels like me. This feels like my life.

"Keep going." I nod.

"Okay. We play table tennis. It's pretty brutal. You're two games ahead, but I think you're about to crack."

"I am *so* not about to crack," I retort automatically.

"Oh, you are."

"Never!" I can't help grinning. "Keep going."

As WE drive through the Kent countryside, Jon has exhausted all the details he can give me about our relationship, and I'm watching the GPS screen in a trance. Suddenly it reminds me of my conversation with Loser Dave, and I heave a sigh.

"What's up?" asks Jon.

"I just still keep wondering what made me go after my career, get my teeth done, turn into this . . . *other* person?" I gesture at myself.

"Well," says Jon, squinting up at a sign. "I suppose it started with what happened at the funeral. The thing with your dad."

"What about my dad?" I say, puzzled.

"Didn't your mother tell you about the funeral?"

"Of course she did! Dad was . . . cremated or whatever."

"That's it?"

I rack my brain. Mum didn't say anything about the funeral. She changed the subject when I brought it up, I suddenly recall. But that's normal for Mum. She changes every subject.

"Well, tell me! If it's so important."

Jon shakes his head. "Your mum has to tell you this one." He pulls into a gravel drive. "We're here."

So we are. I hadn't even noticed. The house is looking pretty much as I remember it: a redbrick house dating from the 1900s. The place hasn't changed since we moved in; it's just got more crumbly.

"So, you're saying Mum lied to me?"

"Not lied. Edited." Jon opens the car door. "Come on."

"OPHELIA! Raphael!" I can just about hear Mum's voice over the scrabbling and yelping. "Get down! Lexi, darling! You really did rush down here. What is all this?"

"Hi, Mum," I say breathlessly, manhandling a dog off me. "This is Jon. My . . . friend." I gesture at Jon.

"Well!" Mum seems flustered. "If I'd realized, I would have rustled up lunch. *How* you expect me to cater at this late notice—"

"We don't expect you to cater. All I want is that folder. Is it still there?"

"Of course." She sounds defensive. "It's perfectly all right."

I hurry up the stairs and into my bedroom. This place *stinks*. I can't tell if it's the dogs or the damp or the rot, but Mum should get it sorted. I spot the folder on top of a chest of drawers and grab it— then recoil. It totally smells of dog pee. Wrinkling my nose, I gingerly extend two fingers and open the folder. I scan the first page, trying to glean as quickly as possible what I was planning. I turn the page, then another. And that's when I see the name.

In an instant, I understand. That is *such* a good idea. I can already see the potential. It could be huge; it could change everything. . . .

Filled with adrenaline, I grab the folder and rush out of the room.

"Got it?" Jon is waiting at the bottom of the stairs.

"Yes!" A smile licks across my face. "It's a brilliant idea!"

"It was your idea."

"Really?" I feel a glow of pride that I try to quell.

"Now!" Mum is approaching bearing a tray of coffee cups. "I can at least offer you a cup of coffee and a biscuit."

"Really, Mum, it's okay," I say. "I'm afraid we have to dash off."

"I'd like a coffee," says Jon pleasantly.

He *what?* Shooting him daggers, I follow him into the sitting room. Jon takes a seat as if he feels totally at home. Maybe he does.

"So, Lexi was just talking about piecing her life together," he says, crunching a biscuit. "And I thought, maybe knowing the events that happened at her dad's funeral would help."

"Well, of course, losing a parent is always traumatic. . . ."

"That's not what I'm talking about," Jon says. "I'm talking about the other events."

Mum looks vague. "Now, Raphael, that's naughty!"

The dogs are all over the biscuit plate, slobbering and grabbing.

"Lexi doesn't seem to have the fullest of pictures," persists Jon.

"Smoky, it's *not* your turn—"

"Stop talking to the dogs!" Jon's voice makes me leap off my seat. Mum looks almost too shocked to speak. Or even move.

"*This* is your child." Jon gestures at me. "Not that." He jerks a thumb at a dog. "Maybe you want to go through life in a state of denial. Maybe it helps you. But it doesn't help Lexi."

"What are you talking about?" I say helplessly. "Mum, what happened at the funeral?"

Mum's hands are fluttering. "It was rather . . . unpleasant. The bailiffs came!" Her cheeks are growing pink with distress. "Right in the middle of the party."

"Bailiffs? But—"

"They came with no warning. Five of them. They wanted to re-possess the house. Take all the furniture, everything. It turned out your father hadn't been totally honest with me. Or anybody."

"Show her the second DVD," says Jon.

There's a pause; then, without looking at either of us, Mum gets up, roots in a drawer, and finds an unmarked, shiny disc. She puts it into the machine, and the three of us sit back.

"Darlings." Dad is on the screen again. "If you're watching this, I've popped it. And there's something you should know. But this one's not for public consumption. There's been a bit of a catastrophe on the old moola front. Didn't mean to land you in it. You girls are clever; you'll find a way to sort it out. Cheers, m'dears." He lifts his glass up—then the screen goes dark.

I wheel around to Mum. "What did he mean, 'catastrophe'?"

"He meant he'd remortgaged the entire house."

"So what did we do?"

"We would have had to sell. Amy would have been taken out of school." Her hands are fluttering again. "So my brother very kindly stepped in. And so did my sister, and . . . and so did you. You said you'd pay off the mortgage. As much as you could afford."

"*Me?*" I sink back in the sofa. "Is it an offshore mortgage?" I say suddenly. "A bank called Uni . . . something?"

"Most of Daddy's dealings were offshore." She nods. "Trying to avoid the tax man. I don't know *why* he couldn't just be honest—"

"Mum, you didn't tell me *any* of this. Can't you see how it might have made things clearer for me? I had no idea where that money was going."

"It's been very difficult!" Mum's eyes are swiveling from side to side.

"But—" I break off as something else even darker occurs to me. "Mum, I have another question. Was Dad ever in prison?"

Mum winces. "Briefly, darling. Let's not dwell on that."

"No!" In frustration, I leap to my feet and stand right in front of her, trying to get her single-minded attention. "Mum, listen! You can't just live in a bubble, pretending nothing's happened. Amy *heard* about Dad going to prison. She got the idea it's cool. No wonder she's been getting into so much trouble." Suddenly the pieces of my life are slotting together. "*That*'s why I suddenly got ambitious. That funeral changed everything."

"When the bailiffs arrived, she went to bits." Jon glances scornfully at Mum. "You had to make the decisions."

"Stop looking at me as though it's all my fault!" Mum suddenly cries out, her voice shrill and quivering. "Your father, that *man*—"

She breaks off, and I catch my breath as her blue eyes meet mine. For the first time that I can remember, my mother sounds . . . true.

"Mum, please. What were you going to say?"

"I was *simply* going to say that before you start blaming me for everything in your life, Lexi, that chap had a lot to answer for. That boyfriend of yours at the funeral. Dave? David?"

"Loser Dave?" I stare at her, thrown. "But Loser Dave wasn't at the funeral. He told me he offered to come but I turned him down. He said . . ." I peter out as I see Jon just shaking his head.

"What else did he tell you?"

"He said we broke up that morning and that it was beautiful and that he gave me a single rose." What was I thinking, even *half*-believing him? "Excuse me."

I march outside into the drive and direct-dial Loser Dave's office.

"Auto Repair Workshop," comes his businesslike voice.

"Loser Dave, it's Lexi," I say, my voice steely. "I need to hear about our breakup again. And this time I need to hear the truth."

"Babe, I told you the truth." He sounds supremely confident.

"Listen, you idiot," I say in slow, furious tones. "I'm at the neurological specialist's office right now, okay? They say someone has been giving me wrong information, and it's messing up my neural memory pathways. And if it isn't corrected, I'll get permanent brain damage."

"Blimey." He sounds shaken. "Straight up?"

He really is stupider than one of Mum's whippets.

"Yeah. So maybe you want to try again with the truth? Or maybe you'd like to speak to the doctor?"

"No! Okay!" He sounds unnerved. "I was trying to protect you."

"Protect me from what? Did you come to the funeral?"

"Yeah, I came along," he says. "I was handing out canapés. Being helpful. Giving you support. Then I . . ." He clears his throat.

"What?"

"Shagged one of the waitresses. It was the stress!" he adds defensively. "It makes us all do crazy things. I thought I'd locked the door—"

I caught Loser Dave two-timing me. I'm not even that surprised.

"So how did I react? And *don't* say I gave you a rose and it was beautiful."

"Well." Loser Dave breathes out. "To be honest, you went ballistic. You started yelling that your life had to change, it was all crap, you hated me, you hated everything . . . You stormed out."

"Then what?"

"Then I didn't see you again. Next time I clapped eyes on you, you were on TV, looking totally different."

"Right." I watch two birds circling in the sky. "You know, you could have told me the truth, first time around."

"I know. I'm sorry." He sounds as genuine as I've ever heard him. "And I'm sorry about that girl. And I'm sorry for what she called you; that was well out of order."

I sit up, suddenly alert. "What did she call me?"

"Oh. I don't remember," he says hastily. "Er . . . I gotta go. Good luck with the doctor." He rings off.

I march into the house to find Jon still sitting on the sofa, reading a copy of *Whippet World*.

"What did the waitress call me at the funeral?"

Jon sighs. "Lexi, it's a tiny detail. Why does it matter?"

"Tell me what that waitress called me. *Now*." I glare at him.

"All right!" Jon lifts his hands as though in defeat. "Dracula."

Dracula? In spite of the fact that I *know* my teeth aren't snaggly anymore, I can feel my cheeks staining with mortification.

"Lexi—" Jon's wincing as he reaches for my hand.

"No." I shake off Jon's hand. "I'm fine." My face still hot, I stand up and head over to the window, trying to put myself back in my own chewed-up, flat-heeled Lexi shoes. It's 2004. I didn't get a bonus. It's my dad's funeral. The bailiffs have just arrived to bankrupt us. I come across my boyfriend with a waitress . . . and she takes one look at me and calls me Dracula. Things are starting to make sense.

On the way back, I sit in silence for a long, long while. "At least I *get* myself a bit more," I say at last. I chew on my thumbnail. "Did I ever talk to you about it? The funeral?"

He takes a hand off the wheel and squeezes mine briefly. "One day, really early on, when we were still just friends, it all came out. The whole story. How you took on your family's debt, booked a cosmetic dentistry appointment the next day, went on a crash diet, decided to change everything about yourself. Then you went on TV, and everything became even more extreme. You rocketed up the career ladder, you met Eric, and he seemed like the answer. He was solid, rich, stable. A million miles away from—" He breaks off.

"My dad," I say eventually.

"I'm no psychologist. But I would guess."

"You know, when I woke up, I thought I'd landed the dream life," I say slowly. "I thought I was Cinderella. I was *better* than Cinderella . . ." I trail off as Jon shakes his head.

"You were living your whole life under strain. You went too far too soon. You didn't know how to handle it; you made mistakes. You alienated your friends. You found that the hardest of all."

"I don't understand why I became a bitch," I say helplessly.

"Lexi, give yourself a break. You were thrust into this boss position. You had a big department to run; you wanted to impress senior management, not be accused of favoritism . . . and you'd built up this tough persona. It was part of your success."

"The *Cobra,*" I say, wincing. I still can't believe that nickname.

"You once said to me, if you could go back in time and do everything differently, you would. Yourself . . . your job . . . Eric . . . Everything looks different when the gloss is gone."

"Look, I'm not some shallow gold digger, okay?" I say hotly. "I must have loved Eric. I wouldn't just marry a guy because of the gloss."

"At first you thought Eric was the real deal," Jon agrees. "He's charming; he ticks the boxes. In fact, he's like one of the intelligent systems from our lofts. Put him on 'Husband' setting and away he goes."

"*Stop* it." I'm trying not to laugh. "Look. Maybe we did have an affair. But maybe I want to make my marriage *work* this time around."

"You can't." Jon doesn't miss a beat. "Eric doesn't love you."

"Yes, he does." I fold my arms. "He said he fell in love with my beautiful mouth and my long legs. It was really romantic."

"So would he love you if your legs *weren't* long?"

I'm momentarily stumped. "I . . . don't know. That's not the point." I jut out my chin. "So what do *you* love about me?"

"I don't know. The essence of you. I can't turn it into a *list.*" There's a long pause. "Okay," says Jon finally as we draw to a halt in a queue of cars. "I like the way you squeak in your sleep."

"I squeak in my sleep?" I say disbelievingly.

"Like a chipmunk. Cobra by day. Chipmunk by night."

I'm trying to keep my mouth straight and firm, but a smile is edging out. As we crawl along the dual highway, my phone bleeps.

"It's Eric," I say after reading the text. "He's arrived in Manchester. He's scoping out some possible new sites for a few days."

"Uh-huh. I know." Jon swings around a traffic circle. We're into the outskirts of the city now. "You know, Eric could have paid off your dad's debt in his sleep," he suddenly says, his voice matter-of-fact. "But he left you to it. Never even mentioned it."

I feel at a loss. I don't know what to think. "It's his money," I say. "Why should he? And anyway, I don't *need* anyone's help."

"I know. I offered. You wouldn't take anything. You're pretty stubborn." He draws up behind a bus and turns to look at me. "I don't know what you're planning for the rest of today if Eric's away."

Deep within me, something starts stirring. "Well." I try to sound businesslike. "I wasn't planning anything. Why?"

"It's just there's some stuff of yours at my flat you might want to pick up."

"Okay." I shrug noncommittally.

Jon lives in the most beautiful flat I've ever seen. Okay, it's in a daggy street in Hammersmith, but the house is big, with massive old arched windows, and it turns out the flat runs into the next-door building, too, so it's a million times wider than it seems from the outside.

"This is *amazing*." I'm looking around his workspace, almost speechless. The ceiling is high, and the walls are white, and there's a tall, sloped desk. In the corner is a drawing easel, and opposite is an entire wall covered in books, with an old-fashioned library ladder on wheels.

"This whole row of houses was built as artists' studios." Jon's eyes are gleaming as he walks around, picking up about ten old coffee cups. "Your stuff's through here."

I walk where he's pointing, through an archway into a cozy sitting room. It's furnished with big, blue-cotton sofas. Behind the sofas are battered wooden shelves, haphazardly filled with books and magazines and plants and . . . "That's my mug." I stare at a hand-painted red pottery mug that Fi once gave me for my birthday.

"Yeah." Jon nods. "That's what I mean. You left stuff here."

"And my sweater!" There's an old ribbed turtleneck draped over one of the sofas. I've had it forever, since I was about sixteen. I look around in disbelief as more things spring into my vision. That furry fake-wolf throw that I always used to wrap around myself. Old college photos. My pink retro *toaster?*

"You used to come here and eat toast like you were starving."

I'm suddenly seeing the other side of me. For the first time since I woke up in the hospital, I feel as if I'm at home. There're even my fairy lights draped around the plant in the corner.

All this time, all my stuff was here. Suddenly I have a memory of Eric's words, that first time I asked him about Jon. *You'd trust Jon with your life.* Maybe that's what I did. Trusted him with my life.

"Do you remember anything?" Jon sounds casual, but I can sense the hope underneath.

"No." I shake my head. "Just the stuff that came from my life before . . ." I break off as I notice a beaded frame I don't recognize. It's a photo of me. And Jon. We're sitting on a tree trunk, and his arms are around me, and my head is tossed back. I'm laughing as though I'm the happiest girl there ever was.

It was real. It was really real. All this time, he had proof.

"You could have shown me this," I say, almost accusingly.

"Would you have wanted to believe me?" He sits on the arm of the sofa.

Maybe he's right. Maybe I would have explained it away, clung on to my dream life. I walk over to a table cluttered with old novels belonging to me and a bowl of seeds. I grab a handful. "I love sunflower seeds."

"I know you do." Jon has the oddest expression on his face.

"What?" I look at him in surprise, seeds halfway to my mouth.

"It's nothing." He shrugs. "We just had this . . . tradition. The first time we made love, you'd been munching on sunflower seeds. You planted one in a yogurt pot, and I took it home. We started doing it every time. As a memento. We called them our children."

"We planted sunflowers?" That rings a tiny bell.

"Uh-huh." Jon nods. "Let me get you a drink."

"So where are they?" I say as he pours out two glasses of wine.

Jon gestures for me to walk along a small corridor. We head through a sparsely decorated bedroom to a wide, decked balcony. And I catch my breath.

There's a wall of sunflowers all the way around. From huge yellow monsters reaching up to the sky, down to spindly green shoots in tiny pots, just starting to open. My throat is suddenly tight as I gaze around at the sea of green and yellow.

I sit down and gulp at my wine, feeling totally overwhelmed.

"How did it all start?" I say eventually.

"It was that weekend Eric was away. I was over, and we were chatting. We were out on the balcony, drinking wine. Kind of like we are now. And then halfway through the afternoon, we fell silent. And we knew."

He lifts his dark eyes to mine, and I feel a lurch, deep inside.

Gently he removes the wineglass from my hand. "Lexi." He brings my hands up to his mouth, closing his eyes, gently kissing them. "I knew . . ." His voice is muffled against my skin. "You'd come back. I knew you'd come back to me."

"Stop it!" I whip my hands away, my heart thudding in distress. "You don't . . . you don't know anything!"

"What's wrong?" Jon looks shell-shocked, as though I'd hit him.

I don't know what's wrong myself. I want him so badly. But I can't. "What's wrong is I'm freaked." I gesture at the sunflowers. "You're presenting me with this fully fledged relationship. But for me, it's just the beginning."

"I'll go back to the beginning, too," he says quickly.

"You can't go back to the beginning!" I thrust my hands hopelessly through my hair. "Jon, I really like you. But I don't love you. How could I?"

"I don't expect you to *love* me—"

"Yes, you do. You do! You expect me to be her."

"You *are* her." There's a sudden streak of anger in his voice.

"I don't *know* if I am, okay?" Tears are streaming down my cheeks. I want to be the girl laughing on the tree trunk. But I'm not. "I look around at these sunflowers." I swallow hard. "And the photo. And all my things here. And I can see that it happened. But it looks like a wonderful romance between two people I don't know."

"It's you," says Jon in a quiet voice. "It's me. You know both of us."

"I know it in my head. But I don't feel it." I clench a fist on my chest, feeling the tears rising again. "If I could just remember *one thing*. If there was one memory, one thread . . ." I trail off in silence.

"So, what are you saying?"

"I'm saying I need time. I need . . ." I break off helplessly.

Spots of rain are starting to fall on the balcony.

At last Jon breaks the silence. "A lift home?"

"Yes." I wipe my eyes and push my hair back. "Please."

IT TAKES fifteen minutes to reach home. Jon pulls the Mercedes into my parking space. Rain is thundering against the roof by now.

"You'll have to run straight in," says Jon, and I nod.

"How will you get back?"

"I'll be fine." He hands me my keys, avoiding my eye. "Good luck with that." He nods at the blue folder. "I mean it."

I pelt through the rain to the entrance, nearly dropping the precious folder, then stand under the portico, gathering the papers together, feeling a fresh spasm of hope as I remember the details.

And all of a sudden, I sag as the reality of my situation hits home. Whatever I have in this folder, Simon Johnson's never going to give me another chance, is he? I'm not the Cobra anymore. I'm the memory-challenged embarrassment-to-the-firm. He won't even give me five minutes, let alone a full hearing. Not unless . . .

No.

I *couldn't*. Could I?

I'm frozen in disbelieving excitement, thinking through the implications, Simon Johnson's voice running through my head. *If you'd recovered your memory, Lexi, then things would be different.*

I pull out my mobile phone and direct dial. "Fi," I say as soon as it's answered. "Don't say anything. Listen."

Seven

THINK boss. Think Cobra.

I survey myself in the mirror. My hair's scraped back, and I'm wearing the most severe outfit I could find in my wardrobe. I spent two hours with Jeremy Northpool yesterday, at his office in Reading, and everything's in place. Now it's up to me.

"You don't look mean enough." Fi, standing by my side in a navy pantsuit, surveys me critically. "You used to have this really chilling stare. Like, 'You are an insignificant minion. Get out of my way instantly.' " She narrows her eyes and puts on a hard, dismissive voice. "I'm the boss, and I'll have things done *my* way."

"That's really good!" I turn in admiration. "You should do this."

"Yeah, right." She pushes my shoulder. "Go on, do it again. Scowl."

"Get out of my way, you minion," I snarl in a Wicked Witch of the West voice. "I'm the boss, and I'll have things done *my* way."

"Yes!" She applauds. "That's better. And kind of flick your eyes past people, like you can't even waste time acknowledging they're there."

I sigh. This bitchy behavior is exhausting. Fi has been coaching me for the last twenty-four hours. She took a sick day yesterday and came over; she stayed all day and the night. And she's done the most brilliant job. I know *everything*. My head is so crammed full of facts it's ready to burst. And the most important bit is that I come across like the old Lexi and fool everyone.

"Fi . . . thanks." I turn and give her a hug. "You're a star."

"If you pull this off, *you'll* be a star." She hesitates, then adds a little gruffly, "Even if you don't pull it off. You didn't have to make all this effort, Lexi. I know they're offering you a big job."

"Yeah, well. That's not the point. Come on, let's go."

As we travel to the office in a cab, my stomach is clenched with nerves. I'm crazy, doing this, but it's the only way I can think of.

"I don't know *how* I'm going to keep a straight face in front of Debs and Carolyn," murmurs Fi as we draw up. We haven't told the others what I'm up to. We reckon the fewer who know, the safer.

"Well, Fi, you'll just have to make an effort, okay?" I snap in my new-Lexi voice and nearly giggle as her face jerks in shock.

"God, that's scary. You're *good*."

We get out of the cab, and I hand the driver the fare.

"Lexi?" A voice comes from behind me. I look around.

"*Amy?* What the hell are you doing here?"

"I've been waiting for you. I'm here to be your intern."

"Amy. Today isn't really a good day. . . ."

"You said!" Her voice quivers. "You said you'd sort it out. I've made a real effort to get here. I got up early and everything."

"She might be a distraction," says Fi. "Can we trust her?"

"Trust me?" Amy's voice sharpens with interest. "With what?"

"Okay." I make a snap decision. "Listen, Amy." I lower my voice. "You can come in, but here's the thing. I'm telling everyone I've recovered my memory, to get a deal done. Even though I haven't. Got it?"

Amy doesn't bat an eyelid. There are some advantages to having a scam artist as a sister. "So you're trying to make out you're the old Lexi."

"Yes."

"Then you should look meaner. Like you think everyone is just a worm."

"That's what I said," agrees Fi. "Come on."

As I push open the glass doors to the building, I adopt my meanest scowl. "Hi," I snarl at Jenny on the reception desk. "This is my temporary intern, Amy. Please make her out a pass. For your information, I'm fully recovered, and if you've got any mail for me, I want to know why it isn't upstairs already."

"There's nothing for you, Lexi." Jenny seems taken aback as she fills out a pass. "So . . . you remember everything now, do you?"

"Everything. Come on, Fi. We're late enough already."

I stride away, toward the lifts. A moment later, I can hear Jenny behind me, saying in an excited undertone, "Guess what? Lexi's got her memory back!" I glance over. Sure enough, she's already on the phone.

The lift pings. Fi, Amy, and I walk in—and as soon as the doors close, dissolve into giggles. "High five!" Fi lifts her hand. "That was great!"

We all get out at the eighth floor, and I head straight to Natasha's desk outside Simon Johnson's office, my head high and imperious.

"Natasha," I say curtly. "I assume you got my message about my memory returning? I'll need to see Simon as soon as possible."

"I'm afraid Simon's quite booked up this morning—"

"Then juggle things around! Cancel someone else!"

"Okay!" Natasha types hastily at her keyboard. "I could do you a slot at ten thirty?"

"Fantast—" I stop as Fi nudges me. "That'll be fine," I amend, shooting Natasha my meanest scowl. "Come on, Fi."

"Where do we go now?" says Amy as we get back in the lift.

"To the Flooring department." I feel a stab of nerves.

I arrive at the main office door and stand there for a few moments, surveying the scene before me. Then I draw a breath.

"So." I summon a harsh, sarcastic voice. "Reading *Hello!* magazine is work, is it?"

Melanie, who had been flicking through the magazine, jumps as though she's been scalded and flames red.

"I'll be speaking to you all about attitude later." I glare around the room. "And that reminds me. Didn't I ask everyone to provide full written travel-expense breakdowns two months ago? I want to see them."

"We thought you'd forgotten," says Carolyn, dumbstruck.

"Well, I've remembered." I give her a scathing smile. "I've remembered everything." I sweep out, almost straight into Byron.

"Lexi!" He almost drops his cup of coffee. "What the hell—"

"Byron. I need to talk to you about Tony Dukes," I say crisply.

"How did you handle the discrepancy in his calculations? Because we all know his reputation for pulling a fast one. Remember the trouble we had in October last year?"

Byron's mouth is hanging open stupidly.

"And where are the minutes of our last product meeting? You were doing them, as I remember."

"I'll . . . get those to you." He looks utterly gobsmacked.

Everything I'm saying is hitting right home. Fi is a total genius!

"So are you recovered?" Byron says as I open my office door.

"Oh yes." I usher Amy in and slam the door. I count to three; then I look out again. "Fi, can you come in here?"

As Fi closes the door behind her, I collapse on the sofa, breathless.

"You should be on the stage!" Fi exclaims. "That was so great! That's just the way you used to be!"

I'm still cringing inside. I can't *believe* I said those things.

"So now we just have to sit it out till ten thirty."

THE door of Simon Johnson's office is closed as Fi and I arrive upstairs, and Natasha gestures to us to take a seat. A moment later, the phone rings and Natasha listens. "All right, Simon," she says. "I'll tell her." She puts down the receiver and looks at me. "Lexi, Simon's in with Sir David and a few other directors."

"Sir David Allbright?" I echo apprehensively. Sir David Allbright is chairman of the board. He's the total bigwig, even bigger and wiggier than Simon. And he's really fierce.

"That's right." Natasha nods. "Simon says you should just go in, join the meeting and see all of them. In about five minutes. Okay?"

Panic is sending little shooters through my chest.

"Of course! Fine. Um . . . Fi, I need to powder my nose. Let's just continue our discussion in the ladies' room." I push my way into the empty bathroom and sit down on a stool, breathing hard. "I can't do this. How am I going to impress Sir David Allbright? I'm no good at giving speeches—"

"Yes, you are!" retorts Fi. "Lexi, you've given speeches to the whole company. You were excellent."

"Really?" It doesn't chime in my brain. "I don't know." I rub my face. "Maybe I'm just not cut out to be a boss."

"No! You're totally meant to be a boss!"

"How can you *say* that? When I was promoted to director, I couldn't cope! I alienated all of you. I screwed it up."

"Lexi, you didn't screw it up." Fi speaks in a rush, almost brusque with embarrassment. "You were a good boss. We . . . weren't fair. We gave you a hard time." She hesitates. "Yes, you were too impatient some of the time. But you did some really great things. You are good at motivating people. Everyone felt alive and kicking. People wanted to impress you. They admired you."

As I take in her words, I can feel an underlying tension slowly slipping off me. "But you made me sound like such a bitch."

"You were a bitch some of the time." Fi nods. "But sometimes you needed to be. Thing is, Lex . . . we were jealous." She looks at me frankly. "One minute you were Snaggletooth. Next thing, you've got this amazing hair and perfect teeth, and you're in charge and telling us what to do."

"I know." I sigh. "It's mad."

"It's not mad." Fi crouches down and takes both my shoulders in her hands. "Lexi, remember when we were at primary school? Remember the sack race on sports day?"

"Don't remind me." I roll my eyes. "I screwed that up, too."

"That's not the point." Fi shakes her head vigorously. "The point is, you were winning. You were way out in front. And if you'd kept going, if you hadn't waited for the rest of us, you would have won." She gazes almost fiercely at me, with the same green eyes I've known since I was six years old. "Just keep going. Don't think about it; don't look back."

The door opens, and we both start. "Lexi?" It's Natasha. "Are you ready?"

I get to my feet and lift my chin high. "Yes. Ready."

"LEXI." Simon beams. "Good to see you. Come and take a seat. So, your memory is recovered! Tremendous news."

"Yes. It's great!"

"We're just going through the implications of June '07." He nods at the papers spread over the table. "This is very good timing, because I knew you had some strong views about the amalgamation."

"Actually . . ." My hands are damp, and I curl them around the folder. "Actually, I wanted to speak to you about something else."

David Allbright looks up with a frown. "What?"

"Flooring."

"Lexi." Simon's voice is tight. "We no longer deal in Flooring."

"But I've done a deal! That's what I want to talk about!" I take a deep breath. "I've always felt the archive prints that Deller owns are one of its biggest assets. For several months, I've been trying to find a way to harness these assets. Now I have a deal in place with a company that would like to use one of our old designs. It'll raise Deller's profile. It'll turn the department around!" I can't help sounding exhilarated. "This can be the beginning of something big and exciting!" I stop breathlessly and survey the faces. I can see it at once. I have made precisely no impact whatsoever.

"I thought the decision on Flooring had been made," says Sir David Allbright testily to Simon. "Why are we raising it again?"

"It has been decided, Sir David," he says hurriedly. "Lexi, I don't know *what* you're doing—"

"I'm doing business!" I retort with a clench of frustration.

"Young lady," Sir David says. "Business is forward-looking. Deller has to move with the times, not cling on to the old."

"I'm not clinging!" I try not to yell. "The old Deller prints are fabulous. It's a *crime* not to use them."

"Is this to do with your husband?" Simon says, as though he suddenly understands. "Lexi's husband is a property developer," he explains to the others, then turns back to me. "Lexi, with all due respect, you're not going to save your department by carpeting a couple of show flats."

One of the men laughs, and I feel a knife of fury. Carpeting a couple of show flats? Is that all they think I'm capable of? Once they hear what this deal is, they'll . . . they'll . . .

And then, all of a sudden, I change my mind. "So you've really made your decision?"

"We made our decision a long time ago," says Simon.

"Right. Well, if you're not interested, maybe I could buy the copyright of the designs? To license them as a private venture."

I can see the directors exchanging glances.

"She had a bump to the head in a car crash," Simon murmurs to a guy I don't recognize. "She hasn't been right since."

"Let's just sort it out." Sir David waves an impatient hand.

"I agree." Simon heads to his desk, lifts his phone, and punches in a number. "Ken? Simon Johnson here. One of our employees will be coming to see you about the copyright of some old Deller carpet design. Work out a nominal fee for the license and the paperwork, could you? Thanks, Ken."

He puts the phone down and scribbles a name and number on a piece of paper. "Ken Allison. Our company lawyer. Call him to make an appointment. And Lexi, I know we talked about a three-month leave. But I think that your employment here should be terminated."

"Fine." I nod. "I understand. Good-bye. And thanks."

Somehow I get out of the room without skipping. Fi is waiting for me as I step out of the lift at the third floor. "Well?"

"Didn't work," I murmur. "But it's not all over." I've arrived at the door to the main office. "Hi," I say as everyone looks up. "I just wanted to let you know, I haven't got my memory back; that was a lie. I tried to pull off a massive bluff to try to save this department. I did everything I could, but . . ." I exhale sharply. "Anyway. The other news is, I've been fired. And to all of you who thought I was a total hard-as-nails bitch, I'm sorry. I know I didn't get it right. But I did my best. Cheers, and good luck, everyone."

"Thanks, Lexi," says Melanie awkwardly. "Thanks for trying, anyway."

"Yeah, thanks," chimes in Clare.

To my astonishment, someone starts clapping. And suddenly the whole room is applauding. "Stop it." My eyes start stinging, and I blink hard. "You idiots. I didn't do anything. I *failed*."

I glance at Fi, and she's clapping hardest of all.

"Anyway." I try to keep my composure. "As I say, I've been fired, so I'll be going to the pub immediately to get drunk. I know it's only eleven o'clock . . . but anyone care to join me?"

BY THREE o'clock, my bar bill is over three hundred quid. It was one of the best parties I've ever been to. Everyone had a great time; in fact, the only one who didn't get totally drunk was me. I couldn't, because I have a meeting with Ken Allison at four thirty.

"So." Fi lifts her drink. "To us." She clinks glasses with me, Debs, and Carolyn. It's just the four of us sitting around a table now. Like the old days. Most of the Flooring employees have drifted back to the office.

"To being unemployed," Debs says morosely. "Not that we blame you, Lexi," she adds hastily.

I take a swig of wine, then lean forward. "Okay, you guys. I have something to tell you. But you can't let on to anyone. I've done a deal. That's what I was trying to tell Simon Johnson about. This company wants to use one of our old retro carpet designs. A special, high-profile limited edition. They'll use the Deller name; we'll get huge PR. It'll be amazing! The details are all sorted out. I just need to finalize the contract."

"That's great, Lexi," says Debs, looking uncertain. "But how can you do it now you're fired?"

"The directors are letting me license the old designs as an independent operator for practically nothing. Then all the profits will come to me. And . . . whoever works with me."

I look from face to face, waiting for the message to hit home.

"*Us?*" says Debs. "You want us to work with you?"

"If you're interested," I say a little awkwardly.

"I'm in," says Fi firmly. "But Lexi, I don't understand. Didn't they get excited when you told them who the deal was with?"

I shrug. "They assumed it was one of Eric's projects."

"So who *is* it?" asks Debs. "Who's the company?"

I glance at Fi—and can't help a tiny smile as I say, "Porsche."

SO THAT'S IT. I AM THE OFFICIAL licenser of Deller carpet designs. I had a meeting with the lawyer yesterday and another one this morning. Everything's signed. Tomorrow I meet with Jeremy North-pool, and we sign the contract for the Porsche deal.

As I arrive home, I'm still powered up by adrenaline. There are voices coming from Eric's office. He must have arrived home from Manchester while I was with the lawyer. I peep around the open door to see a roomful of his senior staff grouped around the coffee table, with an empty cafetière at the center. Clive is there, and the head of HR, Penny.

"Hi!" I smile at Eric. "Good trip?"

"Excellent." He nods, then frowns. "Shouldn't you be at work?"

"I'll explain later. Can I bring you all some more coffee?"

I head into the kitchen, humming as I make a fresh pot, sending quick texts to Fi, Carolyn, and Debs to let them know all went well. We're going to make a good team; I know we are.

I head back to Eric's office with a full pot and discreetly start pouring it out while listening to the discussion. Penny is holding a list of names with figures scribbled in pencil at the side. "I don't think Sally Hedge deserves a pay raise *or* a bonus," she's saying as I pour her a cup of coffee. "She's very average."

"I like Sally," I say. "You know her mum's been ill recently?"

"Really?" Penny makes a face as though to say "So what?"

"Lexi made friends with all the junior staff when she came into the office." Eric laughs. "She's very good at that kind of thing."

"It's not a 'kind of thing'!" I retort, a little rankled by his tone.

"Anyway." Penny turns quickly back to her paper. "We're agreed, no bonus or pay raise this time."

I know this isn't my business. But I can't bear it. I can just imagine Sally waiting for the news of the bonuses. "Excuse me! Can I just say something? The thing is . . . a bonus may not be much to the company, but it's huge to Sally Hedge." I look around at Eric's managers, all dressed in smart, grown-up clothes with their smart, grown-up accessories. "Do *any* of you remember what it was like to be young and poor and struggling? Because I do."

"Lexi, we know you're a tenderhearted soul," says a guy named Steven whose role I've never been able to work out. "But what are you saying—we should all be poor?"

"I'm not saying you have to be poor!" I try to control my impatience. "I'm saying you have to remember what it's like, being at the bottom of the ladder. It feels like it was only six weeks ago that I *was* that girl. No money, hoping for a bonus, wondering if I'd ever get a break, standing in the pouring rain . . ." Suddenly I realize I'm getting a bit carried away. "Anyway. I can tell you, if you give it to her, she really will appreciate it."

There's a pause. Eric has a fixed, livid smile on his face. I pick up the coffeepot and try to creep out of the room silently.

I pick up the paper and am just flicking through to see if there's an "Offices to Rent" section when Eric appears out of his office. "Lexi. A word." He walks me swiftly to my bedroom and closes the door, that horrible smile still on his face. "Please don't interfere with my business."

"Eric, I'm sorry," I say quickly. "But I was only expressing an opinion."

"I don't need any opinions."

"But isn't it *good* to talk about things? Even if we disagree? I mean, that's what keeps relationships alive! Talking!"

"I don't agree." He's still got that smile on, like a mask, as if he has to hide how angry he really is. And all of a sudden, it's like a filter falls off my eyes. I don't know this man. I don't love him. I don't know what I'm doing here.

"Eric, can I ask you a question? What do you really, genuinely think? About us? Our marriage? Everything?"

"I think we're making good progress." Eric nods, his mood instantly better, as though we've moved on to a new subject on the agenda. "We're becoming more intimate . . . I think it's all coming together. All good news."

How can he believe that when he's not interested in what I think or any of my ideas or who I really am? "Eric, let's face it; it's not working out, and I can't do it anymore."

Eric switches instantly into concerned-husband-of-deranged-invalid mode. "Maybe you've been pushing yourself too hard. Take a rest."

"I don't need a rest! I need to be *myself!* Eric, I'm not the girl you think you married. I don't know who I've been these last three years, but it hasn't been me. I like color. I like mess. I like . . . pasta! All this time, I wasn't hungry for success; I was *hungry*."

Eric looks bemused. "Darling," he says carefully. "If it means that much to you, we can buy some pasta. I'll tell Gianna to—"

"It's not about the pasta!" I cry out. "I've been acting for the last few weeks. And I can't do it anymore. I'm not into all this high-tech stuff. To be honest, I'd rather live in a house."

"A *house?*" Eric looks as horrified as if I've said I want to live with a pack of wolves and have their babies.

I suddenly feel bad for criticizing his creation. "This place is stunning, and I really admire it. But it's not me. I'm just not made for . . . loft-style living." Aargh. I can't believe it. I actually did the sweeping, parallel-hands gesture.

"I'm shocked, Lexi." Eric looks truly poleaxed.

"But the most important thing is, you don't love me. Not *me*."

"I do love you! You're talented, and you're beautiful . . ."

"You don't think I'm beautiful. You think my collagen job is beautiful," I correct him gently. "And my tooth veneers and my hair dye." Eric is silenced. I can see him eyeing me up incredulously. I probably told him it was all natural. "I think I should move out."

"Maybe a break *would* be a good idea," Eric says at last. "After a week or two, you'll see things differently."

"Yeah." I nod. "Maybe."

I'M STUFFING the absolute minimum into a suitcase—some underwear, jeans, a few pairs of shoes. I don't feel I have any right to all the beige designer suits. Nor, to be honest, do I want them. As I'm finishing, I look up to see Eric in the doorway.

"I have to go out," he says stiffly. "Will you be all right?"

"Yes, I'll be fine," I reply. "I'll take a cab to Fi's house. She's coming home early from work." I zip up the suitcase.

"I care for you deeply. You must know that." There's genuine pain in Eric's eyes, and I feel a stab of guilt. But you can't stay with people because of guilt. Or because they can drive a speedboat. I survey the massive, immaculate room. I'm sure I'll never live in such a luxurious place again in my life. I must be crazy.

As my gaze sweeps over the bed, something crosses my mind. "Eric, do I squeak in my sleep?" I ask casually.

"Yes, you do." He nods. "We went to a doctor about it. He suggested you douche your nasal passages with salt water before retiring and prescribed a nose clip." He heads to a drawer and produces a gross-looking plastic contraption. "Do you want to take it with you?"

"No," I manage. "Thanks." I'm making the right decision.

Eric hesitates—then comes over and gives me an awkward hug.

"Bye, Eric," I say against his expensive, scented shirt. "I'll see you." Ridiculously, I feel near tears. Not because of Eric, but because it's over. My whole, amazing, perfect dream life.

At last, he pulls away. "Bye, Lexi."

AN HOUR later, I really have finished packing. In the end, I couldn't resist stuffing another suitcase full of La Perla and Chanel makeup and body products. And a third full of coats. I mean, who else will want them? There's still a few minutes till the taxi's due. I feel as if I'm checking out of a posh, boutique-style hotel. It's been a great place to stay, and the facilities were amazing. But it was never home. Even so, I can't help a massive pang. I can remember arriving here and thinking I'd landed in heaven. I guess I didn't have the perfect life handed to me on a plate, after all.

The doorbell rings. "Hi," I say into the entry phone. "Can you possibly come up to the top floor?"

I might need some help with my cases. I head to the outside landing and listen to the lift coming up to the penthouse floor.

"Hello!" I begin as the doors start opening. "I'm sorry, I've got quite a lot of—" And then my heart stops dead.

It's not the taxi driver standing in front of me. It's Jon. He's wearing jeans and a T-shirt. His dark hair is sticking up unevenly, and his face looks crumpled. He's the opposite of Eric's Armani-model groomedness.

"I called you at work," he says. "But they said you were at home. I need to say something to you, Lexi." He takes a deep breath, and every muscle in my body tightens in apprehension. "I need . . . to apologize. I shouldn't have pestered you; it was unfair."

I feel a jolt of shock. That's not what I was expecting.

"I've thought about it a lot," Jon continues rapidly. "I realize this has been an impossible time for you. I haven't helped. And you're right. I'm not your lover. I'm a guy you just met. What I want to say is, don't beat yourself up. You're doing your best. That's all you can do."

"Yeah. Well . . . I'm trying." Oh God, I'm going to cry.

Jon seems to realize this and moves away as though to give me space. "How'd it go at work with the deal?"

"Good." I nod.

"Great. I'm really pleased for you."

"I'm leaving Eric." I blurt it out. "I'm leaving right now."

I don't mean to look for Jon's reaction, but I can't help it. And I see it. The hope rushing into his face like sunshine. Then out again.

"I'm . . . glad," he says, carefully measured. "You probably need time to think everything over. This is all still pretty new for you."

Through the glass behind Jon, I suddenly see a black taxi down below, turning into the entrance. Jon follows my gaze. "I'll help you down."

When the bags are all packed into the taxi, he touches my hand briefly. "Look after yourself."

"You . . ." I swallow. "You, too." With slightly stumbling legs, I get into the cab. "Jon." I look up to where he's still standing. "Were we really good together?"

"We were good." His voice is so low and dry it's barely audible, his face full of mingled love and sadness. "Really, really good."

And now tears are spilling down my cheeks; my stomach is wrenched with pain. I'm almost weakening. I could fling open the door, say I've changed my mind ... But I can't. I can't just run straight from one guy I don't remember into the arms of another.

I pull the heavy door shut. And slowly, the taxi pulls away.

Eight

THE world has gone mad. This is the proof. As I walk into Langridge's department store and unwind my bright-pink scarf, I have to rub my eyes. It's only October 16, and already there's a Christmas tree covered in baubles.

"Special-offer festive Calvin Klein pack?" drones a bored-looking girl in white, and I dodge her before I can get sprayed. Although, on second thought, Debs quite likes that perfume. Maybe I'll get it for her.

"Yes, please," I say, and the girl nearly falls over in surprise.

As she ties up the parcel, I survey myself in the mirror behind her. My hair's still long and glossy, though not quite as bright a shade as before. I'm wearing jeans and a green cardigan, and my feet are comfortable in suede sneakers. My face is bare of makeup; my left hand is bare of a ring. I like what I see. I like my life.

I'm not a millionairess living in penthouse glory, but my office is on the floor above my flat, so I have the world's shortest commute. Four months on, the business has all worked out well. The Porsche contract is happening. We've done another deal supplying carpet to a restaurant chain, and just today, Fi sold my favorite Deller design—an orange circle print—to a trendy spa. That's why I'm here shopping. I reckon everyone on the team deserves a present.

I walk on through the store. As I pass a rack of teetering high heels, I'm reminded of Rosalie and can't help smiling. As soon as she heard Eric and I were splitting up, Rosalie announced that she wasn't going to take sides and she was going to be my rock, my absolute *rock*.

She's come to visit once.

Still, she's done better than Mum, who's managed to cancel each planned visit with some dog ailment or other. But Amy's kept me posted. Apparently, the day after I visited, Mum got a man in to sort out the dry rot. I know it doesn't sound like very much. But in Mum's world, that's huge strides.

And on the completely positive and fantastic front, Amy is doing spectacularly at school! She's wangled a place on Business Studies A level, and her teacher is bowled over by her progress.

As for Eric . . . I've contacted his lawyer about a divorce. The thing is, there's no point dwelling on the past. It's like Fi said, you have to keep looking forward.

I pause in the Accessories department and buy a purple patent bag for Fi. Then I head upstairs and find a cool T-shirt for Carolyn. As I wander on, I realize I seem to have strayed into Menswear when a bright voice greets me. "Hello again!"

It's coming from a woman with a blond bob who's folding pastel-colored sweaters in the Ralph Lauren men's department.

"Er . . . hello," I say uncertainly. "Do I know you?"

"Oh no." She smiles. "I just remember you from last year. You were in here, buying a shirt for your chap." She glances at my hand. "For Christmas. We had quite a long conversation as I gift-wrapped it. I've always remembered it, because you seemed so *in love*."

"This might seem . . . odd, but did I say what his name was?"

"No." The woman eyes me curiously. "You just said he brought you alive. You hadn't been alive before. You were bubbling over with it, with the happiness of it. Don't you remember?"

"No." Something is clenching at my throat. It was Jon. Jon, whom I've tried not to think about every single day since I walked away. "What did I buy him?"

"It was this shirt, as I recall." She hands me a pale green shirt.

I hold the shirt, trying to conjure up the happiness. Maybe it's just the end of a long day, but I can't seem to let go of this shirt. "Could I buy it, please?" I say. "Don't bother wrapping it."

I DON'T KNOW WHAT'S WRONG with me. As I walk out of Langridge's and hail a taxi, I've still got the green shirt, clasped to my face like a comfort blanket. My whole head is buzzing.

A taxi draws up, and I get in, on autopilot. "Where to?" asks the driver, but I barely hear him. I can't stop thinking about Jon. I'm humming . . .

I'm humming a tune I don't know. And all I know is this tune is Jon. It means Jon. It's a tune I know from him.

I close my eyes desperately, chasing it, trying to flag it down. And then, like a flash of light, it's in my head. It's a memory.

I have a memory. Of him. Me. The two of us together. The smell of salt in the air, his chin scratchy, a gray sweater . . . and the tune. That's it. A fleeting moment, nothing else. But I have it. I *have* it.

"Love, where to?" The driver has opened the partition.

I can't let anything else into my mind; I have to keep hold of this memory. "To . . . to . . . Hammersmith."

As the taxi moves through London, I sit bolt upright. I feel as though my head contains a precious liquid and if it's jolted, it'll be spilled. I have to keep this memory intact. I have to tell him.

As we arrive in Jon's road, I thrust some money at the driver and get out. I ring the bell. The next minute, the front door swings open at the top of the steps, and there he is, in a turtleneck and jeans, old Converse sneakers on his feet.

"I remembered something," I blurt out before he can say anything. "I remembered a tune. I don't know it, but I know I heard it with you, at the beach. We must have been there one time. Listen!" I start humming the tune, avid with hope. "Do you remember?"

"Lexi . . ." He pushes his hands through his hair. "What are you talking about? Why are you carrying a shirt?"

I'm babbling, but I can't help it. "I can remember the salty air, and your chin was scratchy, and it went like this." I start humming again, but I'm getting more inaccurate, scrabbling for the right notes. Jon's face is screwed up, perplexed.

"I don't remember," he says.

"*You* don't remember?" I stare at him in outraged disbelief.

"Come on! Think! It was cold, and you hadn't shaved; you had a gray sweater on."

Suddenly his face changes. "The time we went to Whitstable." He's nodding. "To the beach. It was freezing, so we wrapped up and we had a radio with us . . . Wait. Is it that song that was everywhere? 'Bad Day.' " He starts humming, and it's like a dream coming to life.

"Yes!" I say eagerly. "That's it! That's the tune!"

Jon looks bemused. "So that's all you remember? A tune."

When he says it like that, it makes me feel utterly stupid for dashing across London. Cold reality is crashing into my bubble. He's not interested anymore. He's probably got a girlfriend by now.

"Yes." I clear my throat. "That's all. I just thought I'd let you know that I'd remembered something. So . . . um . . . anyway. Nice to see you. Bye." My cheeks are flaming miserably as I turn to leave. This is so embarrassing. I don't know what I was *thinking*—

"Is it enough?" Jon's voice takes me by surprise. I swivel, to see he's come halfway down the steps, his face taut with hope. "You said you needed a memory. A thread linking us." He takes another step down toward me. "Now you have one."

"If I do, it's the thinnest thread in the world. One tune. It's like . . . cobweb. Gossamer thin."

"Well then, hold on to it." He's coming down the rest of the steps. "Hold on, Lexi. Don't let it snap." He reaches me and wraps me tightly in his arms.

"I won't," I whisper, and grab on to him. I don't ever want to let him go again. When at last I resurface, three children are staring at me from the next-door steps.

"Ooh," says one. "Sex-eee."

I can't help laughing, even though my eyes are shiny with tears. "Hey, Jon. Guess what? I suddenly remember something else."

"What?" His face lights up. "What do you remember?"

"I remember going into your house . . . taking the phones off the hooks . . . and having the best sex of my life for twenty-four hours solid," I say seriously. "I even remember the exact date."

"Really?" Jon smiles but looks a bit puzzled. "When?"

"October the sixteenth, 2007. At about"—I consult my watch—"four fifty-seven p.m."

"Aaah." Jon smiles in comprehension. "Of course. Yes, I remember that, too. It was a pretty awesome time, wasn't it? Come on." He leads me up the steps to the cheers and jeers of the children.

"By the way," I say as he kicks the door shut behind us. "I haven't had good sex since 2004. Just so you know."

Jon laughs. He peels off his turtleneck in one movement, and I feel a bolt. My body remembers this, even if I don't.

"I'll accept that challenge." He comes over, takes my face in his two hands, and just surveys me for a moment, silent and purposeful.

I can't hold out anymore. I have to pull his face down to me for a kiss. And this one I'll never forget; this one I'll keep forever.

A Conversation with
Sophie Kinsella

WE CAUGHT up with author Sophie Kinsella not too long ago, during the filming of *Confessions of a Shopaholic.*

SELECT EDITIONS: Can you tell us a little about yourself?

SOPHIE KINSELLA: I was born in London. I studied music at New College, Oxford, but, after a year, switched to Politics, Philosophy and Economics and gained a first [honors degree] after only two years of studying. I then worked as a teacher and a financial journalist.

SE: When was your first book published?

SK: When I was twenty-four. It was called *The Tennis Party* and was published under my real name, Madeleine Wickham.

SE: After writing seven books as Madeleine Wickham, why did you change your pen name to Sophie Kinsella when you started to write your Shopaholic novels?

Vital Stats

RESIDENCE: London, England
FAMILY: Husband and three sons
LATEST ADDICTION: Cadbury's Giant Chocolate Buttons
NUMBER OF SOPHIE KINSELLA NOVELS SO FAR: 8
NUMBER OF MADELEINE WICKHAM NOVELS SO FAR: 7
PROUD HOME POSSESSION: Shoe museum (or "Shoe-seum")
WEBSITE: www.SophieKinsella.com

SK: When I had the idea for Shopaholic, it was as though a light switched on. I realized I actually wanted to write comedy. No apologies, no trying to be serious, just full-on entertainment. The minute I went with that and threw myself into it, it felt just like writing my first book again—it was really liberating. I chose to publish the first Shopaholic book under a pseudonym because I wanted it to be judged on its own merits. I knew that if I tried to pitch the idea to my publishers, they might be dubious, because it was very different from what I'd written before. So I thought I'd just present them with the finished novel under a different name. They could either like it or not like it.

SE: How long does it take you to write a novel?

SK: Usually about nine months in total. I have two stages: The first is the coffee-shop stage, where I sit down, order a coffee, make notes, and plan it all. I do that for weeks before I actually start to write. The second is sitting upstairs alone, writing intensely and listening to very loud music. It's like soundproofing, because it blocks out the rest of the world and allows me to focus.

SE: Where did you get the idea for *Remember Me?*

SK: Just me thinking, What if you woke up and everything in your life was perfect? It's never going to happen to most of us but . . . Also, I've always been fascinated by memory, so having a heroine with amnesia was the obvious way to tell the story.

SE: You are involved in the filming of your Shopaholic novels. What's that like?

SK: The film options were bought seven years ago and now,

"Unforgettable"

When it comes to great plot setups, memory losses like Lexi Smart's are right at the top. Tom Cruise suffered one in *Vanilla Sky*. Alfred Hitchcock tried more than one variation, in *Spellbound* and *Marnie*. And Matt Damon has spent three whole movies learning about himself and his mysterious past in the Bourne series. Perhaps the ultimate amnesia story is James Hilton's *Random Harvest*, where a young man's memory loss also brings the loss of the love of his life, but in the end we find out that he's been married to her all along!

A Field Guide to Chick Lit

Ranging from Candace Bushnell's *Sex and the City* to Sophie Kinsella's Shopaholic titles, there's a whole new book genre out there known as chick lit. These books usually have hip, stylish young female heroines, and their plots revolve around their heroines' successes and failures both in love and in their chosen professions. If you're wondering how to recognize these books, here's a handy field guide.

- Heroine's tone is funny, irreverent, and saucy.
- Heroine, as often as not, wouldn't mind losing a few pounds.
- Heroine works in a really chic job in fashion or the media, and often has talents unrecognized by her superiors.
- Heroine owns, or would like to own, shoes—a lot of shoes.
- Heroine's best friends for life are really best friends for life.
- Heroine is not good at recognizing the best men, although this usually works out okay for her in the end.

---

at last, it's actually happening. Disney is making the movie, which is called *Confessions of a Shopaholic.* It's being re-set in the States, and Isla Fisher is playing Becky Bloomwood and Hugh Dancy is Luke. During the last few weeks, I've been with the film crew in New York. The sets are fantastic, and I love Becky's room. And her shoe collection is amazing!

SE: Do you love New York or hate it?

SK: I love New York, so I was thrilled that the film would be shot here. We've been shooting in a fabulous boutique the last couple of days, so I've even managed to do some shopping between takes!

SE: How do you cope with being a successful writer and mother to three young sons?

SK: I'm very lucky. I have a really supportive husband in Henry, and there's my mum, too. I couldn't have a career and manage the kids' routines and household things single-handedly. I'd just go crazy. I know what my strengths are: making up and writing stories. I'm not so good at remembering to send back the school letters with boxes ticked and signed. Luckily, Henry is brilliant at that. ∎

THIS IS MY SECRET

DON'T TELL
A SOUL

A THRILLER

DAVID ROSENFELT

PROLOGUE

FRIENDS have asked me why I'm telling this story, and for a long time I had no intention of doing so. For one thing, it's already been told so many times. Television has covered it endlessly, newspapers and magazines have made it a staple on their covers, and the inexhaustible blogosphere has grown exhausted in the rehashing.

Everyone remembers where they were the day it all went down. It is seared into the public consciousness, and nothing I can write will change that. Nor would I want it to.

But I have something new to tell, information that citizens perhaps can benefit from hearing. I was there; I had a front-row seat, and that separates me from other chroniclers.

After having told my story for months to every imaginable branch of the federal government, they have mysteriously insisted I maintain a public silence. This I will not do.

I will tell it as it happened, and be, I hope, as unbiased as possible. It will be daunting for me, or painful, or cathartic, or a great relief. Probably all of the above.

So why am I telling the story? I guess I just feel like you should know the truth.

1

"IT'S the little things that change your life. They change your life, Timothy Wallace."

Whenever Tim Wallace's mother, Carol, had something important to tell him, she ended it with "Timothy Wallace," as if his formal name would lend it additional credibility and significance. The sadness in her eyes would make Tim want to look away, but to the best of his recollection he never did.

"The little things can change your life, Timothy Wallace."

What she was really talking about was fate, and how fate was dictated by moments you could neither expect nor control. And then she followed it with the story he had heard so many times. If her friend Donna hadn't taken a bus downtown that day, if she had taken a cab instead, Donna wouldn't have met Charlie, the man she married. And then Charlie could never have fixed Carol up with Kenny Wallace. And Carol and Kenny would never have had their son, Tim. And Kenny couldn't have abandoned them when Tim was only six months old, never contacting them in the years since.

That was what was strange about the "little things," and how they changed your life. They could be good or bad, and sometimes you didn't always know right away.

For Tim and especially for Maggie, the "little thing" was the hat.

IT WAS an important, even symbolic, moment for both of them.

Tim and Maggie had been married for almost five months, and while Tim had sworn "for better or for worse, in sickness and in health," that hadn't as yet included his boat. His pride and joy. His sanctuary.

He had owned the modest thirty-foot motorboat for six years, having bought it on his twenty-fourth birthday. It was his place to decompress, to read, to be alone, to get away from whatever might be bothering him, to focus and reflect on that which was good.

Tim's close friends, Danny and Will, had been out on the boat with him a few times, but never a woman. Not even Maggie.

Not until that day.

The fact that this milestone didn't happen for the first four months after their marriage was more a function of the calendar than anything else. It isn't until early May that things start warming up on Long Island Sound.

"Why don't you keep it docked down here?" Maggie had asked on more than one occasion, pointing down at the Hudson River from the window of their twenty-third-floor apartment in Fort Lee, New Jersey.

Fort Lee wraps around the New Jersey side of the George Washington Bridge and is wildly valued as real estate for its proximity to, and view of, New York City. Tim and Maggie lived in Sunset Towers, as prestigious an address as Fort Lee possesses, and used that vantage point to take advantage of the theater, restaurants, and energy that New York provided better than any city in the world.

They were just leaving their apartment when Maggie unveiled the hat. He assumed it had to be a hat, but in reality it looked like a manhole cover on steroids, with a brim so large that the Third Infantry could find shade under it.

"What the hell is that?" he asked, when she put it on her head. That sounded a little harsh, so he added, "Honey."

"My new hat," she said, turning slightly to show it off in its full glory. "They only had one left."

"So other people beat you to that?"

She nodded. "Isn't it great?"

"And your plan is to carry that around on your head all day?"

"I'm sensing that you don't like it."

"No, I like it," he said, smiling. "It's just that it's among the ugliest things I've ever seen."

"That's good; I was afraid you'd want to borrow it."

The drive out to the pier, with no traffic, was about forty-five minutes. Of course, since there had never yet been a day in New York without traffic, on this particular day it took an hour and fifteen minutes. During the ride, Tim suggested Maggie hold the hat in her lap in deference to the fact that they were in Tim's convertible. Were it to blow out into the open road, he opined, it could take out a tractor trailer.

So instead Maggie's hair blew in the wind, and she was characteristically unconcerned about it. Maggie had dark, curly hair, and in Tim's view it would look good even if she put her head through a car wash. In fact, he thought she looked best when she got out of the shower, when her hair was wet and unbrushed. Of course, she was also naked then, and that may have contributed to his bias.

Halfway into the ride, Maggie reached out, took his hand, and squeezed it. "Did you tell Danny and Will you were taking me on the boat today?" She was referring to Danny McCabe and Will Clampett, Tim's best friends, who often mocked his "sanctuary" concept.

He shook his head. "No, I didn't tell anyone. I figured I'd surprise people after the fact."

Once they arrived at the pier, Maggie was so anxious to see the boat that she kept walking ahead of Tim. There were hundreds of boats lined up, vertically parked along the pier, so she had no idea which one it was. She had to keep waiting for him to catch up, since he was carrying lunch.

But when she happened upon it, she recognized it instantly. He hadn't told her he'd renamed the boat *The Magster*. She stood there staring at the inscription on the hull.

Finally she said, "You think I'm going to cry? Well, I'm not. I love it, and I love you, but I'm not going to cry."

"I wouldn't expect you to," he said. Maggie had a thing about crying; she wanted to save it for the "really important stuff." Which had always been fine with him.

As soon as they got on the boat, Maggie made it very clear that she wasn't there as a passenger. She wanted to know how it all worked, and insisted on doing everything from starting the motor to steering out into the Sound.

After the first hour, they just relaxed out on the water, drifting with the motor off, and reading the Sunday *Times*. Not long after, the wind started to pick up, and knowing what Tim did about weather patterns on the Sound, he was aware there was a chance the day would have to be cut short. He suggested they have lunch, and Maggie got up to prepare it.

Tim was the type that could happily eat his dinner standing next to the refrigerator, but to Maggie each meal was an event. It always amazed him; he had a constant struggle with his weight, stuffing 180 pounds onto his five-foot-eleven frame, while the five-foot-seven Maggie wouldn't weigh 120 pounds if she were carrying a barbell.

Within five minutes the small table was set with a dazzling array of dishes, each in its own special serving piece. Maggie even brought champagne to toast a new, substantial federal contract that Tim's construction company had won.

She looked at the table with satisfaction. "What do you think?"

"I think it should be enough," Tim said. "Actually, if a navy destroyer floats by, we can invite the crew to lunch."

"What about them?" Maggie asked, pointing to a large boat about five hundred yards away. She waved in its direction, but there didn't seem to be anyone out on the deck. Tim had seen it periodically during the morning. It was a ninety-foot Oceanfast 360, retail price close to two million five.

"Anybody who would paint a boat like that such an ugly green color doesn't deserve lunch," he said. "Besides, they're rich enough to buy their own. Let's eat."

Eat they did, and after Tim had consumed enough food to sink *The Magster* from his weight, Maggie asked, "Want some dessert?"

"I can't. I don't have a cubic inch of internal space left."

"That's a shame. I made crème brûlée."

"Unless I use my emergency space. That's always an option."

She nodded her understanding. "If this isn't an emergency, what is?" She got up and walked to the cooler to get the dessert, but as she leaned over, a gust of wind blew the hat off her head. "Damn!" she yelled, as she just missed catching it.

"Don't worry," Tim said, looking at the huge hat floating on the water. "A freighter will find it and tow it back to shore. Or I'll get you another one."

"I like that one."

He nodded. "And it was indeed beautiful. But as you can see, it's going off on its own. All we can do is wish it well."

"Tim, it's right over there." She pointed to the hat, which was already almost thirty yards away.

He tried to put on his most incredulous look. "You mean you want me to go out there to get that ridiculous hat?"

"Of course, I do. Come on, Tim, it's drifting away."

"Maggie . . ." he said, though he was going to have to come up with something a lot stronger if he was going to get out of this. He looked up at the gathering clouds as if for inspiration. "It's going to start raining soon."

She nodded. "Don't worry; you'll be wet from getting the hat anyway." And then she came in with the clincher. "I'll give you my undying love."

He muttered, "I thought I already had that." This was not a battle he was going to win. He restarted the engine and was not happy that it made a strange noise. He made a mental note to get it checked once they went back to the pier. He then pulled the boat ten yards from the hat and prepared to go in to get it.

"Put on your life jacket," Maggie said.

"What for? I can swim like a fish."

"Tim, please put it on."

He sighed and put on the jacket under her watchful eye. He jumped in the water, which sent a cold chill through him, and swam with powerful strokes toward the hat. It had already moved another fifteen yards away. In the distance he could see the Oceanfast 360 and hoped that the people on board did not see him. This was not his finest moment on the high seas.

When Tim finally reached the hat, he put it on his head so Maggie could see him wearing it. "What do you think?"

Maggie wasn't looking at him; she was standing near the side of the boat. "Tim," she called out, "I think there's something . . . there's something wrong with the motor!"

"TURN IT OFF!" he yelled. "TURN IT OFF!"

"It's smoking!"

"MAGGIE! TURN—"

The next thing he saw was a flash of white, so quick that it almost didn't register.

And then nothing.

2

"It went South."

That was the entire message in the handwritten note slipped to Roger Blair in the prison mess hall during dinner. He looked around at the other inmates seated at the long table. No one seemed to be interested, which was not surprising. In this place, it took all available energy to worry about yourself.

"It went South." That's all it said, but Roger realized immediately that it meant something had gone terribly wrong. It also meant something else that he understood very well.

He was going to die.

It was the kind of death sentence from which there was no appeal. There was nowhere to go for help, no stay of execution that could be granted. Going to the prison authorities would, if anything, hasten his demise.

The only remaining questions were when and how. Roger hoped it was soon; days spent in prison waiting to die were days not really worth living. The "how" was almost certain to be a sharp blade in the back or a garrote. For the rest of the day, he looked around warily, waiting for them to make their move.

For the first time in a very long while, he thought about his wife and felt the urge to talk to her. She had stopped coming to see him. He wasn't feeling resentful; he just wanted to say good-bye.

Nothing happened the entire afternoon. These things were better done in darkness. As always, lights went out at ten o'clock. Roger lay on his bed and listened for an approach, but it was not forthcoming, and he drifted off to sleep.

The cell was seven by ten, and completely dark. Roger did not know what time it was when he heard the door rattle slightly. Within moments he could sense that his executioner was inside.

"Took you long enough," Roger said. "You even know why you're doing this?"

He heard a slight laugh of surprise. "Yeah. For money." There was a click, and a beam of light appeared out of the intruder's hand.

Roger said, "I don't mean that. I mean—"

The blade swept across his neck, ending his sentence and his life. A life that had long ago gone South.

FROM the moment he heard the facts, Detective Jonathon Novack realized exactly what he had. It was a cold-blooded murder, and he knew who'd done it. He knew it in his gut, and he could count the times his gut was wrong on very few fingers.

There are a bunch of things that homicide cops in urban areas do not have, at least not in Novack's experience. They don't have long weekends off; they don't have secure, happy marriages; and they don't have coincidences in their work.

Novack had long ago learned to strip away the bull and focus on the facts, and in this case the facts were clear. Tim Wallace had taken his wife, Maggie, out on his boat, a boat he had been on, without incident, at least a hundred times. While drifting on Long Island Sound, he turned on the motor and swam to retrieve a hat his wife had lost overboard. At that very moment, the motor blew up in a massive explosion, obliterating the boat and his wife.

Quite a coincidence.

And a slam-dunk, no-doubt murder if ever there was one.

Except it didn't turn out quite that way, and if there was a more frustrating case, Novack couldn't remember it.

The Coast Guard had been on the scene within minutes, and they found Wallace floating, held up by his life jacket, in a state of what the doctors called convulsive shock. That lasted ten days, long enough to miss his wife's funeral, or more accurately her service, since the body was never recovered. When he finally regained full consciousness, he claimed not to remember anything after reaching the hat and seeing the flash of white.

Unfortunately, experts determined that the blast could conceivably have been an accident, based on a defect in a similar motor that caused an explosion off the coast of Florida.

That was followed by a surprising willingness on the part of Wallace to take a lie detector test, and his just as surprising refusal to hire a lawyer. He passed the test with flying colors, and while that is not admissible in court, it certainly had an effect on both Novack's boss and the district attorney.

To complete the annoying trifecta, Novack could find no evidence of problems in the marriage. They had met eighteen months before, had had a whirlwind courtship, and no one would say anything other than they seemed completely in love.

The media jumped on the case, immediately joining Novack in

the suspicion, almost the certainty, that Wallace had engineered his wife's death. Half of Larry King's panel all but had Wallace convicted, and Nancy Grace accused the police of incompetence for not having Tim in jail on day one. But as day one became month one, the pundits ran out of unsubstantiated charges, and there were simply no revelations to add fuel to the fire.

The simple fact was that Novack had uncovered nothing. And while his gut didn't require any evidence, his bosses and the courts did. It was enough to make him, and his gut, nauseous.

But not enough to make him stop. This case would never get cold, not in Novack's mind. He would work it whenever he could, until he put away the son of a bitch who literally blew his young wife out of the water.

DECEMBER thirty-first held absolutely no special significance for Tim Wallace. It was simply another day to be in pain over the loss of Maggie, a sorrow that was not about to be affected by the fact that it happened to be a holiday.

The aching had not lessened in the months since that awful day, and if truth be told, Tim didn't really want it to lessen. In his mind it would be stupid and illogical to be happy, or content, or pain-free. Maggie was dead, blown to bits, and the knowledge of that was supposed to hurt. He wanted it to hurt.

He also wanted to work; it represented an impersonal world, a place he could be without feeling Maggie's constant presence, or more accurately, lack of presence. And here he caught a break; the small construction company, Wallace Industries, that he began six years prior was thriving.

Soon after 9/11, Tim was among the first to recognize the boom that was about to hit in security construction. Many buildings, especially those owned by the government, were found in need of reinforcement and specially constructed concrete perimeters. They simply had not been built in the expectation that they would someday be bombed, or that a plane might be flown into them.

Tim was shrewd enough to declare his company expert in this

area, and it did not take long for him to start receiving very healthy contracts. The federal government had money to spend. Now Wallace Industries was nearly finished with its part of a massive complex in downtown Newark called the Federal Center, costing in excess of three billion dollars. It would be a model of its type, with each building possessing state-of-the-art security, and was planned as the forerunner for similar projects around the country. They were virtual federal cities within cities, the idea being that it was easier to provide security for one large complex, rather than for buildings spread out in different locations, as was currently the case.

Almost two years ago, Tim had brought Danny McCabe in as his partner. They had met when first starting out at a large construction company and became fast friends.

Danny was both hardworking and talented, a problem solver in a business that had round-the-clock problems. But the most significant asset he brought to the company was a crucial contact. His uncle was Fred Collinsworth, senior United States senator from New Jersey and the ranking member on the Senate Appropriations Committee. Uncle Fred had proven invaluable in steering federal work to his nephew's company, most notably the Newark project, and that was a huge factor in the company's growth.

Granting the project to Danny and Tim's company was not strictly nepotism. Many smaller construction companies were given substantial contracts, and the senator pointed to it as a new way of doing business, as opposed to the recent practice of enormous companies controlling everything.

It was a politically wise move on his part, both because he could claim that he was helping small business, and because in reality it was creating a large group of businessmen who were beholden to him, and who would show their appreciation in campaign contributions. It also earned him the enmity of the Franklin Group and its chairman, Byron Carthon. Franklin was a huge, multinational corporation that was used to getting these kinds of gigantic government contracts.

But Collinsworth was unconcerned with Carthon or the Franklin Group. He was well aware that when the contracts were granted to small companies for similar Federal Center complexes around the country, he would immediately have a huge base of political and financial support, the kind of situation that could help propel a politician to the highest of national offices. And Collinsworth was nothing if not ambitious.

Danny and Tim's other very close friend, Will Clampett, worked for them as an independent contractor handling computer issues vital to modern construction. Danny and Will frequently attempted to draw Tim back into the social world. They felt it would be better for him to get out more, take his mind off things, even if he had no interest in dating.

Tim's efficient, thirty-one-year-old assistant, Meredith Tunney, shared this feeling and joined in the gentle persuading, but Tim remained firm. He was not going to do anything until he was ready, and "ready" seemed light-years away.

But New Year's Eve, while of no significance to Tim, was considered very significant by Danny, Will, and Meredith. They were plainly worried that it would be a particularly difficult night for Tim, despite his protestations that he'd be fine.

Meredith had been a godsend for Tim and the company. Hired just two months before Maggie's death, she had kept Tim's life in order ever since. Whether this was paying his bills, or making all of his appointments and reservations, it enabled him to keep his life only on the brink of chaos, without crossing the line.

So Meredith spent the day with Tim in his Englewood office, stealing glances at him and wondering how she could broach the subject of New Year's Eve. She was going out with friends and had already pronounced it unacceptable that Tim stay home alone.

By three-thirty in the afternoon, she wanted to take off to get ready for her own evening, so she took a deep breath and plunged ahead. Tim was at his desk doing paperwork when she walked in and said, "So, what have you got going on for tonight?"

He didn't even look up. "A couple of parties, then into the city to watch the ball drop, then clubbing until morning."

She frowned. "Come on, really. You're not going out?"

He finally looked up. "No, this year I think I'm going to go in. Everybody else will be 'out,' so I'll have 'in' to myself. Pizza, half pepperoni, and *Godfather I* and *II.*"

She shook her head sadly. "Well, I've gotta go; anything you need before I leave?"

"Can you track Danny down? I need to talk to him."

"He went home an hour ago, Tim." Then, pointedly, "It's New Year's Eve; he has plans. Plans that he'd love to include you in."

Meredith got nowhere with that and left, while Tim did a couple of more hours of work. He stopped for a take-out pizza before heading home.

His apartment felt as barren and unwelcome as always, except for the incredibly soothing presence of Kiley, his golden retriever. Kiley missed Maggie terribly, but she seemed to try and compensate by providing comfort for Tim.

Danny and Will had suggested repeatedly that Tim move out of this apartment, as a way of putting the memories behind him. He hadn't done so, partially out of a vague feeling that it would be disrespectful to Maggie. This same feeling had caused him not to change a single thing about the place. He realized that he was living in the past, but the past seemed a lot better than the present.

Kiley and Tim shared the pizza, though she only liked the crusts. He popped in the *Godfather* DVD. On his large plasma screen, it looked at least as good as it had looked in any theater.

Close to nine o'clock, he was making his nightly decision as to whether to fall asleep on the couch or trudge into the bedroom when the doorbell rang.

"This can't be good," he said. Kiley seemed to nod in agreement. Tim opened the door.

Danny and Will came barging in. "Happy damn New Year," said Danny. "Let's go."

"Go where?" Tim asked, though he knew exactly where they were talking about.

"Oh, I don't know," Will said. "Maybe the same place we go every New Year's Eve."

Will and Danny were fully aware that their friend was in agony, and somehow instinctively felt that if they were in an obvious good mood, it would brighten him up as well. The fact that it hadn't worked all these months somehow never led them to a conclusion that their strategy was ineffective. Tim knew that Will was talking about a bar in nearby Teaneck called the Purple Rose, a place that was always comfortable. They never considered going anywhere else, but Tim had not been back to the Rose since Maggie died.

"It's not going to happen, guys," he said.

"Tim, here's the deal," Danny said. "You're my partner and my friend, and even though you're a complete pain in the ass, I love you. But tonight you walk into the Rose under your own power or get carried in under ours."

"Try and understand this," Tim said. "I don't want to go. It doesn't feel right yet, and I don't want to do it."

Danny nodded. "We know that, Tim. And we know how hard it is. But tonight's the night we give you a push."

"Guys, I appreciate this, okay? You think it will make me feel better, but it won't. It really won't."

Will had already nudged himself into the recliner chair with Kiley and was petting her head. "If you're miserable, you bail out," he said. "Besides, everybody will be so drunk, they won't even know you're there."

"And the French fries," Danny added. "Remember the fries?"

The Purple Rose had the world's greatest French fries, thin and crisp. "I remember," Tim said. "Someday in the future, I will have them again."

"Tonight," said Danny. "Tonight is the night."

Will came in for what he hoped would be the clincher. "Tim, until now I haven't said this to you, and Danny hasn't either, but it's time to put it out there. Tim, Maggie would want you to do this. She would want you to go out and have some fun."

Tim would ordinarily have rejected that out of hand, but for some reason, he'd recently been thinking about the possibility of spending a night with the guys at the Rose, and been annoyed at himself for even the thought. He also knew that what Will said was the absolute truth; Maggie would want him to go.

He finally nodded. "Okay . . . you're right."

Danny put his arm on Tim's shoulder. "This is great. And by the way, since this is your coming-out party, you're buying."

3

THE Purple Rose apparently never got the memo that everything had changed since Maggie's death.

Tim found it somehow jarring that the place was the same as always, sawdust on the floor, wooden tables carved with every possible initial, central wood-burning fireplace, Wurlitzer jukebox, and at least thirty televisions, usually showing sports. Of course, the televisions were tuned to the Times Square festivities, though on a human-per-square-foot basis, the place was every bit as crowded as the streets on which the ball would drop.

Tim, Danny, and Will had their own reserved table, in deference to their years as loyal patrons. They ordered food and beer, and Danny and Will headed off to try their luck with the countless single women milling about.

Tim was at the table for less than a minute when he realized that he simply was not ready for this. He just sat and watched everyone else celebrate having made it through another year, an observer of the human condition from an outsider's perspective.

Danny and Will occasionally came by to check on him, and Tim told them he was fine. He looked at his watch repeatedly. There was a half hour until midnight, but it was going to feel like forever.

"Hi. Happy New Year."

Tim looked up and saw an attractive woman standing right in front of him. "Mind if I sit down?" she asked, but did so without waiting for him to answer.

"Which one of them sent you over?" he asked.

She smiled again. "The drunk one in the blue shirt; I think his name is Danny. He said you needed cheering up."

"Trust me, it's not a job you want to tackle. Don't take this wrong, but I've never been one for opening up to strangers at bars."

"I'm not a stranger," she said, holding out her hand. "I'm Janice."

Tim shook her hand. "Hello, Janice. I'm Tim."

"Nice to meet you, Tim. So will you tell me what's wrong?"

"My wife died," Tim said, and immediately regretted it.

"Oh, I'm sorry. That must be so hard for you."

"It was harder on her." Tim stood up. "Excuse me a second?"

He left the table and headed toward the back of the bar. He wasn't sure where he was going; he just had to get away from Janice and her sincerity. There was a phone booth near the restrooms, and he got in it and closed the door. He leaned his head against the phone and took deep breaths to try to get control of himself. He was scared he was losing it, hyperventilating, and had no idea how long he was in there. Slowly he got himself together.

"You making a call?"

He looked up and saw a guy with his face pressed to the glass, signaling his desire to use the phone, so he let the intruder take his place.

Tim headed back into the main room and saw Will standing near the bar, his left arm around a woman and his right arm around a beer. He made his way over to him. "I'm going to take off, Will."

Will looked at his watch. "It's five of. Just give it ten minutes, okay? Start the New Year with friends."

Tim felt wiped out, too much so to even argue. He found a place at the end of the bar, alone in a room full of people. Unfortunately, this solitude lasted less than a minute, when a man came over to him. He was probably forty, tall and good-looking, with one of those square jaws that projected authority. His tie was loosened at the neck, as if he had just gotten off from work and stopped by for a drink. Except it was many drinks. As he held out his hand, Tim thought that if he didn't take it the man could fall over.

"Hey, how's it goin'? Name's Jeff. Jeff Cashman."

Tim tried to make his response unenthusiastic, though Cashman was in no condition to detect subtlety. "Tim," he said.

"Good to meet ya, Timmy. Happy damn New Year."

"You, too."

Tim hoped Cashman would move on to meet other new friends, but instead he leaned in. "You a good guy?"

Tim looked up at the closest television as if he couldn't hear him. They seemed to be ready to drop the ball on the freezing Times Square crowd. Unfortunately, when Tim looked back, Cashman was still there.

"Hey, Timmy," he said again, "you a good guy?"

Tim nodded with resignation. "Yeah."

"Can you keep a secret? A really big one?"

"No, I think you should tell someone else."

"No, I wanna tell you. I wanna tell someone this year." He looked at his watch exaggeratedly. "So I gotta hurry."

"Look, Jeff, I'm not the guy you—"

"You know where Kinnelon is?" Tim didn't answer. "Kinnelon! You know where it is?"

Kinnelon, a town in northwest Jersey, was about thirty miles from where they were standing. "Yes, but—"

"I murdered somebody there. A girl . . . three months ago."

"That's not funny," Tim said.

Cashman nodded, as if he could see that truth through his alcohol-induced haze. "No, it's not funny," he said. Then he paused. "Well, it's sorta funny. Before I killed her, I cut off her middle finger. Then I buried her behind the swing set at this little park on Maple Avenue."

Cashman had finally accomplished what no one else had been able to. He had cut through Tim's funk and ticked him off. "What the hell is the matter with you?" he asked.

All Cashman did was laugh. "Nothing. Not anymore. I actually feel much better now. Now it's your problem."

Suddenly the entire place was counting down. "TEN . . .

NINE ... EIGHT ... SEVEN ... SIX ... FIVE ... FOUR ...
THREE ... TWO ... ONE ... HAPPY NEW YEAR!"

Everybody started screaming and hugging and kissing each other.
Everybody except Cashman and Tim. Cashman finally got up to
leave but put his finger to his mouth in a signal that Tim should
keep quiet. "This is our secret, okay, Timmy?" he asked. "Just you,
me, and Sheila with the nine fingers. Don't tell a soul."

He laughed again as he walked away, but it was a silent laugh,
drowned out by the noise of all the normal people having fun.

"TRUST me, I freaked him out, totally freaked him out," said the
man who twenty minutes before had pretended to be Jeff Cashman.
He was talking to his employer for the evening.

The employer laughed. "But he believed you?"

"Damn straight. You should have seen his face."

"I wish I had. Was he scared or annoyed?"

They stood talking at a rest stop near exit 156 on the Garden
State Parkway. "Cashman" could see there was someone in the employer's passenger seat. It looked like a woman, but it was dark and
hard to tell. Other than that they were alone, because at that hour,
with the temperature near fifteen degrees, nobody else seemed inclined to stop.

"Scared. I don't know what you have planned for him, but this
part of it worked."

"That's great. Nice work."

"Yeah. So if you'll give me my money ..."

"In the trunk."

"You mean cash? You could have given me a check."

"Sorry," the employer seemed amused over the misunderstand-
ing. "I want you to get in the trunk."

"What are you talking about?" Cashman asked.

The man's voice took on a hard edge. "Get in the trunk. Now."

"Come on, what's going on here?" asked Cashman, fear creeping into his voice. "Quit joking around."

"In the time you've known me, have I ever joked around? I want to kill you while you're in the trunk. Otherwise I have to do it here, then lift you in."

"Cashman" panicked and turned to run. He made it about a foot and a half before an incredibly powerful hand grabbed his neck.

The last thing he heard was the snap from behind.

IF THE night out was meant to ease Tim's entry back into the world, it didn't quite go according to plan. It was a completely uncomfortable experience, capped off by an encounter with a lunatic.

At least Tim hoped he was a lunatic, because the alternative was that he was a brutal killer. He didn't look like the killer type, but then again Tim had never really met one in the flesh.

Tim had turned his phone ringer off when he got home, and in the morning the message light was flashing. That light represented the outside world, so he showered, dressed, and had breakfast before pressing the button.

It was Will, saying, "Hey, Tim, I hope last night wasn't too painful. Danny and I are going down to the Rose to watch the Bowl games. How 'bout meeting us down there? Just beer, burgers, and football; I promise."

Spending New Year's Day watching the games was another tradition that Danny, Will, and Tim observed religiously, and Maggie was there last year as well. But Tim certainly had no desire to go back to the Rose, at least not in this decade. He Googled the terms "Sheila," "murder," "missing person," and "Kinnelon" in various combinations and came up empty. This was probably more reassuring to him than it should have been; like many other people, Tim had come to believe that if something wasn't on Google, it didn't exist. Having performed that cursory investigation, he turned off the computer, put Kiley in the car, and drove to the dog park.

Dog parks are a creative invention of the late twentieth century, which basically provide dog parents a chance to arrange a mass canine playdate in a very large enclosed area. Their human owners, mostly female, stand off to the side, and occasionally tennis balls are thrown, creating an absolute frenzy.

Not all dogs like it, and Tim suspected that Kiley had mixed feelings. She had always seemed reserved in her enthusiasm, not joining in with the main crowd, but occasionally sniffing and being sniffed by certain dogs that she knew and liked.

Maggie and Tim used to come here every Sunday morning, and it didn't seem fair to deprive Kiley of enjoyment and exercise, so Tim continued to take her there every week.

When Maggie was there, she did most of the socializing, and Tim became the designated tennis ball thrower. There were a few people he spoke to regularly, one of whom was Eden Alexander, a woman two years younger than him.

As always, Eden was there when Tim and Kiley arrived, and she greeted them with her ever-present smile. Tim had a tendency to think that people who were relentlessly upbeat were probably not all that bright, but Maggie told him once that Eden had a Ph.D. in art history from Stanford. She had a blond ponytail and always wore a Mets cap.

Kiley made no secret of her friendship with Eden's German shepherd, Travis. Her tail started wagging the moment she saw him. Human smiles and apparent warmth can be insincere, but Kiley's tail-wag could be taken to the bank.

Eden had been helpful to Tim in the weeks after Maggie's death. She came by his apartment occasionally, just to say hello and ask if he needed anything. He was almost obsessive in not letting friends help, yet he'd let Eden take Kiley to the park. She was there without being intrusive, a talent Tim learned not to take lightly.

"Really cold today, huh?" he asked.

Eden did a double take. "Wait a minute. Was that chitchat?"

"I'm making conversation. It's a New Year's resolution."

"No, that wasn't conversation," she said. "That was chitchat. And since I've never heard you chitchat before, there must be something going on."

"Nothing's going on."

She didn't believe him. "Come on, talk to Auntie Eden."

For some reason, he did feel able to talk to her. "Something weird happened last night," he said. "Actually, beyond weird."

"You mean besides my date?"

"I went to the Purple Rose with some friends. . . ."

She nodded her approval. "Good. Did you have fun?"

He shook his head. "Not even a little, but I didn't expect to. What was a surprise happened just before midnight. Some guy I never met before told me he committed a murder three months ago."

"Oh, my God!" she said, and a few women looked over. Eden smiled and lowered her voice. "Just like that?"

"Just like that. He asked if I could keep a secret, then told me about it. Like he was getting it off his chest onto mine."

"Was he drunk? Maybe it was the alcohol talking."

"I hope so."

"Did he tell you who the victim was?"

"He said her name was Sheila, and that he killed her in Kinnelon. I'll spare you the gruesome details."

Eden thought about it for a few moments. This was not an area in which she had a great deal of expertise. "You think he could have been telling the truth?"

Tim shrugged. "I Googled it, but I didn't find anything."

"Are you going to go to the police? Just in case?"

"I don't know; it's probably just a drunk in a bar spouting off. I was thinking I could check a little more on my own. Maybe drive out there. Today."

"You're going to go try and dig up a body?"

"You think I'm nuts?" he asked.

She smiled. "Pretty much; just be careful. Hey, why don't you leave Kiley? She'll have a great time with Travis."

It was a good idea, and Tim accepted the offer. Eden said that they could meet back at the dog park at four o'clock, and promised that Kiley would have a wonderful day.

While Tim went looking for a body.

4

KINNELON is in the most rustic part of New Jersey. It's an affluent residential community that borders the state's ski resorts and is particularly beautiful in the winter. As a teenager, Tim used to ski about twenty minutes down the road, at Great Gorge. He figured he'd just drive along Maple Avenue looking for a park with a swing set, and maybe a headstone that said HERE LIES SHEILA. MURDERED BY CASHMAN. That was pretty much the extent of his plan.

The route took him through the center of the quaint town, which, while never bustling, was particularly quiet on the holiday. He saw that there were two cars in front of the small town hall, and decided to park, just in case anybody was there. The front door was open, and there was a woman at the general information desk.

Tim walked over to her. "Happy New Year. I was wondering if you had any information on missing persons in Kinnelon within the last six months."

She looked at him as if he were insane. "We don't keep records like that here. That would be a police matter."

"Right. Of course. I'm not asking for official information. But are you yourself aware of a missing young woman, or a recent murder?"

"I should say not," she huffed.

Tim smiled pleasantly and left, actually feeling he had learned something. He got back in his car and drove slowly, only going about four blocks before he saw the park. He got out of the car. It was cold enough that the snow barely showed indentations when he stepped on it, and five kids playing on the swing set were bundled up in ski jackets. Four women stood nearby.

Tim smiled and gave the women a little wave. When he walked behind the swing set, they all walked closer in a protective, synchronized movement. "I dropped something around here. . . . I figured maybe I'd look for it," he said lamely.

Actually, there was no need for him to be there at all. It wasn't like he was going to take a pick and shovel and dig up the area. In the unlikely event a woman was buried underground, there was no way to know where.

He stared at the ground for a minute or so, then got in his car and drove back home, thankful no one he knew had witnessed his investigative prowess in action. The only one who was even aware he was going there was Eden, and his plan was to give her a recounting that would make it sound less pathetic than it really was.

He drove to the dog park, where Eden was waiting for him. "So?" she asked.

"So, what?"

"Was there a murder or wasn't there?"

Tim proceeded to tell her the events of the day.

"So what do your instincts tell you?" she asked, after he finished.

"That a drunken ass sent me on a wild-goose chase."

"You don't think you should at least tell the police?"

He knew that he probably should do exactly that, but didn't want to. "If I thought there really was a Sheila . . . but there's no evidence of any kind that Cashman was telling the truth."

"Except for the fact that there is a park with a swing set on Maple Avenue in Kinnelon."

She was right, of course. He felt a need to defend his reluctance to bring the story to the police. "My recent experience with law enforcement was not the most pleasant."

Eden knew of at least some of his dealings with the police after Maggie's death and their clear suspicion of him, so she didn't press the issue. "You'll make the right decision," she said, then smiled. "Or maybe you won't."

LEAVING for work in the morning, Tim was five feet out the front door when he saw it. Stapled eye-level to a telephone pole, it was a missing persons flyer, with a picture of a young woman. Sheila Blair, last seen in the Kinnelon area, had been missing for three months. Anyone with information was to contact the state police.

It had to be Cashman's Sheila, Tim knew. There are no coincidences that enormous.

He took down the flyer and put it in his briefcase. Danny had beaten him in to work, and Tim brought him up to date on his weird conversation with Cashman and fruitless trip out to Kinnelon.

"So you think it was bull?" Danny asked.

"I did until I found this." Tim took out the flyer. "It was tacked to a telephone pole in front of my apartment."

"That's her?" Danny asked.

"He didn't give me her last name, but the first name, and the time, and Kinnelon . . . how could it not be her?"

"You've got to talk to the cops about this," he said.

Tim nodded. "I know; I'm dreading it."

"It doesn't have to be Novack. There are other cops."

"Yeah," Tim said. Danny knew all about Novack, the cop with the relentless certainty that Tim was Maggie's murderer. In the months since, Novack had called Tim occasionally to ask about some innocuous detail of that awful day. It was his way of telling Tim that he was still on the case.

"You want me to go with you?"

Tim shook his head. "No, I'm just going to get it over with."

He decided to avoid any chance of dealing with Novack by going to the local Fort Lee police precinct. He told the desk sergeant there that he had information about a possible murder and was immediately whisked in to see Joanie Patrick, an attractive, petite woman about thirty. If you gave Tim five hundred guesses as to her occupation, homicide detective wouldn't be on his list.

He told Detective Patrick the story, concluding with the flyer. She was quiet and mostly expressionless. When he finished, she asked, "Could you identify Jeff Cashman if you saw him again?"

He nodded. "Definitely."

"But you never met him before?"

"If I did, I certainly don't remember it."

"Your wife never mentioned him?"

The question hit him like a punch in the gut. She knew who Tim was, had known it all along, and was already considering the possibility that this new situation was somehow related to Maggie's death. "No, my wife never mentioned him. Are we finished here?"

She let him go after finding out how to reach him if she had further questions.

"What are you going to do about this?" Tim asked.

"We'll contact you if we need you," she said.

THE van was a three-year-old Chevy Caravan, and it looked exactly like tens of thousands of others. Like everything else involved in this process, that was by design. Nothing would be done to attract attention or stand out in any way.

The drive up from Florida had so far taken three days. Ricardo Vasquez had been instructed not to exceed sixty-five miles per hour and to obey every traffic law to the letter. On the New Jersey Turnpike, sixty-five seemed like walking. Ricardo watched the world whiz by. That's okay, he thought. He'd get the money from this trip and buy a Porsche; then they could eat his dust.

Until then he would be very careful. Only Lucia had any idea where he was, and she wasn't smart enough to know what he was doing. She wouldn't tell anybody anyway; she knew what he would do to her if she did.

Ricardo had been on the road since seven o'clock and hadn't had breakfast before he left. As it was approaching eleven, he was starving. His specific instructions were to get all his meals at fast-food places along the highway and eat them in the car, but he was getting sick of it. He wasn't looking for anything fancy, maybe just some blueberry pancakes, with sides of bacon and hash browns. Off the turnpike near a town called Cedar Grove, he found a perfect place called Grandma Patty's Pancake House.

Ricardo didn't bother to look around when he got out of the car. Even if he had, he would not have noticed the gray minivan that had been following him since he entered New Jersey. Its GPS transponder made following at a distance easy. He did make sure his van was locked. This seemed like a sleepy little town, but he imagined its citizens would wake up pretty quickly if they learned barrels of illegal drugs worth many millions of dollars were sitting outside Grandma Patty's.

Patty proved to be a disappointment. The portions were large, but tasteless and greasy. The blueberries were not even mixed in the pancakes. Ricardo would have complained, but he was not about to draw attention to himself. He even left a tip.

Annoyed that he had wasted time, Ricardo got back in the van and pulled out onto the road without really seeing the teenaged boy stepping into the crosswalk with his five-year-old brother. He felt the thud and watched in horror as the little boy was thrown off the fender. The teenager ran to his brother, lying dazed in the grass.

Ricardo had only a moment to decide what to do. To stop and get out was to invite disaster; the cops would find out that the van was stolen, and would then impound and examine it. Ricardo would be finished. To take off was his only chance. Even if bystanders had witnessed the accident, the van had fake plates, and he would steal new ones at the next rest stop.

So his decision was an easy one, no matter how it turned out. And within a minute, it was obvious that it was not turning out well. He heard the siren before he saw the police car in his rearview mirror. The van was not about to outrun it in its loaded-down condition. Ricardo did not head back for the turnpike; that would draw in the state police and choppers. Instead he wanted to make it through the town to back roads. He was nearing eighty miles an hour when he reached into the glove compartment and took out the .44 Magnum.

The sound of the siren was getting louder, and Ricardo realized that an additional police car was coming at him from a different direction. His senses keenly tuned, he waited for his chance as he flew down the streets.

Suddenly, as the cars were closing in, he saw a narrow alley. Hitting the brakes and taking the turn on two wheels, he made it into the opening, then headed back toward the turnpike, just minutes away.

The first bullet ripped through the base of his neck and severed his spinal column. For all intents and purposes, he was dead by the time the second bullet tore through the van.

Ricardo was obviously not able to witness the resulting explosion. He was therefore not aware that it was powerful enough to level half a city block and blow out windows in a paper factory three blocks away. He was also not aware that the plan was for him not to make it to New York alive anyway and that the chase only hastened his demise by less than an hour.

The timing and manner of Ricardo's death also prevented him from having the surprise of his life, which would have been the discovery that the size of the explosion meant that what he was carrying in the van wasn't drugs at all.

FOR Jonathon Novack, the phone call was the best Christmas present he had gotten. Ever. It was far too soon to know how Tim Wallace's trip to the Fort Lee police fit into his wife's murder, but it certainly had to be connected. And whatever this latest twist was, Novack was going to use it to nail Tim's ass.

Novack was at his ex-wife's house in Fair Lawn when he got the call from Lieutenant Patrick. Cindy had divorced him three years ago, but in some bizarre way the divorce hadn't taken. Even though Novack had moved out, he came around every chance he could.

Cindy had initially viewed this as a significant problem. Potential suitors were less likely to visit knowing that her six-foot-three detective ex-husband was on guard. But over time she'd gotten used to the arrangement. Novack could still be a major pain, but he was more attentive, and she could more easily throw him out of the house than when he lived there. Cindy had finished her master's in speech therapy, gotten a job in the local school system, and started a private practice, so she was making more money than he was. Even the sex, while never a problem between them, had gotten better. So all in all, the divorce had done quite a bit for their marriage.

Within thirty seconds of getting the news about Tim, Novack was in the car and on the way to pick up Detective James Anders. Anders had only been partnered with Novack for four months, but he sure as hell had heard about the Wallace case; Novack saw to that.

They went to Tim's office, and since Meredith said he was out to lunch, they decided to wait. Meredith was not happy about this, but there was nothing she could do.

Tim was not surprised to find them there when he arrived. Novack introduced Anders, and Tim brought them back to his office.

"So tell us all about this Cashman guy," Novack said.

It was a story Tim was getting tired of telling, but he went through it one more time. Neither Novack nor Anders interrupted, just as Lieutenant Patrick hadn't. Tim chalked that up to a police listening technique.

When he finished, Novack asked, "And you're sure you never met him before?"

"Sure as I can be. And I haven't seen him since that night."

"So he comes up to a perfect stranger and confesses to a murder. Any idea why he would do that?"

"He said it was his way of getting it off his chest. That now it's my problem, which I'm starting to believe is the truth."

"Tell me about the flyer," Novack said. "Where did you find it?"

"I told you. On a telephone pole in front of my apartment."

"Right. Have you seen others, or just that one?"

"Just that one." Even as Tim said this, he knew how ridiculous it sounded. The only flyer for the murder Cashman had told him about happened to appear in front of his apartment. "Look—"

Novack interrupted him. "Did you see any flyers in Kinnelon?"

"No, but—"

"So somebody in Kinnelon goes missing, they wait three months, print one flyer, and post it thirty miles away in front of your apartment?"

"Maybe they printed ten thousand flyers and posted them everywhere; I don't know. Maybe Cashman posted the one I saw; why don't you catch the slimeball and ask him?"

"You seem nervous," Novack said.

"I'm not nervous; I'm annoyed. I did what I was supposed to do and reported this. You can do with it whatever you want."

"And we appreciate your cooperation," Novack lied. "Right now I'd like you to come with us. You don't have to, but it would be helpful if you did."

"Where to?" Tim asked.

"Kinnelon. To look for Sheila."

"What do you need me for? I've told you everything I know."

Novack shrugged. "Maybe you'll think of something else."

The drive in Novack's car out to Kinnelon was an uncomfortable one for Tim. He couldn't see how he could be of any real value; they had to be harboring the ridiculous hope that he'd somehow trip up, make a mistake, and in the process reveal himself to be a murderer.

Anders drove, and Novack sat in the passenger seat, with Tim in the back. They didn't ask him for any directions, just drove directly to the park, further proving that they were not seeking any help from him whatsoever.

The park looked nothing like it did the last time Tim was there. Replacing the women and their kids were six police cars, at least fifteen officers, and some digging equipment. Since it had only been about five hours since Tim told his story to Lieutenant Patrick, it was an impressive mobilization.

Novack directed Tim to stay nearby, and he and Anders headed for Sergeant Conway of the Kinnelon police.

Conway was not happy to be there. The temperature was hovering in the mid-teens. "You're late," he said.

"That's because we drove all the way here from civilization," Novack said. "Find anything?"

Conway shook his head. "No, but then again, there's nothing to find. Nobody's heard of this woman or reported her missing. And there's not a damn flyer within fifty miles."

They started walking, and Tim followed along. "Is this the only swing set around here?" Anders asked.

Conway nodded. "It is, but we can dig up the entire town if you'd like."

"You think we shouldn't have called you?" Novack asked.

Conway shrugged. "We're small-town. We just keep our shovels ready and dig when you big-city guys tell us."

Novack nodded. "And don't think we don't appreciate it."

They all stood off to the side, about twenty feet from where the digging was going on. After about thirty minutes, none of them had any feeling in their extremities.

"Sergeant, over here," one of the diggers called urgently.

Conway, Novack, Anders, and Tim hobbled over on frozen feet. An officer pointed down into the ditch.

It was the skeletal remains of a hand, pointing up out of the frozen ground, the middle finger missing.

"Holy hell," Novack said.

5

THE discovery of the body immediately turned the park into a crime scene.

Anders led Tim away and into the back of the car, where he was forced to wait almost two hours by himself. Tim did not get to see what was going on, and when Novack and Anders finally began the drive back, they weren't saying anything to each other, and certainly not to him.

When they got back to the station house, Novack brought Tim to the office of Sergeant Robert Taveras, the sketch artist for the department. Taveras's office, rather than have a chair behind a desk, had one facing an easel.

Taveras had an easygoing way about him and went to some lengths to get Tim to remain calm. "I want you to tell me everything you remember about Cashman's face, but don't try too hard. Just relax and remember him as you would anyone else."

Tim had always been very visual and attentive to detail; he'd trained as an architect before moving into construction. He directed Taveras confidently and expertly, and a likeness of Cashman immediately started to take shape.

"Square off the chin a little . . . not too much," Tim said.

Taveras did as he was told. "Like that?"

"Almost. Can I show you?"

Taveras gave him the pencil, and Tim made a slight adjustment. "That's it, except the cheeks were a little fuller."

Taveras did a little work on the cheeks. As far as Tim was concerned, he was looking at Jeff Cashman. "That's him."

"You sure?" Taveras asked.

"Well, I only met him once, but I don't think you could get a much better likeness. It gives me the creeps all over again."

Taveras sprayed the canvas to prevent it from smearing, and then called Novack, who came right in.

"So, how's it going?" Novack asked.

"We need more witnesses like this guy," Taveras said.

Novack looked at the drawing. "So that's your Jeff Cashman?"

Tim didn't like Novack's use of the word "your." It implied that Cashman was Tim's creation. "That's Jeff Cashman. Can I go home now? Do you need me any more?"

"Are you planning any trips?"

The question, like pretty much everything Novack said, got under Tim's skin. "What if I was?"

"Then I would tell you to change your plans," Novack said.

"Why?"

"Why? Because we just dug a woman out of the ground. She was killed and very probably tortured. And if I decide it'll help me catch the scumbag who did it by talking to you, I don't want to have to go looking for Club Med."

"I'm not planning any trips."

"It's refreshing to meet such a concerned citizen. You're free to go."

Once Tim left, a copy of the Cashman drawing in hand, Novack went into Anders's office to rehash the events of the day. "He killed her," Novack said. "He killed her, and he's rubbing our noses in it."

"Why would he do that?" Anders asked.

"How the hell do I know? Maybe he's a sicko." The truth was that the recent events didn't fit with Novack's view of Wallace, which was not of a serial killer.

"Sicko? That's the technical term?" Anders grabbed his jacket.

"Where are you going?" Novack asked.

"Home. Just in case my girlfriend still lives there." Anders had a girlfriend he mentioned occasionally, but that no one in the department had ever met. "Aren't you going to Cindy's?"

Novack shook his head. "Nah, it's Tuesday."

"So?"

"So lately she doesn't want me to come over on Tuesday."

"Maybe she has an emotionally stable, nondegenerate guy come over on Tuesdays. Just for a change of pace."

Novack shook his head again. "Nah . . . last Tuesday I hid out in the bushes by her house, just to make sure."

TIM made a quick stop home to walk Kiley before heading back out. His destination was the Purple Rose, a place he hadn't planned to frequent again for a very long time. But Tim didn't like where this Cashman situation might be headed, and he certainly didn't trust what Novack would do with it.

It was not a time to sit back and wait.

Danny and Will were at their regular table when he arrived; it would have been a news event if they weren't. But Tim's first stop was the bar, to talk to Frank Lester, a man who always had a smile on his face, no matter how chaotic the place got.

"Hey, Tim, good to see you. We miss you around here."

"Thanks, Frank. I was here New Year's Eve."

"You were? I didn't see you. Wild night, huh?"

"Yeah. I was the one hanging from the chandelier." Tim reached into his jacket for the drawing of Cashman. "Were you here all night?"

Frank nodded. "Until around three in the morning."

Tim put the picture on the bar. "Did you see this guy?"

Frank stared at Cashman's face. "It's possible. He looks a little familiar. But there were so many people here."

"So you don't know who he is?"

Frank shook his head. "No. I don't think so. You want to leave it here and I'll ask some other people?"

"No, that's okay. Thanks."

"Buddy, it's really good to have you back."

Tim nodded his thanks and continued on to the table to see his friends. Their surprise and delight at his arrival was obvious. They made a big show of bringing over another chair for Tim, affording him the best view of the televisions. As shallow males go, it was a poignant and heartfelt gesture of friendship.

"What happened with Novack?" Danny asked.

Tim proceeded to tell them about the trip to Kinnelon and the discovery of Sheila's body.

"No way!" Will said, amazed. "She was where Cashman said she'd be?"

Tim nodded. "Yeah. With a middle finger missing." He took out the picture. "You guys recognize him?"

Neither Danny nor Will did, but both admitted they were drunk that night. "Do they know who this Sheila was?" Will asked.

Tim shrugged. "I don't think so, but Novack's not exactly confiding in me. He doesn't believe a word I say."

"Cops aren't supposed to believe people," Will said.

"I just feel like I owe Sheila more than this," Tim said. "Hey, what about the women you guys were with? Maybe they'll recognize the picture."

"Tim, it was New Year's Eve, remember? Alcohol . . . ?"

"So was I the only sober one in the place that night?"

Will raised his glass. "Soon you'll be the only one tonight."

"I think it's subject-changing time," Danny said. "Did you catch the news today?"

"No. Why?"

"Some guy crashed his car after a police chase down in South Jersey. It exploded and took out windows three blocks away. They think it was Cintron 421, at least a hundred pounds."

"Jeez . . . where was he going?"

"North."

The partners didn't need to verbalize why this was especially meaningful to them. Their job was to construct buildings that could withstand significant explosives, and Cintron 421 was about as significant as you could get without a mushroom cloud.

"Did you find out any of the particulars?"

"Not yet, but I called my uncle. If we're lucky, he'll call back." Senator Collinsworth would certainly get information faster than they would, but he was not exactly quick to respond to requests.

"Let me know what you hear," Tim said.

Danny got up and headed for the bathroom, and Will said, "Hey, Tim, I'm sorry about the other night. We were just trying to get you to have some fun, and—"

"Not your fault, Will. You couldn't have known."

A genius with computers, Will designed the programs for Wallace Industries that governed temperature control and ventilation and alarm systems. While outwardly professing to be rigidly self-ruled by logic, of the three friends he actually possessed the most sensitivity. "Yeah, but now you've got all this crap to deal with. I'm just sorry about it, you know? You of all people shouldn't have the aggravation."

Danny returned, and Tim said his good-byes and went straight home. When he got there, the phone was ringing. "You get it," he said to Kiley. "It's probably Novack."

Kiley was not inclined to answer the phone, so Tim did. "Hello?"

"You told them, Timmy."

The voice was filtered through a computer and therefore not recognizable, but Tim knew what the words meant. "Cashman?"

"I trusted you. It was our secret."

"You murdered her."

"Right. Just like I said. But you shouldn't have told them, Timmy. It was our secret. I'm very disappointed in you."

"I'm sorry. Why don't we meet somewhere to talk about it?"

"Oh, we'll definitely meet again. Pleasant dreams, Timmy."

Click.

"IF CASHMAN lived within two hundred miles of here or Kinnelon, he changed his name," Novack said, as he paced around the office of his boss, Captain Mark Donovan. He and Anders were there to bring Donovan up to date on events so far, and what they had learned about them.

Donovan represented everything that Novack ordinarily would have expected not to like in a cop. The son of former commissioner Stanley Donovan, he was groomed from day one to move to the top of the department. Everyone knew that this precinct captain position was just another check mark on a résumé. What made this surprisingly palatable was that Donovan was open about his political ambitions, and agreeably deferential to cops. He gave respect and in turn received it, even from the normally disrespectful Novack.

"Jeff Cashman doesn't seem like an unusual name," Donovan said.

Novack nodded. "It isn't; there are seventeen of them in the target area, but none are our boy."

"What about the victim?"

Anders provided the information. "Just as dry; if her name really was Sheila Blair, nobody's reported her missing. It's possible that Cashman just made her name up."

"DNA?" asked Donovan.

Anders nodded. "Running it now."

"You want to go public with the sketch?" Novack asked.

Donovan thought about this for a moment. "No, I don't want to let him know we're looking for him yet."

"That's if he exists," said Novack.

"You think Wallace is lying?"

"Damn straight. I think Cashman is Santa Claus and the Tooth Fairy," Novack said. "Look, you're Cashman. You commit a murder months ago, you get away with it, and then you give it up to some stranger in a bar? Does that make sense?"

Donovan noticed that Anders could not conceal a slight grimace. "You don't agree?"

Anders shook his head. "I look at it a different way. You're Wallace. You commit a murder, get away with it, and go to the police with a made-up story about some guy confessing in a bar? That make any more sense?"

"Maybe Wallace felt guilty, had to let somebody know where she was," Novack said. "So he makes up this story."

"The same could be true of Cashman," Anders said. "But if I'm Wallace, I know you've been after me for months. I make an anonymous phone call."

"Not if Wallace wanted to mess with my mind," Novack said.

"Come on, you're the one who's obsessed here. Not him," Anders said.

Despite his respect for Novack's instincts, Donovan had known for a long time that Novack was overboard in his unrelenting focus on Wallace. Nevertheless, he decided to jump in for the moment on Novack's side. "The flyer is a significant piece here."

Novack nodded vigorously. "That's right; the only flyer gets posted outside Wallace's apartment. And only Wallace's prints are on it. And we can't even find anybody who's ever heard of Sheila, so who printed it? The state police know nothing about her. Wallace printed and hung the damn thing himself."

"Maybe Cashman did it, but he's setting up Wallace," Anders said. "Maybe he has a grudge against him."

"Did you go to the police academy?" Novack asked. "Or did you just see the movie?"

Before Anders could respond, Donovan's intercom buzzed, and he answered it. He listened for a moment and then hung up. "Wallace is here to see you," he said, to Novack.

Anders was surprised. "He's here again?"

"Sicko." Novack stood up and grinned.

Tim was waiting in Novack's office when he and Anders got back. "Well, good morning. Glad you stopped by," Novack said.

Tim was not in the mood for chitchat, particularly when it was of the insincere variety. "I'm in a hurry to get to work, but there's something I had to tell you."

"You want some coffee?" Anders asked.

"No. He called me."

"Who called you?" Novack asked.

"Cashman. His voice was filtered through a computer, but it had to be him. He knew that I told you about him, and about Sheila."

"How did he know that?" Anders asked.

"He didn't say, but he was angry. He said he was disappointed in me, that we'd meet again, and to have pleasant dreams."

"The animal," Novack said, shaking his head in mock horror.

Tim was immediately annoyed. "Hey, this isn't funny, you know? We're talking about a murderer here."

"That's for sure. We're definitely talking about a murderer."

It was a veiled reference to Novack's suspicions of Tim, and it did not escape him. "You think I'm making this up? Maybe you think I killed Sheila?"

Novack was not about to back down. "I'm still working on what I think, so for now I'll just tell you what I know. I know you've been involved with the violent death of two women in less than a year."

As always, the reference to Maggie's death in a criminal light angered Tim, and he started to object, but Novack cut him off.

"Two in one year; that's pretty unusual. You can go on the street and check out a thousand people . . . fifty thousand . . . and none of them will have that track record. Two murder cases is a lot."

"My wife's death was not a 'case.' It was an accident."

"Yeah, well . . ." Novack had a slight smile on his face.

"Check his notes," Tim said to Anders. "I answered every stupid question he had ten times hooked up to a lie detector. Look, am I being held here? I have work to do; can I leave?"

"This time you can leave," Novack said.

Tim stood up and went to the door. "There's a maniac out there. He kills women and cuts off their fingers. I don't know why he drew me into this, but you might stop wasting time and find out."

TIM'S NEXT FEW DAYS WERE "Cashman-free," which is to say that he heard nothing from either Cashman or Novack and was able to mostly block it from his mind as he went about his business.

Tim usually spent the bulk of his time in his office, leaving Danny to supervise most of the work at the Federal Center site, but lately they were in crunch time, with the center scheduled to be opened in just four weeks with a gala reception. It would be rather embarrassing if everyone showed up and the building had no roof.

As it came together, the Federal Center was an immensely impressive project, a crowning achievement for Senator Collinsworth, bringing in a huge amount of money and jobs to the state. Tim and Danny's company had a big stake in that success, and if things went according to plan and budget, they could expect a substantial amount of work when the complexes went national.

The car explosion in South Jersey had no direct effect on Tim's work, but it had a psychological effect on anyone involved with combating terror. After two days, it had succumbed to the ever-changing news cycles and the lack of new information, so the media moved on. But for people in the know, it was scary as hell.

Federal authorities had identified Ricardo Vasquez as the ill-fated driver of the car but had so far failed to connect him to any terrorist cells. If the media reports were to be believed, they also had no idea where he got the explosives, where he was taking them, or what triggered the detonation. This lack of knowledge sent spasms throughout the security industry.

The truth was that the Federal Center buildings under construction could conceivably handle the amount of explosives Vasquez was transporting. The construction mandate was to build a structure that could withstand a powerful explosion from outside, perhaps in a car bomb, with relatively minor damage. If the blast was to take place inside the building, then the essential task was to contain it and prevent it from bringing the building down.

Probably the center's most unique security feature was its "lockdown" ability. If there was a perceived danger from outside, the capability existed of encasing the building openings with movable steel doors and reinforcements, creating a virtually impregnable barrier to protect the people inside.

Tim was on site because a number of decisions had to be made quickly, but Danny had far more knowledge of the nuts and bolts of construction. Tim saw the big picture, but Danny knew how to build it.

Danny was in a meeting, so Tim went into the computer room, where he knew Will would be working. Tim hadn't been there since it was finished, and it was a truly extraordinary place. Two entire walls were covered with computer equipment and monitors. Will was hunched over a keyboard as the machines were responding to his commands.

"Damn . . . it looks like you could control the world from here."

Will looked over and smiled. "Probably. But right now I'd rather be out in the world and let somebody else do the controlling."

"Having a rough time?"

Will shrugged. "Just the usual. It'll be ready."

"Can I help?" asked Tim, a question they both knew to be ridiculous, since Tim barely had the technical expertise to master e-mail.

Will smiled. "I'll call you if I need you."

As Tim was getting ready to leave the site, he saw that Danny was out of his meeting. "Are you sure you need me here tomorrow?" he asked. "There's plenty for me to do at the office, and you've got things under control."

"Damn straight I need you," Danny said. "Without you, I'd have to bring the doughnuts."

Once Tim got in the car, Meredith called to say that Eden Alexander had called and wanted to take him and Kiley to dinner.

"You have her number?" Tim asked.

Meredith gave it to him. "And who might she be?"

"I didn't tell you? I got married yesterday during lunch."

"Are you going to have dinner with her?" Meredith asked.

"Bye, Meredith. Take the rest of the day off."

Tim would have expected to be dismissive of the idea of having dinner with Eden, but instead his reaction was somewhat unsure.

He called her, and she sounded surprised to hear from him. "I didn't think your assistant would give you the message."

"Meredith? Why?"

"Have you noticed she's rather protective of you? She was pumping me for so much information. . . ."

He laughed. "Sorry. She considers me rather helpless out in the real world."

Eden suggested that they go to a local restaurant called the Firepit, since it allowed dogs. The idea held some appeal for Tim, but he hesitated.

Eden picked up on it. "Tim, relax. I'm not inviting you to a weekend in the Poconos in a heart-shaped tub. It's not even a date."

"It's not that. I—"

"I'll tell you what; we can be at different tables, with a wall between us," she said. "And you can sit in a soundproof booth."

"That might work," he said.

"I just thought it would be nice, for us and for the dogs, and I wanted to hear where things stand with the police and that poor woman in Kinnelon."

"Sounds good," Tim said, surprised to hear the words come out of his mouth. "Meet you there in an hour?"

"Great," she said, and hung up.

Eden and Travis were waiting for Tim and Kiley when they arrived, and Eden had already secured two water dishes.

"Sorry we're late," Tim said. Kiley offered no such apologies. "Did I miss anything?"

"Not so far."

Tim ordered a burger, while Eden opted for a vegetable plate, and they both had a beer. They also ordered steamed asparagus for the two dogs, Kiley's all-time favorite.

Once they were settled in, Tim recounted the phone call from Cashman, as well as his encounters with Novack.

"What is his problem?" Eden asked. "Would he rather people didn't report these things?"

"He thinks I killed Maggie," Tim blurted out.

"That's outrageous," she said. "How can that be?"

"He always has. This just confirms it for him: I'm sure he thinks I killed Sheila as well. Tim Wallace, serial killer."

"So what are you doing about it?" It was a demand; she expected him to come out fighting.

"There's nothing I can do. He couldn't find any evidence before, and there's nothing to find now. The only consolation is that it drives him crazy."

"You think only guilty people get charged with crimes?"

"I don't really think about it much at all."

"You're in denial," she said.

He smiled. "I won't deny that."

"Tim, I think you should get yourself a lawyer."

"You think Novack is more dangerous to me than Cashman?"

"Probably, but maybe you should get a bodyguard, too."

"You know a lawyer?" Tim had only dealt with corporate types; he couldn't picture them in a room with Novack.

"As a matter of fact, I do. My brother is a criminal attorney. Nick Alexander."

"Nick Alexander is your brother? The guy who defended Billy Scarborough?" Scarborough was the CEO of an energy trading company charged in fraud scandals with what seemed like a thousand counts of fiscal crimes. Alexander got him acquitted of every single count.

"That's him. He's had some big cases. He's on television all the time and can attract attention to how unfairly you're being treated."

"The last thing I want is media attention." Tim let it stand at that, without mentioning the danger such attention could cause to his business. Someone receiving government money to protect the country from murderous terrorists does not want to be portrayed in the media as a potential serial killer.

Tim decided this was a good subject to change. "So what do you do for a living?"

She laughed. "You have a driving curiosity about me?"

"What do you mean?"

"I mean we were talking about something that made you uncomfortable, and all of a sudden you asked the first question about me that you've ever asked."

He nodded. "Guilty as charged. I'm afraid I've been a little self-centered this decade. But I really want to know what you do."

"I'm a professor of art history at Montclair State."

"Really?" he asked. "So am I. I'm surprised we haven't run into each other on campus."

They lingered after coffee for more than an hour, talking normal, non-Cashman talk, and decided to leave only when Kiley and Travis were getting bored. "I enjoyed this. Thank you," Tim said.

"So I was right not to tell you about my biological clock?"

"You didn't have to. I heard it ticking."

NOVACK could feel the frustration setting in already. So far everything was coming up empty, much as it had when Tim Wallace killed his wife. Novack felt like he was running in place, a hamster in a cage designed by a murderer who was toying with him.

Cashman was nowhere to be found, but that was to be expected. As far as Novack was concerned, Cashman didn't exist. He was created by Tim as part of the game, a game he consistently left Novack no opportunity to win. The fact that Tim was playing this game at all came as a surprise to Novack and represented a misjudgment on his part. He had Tim pegged as a garden-variety wife killer; this elevated him to a higher plane of evil.

"Are you okay?" Cindy looked at him sitting at the kitchen table. She was preparing his favorite dish, chicken parmigiana.

He didn't answer, since he was in something of a trance, lost in his own thoughts. It's why she asked the question in the first place. "Earth to John, come in, please."

"What? I'm sorry . . . what?"

"Are you all right? You seem tense and distracted."

"Why do you say that?"

"Well, for starters, you're grinding your teeth and your hands are curled into fists."

He looked at his fists. "It's just something at work."

"You're kidding!" Cindy exclaimed in mock surprise. "I thought you were upset that the ballet left town."

"Wallace killed another woman. He's rubbing my nose in it."

Her instinct was to walk over and put her arms around him. She didn't do it because she knew he hated to be touched when he was upset. It was one of the hundred thousand ways they were different. "Who did he kill?" she asked.

"We haven't even been able to identify her. But Wallace led us to the body." Novack told her about Cashman and the alleged conversation on New Year's Eve.

"It couldn't have happened that way?" she asked. He just stared at her, and she smiled. "You'll get him this time."

He thought about it. "Hey, want to go get something to eat?"

She smiled. "John, I've been making dinner, in the kitchen where you're currently sitting, for the last half hour."

"I knew that," he lied. "It smells delicious."

6

RICARDO Vasquez was completely unaware of just how significant he had become. That lack of awareness was understandable, since his body had been reduced to a cream sauce spread all over South Jersey. But the truth was that he had become a hell of a lot more important in death than in life.

FBI Special Agent Carl White, assigned to Homeland Security, was in charge of finding out all there was to know about Vasquez. It was an assignment for which he was uniquely qualified, having worked undercover with Miami PD before joining the bureau. He knew the area Vasquez was from; he could get whatever information was to be found. Smart, instinctive, and comparatively fearless, he had worked his way up in the department. Advancement for African-Americans was a Miami PD goal, but Carl saw the FBI as the place to make a difference and get national notice.

Homeland Security was in a panic over the explosion, and they were right to feel that way. Vasquez was not carrying garden-variety explosives; this was stuff that the U.S. military used in Afghanistan. No one knew where Ricardo was headed with his cargo, but there is no Afghanistan exit on the New Jersey Turnpike.

Carl was promised whatever manpower he needed, and was assigned four agents. They spent the four days after the explosion turning Ricardo Vasquez's life upside down.

They came up empty.

Ricardo was simply a small-time punk, with plenty of connections to other punks, but none to terrorists. There seemed to be no chance that Ricardo could have been a strategist in any plot; he just wasn't bright enough. And any terrorist that would have entrusted Ricardo to transport such a valuable and important cargo couldn't have been very smart either.

But he had had the explosives, and he was taking them somewhere. Those are facts that could not be challenged, yet Carl had absolutely no explanation for them.

That, he knew all too well, was a recipe for disaster.

DIFFERENT people relax in different ways, and the best way for Tim was to play racquetball. It required energy and concentration, and enabled Tim's competitive nature to kick into high gear. Which meant at least a brief vacation from unwanted thoughts.

He and Danny had a regular game every Saturday morning. Danny was nearly as good as Tim, and the matches were almost always close. They played at the Englewood Racquet Club and kept a standing eight o'clock reservation for court four.

This was the first time they had played since Cashman entered Tim's life, and he made a conscious effort to go all out. After one particularly grueling point, Danny stopped playing and started laughing. "Did we bet on the game, and you forgot to tell me?"

"What do you mean? What's the matter?" Tim asked.

"You're like a maniac today. Relax, or you'll have a heart attack. You're an old man."

"I'm a week older than you," Tim said, which they both knew was true. "Although this has been a long week."

Their normal routine was to play the best of three games. This time Tim won the first two in record time. "You want to play another one?" he said.

"You haven't humiliated me enough?"

"Not even close."

Danny pointed his racket at him. "You just made a big mistake, pal. You ticked me off."

Danny played the next game with considerably more intensity, losing by a closer score. "One more?" Tim asked.

Out of breath, drenched in sweat, Danny said, "No más."

They turned to leave, when Tim noticed something in the clear fiberglass compartment recessed in the back wall. It was where players usually put their jewelry, money, or other valuables while they played. Tim and Danny never used it, because they changed and kept their things in the locker room. "What's that?" Tim asked.

"What?"

Tim pointed. "Something's in there. Like a jewelry box."

They both walked toward it, and Danny opened the door. The box had a Tiffany insignia. "You planning on proposing to me? You buy me a ring?"

"See if there's anything in it," Tim said.

Danny opened the box. His puzzled expression was followed by a look of pure shock. Suddenly he started to scream.

"What the . . ." Tim started to say but stopped as the box dropped to the floor and its contents fell out. It was not a ring, but a ring could have fit on it.

It was a severed human finger.

Within ten seconds, at least half the people in the club had come running to see what could have prompted Danny's awful scream. As each person saw the finger, the screams became a chorus, which brought the latecomers over. By the time the police arrived and cordoned off the court, at least thirty people had entered the area, though nobody touched the finger or the box. Tim and Danny were brought back to the manager's office.

Stan Mullins, a detective with the Englewood police, came in to question Tim and Danny. Aware of how this was going to play out, Tim asked, "How about if we wait until Novack gets here?"

"Who's Novack?" Mullins asked.

"He's with the state police. He'll be taking over this case."

Mullins's annoyance was obvious. "Nobody is taking this case from me," he said, and then turned to Danny. "We'll start with you. Tell me exactly what happened. From the beginning."

A shaken Danny said, "Well, we finished our game, and—"

He was interrupted by Mullins's cell phone ringing, which he answered. "Mullins." After a pause, he said, "That's bull. You . . . yeah. But it's still bull."

Mullins hung up and without another word walked toward the door. "I'll give Novack your regards," Tim said.

It was twenty minutes before Novack and Anders arrived, and another two hours before Tim and Danny were allowed to leave. They were separated for the questioning, and Tim was surprised that Novack left Anders to deal with him. Anders kept forcing him to repeat the story over and over, but even at that, Tim finished first and waited in the office for Danny to be brought back.

Once they were together, Danny started to relate what had happened in his session with Novack, but a glance from Tim told him to wait until they were alone, and he picked up on it.

As soon as they got in the car, Danny said, "Tim, Novack is trying to pin it on you."

Tim nodded, not at all surprised to hear that. "What did he say?"

"All he wanted to know was stuff like, were you ever alone on the court, did you carry anything in that could have concealed the jewelry box. He was hoping I'd nail you."

"You didn't have to. Cashman is doing it for him."

"Tim, this is moving way past weird. You think Cashman followed you to the bar that night? Or were you just in the wrong place at the wrong time?"

"He came after me; he knows too much about me to have put this all together on the fly. He may even have killed Sheila for no other reason than to pin it on me."

"You can't just sit back and let this happen to you."

Tim had come to that conclusion the moment he saw the finger on the court. "I'm going to get a lawyer."

Danny was quiet for a moment. "Hey, I think that's a good idea, but be careful. We don't need publicity about this."

"I know."

"I mean, my uncle is way out there on a limb for us, but he'll saw it off if he has to. You remember last time."

Senator Collinsworth had been upset at the public suspicion of Tim following Maggie's death. Danny had calmed him down, and Tim's subsequent exoneration defused the situation, but it was a close call. "I'm not hiring a press agent, Danny. I'm hiring a lawyer."

Danny pulled into the driveway in front of Tim's apartment. "You know anybody that handles that kind of stuff?"

Tim was surprised to see Eden, standing in front of the building. He pointed to her. "No, but she does."

"Who the hell is she? You got a life you're keeping from me?"

Tim didn't answer, just got out of the car and went over to Eden. "What are you doing here?"

"I heard about what happened at the racquetball club. It's the top story on the news."

"With my name attached?" Tim asked, cringing.

"No, but when I heard about the . . . finger . . . it wasn't hard to make the connection."

He nodded. "Come on up."

When they got upstairs, Tim briefly told Eden what had happened. "I need you to call your brother for me, if you feel comfortable with that," he said.

She nodded, went directly to the phone, and within two minutes had an appointment set up for Tim at ten Monday morning. Then she wrote out the name of the firm and address and gave it to him.

Tim was surprised when he looked at the paper. "He works for Hammond, Simmons, and Carcher?" It was one of New Jersey's largest and most prestigious firms.

"Yes, they brought him in to start a criminal law division last year, but it may not be the greatest fit."

"Why not?"

"You'll understand when you meet him."

WHEN Anders came into Novack's office, he had that look on his face. Novack had no trouble recognizing it; it said that Anders had something important, positive or negative, to tell him.

"Tell me something good," Novack said.

"Something good?"

"Yes, as in the exact opposite of bad."

Anders smiled. "We got a DNA hit. We ID'd Sheila."

It was all Novack could do not to jump out of his chair. "Who was she?"

Anders opened a folder. "Her name was Carol Blair, middle name Sheila. She lived in Carson, Wyoming, but would go away for months at a time. That's why nobody considered her missing."

"Why was she in the DNA registry?" A person's DNA is on file almost always as a result of criminal activity.

"She had an armed robbery conviction, part of a husband-and-wife team that held up a bank. 'Armed' is probably understating the case. He had a bomb he threatened to detonate if they didn't cough up the cash. She was waiting in the car. Local cops made the collar three days later."

"So she served time?" Novack asked.

"No." Anders flipped through papers. "Just probation. She and Roger Blair copped a plea. Eight months ago, she walked, and he got three years."

"That's all? For robbing and threatening to blow up a bank?"

"Looks like it. Not exactly frontier justice, huh?"

"So the husband is still inside?"

"He had his throat slit a couple of months after he went in."

Novack smiled. "Saddle up, pardner. We're heading out west."

"You think Donovan will spring for two plane trips?" Captain Donovan was notoriously cheap. "Sheila was from Wyoming and killed in Kinnelon. We're not swimming in jurisdiction here."

"When I get finished, he'll throw in tickets to the rodeo."

While Novack went off to talk to Donovan, Anders called Keith Rivers, Senator Collinsworth's right-hand man, to tell him about this new development in Wyoming.

Collinsworth and Rivers had tentacles that reached everywhere, and they'd had no trouble getting to Anders, offering him substantial considerations for information about the investigation. Anders had hesitated but finally came to the rationalization that much of the information would be harmless, and that he would judge it on a case-by-case basis.

The Wyoming information was an easy call to make, and he had no hesitation in contacting Rivers and sharing it. He accomplished that before Novack came back with the news that Donovan had approved the trip. They were going to Wyoming.

HAMMOND, Simmons, and Carcher had their own four-story building off Route 17 in Ridgewood, a dazzling mixture of glass and chrome. Tim had seen less sterile hospital operating rooms. But the overall effect was one of modern wealth and confidence, no doubt exactly what they were trying to project.

The receptionist in the lobby looked like she came with the building, perfectly put together and a model of efficiency. She juggled four calls while Tim was at her desk, yet within three minutes she had ushered him into Nick Alexander's office.

It was hard to believe Nick's office was in the same building. It was a mess, papers strewn everywhere, sports memorabilia hanging at awkward angles on the wall, soda cans and Popsicle sticks on the tables. With all the reflections from the chrome and mirrors, the room felt like a carnival maze constructed out of trash.

Nick was in sneakers and jeans, with a pullover shirt half tucked into his pants. "Hey, come on in," he said after they shook hands. "Just move that stuff off the chair."

"Okay . . ." Tim said hesitantly. "Thanks for seeing me on such short notice."

"No problem, any friend of Eden's . . . hey, want something to drink? Diet Pepsi, Yoo-Hoo?" He reached in his pocket and took out something grayish. "Maybe a mint?"

"No, thanks."

"It's hot in here, huh? They turn the heat up so high, and you can't open the windows. You believe that?"

Tim nodded. "A lot of buildings, you—"

"I know; it drives me crazy. My old office, I had the windows open all the time. You could smell the food from the Chinese restaurant at ten in the morning. You remember the *Honeymooners* episode where Norton could tell the time based on when the egg foo yong smell reached his window?"

"No, I'm afraid I don't."

He looked surprised. "Really? It was a TV classic."

"I'll have to check it out. So, I'm here because—"

Nick finished the sentence for him. "The police, most notably Detective Novack, think you murdered two people." He twisted the top off a bottle of Yoo-Hoo and handed it to Tim.

"How did you know that?" Tim asked. "Did Eden tell you?"

"No. I asked around a bit. Believe me, it's not a major secret."

"With all due respect, I haven't hired you yet."

Nick smiled. "With just as much respect, I haven't accepted you as a client yet. You can be sure I didn't reveal to anyone that I had a professional interest in this case. In fact, at this point I don't."

Tim nodded. "Sorry."

"No problem. Tell me your story, leaving nothing out."

Tim spent the next half hour doing just that, and Nick's occasional probing questions brought out more detail and fresh perspective. It didn't take Tim long to realize that Nick was a lot smarter than his first impression had led him to believe. In previous recountings, Tim's dominant emotions were frustration and anxiety; this time he felt a growing anger at what was happening to him. By the time he finished, he knew he was in desperate need of help.

"Now tell me about your wife," Nick said.

"What about her? She has nothing to do with this."

Nick shook his head. "Of course she does. Her death is the reason Novack is after you. And Novack is the guy I'd be defending you against, so I have to know what he thinks he knows."

"Of course. It just bugs the hell out of me when people talk about Maggie's death as if it were a murder case." Tim related the events of that awful day as best he could remember, as well as his dealings with Novack. "After a lie detector test, I never heard from them again. The talking heads in the media stopped jabbering as well."

Nick laughed. "I was one of those talking heads; somehow I've gotten on the list of defense attorneys they call."

"I never watched the coverage. What did you say?"

"I don't remember; I knew absolutely nothing about it. That never gets in the way; I just jabber about the presumption of innocence and holes in the prosecution's case. Have you told me everything?"

"I think so. But I have a question." Tim pointed toward the rest of the offices. "You just don't seem to fit in this place."

Nick grinned. "About eight months ago, the geniuses here decided they wanted to get into criminal law, maybe because most of their corporate clients are crooks. They went out to hire the best, threw a ton of money at me, and gave me autonomy."

Tim laughed. "Obviously, you're exempt from the dress code."

"Hey, I dress up pretty nice when I have to go to court. Which is one place we don't want you to wind up."

"So you'll take the case?"

Nick thought a few moments. "I'll draw up an agreement; among other things, it will detail the fee structure. You have money? Somebody's got to pay for this chrome."

"It's not a problem."

"Okay. If you sign the document, I'm your lawyer."

"You're my lawyer," Tim said.

Nick raised his bottle of Yoo-Hoo in a toast. "Cheers."

7

CARSON, Wyoming, was everything that Anders and Novack expected, and less. Forty-five hundred citizens were spread out over an area probably as large as Manhattan, and the closest thing to a high-rise was a tree house some kids had built. Basically, half the residents were involved in farming, while half worked twenty miles away at the prison at Lampley, putting Carson's economy simultaneously at the mercy of the weather and the state crime rate.

The two detectives arrived at four in the afternoon. The outside temperature gauge on their rental car showed eight degrees, which felt generous. Carson, Wyoming, made New Jersey feel like Guatemala. Their hotel, a dive out near the highway, had fourteen tractor trailers in the unpaved parking lot.

They dropped their bags in their tiny room and left, arriving promptly at five o'clock at the police station, a two-room building that had them longing for the spacious luxury of the hotel. The entire police force was there, consisting of a receptionist, a deputy, and the chief himself, Matthew Drew.

If Novack and Anders were expecting Andy Taylor and Barney Fife, they were in for a surprise. Chief Drew was an experienced police officer, having spent eleven years in Reno PD. "This is a nice, quiet place to live," he said after the hellos. "I guess you guys have come to change that?"

Novack smiled. "Nah . . . we're just working the job. One of the perks is to visit nice, quiet places."

Novack had sent information ahead for Drew to review, including the sketch of Cashman. "I showed the sketch around," Drew said. "Nobody here has ever seen that guy."

"What can you tell us about the victim?" Novack asked.

"Born and raised here; a little wild by our standards but no real problems. She left to go to L.A. and be a cocktail waitress when she was nineteen."

"When did she come back?" Anders asked.

"About two years ago. She brought a boyfriend with her."

"Roger Blair?"

Drew nodded. "Right. They lived in a trailer, about five miles out, kept to themselves. He was a mechanic but made most of his money blowing stuff up."

"What does that mean?"

"He was an explosives expert; learned it in the army. The guy was amazing; give him a glass of water and a tube of hair gel, and he could incinerate South Dakota."

"He made that into a business?" Novack asked.

"You'd be surprised how much use there is for explosives. Irrigation, clearing land, demolishing unwanted structures. He seemed to do okay for himself."

"What did she do?"

"She was like his assistant. It was like he was a chef and she brought him the ingredients."

"How come he and his wife got off so easy? What the hell is armed robbery out here, a misdemeanor?" Novack asked.

Drew shrugged. "Yeah, I was surprised at that myself. Judge said it was a first offense; nobody got hurt. He may have been pressured, but I don't have a clue where it came from."

"What did the wife do when Blair went inside?"

Drew shook his head. "I don't know, but whatever it was, she wasn't doing it here. Far as I know, nobody had seen her since."

They spent the better part of another hour asking Drew questions, but got no closer to Sheila's killer. "Do you know the warden at Lampley?" Novack asked.

"Sure. Name's Luther Marshall. I know him real well."

"Any chance you could get him to meet with us?"

Drew called out to his receptionist. "Hey, Bryna, they want to know if I could get Luther to meet with them."

She laughed. "That depends. You guys like beer?"

"On occasion," Novack said.

"Luther and I are having a few tonight," Drew said. "If you bring your big-city wallets, you can come along."

DANNY'S drive to Montclair took about forty-five minutes, but if he had his preference, it would have been forty-five days. He had been summoned to meet with his uncle, back for a few weeks while the Senate was on recess.

The invitation came in the form of a phone call from the senator's chief of staff, Keith Rivers. That in itself was fairly ominous. When Collinsworth had good news to share, he picked up the phone himself. And that the invitation was for a drink, not dinner, was another danger sign. This was going to be quick.

The senator always referred to his home as "the estate." The house included a screening room, tennis court, swimming pool, and a pair of bowling alleys. His third wife wasn't in town, but when Danny was brought into Collinsworth's spacious study, he wasn't surprised to see Rivers standing unobtrusively off to the side.

Danny started with, "Uncle Fred, it's great to see you."

Collinsworth was sitting behind his desk. He spent a great deal of time there, though Danny had never seen so much as a piece of paper on that desk. He was sipping from a glass of chardonnay, as he seemed to do twenty-four hours a day. Watching him speak on the Senate floor on C-Span, Danny assumed it was hidden behind the lectern. The senator seemed undressed without it.

"Danny, my boy, this is nice . . . communicating like this."

"I always enjoy talking with you, Uncle Fred."

"That's good, because I'm easy to chat with, aren't I?"

Danny nodded. "Very easy."

"Then why the hell didn't you mention that the police are after your psycho partner for another murder?"

"He didn't do it. He—"

"Oh, so you figured I'd only care if he actually got convicted? You were waiting for the jury to come in before telling me?"

"I'm sorry, but this time it's really ridiculous. There was a murder, but he knows who did it. The guy confessed to him," Danny said.

The senator waved this off. "I heard the whole story. The police don't believe it, and I don't blame them."

"Uncle Fred, I swear, they don't have anything on Tim, because there's nothing to have," Danny said. This was going to be painful; the senator was said to be pondering a run for the White House, and anything that stood even a remote chance of derailing him was going to be dealt with severely.

Collinsworth shook his head sadly and turned to Rivers. "I wish I didn't have a weakness for family." Then, to Danny, "Did you know they identified the victim?"

Danny's silence indicated that he didn't.

Collinsworth decided to reveal an important piece of information in order to scare Danny, but of course without revealing that Anders was his source. "Did you know that Novack and his partner are out in Carson, Wyoming, right now, following up on it? Does that sound like cops who are floundering around?"

"I swear, this will blow over. I know Tim as well as I know myself; there's no way he could kill anyone."

"Let me tell you something. Right now he's in the process of killing your career."

THEY shouldn't have agreed to buy the beer. That's the first thing that went through Novack's mind when he and Anders met Warden Luther Marshall. They were at a bar/restaurant called the Big Barn, one enormous room, with wood-burning stoves strategically positioned to warm patrons.

Luther was sitting with Drew, and there were already four empty beer bottles on the table. When he stood up to shake hands, it seemed to take twenty minutes to unfold his entire six-foot-eight, 290-pound frame. It was unlikely, thought Novack, that there needed to be guards working at Luther's prison. No prisoner would dare piss Luther off by trying to escape.

But Luther proved to be an affable sort, and he and Drew were good guys to drink with, so much so that by the time they got around to why the East Coast detectives were there, Luther had enough beer in him to flood an average-sized basement.

In fact, it was Luther himself who finally brought it up. "So I hear you guys want to know something about Roger Blair?"

Novack nodded. "Whatever you can tell us."

Luther shrugged. "I can't tell you much; he pretty much stayed to himself while he was inside."

"Did his wife come to visit him?" Anders asked.

"A couple of times early on. After that, nobody came."

"What about phone calls? In or out."

"Hard to know. Nothing on the prison phone, but they get cell phones in there, so there's no sure way to keep track."

"Any idea why he was killed? Or who killed him?"

"No, but it was a contract job, for sure. Chances are the guy who did it didn't even know who was paying him."

Anders took out Cashman's picture. "You ever see this guy?"

Luther looked at it intently. "No . . . don't think so."

Novack took Tim's picture out of a folder. "What about him?"

Luther looked and said, "No, can't say as I have."

Novack had started putting Tim's photo back in the folder when Drew grabbed it and put it back on the table. "I know that guy."

"How?" a stunned Novack asked.

"He was here in Carson. Last year."

Novack looked at Anders and smiled. "Small world, huh?"

As SOON as Danny told him the news, Tim called Nick Alexander. "I think we have a problem. Novack is out in Wyoming. That's where the victim is from."

"What's her name?" Nick asked.

"I don't know. All I know is that she's from Carson."

"How did you find this out?"

Tim hesitated. "I'd rather not say."

"I probably should have explained this more clearly. It doesn't matter what you would rather say or not say. What's important is that you tell me everything, or this is not going to work. Once I hear it, I'm the one who can't talk about it, or I'd be violating my oath of confidentiality."

"Okay. My partner Danny's uncle is Senator Collinsworth. He told Danny about it, and Danny told me."

"How did Collinsworth get the information?"

"I don't know," Tim said. "But he has ways of finding out pretty much everything."

"Why was he interested?"

"He's been helpful in getting our company some major work on the Federal Center in Newark. If it turned out he was getting the work for a murderer, that wouldn't look great for him. Especially if he runs for president."

"Okay, let's back up for a minute. You said Novack's being in Wyoming was a problem. Why do you see it that way?"

"Carson is a small town. I was there last year. This just seems like another one of those things that can't be a coincidence."

"What were you doing there?"

"There's a quarry about twenty minutes outside of town. We had gotten word that competitors were getting quality materials there. We're in a very competitive business, so we have to check these things out. But there was nothing special about the stone or the price. And then my car was vandalized; I was stuck there for a day while it was being fixed."

"So people in the town would remember you?"

"Somebody might. I filed a police report. Hell, this is unbelievable. Why are they doing this to me?"

Nick was wondering the same thing. He spent another ten minutes questioning Tim about whether anything unusual happened in Carson.

"Not that I remember," Tim said. "I mostly stayed in the hotel, and when the car was ready, I was out of there. As far as I know, they never caught whoever vandalized it."

"And you don't remember seeing anyone there who looked like the woman on the flyer?"

Tim racked his memory. "I don't think so."

"Think some more. Write down everything you did, who you spoke to. Every detail."

"Okay. You think we should be worried about this?"

"Generally the best approach is to worry about everything."

NOVACK and Anders were back in Chief Drew's office at nine a.m. to question Bryna Keller, Drew's receptionist.

"Let me guess," she said when she arrived at nine-fifteen, and noticed Drew, Anders, and Novack staring at her. "None of you could figure out how to make coffee."

"That's true," Drew said. "But it can wait. These gentlemen need to talk to you."

"What about?"

Anders handed her the picture of Tim. "Him."

She looked at the picture with no sign of recognition. "Who is he?" Then she suddenly brightened. "Wait a minute. . . . That guy was here last year."

Novack was delighted. "Why was he here?" he asked.

"I'm not sure. He was on some kind of a business trip. He came in here because his car broke down, and Roger said something was poured in the gas tank. . . ."

"Roger Blair?" asked Novack.

Bryna looked surprised. "Right, the mechanic. It was before he went to jail. You knew him?"

Novack shook his head. "That isn't what's important. What's important is whether Wallace knew him."

"Well, he serviced his car."

"You can definitely place them together? In the same room?"

"Yes. In fact, it was this very room."

"WE'VE got enough, Captain. More than enough." Novack and Anders had gone directly from the airport to the precinct to meet with Donovan. Novack was hoping for a positive reaction to his request to arrest Tim, but wasn't getting it.

"You've got logic," said Donovan. "You have Wallace's story about

Cashman, his knowing where Sheila was buried, his showing up with the flyer, his having been in Carson. But there's no evidence."

"What about the finger?" Novack said.

"You got anybody that saw him plant it?"

"Come on, if it walks and quacks like a duck, it's a duck."

"But you've got to prove it's a duck, beyond a reasonable doubt. And there's no way McDermott would think you're there." Donovan was talking about the district attorney, who would make the ultimate decision whether to bring the case to trial. Lee McDermott was widely scorned by the police for his refusal to take anything but sure things before a judge, but his caution helped remove the chance that Donovan would approve a very public arrest that went nowhere.

"He's killed two women, Captain. When he kills a third, you gonna tell the victim's family that McDermott would have given you a hard time?"

"Don't hand me that crap, Novack." Donovan turned to Anders, who had been largely silent. "What do you think?"

"I think we need to get him off the street. Things are starting to break our way, and as the pressure mounts on him, I don't want to give him a chance to do something stupid."

Donovan was surprised at Anders's about-face. He thought that Anders still disagreed with Novack's certainty of Tim's guilt. That caused him to pause and briefly reconsider his decision, but there was still no upside to be found in moving precipitously.

"No, not yet. But we're close. Get me something else."

Novack was not about to let it drop. "Something else? Wallace gave us the body; then he gave us the missing finger. If you find a head in my freezer, you can arrest me."

"Arresting you is something I would look forward to," Donovan said. "Now get out of here and nail the bastard."

THE New Jersey state crime lab was state-of-the-art, and it owed a good deal of its fine reputation to Dr. Robin Miller, who ran the DNA department. New Jersey law enforcement liked to use the state lab as much as possible, rather than relying on the FBI, and for that reason Dr. Miller and her staff were constantly overloaded.

Dr. Miller showed no interest in the particulars of the cases and ran her tests without any prejudice, like a good scientist should. Her job was simply to determine the facts. Her administrative assistant, Stephen Cowlings, was left to prioritize the samples and deal with the law enforcement agencies eagerly waiting for results.

Cowlings was, in fact, the main reason the finger found at the racquetball court was tested before samples that had come in earlier. Novack's people had put in an urgent request, but Cowlings had another reason for rushing this.

Dr. Miller had determined the type of preservative used to keep the finger in such pristine shape. She then achieved a DNA type, which was run through the computers to see if a match could be made with samples in the database. If no match was found, the larger FBI database could take up to three weeks.

The results would come to Dr. Miller's office, but Cowlings would read them and know who needed the information first.

Somebody who would pay for it.

"WE NEED to talk. Immediately."

Nick Alexander's words sent waves of panic through Tim's gut. This could not be good news. "What's the matter?"

"Not over the phone."

"You want to come here, to my office?"

"Where do you live?" Nick asked, and when Tim told him, he said, "I'll meet you at your apartment in twenty minutes."

Tim left the office hastily as Meredith came into the hallway.

"Tim? Are you all right?" she asked.

"I'm fine. Something came up that I have to deal with."

"Anything I should know about?" she asked uncertainly. "When should I tell people you'll be back?"

"I'll call you."

When he arrived at his building, Nick was in the lobby. They rode up in the elevator without a word, and by the time they got into the apartment, Tim was beyond worried.

"I just learned the results of the DNA tests on the severed finger," Nick said.

"From Novack?" Tim asked, and was immediately sorry he did. It would only delay his hearing the news.

Nick shook his head. "No, I have someone on my payroll at the state lab; it often comes in handy. Like now."

"What did the tests show?"

Nick didn't pull the punch. "It was your wife's finger."

THIS time there was no internal debate.

Within minutes of getting the news of the DNA match, Captain Donovan had agreed to arrest Tim. An hour later, DA McDermott signed on, and a half hour after that, they secured a signed arrest warrant, and another warrant to search Tim's office and home.

Undercover officers were sent to confirm that Tim was at his office, and Captain Donovan started to rearrange his officers so that the arrest would be done with sufficient manpower. Novack and Anders were to lead a group of six into the office, all exits and stairwells were to be guarded, and every detail of the plan was to be presented to Donovan, utilizing a diagram of the building.

Donovan looked at it from every angle. "It works for me," he finally said. "Just don't screw it up."

"It'll go down perfectly," Novack said, smiling.

At that moment a call came in from one of the undercover officers saying that Tim was not, in fact, at his office. Pretending to be a potential client, the officer was told by Meredith that she expected Tim back shortly.

The decision was made not to change the plan. They would wait until Tim got back to his office, and then move in.

IT WAS unlikely that any news could have devastated Tim as completely. It was his worst nightmare. He sank to his knees. "It can't be," he said. "It just can't be."

"I'm sorry, but it's a fact," Nick said. "The chance of these things being wrong is one in billions."

"Maggie died in the explosion. I was there."

"But you didn't actually see it. You said you saw a flash of white and then you lost consciousness."

"We were alone out there in the water. It's not possible."

"We'll need to talk this out, but this is not the time. We've got more pressing stuff to deal with."

Tim was lost in his own thoughts. "Are you saying she survived and then was tortured?" The words came out as a plea, as if begging Nick for another explanation. "Could she be alive? If that is her finger, and her body wasn't lost at sea, could she still be alive?"

Nick had to get through. "Listen to me, Tim. There is no doubt you are going to be arrested."

"What?"

"You are going to be arrested. It's best to turn yourself in. We'll avoid some press coverage, maybe cut out the perp walk."

"When . . . when do you want to do this?"

"Soon. In an hour."

Tim was responding slowly, still trying to make sense out of this in his mind. "What should I do?"

"Pack a bag, get someone to take care of your dog. Once you're ready, I'll call Novack and offer to bring you in. I'll be back in an hour."

Tim nodded. "Okay."

Nick left, and Tim was alone with his agony. It was a good half hour before he could think clearly. His phone rang, and he considered not answering it, then saw it was his office. "Hello?"

It was Meredith, and she sounded extremely scared. "Tim, there are police all over the building. They think I don't know who they are, but I'm not stupid."

"It's okay, Meredith." He didn't have the time to console her.

"Tim, I overheard them talking. One said he'd love to take a shot at you. The other talked about what would happen to you in prison."

"Meredith, just stay in the office. I have to go."

Meredith's call had further shaken him, if that were possible. One thing was all too obvious; whoever was doing this to him had won.

It was planned to perfection, and when he was taken into custody, he would never come back. The worst pain of all was that he was the only person who could avenge whatever happened to Maggie.

He was positive of only one thing. He had to run.

8

LUCIA Angelos had no idea two cameras and three agents were watching her every move. No one had been around when she arrived at Ricardo Vasquez's apartment, and she had a key. Entering was neither particularly poignant nor upsetting. She had stayed overnight dozens of times before Vasquez had been blown to bits, but it had not been an idyllic romance.

Lucia took her time in the search; she knew that if Ricardo had hidden something of value there, he would have done a very good job of it. Burglaries were commonplace in this neighborhood, and Ricardo had committed many of them.

In watching Lucia search the apartment for over two hours, FBI Agent Carl White was showing remarkable patience. Ever since he had been assigned the case, he had gotten nowhere in figuring out what Vasquez was doing with the Cintron 421. His instincts told him that Lucia was going to change all that.

There was no harm in letting Lucia search the apartment; forensics had long ago turned the place upside down. But Carl sent in the agents to frighten her. Scared people are more likely to talk.

Six agents burst into the apartment, guns drawn and screaming at Lucia to hit the floor. Carl had them cuff her and read her her rights, though she hadn't done anything to warrant arrest. He knew she'd be more uncomfortable in a downtown holding cell, so he arranged for this with Miami PD, and they took her possessions and cell phone, then let her stew in jail for hours before bringing her to an interrogation room.

"What were you looking for?" he asked as he walked in.

"My stuff," she said.

"What kind of stuff?"

"Just clothes and things, shoes. Stuff, you know?"

"You were looking inside the mattress. That's where you keep your clothes and shoes?"

"Jewelry . . . I hide stuff in there," she said.

"The jewelry stuff in the mattress, let me see it."

She shrugged. "It wasn't there. Must have been stolen."

Carl smiled a cold smile and pulled up a chair at the table. He leaned in and spoke softly. "Here's the thing, Lucia. You think you'll jerk me around for a while and I'll let you go. But this is a bigger deal than you can handle. Whatever Ricardo was doing, it was a threat to this entire country, and if you don't help me, I am going to bury you so far down you'll never come up for air."

"I didn't do nothing wrong."

"Then it's a shame that the next time you see your little Carmela she'll have three grown kids and gray hair."

In just a couple of hours, they already knew about her infant daughter. Lucia was afraid of them, but not as afraid as she was of the man who'd sent her to the apartment. "Does my mother know about this?"

Carl looked at his watch. "The agents will be at her house in twenty minutes. Is she afraid of guns?"

Game, set, and match. "I was looking for money."

Carl gave a slight nod. "Which money might that be?"

"Ricardo said he was being paid a lot of money, and he would buy me stuff when he came back. Since he ain't around to use it, I went looking for it."

"Who was paying him?"

"I don't know his name; Ricardo never talked about it."

"So you never saw this guy?"

"No," she lied, "but Ricardo was scared of him, I can tell you. Every time he talked to him, he got all nervous."

"You were there when they talked?"

She nodded. "A couple of times. He talked soft into the phone, and I pretended like I was asleep."

Every call from the apartment phone and Ricardo's cell phone had been checked and rechecked, turning up nothing suspicious. "What phone did he use?"

"A cell phone he thought they wouldn't connect to him."

"We checked all the calls he made," Carl said.

She nodded. "What do I have to do to get out of here?"

It was time to appear sympathetic. "Lucia, you didn't start all this. We don't want you; we want what you know."

She nodded again. "Okay. Ricardo didn't use his cell phone."

"Which one did he use?"

"He used mine. The one your people took from me."

TIM had to take deep breaths and tell himself not to panic.

He knew that the actions he took now would set the stage for all that would follow, and he had to think and act deliberately, even if he was operating in an area in which he had no experience.

His estimation was that he'd have a five-hour head start. When Nick realized he'd left, it was unlikely that he'd immediately notify Novack. He'd give Tim time in the hope that he would come back.

He filled two suitcases with clothes and put them in his car. He also took what he'd come to think about as "the file." He'd never opened it and had thought he never would, but he recognized the possibility that it could be crucial to his current situation.

Tim went back in to get Kiley and write a note to Nick, which he left in an envelope on the door. It said that he needed time to think, and anything Nick could do to arrange that would be very much appreciated. Tim regretted deceiving him, but he had no real choice.

Just before he left, he went to the top of his bedroom closet and opened a box. Tim had gotten the handgun after Maggie's death, when the media uproar resulted in his receiving a number of death threats. He thought he should take it, though he recognized that it might prove more dangerous than helpful.

With Kiley in the backseat, Tim's first stop was his bank to get money. He had twenty-one thousand dollars in his checking account, which he withdrew. He also took the maximum cash advances off his credit cards, smiling and telling the curious bank assistant manager that he was headed to Vegas. By the time he left, he had almost thirty-five thousand, and half the employees were staring at him. He knew that the police would soon be talking to each and every one of them.

The next issue was Kiley. Much as he wanted to, he couldn't take her with him. He briefly considered asking Danny or Will to care for her, but decided that Eden would be a better choice. He felt that Kiley would enjoy being with her and Travis more than alone in Danny or Will's apartment all day.

Tim did not think that leaving Kiley with Eden would result in any legal difficulties for her. He was not yet technically a fugitive, and she could say that she was simply doing a favor for a friend.

He headed for Eden's house, hoping that she was home.

She saw him through the window and came out to greet him. The look on his face told her something was very wrong, and she said, "What is it?" and brought him inside.

"I was hoping you could take care of Kiley," he said. "I'm going to go away for a while."

"Where are you going?"

"I'm not sure. Will you watch her?"

"Of course I'll watch her. Tell me what's going on."

"The finger in the box . . . it was Maggie's."

Eden put her hand to her mouth. "Oh, my God. No."

"They're planning to arrest me, but I can't let them do it. If they take me in, I'll never get out."

"How could they know it was—"

"The DNA test. According to Nick, there's no doubt. But then I don't see how she could have died in the explosion, and that raises terrible possibilities."

"Oh, Tim, I'm so sorry."

"Thank you. And I appreciate your doing this more than

you know. If they find out, just tell them you've watched my dog before. You had no way of knowing I was running from the police."

"But where are you running to?"

"I honestly don't know. Someplace out of the way."

"Stay here."

Tim's answer was immediate. "No. Thank you, but no."

"They would have no reason to look here. Nobody except Nick even knows we're friends."

"Eden, you could go to jail. This is not a game."

She got angry. "You think I consider this a game? Two people have been murdered, and I think this is a game?"

"I can't involve you in this any more than I already have."

"I'm not talking about permanently. Just until we figure out your next step. And I can help."

He knew she was right. To learn who was behind this nightmare as a fugitive, alone, seemed an impossible task. "Just for tonight. One way or the other, I leave tomorrow."

NICK knew even before he saw the note that Tim had run. It was an intuition he had, the kind that was always right.

Tim's running was understandable, but Nick knew it to be ill-advised. Tim was not Osama bin Laden; he was a businessman from New Jersey. Nick had decided not to call Novack until he had Tim in hand, and since neither Tim nor Nick had officially been notified of an arrest warrant, Tim would not immediately be classified as a fugitive. But that was a short-term respite, and if Tim tried to contact Nick, he wouldn't like what he would hear.

Nick had nothing to gain by hanging out at Tim's apartment, so he drove back to his office, then called Eden. She was sitting with Tim in her living room when she saw who it was on caller ID.

"It's Nick," she said to Tim.

"Please don't tell him you've seen or talked to me."

She nodded and picked up the phone. "Hello?"

"It's Nick. Has Tim contacted you?"

"No. Why?"

"Eden, if you talk to him, tell Tim to call me. Tell him it's not too late, but pretty soon it will be. Do you understand?"

"Yes."

With that one-word answer, Nick knew that she'd seen Tim. If not, she would have questioned him about his cryptic message. "Eden, stay as far away from this as you can. Don't make the worst mistake of your life."

"Thanks, big brother."

"I mean it. You can wind up in prison." He could have added, "or worse." The fact was, based on the evidence he was aware of, Tim was very possibly a killer of women.

As it was the job of a defense attorney to provide the best possible representation, Nick spent no time wondering if clients were innocent of the crime of which they were accused. But this was personal. If Tim was guilty, Eden was in more danger than she could handle.

Nick got off the phone feeling less in control than at any time he could remember. His client was perched on the edge of a cliff, and his sister was out there with him. And it was a long way down.

"I KNOW where you can stay, Tim," Eden said. "I can't believe I didn't think of it before."

She said it after an hour of discussion punctuated by periodic silences, as each of them tried to grapple with his predicament. They were sitting in her den, petting the dogs as they talked. It could have been a perfectly normal scene, except for what they were discussing.

"Where?"

"There's a house in Lincoln Park, set in the woods. The school owns it; we use it for visiting professors, graduate exchange students, that kind of thing." She stood up to go through her desk for her address book.

"And it's empty now?" Tim asked.

She nodded. "For at least the next six weeks. A colleague of mine has been living there, but he's on sabbatical."

"If I was found there, it would be obvious to the police that you arranged it."

"No, I could have told you about it long ago. Look, it's the perfect situation; any neighbors would be used to seeing different people in the house. There's even a car you could use."

"That's good, because I'd have to come and go. Somehow I've got to figure out who's done this to me, and I'm not going to call suspects in to be interviewed."

She looked dubious. "You have any experience at this?"

He shook his head. "Of course not."

They lapsed into another silence. "I can help."

"You're already doing much too much."

"I can help you check things out, talk to people."

He smiled. "You have any experience with this?"

"About the same as you."

"No. The more you do, the more jeopardy you're in. I'll bet Nick told you that when he called."

"I'll be careful. But you need help, and I seem to be the only chance you've got. Now we can debate it some more, or we can make concrete plans."

They figured out everything from how they would contact each other to how they would reduce the chance of his being identified. By the time Tim went to sleep, he had closely cropped light brown hair, drugstore glasses, and a plan to grow a moustache and goatee. Even without the facial hair, the difference was dramatic.

"Your own mother wouldn't even recognize you," Eden said.

He nodded. "That's the good news."

"What's the bad?"

"Novack's not my mother."

AT THAT very moment, the man who was not Tim's mother was in Tim's apartment, directing a thorough search of the place. So far it had turned up nothing of obvious value, though forensics was still doing their thing. Novack was by this time all but certain that Tim was on the run; there were no suitcases to be found, and the toiletries had been removed from the bathroom.

He called Nick. "I'm at your client's apartment, counselor."

"Let me speak to him." Nick said this knowing full well that Tim was not there but hoping to maintain the ruse that neither he nor Tim had any idea he was a wanted man.

"That would be difficult. He's not here."

"Then what the hell are you doing there?" Nick asked, though he knew the answer all too well.

"Looking for him, and exercising a lawful search warrant."

"I'm coming over. I don't want you stealing any towels."

"Bring Wallace with you, so I can arrest him."

"On what charge?"

"The murder of Margaret Wallace." They had much more evidence, circumstantial and otherwise, in Maggie's case, and they could hold Sheila's in reserve.

9

THE media was enlisted in the hunt for Tim at six a.m. Novack held a hastily arranged news conference on the steps of the state police headquarters. The temperature outside was sixteen degrees, and the reporters shivered and huddled to ward off the cold.

Like most police at such conferences, Novack adopted the attitude that he was there reluctantly, as if his attendance were compulsory. He treated reporters' questions as unwanted intrusions, and the questioners as if they were there to defeat the cause of justice.

The truth was that Novack hated these moments; public speaking made him uncomfortable, which made him uncommunicative. Since the purpose was to communicate, the situation was not ideal.

"Timothy Wallace is wanted for questioning in the murder of Margaret Wallace. We are asking the public to call a hotline number if they have any information as to his whereabouts."

Since many of the reporters had covered the investigation after Maggie's death, this prompted a barrage of questions.

"I can't discuss the evidence in an ongoing investigation," Novack said. "You people know that by now."

He showed Tim's picture, passed out copies, and announced the number to call. He agreed to answer one or two more questions, incorrectly implying that he had answered the previous ones.

"Do you consider him armed and dangerous?"

"I would advise people not to find out; call the number and let the police handle it. Thank you very much."

The police hunt for Tim was the lead story on every morning newscast, by which time Tim was in the Lincoln Park house. He had been busy in the preceding hours. Among other things, he had rented a prepaid cell phone at an all-night electronics store, using a fake name. He had also stopped and stolen license plates off a car at a shopping mall and put them on his own car. Although he was about to be the subject of an intense manhunt, the theft was the first actual crime he was aware of committing in his life.

Tim had called Danny from a pay phone early in the morning. "What's the matter?" Danny had asked, once he got himself awake.

"They're trying to arrest me for Maggie's death."

"What? You took a damn lie detector test and—"

"It was her finger. At the racquetball club, it was her finger." The thought was so horrifying, he found it jarring to verbalize it.

"Oh, no . . . Tim . . . where are you now?"

"On the way to a motel outside of Philly." It was a lie, a planned one. Tim wasn't sure he told it because he didn't want Danny having to conceal something from the police, or because he wasn't sure he could trust anyone, not even his best friend.

"Tim, if the cops are after you, are you sure this is a good idea?"

"No, but it's the only one I've got."

"So how can I help?"

"Pay my lawyer for me when he comes and—"

"No problem. Whatever's necessary. What else?"

"Nothing. Stay as far away from this as possible."

"What the hell are you going to do?"

"Figure this out."

"I'M SORRY I DID THAT TO YOU," Tim said as soon as Nick picked up the phone. He was worried about Nick's reaction; he needed him as an ally.

"You didn't do it to me," Nick said. "You did it to you."

"I just didn't feel like I had a choice."

"You had a choice, Tim. You made the wrong one. You felt the pressure and threw up a damn air ball."

Nick's blunt assessment simultaneously annoyed and scared Tim. "Where do we go from here?"

"I'm under a legal obligation to advise you that you are committing a felony by avoiding arrest, and to advise you to surrender to the proper authorities immediately."

"And if I don't?"

"Then you don't. You're calling the shots, at least for now."

"Will you continue to help me?"

"Of course I'll help you; I'm your lawyer."

"Thank you. You don't know how much I appreciate that."

"Before you say anything, I do not want you to tell me where you are. If you do, I'm obligated to reveal it to the police."

"Okay. What am I allowed to tell you?"

"Any ideas you have that might help your situation. Anything you want me to follow through on. Things like that."

"The only thing I have to go on is that Cashman is behind this. Or at least involved in it."

"But you don't know who he is. Or why he targeted you."

"No. But I saw him; I spoke to him. And we have his picture."

Nick jumped on this. "The media will eat it up. I've probably had fifty calls for information; when they get the sketch, they'll go crazy."

"Somebody has to know him. Should we offer a reward? My partner, Danny McCabe, will front money from the company for this and for your fees." Tim paused. "Is he allowed to do that?"

"Sure. Everybody's entitled to an expensive defense. I'll get right on it."

"Can I keep calling you?" Tim asked. "I mean, would they tap your phone or anything like that?"

Nick had thought of this. "Not now. The chance that they'd risk destroying their own case by breaking attorney-client privilege would scare them off. Maybe later when they get desperate."

"Listen, Nick . . ."

"What?"

"I've been trying to look at this a little bit from your point of view. You probably think I'm guilty. But—"

"You're not going to tell me you're innocent, are you?"

"Actually, I was."

"Save your breath. For the moment it's irrelevant."

"This is Carl White, special agent with the FBI, from the Miami office," Captain Donovan said.

"Good to meet you," Anders said, shaking White's hand.

"Uh-oh," said Novack, aware that this wasn't a social visit. FBI agents don't just show up; they often come in and take over cases. "What's going on?"

"Agent White is interested in our investigation of Tim Wallace."

"Why is that?" Novack asked.

"Remember that van that exploded near the turnpike?" Carl asked. "The driver called Wallace's office twice in the ten days before his death."

"Any idea why?" Anders asked.

"Not yet."

"It doesn't make sense," Novack said. "I don't see Wallace as a terrorist. He does his killing up close and personal."

"But I understand his wife was killed in an explosion?"

Novack nodded. "She was. And we've also connected him to a now deceased explosives expert in Carson, Wyoming. We believe his wife was Wallace's second victim."

"I've agreed with Agent White that we will share all relevant information from both investigations," said Donovan.

"With who determining relevance?" Novack asked. Donovan would have no stomach for a fight with the Feds. That wasn't how careers were made.

Donovan let a harder edge creep into his voice. "That will be determined jointly."

"This is the man we are looking for. He goes by the name of Jeff Cashman, but that is probably an alias." Nick held up the sketch so that Larry King's audience could get a good look at it. It was his fifth television appearance of the day, so if anyone had not seen Cashman's picture by now, that person likely was one of the few remaining Americans still resisting the advance of cable television.

Nick was sitting in a studio on West Fifty-fourth Street in Manhattan, from where he had done all of the interviews with the various networks. He had not actually met a single person he was questioned by all day.

"And why are you looking for him?" Larry asked.

"Unlike the police, I do not intend to talk publicly about the evidence, but it would be fair to say that Mr. Cashman is a person of interest."

"Is he of interest to the police as well?" King asked.

"He should be," Nick said. "They've known about him for weeks, yet they've refused to release this sketch publicly. If anyone has seen this man or knows who he is, please call me at 201-525-3176. We are offering a reward of twenty-five thousand dollars for information that leads to him."

"Your client, Timothy Wallace, has a warrant out for his arrest. Do you know where he is?"

"I don't have the slightest idea," said Nick. "Very dangerous people have targeted him, and he is justifiably frightened."

"So you've spoken to him?"

"That is not a question I would answer whatever the facts were. I know you understand attorney-client privilege, Larry."

For Tim, sitting in a strange house watching Nick was surreal. Hearing himself talked about on television, in a predicament that was both bewildering and frightening, was almost too much to bear.

He turned off the TV and got into the strange bed. He'd never felt so alone. He missed Maggie more than ever and now feared for her in death as much as he ever had in life. What had she endured? How much had she suffered? How could he have left her so unprotected from whatever evil had entered their lives?

With Maggie gone, there was no one he could trust. Someone with intimate knowledge of him was conspiring against him right now. How else could his life have been so thoroughly destroyed? Someone who'd known which boat was his and when he would be on it. Where he would go on New Year's Eve, where he lived. That he'd been in Wyoming, where and when he played racquetball.

It was disconcerting that the only person Tim could think of who fit that bill was Danny. But what would Danny have to gain? Could it have to do with the business? Perhaps he was stealing money or using the company for illicit purposes? But why go to such lengths? Why kill Sheila? It pained Tim to even consider the Danny he knew doing any of this. But somebody obviously was. Danny had to be at the top of the list of suspects.

A list that at the moment included only one name.

LUCIA Angelos was glad it was over. She'd done as she was told, the FBI was gone, and she'd gotten some money in the process.

It was time to take that money and start living, which was what she told her sister Maria on one of their phone calls. "I'm going to move to New York and get a job."

Maria, who lived in New York herself, said, "You always say that, but you never do it."

"This time I will. In New York at least I have you."

"But I have Orlando." Maria's marriage was not made in heaven.

"So you can leave him, and we'll move in together."

Maria laughed at the absurdity of it. "Of course. We'll go to Park Avenue and have servants."

Lucia was not familiar with Park Avenue and was about to ask about it when there was a knock on her door. "Hold on a sec . . ." She put the phone down and went to answer it.

She opened it and saw the man she hoped never to see again. "Hello, Lucia, nice to see you. You did a very nice job."

"I did what you wanted. I told the FBI everything you said."

"I know you did. I'm just here to make things clean and neat."

He moved toward her, and as he did she looked directly into his eyes. Suddenly she knew why Ricardo had been so afraid of this man.

But by then it was too late.

BY TEN o'clock in the morning, over a thousand tips had come in to Nick's hotline, far more than the firm's investigative arm was equipped to handle. The hope was that anyone with legitimate information would be persistent.

Nick could only passively wait for something to develop, and passive waiting was never his specialty. He wanted to know all the evidence the prosecution had against Tim, but they had no obligation to turn over anything until pretrial discovery, when Tim was in custody and arraigned.

Still, Nick had sources within the department, and he worked them vigorously.

Eden Alexander, who by her own estimation hadn't watched more than ten hours of television in the previous year, sat glued to the set. She cringed every time CNN broke in with a "breaking news" banner. None of them had anything to do with Tim.

She and Tim had agreed that, even though she knew his new cell-phone number, if they had to communicate it would be through e-mail. She had opened a new Yahoo address with the screen name "Kileysfriend." To this point Tim had not sent her any messages.

Eden was not taking Kiley and Travis for walks on the street, instead using the yard behind her house. She tried to be alert and so far had not detected being watched, but she had little confidence that this meant much. For all she knew, they could be tracking her every move, and she was simply oblivious to it.

IT IS a truism in Washington that some of the most powerful people in government are complete unknowns to the public. One such person was Gregory Campbell, who had come from Boise, Idaho, as part of the congressional page program, attended Georgetown

University, then secured a job as a low-level minority staffer on the House Appropriations Committee.

In twenty-five years, Campbell had made absolutely no effort to shed his public anonymity. Working fourteen-hour days, he became a crucial cog in the wheels of government, advancing to lead minority staffer on the Senate Appropriations Committee, where he came under the wing of Fred Collinsworth.

If one had to come under a wing, that was about as good as it could get. Collinsworth could make things happen for people he needed and pretended to care about. He secretly made Campbell a very rich man with the occasional amazingly prescient stock tip, the fortuitous land purchase in an area soon adjacent to new highways. Eventually, the senator had arranged for him to move to the executive branch, specifically the General Services Administration, where he could be even more influential in steering large contracts to places the senator wanted them steered.

The relationship came in handy in dealing with the potential political disaster of Tim Wallace's fugitive status.

As soon as Gregory got the call that he was to meet with Keith Rivers, he knew Collinsworth had a problem. Since people as rich and powerful as Collinsworth rarely solved problems personally, Rivers was always his chosen solver. He was as good a solver as Gregory had ever been around.

They met at a restaurant in northern Virginia, though they could have dined anywhere in Washington and not attracted attention as a "power couple."

Soon after they sat down, the waiter came over. "Would you care for something to drink? Or like to hear our specials?"

"No," Rivers said.

The waiter seemed not to know what to make of this directness. "I'll give you a few moments," he mumbled.

Once he was gone, Rivers asked, "Have you heard about the man wanted for murder in New Jersey?"

Gregory was not a watcher of television, nor did he read about crime in the newspaper. "I don't think so. . . ."

"Daniel McCabe's partner is currently a fugitive."

It started to click into place, Collinsworth's prior embarrassment. "Is that the guy whose wife died on the boat?"

Rivers nodded. "It is. You should familiarize yourself with the media coverage. It can never become public knowledge that the senator had anything to do with awarding the contract to that company. He didn't even know about it until long after the fact."

Gregory nodded in solemn agreement with what was in reality a total fantasy. "Of course."

"The grand strategy of awarding the contracts to small-business people was his; then he left the details to people like yourself. He lets people do their jobs."

"Absolutely. That's one of his greatest strengths."

Rivers got up to leave. "Enjoy your dinner."

CONSCIOUSLY putting Danny to the back of his mind, Tim took a deep breath and opened "the file."

The file included newspaper stories about Maggie's death and the subsequent investigation, the coroner's report, the Coast Guard report, and all the other official documents Tim had received once he had been cleared of the murder.

Tim had never wanted to read any of it, but he had requested that Meredith prepare a file, and now he felt he had to go through it in the hope he might learn something relevant. It was beyond painful, and the worst part was the lack of humanity granted Maggie. In the cold type of this paper world, she was an object, without her smile, her personality, her dreams. Page after page was about her, yet had nothing to do with who she was.

It was awful to read about that day on the boat, in newspaper articles written while he'd still been in the hospital. It was another jolt to realize that he may not, in fact, have had full knowledge of what took place. Tim was finding himself consumed by doubt. Had he not seen what he thought he saw?

He tried to force himself to read the articles dispassionately. The motor apparently caught fire and blew up; then a private plane traveling overhead saw the fire, though based on the size of the blaze it was believed between five and ten minutes had passed. The pilot had called in the emergency, and when a Coast Guard cutter arrived, small pieces of the boat were still floating, but Maggie's body was presumed to have been blown apart and washed away. Tim was found floating unconscious, held up by his life jacket. No other boats were in the area.

The Coast Guard report presented basically the same story, and Tim moved on to the police reports.

Suddenly the realization hit him between the eyes. No other boats? There was an Oceanfast not far in the distance when he went into the water for the hat. It was close all day; he and Maggie had both admired it. It was certainly close enough to see the explosion.

How could the people on that boat not have reported it?

Tim tried to answer that question for himself. Perhaps they were asleep, or they didn't want to be involved, or they were out there for a reason they didn't want anyone to know about.

But none of the answers rang true. They had to have at least heard the explosion, and it was impossible to imagine that in such a situation they would not have tried to help.

Unless they were out there waiting for Tim's boat to blow up.

Despite Nick's stated assurance that his phone would not be tapped, Tim was reluctant to contact him. This time was worth the risk, though, since he needed Nick's help to check out the boat.

Nick's secretary answered the phone, and Tim told her it was Jerry Koosman calling. It was a signal they had arranged: As a huge Mets fan, Nick had suggested using the name of the former Mets left-handed pitcher.

"Talk to me," Nick said immediately, not wanting these calls to last too long.

"I read through all the reports on the day Maggie died. There is no mention of another boat that was nearby. I saw it; it was definitely there, but the people on board never reported the explosion. The fire was called in by a pilot flying over."

"So?"

"So people out on the water take care of each other; it's like a private fraternity. They should have reported it, and there would have to be a damn good reason if they didn't."

"Did you mention it when they questioned you back then?"

"No. I just assumed the people on the boat had been the ones to report the explosion. I never made the connection."

Nick didn't think much of this news, but it wasn't like he had anything better. "Anything distinctive about the boat?"

"It was an Oceanfast 360, worth over two million. Maggie and I were admiring it; we even joked about it."

"How many of them would there be around here?" Nick asked.

"No way for me to know, but this one was painted an ugly green, like army khakis used to be. It also had two white stripes. It would be the only one of its kind, if it hasn't been repainted."

"So let's find out who owns it," Nick said.

"How do we do that?"

"We take one of our investigators off the dead-end hunt for Cashman and put him on this."

"So nothing is happening on Cashman?"

"The only thing happening is that every crackpot east of Maui is trying to get the reward."

"He's out there, Nick," Tim said. "I'm not making him up."

SITTING at a corner table at Spumoni's, a fashionable, overpriced D.C. restaurant, Jimmy Lee Curry was glad Professor Richmond wasn't there to see him. Richmond was the man who had taken Jimmy under his wing at the University of Alabama, and who basically shepherded him all the way to a master's in journalism. Richmond had seen in Jimmy the makings of a crack investigative reporter, and he had instilled in him the need to be unbiased, ethical, and relentless. Twenty-five years later Jimmy Lee Curry's byline was respected and feared. But as he became more and more successful, the very qualities that got him there became less essential.

Jimmy Lee was not the first reporter this had happened to. There were maybe a dozen journalists big enough to limit their investigative efforts to picking up the phone. People who had news to spread called Jimmy Lee, and if he wrote a column on it, people fawned all over him.

At this stage of his life, Jimmy Lee figured, sitting in this restaurant, waiting for Susan Moreno to slip him an important story, was pretty much as good as it got.

Susan was in her mid-thirties, a strikingly beautiful woman, top assistant to Walter Evans, the superstar junior senator from Ohio. When Senator Evans wanted something to happen, he sent Susan.

She performed basically the same function for Evans that Keith Rivers did for Senator Collinsworth; she just weighed 150 pounds less and had a higher-pitched voice.

Susan always waited until coffee was ordered before delivering her message, and this time was no exception. "Have you heard about Tim Wallace, the guy in New Jersey who the police are after for killing his wife?"

"Of course."

"Did you know his company was doing security construction work on the Newark Federal Center?"

"Why is that important?" Jimmy Lee asked.

"Because he got the work through Senator Collinsworth."

"Really? What is Collinsworth's connection to Wallace?"

"Wallace's partner is Collinsworth's nephew," she said.

This was moderately interesting to Jimmy Lee, but not the kind of bombshell that someone like Susan Moreno would spend an entire lunch waiting to detonate. "I assume there's more to this? Something that more directly benefits you and your boss?"

She smiled. "Pending our negotiations; we have to come to agreement on the terms."

"Which are?"

"You write this story, and then in two weeks, the day after the Federal Center opens, you write the follow-up piece."

He nodded; here it comes. "And that includes . . ."

"You of course remember the explosion on the Jersey Turnpike a while back? The driver of the van that blew up had called Wallace a few times before he died. So we have Collinsworth getting major security construction work for someone dealing with a guy with a truckload of Cintron 421."

This was, in fact, a potential bombshell, and the question of what Susan's boss would gain from this story was now amply answered. Evans and Collinsworth were bitter rivals, a situation exacerbated when Collinsworth got the nod as head of the Senate Appropriations Committee. They were also expected to play out their rivalry in the presidential election two years away.

Jimmy Lee smiled. "Now you're talking."

Susan took a leisurely sip of her coffee. "So, Jimmy Lee, you think this might be a decent story?"

"Do I need a second source on this?"

Susan shook her head. "This is rock solid."

"Why wait two weeks for the second piece?" he asked.

She leaned forward, lowering her voice. "It's just been decided that the dignitaries the night of the opening will include the president of the United States. Security will be tripled, so there's no danger, but your story will say that President Markham spent the evening in a building built by Senator Collinsworth's mad bomber."

"YOU have no idea where he is?" Danny asked.

"Of course not," said Meredith. "You think he would tell me and not you?"

"I don't think he'd tell anybody. But that's not what I mean. Can you figure out where he might be? You run his life, for Pete's sake."

"Not this part of it. This part scares the hell out of me."

"He didn't do anything wrong, and he's going to be fine."

"Is it having any effect on the business?" she asked.

He nodded. "Probably. The FBI has been at the site, and Homeland Security's been going over the place, although they might have been doing that anyway."

"Any chance they're going to cancel the opening?"

"Zero. Too many big shots are going to be there."

"Have the police talked to you?" she asked.

"Twice, and the FBI once. I told them I don't know where he is, and that he'd never do anything like they're saying."

Meredith nodded; she had pretty much said the same thing. Of course, if she knew where Tim was, she would never tell the police anyway. She was not sure she could say the same for Danny.

"There was this woman I saw him with recently. Tall, blond hair . . . you have any idea who she is?" Danny asked.

"No, he never mentioned anyone," Meredith lied, neglecting to say that Eden Alexander had invited Tim to dinner.

Eden Alexander. That was a name she was not about to share with Danny.

GEORGIE Silvers had no illusions about the opportunity that had presented itself. What he had to say might get him special considerations, but no way was it going to let him walk.

Still, it was better going to the cops than going after a reward he'd never see in this New Jersey state prison. Even if these cops didn't even seem that interested.

Novack put the sketch of Cashman on the table. "So you know this man?"

Georgie nodded. "Yeah. I know him. I was on the inside with him up at Lampley."

"What's his real name?" Anders asked.

George couldn't help laughing. "What's his name? Come on, you guys know that ain't the way this works."

"You want something for the name?" Novack asked. "Maybe a villa in the Caribbean? A suite at Caesar's Palace?"

"Come on," Georgie said. "I'm a reasonable guy."

"Who said we want the name?" asked Anders.

"You didn't come here to shoot the breeze. I could have gone to that lawyer and collected the reward, but I'm being a good citizen."

"Your country salutes you," said Novack. "What do you want?"

"A job in the library. In the kitchen, I sweat my ass off."

"You think we're here from the employment agency?"

"And in July, when they do the reassignments, I want to go to

Milford." Milford Federal Prison was a major step up in comfort level, but not a place where repeat breaking-and-entering offenders like Georgie Silvers wound up.

"Milford?" asked Novack, making no attempt to conceal his amusement. "That's minimum security. You want to go there? Run for Congress and take a bribe."

It was a long shot, and Georgie knew it. "I'll tell you what; if this guy turns out to be somebody important, then try and get me to Milford. Is that fair? Meanwhile, get me the library job."

Novack nodded. "Okay, deal. Now what's his real name?"

"Billy Zimmerman. We used to call him Dollar Bill, 'cause he was in for forging checks."

Dollar Bill, renamed Cashman. "And he looked like this?"

"Nah. That's what he told me he was going to look like. If he ever had to go into hiding, you know?"

Novack shook his head in annoyance. "No, we don't know. Why don't you tell us?"

"His girlfriend was a makeup artist or something; I think for one of those Broadway shows that goes on the road. She—"

"What was her name?"

"Denise. I don't know her last name. She was working in Buffalo on that musical about the French guys."

"Les Miz?" Novack asked.

"Yeah, I think that was it. Anyway, she taught Billy how to do the makeup, but they arrested him in bed in the middle of the night. He said if he ever escaped, or if the cops were after him, he was going to change his appearance. He even had his girlfriend draw a picture of what he could look like."

Novack pointed to the sketch. "And that's it?"

Georgie nodded. "That's it."

10

THE man who killed Jeff Cashman didn't care for his latest assignment. Following someone was tedious work, the kind dumb cops were invented to do. Following Eden Alexander was beneath him; the only thing worse than her boring life was watching her lead it.

It also made no sense at all. If they wanted to know where Wallace was, the way to go about it was to grab this broad and start inflicting some pain and fear.

The worst part was when she went to school to teach. He would look too out of place on campus, so he parked near the front gate and waited the five or six hours it took for her to come out.

The only positive was that he wouldn't have to do this for more than two weeks. That's when his employers needed to know where Wallace was hiding, and if she hadn't led him to Wallace by then, he would simply grab her and extract the information. It gave him something to look forward to.

After that he would make his own move. Instructing him to kill Cashman and the broad in Florida was a mistake his employers would come to regret. It showed him how they treated their partners, and led him to believe they probably had the same fate planned for him. But no matter how much money and power they had, they'd find out soon they were not in his league.

EDEN Alexander had never seen the car nor the man behind the wheel before. It was a gray minivan parked at the end of her street, and the man was blond, early thirties, and so large that the car seemed filled to capacity.

She knew she was being watched, and that he was watching her. It was an instinct she had, and she trusted it completely.

Eden avoided staring at the car or the man, as she went to her own car. She drove to her job at the university, waving to the guard at the gate as he let her in. She did not see the minivan behind her at any point, but she would have bet a week's pay it was there.

Going straight to the faculty room, she was relieved to see Andy Miller, a colleague, having coffee. "Andy, I need a favor."

"Shoot."

"I'd like you to walk out past the gate. If a gray minivan is near there, I want you to get the license plate number."

"What's going on?" he asked. "You okay, Eden?"

She smiled. "I'm fine. Really."

He stood up. "Okay, gray minivan. I'm on the case."

Andy left and was gone about ten minutes. He came back and said, "WKT-535."

"Was there anybody in the car?" she asked.

"Big guy, blond hair. I didn't look too closely."

She forced a smile. "Great, Andy. I really appreciate it."

"Anything else I can do? You're sure nothing's wrong?"

"Really, Andy, everything is fine," she lied, fighting panic. That had to be a police officer in that car, and he would only be following her if he thought she might lead him to Tim.

Which meant they were both in big trouble.

TIM was going crazy.

Just sitting around the house was getting him nowhere, and by now his grown-in facial hair had made him confident he wouldn't be recognized by a media-alerted citizen. So he was willing to go out; the problem was he had nowhere to go.

Tim decided he would make his first foray into the outside world by going to the library. He wanted to use the library computer to contact Eden.

Just walking out the door of the house was an uncomfortable experience. He knew the police were not out there waiting for him; if they were, they would have long ago barged in. But he still looked around warily and continued doing so even after he pulled away.

The Lincoln Park library was surprisingly large and even at this early hour had close to fifteen people in it. He was relieved to discover that he did not have to have a library card to use the computers; all he had to do was sign in. He did so, using a fake name.

Tim had asked Eden to create a Hotmail address for him, and he signed on to it. He was surprised to see that he had seven e-mails waiting for him. As it turned out, six were spam, and one was from "Kileysfriend," the address Eden had created for herself.

He opened the e-mail and read:

> I'm being followed. I don't know who it is, but I'm afraid it's the police. I have the license number of the car. What should I do?

Tim was stunned by the message. He had the sensation of wanting to get up and pace, to relieve some of the pent-up anxiety and perhaps think more clearly. But he couldn't do anything that might attract attention from the other patrons.

He typed a reply, hoping she was near a computer to receive it:

> Go see Nick. Tell him what you think and give him the plate number. Not over the phone.

He pressed SEND and waited. A minute later, her reply appeared:

> I will; I'll write back and tell you what he said. Are you OK?

He wrote back:

> Yes. If you ever get into danger, tell the truth about where I am. Please don't take any unnecessary chances.

Her reply:

> Same to you, buddy.

It made Tim smile. He wished he could be with her, to spend a normal day, but that really was impossible under the circumstances.

DENISE Wagner's career was not exactly taking off. She was no longer working on theatrical road shows. The fact that her drinking caused her to miss an average of three shows a week had made her less than sought after. Denise was now in the ignominious position of working for Salon 37 in Manhasset, Long Island, as a makeup consultant.

As far as Novack could remember, this was the first beauty salon he had ever been in. It was a relatively frightening sight, women camped under enormous machines, reading magazines while sporting a head full of tinfoil. Not the place to be in a lightning storm.

Novack stopped at the front desk and asked where he might find Denise Wagner. The receptionist pointed toward the back but said that Denise was busy.

"Aren't we all?" asked Novack, heading for Denise.

She was applying eye shadow to a customer when she saw him coming. He noticed the flash of fear in her eyes, followed by resignation. "Denise Wagner?" He took out his shield.

"Yes."

"I'm Detective Novack." He turned to the customer. "I think she's done as much as she can for you."

Momentarily speechless, the customer obliged.

"This is about Billy," Denise said. "I saw his picture on TV. I haven't seen him in over a year. He's out of my life."

"But you're sure it was him?"

She nodded. "I'm sure."

"Do you know where he is?"

"No."

"What can you tell me about him?" Novack asked.

"I really don't know anything. I met him in a bar out west. We were together less than three months before he went to jail on some kind of parole violation."

"You showed him how to make himself look different?"

She nodded. "He made me show him."

Novack questioned her for another fifteen minutes but got few details that might lead him to Billy Zimmerman, the man that Tim Wallace knew as Cashman.

This was very disconcerting to Novack. He had been positive that Cashman did not exist. What else had he been wrong about?

SUCH were the extent of Nick's connections with the police department and prosecutor's office that he knew about Billy Zimmerman three hours after Novack did. He didn't yet know Denise had confirmed Billy's existence, but he'd know that before long.

Either way it was the first piece of good news that the defense had gotten since this whole thing had started. Nick didn't expect Novack to do anything with it, but Cashman's existence, and especially his incarceration at Lampley, confirmed a piece of Tim's story. Unfortunately, that brought the pieces of Tim's story that had been confirmed to a total of one.

Nick was a little uneasy over the phone call he'd received from Eden a few minutes earlier. She sounded scared and said that she needed to talk to him in person.

When she arrived, she looked even more worried than she had sounded. "I'm being followed, Nick. I'm sure of it."

"Do you know who it is?"

"No, but it's a big guy with blond hair driving a gray minivan." She handed him the plate number.

He walked to the window, though from that height it was difficult to see the street. "Did he follow you here?"

"I didn't see him, but I didn't want to be too obvious. Do you think it's the police, thinking I'll lead them to Tim?"

"I doubt it. They usually travel in pairs. And the gray minivan doesn't fit." Then he said pointedly, "Eden, why would anyone think that you might lead them to Tim?"

"I don't know, Nick. I haven't mentioned Tim to anyone but you. And I don't walk his dog out on the street."

"Have you had any contact with him?"

She decided to tell the truth. "We've e-mailed."

"Hell."

"Is that your considered legal opinion?" she asked, not backing down.

"Eden, have I mentioned that you are digging a hole for yourself that you may not be able to climb out of?"

"Yes, repeatedly. Now, will you find out who's following me?"

He nodded with resignation. "Yes."

"Thank you, big brother."

"SO CASHMAN is real? I thought you said Wallace made him up."

Novack could have responded defensively to what amounted to a challenge by Captain Donovan, but he didn't. "That's what I thought, but I'm not so sure anymore."

Anders was in the room as well but wanted no part of this conversation. He was going to let Novack take the heat.

"So where the hell does this leave us?" Uncertainty was disconcerting to Donovan, and coming from the supremely confident Novack, it was particularly unnerving.

"In exactly the same place we were before. There's absolutely no evidence to make us believe Cashman set Wallace up on this."

"But Cashman is real."

Novack nodded. "Right, and it's possible he helped Wallace in some way, and Wallace turned on him. But Cashman sure as hell wasn't out on the water with Maggie Wallace. And it was her finger at the racquetball club."

Donovan seemed far from convinced. "I don't like this. We're acting like we know what's going on, and we don't know squat."

"When we find Wallace, it will fall into place," Novack said, without fully believing it.

"And when might that be?" Donovan asked. "I've got the brass coming down on me about this."

Anders felt he should say something. "It'll be soon."

"You a fortune-teller, or have you seen something I haven't?"

"This is not a guy at home on the streets," Anders said. "He's holed up somewhere, but when he comes out, he won't last twenty-four hours."

Donovan turned back to Novack. "We're starting to look stupid for not being able to catch him. But nowhere near as stupid as we're going to look if he's not our man, if Cashman set this up."

"There's nothing to worry about," Novack said.

"Then why the hell am I worried?"

TO SAY the Passaic River was not as polluted as it once was is to damn it with faint praise. A lot of effort had taken what was not much more than an aboveground sewer and turned it into an acceptably clean waterway. There were even a few places where people went to fish. The Morlot Avenue Bridge, between Paterson and Fair Lawn, was where Jason Durant took his eleven-year-old son, Robbie, early on Saturday morning.

They stood on the bridge, dropped the bait in the water, and leaned forward so as not to be too close to the passing cars. After an hour of nothing, Robbie said, "Doesn't seem like our day, huh?"

Jason looked at his watch. "It's seven-thirty."

"You think the fish are still asleep?"

"They'll wake up hungry, and that's when we'll get 'em."

After another forty-five minutes, Robbie figured the fish must have forgotten to set their alarm. "I don't know if the fish are hungry, but I am."

"Might as well get the food," Jason said. They had parked near the riverbank. "Call me if you get a bite."

Jason walked to the end of the bridge, reached the car, and took out the cooler of food his wife had prepared. But he slipped on a stretch of mud, and the cooler fell from his hands and tumbled down to the edge of the river.

Balancing himself, Jason made it down the ten feet. The cooler had not gone into the water. It was wedged up against something.

A human arm.

Jason screamed, loud enough so that if there were really any fish still asleep, their day had officially begun.

NICK was starting to feel slightly better about the case. There were six Oceanfast 360s in the New York area, and he had the preliminary investigative report that listed the corporate and individual owners, though none of the names meant anything to him.

And when Tim called asking if there was anything to report, Nick had some more news.

"The police know who Cashman is. His real name is Billy Zimmerman, and he was in prison in Lampley."

"That's great! Do they know where he is now?"

"Apparently not, though that could change any time."

"So we wait?"

"No, our people are all over it. But the cops have easier entry. Meanwhile, I've got the list of boats."

Nick read the names of the boats, as well as the owning people and companies.

"I've never heard of any of them," a disappointed Tim said. "Can you find out where the boats are? I can check them out."

"You want to take that chance?" Nick asked.

"I look different; I think I can get away with it."

"If you're wrong, and you encounter the police, do not resist arrest. They consider you armed and dangerous."

"I am armed, but I'm not dangerous."

"You have a gun?" Nick asked, his surprise evident.

"Yes. There are murderers after me. I'm not going to use it against the police. It's not even loaded yet."

"Don't bring it with you when you check out the boats."

"I won't. I'm afraid of it."

CARL White received the information first, which reflected his higher status as a federal agent. It was another jagged piece of a puzzle that did not seem to fit anywhere. He had his assistant place a call to Novack and ask him to come right over.

Novack was not the type who liked to be summoned by an FBI agent, and he only agreed to go when he was assured there was significant news.

He and Anders were ushered right in. White didn't spend any time on small talk. "On Saturday morning, a resident of Fair Lawn found the arm of a white male in the Passaic River. Divers located the body, and DNA testing was done. It was Billy Zimmerman."

Novack had to suppress his annoyance that White obviously had been made privy to evidence of a local crime before Novack.

"Do we know when he died?" asked Novack.

"Too soon to tell. The autopsy's being done today."

"You could have told us this over the phone," said Anders.

White nodded. "But then I couldn't have picked your brains."

"About what?" asked Anders.

"The Federal Center opens a week from Wednesday night with a big dinner, speeches, the whole bit."

"We've known that for a while," Novack said.

"Did you know the president is going to be there?"

"No," said Novack. "Lately he hasn't been checking in with me when he's making up his schedule."

The comment annoyed White. "So you don't see this as your problem?"

"I gotta be honest," Novack said. "I don't even see it as your problem. Because I don't see Wallace as a terrorist. I see him as a sicko who kills women for fun, not a guy with a political agenda."

"So Zimmerman was a woman Wallace killed for fun?"

"I don't know where Zimmerman fits in," Novack admitted. "But if Wallace was going to blow up the Federal Center, he wouldn't have told us about Cashman and Sheila."

"Unless he also kills presidents for fun. By the way, we questioned the girlfriend of the guy blown up on the turnpike."

Novack nodded. "Yeah. We saw the interview report."

"But you didn't know that an agent later went back to her apartment to ask her a few more questions. She was gone, but all her clothes were still there. She'd been talking on the phone, got up to answer the door, and hasn't been heard from since."

"So she's dead," Novack reasoned. "There's no way Wallace went down there; it would be too risky. He's in hiding."

"And I don't see how he could have known about her in the first place," White said. "So it was somebody else. Which means you've got more going on here than you think."

Novack nodded; he had known that ever since learning that Cashman was not a creation of Tim's imagination. "Yes, it does."

CONSIDERING the circumstances, both Danny and Will found it more than a little weird to be at the Purple Rose. They had only gone there twice since Tim's disappearance, and that was more out of a desire to try and restore normalcy to their lives, rather than a hope they might have fun.

The two friends had agreed in advance not to talk about Tim, but that resolution broke down before the first beers arrived. "I just wish there was a way to help him," Danny said. "If I knew where he was, I could get him money."

"He cleaned out his checking account. It was in the paper."

"Yeah, I know. He must be scared out of his mind."

"He should be," Will said. "The cops are acting like he's Al Capone. They've questioned me three times."

Danny nodded. "You speak to the FBI agent? White?"

"Yeah. He had a million questions about the buildings. Like Tim's gonna show up with an army and attack."

"The security down there is unbelievable," Danny said.

"I know. I spent five hours teaching the computer setup to a government guy. You know who's coming to the opening?"

"Not really. A bunch of congressmen, my uncle . . ."

"He giving you grief about Tim?"

Danny nodded. "Every hour on the hour. He has his right-hand guy, Rivers, call me. Like there's something I can do about it."

"If one of us finds out where Tim is, we tell the other, okay?" Will asked. "And we figure out a way to help him."

Danny held out his hand, and Will took it. "It's a deal."

11

THE Oceanfast 360s were spread out through the metropolitan area. Three were on Long Island Sound, one was on the Hudson River, and the remaining two were in New Jersey. Tim knew some of the locations; they were upscale, high-end piers that charged exorbitant fees and provided excellent access.

Tim fully understood that the risks involved in checking out the boats himself were heightened by the fact that he was at least casually familiar with many people in the boating community. But working in his favor was that, with many boats in winter dry dock, not many owners would be around, unless they were doing work on their boats. The flip side of that, of course, would be that Tim would stand out even more.

Though the Jersey piers were significantly closer, Tim decided to check out Long Island first. Two of the Oceanfasts were said to be on the North Shore on Long Island Sound, where Tim's boat had been that fateful day.

Even the drive there was intense. Tim was sure that everyone in each car was staring at him; when one driver alongside took out a cell phone, it took all his self-control to not turn around. He was glad he used the car at the house, and not his own.

His first stop was at Mill Neck. He parked as close as he could to the pier and left the car unlocked in case he wanted to leave quickly. It was almost thirty degrees out, but he still pulled his ski cap low and bundled his coat upward, exposing a small amount of his face.

The dock area was fairly desolate. There were at least four hundred boats, and a fence around the entire property, but three gates were open. Even though he didn't see anyone around, Tim tried to make it appear that he knew where he was going, as if he had his own boat there. The boats were set up in aisles, and he figured that walking quickly he could see all of them within five minutes. He walked down the first aisle and turned up the second aisle.

"Hey, can I help you?" The words sent a wave of panic through him that he attempted to conceal as he turned to a short, stocky man, who seemed to be an attendant.

Tim smiled. "Nah, just looking around. I'm gonna buy a boat, and I'm trying to get some ideas."

"This ain't a showroom, pal."

Tim laughed, as if the man had made a joke. "I know, but I heard there was an Oceanfast 360 here, and I wanted to get a look at it."

"You know what those things run?"

"Pretty steep, from what I hear. Me and a couple of friends, we're thinking of going in on it together."

The attendant thought about that for a moment, then finally shrugged and pointed. "Third aisle. But don't try and board it."

Tim nodded. "Gotcha. Thanks."

Tim walked away, literally shaking from the encounter. He could feel sweat drenching his clothes. He'd have to get himself under control; if he was going to react this way to a nonincident, he would likely die of stress when he had a close call.

Halfway down the aisle, he saw the Oceanfast 360 and instantly felt a wave of disappointment. It was the smaller version. The boat was made in two basic lengths, and this seventy-footer was not the one he was looking for.

He put his head down and walked briskly back to the car.

THE license plate on the car following Eden was stolen. It had been the property of an eighty-one-year-old grandmother in Cherry Hill, New Jersey. Nick called Eden to tell her what he'd learned. She sounded less worried. "I haven't seen him in days."

"Maybe he's just being more careful."

"Is it the police?"

"Not unless they're into stealing license plates."

"So who is it?" she asked

"I have no idea, Eden. But only go to very public places. When you're home, make sure the doors and windows are locked and the alarm is on. And if you see him again, call me immediately."

TIM knew it was the same boat the moment he saw it. Not just the color, but the stripe design. It was highly unlikely that there could be two such boats.

It was one of at least a hundred boats at the pier in Southold, but it was the only one surrounded by its own fence, a silent statement that it was more expensive and more important than the others. It was in the water, and Tim could see a jet underneath it—a machine to keep the water from freezing.

From his vantage point, he could make out only the last three letters of the name on the hull, *e-a-s*. He basically just stood there letting the memory of that day on the water once again roll over him.

"Not bad, huh?"

Tim turned and saw a young woman dressed in work coveralls under a ski jacket. She held a sander in her hand; she was obviously there working on a boat. She had a welcoming smile on her face.

Tim gave the Oceanfast another quick glance. "Beautiful, though I might go with a different color."

She laughed. "That's for sure. Have you ever been on one?"

"In a showroom once. Is it yours?"

Another laugh. "Afraid not. Mine's over there. You could fit mine in one of the bedrooms on this one."

"Do you know who owns it?"

She shook her head. "I tried to talk to a guy doing work on it the other day, but he blew me off."

"People come on this time of year?"

She nodded. "Yeah, but he wasn't one of the owners; he was there doing work. The owners are definitely big shots."

"Because it's so expensive?" he asked.

"Well, sure, but also because of the people that have been on it. A lot of Washington types, even some senators and congressmen."

"Is that right? Which ones, do you know?" He smiled. "I'm sort of a political junkie."

She thought for a moment. "Well, I definitely know Senator Collinsworth was on it at least once 'cause I recognized him."

The news that Collinsworth had been on board was jolting to Tim and instantly reestablished his suspicions about Danny. "Wow," he said. "When was Collinsworth on?"

"Last summer. There were a whole bunch of people in tuxedos. Imagine putting on formal clothes to go out on a boat."

"Hard to believe," he agreed. He gently tried to coax more information out of her, but she didn't seem to have any. She wished him a good day and went back to her work.

JIMMY Lee's story didn't set the world on fire, but that didn't concern him. He knew that the reaction to the second part would be far greater. And he knew that timing was everything.

For Senator Collinsworth, the story was a potentially major problem. Not so much because he had steered work to a company owned by a relative; that was understood to be business as usual in Washington. Besides, there was no allegation that the company was incompetent or unable to perform the work they contracted to do.

Collinsworth was upset because of what it portended for the plans he had laid so painstakingly. Once the Federal Center in New Jersey was judged a resounding success, it would be duplicated in virtually every state. Hundreds of billions of dollars would be involved, and with Collinsworth's plan of spreading the contracting work to many small-sized businesses, he could build a network of beholden contributors that could fill his campaign war chest.

If the story about Wallace damaged that plan, it would be an unmitigated disaster. So he had Keith Rivers plant the competing story, one that said that while Collinsworth had had the grand idea for these complexes, he stayed out of choosing contractors.

Collinsworth did not bother calling Danny. There was nothing to be gained; Danny would be smart enough to know that his days of his uncle getting him work were officially over. He might as well disappear along with his murdering partner, because as far as Uncle Fred was concerned, he no longer existed.

NICK MENTIONED THE Collinsworth story when Tim called him, but the last thing on Tim's mind was future business prospects.

"I've got more interesting news about Collinsworth," Tim said.

"Oh?"

"I found the boat that was out on the water that day; it's the one docked at Southold. And I found someone who told me that Collinsworth has been out on it."

Nick checked through his paperwork. "The boat is owned by Bennington, Inc. I'll have them checked out. In the meantime, I've got something to tell you that you're not going to like."

Tim braced himself. "What is it?"

"I found out from my sources that there's an FBI agent up here from Florida, assigned to this case. Remember the car that blew up on the Jersey Turnpike?"

"Of course," Tim said. "It was carrying Cintron 421. Danny and I were worried about it."

"Well, now you've got a bigger reason to worry. The driver apparently called your office a few times in the week before the explosion. They think he talked to you."

Tim exploded. "Now they think I'm a terrorist? What'll it be next? Maybe I killed Kennedy!"

"So you know nothing about it?"

"Of course not. I—" He paused for a few moments.

"What's going on?" Nick asked. "You still there?"

The frustration in Tim's voice was suddenly replaced by excitement. "It all fits! Damn . . . it all fits!" Tim went on to explain his suspicions about Danny. "So this guy may have called our office, but he must have talked to him. It has to involve the business. Danny must want me out of the way."

"Do you know why?"

"I'll figure it out. First he tried to have me killed, then—"

"Tried to have you killed?"

"Absolutely. I was the only person who knew Maggie was going out on the boat. That explosion was meant to kill me, not her."

"How did her finger wind up at the racquetball court?"

"Hell. I don't know; there are a lot of pieces we don't have, but every one we do have involves Danny. And Collinsworth has to be involved as well."

CINDY could tell that something was bothering Novack. This didn't qualify as a stunning insight; something had been bothering him pretty much every day for as long as she had known him. It always had to do with his work, but she had never gotten used to it and was always frustrated by her inability to make him feel better.

On this particular night, he seemed more troubled than usual. He was drinking coffee in the dining room after a dinner during which he had hardly said anything, and she was clearing the table. "Is it the Wallace case?" she asked.

"What?" he asked, obviously distracted.

"Is it the Wallace case?"

"Is what the Wallace case?"

"Whatever it is that has you so upset."

"I tried to hide it."

She smiled. "Good job."

"I don't like where it's going," he confirmed.

"I saw the story about the senator getting him the contract."

"Are you really interested in this?" he asked. "Or just trying to make me feel better?"

She smiled. "Both."

"Okay, but it won't work. I simply refuse to feel better."

"I know."

"I couldn't care less about the story. That's just political crap."

"Then what's wrong? Is it that you haven't found Wallace?"

"That ain't helping, but there's something else. The FBI's tied him to that car that exploded on the turnpike," Novack said.

"A terrorist?" she asked, surprised. "Are they right?"

He shook his head. "No way. It just doesn't ring true."

"But you still think he killed his wife?"

He half whirled to face her. "He killed his wife. No doubt about it. And he killed that woman in Kinnelon."

"Okay, okay. Don't take it out on me. What about that guy Cashman? Did Wallace kill him, too?"

"I don't know. I don't know where the hell he fits in." Then, "There's too much about this case I don't know."

"And that bothers you," she said.

He smiled. "No kidding, Sherlock."

"I think we should go into the bedroom and make love."

He shrugged. "Might as well; nothing else to do," he said, then ducked as she threw the expected dish towel at him.

EDEN sensed the gray minivan was back before she saw it. She was in the supermarket, and as she walked toward the front of the store, she looked into the parking lot. There it was, near the back, with a vantage point to the store exit.

She left her cart in a corner, went into the restroom, and called Nick's office from her cell phone. His assistant said that he was in court. Eden then went to a pay phone and called Tim.

Just the ringing of the cell phone scared him; he had never heard it ring. The caller ID showed a number he didn't recognize, and he debated whether to answer it. "Hello?"

"Tim, it's me, Eden. I'm sorry to call you—"

"It's okay," he said. She sounded upset. "What is it?"

"I'm being followed again by the same car. What do you think I should do? Nick's in court."

Tim was worried. "I think you should drive to the police station. Tell them you have my dog, and that the guy following you must have something to do with me."

"Are you sure about that? It might help them get to you."

He thought about it a moment. "Where are you now?" he asked, and she told him.

"Okay. Stay where you are for about fifteen minutes, then drive to Paramus Park Mall," he said. "It won't be crowded now; it's too early. Park in the rear parking lot and go into any store. I think there's still an Ann Taylor."

"Then what?"

"Stay inside for at least a half hour, then get back in your car. The guy won't be following you at that point. Call and tell Nick what happened when you get home."

"What are you going to do?"

"I'm going to start taking my life back."

EDEN was not happy about following Tim's instructions. She wasn't concerned for her own safety; the Paramus Park Mall was a very public place. But she was very worried. If the man was no longer out there when she returned to her car, then it would have to mean that Tim had intervened.

She had the feeling that intervening with people like this was not Tim's specialty. But she had no real option other than to do as he requested; it was Tim's life that was at stake, and he had to do whatever he could to save it. So she headed for Paramus Park, sure the minivan must be behind her.

Tim had little more confidence in his ability to handle this than Eden. But the clock was ticking on how long he could elude the police, and he still instinctively felt that if he didn't create something positive, his prospects for exoneration were nil. So he too headed for Paramus Park. And he brought his gun.

He got to Paramus Park before Eden and positioned himself in a place where he would be able to see her drive in. It was almost ten minutes before she parked toward the front of the rear lot, near the entrance to Ann Taylor.

There were cars at the very rear of the lot, bordering the woods. Tim had worked at Men's Wearhouse one college summer break and remembered that this was the area in which employees of all the stores were told to park. Tim assumed that the gray minivan would park among these cars, so as to stay a safe distance from Eden, yet not stand out in an otherwise empty area.

For Tim's plan to have any chance of success, the man would have to park in this area.

He did.

Once the minivan was settled in, and it was apparent that the driver was staying put, Tim waited five minutes and then parked two rows behind it. He walked up toward the passenger side of the minivan and felt a wave of fear when the driver looked up, but by then the die had been cast. Pulling the gun from his pocket, he yanked the passenger door open.

The large blond man whirled and started reaching for his inside jacket pocket but stopped when he saw Tim point the gun with two hands and scream, "DON'T MOVE!"

The man seemed unruffled but partially raised his hands, palms upward, "No problem, pal. Whatever you say."

Tim got into the car and closed the door, keeping the gun pointed. He spoke in a calm voice that even surprised himself. "Reach into your pocket slowly and take out your gun. Place it on the seat, pointed at yourself. If it isn't, I'm going to shoot you."

The man did as he was told. Tim pulled the gun toward himself but did not pick it up. "Okay. Drive," he said.

The man pulled out of the lot, and Tim directed him up Route 17, getting off at Route 202 and heading toward Rockland County. The ride took twenty minutes. Tim's arms ached, but he was not about to lower the gun. Feeling an almost surreal sense of alertness, he directed the man down a long dirt road to an area where he and his friends had played sports years ago.

"Okay, turn the car off but leave the key in the ignition," he said. "Now put your palms on the dashboard. I'm going to walk around the car. If you move your hands, I will shoot you in the head."

Tim walked around the car at the front, pointing the gun at his captive. He opened the driver's door. "Get out and stand with your hands clasped behind your head," he said.

The man got out slowly and did as he was told.

"Why are you following that woman?" Tim asked.

"I wanted her to lead me to you. So I could kill you."

"Why do you want to kill me?"

The man smiled confidently. "None of your business."

"Who are you?"

"None of your business," the man repeated. "I'm getting tired of this. I'm leaving, and the only way you're going to stop me is to shoot me. And I would be surprised if you had the balls for that."

"Try me," Tim said, desperately hoping that he wouldn't.

The man took a half step forward. Tim tensed, but when he didn't shoot, the man smiled and took another step.

So Tim shot him.

He wasn't even sure he did it intentionally. The shot went off to the right, grazing the man's shoulder.

The man reached for his arm and put his hand on a growing spot of blood. The look on his face was one of such rage that Tim's blood ran cold. The man recovered quickly and smiled. "You think things have been bad lately? They just got ten times worse."

With that he did an about-face, walking away from Tim and toward the woods. He had determined that Tim would shoot him again if he felt threatened, but would never shoot him in the back.

Tim waited until the man was a couple of hundred feet away, and then got back into the car on the driver's side. He was profoundly shaken by the encounter.

On the way back to Paramus Park, Tim called Nick and was relieved when he answered the phone. He told him as concisely as he could what had happened, then said, "Go to Paramus Park; there'll be a gray minivan parked in the back of the rear parking lot. It will have a gun on the front seat, which will have the fingerprints of the driver. In fact, both of our fingerprints will be all over the car."

"Where is Eden?" Nick asked.

Tim was pulling into Paramus Park at the moment and was relieved to find that her car was gone. "I assume she's home; can we get someone to protect her?"

"Yes. Now get out of there quickly; in a little while that place is going to be crawling with cops."

12

NICK knew exactly what it meant when he got an 8 a.m. call from Novack, asking him to come for a meeting as soon as possible. It meant they had hit pay dirt on the fingerprint, and that Novack wanted to know everything that Nick knew.

Nick had been cryptic the day before, telling Novack about the gray minivan with the gun on the seat, and mentioning that it had a direct relevance to the Wallace case. The police had descended on the place, but Nick stayed away.

Novack and Anders were waiting for Nick when he arrived. "You want coffee or something?" Anders asked.

"I'll have black coffee," said Nick.

Novack poured Nick a cup. "So tell me where the car with the gun came from."

"So tell me that Jeff Cashman is really Billy Zimmerman."

"Was. His body was fished out of the Passaic a few days ago."

Nick was surprised to hear this news, but he took it in stride. "I suppose you think Tim came out of hiding to do that? You think he runs a murder factory? The General Motors of homicide?"

Novack smiled. "Let's just say he's a person of interest."

"Okay," Nick said. "Moving on. Whose prints were on the gun?"

Novack exchanged a glance with Anders. "I'll tell you what. For the purpose of this conversation, you tell us what you know, and we'll tell you what we know."

"That works. Until it butts up against client confidentiality."

"Fair enough. You start," said Novack.

"Okay. My sister is a friend of Tim Wallace's; that's how he came to call me for representation. Wallace left his dog with her before he ran off. She discovered that someone was following her in recent days, maybe thinking she would lead him to Wallace. Which she could not do."

"Because she doesn't have the slightest idea where he is," Novack said dryly.

"Right. And did I mention she's on my staff?" Nick had told Eden he was "hiring" her, at one dollar a month, so she could hide behind client confidentiality as well.

"What a surprise," Anders said. "Keep going."

"I received a phone call saying that the car was there, with the gun on the seat. I have a description of the man as well."

"A call from who?"

"Sorry," Nick said, tacitly citing confidentiality. "But I can tell you that the man was slightly injured in the encounter; a bullet grazed his left arm. I believe it's your turn. Who was the driver?"

"His name is Richie Patrick. He's thirty-one years old, born in Bloomington, Indiana. He was wanted in three different states for three different murders."

"A hit man?"

Novack shook his head. "That's too limiting. He's available for hire to do pretty much anything, but murder is his specialty."

"So there's a hit man involved in this case, but you make Wallace for all these murders? How does that make sense?"

"Wallace is charged with his wife's murder, and he's guilty."

"You said Patrick 'was wanted,' " said Nick.

Novack nodded. "Right. He was identified as killed in a plane crash eighteen months ago in Minnesota."

"Well, he's apparently made a comeback. There's something else I want to tell you guys," Nick said.

"We're all ears," said Novack.

"There was a boat out on the water that day, not far from Wallace's boat, when the explosion happened. The people on board never reported it and left the scene before the Coast Guard arrived." Nick proceeded to talk about the Oceanfast 360, and how Tim and Maggie had seen it moments before the explosion.

"Why should we care about this?" asked Novack.

"Because I now know which boat it was, what company owns it, and who has been on it in the past."

"Who might that be?"

"Senator Fred Collinsworth."

IT SEEMED as if there were more dogs than people at the Federal Center in Newark. Every square inch of the building was being sniffed and examined, over and over again.

One of the features of the building in which the dinner party was to be held was an ability to lock it down in the event of an outside threat, closing it up into an airtight, virtually impregnable fortress.

The computers that controlled such a lockdown, and the ventilation system that was triggered to provide oxygen, were checked and rechecked. Once again Will was called in to provide a detailed description of the system, albeit to a different Homeland Security computer expert.

This one's name was Teri Berman, an attractive woman who looked incredibly familiar to Will. He had a hunch that she'd shot him down at the Purple Rose one night, but didn't want to bring it up, in case another opportunity presented itself.

This wasn't such an opportunity. She came into the computer room at the Federal Center building with a no-nonsense attitude, asking that he show her everything about the system, starting at the beginning. "Leave nothing out."

Will was slightly annoyed at having to go through this again. "Don't you guys ever talk to each other down there?" he asked.

"What does that mean?"

"I went through this with one of your colleagues two weeks ago."

She shrugged, not knowing what he was talking about, and not really caring. Inefficiency in the bureaucracy was not exactly a news event. "So you should have it down pat by now."

When they were finished, Teri made it very clear to Will that he would not be on the scene on the big night. She and other government operators would be running the computer room. He was to provide them with all applicable passwords and codes, which he did. It wasn't that they didn't trust Will; it was simply that they didn't trust anyone.

The outside of the building was scrutinized just as thoroughly. There was no way a vehicle could get close enough to damage the building, even with Cintron 421. Airspace would be off-limits, and fighter planes would be enforcing that restriction. Additional security would be fanned out into surrounding neighborhoods.

Everything was confirmed repeatedly by the Secret Service to be as it should be. The word was communicated to an anxious White House that all was secure.

The fact that they were wrong would not be known until it was too late.

"I THINK we should go to Donovan with this," Novack said. In addition to all the other new information they had received, they had just learned that the Oceanfast in question was registered to a holding company whose ownership could not be determined. However, the listed name on the documents was Keith Rivers, right-hand man for Collinsworth.

"Why?" asked Anders.

"Because this is way past what we thought. And I'm not sure Wallace is behind it."

"You've got to be kidding."

Novack had been slowly moving toward this position for a while. "I was positive he killed his wife. But he's not a terrorist, he didn't hop down to Florida to kill that woman, he didn't create Zimmerman out of thin air, and he didn't tie that boat to Collinsworth."

Anders played devil's advocate. "Maybe Collinsworth's nephew told him, and he made up the story that it was out there the day he killed his wife."

Novack wasn't convinced. "The finger doesn't fit in either. Why, if he was behind all this other stuff, would he have saved the finger and planted it?"

"He's a sicko, remember?"

"I don't think so, not anymore."

"Come on, Novack. You saying some mysterious bad guys kill his wife, then wait almost a year to—"

"But that's the point. If he didn't do it, then the wife probably wasn't the target. It was the first time she was on the boat. What if he was supposed to die?"

"Then why not kill him now? Why go through all this stuff?"

Novack shrugged. "Beats me; I'm just a dumb cop." He looked at his watch and stood up. "Call Donovan and set up a meeting."

"Donovan will think you're nuts."

Novack shrugged. "It won't be the first time."

FOR Senator Collinsworth, the worst was apparently over. Jimmy Lee Curry's story had run about his connection to Tim's company, and while it was a short-term embarrassment, the damage appeared to have been minor. Collinsworth had commissioned a poll to be taken on the subject and was relieved to find that eighty-one percent of Americans were not even aware of it.

The best news was a phone call Detective Anders had made to Keith Rivers, informing him of recent developments, which were so significant that Novack had doubts about Tim's guilt. Putting Anders on the payroll was one of the smartest moves he had made.

Collinsworth would have Rivers contact Danny and tell him about Novack's doubts, which might even lead to Tim's coming out of hiding. This was dependent, of course, on Danny knowing how to contact him, as Collinsworth suspected he did.

The recent events would allow the senator to focus on the weekend's opening of the Federal Center. As the home state senator and a man directly responsible for the project, Collinsworth was going to make the welcoming speech. With the president in attendance, every major media outlet in the country would be there.

It would be a platform and a moment that Collinsworth would not let go to waste. He had three speechwriters working on it, and he was torturing them to get it exactly right. It was to focus on the project's concept as a way to defeat terrorism and protect Americans; that was how Collinsworth wanted to be viewed.

"I NEED TO SPEAK TO NOVACK" were the first words Cindy heard when she picked up the phone.

"I'm sorry, but he's not here," she said.

"It's important that I see him. It's a matter of life and death."

"Who is this?" she asked.

"Tim Wallace. Can you please give him a message for me?"

The name sent a shock wave through her, and it never entered her mind to be worried by the fact that he knew her number. "Yes, I will," she said. Novack was due to come over at any time.

"Please tell him to meet me at Squires Delicatessen in Fort Lee. Tell him to take a seat at a booth in the back, and I'll be in five minutes after he arrives."

"He'll want to know what this is about."

"It's about me giving him information that will blow this case wide open, and then turning myself in after I do."

"I'll tell him, but I'm not sure how long it will take."

"That's okay; I'll wait. He's the only one I'd tell this to."

Click. The call was disconnected, but Cindy only stopped staring at the phone when she heard the front door open.

Novack came in and saw the look on her face. "What's wrong?"

"Tim Wallace wants to see you right away." She described the conversation in as much detail as she could remember.

"Did he say I needed to come alone?" he asked.

"No, but he said it had to be you."

"Did you use that phone?" He asked, pointing to the phone on the desk.

"Yes."

"Don't use it again. Make any calls on your cell." He wanted to preserve the possibility of calling back the number by using *69, should that become necessary.

Novack took out his own cell phone and called Anders. He described what had happened, and in three minutes they had a plan to place officers strategically on the blocks surrounding the deli, also two in the deli in plainclothes, posing as customers. Novack would delay leaving for fifteen minutes to give it time to set up.

"Are you sure you should go?" Cindy asked when he got off the phone. "You said yourself he's a murderer."

"Maybe," Novack said. "Either way we'll have cops everywhere. We can play by his rules for now."

The fifteen minutes spent waiting were among the longest Novack had ever endured. There was always the danger that Wallace would change his mind.

The truth was that Novack was suspicious of Wallace's motives; if he had crucial information to impart, he could have done so through his lawyer. He briefly considered whether to call Nick Alexander, but it was entirely possible that Wallace was doing something contrary to his own best interests, and Novack didn't want him talked out of it.

He went to the bedroom to change his clothes. He called Anders to confirm that everything was ready. Satisfied that it was, he went back downstairs.

Then something hit Novack. "Did he say how he got this number, or why he thought I'd be here?"

Cindy shook her head. "No."

The idea of Wallace knowing where Cindy lived was discomforting. He said, "Make sure the windows and doors are locked. Don't open it for anybody. If I want to get in, I'll call you first."

"You really think he might come here?"

"No, just covering every base."

She hugged him, and he left the house. He was halfway to his car when he heard her through the partially open door. "Call me as soon as it's over," she said.

He turned to tell her that he would do exactly that, and the turn caused the bullet to miss his heart and hit below the right shoulder. His bulletproof vest did not provide full protection from the "cop-killer" bullet, and he was blown back five feet from the impact.

He saw Cindy scream and rush toward him. He wanted to yell at her to go back, but he couldn't form the words.

TIM was watching CNN when he found out that he'd shot Novack. It started out as an alert that said Novack was shot in front of his house, and identified him as the lead detective in the Tim Wallace murder case.

Within five minutes, coverage became wall-to-wall. There was open speculation that Tim was responsible, followed by a vaguely worded statement from the state police public relations office that seemed to confirm that he'd been the shooter. There was no word on Novack's condition, only that he was still alive.

As bizarre as the preceding weeks had been for Tim, this was way beyond all that. He watched as if disembodied, and even wondered if there was another Tim Wallace, an alter ego of himself, that had set out to destroy the world.

None of it made sense. Somebody had done this as part of the grand scheme, but why bother ratcheting up the pressure? And why Novack, the commander of the anti-Tim forces?

Tim called Nick's cell phone, and he was relieved when he answered. "Nick, what the hell is going on?"

Nick was standing behind police barricades outside Cindy's house. "Somebody shot Novack; they think it was you."

"Why?"

"Did you call him tonight?" Nick asked.

"Novack? Of course not. Are they saying I did?"

"Somebody called saying it was you and asking to meet Novack. When he walked out of the house, he was shot."

"I swear, it wasn't me. Can't they trace the call?"

"I'm trying to find out more, but they're saying very little."

Tim was watching television while talking, and suddenly there was a panning shot of the street, and he saw Nick on camera. "You're there. . . . I can see you on TV."

"Are they showing my good side? Call me later; I gotta go."

NOVACK regained consciousness within minutes of arriving at the hospital. He had lost considerable blood and was given a massive transfusion. It took a few hours for him to stabilize sufficiently to be relatively clearheaded.

At that moment, he was the only person in the police department, and one of the few in America, who did not believe he was shot by Tim Wallace.

His reasoning was simple. Wallace had called Cindy before Novack got home, and the message was for Novack to leave immediately for the meeting. He therefore already had to have been in position at the house, waiting for Novack to leave, so he could shoot him. But if he were there, he would have shot Novack on the way in. There wouldn't have been any reason to wait; he couldn't have been sure that Novack would take the bait to meet him.

And Novack finally, instinctively, knew one other thing with certainty. Not only was Wallace not the shooter.

He was not a murderer at all.

SENATOR Walter Evans could feign outrage with the best of them, and when he took to the Senate floor the next morning, he was in rare form. Evans was only a freshman senator, but his charisma had vaulted him into the group of politicians considered presidential timber. The chamber was mostly empty, but with the C-Span cameras rolling, he could be sure that his words would reverberate on cable news.

Evans never mentioned Collinsworth by name. He acted as if saddened that he had to address the issue at all, and in the process implicitly criticize a member of his own party. Railing against the "old way of doing business" that wasn't good enough in "this era of terror," he took full advantage of Jimmy Lee Curry's revelation that Collinsworth had put a murderer on the government payroll.

Susan Moreno enjoyed the speech immensely. She thought that her boss was doing a great job, avoiding specifics to make a very specific point, and readied herself for calls asking for his appearance on Sunday talk shows. She couldn't help smiling over the knowledge that her counterpart on Collinsworth's staff, Keith Rivers, must be furious and seeking revenge.

It was just one of the things she couldn't have been more wrong about.

THERE WAS A STEADY STREAM of visitors to Novack's room during the next twenty-four hours. A parade of fellow detectives came by to show their support for a downed colleague, and they were delighted to find that Novack was doing very well. So well that by late morning he was being insulted and ridiculed with regularity.

Novack expressed to Anders and Donovan his feeling that Tim had not been the one who shot him.

"Maybe you showed up before he could get a good line of fire," Anders said.

"I can prove it wasn't him."

"Then go right ahead," said Donovan.

Novack turned to Anders. "Cindy's out in the hall. Ask her to come in."

Anders went to get Cindy, who'd been at the hospital virtually every moment, except for running a crucial errand.

"Tell these guys what you did this morning."

"I listened to some interviews in your Wallace case file."

Donovan turned to Novack. "You realize you just broke about ten departmental rules by having her do that."

"Oops. My bad," said Novack. Then, to Cindy, "Tell them what you found out."

"It wasn't Wallace on the phone," Cindy said. "Not even close."

"How can you be sure of that?" Donovan asked.

"Captain, she's a speech therapist."

"I can go into specifics about speech patterns and accents, if you want," Cindy said. "But there's not a doubt in my mind. The person who called was a Midwesterner; maybe Michigan, maybe Indiana. He's also older than Wallace."

"Richie Patrick," Donovan said, since the hit man whose fingerprints were all over the car was from Indiana.

Novack nodded. "I also talked to Kelly in forensics; they think the shooter was in the alley adjacent to the house across the street. It was no easy shot."

"Have we been wrong on Wallace all along?" Donovan asked.

"You weren't. I was."

The most worried man in the room at that moment was Anders. He believed it possible that the reason Novack was shot was because he was starting to believe in Tim's innocence. And Anders had not kept that information confidential.

He had told it to Keith Rivers, which was the same as telling it to Senator Collinsworth.

IT HAD been a while since Eden had heard anything from Tim, and she was going crazy. The media had already tried and convicted him of the Novack shooting. At least Nick had assured her that Tim had had nothing to do with the shooting, and for the first time he admitted sharing her feeling that Tim was innocent of all other charges as well. She could use all the comfort she could get.

Eden hadn't been going out much, out of concern that Richie Patrick might reappear. She hadn't seen him since that day at Paramus Park. Perhaps he was deterred by the police officer Novack had assigned to sit in a squad car in front of her house.

But while Eden felt fairly personally secure, she was in constant fear for Tim, and she checked her e-mail every few minutes, hoping that he would contact her. It was almost dinnertime when Eden received the e-mail. It read:

> I hate to ask you this, but I need you to tell Danny that I have to see him. Don't call; tell him I need his help, and that he should meet me tomorrow morning at ten o'clock, where we used to play touch football. Thanks, and be careful.

Eden e-mailed back asking where Danny lived. She waited for an hour, but there was no response. Eden had no way to get Danny's address online or through the phone book; she didn't even know his last name. She had two choices. One was to go to the company office in the morning and hope that Danny came in early enough to still be able to meet Tim at ten o'clock. The other alternative was to go to the Purple Rose. Tim had told her that his friends used to hang out there almost every night, and if Danny wasn't there, maybe somebody would know how to contact him.

She went outside and told the police officer out front that she was leaving to have a drink with a friend, and he nodded and said he would follow her. When she drove to the Purple Rose, he just pulled into the parking lot behind her and waited in his car.

The Purple Rose was fairly crowded, and since Eden had never met Danny, she went to the bartender for help. "Excuse me, can you tell me if Danny is here? He's a friend of Tim Wallace's."

"Danny? Sure, he's right over there." He pointed to a table across the room, where Danny was sitting with Will. "In the blue shirt."

"Thanks," Eden said, and headed for the table.

As she and Danny made eye contact, he noticeably tensed. He had seen her in front of Tim's apartment, after the finger was found at the racquetball club. It couldn't be a coincidence.

He stood up, and she said, "Danny?"

"Yes."

"I need to speak to you about something. In private."

"Sure, of course. Will, can you give us a couple of minutes?"

Will had never met Eden, and it took him a moment to register that he was being asked to leave. Then, "Yeah . . . no problem."

He got up and took a walk toward the back of the restaurant.

"Have a seat," Danny said. "I'm sorry, what's your name?"

"That doesn't matter. I have a message for you from Tim."

"How is he?"

"Fine. He wants to meet you tomorrow morning at ten."

Danny instinctively looked around to make sure no one was close enough to hear what they were saying. "Where?"

"At the place where you used to play touch football. He wants you to come alone, without telling anyone else."

"Why does he want to meet with me?"

"I don't know."

"Do you know where he is? Can I reach him tonight? Maybe he wants me to bring money—"

"I've already told you everything I know."

She turned to leave, and saw Will walk back. She hoped that Danny would keep her message to himself, but she had her doubts.

Once she left, Will asked, "Who the hell was that?"

"A friend of a friend," Danny said.

"This have something to do with Tim?"

"No."

"Thanks for sharing," Will said, reaching for his beer.

Eden called Nick, thinking that Tim would be fine with her doing so. Nick wasn't in, so she left a message on his machine to call her. She signaled to the officer as she was approaching her car, and he nodded and pulled out behind her.

13

RICHIE Patrick was waiting for Eden when she entered her house. He sat calmly on the couch, petting Travis with one hand and casually holding a handgun in the other. "If you scream, it will be the last sound you ever make," he said.

Her panic was such that she couldn't catch her breath. All she could think about was the police officer outside and how she might alert him. "What do you want?"

He laughed. "More than you've got, but you'll have to do for now."

"The house is surrounded by police."

"You mean that clown in the black-and-white outside? Where is Wallace?"

"I have no idea."

"Sure you do. But we've got time for that later. Let's go."

"Where?"

"Let's make some ground rules." His sudden intensity was chilling. "Don't . . . ask . . . another . . . single . . . question."

He took her by the arm and led her out the back door.

NICK got Eden's message around ten o'clock, having just returned from dinner out. He returned the call, but there was no answer. He assumed that she was out and wasn't very worried, because she had the police officer to follow her. He left a message for her to call him back.

Waking up briefly at four in the morning, he reflected on the fact that she had not called him back, and assumed she got home late. He still wasn't particularly worried, so he went back to sleep.

THE meeting was at the same location in Rockland County where Tim had taken Richie Patrick. He chose it because there was only one entrance in by car, a long, winding road that he could observe from the hill above. If Danny was not alone, he could be out long before anyone would even know he was there.

He was in position well in advance. At five to ten, Danny's car started up the road. He appeared to be alone.

Danny stopped his car on the field where they had played touch football all those years before, got out, and looked around. He whirled in surprise when he heard words yelled from up above. "Start walking up the hill!"

Danny looked up and shielded his eyes. "Tim?"

"Start walking up the hill!"

Danny walked up the only path that would take him there. Tim kept his eyes on the road but saw no sign of anyone. He let Danny get three quarters of the way up before starting down to meet him.

Danny heard Tim before he saw him, and was pretty much blinded by the sun over Tim's shoulder. "Tim, is that you?"

"It's me."

Danny again shielded the sun with his hand, which was how he saw that Tim was pointing a gun at him. "What's that for?"

"We need to talk, Danny."

"So let's talk. Why do you have a gun? Is that thing real?"

"Why are you doing this to me, Danny?"

"Doing what?" Danny said, his voice cracking slightly, his fear evident. "Come on, Tim, it's just me here."

"You set me up from the beginning. You killed Maggie."

"No, no—"

"Danny, tell me the truth, or I'll kill you right here."

"I swear I don't know what you're talking about. Please—"

"I'm talking about you knowing I was going to be on the boat that day. I'm talking about you knowing I was in Wyoming, about you being at the racquetball club."

"Of course I knew where you were; we're partners. You always know where I am, too."

"Danny, all I want to know is why you did it."

"Tim, I swear—"

"There was another boat out there the day Maggie died. I found it. You know who's been out on that boat? Your uncle."

Danny seemed unable to process all of this. "My uncle?"

"Right. Keith Rivers signed for the license. Were you out there that day, Danny? Waiting for the explosion?"

"Yours is the only boat I've ever been on, Tim. I swear it."

"What does your uncle get out of ruining my life, Danny? What do you get out of it?"

"Tim, we're friends since we were kids. Why would I do this to you? Why would my uncle do it? He's pissed off about it."

Tim walked toward him, until he was about ten feet away. He was pointing the gun with two hands. "Danny, you're going to tell me the truth by the time I count to three, or I'm going to shoot you. One . . . Two . . ."

The fact that Danny didn't confess to anything did not come from some place of courage, or principle. He was so confused, so frightened, that he did not even have the capacity to make up a story.

"Tim, I have told you the truth," he finally said, and braced himself. "Please . . . there's nothing else I can say."

Tim lowered the gun. "Danny, I need help."

EDEN had absolutely no idea where she was. Patrick had tied her hands and placed a gag over her mouth and a blindfold over her eyes, then put her in the back of what seemed to be a van. She tried to figure out how far they drove, but that proved impossible. Instead she tried to get her fear under control.

When they arrived at their destination, he led her over what seemed almost like a footbridge, took her down some stairs, and cuffed her to what felt like pipes. She was surprised he took off the gag but left the blindfold on.

"This is gonna be your home for a while," he said. "Depending on your behavior, it could be the last one you ever have."

She didn't answer him.

"I'll be back tomorrow. No one can hear you anyway, but an intercom system records any sound. If I find that you've screamed, even spoken, I will cut open your throat and rip out your larynx. Understand?"

She nodded.

"Good. Tomorrow you'll tell me where your friend is."

He left, and she willed herself not to cry. The microphones would pick it up, and she didn't want to give him the satisfaction.

NICK tried Eden three times between seven and eight in the morning and then went to her house. He saw the officer parked in front of her house, identified himself, and asked where Eden was.

"She's inside," he said.

Nick could hear the dogs barking inside. "She's not answering her phone."

The officer got out of the car and followed Nick. They rang the bell a few times and pounded on the front door; then the officer broke its small window and reached in, unlocking it.

Eden's bed was still made, and it did not appear that the dogs had been fed. Nick knew there was no benign explanation for this.

She was in desperate trouble.

DANNY and Tim talked for almost three hours. It was unlike any conversation they had ever had; no sports, no business, no women. They were trying to figure out how Tim's life had been taken away from him, and how to get it back.

Much of the conversation was Tim filling in Danny on what he had learned, about the Oceanfast, about Collinsworth, about Wyoming, about Vasquez calling their office, and about Richie Patrick. He hoped something would trigger a thought in Danny's mind.

But Danny's reaction was primarily astonishment, especially about Collinsworth's possible involvement. "It doesn't compute," he said. "Your situation only makes him look bad."

"He's got an angle we haven't figured out," Tim said. "This somehow gets him what he wants."

"He really wants to be president, so how can this help?"

Tim had no answer for that, so he once again changed the subject, trying to stumble on something that made sense. "There has to be a bigger picture than we're seeing, another shoe that's going to drop. I'm the fall guy for something that hasn't happened yet."

"The Federal Center?" Danny asked. "The opening is Saturday night; the president is going to be there. The FBI has talked to me twice, and the Secret Service once. Maybe that's where the Cintron 421 was going."

"Well, it's not going to get there now," Tim said. "That place will be swimming with security; nothing is getting near there."

"But that guy called our office?"

Tim nodded. "Yeah, I thought he was calling you. What he must have been doing was pretending to be somebody else, maybe a salesman or something, just so my number would show up on his phone. The bastards have covered every base."

"I hope you don't mind my bringing this up, but what I don't understand," Danny said, "is how that could have been Maggie's finger. I mean, you saw the explosion, right?"

"All I remember was a flash of white. I assumed it was an explosion, and I believed them when they said Maggie's body was never found."

"But they were sure? I mean the DNA tests . . ."

"They said it's one in billions it could be wrong. And the labs aren't police labs, so . . ."

Tim's voice trailed off. Something was bothering him, something didn't make sense, and he couldn't quite put his finger on it.

"What is it?" Danny asked.

Tim was still silent, trying to focus on it.

"Tim?"

"Danny, I just thought of something; I've got to go."

"Okay; can I help?"

"I don't think so, but if you can, I'll get in touch."

They walked up the hill to Tim's car, so that he could drive Danny back to where he left his.

As soon as they got in the car, Tim turned the radio on to the local news, and it was the first story they heard. A woman named Eden Alexander was kidnapped, and it was believed to be tied to the Tim Wallace case.

"Oh, my God," Tim said, devastated. "It has to be Patrick. . . ."

"What would he want from her?" Danny asked.

"Me."

THE ceremony that would officially open the Federal Center was forty-eight hours away, and it could be said that the preparations were both complete and ongoing. Everything had been gone over countless times, yet things were being checked and rechecked. The U.S. Marshal's Office and Secret Service were running what amounted to a dress rehearsal with staffers from the White House and various senator's offices.

The evening was to be fairly simple. There would be a cocktail party, lasting ninety minutes. The president would arrive fifteen minutes prior to its end, then join the dignitaries as they moved into a large room where dinner would be served and speeches given.

That room was chosen because of the uniqueness of its security. In the event of danger, a computer would totally lock it down, closing impregnable metal doors, and simultaneously start an emergency ventilation system utilizing oxygen tanks in the basement.

The theory was planned for use in subsequent Federal Centers. Buildings would no longer have to be evacuated in an emergency, an often panic-filled process that by itself could result in injuries. A safe haven would be created within the structure itself.

Before dinner, short speeches would be given by Newark Congresswoman Nancy Fellows, Senator Evans, and Senator Collinsworth. As his remarks concluded, Collinsworth was to introduce the president for a short speech. Once dinner was finished, the president and his entourage would clear the building. The entire evening was scheduled to take three and a half hours.

Carl White spent virtually all of his time on the scene. His investigation into Ricardo Vasquez had run cold, but his instincts told him that Wallace's connection to the case meant it was tied to the Federal Center. He had warned his boss that the president's visit was a chance he shouldn't be taking, but with all the triple vigilance and maximum security, his boss claimed that the Federal Center that night would be the safest place on earth. So White was rapidly becoming an annoyance to Secret Service Captain Steven Radford, the man in charge for the evening. Radford tolerated White's constant presence, but he knew he had things under control.

TIM knew he could no longer go back to the house where he'd been staying. He'd told Eden that if she got into trouble she should give up his location, and he could only hope it would save her, but he knew that if she could identify Patrick, he would not let her live.

His focus had shifted completely. It was a new kind of agony. There was no escaping the truth that if not for him, this evil would not have entered Eden's life. He had to silently scream at himself to use it as a motivation to find a way out for both of them.

Tim checked into a place called the Village Motel in downtown Hackensack. It was the kind of establishment that did most of their room renting by the hour, but did not require ID or a credit card.

He called Nick, who was distraught, blaming himself for not doing more to protect his sister. Unfortunately, Nick had little more to offer about Eden's situation. No ransom or demands of any kind had been made.

After leaving Kiley and Travis with his assistant, Nick had been to see Novack, who was chafing to get out of the hospital. "For what it's worth, I think he's done a one-eighty on you," Nick said.

"What does that mean?" Tim asked.

"He wouldn't say so directly, but I've got a hunch he thinks you've been set up for something all along. Too bad he can't convince his captain and the district attorney."

"Will he see me?"

"Now you're turning yourself in?"

"No, I mean will he talk to me without arresting me? There are things he knows that I need to know. I think together we might have a chance to figure this out."

Nick thought about it. "I could talk to him," he said. "If he gives his word, we can take it to the bank."

PATRICK arrived at 7 a.m., though Eden had no way of knowing what time it was. He untied her but kept her blindfold on. It wasn't that he was afraid she would see where she was, since he was going to kill her anyway. It was just that he knew she would feel more vulnerable not being able to see, and he wanted her to give him the information quickly, so he could move on.

He grabbed her by the arm and took her to the bathroom. "If I find out you took the blindfold off, I will take a candle and burn out your eyes," he said, matter-of-factly. A few minutes later, he led her back out, sat her in a chair, and put a box of crackers in her hand. She ate a few, and he gave her a glass of water to drink.

She sat there, waiting, not knowing if he had left. Her fear and hatred were palpable. She knew that if she had the opportunity she would kill him without a moment's hesitation.

"There's a table in front of you," he said. "Put your hands on it, palms down."

She did as she was told.

"I'm going to ask you a question. Answer it correctly. Every time I have to ask it again, I'll cut off one finger."

She started to sob and shake, momentarily gripped in a fear beyond anything she could have imagined.

"Ready?" he said. "Where is Tim Wallace hiding?"

Tim had told her to reveal what she knew, and this kind of fear was not something she was equipped to deal with. She told Patrick where the house was, and answered a few specific questions about how to get there. He could tell she was telling the truth.

"Okay, you can take your hands off the table," he said. He debated whether to kill her then, but he decided to wait until afterward, when no cleanup would be necessary. Besides, if things went wrong, there might be a need for bargaining chips, and Eden alive was worth more than Eden dead. He tied and gagged her and left her in darkness.

Patrick drove immediately to the house in Lincoln Park. He no longer expected Tim to be there; once Eden's kidnapping was reported in the press, Tim would have found another place to hide.

Patrick had known he'd waited too long to get this location from Eden, but he had other plans to make. His employers would be unhappy, because having Tim in their custody was vital to their plan. But not having Tim would soon be the least of his employers' problems. Things were going to go very wrong for them, and by then it would be too late.

14

NICK and Novack quickly negotiated the terms and details of the meeting with Tim. Present would be Tim, Novack, and Nick, all promising in advance not to reveal that the meeting ever took place.

The location was to be Tim's motel, chosen because patrons could park in front of their own rooms. Nick and Novack pulled up in Nick's car, determined there was no one around, and quickly went in.

Tim was standing across the dingy room when they walked in. Nick closed the door behind them, and Novack and Tim just stared at each other. Both were so used to hating the other that it seemed to take time to digest that they were there for a common purpose.

"Nice place you've got here," said Novack.

Tim nodded. "Yeah. I appreciate your coming. I've had a lot of time to think about what's happened. You can believe me or not.

Nobody would go to all this trouble just to ruin my life. That doesn't make any sense. Plus I don't have those kinds of enemies. I didn't know Richie Patrick until the day I shot him."

"So why you?" Novack asked.

"Because it's about something much bigger. I was supposed to be the one killed on that boat that day. There was no way anyone could have known Maggie would be out there. I was supposed to be blown up, and they were out there on the Oceanfast watching, probably ready to finish the job if I somehow survived. The sun was behind us; they would have been looking into it. I doubt that they realized I was in the water, still alive."

Nick spoke. "So why haven't they killed you since?"

"Because they figured out a better way for them. I was going to be killed to get me out of the way so they could do something crim-inal; I must have been in their way without my knowing it."

"So instead of getting rid of you so they could do it, they decided to do it and blame you for it," Novack said.

"Right. They manipulated me like a damn puppet."

"Who knows you that well?"

"That's why you're here," Tim said. "To tell me. You told me that it was Maggie's finger at the club. How did you know that?"

Novack said, "We ran a DNA test. It came back conclusive."

"Matched against Maggie's DNA?"

Novack nodded. "Of course."

"Where did you get it?"

"Her DNA? We've had it since we opened the investigation into her death."

"But where did you get it? Maggie's body was lost at sea. And it's not like she was a convicted felon, somebody whose DNA would be on file. Where could you have gotten it?"

Novack slowly nodded his head. "Hell. I don't know."

He took out his cell phone and dialed a number. "Sam, about the Wallace case . . . I need you to get the file out. I want to know who collected the DNA, and how we got it. I'll wait."

Novack put his hand over the mouth and said to Tim and Nick,

"Sam's our forensics guy." He held the phone to his ear for almost ten minutes. Everyone in the room was silent, waiting for the answer. "I'm here," Novack said, as Sam came back on the line. "What did you come up with?" Another pause. "You're sure? Okay, thanks."

Novack hung up the phone. "Sam collected the DNA himself. He checked the file to make sure. You were in the hospital, and your assistant, Meredith Tunney, took Sam to your house. He got the DNA off your wife's toothbrush. Meredith gave it to him."

"Of course; why haven't I seen it? She ran my life. She scheduled our racquetball games; she knew when I'd be on the boat. . . . She knew absolutely everything."

"How long has she worked for you?" Nick asked.

"Since a few months before Maggie died." Tim sat down, trying to digest it. His dominant feeling was relief that Maggie had in fact died instantly and painlessly on the boat. "I'm not sure, but I think Meredith may have told me about the stone quarry near Carson."

"Where they were waiting for you."

"Right. Once Maggie died, and you told the world how guilty I was, they figured I'd have more value as someone to set up for what they were going to do in the future. But if it wasn't Maggie's DNA and Maggie's finger, whose was it?"

"We'll probably never know," Novack said. "They could have killed a woman who lived on the street just for that purpose. Now that we know how they got to you, we need to figure out why."

"It has to be about the business and Collinsworth."

Novack shook his head. "This is not some white-collar crime. We're looking at a bunch of murders, an exploding car, a kidnapping. That would be pretty dirty, even for a U.S. senator."

"It's the Federal Center," Tim said. "Something must be planned for that, and I'd bet it's tomorrow night. Meredith was in a position to give out passes during the construction. She could have gotten people in there."

"But why plan something and do all this to alert the opposition?"

"Because they're not worried about the opposition. They don't think they can be stopped."

"IT'S MEREDITH. I NEED TO talk to you about Tim."

"Do you know where he is?" Will asked.

"I don't want to talk about it on the phone, but it's very important. I couldn't reach Danny, and I need to talk about it with someone right away."

"Okay . . . sure," he said. "Should I come to the office?"

"No, I'll come to you." Will was in Ridgewood, so they made arrangements to meet in front of a small park on Ridgewood Avenue. "I'll be in my red Toyota. We can talk while I drive. That way no one can listen in."

Will had been waiting for ten minutes when he saw her pull up. She reached across and opened the door for him.

"What's going on with Tim?" Will asked.

She pulled off. "Not much. What's going on with you?"

Her answer confused him. "You wanted to talk about Tim."

"If I were you, I'd be more worried about yourself."

"What? Why?"

"Well, for one thing, at least Tim doesn't have a gun pointed at the back of his head."

Will turned and saw Richie Patrick pointing a gun at him. "What the hell is going on?"

Patrick smiled. "Well, I'd say you've got a bit of a problem."

It didn't take more than a few moments for Will to realize where he had seen Patrick before. "You're the guy from Homeland Security, the guy I took through the computer system in the building." As he was saying it, he realized why he was subsequently asked to do so a second time, with a different person. Patrick had been there under a false identity, with a pass provided by Meredith.

Patrick smiled again. "And you have no idea how much I appreciated it."

NOVACK left Tim in the hotel room with instructions to stay put. He was officially a fugitive; Novack didn't want him shot by some cop looking to make a name for himself.

Novack did make the concession that he would attempt to keep

Nick informed of developments. He called Anders and Donovan and downloaded them on what he'd learned, leaving out the fact that he'd met Tim in person, then picked up Anders and went to Wallace Industries, backed up by four other officers.

Meredith was not there, but Danny was in his office. He told them Meredith had not been in that day and had not called. He said it was very out of character for her to do that.

"Where does she live?" Novack asked.

"In Leonia." Danny got up to look her address up in the file cabinet. "Any chance you'll tell me what's going on?"

"Zero. If she calls in, do not tell her that we were here," Novack said, knowing all the while she wouldn't be calling.

The subsequent raid on her house failed to apprehend her, mainly because the address on file was a vacant lot.

Meredith was long gone.

DONOVAN took on the job of communicating events to Carl White. Danny provided Novack with a picture of Meredith, taken at a company outing, and White turned it over to the Secret Service.

Facial-recognition monitors were posted at twenty-one locations surrounding the Federal Center, and the pictures of Patrick, Meredith, and Tim were added to the terrorist data bank. If any of them came within five blocks, authorities would know in a split second.

Steven Radford, the Secret Service agent in charge, was not unduly worried. The fact that there were dangerous people who might be intent on killing the president was no surprise; such people are out there in droves. What was important to Radford was that the location was secure, and he felt confident that it was.

EDEN heard them upstairs. It was a woman and two men, and one of the men was Patrick. She couldn't make out what they said.

Their arrival came at a particularly inopportune time. She was making ever so slight progress on loosening the rope that was tying her hands to the metal bar. If Patrick came downstairs quietly and caught her, he would do something horrible.

But Eden was by nature a realist, and she had to force herself to be one now. When this was all over, Patrick was going to do something horrible anyway.

So she continued working on the ropes. Patrick did not come down, and after a long time there was only a little more to be done.

IT WOULD not have been a surprise to anyone to know that Keith Rivers was giving the senator crucial advice. What would have rocked Washington was the fact that the advice he was giving was not to Senator Collinsworth, but to Senator Evans.

The conversation was over the phone; the men could not have taken a chance being seen together. Rivers was making sure Evans knew every detail of what was to take place. "The timing is crucial," he said.

"Just make sure our friends know what they're doing."

"They're professionals," Rivers said, the clear implication being that Evans was not, at least in matters of this type.

"I hope so," Evans said. "When was the last time you spoke to your boss?"

Rivers knew who he was talking about, and it certainly wasn't Collinsworth. "Last night. He's out of the country."

"Maybe I should speak with him," Evans said.

"He's not reachable until well after this is over."

"Fine," Evans said, thinking that when this was over, he would talk to whomever he wanted, whenever he wanted.

Then even Rivers's boss could kiss his ass.

"THE frustrating thing about money is that it's impossible to own all of it," Byron Carthon said, then waited for the laughter to subside. He enjoyed the sound of it, even though he knew it was not merited by the joke, but rather by the fact that he owned his audience, lock, stock, and barrel.

There were seventy people in the audience, the top thirty-five employees of the Franklin Group and their spouses. They had come from Franklin subsidiaries all over the world to this outing on the Crystal Line cruise ship *Serenity,* as it sailed the South Pacific.

The purpose of the gathering was to relax, talk, and strategize about future growth. Byron's goal was to grow his company over the next ten years at a greater rate than the previous ten. That would be a tall order, as Franklin had no peer as the leading construction, mining, and oil and gas company in the world. Ironically the only blemish on the business was its American operations.

Franklin had come out on the short end of what Byron Carthon considered petty American politics. Certain politicians had used the company as a convenient whipping boy, and government contracts had become less frequent and lucrative than in the past. Franklin had more than made up for it through its international operations, but that was not good enough for Byron. The U.S. market was still the most important, and Franklin would once again reign supreme.

What Byron did not tell his guests was that the real reason for being on the ship was simply to be on the ship when his plan was executed. And it was totally his plan, although history would never record it as such. It would leave Byron Carthon wealthy beyond even his imagination, and in control over everything, including the next president of the United States.

"You all have the agenda," Byron said. "There are no meetings until Monday, so take the weekend to relax and rejuvenate. For the next two days, the world will go on without us."

He neglected to mention that after tonight the world would never be the same.

TIM had the awful sensation that he was being dragged toward the edge of a cliff, a long, slow process that would result in his plunging off in about two hours. That was when the gala event was to start at the Federal Center.

He was going insane cooped up in the motel room, but he couldn't figure out where to go. How could the center be so secure, yet so vulnerable? Something had to be accomplished from the inside. Yet everyone would have to go through security to get in.

Unless it was an inside job controlled from the outside.

Tim grabbed the phone and called Danny on his cell. "Danny, it's me."

"Tim, are you okay?"

"Where is Will? I've got to talk to him."

"I wish I knew. I've been trying to reach him since yesterday. Home, cell, even his new girlfriend."

Will would never leave without letting Danny know where he could be reached. To do so the day of the big opening was completely inconceivable. "Danny, keep trying to find him." Tim gave Danny his cell-phone number; there was no hiding any more.

He hung up and called Nick. "Nick, it's the computer."

"What are you talking about?"

"Will Clampett did the computer security work at the Federal Center. He's been missing and can't be reached."

"So you think he's on the other side?"

Tim had considered that possibility. "I doubt it. But whoever wanted to control the computers could do so through him. From a remote location. Nick, that building has got to be shut down now."

As soon as Nick got off the phone, he called Novack and told him what Tim had said. Novack had interviewed Will during the investigation and did not see him as the type to take off without regard to his job. He called Danny and asked him to locate a picture of Will, then called Carl White at the Federal Center, where the guests had not yet started to arrive. Novack quickly filled him in on what he knew. "They could be making their move through the building computer somehow," he said.

"I don't see how," White said. "Secret Service techs are running the thing. I was in the room with them a little while ago. Everything seemed fine."

"At least alert them to the possibility that something might happen. And make sure that room is secure."

THE president of the United States is the elephant in every room he is ever in. That's a given. But equally true is the fact that he is also the elephant in every room he is planning to enter.

This was obvious to everyone at the cocktail party at the Federal Center. Everyone was already jockeying for position, so as to have access to him. This was made slightly more complicated by the rivalries in the room, most notably the one between Senators Collinsworth and Evans. They and their staffers were determined to stay apart, yet equally determined to be near the arriving president. It made for interesting theater, sort of a senatorial Kabuki dance.

CARL White was getting nowhere with Radford. The Secret Service captain had listened patiently to White, but this was showtime, and he had no time for wild theories. The computers were firmly in the hands of men with top security clearances, men whom Radford trusted completely. Besides, what real damage could the computers cause? The building was secure; Radford saw no way that hackers could be any more than an annoyance. Surely there was no way they could pose a physical danger to the guests.

So Radford was too circumspect to say it straight-out, but he basically implied that Carl should have an hors d'oeuvre and leave the Secret Service alone to do their job.

RICHIE Patrick thought it was damn nice of CNN to act as his accomplice. One pool camera would cover the dinner speeches, and CNN would show them on the air.

The timing had to be just right, and Richie could just turn on the television and be perfectly well informed. Then, once he triggered the event, his computer monitors would tell him all he needed to know. But for now, CNN would do just fine.

TIM would be watching television as well, but he was watching with a feeling of foreboding. He knew in his gut that something awful was going to happen, and it would involve the computers.

At that point he would understand what he had been trying to understand for all these months. He would know what they were doing, and how they were blaming him for it.

Of course, by then it would be too late.

15

PRESIDENT Markham arrived promptly fifteen minutes before the end of the cocktail party. Every movement was perfectly coordinated by his staff. He managed to take pictures with everyone he was supposed to during that time, and was a master at making personal comments to make them feel good.

The president separately spent a little extra time with Collinsworth and Evans. He knew both senators had ambitions to succeed him, and he had been holding out the carrot of his future support to each of them. The truth was he considered Collinsworth a pompous ass and thought Evans overly aggressive. He had told his wife that if he thought one of them might someday be moving into the White House, he'd burn it down first.

The assembled guests moved into the main hall for the dinner. The room lacked the elegance that the evening called for, but the tables were set ornately, and the flowers alone cost more than any five of the waiters earned in a year.

After all, the nation was watching.

ONE of the few people not watching was Eden Alexander. She could still hear Patrick and other people upstairs, but it had been so long since he'd come down, she felt confident he was not going to.

She was almost out of her bonds; there was only a little more to be done, and then she would be free. She hadn't yet figured out what she would do with that freedom, but at least she would be giving herself a chance to survive, where previously she had had none.

It wouldn't be long now.

"I'VE been in this business a long time," Senator Collinsworth began. "And I've learned that you have to dream big, then compromise. Nothing happens exactly as you hope; everyone has agendas to take into consideration. All you can do is your best, and hope that the end result includes as much of your vision as possible.

"But tonight is very, very different. This glorious Federal Center is exactly how I and others envisioned it just two short years ago. It is the perfect model for other Federal Centers all over this great country and will come to symbolize the strength and ingenuity that we are, and the security that we are entitled to. In short, truly a dream that has come true."

Collinsworth went on for another seven minutes, claiming full credit for the center while trying to appear gracious and modest to all those who did not know he didn't have a gracious or modest bone in his body.

"And now it is my pleasure to introduce the man who ultimately made this all possible. A leader without whose leadership all the dreams in the world wouldn't have been enough. Please welcome the president of the United States, Christopher Markham."

The crowd rose to a standing ovation. They had no idea that Richie Patrick had just typed in a code on his computer that effectively gave him control over their lives.

AT FIRST, almost nobody in the hall realized what was happening. The standing ovation prevented people from noticing what was going on behind them.

Large reinforced steel doors were closing in from both sides, and reinforced steel panels were covering the windows, but since it was nighttime, the lighting in the room did not change. Carl White immediately started looking for Captain Radford, and he was not about to find him. Radford was in an outer hallway, checking perimeter security, when the closing doors locked him out.

White ran to the computer room, where there was chaos, as the computer operators realized they no longer had control over the system. Their monitors had gone dark, after which a typed message appeared.

This building is under my control. No one can get in or out, and those inside will live or die depending on their actions. Oxygen tank number three contains one-fiftieth of one ounce of thallium, enough to kill every person in the building a hundred times over. By pressing a button, I can instantly release it.

This computer has been programmed to treat any interruption of power as an enemy attack. It will similarly regard any attempt to enter the room or breach the barricades. In a matter of seconds, all present will be inhaling thallium.

There is to be no contact between those inside and outside. You will have my nonnegotiable demand in five minutes. I can see through every camera in the room.

Timothy Wallace

The message was simultaneously sent to every mainstream media outlet in the country, and Captain Radford himself read it on one of the outside media monitors.

A safe haven had become a prison, and possibly a tomb.

"HOW am I doing?" Patrick asked Will, who watched in horror.

"How did you get thallium into that tank?" Will asked. He knew thallium was a radium poison that caused a slow and unpleasant death.

Patrick smiled. "When you have a pass, you can do anything."

Will looked over at Meredith, who as office manager had provided the construction passes. She smiled, obviously having no second thoughts. "So how's he doing?" she asked.

Will turned his attention back to Patrick. "They'll figure out a way to take it back."

"You know something?" Patrick said. "They just might. But not in twenty minutes, and that's all they have."

THERE was obviously no way for Tim to be sure he was right. He knew enough about computers to realize that the people controlling the building could be anywhere; when they accomplished whatever they were doing, they would want to disappear without leaving a paper or electronic trail. And the woman at the Southold marina had said that people had been on the Oceanfast 360 recently doing work and that they had blown her off when she tried to be friendly.

The boat was in the water, and there would be nothing to stop it from sailing away, silently and anonymously.

Tim tried to reach Nick but had to leave a message telling him where he was going and why. He was still twenty minutes away from the pier, when he realized he'd forgotten to bring his handgun.

INSIDE the building, the guests were slowly learning what was going on. Secret Service agents were at an uncharacteristic loss as to how to proceed. Generally the protocol was to take the president to a safe haven. In this situation they shepherded him to a corner and hovered around him like human shields, though their bodies would obviously be of no benefit against an airborne poison.

When Senator Collinsworth was informed what was happening, he saw his political life flash before his eyes. Meanwhile, Senator Evans didn't need updates; he knew exactly what was going on, and therefore was not worried about any terrorist threats. Instead he stared at a window, fifteen feet up at the east side of the room. He could not see the place where the steel covering was not fully closed, but he knew it was there.

In eleven minutes he would pretend to see it, and climb up to it, in apparent disregard of his own personal well-being. Then he would pry it open and heroically lead the people in the room to safety. He would be hailed as an American hero.

And then there would be no stopping him.

THE next set of instructions came exactly on time, as promised:

You will immediately wire five billion dollars to the Bank of Zurich, account number 327-548-6999873-24, informing them that the United States Government insists they follow the separate instructions I sent them. All transactions must be accomplished within the next fifteen minutes, or I will release the thallium. No excuses will be tolerated.

THE late-night piano player in the ship's main bar was better than Byron Carthon expected. He was doing a long medley of Broadway songs, and Byron had always been a sucker for show music. The man was moderately talented, but not quite deserving of the hundred-dollar bill that Byron placed in his tip jar.

Byron wanted to be noticed, which was why he had brought a bunch of his executives to the bar with him. Usually early to bed, Byron chose to stay up late, so he could be seen having absolutely nothing to do with the chaos that he knew was going on at that moment, thousands of miles away, at the Federal Center.

His work was finished long ago. He had used his contacts, separated by many layers, to procure the thallium and secure the route that the money would take. He had placed the best people available in place, paying exorbitant money to do so. Of course, it wasn't exorbitant when compared to the ultimate payoff, and this was an operation that would never stop paying off.

So Byron ordered another round of drinks and requested a rendition of "If I Were a Rich Man," from *Fiddler on the Roof*. The idea of Byron Carthon yearning to be a rich man drew a laugh from the others in his party, and Byron laughed along with them.

It was obvious he didn't have a care in the world, and there was an entire bar full of witnesses to swear to it.

FRANTIC conference calls were conducted among the vice president, the attorney general, the chairman of the Joint Chiefs of Staff, and the directors of Homeland Security, the Secret Service, FBI, and CIA.

The first thing to be determined was whether the threat was credible. The chairman of the Joint Chiefs and the CIA director both reported that their biological warfare experts were confirming that the thallium could easily have gone undetected in the tanks. The quantity necessary to be deadly would have made detection almost impossible.

Next to be examined was the likelihood of entering the building by force. This was quickly rejected as impractical. The building was incredibly well fortified, and explosives powerful enough to penetrate it might kill or injure the hostages.

The question of the money was the easiest. Despite President Markham's many pronouncements that the United States would never negotiate with terrorists, if they could get out of this for five billion dollars, they would feel they got off cheap.

The approval was given, and the money was sent.

SENATOR Evans knew that his moment had come. This was an operation entirely based on precision timing, and he couldn't risk deviating from it in any way. He glanced over and made eye contact with Keith Rivers. He thought that Rivers nodded ever so slightly, but it didn't matter either way. It was time to act.

Evans looked up to the window at the side of the room. "Look at that," he said, loudly enough that half a dozen people could hear.

"What?" someone asked, but Evans was already up and walking, as if intent on whatever he had seen.

He stood under the window. "Give me a hand with that table," he said to those nearby, and they helped him drag it over, then put a chair up on it.

RICHIE Patrick laughed in gleeful anticipation, watching Evans's every move on his computer monitors. "Watch this," he said to Meredith and Will. "This is going to be great." Patrick's only regret was not being able to see Carthon's reaction when he learned the president he was going to control was dead.

Evans got up on the chair, from where he could barely reach the window ledge. He would pull himself up, which was a bit of a strain, but he had practiced this many times. He would reach the window, then drop back down and secure a piece of metal, which he would take back up to insert into the opening he found, pry the panels open, and, with the help of rescuers outside, bring everybody to safety.

He made it up there but then experienced the most crushing moment in his life. All he saw was steel. No opening. No way out.

He understood instantly that he'd been betrayed, and that he and everyone else in that room were going to die.

Richie Patrick knew exactly what was going through Evans's mind. He had no sympathy for him, because Evans was stupid. He should have realized that in an operation of this magnitude, with the largest law-enforcement effort in history certain to follow, Patrick could not afford to leave anyone alive.

They were all going to die . . . Evans, Rivers, Eden, Will, Tim, and even Meredith, though she didn't yet realize it. She thought they would marry and sail off into the sunset, but she was in for a rather rude, and deadly, awakening.

He would even kill Carthon, though that would be a little more difficult, and much more dangerous.

But he would do it, no matter what. Because the truth, as Patrick knew it, was that you have to kill to stay alive.

It was the cost of doing business.

TIM arrived at the pier and parked where he could not be seen from the Oceanfast yacht. He realized as he got out of the car that it might well have already gone out to sea.

He ran toward where it had been and was relieved to find it still docked there. He then made his way cautiously, trying to avoid being seen by anyone on the boat who might be watching. Detecting no movement or activity, he recognized the distinct possibility that he was wrong about all of this, but he had to act as if he were one hundred percent right.

Tim quietly walked onto the boat, and for the first time he could hear someone talking. He edged along a corridor past a kitchen and two bedrooms, to a partially open door. Inside he could see Patrick sitting in front of an elaborate computer setup, and Will and Meredith across the room on a couch. Will seemed to have his arms bound behind him.

Tim backed away and went into the kitchen, picked up a knife and a coffee mug, then positioned himself in an adjacent bedroom.

He held out the coffee mug and dropped it on the floor.

PATRICK heard a noise that seemed to be coming from near the kitchen; it sounded like something fell to the floor. Since the boat was rocking in the water, it was likely this meant little. Still, he wasn't about to take chances. "Check that out," he said to Meredith.

She left the room and walked down the hall. Tim let her walk by, trying to figure out what to do.

He made his decision while she was on the way back, waiting until she was at the doorway before coming out just behind her. He punched her as hard as he could in the right temple. Hitting a woman would have previously seemed inconceivable to him, but this was a person who had helped to kill Maggie.

He caught the unconscious Meredith before she reached the floor.

PATRICK didn't need to wait for her return. As Will watched in horror, he pressed the code numbers that would release the thallium-tainted oxygen into the room at the Federal Center.

Only then did he go to find out what the hell was keeping her.

In the Federal Center, the guests had no idea that poisonous air was slowly making its way into the room. It was as colorless and odorless as it was deadly.

By the time Patrick came down the hall, Tim had pulled Meredith's body into the bedroom. He heard Patrick coming, and as he walked by, Tim jumped out at him and swung the kitchen knife.

He slashed Patrick between the shoulder and the neck, and blood started gushing. Patrick staggered and fell. Tim saw him go down, and started toward the computer room.

The bullet hit him in the upper back and sent him sprawling. He fell to the ground and rolled over, pain shooting through him. He looked back and saw Patrick raise his gun to fire again.

Tim also saw Eden come up behind Patrick and smash him over the head with a heavy lamp. It crushed his skull, killing him.

Eden rushed to Tim, who was conscious but covered in blood. "Untie Will," he said. She hesitated a moment before rushing off.

Once untied, Will went straight to the computer and shut off oxygen tank three, at the same time opening the doors and windows of the building. The guests, not even aware that they had been exposed to the thallium, rushed out of the room and fled.

Eden went back to where Tim was lying. He was unmoving, apparently unconscious. She heard a noise and looked up to see Novack running toward them, handgun drawn.

"It's over," she said. "But Tim . . ."

Novack went to Tim's side and saw that his eyes were closed. He felt for a pulse, as Tim opened his eyes and looked up at him.

"I'm gonna live," Tim said.

"Damn . . . I can't catch a break," Novack said, and then smiled.

He took off his jacket and wrapped it around Tim's back and shoulder to stem the flow of blood. "You owe me for this jacket."

EPILOGUE

IF THERE'S one thing I do not have to educate the public about, it is the devastating effect of thallium. Thirty-one people in that room that night have since died, cruelly chosen by fate according to their unwitting proximity to air vents.

Included in the fatalities were Senator Collinsworth and Keith Rivers, while Senator Evans has suffered but survived, though he surely will live out his days in prison. Among the lucky ones were President Markham and Carl White, both of whom were far away.

Evans and Meredith have provided much of the details of the conspiracy, though they will receive no benefit from the courts or public opinion for doing so. Byron Carthon is in Venezuela, successfully fighting extradition. There is speculation that if the Venezuelan government refuses to send him back, Special Service commandoes will render a more immediate form of justice.

Tim Wallace suffered substantial injuries, but physical therapy has gotten him back to almost full strength. He has been called a hero by various government agencies and will soon be awarded the Congressional Medal. He has not gone public with his thoughts about his experience, preferring to get on with his life.

Amazingly, there are those, conditioned by earlier media reports and current conspiracy theorists, who still believe Tim to have been a leader in the criminal operation. Those in the know are very public in correcting this allegation, and Detective John Novack has been the most vocal of all in defending Tim's role.

Tim and I are spending a great deal of time with each other. To live our lives privately is mostly impossible with the media, but we still go to the dog park every Sunday. I socialize, and Tim throws the tennis balls, though not as far as he used to.

We're planning on moving in together next month. Kiley and Travis seem very much in favor of it; they wag their tails whenever the subject is mentioned.

Tim is upbeat and looking forward to the new life we are starting together.

The nightmare is officially over.

The Eccentricities of
David Rosenfelt

Vital Stats

BORN: March 31, 1949, New Jersey
RESIDENCE: Southern California
SERIES CHARACTER: Andy Carpenter
OBSESSION: Golden retrievers
FAVORITE AUTHORS: Lee Child, Robert B. Parker, Michael Connelly
WEBSITE: www.DavidRosenfelt.com

RECENTLY, Select Editions asked David Rosenfelt about his early days in the movie biz, his eccentricities, and his love of dogs—lots of them!

SELECT EDITIONS: You worked as president of marketing for Tri-Star pictures for many years. How did you get into the movie business?

DAVID ROSENFELT: I took the route that I would recommend to everyone: My uncle, who was the head of United Artists, hired me.

SE: What was it like?

DR: It was an exciting place to be, as each movie offers a unique marketing opportunity. I can't think of any other product that can achieve great success or devastating failure, literally overnight. Movies open on a Friday, and by Saturday you know whether they're a triumph or a disaster. I miss it, but being an author is a much better lifestyle.

RD: How long have you been writing novels?

DR: I started in 2002. I was writing television movies, and I wanted to create a courtroom drama. The studios weren't making them at the time, so I decided to try my idea as a novel, *Open and Shut*.

SE: You describe yourself as "a novelist with thirty-seven dogs." Can you tell us about that?

DR: My wife and I rescue dogs, and we've set up a sanctuary for them at our home. The numbers fluctuate between twenty-five and thirty-eight. Right now, we have twenty-seven.

SE: Where did you grow up?

DR: I grew up in New Jersey, and for me it was the best place in the world. Now I live with my family just south of Los Angeles.

SE: On your website you express gratitude that neither of your children has inherited your "eccentricities." Are you willing to share those publicly?

DR: I just have a peculiar, often bizarre, view of the world. I'm highly skeptical, absurdly logical, and I see humor in things when it probably isn't there.

SE: Which has been the most challenging and/or rewarding role of your life—being a movie mogul, a dad, a dog rescuer, or an author?

Safe Skyscrapers

While the plot of *Don't Tell a Soul* may be appealingly fictional, the concept of terror-proof buildings is a reality.

An example is the new building at 7 World Trade Center, one of the safest skyscrapers in the world. The 52-story glass structure boasts a concrete core built to act like a bunker in the event of an emergency. The structure around the core can be damaged in any number of ways—fire, explosion, a biological or chemical problem—but the core itself will be protected.

Similar skyscrapers are planned or under construction in farflung locales such as Chicago, Taipei, Korea, and Russia.

DR: I should point out that I was never a mogul. Being a dad and dog rescuer were easily the most rewarding. I've been blessed with great kids, so dog rescuer is probably the toughest.

SE: If your family had to pick just three adjectives to describe you, what would they be?

DR: Self-deprecating, and that would preclude my mentioning the other two. ∎

LEAVING JACK

JACK

GARETH CROCKER

They were ordered to leave their dogs behind
One man refused

Based on actual events

⌒ PROLOGUE

Chicago
January 11, 1972

THE wind sulked around Hampton Lane cemetery. It stirred the leaves lining the cobbled paths but did little more than slowly tow them along, like condemned souls being dragged to the afterlife.

Standing among the rolling fields of dead in a sea of granite and marble tombstones, Fletcher Carson slowly made his way to the foot of a tree where his life lay buried under two stark white crosses. His wife, Abigail, had been such a positive person that she had seldom discussed death. Only during the drawing up of their wills did it emerge that she wished to be interred under the shade of a maple tree with only a simple white cross to mark her final resting place. Her epitaph was every word as humble as the two plain wooden planks that bore its inscription. It read:

> HERE RESTS ABIGAIL CARSON,
> LOVING WIFE AND MOTHER.
> MAY HER LIGHT NEVER FADE
> FROM OUR HEARTS.

Kelly's cross was half the size of her mother's. It carried only her name and the dates denoting her short life. Fletcher had been a writer for most of his working life. He was certain the right words did not exist.

"Fletcher." A voice drifted toward him. "I thought I'd find you here."

Fletcher recognized the broad southern drawl. It was Marvin Samuels, his editor and only remaining friend in the world.

"You look good," Marvin continued, but the inflection in his voice suggested otherwise. Fletcher Carson was just under six foot, but there was a stoop in his posture that belied his true height. He was blessed with smooth olive skin, thick black hair, and hazel eyes. At twenty-nine he was in his prime, but the burden of recent months weighed heavily on him. His athletic build remained, but his face carried the expression of a man who had wandered into a dark labyrinth and had long since abandoned hope of ever finding his way out.

"I read somewhere that the dead can hear you," Fletcher said, staring at the ground. "If someone they really loved visits their grave, they can hear that person's thoughts. It can be raining or blowing a gale, but just around their grave, everything becomes still. That's when they're listening."

"I hope it's true."

Fletcher nodded tokenly. "Why'd you come here, Marvin?"

"Why do you ask questions you know the answers to?"

"We've been through this. There's nothing left to discuss. I'm leaving tomorrow."

Marvin folded his arms and looked up at the sky. "Sure. I'll just stand around and watch while you try and get yourself killed."

"I'm asking you to respect my decision."

"Do you think this is what your girls would've wanted?"

Fletcher snapped his head around. "You're in no position to ask that! Do you know what the last few months have been like?"

"No. But going off to fight in Vietnam isn't the answer."

"What if it were Cathy or Cynthia? What would you do?"

"I'd try to get over their passing and carry on with my life."

"Really?" Fletcher pointed to his daughter's grave, his hand trembling. "Kelly was seven. How do you get over that?"

"Fletcher—"

"Tell me something," he continued, his voice faltering. "Do you know where the line is?"

"The line?"

"Where you end . . . and your family begins?"

"C'mon, don't do this."

"I'll tell you. There is no line. You're one entity, and when a part of you is cut away, the rest of you slowly dies."

"Fletcher."

"Our soldiers are being massacred in Vietnam. Most of them are still kids. They've got their whole lives ahead of them. It makes sense that people like me enlist."

"People like you," Marvin whispered. "You mean, people who want to die. You need help, Fletcher. You need to speak to a professional."

"A shrink? Will that bring back my girls?"

"It might help you learn to cope without them."

"That's just it," Fletcher replied, shaking his head. "I don't want to cope without them."

"Just let me—"

"Please," Fletcher said. "I appreciate you coming and all that you've done for me, but I think you should leave. Just go."

Marvin began to walk away, then stopped. "Do you remember

that piece you did on suicide about two years ago? In the end, you wrote that if only the sufferers had been able to see past the moment of their pain, they could claw their way back to life."

"What I didn't realize," Fletcher replied, "is that you can never truly understand things that haven't happened to you."

Marvin shook his head. "I've stood by you through this nightmare. From the moment the plane went down to the day you left the hospital. If you go tomorrow, I've just been wasting my time."

"I'm sorry Marvin, but this isn't about you."

"Fine. But know that this is the last thing your girls would've wanted for you. You're making a terrible mistake."

"Maybe . . . but it's mine to make."

Marvin turned away, still shaking his head. "Then go to hell."

Fletcher nodded slowly. "Already there."

When Marvin was gone, Fletcher knelt down between the two graves. He reached into his pocket and pulled out a silver frame Abigail had kept on her bedside table. It held one of her favorite photos of the three of them in Yellowstone Park. He gently placed it down on her grave. From another pocket, he withdrew a small wooden box that he rested against Kelly's cross. In it was a crystal sculpture of the dog he had promised to buy her. She had died three days before her seventh birthday.

It was the present she would never have.

 # ONE

Death Valley, Vietnam
July 6, 1972
ONLY the top half of Fletcher's head was visible above the murky water. The rest of his body was submerged beneath the mud and thick reeds alongside the riverbank. He was drawing short, shallow breaths. From his position, he could make out three members of his

platoon. Point man Mitchell Lord, radioman Gunther Pearson, and his lieutenant, Rogan Brock were hidden in a classic L-shaped ambush awaiting an enemy patrol. They had been hiking up to a site three kilometers away to set up a landing zone when they were warned about the patrol.

Fletcher blinked away the sweat around his eyes and checked his rifle. As a sniper, his job was to pick out the ranking officer and take him down first. *Cut off the head, and the body will fall,* the army taught them.

Both the North Vietnamese Army and the Vietcong, or *Charlie,* as U.S. soldiers nicknamed them, were smart and elusive. Their tactics were to attack and retreat—basic guerrilla warfare. No helicopters, gunships, or bombing campaigns. Just cunning *and cutting.* Charlie would stab you, then withdraw into the shadows. He was a ghost that never slept. He made traps that intended to maim, not kill. This would slow down platoons and gnaw away at their spirit.

Faint voices.

Fletcher remained perfectly still, the area around him disturbed only by a swarm of flying insects breaking the surface of the soupy water with their wings in an attempt to lure out prey.

It seems everyone's hunting, he thought grimly. The body of his gun was covered with mud to guard against reflections. Only the open barrel—the killing eye—was visible to the trail.

Footsteps and voices. Louder now.

Charlie was close. Fletcher could almost smell him.

A soldier, barely five feet tall, emerged over the rise. Fletcher curled his finger around the trigger of his M-16.

Waiting . . . *waiting.*

Fletcher flinched at what he saw next. An American soldier wearing the emblem of the First Air Cavalry Division appeared. His arms were bound over a wooden pole behind his back. As he limped forward, he was kicked in the back by one of his captors.

Fletcher looked to his lieutenant. Through a series of hand signals, Rogan ordered him to take out the two soldiers directly in front of and behind the hostage. He signaled for the rest of the platoon to switch from automatic to single fire. He looked back at Fletcher and held up his fist, waiting for the right moment.

A bead of sweat rolled down Fletcher's nose, then dropped into the water. With one eye on Rogan and the other straining toward his two marks, he held his breath. C'mon . . . c'mon . . .

Rogan dropped his hand.

Fletcher squeezed off two rounds in quick succession. Before the second soldier even hit the ground, the rest of the platoon opened fire. The sound was devastating. As Charlie tried to return fire, point man Mitchell Lord burst out of his hiding place, tackled the U.S. hostage, and dragged him down an embankment. It was typical Lord. He was as brave as he was crazy. In less than a minute, twenty-three Charlie lay dead in the burning sunshine of Vietnam.

After a quick sweep of the area to ensure that there were no splinter patrols nearby, Fletcher's closest friend in the platoon, infantryman Travis Tucker, untied the hostage. He appeared badly dehydrated; his tongue was so swollen he could barely speak. Only after several sips of water was he able to relay some information. He was a helicopter pilot who had been shot down as he was dropping a platoon into a hot zone. He had been held hostage for more than a week and had been interrogated and tortured. His hands were shaking so badly he could barely hold the canteen up to his mouth.

"Easy with that," Rogan warned, throwing Travis a glance. "He'll throw it all up." From a physical perspective, few men registered a more imposing presence than Rogan Brock. Tall and heavily built, there was something deeply unsettling behind his stare, a sense of raw aggression that struck fear into people. His shaven head and pitted face added additional threat to his appearance.

The pilot wiped his mouth with the side of his torn sleeve. "I can't tell you how grateful I am. I'm pretty sure they were going to kill me today. One more interrogation and they were going to put a bullet in my face. How'd you know where to find me?"

The question saddened Fletcher. In his delirious state, the pilot believed that what had just transpired was a planned rescue. The truth was that the United States was having enough of a battle just trying to keep a foothold in the war without having to coordinate rescue attempts for POWs.

"Forget about that. The important thing is that you're safe now. We'll have you back at base tomorrow morning, where you can get some rest. The name's Travis, by the way. Travis Tucker."

"Will Peterson," he replied, accepting Travis's hand.

"Let me introduce you to the rest of the Fat Lady."

"The Fat Lady? I've heard of you guys. You were part of the company that survived Kon Tum. The story I heard had you outnumbered eight to one."

"More like four to one, and we didn't all survive. We lost three men that day," Rogan replied abruptly. "You shouldn't believe everything you hear."

Travis quickly defused the moment. "This, as you might've already guessed, is our lieutenant, the charismatic Rogan Brock. The man sitting next to you is probably the third best sniper within a hundred yards from here—Fletcher Carson."

"Definitely top ten." Fletcher nodded.

"Radio man Gunther Pearson . . . squad leader Wayville Rex . . . weapons specialist Kingston Lane . . . infantryman Arnold Keens . . . medic Edgar Green . . . and infantryman Craig Fallow."

More handshakes and nods.

"And this," Travis continued, "is the madman that dragged you down the embankment. The finest point man in all of Vietnam, Mitchell Lord."

"All right, ladies. Now that we've exchanged phone numbers," Rogan said, "we need to get moving. There's a war going on."

They picked up their gear while Fletcher and Travis helped Will to his feet.

"Why do you call yourselves the Fat Lady?" Will asked.

"Wayville, why do we call ourselves the Fat Lady?" Fletcher called out.

"Because Vietnam ain't over baby . . . 'til the Fat Lady sings!"

They all laughed, until Rogan spun around. "We having fun, platoon? Should we light a few flares to make the VC's job a little easier? I don't want to hear another word until we hit the LZ."

THE platoon dug foxholes and rigged the area with trip wires linked to mines and flares. The soldiers constructed hooches above their foxholes—makeshift tents created by zipping two ponchos together. Once the work was done and their coordinates radioed in to base for the morning pickup, Rogan called the platoon together for a debriefing. Afterward he turned his attention to guard duty. "Fallow and Green, you're on watch until twenty-two hundred. Carson and Tucker 'til oh three hundred. Rex and Lane, you relieve them 'til sunrise."

Fletcher shook his head. "Graveyard again, damn it!"

Mitchell Lord stood up and ran his fingers through his long black hair. How he was allowed to keep it that length was something of a mystery. "I'll take over for you guys."

"Thanks, Mitch, but if Rogan finds out you're covering for us, there'll be hell to pay," Fletcher replied.

Mitchell was hardly ever assigned to guard duty, not because Rogan favored him, but as point man they couldn't afford to have him tired. Running point required skill and concentration. It entailed going ahead of the patrol, checking for traps, ambushes, enemy patrols. It was also physically taxing because he had to navigate and hack his way through long stretches of dense jungle with a machete. One of the reasons they had suffered relatively few casualties was because of Mitchell's ability to sniff out danger.

At their foxhole, Travis removed his boots and sat down next to Fletcher. He pushed his glasses onto the top of his head, which apart from a sprinkling of brown hair was largely bald. He had piercing blue eyes and a kind and open face that people responded to. For a while they spoke about Will Peterson and the firefight, but gradually their conversation meandered away from the day's events. For months, Travis had wanted to find out more about the plane crash that had claimed Fletcher's wife and child, but he was afraid to ask. Finally, when there was a lull in the conversation, he broached the subject. "Fletcher, I'll understand if you don't want to talk about it. You can tell me to mind my own business, but . . ."

"You want to know about the crash?"

Travis nodded hesitantly.

Fletcher propped his rifle against the side of the hole and stared out over the jungle. "The plane—*The Odyssey,* they called it—was billed as a revolution in passenger air travel. It took ten years to build and was capable of holding almost six hundred passengers."

"I remember," Travis replied softly. "It was all over the news."

"You should've seen her, Trav. She was as big as a ship, with a wingspan as wide as a football field. She was designed to fly supersonic at a range of ten thousand miles. Although . . ." he said, trailing off, "they never did prove that."

"Did they ever find out what brought her down?"

"A design anomaly in the fuel system. There were three hundred and twenty-seven passengers on board, and only nine of us survived."

Fletcher paused. When he spoke again, his voice was flat. "As one of the journalists invited to the launch, I was allowed to bring my family along for the ride. We had just reached cruising altitude when the pilot invited all the children to the flight deck. Kelly was about to step into the cockpit when the children were rushed back to their seats. The crew told us to put on our safety belts. A minute later an engine on the right wing failed; it felt like a cough, and then it exploded. Another two on the left wing followed moments later. I held on to Abby and Kelly as the plane fell, telling them that everything was going to be okay, but I knew the wings had been damaged. And then there was nothing. I woke up still strapped to my seat, lying in someone's backyard. I could see what was left of the plane's fuselage. It was lying in a field. The flames were as high as church steeples. I knew then that my girls were gone."

Travis failed to find anything meaningful to say. But he pressed on with the question that had been needling him.

"Except for Rogan, you and I are the oldest here. I think I know the answer, but what made you come to Vietnam?"

"The day after the funeral, I decided to kill myself," Fletcher replied matter-of-factly. "I threw myself off the sixth floor of the hospital where I was being treated. A passing truck broke my fall, and I survived, but a few weeks later I was back on the same balcony. Then a strange thing happened. As I was standing there preparing to jump, a news broadcast came on the radio about Vietnam and how hundreds of American GIs were being killed every week. The mother of two boys who had both been lost in the space of a weekend spoke of their passing. Her voice jarred with pain. The report went on to describe how the average age of the dead hovered at around nineteen. Still teenagers, still *boys*. Suddenly suicide seemed like such a waste. That's when I decided to enlist."

"Well, considering the alternative, I'm glad you made it here."

Fletcher smiled. "Try to get some rest Trav."

"You, too," he replied, then yawned like a man who hadn't truly slept in a long time. "I know how hard that must've been for you to tell me. Thank you. We never have to speak about it again."

"That's the first time I've told anyone the story."

"I'm privileged, then."

Within a few minutes, Travis was fast asleep, most likely to dream about his own dead wife, Fletcher thought. He had lost his wife a year before coming to Vietnam. She was driving to work one morning when a car ran a traffic light and plowed into her. She was in a coma for over a month but died the day after their wedding anniversary. Blood tests revealed that she was pregnant—it would have been their first child.

While Travis slept, Fletcher removed his friend's glasses and placed them in his top pocket. He leaned forward and folded his arms on the edge of the foxhole. The sun was a fiery mirage on the horizon. Vietnam sunsets were beautiful while they lasted but gave way to sudden darkness—something that soldiers dreaded. They were at their most vulnerable under the cover of dark. It was the time when soldiers were truly alone with their thoughts and fears.

BY MID-MORNING, Gunther Pearson had confirmed their coordinates via radio and ordered their pickup within the half hour. Other choppers would soon follow to secure and develop the area, but their job was over. Squad leader Wayville Rex and Kingston Lane were instructed to set up three separate smoke canisters surrounding the landing zone that would be deployed once the helicopter was within range. Each canister contained a different color smoke. The pilot would then have three potential pickup points, of which only one was correct. Gunther would reveal which one they were positioned next to only at the last moment. This was done so that if Charlie was nearby, he would have to guess their location and consequently where the pickup zone was. Once down, the helicopter would hover just above the ground, and the men would clamber on board as quickly as possible. This was the most vulnerable time of the operation. Scores of U.S. HU-1 helicopters—or Hueys, as they were known—had been brought down by rocket launchers as they waited to either pick up soldiers or drop them off.

Waiting anxiously, the Fat Lady listened for signs that their lift was approaching. As usual, Mitchell was the first to hear it. "Flapping bird. Flying from the east."

As the helicopter's drone grew louder, Rogan gave the order to deploy the canisters. Ribbons of red, blue, and white smoke billowed into the sky.

The command of *red* was given to the pilot in a simple code. It was an inside joke, as the Fat Lady only ever waited under red smoke. Within seconds, the Huey swooped down over the trees.

The Fat Lady hurried toward the chopper and scrambled on board. As always, Rogan was at the rear, looking for any signs of activity behind them. He turned around for the last few yards and launched himself up into the cabin. He raised his hand, extended his index finger, and swung his wrist around in a circular motion, signaling the pilot to fly. His hand was still turning when something caught his attention. A flash, smoke, and a series of hollow thuds.

"Shooter at one o-clock!" he shouted, immediately returning fire. Mitchell, Travis, and Wayville joined in. They sprayed hundreds of rounds into the trees until they were out of range. "Is everyone all right?" Rogan asked.

"We're good," Travis replied, "but Gunther's going to need a new radio."

"What?" Gunther frowned, removing the radio off his back.

Smoke wafted out from a burned hole in the middle of the pack.

"Damn! I knew there was a reason I signed up for comms!"

He bent over and kissed the scorched canvas.

"Pity we don't use handheld radios," Travis smiled.

"Real funny." Gunther smirked.

The men all laughed, but the incident was a sobering reminder that as long as they were in Vietnam, death shadowed them.

～ TWO

THE Strip, as it was affectionately known by the soldiers, was located thirty kilometers north of Dak To in a mountainous area near the Laos border. Situated on top of a hill, it was home to some six hundred troops. It contained the usual spattering of tents and pre-fab buildings, several munitions stores, bunkers, watchtowers, a mess, and of course, base headquarters. It was surrounded by barbed wire and protected by mines linked to large oil drums brimming with *fugas*—a lethal combination of diesel and napalm. If Charlie wanted to get up close and personal with them, he would first have to tiptoe his way through the Strip's tricky dance floor.

Fletcher plodded toward his tent, which he shared with Travis Tucker and Mitchell Lord. He slipped off his boots and settled into his stretcher. He made sure he was alone before pulling out a photograph he kept in his back pocket—a picture of his wife and daughter taken in their living room a year before the crash. The camera had a self-timer that allowed him to be included in the photo. However, in his haste to get into place alongside his girls, he had slipped and fell headfirst into the couch. The photograph showed Abigail and Kelly in hysterics, watching wide-eyed as he lunged comically across the bottom half of the frame. They looked so happy, *so perfect.* Abigail, with her long black hair and sultry blue eyes, and Kelly, with a thick mop of mahogany hair and bright green eyes, were incandescent on the small square of film.

If only he had known they were living on borrowed time, he would've made more of their days together. He would've held hands longer. He would've pushed Kelly on her swing until it was dark. But most of all, he would've told them both how much he cherished them every single day.

He stared at the photo for as long as he could bear before slipping it back into his pocket.

THAT night, like most evenings after an excursion, the Fat Lady gathered at the Soup to blow off some steam. The pub was little more than a tent furnished with a few tables and benches, a string of old Christmas lights, and a dilapidated fridge.

Although the tone of their conversation had been jovial enough, Fletcher sensed there was something bubbling beneath the surface. Wayville, in particular, had the look of a man who wanted to get something off his chest.

"Hey, Wayville," Fletcher said. "What's on your mind?"

"This war," he replied, staring down into his glass. "Am I the only one who sees that we're getting our arses kicked out there?"

"Easy," Mitchell warned, his eyes barely slits in the soft light. "Leave it alone."

"We're getting slaughtered out there. We're losing this war. I want to know when it's going to stop. When will there be enough body bags before those guys in Washington finally pull the plug?"

"Don't do this to yourself," Travis said. "This kind of talk will drive you insane."

"So are we just supposed to sit back and wait until the bullet with our name on it finally ends our involvement in this twisted puppet show? I'm sick to hell of—"

"Of what?" Rogan interrupted. He was standing at the entrance to the Soup. "Finish your sentence, Rex."

Wayville paused, then lowered his voice a notch. "C'mon, Lieutenant, we're risking our necks, and for what? To delay the inevitable? The war will soon be over."

"You don't know that."

"Maybe not, but I don't want to get shot while the politicians try to figure out how we can get out of this mess."

Rogan slammed his fist into the table. "Let me make this clear. We're all part of a bigger machine. Our role is to execute our orders. If Lord's mind begins to wander while he's at point, we die. If Pearson radios in the wrong coordinates for support fire, we die. If Green decides not to be a medic but instead to scratch himself and wonder how many days he has left here, we die. And if we die, the men behind us die! Do you get me Rex?"

The room fell into a deep silence.

Rogan glared at each of the men, demanding their buy-in.

Finally satisfied, he took a deep breath. "While you're all together, you may as well know we've got orders for a recon mission the day after tomorrow. We spread our wings early—two hours before first light." He scanned the room, waiting to be challenged. When no one spoke, he turned and walked away.

FOR the first time that Fletcher could remember, the Fat Lady flew in total silence, except for the sound of the helicopter's rotors and the wind swirling through the cabin.

They were headed to one of the most dangerous areas in Vietnam: Lao Trung. Their job was to pinpoint Charlie strongholds. The coordinates would then be radioed back to base, and the area would later be bombed with daisy cutters. Tainting everything, though, was the unshakable feeling of futility at what they were doing. The little that remained of the war would almost surely be played out in weeks or months, not years. They all knew it. To exacerbate matters, tension still lingered between Rogan and Wayville.

"Someone say something," Gunther eventually said.

"All right. . . . You're an idiot," Kingston replied casually.

A smile tugged at Gunther's mouth. "Screw you clowns!"

Even Rogan managed a smile, but it was short-lived. Moments of levity in Vietnam seldom lasted.

They were approaching the drop-off zone.

JUMP, land, roll, and run for cover—basic military training. What the army couldn't equip you for, Fletcher thought, was the sickening feeling that Charlie might be waiting behind you in the trees, his AK-47 trained on your back. It never failed to prick up the hairs on his neck.

As Fletcher hit the ground, he rolled and tried to get onto his feet in one fluid motion but slipped and fell. The weight of his pack pinned him briefly to the earth.

"Carson, get on your feet," Rogan yelled, grabbing him and wrenching him up. Together they scrambled to a nearby rock. They all held their positions as the Huey disappeared over the treetops.

The key now, Fletcher knew, was to get moving as quickly as possible. The helicopter would have alerted Charlie to their presence. As of now, they were being hunted.

Rogan called everyone in. "Fallow, what business are we in?"

He always asked the same question at the start of an operation.

"The business of survival, sir."

"That's right! Let's remember that. Get your minds focused." A minute later they were moving. They mostly traveled in the same formation: Mitchell at point, followed by Rogan, Wayville, Gunther, Kingston, Fletcher, and Travis. The three teenagers—Edgar Green, Craig Fallow, and Arnold Keens—always brought up the rear. Rogan insisted on it. Although he never offered an explanation, Fletcher knew why he did it. The young men were safer at the back, shielded from traps and ambushes.

By late morning, they had made good ground. They had been able to move quickly, encountering nothing more sinister than the jungle's wildlife.

They had just stopped to eat and tend to blisters and insect bites when Mitchell Lord raised his hand as a sign of danger. Back on the Strip, they often joked that he was two parts bloodhound, one part human. But there was no laughter now. His ability to detect danger continued to keep them from harm's way.

Without saying a word, he lowered down onto his stomach and began to crawl up a hill. Rogan and Fletcher followed behind. At the top, they carefully parted the tall grass, and Fletcher eased his rifle through the gap. There were four men, moving slowly, less than two hundred yards away.

"What're they holding?" Fletcher whispered, squinting.

Rogan reached for his binoculars. "Bow and arrow . . . and a spear. . . . They're hunting." He panned the binoculars away from the men and saw what they were after. "Wild pig."

"Soldiers?" Fletcher asked.

"Looks like . . . montagnards. Jungle people," Mitchell said. "Not many of them left. Some believe they're also cannibals."

Fletcher watched as the four men closed in on their prey. With unnerving precision, the man in front drove a long spear into the animal's back. The pig squealed briefly, then fell silent.

"All right, no need to sound the alarm. Let's just get moving," Rogan decided. They retreated quietly down the embankment, collected their gear, and moved out.

After a few minutes, Fletcher pulled up alongside Mitchell. "Those men were almost two hundred yards away. How the hell did you hear them?"

"I didn't. I could smell pig in the breeze."

The jungle was a bouquet of different smells whose recipe included plants, herbs, dead animals, mud—yet Mitchell had still managed to discern that something was amiss. "Unbelievable," Fletcher said.

"It's because he used to sleep out in the barn back home," Wayville commented from behind.

Mitchell didn't take the bait. He never did out in the field.

Three hours later they were nearing the area where they planned to hole up for the night, when Mitchell lowered down onto his haunches and inspected the path ahead of him. It was covered with banana leaves. He carefully pried them up.

Rogan knelt down beside him. "What've you got?"

"Possible soldiers on a skewer." ·

The leaves disguised one of Charlie's most devastating traps: a Punji Pit. Sharpened bamboo sticks lined a deep cavity in the ground. The rest of the platoon gathered around.

"That's the first one I've ever seen," Arnold Keens said.

Mitchell shook his head. "Something's wrong."

"What is it?"

"Too easy.... They wanted us to find it. They used banana leaves. Proper Punji Pits are concealed with mud and small leaves."

"Stop!" Rogan called out to Arnold Keens who had wandered around the side of the pit. "Don't move!" He walked over to the young infantryman and knelt down. He pressed down on the foliage at his feet. The ground gave way, revealing a second Punji Pit. This was the one intended for them.

Arnold slowly stepped back. "That was close."

Rogan grabbed the youngster by his collar. "Who told you to break formation? You need to think about what you're doing!"

"Yes.... Sorry, sir."

"What are we in the business of?"

"Survival, sir."

Rogan pulled him closer. "Arnold, I'm tired of writing letters to mothers explaining how their sons died."

"I'm really sorry, sir. It won't happen again."

"It better not," he replied, letting him go. *It better not.*

It was the first time Fletcher could remember the lieutenant calling one of them by their first name. Perhaps he was human, after all.

ANOTHER night in hell, another hastily dug foxhole.

Travis had managed to fall asleep with relative ease, but Fletcher was again left grappling with the oppressively dark night.

For his earlier lapse, Arnold Keens and his foxhole-mate Edgar Green were pulling watch. Fletcher listened as the two quietly discussed topics natural to men of their age—cars, music, and women.

After a while, Fletcher tuned out their conversation and turned to his own thoughts. The prospect of the war coming to an end left him feeling conflicted. He was happy that American troops would soon go home, but he felt for the South Vietnamese. Without support, they would succumb to the North within a matter of weeks.

For him, the end of the war would leave him adrift. He had hoped Vietnam would've somehow provided him with renewed purpose. But all the war had done was darken the nightmares that plagued his nights. If he made it out, what would he do with the rest of his life? Return to Chicago? Not likely. He doubted he would be able to face anything from his earlier life. He would have to relocate. Change jobs. Meet new people. *Try to outrun his past*. If he couldn't, there was always a balcony he could revisit.

Fletcher woke up to the sound of rain pelting down.

"Just a week without getting wet, that's all I ask," Travis said, his eyes still closed. "Tell me I'm dreaming the rain." Their hooch was covering their bodies well enough, but water was pouring down the sides of the pit.

"You're dreaming the rain."

"Tell me the Cubs won the World Series."

"Sorry, but even dreams have a toehold in reality."

Travis sat up and rubbed his eyes. "Did you get any sleep?"

"About an hour if you include all the blinking."

"That's pretty good for you these days."

"Yeah. But I'm thinking of giving it up altogether. Every time I fall asleep, I keep waking up in Vietnam."

"I know what you mean. I have the same dream."

Fletcher paused, then adopted a serious tone. "What're you going to do with your life when you get out of here?"

"I'm not sure. But I do know the *first* thing I'm going to do."

"What's that?"

"Fly to Miami. Book into a hotel with clean, crisp white sheets and a view of the beach. I'll spend my mornings swimming in the ocean and my afternoons watching it from my balcony. At night, I'll let the tides lull me to sleep."

Fletcher smiled warmly. He could imagine Travis sitting on a balcony with a drink in his hand gazing out over an azure ocean.

"What about you?"

For a while, he was quiet. "Go visit my girls. Tell them about this place. Remind them how much I miss them."

"And after that?"

"Who knows? Maybe I'll fly to Miami. Spend some time with a friend."

"I do need someone to mix my drinks," Travis said, watching muddy water pool at their feet. "Come with me, Fletch. We'll stay a couple of weeks, then decide what to do with the rest of our lives."

Outside their foxhole, the jungle was now a solid gray sheet of rain. "What? And give up all this?"

～ THREE

FOUR days later the Fat Lady was finally on its way to the extraction point. Drained both physically and mentally, they had gathered information and plotted the coordinates of numerous enemy bunkers, field bases, and a bridge that, once taken out, would hamper the NVA's supply line. Fletcher was startled at just how quickly Charlie was advancing and how strong he had become. All they could do now was try to slow him down.

They had narrowly missed being intercepted by NVA patrols and had twice been forced to separate. Now, with only two kilometers left to hike, the men had become quiet. Having survived a week in the enemy's basement, they were anxious for fresh air. Mitchell, still at point, was completely wired. He regarded Charlie's traps not so much as weapons of war, but more as personal affronts to him. He would shuffle forward a few steps, then stop, breathe deeply, scan the area in front of him, then dart forward again. Sometimes he would rub his hands on the ground and lick the tips of his fingers.

As was typical toward the end of an assignment, Rogan dropped to the back to shepherd his men from the rear. Within hours, their entire area of operations would be the subject of an intense bombing campaign. Most of the men they had stolen past, laughing and drinking cheap alcohol outside huts, would soon be dead or wishing they were. The thing about war is that you could be on the winning side before breakfast but still be dead by nightfall.

The thought brought no joy to Fletcher.

"Halt!"

"What is it?" Kingston asked.

Mitchell shook his head as if his eyes deceived him. "A dog."

Fletcher turned to his right. In the distance, a yellow Labrador, with its tongue lolling out of its mouth, emerged from the trees. The animal was moving badly, favoring its left side. What appeared to be a large cut ran from the top of its back down its front leg. Flies hung over the wound. A swollen mass of dried blood was caked under its neck. "What the hell is a dog doing out here?"

Rogan briefly studied the animal, then gestured to Fletcher. "Take him out."

"What?"

"You heard me, Carson."

Fletcher was taken aback by the order. He watched as the dog slipped on the wet undergrowth and then struggled to get back up. He looked weak and hungry. "What are you talking about?"

"Are you deaf? Kill the dog. That's an order. There's something around its neck—probably a mine."

Fletcher raised his rifle and looked through the scope. "It's just blood and dirt."

"This isn't a debate. Take your shot."

Fletcher followed the animal in his sights as it approached them. In his first days in Vietnam, he'd spent some time at a base that had a dog unit attached to it. All the animals there had been German shepherds, but he had heard that there were Labradors working as scout dogs throughout Vietnam. "I'm not doing it."

Rogan withdrew his sidearm and pressed it against Fletcher's head. "Take the shot."

"You first."

"What is wrong with you? It's just a damn dog!"

"He's one of ours! The only Labradors in Vietnam belong to us. He must've got separated from his handler. Besides," Fletcher bargained, "if I shoot, we'll concede our position—"

"I'm warning you. This is your last chance."

"Do you think I give a damn about dying? Go ahead. Pull the trigger. I'm not shooting him."

The Labrador was less than a hundred yards away and closing.

"Keens . . . take the shot," Rogan instructed, still holding the gun against Fletcher's head.

Arnold Keens, who'd been watching their exchange in disbelief, recoiled at the sound of his name.

"Your rifle, Keens! That metal thing strapped around your skinny neck. Use it! Take out the dog!"

Reluctantly, Arnold raised his gun and took aim.

"Don't do it, Arnold. Let him come to us. He's hurt. He recognizes our uniforms. He's one of us. There's no danger—"

"Shut your mouth, Carson."

Fletcher turned to face the teenager. "Arnold, look at me. Please, don't shoot him."

"Discharge your weapon or I'll have you thrown in prison!"

The Labrador, sensing something was wrong, stopped walking.

"Forgive me," Arnold whispered, and squeezed off two rounds.

The first shot punched into the dog's chest and the second into the top of his front leg. He collapsed onto his side and immediately tried to stand up, but his legs buckled.

Something unraveled in Fletcher's mind.

He threw off his pack and launched himself at Rogan.

"Fletcher, no!" Travis yelled, scrambling toward them.

Fletcher hit Rogan in the stomach. The force of the blow sent him hurtling. Fletcher charged after him and started swinging his fists wildly, connecting with his face and chest.

Wayville and Kingston pulled Fletcher away. Blood flowed from Rogan's nose. "Have you lost your mind, Carson?"

Fletcher didn't reply. He couldn't. His mind was teetering on the edge of a breakdown. He had rarely felt such anger, such hatred. He turned away and ran toward the dog.

"No," Gunther warned. "There could be traps."

But Fletcher could only think of getting to the animal's side. By the time he reached the dog, it was clear he was dying. His chest was heaving. Blood had formed a half moon around his body. Kneeling down, Fletcher carefully placed his hand on the Labrador's side to try and comfort him. As he touched his coat, the dog lifted his head and looked at him. Instead of fear, his eyes conveyed a look of sadness, a glimmer of betrayal. Fletcher felt his stomach tighten. "You were coming to us for help, weren't you?"

The dog tried to lick his hand but was slipping away.

Fletcher gently stroked the side of his face. "I'm sorry, boy." He withdrew his sidearm. With his hand shaking and his vision blurred, he took aim. "Close your eyes. Your suffering ends now."

Slowly the dog's tail swept across the ground.

Fletcher was about to pull the trigger when he heard a voice over his shoulder. "Don't do it," Travis said softly, covering the gun with his hand. "He deserves a chance to live."

FLETCHER carried the critically wounded Labrador to the pickup point. He should have weighed sixty or seventy pounds, but in his malnourished state was little more than half that. Edgar, their medic, applied tourniquets, but the dog continued to lose blood. As they waited for the chopper, Fletcher tried to funnel water into his mouth, but he could barely swallow. "C'mon, boy, just a few sips."

The dog looked at him, blinked, then closed his eyes. For a moment, Fletcher thought he was gone, but his chest continued to rise and fall in an uneven rhythm. He was hanging on, but only just.

Sitting opposite Fletcher, Travis gently patted the dog's face. "There's something about him. He's going to make it. I know it."

Fletcher nodded but couldn't reply. Something deep within him had given way. He knew his actions would have severe repercussions when they returned to base. There would be a hearing, and he would most likely be court-martialed and imprisoned. But all that concerned him now was trying to save the dog.

Edgar knelt down beside the Labrador and listened to his chest. "Look, I can't be sure, but I think he's punctured a lung."

"Will he make it back to base?" Fletcher whispered.

"His wounds are very serious."

A few minutes passed by.

"Bruno Ship," Fletcher finally said.

"Who?" Travis asked.

"Bruno Ship. He's a chef in the officers mess."

"Yes . . . bald guy. Friendly. What about him?"

"He was studying to become a vet. He'll help us. He'll operate on the dog."

"Fletcher," Edgar said. "The army's going to come down hard on you for what you've done. I'm not sure Bruno is going to want to jeopardize himself to help you out."

"He'll help. I *know* it. But we need supplies. As soon as we get back, can you source whatever you think we might need? Antibiotics, bandages, disinfectant."

"It shouldn't be a problem. I have a key to the supply room. No one keeps a real inventory, anyway."

Fletcher looked down at the Labrador and gently traced his fingers down the length of his nose. Each ragged breath seemed certain to be his last. "Hold on, boy. *Hold on.*"

In the distance, the sound of rotor blades whooped toward them.

BRUNO Ship massaged his temples as if trying to ward off sleep. He was standing at the entrance to Fletcher's tent, where the dog lay sprawled out on a stretcher.

"I've been trying to save animals since I was four years old. Of course I'll help."

Fletcher felt his throat constrict. "Thank you. Once the operation is over, no one will know you were involved. You have my word on that. So when do you want to operate? Tonight?"

"No time. Edgar was right. Our friend has punctured a lung, and there's a lot of internal bleeding. We need to drain the chest cavity and do what we can to repair the damage."

"Now?"

Bruno shook his head. "As in half an hour ago."

He instructed Fletcher and Travis to boil two large pots of water and find a new mosquito net under which he would perform the operation. To make the environment as sterile as possible, the net would be doused in disinfectant.

"I've got a net I've never used," a voice said, drifting into the room. "It's yours if you want it."

It was Mitchell. And Wayville, Kingston, Gunther, and Craig Fallow were standing beside him. "What can we do to help?"

Fletcher raised his hands. "Thanks, guys, but there're enough people in the firing line as it is. And there's nothing else to do. Bruno is performing the operation, and Edgar's organizing the supplies. I will, however, take you up on that mosquito net, Mitch."

"Done."

"How's he doing?" Kingston asked, moving to the stretcher.

"He's holding on, but not by much."

"If he survives, we'll make him our mascot."

Fletcher agreed but knew that if the dog somehow did recover, he would soon be reunited with his unit.

"How long do you think you've got before they haul you down to headquarters?" Wayville asked.

"Hopefully enough time to get the tent set up for the operation."

Then Fletcher and Travis noticed Arnold Keens sitting on his own. He had the look of a man at conflict with himself.

"I've got this," Travis whispered. "Go talk to him."

"ARNOLD, are you all right?"

The infantryman flinched. "Fletcher . . . I'm so sorry. This is all my fault," he blurted out, his eyes red and swollen.

"No. It's me who owes you an apology. You were given a direct order, and you obeyed it. You were right to do what you did."

A sob wracked through Arnold's body.

"Arnold, listen to me. I'm the one to blame here. What I did placed the entire platoon at risk. I wasn't thinking clearly."

"What's going to happen to you?"

"I'm not sure, but they'll soon be coming for me."

They were quiet for a while as Arnold tried to collect himself. "How's he doing? Is he going to make it?"

"I don't know, but there's a few good people pulling for him. That's got to make a difference, don't you think?"

"I hope so," he replied. "Why'd you make a stand, Fletcher? Why risk yourself?"

"I don't know, really. I can't explain it. Something inside of me just reacted. I couldn't bear the thought of the dog being shot. He recognized our uniforms. He was coming to us for help, and we were going to kill him. I just couldn't abide by it."

"Do you think he's one of ours?"

"I haven't noticed any markings, but I'm pretty sure he is."

"Let me do something, Fletcher. Let me help in some way."

"Well, there are so many people involved now, what's another name on my conscience?"

Arnold smiled warmly despite the scarlet rings around his eyes.

"I'M READY," Bruno announced, snapping on a pair of latex gloves. He was standing in front of Fletcher's tent.

"I know you're risking a lot," said Fletcher. "Thank you."

"You can thank us afterward. Come on, Edgar. Let's get moving," Bruno replied, and disappeared into the tent.

"Where're you going?" Mitchell asked Fletcher.

"To the Soup. I'll lose my mind if I wait around here."

At the Soup, Fletcher sat at a table with Wayville and Travis.

"Still not incarcerated, I see," Kingston joked, entering the pub. He was followed by Gunther and Craig Fallow.

"Not yet, but it shouldn't be long now."

"Well, they're taking their time. I wonder what's going on."

"I'm trying not to think about it. Have either of you been past the tent? Are they still operating?"

"Yeah. They're still working on the slug in his chest. They haven't even got to the one in his leg yet."

"This is taking forever."

"Relax, Fletch," Gunther said. "Maybe this'll cheer you up. I radioed a dog unit in Dak To. Their squad leader is willing to help and has set aside medicine and food for our patient."

Fletcher's expression brightened. "That's great, but how're we going to get it here?"

"Remember our pilot friend we rescued?" Craig cut in. "The good Will Peterson? Well, as Lady Karma would have it, he's now based in Dak To and has agreed to run the stuff over to us this afternoon. They're loading up the supplies as we speak."

Fletcher was visibly moved by his friends' efforts. "This is unbelievable. I don't know what to say."

"Hey, this isn't your personal crusade," Wayville replied. "None of us wanted to see the dog shot. You just showed more guts than the rest of us."

"Nothing gutsy about it. I saw the dog coming toward us needing help, and we were going to shoot him. It didn't seem right."

"At one point, I thought Rogan was going to tear your arms off."

"If you guys hadn't separated us, he probably would've."

"You didn't do too badly."

Fletcher allowed himself a wry smile. "The lieutenant's not the bad guy in this. He was just trying to protect us."

"How's Arnold doing?" Kingston asked.

"I had a chat with him. He feels really bad. I think he'll be all right, though. I explained that he was right to follow orders, and I apologized for what I did."

"Carson!" a voice suddenly called out. Three armed soldiers were standing outside the entrance to the Soup.

FLETCHER was escorted to the officers pub. Inside, a single patron occupied a table. The three officers walked Fletcher across to him, then turned and strode away.

Fletcher pulled out a chair and sat down.

"Do you know how long I've been in Vietnam?" Rogan asked. "This is my third tour. Seen a lot of death on both sides. Most of the men out here are terrified and will do whatever they can to get back home in one piece. But the Fat Lady is different. I have witnessed exceptional courage. Everyone looks out for one another. The Fat Lady is something special. Something rare."

"I agree."

"Then why did you choose to threaten what we have today? What made you decide to jeopardize all that we are?"

"I don't know. I just couldn't let the dog die."

"Do you understand why I gave the order?"

"Yes, because Charlie has been known to booby-trap animals with grenades and mines," Fletcher replied. "But there was nothing tied around his neck, I told you—"

"Not around his neck, Carson!" Rogan shouted. "Inside it! They stitch handmade bombs no bigger than your fist into the skin under their necks. The bombs blow the animal to pieces and send a cloud of napalm fifty feet into the air. I've watched it happen."

Fletcher sat upright in his chair. Sweat rolled down the side of his face. He thought back to how the dog's neck was caked in blood. "Lieutenant, I didn't know. I'm sorry—"

"You could've killed us!" he yelled. "You did put everyone's lives in danger. Do you think I wanted to have the dog shot?"

Fletcher was at a loss for words.

"I know why you're here. I know what happened to your family, and I'm sorry for what you've been through. But that doesn't give you the right to impose your death wish on the men you serve with. You display the kind of fearlessness that only a man who has nothing to lose can show. Up until now, it's made you a highly effective soldier, but today it could've cost us our lives. I can't have you on board unless you get your head on straight!"

"You're right," Fletcher agreed, holding up his hands. "Please, believe me. I never meant to endanger the men."

Rogan looked up at the ceiling but did not reply.

For a while they sat in silence.

"What happens now? When is the hearing?"

"There isn't going to be one."

"Are you telling me you aren't taking this any further?"

"Not officially, but I want you to apologize to the men. Especially Keens. You put him in a very difficult position."

"I've already spoken to him. I feel terrible about it."

"What I have to know right now is," he continued, "are you a liability to us? Can I expect any more stupid moves from you?"

"You have my word. I won't go against your orders again."

Rogan took a deep breath, then slowly shook his head. "All right, that's it. This is over. Get out of here."

Fletcher stood up and made his way toward the door.

"Carson, wait. How's the dog doing?"

"They're still operating."

"Operating? Who is . . . Never mind." He sighed.

As FLETCHER left the officers pub, he began to comprehend how his behavior could have cost the lives of his friends. He shuddered at the thought. He cut in front of a jeep and turned toward his tent. He saw Bruno step out, wiping his bloody hands with a towel.

"Bruno . . . how'd it go?"

"We pulled out four slugs. Two of ours and two AK-47 rounds. Theirs were in the back leg and neck. I'm not going to lie to you, Fletcher. He's lost a lot of blood."

"What're his chances?"

"Maybe thirty percent. There's significant muscle and tissue damage. He's got three cracked ribs, a punctured lung, and his front right leg was partially dislocated. My real concern is his breathing and whether or not we've stopped the internal bleeding."

"So what do we do now?"

"We wait. Gunther tells me the proper antibiotics will be here shortly. The sooner I can administer those, the better. We've got him on an IV, and his breathing is still ragged, but it has stabilized."

Edgar pushed through the tent flap and shielded his eyes from the bright sunlight. "This man is a genius. He did a great job. He's given our boy a fighting chance."

Fletcher, fighting back the emotion, thanked both men and made his way into the tent. Mitchell followed behind. The mosquito net, draped over the stretcher, gave the room an ethereal feel. The smell of disinfectant was almost asphyxiating.

Fletcher knelt down next to the dog. A wave of affection swept through him. He felt an almost otherworldly connection to him.

As he stroked the side of the animal's face, Mitchell spoke. "I can't help but notice that you're not in chains."

"Rogan's not taking it any further."

"You're off the hook? What'd he say to you?"

Fletcher briefly took him through their conversation. "I owe everyone an apology. I'll speak to the men tonight. Rogan and I might not get along, but he was right about today."

The tent flap parted and in stepped Travis and Gunther, carrying boxes of medical supplies. Travis placed one of the boxes down and pulled out a letter. "This is for you."

Fletcher quickly unfolded the note and read it out loud:

Dear Corporal Carson,

Your man has told us what you are doing to try and save the life of what you believe is a U.S. scout dog.

Look inside his ears. There should be a letter and number marking his unit. Once you find it, radio the information back to me and I'll trace where the dog comes from.

Thank you for what you are doing. Our dogs are saving hundreds of soldiers' lives.

The medicine comes with our thoughts and prayers. Let us know if there is anything else we can do to help you.

Sincerely,
W. Wallace
Squad Leader, Wolf Pack

Beside his name was a stamp of a German shepherd sitting at his handler's feet. The words "In Dog We Trust" underlined the image.

~~ FOUR

THAT night, while Travis and Mitchell slept, Fletcher shifted his stretcher up alongside the dog. He listened as the animal drew one strained breath after another. He reached under the net to stroke the dog's chest every few minutes. His touch seemed to have a soothing effect, or so he liked to believe. Two IVs hung from the top of the tent, one fighting infection and the other keeping the dog hydrated.

Fletcher checked to see if there were any markings in either of the dog's ears, but there were none. He was wondering how that could be, when he felt a slight change in the air.

"How's our patient?" Bruno asked, entering the tent holding a small plastic box. "I've got a change of dressings and a thermometer. I want to see if his temperature has come down at all."

"He's doing all right, but he's battling to breathe again."

Using Fletcher's flashlight, they changed his dressings and were surprised to discover that his temperature had dropped.

"That's encouraging; it means the treatment's working," Bruno remarked. He dropped to his haunches and gently lifted the animal's jowls to inspect the color of his gums. Satisfied, he then pulled down one of his eyelids to look at the tissue lining.

Fletcher took a deep breath. "How're things really looking?"

"Honestly? Listening to his chest, it's not good. If he makes it through the night, I'm going to have to open him up again."

Fletcher nodded slowly. "Have you ever seen a dog make it through worse?"

"Dogs are amazing creatures, especially Labradors. You'll be amazed at what they can endure. He's got the spirit for a fight."

"I hope you're right."

Bruno looked up at Fletcher and removed his glasses. "If I may ask, why are you so attached to this dog?"

"I've been asking myself the same question. I just feel bonded to him in some way," Fletcher replied. "He can't die, Bruno."

"Then we won't let him," he replied. "Now you get some rest."

TRAVIS wiped the sleep from his eyes. "Tell me you got some rest last night," he yawned.

"Slept like a baby," Fletcher replied.

"Liar," Mitchell whispered, sitting up. "How's he doing?"

"Same as yesterday. Just holding on," Fletcher replied. "Bruno was here earlier to check on him. His circulation has improved, and his temperature has come down, but . . ."

"It's his breathing," Mitchell said softly. "I can hear it."

"Bruno wants to operate again today. Doesn't think he'll make it otherwise."

"Morning, all," Bruno said, entering the tent with supplies in his arms. "I take it our boy made it through the morning?"

"He's still with us," Fletcher confirmed.

Bruno fished out his stethoscope and placed it on the Labrador's chest. He frowned. "Fletcher, what're your duties this morning? I need an assistant."

"When?"

"Right now. We have to operate immediately. He's drowning in his own blood."

"All right," Fletcher said, clearing his throat, "what should I do?"

"HOW long has it been?" Wayville asked, sitting outside the tent.

"Almost an hour and a half," Travis replied.

"Should it be taking this long?"

"How the hell should I know?"

Kingston stood up and stretched. "Let's take a peek."

Wayville quietly lifted the tent's flap. The smell of ammonia wafted out to them. Beyond the mosquito net Bruno was hunched over the dog. Fletcher, standing alongside him, was holding a clamp that disappeared into the dog's abdomen.

"Can we get you guys anything?" Gunther asked.

Neither man replied. They seemed oblivious to the question.

"Let's leave them be," Mitchell said, closing the flap. "If they need our help, they'll ask for it." He turned away and was about to sit back down when the first mortar hit.

"INCOMING!" a panicked voice issued from the base's northern watchtower.

"No kidding!" Gunther yelled, feeling his face for shrapnel.

Wayville instinctively reached for his gun. "Anyone hurt?"

Travis's glasses had shielded his eyes from the dust, and he was able to scan the area. "I don't think so."

"How the hell did Charlie get so close? It's broad daylight!"

Soldiers, half-dressed, spilled out of their tents. Officers barked orders. Jeeps roared to life. Pilots ran for their choppers.

Another mortar whined toward them.

"Get down!" Kingston shouted.

The missile hit less than fifty yards away, taking out a small pre-fab supply hold. Another mortar hit, farther away this time.

The base took close on a dozen hits before it replied with heavy artillery fire. Mitchell, seemingly unaffected by the chaos, stood up and stared out into the jungle.

"What are you doing? Get down, Lord!" Wayville said.

Mitchell breathed in the caustic smell of cordite. His eyes focused on a distant hillside. "Show yourself," he whispered.

His eye caught a puff of smoke. "I see you . . ."

He ran toward the nearest gun battery. The soldier manning it was firing wildly into the air. "Move," he commanded.

Mitchell spun the field gun around and opened fire. The ground shook as the giant rounds tore into the hillside.

Travis crawled up to the tent and threw up the flap. "Fletcher . . . Bruno, you've got to get to a bunker."

"We can't. If we leave now, he's dead."

Suddenly three small holes punched through the tent.

"This is madness!" Travis screamed, diving down.

Both men stood their ground. Fletcher was holding an artery

closed with a clamp. If he moved suddenly and the artery opened, the dog would bleed out in seconds.

Gunther, lying behind Travis, tugged at his pants. "I've got an idea." He pointed to an armored vehicle parked opposite them. "It'll shield them."

Travis's eyes widened in agreement.

Together they ran to the vehicle as puffs of dust exploded at their feet. Gunther leaped into the cabin and reached under the steering wheel. He twisted the key and slammed the truck into gear. Moments later the vehicle skidded to a halt in front of the tent.

"Are you guys all right in there?" Travis yelled.

For a moment there was no reply, then Bruno called out. "Damn it. . . . We're losing him!"

WITHIN minutes, the attack was over. By the time the helicopters had emptied the last of their cannons, it was clear Charlie was gone. A sweep revealed tracks and shells at half a dozen sites, suggesting that the offensive involved as many as fifty soldiers.

Despite everything, Bruno and Fletcher completed the operation. At the height of the mayhem, the Labrador's blood pressure had dropped alarmingly, but they managed to stabilize it.

Sitting outside their tent as the sun dipped over the horizon, Fletcher, Bruno, and Travis nursed a few cold beers. They had spent the afternoon towing away debris and leveling areas where the mortars had hit. "How'd they get so damn close?" Travis asked.

"I think the real question is why," Fletcher replied. "They had no real hope of taking out the base. Why do it?"

"To send us a message," Bruno said. "That they can hurt us whenever they want."

"Just a quick twist of the knife and then gone," Travis added, running his hands through his thinning hair.

"You have to give it to Charlie, though. He is one gutsy, conniving bastard," Fletcher remarked, knowing that in the wrong company, his comment would spark outrage.

"In the end, it all comes down to motivation," Bruno replied.

"All our boys want to do is get back home, preferably with their limbs still attached. Charlie is fighting for his way of life—for his survival. He would rather die than have to march to our tune."

For a long while, they sat in silence, until Fletcher finally spoke. "Bruno, why'd you go through with the operation?"

"It just felt like the right thing to do. If we'd stopped, he would've died. Too many people have invested too much in him for me to just give up when things got a little hairy."

Fletcher handed out another round of beers. "A toast, gentlemen. To friends coming together to help one another. And to those among us who commandeer armored vehicles to protect a crazed surgeon and his deranged nurse."

Fletcher and Bruno raised their cans. "Some things," Fletcher continued, "are still worth fighting for."

DURING the next two weeks, the Fat Lady was involved in a company-size foray into the mountains near the Cambodian border. They operated at point, with Mitchell effectively leading a team of three hundred men on another seemingly futile exercise through the sticky mess of Vietnam. During nine days, they were involved in two firefights. Their exchanges claimed thirty-four Vietcong, but eighteen U.S. soldiers would never see their families again. The Fat Lady, however, emerged intact.

By the time the helicopters arrived to pick them up, Fletcher was desperate to find out how the dog was doing. In the days following the operation, the Labrador's vital signs had shown improvement. His temperature dropped to normal, there was a steady rhythm to his breathing, and it appeared as though he had fought off earlier signs of infection. But he remained in a coma.

The flight back lasted three quarters of an hour. When they touched down, Fletcher jumped from the helicopter and ran toward his tent. Bruno emerged, wiping the back of his neck with a towel. His friend's expression told him the news was not good.

"He's alive, but I'm afraid he's in a deep coma. He hasn't regained consciousness since you left."

Fletcher let his pack drop. "What does this mean?"

"I'm sorry, Fletch. If he hasn't regained consciousness by now, there's a good chance he may never."

Fletcher made no attempt to hide his disappointment.

"I'm afraid the bad news doesn't end there. Wilson has found out about all this, and he's not happy. He wants you, Travis, and Mitchell in his office first thing tomorrow morning. Evidently, he's not aware of my role in proceedings."

"And that's how it'll stay."

Despite feeling responsible for implicating Travis and Mitchell, Fletcher didn't care much what battalion commander Frank Wilson planned to do. Few punishments carried more threat than remaining a soldier in Vietnam. "Thank you for everything."

Bruno nodded and placed his hand on Fletcher's shoulder before stepping aside.

As Fletcher moved into the tent, he was stunned by what he saw. Sixty or seventy letters and cards were pinned to the inside walls of the tent, along with hundreds of dollar bills.

"What the hell is this?"

Bruno shuffled past him. "There's been an outpouring of support while you've been away. It started when three soldiers asked if they could see the dog. I let them in, and they offered to help in whatever way they could. The next day, there were ten soldiers. The day after that, thirty."

Overwhelmed, Fletcher moved away from the money wall and turned his attention to the dog. The mosquito net was still draped over his stretcher. Spreading the gauze, he sat down next to the Labrador. The animal's golden coat looked brighter. He had put on four or five pounds.

"He looks so good," Fletcher said, battling to keep his emotions in check. "He just needs to wake up." He lightly stroked the dog's fur. "How've you been managing with the IVs?"

"We were running out, but one call to our friend and another shipment was with us the next morning. He wanted to know if you found any markings. I didn't know what he was talking about."

"Apparently, all U.S. war dogs have their ID imprinted on the inside of their ears."

"And?"

"Nothing. I can't find any markings."

"Does that mean he's not one of ours?"

"I don't know what it means."

"Anyway, we have enough drips for another five days or so, and the money wall should keep us going with whatever else we need."

Fletcher stepped back and pulled down the mosquito net behind him. Again he surveyed the walls of the tent. "I can't believe this. I never knew we had so many animal lovers."

"I think it's more what our patient represents. Most of the men associate dogs with their lives back home. It gives them something familiar to cling to. Something normal."

"Either way, I'm grateful for their support," Fletcher said, reading the message on one of the cards. "I hope it's not in vain."

FLETCHER lifted Kelly above his head and threw her into a wave as she shrieked with delight.

"Again," she cried, wiping the salt water from her eyes. "Again!"

Fletcher grabbed her and again pitched her into an oncoming swell.

She emerged laughing, her long hair plastered to her face.

"Easy, honey," Abigail warned, joining them in the waist-high water. "That's precious cargo you've got there."

"Yes, Daddy!" Kelly agreed. "I'm very precious, don't you know."

"Precious? More like precocious!"

"Pre what?"

"Precocious. It means fish food."

Kelly put her hands on her hips indignantly, her pink costume shimmering in the sun. "I'm not fish food. I'm a princess—" she began before a wave knocked her off her feet. By the time Fletcher had fished her out of the water, she was laughing again.

"All right, young lady." Abigail smiled. "That's enough for now. Let's go get something to eat."

Abigail reached for Kelly's hand. Fletcher took Kelly's other hand, and together they waded toward the beach. As they trudged forward, Fletcher noticed that the current had grown stronger. Instinctively he held Kelly back. Fletcher noticed that the sky was now overcast. A wind rose up and sprayed sea salt in their eyes.

"What's going on?" Abigail said above a crack of lightning.

"I don't know," Fletcher replied.

"We're going to be sucked out to sea!"

"Don't panic!" he replied, but his words were lost to a gale.

"Daddy, don't let us drown!" Kelly pleaded.

Fletcher looked at the water. What was deep blue before was now black. He searched for the beach, but it was no longer there.

"Somebody help us!" Abigail cried, clinging to her daughter.

The wind cut up the water's surface, and more lightning fired on the horizon. Then came the rain. But instead of water, it was blood. A fiery shower that burned like acid. Where it met the water, it burst into streaks of ruby flame. Then his girls were gone. And the ocean, now a swirling mass of lava, began to pull him under.

Fletcher woke with a pinched-off scream. He sat up and used his sheet to dab away the sweat on his forehead. As he tried to gather his thoughts, he felt a weight pressing down on his right thigh.

He opened his eyes. The dog, lying alongside him, was resting its head on his leg. Fletcher leaned over the animal. Gently he rubbed the Labrador's face. His heart, still racing after the dream, began to pound even harder. He spoke quietly. "Are you awake?"

The dog stirred but remained unconscious.

Fletcher leaned in closer and repeated himself. This time the dog's ears pricked up at the sound of his voice. His front right leg gave a short kick. And then, miraculously, he opened his eyes.

Fletcher felt a surge of warmth rise up in his chest.

The dog's rich brown-and-yellow eyes held Fletcher's stare.

"I never doubted you for a minute," he managed. "What took you so long?"

↶ **FIVE**

"I'LL be damned," Bruno said. "I truly thought we'd lost him."

"We should have," Fletcher replied, gently massaging the Labrador's neck, "but you saved him."

"I think we had some . . . higher help. This dog was meant to survive. Believe me, we're in the league of miracles here."

The dog lifted his head and tried to sit up. "Easy, buddy," Fletcher whispered, helping to prop him up. The dog looked down at the gauze patches on his body, then back up at Fletcher. His eyes were heavy with sleep.

"You're going to be just fine."

He blinked wearily, then nuzzled the side of Fletcher's arm.

Arnold, who had been chronically depressed since the shooting, knelt down next to the Labrador. The dog turned, regarded him wearily for a moment, and then licked his hand.

Fletcher watched as the tears welled up in the young soldier's eyes. In a single stroke, he had been absolved of his offenses.

Gunther screwed open his flask and poured some water into an upturned helmet. "Let's see if he's ready to drink yet."

The dog's ears pricked up. He lapped up the water, splashing it all over Fletcher's legs.

Travis moved toward the dog. "It's so strange that he's a Labrador. Most of the dogs out here are German shepherds."

"There're quite a few Labradors operating as scouts. They pick up enemy tracks and provide early warning of snipers and traps. If he has training, we could actually use him," Mitchell replied.

As the possibility rattled around in Fletcher's mind, Bruno asked, "What're we going to call him?"

The question was clearly directed at Fletcher, and Fletcher had the answer. "Jack. We'll call him Jack."

"That was quick. Why Jack?" Bruno asked.

"I don't know," Fletcher replied. "The name just came to me."

Mitchell cupped his hand over the side of the Labrador's face. "Well, Jack . . . welcome back to hell."

HUDDLED together, Fletcher, Travis, and Mitchell waited to be summoned into Frank Wilson's office.

"What's our plan?" Travis whispered.

"Just leave the talking to me. It's my fault that you're both here."

"If you think we're going to sit back and let you play the martyr, you can forget it." Travis yawned. "Besides, what's the worst they can do? Send us to bed without supper?"

Fletcher was about to respond, when the door to Frank Wilson's office opened.

"Inside, gentlemen. *Now*." Frank Wilson rolled up a large map he'd been studying. "I suppose you know why you're here."

"Yes, sir," Fletcher replied. "Neither of these men—"

Frank held up his hand. "Rogan told me everything. You found the dog. I know it was Rogan's idea to bring him back, that you were acting under orders. I'm not happy with the situation, but we have to deal with it. I've been told that the dog has been placed in your care and that he regained consciousness. Is this true?"

Fletcher could not believe what he was hearing. Not only had Rogan covered up their fight, but he had taken blame for the dog. Fletcher felt a sudden sense of gratitude toward him and, in that moment, every preconceived notion he had of the lieutenant was cast into doubt. "Uh . . . yes, sir."

"Well? Is he going to live?"

Sensing Fletcher had been put off his stride, Travis intercepted the question. "We hope so, sir. He's eating and drinking now."

"I've heard about your tent, gentlemen. I've also noticed what his presence has done for the men. I won't deny that I'm moved by all the support your patient has had, but I have a base to run. Have you checked the dog for any type of identification? We need to get him back to his unit if he's one of ours."

"We have, sir. All U.S. dogs serving in Vietnam have coding inside their ears," Travis replied. "But there's nothing there."

Frank sat back in his chair and folded his arms. "All right, gentlemen. What is your recommendation?"

Fletcher, having regained his composure, recognized his opportunity. "I suggest we keep him here until he is fully rehabilitated."

"And then?"

"We could use a dog here to patrol the perimeter."

"We don't have any facilities to care for dogs here."

"Sir, we've been given support from a nearby dog unit. We have all the supplies we need."

"You're the senior man, Lord. What do you make of this?"

"I think the dog is doing wonders for morale," said Mitchell. "And the base can do with all the good feeling we can muster."

Frank looked up at the ceiling. "I want a plan, Carson. On my desk by the end of today. Where he's going to sleep, a schedule to get him moving again—everything."

"Thank you, sir. I can't tell you what this means to us."

"I'm not blind to what goes on around here. I've seen what this dog has done for the men. All right . . . you're all dismissed."

As they walked toward the door, Frank stopped them. "Carson, wait," he said, offering a wad of dollar bills. "For your money wall."

THE next few weeks were spent largely rehabilitating Jack. At first, his progress was painstakingly slow. They suspected his legs were permanently damaged, because he could barely stand for more than a minute before collapsing. He was eating and drinking better than any dog living in the backyard of American suburbia, but his lack of mobility was a major concern.

Then Jack tentatively began to take a few shaky steps. As the circulation in his legs improved, he progressed to a sure-footed trot. The men took turns walking, feeding, and looking after him, but mostly when Fletcher wasn't able to. The dog may have become the base's mascot, but there were no illusions as to whom he belonged.

Gunther spent hours tracking down dog units in the region, but none of them reported a missing dog of Jack's description. Yet the dog was highly trained. It first became apparent when he reacted to basic commands but was even more obvious one morning when he was taken on a patrol of the base's perimeter. Fletcher noticed a change in him the instant he put on his leash. Jack quickly moved ahead of him, sniffing the ground. Then Jack suddenly dropped down and began to make soft whimpering noises.

"What is it, Jack?" Fletcher asked, moving up alongside him.

A low growl issued from the back of Jack's throat. Not sure what to do, Fletcher gently placed his hand on top of his head to calm him, but the growl only intensified.

Suddenly Fletcher understood. No less than a yard ahead of them, buried alongside the fence, was a live mortar that had failed to detonate. A remnant of the attack they had suffered several weeks before. He tugged at Jack's leash, and the Labrador instantly relented and followed after him.

The mortar was later safely detonated, and the majority of Jack's detractors, if any remained, were permanently silenced. Every morning after that, Fletcher and Jack patrolled the perimeter as part of their daily duties.

It wasn't long before Jack's other talents were discovered. They had received a booklet of basic dog commands from squad leader Wallace. It consisted of typical word and hand commands used out in the field. Jack knew every one of them.

As the memory of his injuries faded, Jack's true personality began to emerge. He was surprisingly mischievous. He would steal food out of the men's knapsacks and chew holes in their boots. He joined them in the Soup, happily lapping up any beer that was offered. In a matter of weeks, he had worked his way into the affections of all on base. All but one.

Despite taking responsibility for Jack's being brought back to base, Rogan seemed uninterested in the dog. Fletcher tried to thank him for what he had done, but Rogan stopped him in mid-sentence. His thoughts were only on the war and the Fat Lady. This, however, was of little consequence to Jack, who continually sought Rogan out as if he sensed the lieutenant's indifference toward him. In meetings, he would sit at his feet. To the amusement of the platoon, he even offered Rogan his paw during a briefing session. But it had little effect. Rogan's mind was totally focused on the war.

A war they were losing.

"THIS isn't a debate," Frank Wilson warned. "The dog is highly trained and could save you out there."

"We're not a dog unit, Frank," Rogan replied. "We're not sure if he's ever operated in the field. He could give away our position."

"The dog follows voice and hand signals. He seems to share half his brain with Carson."

"This is madness."

"No. *Madness* is being forced to send you up the Chi San trail. You're going to be moving through treacherous terrain. You have three days before you go. Carson, Tucker, Lord, and Rex have agreed to do two short patrols with the dog to get a feel. If by then there are concerns, we'll leave him behind. If not, he's going with you. Besides, I don't understand why you're against this. You're the one who rescued him in the first place."

Rogan massaged his eyes with his fingers. "This is different."

"Look, I'm only doing this because I truly believe the dog can help you. This dog, *he can sense things.* He is a wonder."

"Frank, you have the respect of every man on this base, myself included. So I'll take the dog with us. But I want you to know that if he does anything to threaten our mission, I will kill him."

Frank agreed. "Just get in and out as quick as you can."

Frank held out his hand, and Rogan accepted it. "How long, sir?"

"Until what?"

"Until we pull out."

"Could be as soon as a month or two. That's what I'm hearing."

A sardonic grin danced across Rogan's face. "More than enough time to die, then."

"LET ME GET THIS STRAIGHT," Wayville said. "We're going to tip-toe up the Chi San trail into Charlie's heart and pick off two of his top commanding officers, all without any backup?"

"So you *were* listening," Rogan replied evenly.

"And then we quietly sneak out without Charlie seeing us and skip merrily back down the yellow brick road?"

"How far back will the drop be?" Gunther cut in.

"Thirty . . . maybe thirty-five clicks."

"Thirty-five kilometers? That's a two-day hike!"

"More like three," Mitchell corrected him.

"There's something else." Rogan paused, looking at his men. "This base is underground."

"A tunnel complex? Why don't we just kill ourselves now?"

Rogan stepped forward. "I don't like this any more than you do. We're risking our necks for reasons that don't make much sense. However, we've been ordered to go. Now, we can either sit around and whine about it or we can start planning this thing down to the last detail so we minimize our risk. For most of you the biggest risk will be making it to the complex."

"How do you figure that? Once underground, we'll be hunted like rats in a maze," Gunther replied.

"Because *you're* not going *in!* Only Carson, Lord, and myself are. Carson's going in as our assassin, with Lord and myself as his shadow. Our informant produced a sketch of the complex and has shown us where our two targets will be sleeping. We'll infiltrate at oh three hundred and be out within an hour." Rogan paused. "One last thing. Our commander feels that we might need Fletcher's dog and his tracking abilities. I will only take him with us if every man is in agreement. If one of you feels that the dog might in any way compromise us, speak now."

The group exchanged glances at one another but said nothing.

"All right, then. Fletcher will be his handler, and they'll hike at point with Lord. Gentlemen, we leave in forty-eight hours. As of now, there is no more drinking. We're going to be under Charlie's nose, and he'll be able to smell the liquor on your skin a mile away."

~ SIX

ANOTHER week, another tense flight over Vietnam, Fletcher thought as they hovered above the Strip. He knew if he made it back to the outside world, he would never set foot in another helicopter. Holding Jack's leash, he looked down at the Lab sitting between his legs. "Where did you come from?" he whispered.

Despite the drone of the rotors, Jack picked up on Fletcher's voice. He turned and licked him on the cheek.

Travis smiled. "There's something about him, Fletcher. He's different. I don't know how or why, but he just is."

"I know. I feel it, too." The helicopter swooped over the trees, clearing the branches by a few feet.

"All right, men," Rogan called out. "Ten minutes to put down. Get your minds on the game."

OVER the next three days, the Fat Lady's pace was slow as they hid from numerous NVA patrols. Their movement was further hampered by traps along the trail. Mitchell uncovered more than a dozen. Jack repaid the faith shown in him by sniffing out almost half as many.

As nightfall approached after yet another late-afternoon deluge, they were still almost two kilometers away from the tunnel complex. "Lord, Carson . . . we need to get a move on. There's not much light left," Rogan said, marching up behind them.

Mitchell's eyes were red and swollen from the demands of a long day. "We can't go any quicker. The closer we get, the more traps we come across."

"If we don't make it to the complex soon, we lose another day. We *definitely* can't afford that."

"We'll try to shift it up a notch," Fletcher replied.

"You do that."

For fifteen minutes, the platoon increased its pace marginally, but the light was rapidly dwindling. Already telltale streaks of pink and purple stretched across the sky. Again Rogan pulled up behind them. "We need to move faster. Fall back. I'll take over point."

"With respect, Rogan—" Mitchell began.

"This isn't a request, Lord! I'm not asking you to dance. Now fall back. Both of you." With that, he pushed past them.

"He's going to get himself killed," Fletcher said.

They hadn't covered more than fifty yards when Jack suddenly sprinted ahead. His burst of acceleration caught Fletcher by surprise, and the leash slipped out of his hand. "Wait, Jack!"

The Labrador leaped up and bit Rogan on the arm. It was enough to send him crashing to the ground.

"Release, Jack! *Release!*" Fletcher shouted.

Jack, growling now, stood over the lieutenant.

"Retreat!" Fletcher commanded as he and Mitchell drew up alongside them.

Rogan's eyes were reduced to thin slits as he stared at the dog. His right arm, muddied and bleeding just above the elbow, was fully extended, and his gun was only inches away from Jack's face.

Fletcher moved up alongside the Labrador and gently grabbed him by his collar. "Easy, boy. . . . Easy."

Rogan looked at Fletcher, as if disorientated, then began to sit up. Jack suddenly leaped at him. This time he snapped at Rogan's face.

"Pull your dog back! Now!"

Fletcher battled to restrain Jack. Rogan again started to get up, when Mitchell noticed something. "Don't move. Stop!"

Stretched across Rogan's head was a thin trip wire.

"Slide back slowly and keep your head down."

Rogan did as instructed. Mitchell carefully took hold of the trip wire and gently returned it to its position.

Jack immediately relented, the fight gone out of him, and sat down at Fletcher's side. The wire was linked to a cluster of hand grenades fixed to the base of a tree. Another wire connected eight trees down the path, each with their own cargo of explosives. Had the wire been crossed, it was designed to take out an entire platoon.

In his first tour with the Fat Lady, Jack had saved them all.

IGNORING what had just happened, Rogan returned to point and continued to push forward, although this time he moved at a more sensible pace. What little light remained was rapidly disappearing. Within minutes a cloying darkness would descend over them.

The tunnel complex was now just over a kilometer away. They would soon have to find somewhere to hide until it was time to go in. Once their orders had been executed, they would immediately begin their hike back down the path toward the pickup point.

As they rounded a bank of trees, Rogan pointed to a slight declivity that would conceal their position. One by one, they filed down the embankment and settled under the dense foliage.

Rogan, Mitchell, and Fletcher sat down to go over the plan.

"Pearson, we need to review the sketch of the complex. Get over here," Rogan said.

Gunther crawled over and shined his flashlight down onto the creased paper. "The entrance to the complex is four hundred yards ahead. It's marked by a short wooden stake. A trapdoor takes you down twenty feet to a crawl space that feeds the main corridor. This corridor runs some five hundred yards south. Off here, you'll find supply rooms, a kitchen, a hospital room, and the soldiers barracks. The officers dormitory lies behind the barracks."

"Okay," Rogan began, removing his pack. "The best time to infiltrate is around oh three hundred. If we're lucky, we can get into the main corridor without being detected. The problem comes after that. We don't know how many soldiers are in that room or how difficult it is going to be to access the officers dormitory."

"We also can't rely on the fact that they'll all be sleeping like angels. Fletch, you're going to have to be pretty sure that none of the soldiers are awake before you go in," Mitchell added.

"And if they're not?"

"You'll have to wait. We've built in some extra time. You've basically got an hour to get in and out. That gives us an hour head start. We can't risk anything less than that," Rogan replied.

"Where will you guys be?"

"Making sure no one comes up behind you."

Fletcher knew he was asking the obvious, but he proceeded with his question, anyway. "What happens if someone raises the alarm?"

Rogan rested his arms on two hand grenades that were secured to the front of his jacket. "We'll take out as many as we can."

FLETCHER'S cheek brushed up against the side of the tunnel. It felt warm and moist against his skin. Apart from the stench of natural decay, he was able to discern a number of other pungent smells, such as stale tobacco, cordite, urine, and even sweat—although most of the latter was probably his own, he thought. Despite the size of the complex, the crawl space was minuscule; he had to tuck his elbows in tight just to squeeze through the opening that joined the entrance section to the main tunnel. He had expected to encounter some resistance by now, but so far the chamber was empty.

Lying at the entrance to the main corridor, Fletcher remained still, listening for movement. All was quiet. The corridor itself was twice as wide as the entranceway and would allow an average Vietnamese soldier to walk straight up. He, however, had to walk with a stoop. He quietly headed toward the faint glow of a lantern some forty yards away. According to their information, the fourth tunnel off to the right of the corridor was the main soldiers barracks. Behind this area was the officers dormitory.

He moved toward the pale light and was amazed by how clean and well constructed the complex was. Thick wooden struts supported the roof. As he neared the lantern, he realized it was hanging on the wall outside the first room. True to their information, it was a supply room. Farther down the corridor was the kitchen, then almost two hundred yards farther was the soldiers barracks.

Standing alongside the open entranceway, he waited to hear if anyone was talking. A lantern cast a soft yellow silhouette over the sleeping soldiers. There were at least thirty men lying on the floor, side by side. Strangely, not a single one of them was snoring or even stirring. They hardly appeared to be breathing.

There's no room to walk, Fletcher suddenly realized. It had never occurred to him that they would be lying so close together. Staring at the sea of bodies, he weighed his options. He saw a door at the back of the room leading to the officers sleeping quarters. It was some twenty five yards away. He debated trying to step between the men but knew he could get stranded with his path blocked. Or he might lose his balance and step on one of the men. It was too much of a risk. There remained only one other option.

As part of the support structure of the roof, a steel beam with a narrow inner railing, much like a railway track, ran the length of the room, ending a yard or so from the back door. He studied the beam to ensure that there was enough space for him to grip the bar. It seemed sufficient. He would climb over the men.

He glanced down at his watch: 0323. He'd been in the complex for almost a quarter of an hour. He took a deep breath, checked that his gun was properly secured, and grabbed hold of the railing. He hoisted himself up and began to swing forward. It reminded him of how Kelly used to hang from the monkey bars at her school. He quickly banished the image.

He made it almost halfway across the room when the first beads of sweat began to rise up on his forehead. The complex was oppressively hot. A few moments later he could feel the perspiration dripping off his face. His arms and shoulders were showing signs of strain. His shoulders began to tremble.

Below, a soldier stirred and then sat up.

Fletcher lifted his knees to his chest. His fingers were burning with exertion and beginning to slide on the sweat-slicked steel. The soldier looked around the room and lay back down. A few moments later he rolled onto his side and was back asleep.

Fighting away the cramp and pain, Fletcher continued forward. Every new reach sapped away his strength. His legs felt like concrete pillars. But he closed in on the back of the room.

Five yards. Four. Three.

Suddenly he lost his grip. Instinctively, he opened his stance and landed with both feet on either side of a soldier's head. He immediately pulled out his gun and pointed it at the man's face. Miraculously, he remained asleep. Fletcher quickly spun around to check that none of the other men had woken up.

They hadn't.

He straightened up and carefully stepped over the remaining two soldiers. He waited a moment to catch his breath before quietly opening the bamboo door to the officers dormitory. He withdrew his flashlight, covered his shirt over the lens to diffuse the light, and switched it on. The room lit up dimly in a sickly green glow. The chamber was almost as big as the soldiers barracks but housed only the two commanding officers. They were sleeping in a bunk bed at the back of the room.

Perfect, he thought.

As he approached the beds, he was gripped by a terrible sadness. In a matter of months, he'd gone from pushing his daughter on a swing to standing over two strangers he was about to murder. Did they have children? Did they deserve to be gunned down? Fletcher's world was again threatening to spiral out of control.

He cocked the gun and knelt down next to the man sleeping on the lower bunk. He wrapped a small towel around the barrel to further muffle the sound. His last thought was to wonder what the man was dreaming.

He hoped it was a good dream.

Closing his eyes, Fletcher felt his arm recoil and warm blood splatter up his hand. The shot sounded like a heavy book dropping off a table. The second officer shifted in the bunk above him. The sound of his voice thrust Fletcher into action. He dived on top of his first mark, pressed his gun into the mattress above him, and fired twice. Blood seeped through the holes.

Taking short, sharp breaths, Fletcher could feel his pulse gallop.

He was now a murderer. The thought of what he had just done sickened him. For a while, he battled to contain a thick, viscous nausea that churned in his stomach. After what felt like a long time, he lowered his gun. His arm was shaking violently. Wiping the blood off his hand, he checked his watch.

He was out of time. He had to get moving.

He sat up and climbed off the dead man. With his entire body trembling, he hurried out of the room and slipped back into the soldiers barracks. Still the men slept peacefully. He looked up at the railing on the ceiling, then placed his fingers into the thin steel groove and hoisted himself up. Surprisingly, his body felt light and his arms and hands strong—most likely on account of the adrenaline coursing through his veins. He quickly began to swing back across the room.

He was approaching the end of the railing when he noticed there was an open space three or four yards from the front of the room.

A body was missing.

Fear prickled up the back of his neck. One of the soldiers had woken up and probably gone to relieve himself. He'd be returning any minute. Fletcher needed to get out fast.

Move . . . *move* . . . *move.* His mind urged him forward. He reached the end of the railing and dropped down as gracefully as he could.

Still no one stirred—except for the man standing in the doorway.

The soldier blinked and took a step back. He was just beyond Fletcher's reach. The soldier took a breath and was about to raise the alarm when Rogan stepped into view and punched the soldier on the side of his head. He was unconscious even before he collapsed into Mitchell's arms.

Fletcher exhaled like a man who had narrowly avoided falling off a cliff.

"Job done?" Rogan asked.

"The marks are down," Fletcher replied numbly.

Mitchell carried the soldier back to where he was sleeping. If another soldier woke up, it was crucial that everything appeared normal. The Fat Lady needed a head start down the trail.

As they started back down the main corridor, Fletcher felt a fresh wave of nausea pass over him. He cleared his mind and tried to separate himself from his circumstances. After a few seconds, he closed his eyes and swallowed back the sickening feeling.

"You okay?" Mitchell asked.

"No."

"Good. All right, then, let's move."

Within minutes, they were out of the complex. Pushing through the top of the trapdoor, Fletcher filled his nostrils with the sweet scent of the jungle night.

THE darkness made it difficult for the Fat Lady to progress with any speed down the trail. Mitchell had mapped out the remaining traps ahead. The terrain itself prohibited anything more than a brisk walk. Whenever they tried to accelerate, someone would lose their footing. There was a danger of one of them getting hurt and hindering their pace even further.

After a while, Travis pulled up alongside Fletcher. "Do you want to talk about what happened down there?"

Fletcher shrugged. "I don't mind."

"How'd it go?"

"For me," he began, still contesting a lingering queasiness, "okay. For the two officers I murdered . . . not so good."

"It couldn't have been easy."

Fletcher stumbled on a loose rock but reached out for Jack to steady himself. "Taking a man's life in open combat is one thing. This was just plain murder."

"It's not murder, Fletcher. It's war. This isn't the same thing."

"Isn't it?"

"C'mon, Fletch, you know it isn't."

"All I know is this," he replied, raising his arms up to the pale moonlight. The back of his hands and the cuffs of his sleeves were smeared black with blood. "*This* is what's real to me right now."

"We've all got blood on our hands. Yours is no different."

"I don't recognize the man I've become. A year ago I was a different person. Never even thought of owning a gun, let alone firing one. Now I kill people in their sleep."

Travis was about to respond, when the darkness was lit up by an explosion of angry gunfire.

"Down . . . *down!*" Rogan shouted.

Bright bursts of light—the distinctive flairs of machine-gun fire—crackled to their right from behind a small rise.

Mitchell and Rogan were the first to react, returning fire.

How the hell had they wandered into an ambush? Fletcher thought as he fumbled for his rifle.

The sound of their exchange was thunderous. By the time Fletcher had emptied his second clip, he realized they were no longer being fired upon.

"Halt," Rogan instructed. "Hold your fire."

The jungle was quiet, save for the birds that had been disturbed from their nests.

Miraculously, nobody had been shot.

Mitchell and Kingston quickly swept through the area. Once again, and to no one's surprise, Charlie was gone. All that remained in his wake were two small mounds of empty shells.

～ SEVEN

IT WAS late afternoon the following day when they reached the extraction point. The relief of surviving their assignment was eclipsed by their exhaustion. Jack, in particular, looked stiff and sore from the journey. It was the farthest he had traveled since his recovery.

Fletcher closed his eyes and tried to tune out the drone of the helicopter rotors. He imagined he was sitting on a perfect golden beach, the sun shimmering off the crisp blue ocean. The image evoked the memory of a wonderful holiday he and his girls had shared only two years ago. He remembered when Kelly, who had built an elaborate sand castle too close to the shoreline, was working furiously to build a moat to protect her handiwork.

"Mommy . . . daddy . . . help me! Quick! The water's going to wash away my castle!"

Abigail rushed to her daughter's side. "C'mon, Fletch."

Fletcher set aside his newspaper and joined his girls. The three of them dug a moat around the castle, but no matter how hard they worked, the waves kept coming. Eventually the incoming tide overwhelmed the castle, reducing it to a blurred, indistinct mound. Watching her creation being destroyed, Kelly looked up at her father. She never said anything, but Fletcher saw it in her eyes. She was disappointed in him. She was upset that he wasn't able to save something of hers. He was her father. He was supposed to protect her.

That innocently conceived but accusing expression had haunted Fletcher since the crash. The sand castle became a metaphor for her death. Just as he could not protect her sculpture, so he had failed to save her from that nightmarish December morning. Sometimes that single thought threatened to consume him.

A familiar weight pressed against his thigh, rousing him from his daydream. It was Jack. In his first assignment, he had performed far beyond everyone's expectations. Fletcher couldn't help but feel proud of how well Jack had fared. As he watched the Labrador drift off to sleep, familiar questions swirled around in his mind: Where did he come from? Why didn't he have any markings? He couldn't shake the nagging feeling that Jack was somehow lost, as if he had been traveling between worlds and had somehow strayed from his journey.

He felt Jack move away from him. He watched with interest as Rogan fished out two biscuits from his pocket and offered them to Jack. Unsure of the lieutenant, the Labrador edged forward and gently accepted the treats. As soon as they left his hand, Rogan turned away as if the moment had never happened.

THE next two weeks back at base drifted by without incident. Fletcher and Travis spent most of their time training Jack. If he was to accompany them on more assignments, it was important he learn certain new hand and voice commands.

His progress was unreal. Within a few days, they had taught him twenty commands, including an instruction to detach from the Fat Lady and track them down at a later time. The idea was that if they came under heavy fire, it would be safer for Jack to leave the area and return later.

Jack became as much a feature of life on the Strip as the smell of diesel and cordite. He won over all the men. Even those who weren't dog lovers enjoyed having Jack around. The commander became partial to him and ordered a special leather harness for his upcoming patrols.

One morning a few of the men built Jack a special eight-foot-wide steel bath that he could wade around in to cool off. To get him to use it, Fletcher and Travis climbed into the tub and, while trying to coax him into the waist-high water, found it a most agreeable place to see out the afternoon. The next day, they brought beers with them and remained well after sunset. They spent hours sitting on either side of Jack, reminiscing over happier times back home. Their conversations remained light and whimsical, circling the darker areas of their pasts. Jack, like all dogs, was just content to be in the company of his owners.

Fletcher and Jack became virtually inseparable. Wherever Fletcher went, Jack followed. When the Fat Lady was sent on two short assignments, Jack accompanied them. On each occasion, he sniffed out traps that might have otherwise proved fatal.

Jack was no longer a dog they had simply found, or even the base's mascot. He was a soldier.

Theirs.

GUNFIRE ripped through the jungle.

Fletcher grabbed Jack by his harness and scrambled toward a bank of nearby trees. Glancing over his shoulder, he saw Rogan lying on his back, his M-16 bucking against his chest as he returned fire. "Cover . . . *cover!*" he shouted, urging his men to safety.

As Fletcher rounded the trees and reached for his rifle, he realized that he was at the top of a steep embankment. He slid on the mud and slick grass and fell down the slope. As the sound of gunfire continued to punctuate the air, he realized that Jack hadn't fallen with him. In a wild frenzy, he punched and kicked his way back up to the top of the slope.

The first thing he saw was a soldier lying on his side about fifty yards down the trail.

Jack was standing over him, trying to protect him. His hackles were raised, and he was growling and snapping in the direction of the fire, trying to ward off their attackers. The rest of the Fat Lady had managed to find cover and were returning fire.

All except Rogan.

He was running toward Jack and the downed soldier.

Fletcher immediately joined in the chase. He watched helplessly as bullets exploded into the ground around Jack and the soldier. Even when two bullets tore into the man's back, Jack stood firm, refusing to relent. Fletcher's breath caught in his throat when he realized who the soldier was.

"No!"

Another volley tore into Travis's legs. Suddenly Jack bit into Travis's shirtsleeve and tried to drag him away from the fire.

Fletcher's heart lurched at the sight. He held out his rifle in one hand and, without looking, opened fire into the hill.

A bullet tore through a fold in Fletcher's pants, grazing his leg. Another skipped off the back of his helmet. He was a natural athlete and was on Rogan's shoulder the moment he reached Travis. The lieutenant swooped down and grabbed the front of Travis's shirt and lifted him up. Fletcher scooped up Jack, and together they scrambled for cover. They had no sooner collapsed to the ground when the firing stopped.

Mitchell called out to them from the hill. He had flanked their attackers and taken them out. "Hold your fire! All Charlie down."

"Edgar," Rogan screamed. "Get here!"

Fletcher crawled next to Travis and cradled his friend's head in his hands while Edgar checked his wrist for a pulse.

Travis had taken at least five rounds. A thick pool of black blood arced around his legs and waist.

"Travis, can you hear me?" Fletcher asked.

His eyes stirred but remained closed.

"C'mon, man . . . *please.*"

Slowly he opened his eyes. "Fletch . . ."

"Yeah, Trav . . . it's me. It's all over."

The whites of Travis's eyes were outlined in blood.

"Did you see Jack?" he asked quietly, his teeth coated red. "Did you see what he did? He tried to save me."

Fletcher nodded but could not reply.

Edgar was trying to stem the blood flow, but it was useless.

Travis choked, then looked up peacefully at the sky. "It's true what they say, you know."

"What is?" Fletcher replied, feeling his friend's blood spread under his knees.

"How calm everything becomes before you die."

"Please, Trav. . . . *Don't.*"

"It's all right, Fletch. Especially for guys like you and me."

The comment was lost on most of the men, but Fletcher nodded as fresh tears cut a trail through the grime on his cheeks.

"Look after Jack. He deserves to get out of this place. Take him to Miami. Let him run on the beach."

Fletcher began to cry. "I will. You have my word."

"Make sure you have a view of the ocean . . . and crisp fresh sheets."

Fletcher smiled, his lips trembling.

"If I see your girls, I'll tell them how much you miss them."

As Travis took his final breath, Fletcher bent over and whispered to him, "Go to your wife. . . . She's waiting for you."

Travis squeezed Fletcher's hand. Then he was gone.

THE weight of Travis's death pressed heavily on each of the men as they flew back to base. His body was bound in sleeping bags, but blood still seeped through. Jack was sitting alongside Fletcher with his head perched on his knee, staring at Travis's body. The Labrador's expression projected a deep and primal sadness.

"It wasn't our fault, Jack," Mitchell offered, recognizing the look in the dog's eyes. "They were downwind of us almost two hundred yards. There's nothing we could've done. We never had a chance."

Kingston, who had not uttered a single word since the ambush, began to sing "Amazing Grace." He closed his eyes and let his strong voice fill the cabin. He was a deeply religious man, and his faith, which had never wavered despite all the atrocities he had witnessed, gave him an inner strength that Fletcher envied. His own faith, which at its most resolute had not held much conviction, had been eroded away over the past two years. Every death was another wave overwhelming it. He knew he was on the verge of a final breakdown. There were just too many dead faces. Too much loss. While he thought of this and other nightmares, he allowed Kingston's song into his heart.

Before the helicopter even touched down, it was clear something important had happened on base. As they came into land, they could see men running, hugging, and punching the air. One soldier was on his knees, holding his head in his hands.

As the Fat Lady disembarked, Fletcher remained behind. He already knew why they were celebrating. There could only be one explanation.

As the pilot cut the engine and the rotors lost their will, Fletcher watched as one of the soldiers ran up to Wayville and Gunther. Fletcher couldn't hear what he said, but the shape of his words were unmistakable. "It's over!" he cried. "We're going home!"

Fletcher closed his eyes and shook his head. He felt sick.

In the dying embers of the war, Travis might well have been Vietnam's final casualty.

At least among the dead.

THEY had all known it was coming, but few expected the end to arrive as suddenly as it did.

As they disembarked from the helicopter, they learned that a cease-fire had been signed by the United States, South Vietnam, North Vietnam, and the Vietcong. The war was over.

But before they could properly process the news, the Fat Lady had to tend to their own. They carried Travis down to their church to pay final respects. It was little more than a tent featuring a crudely fashioned wooden cross, a spattering of candles, and half a dozen wooden benches, but it sufficed. This was the way they had always bade farewell to one of their own.

Entering the tent, they gently placed his body underneath the cross and all lowered down to their knees. Kingston recited a few psalms as well as a passage from Revelations. After prayer, Kingston began to sing "Abide with Me," but his emotions got the better of him and he could not complete the hymn. Despite the sounds of revelry outside, each of the men remained behind, taking their time to say good-bye. Eventually, one by one, they drifted out of the tent until only Fletcher and Mitchell were left behind.

"I can't believe he's gone," Fletcher whispered.

Mitchell normally spoke sparingly, as if dialogue was vital ammunition that needed to be conserved. But he told Fletcher, "I know how close the two of you were. You were a very good friend to him. And in this place, that really means something."

Fletcher smiled thinly, tears stinging his eyes. "At least," he began, his voice wavering, "he's gone home now. He's back where he belongs."

Mitchell placed his hand on Fletcher's shoulder but chose not to speak. He had no more words left to offer.

THAT night, almost every man, woman, and dog got drunk. Most indulged not only to celebrate surviving the darkness of Vietnam and the prospect of returning home to their families, but to remember those who had been lost.

As Fletcher nursed his beer and looked around the Soup, the soldiers' excitement was plain to see. For so long the horror of Vietnam had been their lives, and now, within weeks, they would all be back home. He imagined wives running into the arms of their husbands, children running to their fathers. He felt a genuine sense of warmth and happiness for them, but this was tempered by the thousands of families who would never again be reunited and by the fate that awaited the people of South Vietnam. Fletcher knew the cease-fire would ultimately break down and the South would soon be overpowered. South Vietnam stood no chance on its own.

"To Travis," Gunther said, raising his beer.

"And to every soldier who died in this hellhole," Wayville added.

"Hear! Hear!" the room chorused.

The drinking never slowed. Fletcher had hoped the alcohol might numb him to the effects of the day, but it seemed only to fuel his depression. He finally decided he'd had enough. As he and Jack left the Soup and made their way toward their tent, he noticed a man sitting on a rock in the open field. There was no mistaking his frame. He had seen it often enough under the cover of night to know who it was. "Getting some air?" he called out.

Rogan turned. "Carson . . . what are you doing out here?"

"The beer tasted off. Want some company?"

"Sure."

Fletcher and Jack sat down a few yards away from the lieutenant, and for a while, they were both quiet.

"I've been out here for almost an hour. So far I've counted over five hundred stars. I wonder how long it took to lose our first five hundred men in this place."

"Forget it, Lieutenant. It'll drive you mad just thinking about it."

"So many lives lost for a failed cause."

"I understand how you feel—"

"I'm not sure you do. I really believed in what we've been trying to achieve here," said Rogan. "Maybe it's why I've lasted this long." He slowly began to shake his head. "We're sending the South to their deaths. You know that, don't you?"

Fletcher shifted onto his haunches, not interested in pursuing a political debate. "Are you going to stay in the service?"

"I don't know. I can't see myself getting a normal job, like selling cars, can you?"

Fletcher smiled at the thought. "For what it's worth, thank you."

"For what?"

"Keeping us alive."

"You've got to be kidding me."

"Without you and Mitchell, none of us would've survived."

"That's not true and you know it. I became reckless. If it wasn't for Jack here, we wouldn't be having this conversation." The Labrador had curled up and was already fast asleep. "If he hadn't stopped me before that wire—"

"That's one incident. How many times have you saved us?"

Rogan looked at the night sky. "I wasn't able to save Travis."

"You did everything you could! What you did today was the most courageous thing I've ever seen. How you didn't get yourself killed, I'll never know."

"If I recall, you were right behind me."

"That's different. You were drawing their fire."

"Bull. You're still trying to get yourself killed." Rogan sighed. "So what're you going to do with your life now? Find another war? Put a gun in your mouth?"

"I couldn't. Who'd look after Jack?"

"Is that what it comes down to? Is the line that thin for you?"

"Isn't it for everyone?"

"You tell me."

"Travis was half an hour away from surviving this place. I'd say that's a thin line."

"Yes, but the difference is, he wanted to live."

Fletcher nodded. "I suppose you're right."

Rogan reached across and rubbed the side of Jack's face. "You know . . . this damn animal really grows on you. I'm really glad he survived. He's going to love America."

"I think so, too," Fletcher nodded. "Do you know when we're scheduled to pull out?"

"There'll be a full briefing tomorrow morning, but the men aren't going to like it. Because of our advanced position, we're one of the last bases to leave."

~~ EIGHT

WHEN Fletcher reached his tent, he tried to ignore Travis's empty bunk, but his eyes were drawn to it. Some of his personal effects—photographs and books, mostly—were stacked on a small bedside table. The sight of them depressed Fletcher. He knew he would have to sort through them and have them packaged and sent home, but just not tonight. He was about to collapse onto his bed, when he noticed a large brown envelope on his pillow.

Lifting the envelope, he immediately recognized the handwriting on its cover. It was the same scrawl that had often blotted his articles. It was Marvin Samuels, his old friend and former editor. He tore it open and removed its contents. There were three back issues of *The Mirror* inside, with highlighted articles about Vietnam, but there was also a second, smaller envelope.

For no particular reason, he felt his pulse quicken.

The envelope contained a letter attached to a document.

Dear Fletcher,

I hope these words find you, and find you well.

You should know that your efforts are greatly appreciated by scores back here, but equally many are against our nation's presence in Vietnam. It saddens me to tell you that some soldiers returning home are being treated like criminals. I hope it's enough for you to know that cowards like myself are very grateful for what you are doing and are indebted to your sacrifice.

I feel sick about the way things ended between us at the cemetery, and I'm truly sorry for my part. Having said that, I fear I have placed an even greater risk on our friendship by what I am about to reveal.

Attached to this letter are thirty-nine pages of a diary your wife kept. Your mother found it in a box during the sale of your home and came to me. She didn't know what to do with it. She felt that if she sent it to you, it might just make what you are going through all that more difficult to endure. Or it might—please let me be right—raise your spirits.

I've kept these pages in my drawer for months under lock and key. Every day I've debated sending them to you, and every day I've found a reason not to.

But they're beginning to burn a hole through my desk, through my heart. Neither your mother nor I have read beyond the first page; its content was never intended for us. I pray that these pages go some way to mending the hurt that you live with. Selfishly, I hope they bring me to a day when I can again be in the company of my friend and tell him how proud I am of him. And how much I've missed him.

May God keep you until that day.

Your friend,
Marvin

Fletcher felt his hands begin to shake. He had no idea Abby had kept a diary. With his heart racing, he unfolded the pages. He managed to read the first few words before he was overcome. Abigail had addressed the diary to Kelly, who at the time of writing had not yet been conceived. It was a mother writing a diary that she one day intended to give to her daughter.

It began: "Kelly, my angel, today I met the man I know I'm going to marry. Today I met your father."

THE weeks that followed were all about packing up supplies and loading them onto helicopters. The sound of choppers taking off and landing became a constant background noise, like great mechanical bees. The men whiled away their extra time playing baseball or touch football. The nights were for drinking.

While under the spell of alcohol, the men often became emotional. They exchanged photographs of loved ones. They got into meaningless fights. They told stories of home.

They were all slowly coming to terms with surviving Vietnam and the prospect of life beyond it. The dark cloud that had hung over them for so long was finally beginning to lift.

With just under two weeks to go until their withdrawal, Fletcher was on his way to the medical tent to set up one final dip for Jack when a man called out to him.

"Fletcher," the voice said behind him. "This came for you."

It was the base mailman, and he was carrying a crumpled brown envelope. For a moment, Fletcher wondered if Marvin had somehow come across another part of Abby's diary.

Was it possible?

He had savored every word of the thirty-nine pages. Her entries were all about their courtship, and they afforded him a precious glimpse back into their early life together. The emotion of her writing was difficult to bear, but he welcomed her words.

He tore open the envelope. Inside was a letter. He unfolded it and instantly recognized the name at the bottom of the page.

Dear Fletcher,

My squad and I enjoyed helping you get Jack rehabilitated and have taken pleasure in hearing of his successes out in the field. However, I am the bearer of bad news.

It appears the price of withdrawing troops and equipment from Vietnam is proving too costly for our government. I'm afraid there is no easy way to say this. Fletcher, our dogs have been officially declared "surplus military equipment" and are not being allowed to return home with us. We've been ordered to hand them over to the South Vietnamese. Those that aren't are being euthanized or just left to die.

It's a nightmare for all us dog handlers. Some four thousand dogs have been fighting, giving their lives to save American soldiers, and they are now being abandoned by our government.

I'm fighting this with everything I have, but I don't hold out much hope. I've been in contact with other dog units, and they've been forced to leave their dogs behind, some at gunpoint. Handlers have been arrested for showing resistance.

If I manage to organize safe passage for our dogs, I'll send for Jack. But it's not looking good. We're due to leave in a few days. If you haven't received word from me by March 13, then I have failed. In which case, I pray you have better luck. I'll be thinking of you and Jack.

Your friend,
W. Wallace

Fletcher's mind was reeling. How could the government do this? How could they just abandon the dogs?

With his hands trembling, he reread his friend's letter. ". . . If you haven't received word from me by March 13, then I have failed. . . ."

The letter slipped from Fletcher's grasp and floated gracefully to the ground. It was March 15.

"THIS is wrong!" Fletcher shouted. "Everyone knows it!"

"I've been given orders right from the top," said Frank Wilson. "I know it's cruel. Damn it, man, I was right behind you in getting Jack on his feet again. But—"

"But what? These dogs are soldiers. How can we leave them behind?" Fletcher began to pace across the room.

"I know this is hard for you. It's difficult for all of us."

"Look, this is the way I see it. Jack is the only dog on base. It'll be easier to sneak him off than it would be if we had a dog unit."

"I'm sorry, but I can't go against senior orders. I'm not jeopardizing a thirty-year career in the military for this. It's ludicrous."

"He deserves a chance, Frank. Please . . . let me try."

"No, Fletcher, it's over. There's nothing more either of us can do. Why don't you focus on the positives? You're going home in a few days. You have the rest of your life to look forward to. Start putting your energies into that."

Fletcher snatched his hat off the table and headed toward the door. "How can you be so damn weak?"

Frank's expression hardened. "I've had about enough of your attitude. Do I need to remind you who you're talking to?"

"Don't worry. I know *exactly* who I'm talking to. The sad thing is that up until today, I had the utmost respect for you."

"We're not finished. This—"

"Oh, we're finished," Fletcher insisted, pushing through the door, "and for what it's worth . . . screw you."

FLETCHER spent his final days in Vietnam trying to devise a plan to smuggle Jack back to America. But there were too many logistical hurdles to overcome. He discovered that the trip home involved four flights and several transfers, and he simply didn't have the contacts to sustain the effort. The obvious temptation was to hide Jack in a crate, but the risk of him freezing to death in the various cargo holds forced him to abandon the idea. He wrote letters, spoke to other dog units, even called old press contacts back home, but one way or another, each avenue soon reached a dead end.

Fletcher spent hours alone with Jack, savoring their time together. How long would Jack survive on his own? What would claim him in the end? Starvation, heat stroke, disease? Or would his life finally draw to a close on the tip of Charlie's knife?

Not since his attempted suicide had Fletcher felt more alone. With only a day left before their withdrawal, he found a secluded place near the base's perimeter where he and Jack could spend the afternoon together. Sitting quietly, they watched as the sun slowly slid across the sky and then finally dipped behind a bank of clouds.

Fletcher knew that just as he had lost his wife and daughter, he was on the brink of losing Jack. He knew that if that happened, then he, too, would be lost.

"THERE'S nothing else we can do?" Rogan asked.

"I'm afraid not," Frank Wilson replied.

"You know how much he gave to this war. Why can't they make an exception? The man is teetering on the edge."

"I've sent special requests right to the top. They feel that if they let Jack come back, there would be no stopping the remaining dog handlers. They're just not prepared to set a precedent."

"This is a travesty."

"I know, but I've done all I can. Believe me."

Rogan paused as a helicopter swooped overhead. "Do you know that the dog saved my life?"

"I didn't, but I'm not surprised."

"In fact, he saved all of us. And now we're just letting him die?"

"I'm sorry, Rogan. I really am," Frank replied as he packed away the last of his personal effects. "Look, I'm scheduled on the next chopper out. Why don't you join me."

"No. I'm going to stay with Fletcher and do what I can to make this easier for him."

Frank stood up and held out his hand. "Something that's always impressed me about you Rogan is how much you care about your men. You're a fine soldier and a great leader."

ROGAN stood at the entrance to the tent and watched as Fletcher brushed Jack.

"He should've died that day," Fletcher said without looking up.

"Maybe so, but you saved him."

"No. He survived because he was meant to live. I'm still convinced of it."

"Fletcher, you've done all you can. You've risked your life for him more than once. You have the strength to get past this."

Fletcher looked up. His eyes were bloodshot. "Without Jack I have nothing left. Don't you understand that?"

"Look, I know you won't be with him, but he might make it out there. He survived before—"

"Alone in this place, he'll be dead in two weeks."

Rogan thought of a reply but could summon nothing honest.

"Everyone's gone, Fletcher. It's just us now. The last chopper will be here any minute. I'll give you some time to say good-bye."

As he turned to leave, Fletcher called out to him. "Wait. Hold on, Rogan." He lifted Jack up and held him against his chest. "They're taking a register of everyone leaving, aren't they?"

"Yes, why?"

"Will you help me?"

"Of course," Rogan replied, wondering what Fletcher meant.

Outside, like the sound of a heartbeat, a final Huey approached.

"FLETCHER Carson? Lieutenant Brock? We're under orders to bring you both out."

Startled, Fletcher looked up at the two men. He hadn't anticipated this. They were both military police.

"What the hell's going on?" Rogan asked. "Who ordered this?"

"That's of no concern to you."

"What have you been told?"

"Shut up!" the second soldier snapped. "The bird's waiting. Go."

Rogan stood up. "Son, how about you put down the M-sixteen."

The senior soldier stepped forward and jabbed his rifle into Rogan's chest. "You can either walk to the chopper or be carried there. Either way, we're leaving right now. Let's go."

"You, too, Carson!" echoed his partner.

Jack, sensing the tension, began to growl.

As they exited the tent, Fletcher instructed Jack to walk ahead of him. The Labrador's hackles were raised, and he was still growling, but he reluctantly followed Fletcher's command.

When Fletcher slowed, one of the soldiers kicked him. "Move!"

Rogan stopped and turned around. "That's enough!"

Both soldiers quickly raised their rifles.

"What's wrong with you men? Why are you doing this?"

"We were warned there might be a problem with you two."

"And they were right," his partner added.

"Look, we're going to get on the damn chopper, but first this man would like to say good-bye to his dog. That's all."

The officer shook his head. "You know what? Let's just shoot your dog and that'll be the end of it!" He aimed his rifle at Jack.

"No . . . *please,*" Fletcher cried out.

"Stand aside, Carson!"

Fletcher knelt down and shepherded Jack behind him. "You'll have to shoot me first."

"Spare me the dramatics. It's only a dog."

Detecting Fletcher's resolve, the soldiers fanned out to create an angle for a shot. As Rogan stepped forward to help Fletcher, the officer let off a round. The bullet skipped off the sand only inches away from his foot. "Stay where you are!"

"Stop this . . . *please,*" Fletcher urged.

"Make this easier on yourself, Carson."

"Have you lost your minds?" Rogan shouted.

Another bullet clipped the bottom of Fletcher's boot.

"You're going to kill him!"

"Then order your man to move away from the dog now!"

The situation had spiraled out of control. Fletcher knew he had to do something drastic. He grabbed a handful of sand and hurled it in the face of the officer. Instinctively, the man dropped his rifle and brought his hands up to his eyes. The incident distracted his partner, and he shifted his rifle away from Rogan for an instant.

It was all Rogan needed. He lunged forward and punched the soldier, sending him crashing to the ground. Rogan quickly disarmed him and ran across to Fletcher, who was wrestling with the officer. "Let him go right now or I *will* end your pathetic life," Rogan screamed.

The officer stopped resisting, and Fletcher pulled his rifle off him. He shoved the barrel under the man's chin. "Why shouldn't I kill you? Answer me!"

"Because I'll take down your lieutenant," a voice intruded from behind them.

It was the pilot. With the sound of the rotors disguising his movements, he had managed to track up behind them undetected. He was standing only five feet behind Rogan, with his sidearm aimed at his head. "Lower your weapons, both of you."

The scene had become surreal to Fletcher. "I just want you to let my dog go."

"I don't care what you want! Return the rifle to the officer and get onto the chopper."

"Will you let my dog live?"

The pilot let off a round only inches above Rogan's head. "Lower the rifle now or I'll blow your lieutenant's head off!"

Fletcher was out of options. Rogan had already sacrificed enough for him; he couldn't endanger his life any further. He took a deep breath and looked at Jack. "Ruush," he whispered, fighting back the tears. "Ruuush."

It was the command for Jack to run.

"Ruush, Jack—now. *Please.*"

Jack took two steps back then stopped.

Fletcher felt as if his heart were being torn out of his chest. "Run, Jack . . . run . . . please. . . . They're going to kill you," he cried.

Eventually, Jack turned and fled.

As Jack disappeared, Fletcher discarded the rifle. The officer quickly retrieved his weapon and swung it at Fletcher. Blood exploded from his forehead.

"Leave him alone, you bastard!"

"Shut up!" the other soldier screamed, reclaiming his own weapon.

The pilot turned away and headed back to the helicopter. "Get them on board and put restraints on them. Think you two clowns can handle that?"

The officer pulled Fletcher to his feet. "In the chopper—now!"

As they moved, Rogan turned to Fletcher. "Are you all right?"

Blood was streaming down Fletcher's face, soaking the front of his shirt. "This wasn't supposed to happen. This wasn't the plan. . . ."

"What plan? What're you talking about?"

Something in Fletcher's mind had finally let go. Rogan could see it in his eyes. They were pushed on board and forced to lie down on their stomachs with their arms held behind them. While the officers searched for handcuffs, the pilot fired up the chopper.

As they lay together facing each other, Rogan continued. "What did you mean this wasn't part of the plan?"

Fletcher didn't reply immediately, but as the helicopter lifted off, he whispered something: "You said you would help me," he uttered. "Please . . . I can't leave him behind."

Suddenly Rogan understood what he wanted. "But you'll die."

Fletcher shook his head. "I'll die anyway."

Reluctantly Rogan nodded. He held Fletcher's gaze for a moment before turning over and, in one fluid movement, tackling the two soldiers.

Fletcher pulled himself to the edge of the cabin. The chopper was rising steeply. Out of the corner of his eye, he saw movement.

It was Jack. He was running after the helicopter.

Just as Fletcher had stepped off a ledge to end his life months before, he again plunged into another abyss. Except this time he was falling to save himself. As he plummeted to the ground, he felt himself turning over. He landed on his back. A jolt of pain drove through his spine. He struggled onto his haunches just as Jack reached him. The Labrador launched himself into his arms.

He held him close, and Jack licked the side of his face. "I was never going to leave you. I never planned to get on that chopper."

The helicopter hovered above them, and Fletcher watched as the two soldiers battled to subdue Rogan. Before they overpowered him, he managed to get hold of a gun and push it out of the cabin.

Then, just as Fletcher had suspected, instead of landing, the helicopter continued to rise. For them, the war was over. As he watched the helicopter disappear, Rogan stretched his arm out of the cabin. He pressed his thumb into the palm of his hand and extended two fingers. It was one of the many dog commands they had taught Jack.

It meant, Find home.

~ NINE

FLETCHER just sat holding Jack until he could no longer hear the helicopter. "Thank God," he kept saying. "Thank God."

As his breathing eased and he checked himself to make sure nothing was broken, he thought of what Rogan had sacrificed for him. Rogan would almost certainly face a court marshal, perhaps even jail time. A sudden swell of gratitude rose up within him. Despite their problems initially, in the end, Rogan had stood by him.

Jack shifted in Fletcher's arms and nuzzled his hand. He was just happy that they were together again.

"It's just us now, Jack. All alone in hell."

He lifted to his feet and scanned the deserted base. It was an eerie scene. Half a dozen tents remained, as well as two supply rooms and an empty munitions depot, but without the constant throng of soldiers, it felt like a foreign landscape.

"Surplus military equipment," Fletcher whispered cynically.

Nursing his lower back, he slowly made his way toward the closest tent. He walked inside and headed to the far corner, where he knelt down and dug through the soft sand. A moment later he pulled out a map and compass wrapped in a plastic bag.

"I told you I never meant to get on that chopper."

Jack tilted his head as if unsure of what was happening.

Fletcher had never intended to abandon Jack, although the arrival of the two MPs almost derailed his plan. Unfolding the map, he used his finger to trace a line from their base westward, out of Vietnam, across Laos and into Thailand—a country friendly to the United States. The route constituted some three hundred and fifty miles of hostile territory.

He looked down at Jack. "I know we can do this."

They were going to hike their way out.

THE Strip had been one of the last U.S. bases to pull out of central Vietnam. There wasn't another American for a hundred and fifty miles. Not that it mattered. Fletcher had no intentions of traveling south. Their journey lay west to Thailand. There he would find a way to get them home. A three-hundred-and-fifty-mile walk on an open road would take upward of ten days. Their journey was likely to take a month.

With Jack following closely behind, Fletcher began to gather the supplies he had stowed away. He had four canteens, two boxes of matches, two loaves of bread, sixteen soup powders, and a pile of exactly one hundred and fifty-seven dog biscuits. The canteens were important because although there were likely to be numerous water sources along their route, not all would be safe to drink.

The biscuits would become their staple diet, by far their most nutritious food source. They could survive on a handful of them a day. If things got desperate, he could always hunt for food using the gun Rogan had thrown out of the chopper, but at the risk of bringing unwanted attention to themselves, it would be only as a last resort.

Picking up an old, worn knapsack, Fletcher loaded up their supplies. He wondered what their chances were. They would have to negotiate traps and pass undetected for weeks. His navigating would also have to be extremely accurate. Laos was still hostile territory. He would also have to traverse Charlie's infamous supply route to the South—the Ho Chi Minh Trail.

As he packed the knapsack, he felt a small bulge near the bottom. He reached down and withdrew the object. It was a small first-aid kit, with scissors, bandages, a needle, and three vials of penicillin.

"Let's hope we don't need this."

That night, Fletcher battled to fall asleep. The Strip, which had been their sanctuary for so long, was now a dangerous place to be. Charlie would be coming soon, sweeping through the deserted camps like scavengers picking at the wet bones of a rotting corpse.

Just not tonight, Fletcher hoped.

"WHO'S there?" Fletcher mumbled, startled. He had no idea what had woken him, but something felt wrong. The flap of the tent swayed gently in the breeze. A shadow appeared on the canvas wall beside him. He snatched at his gun. The figure was stooped over, but the pose seemed exaggerated.

"Jack," he said as the Labrador poked his head inside the tent. "Where've you been?"

Jack wagged his tail and flopped down.

"Don't get too comfortable," he warned, noticing the darkness beginning to lift on the horizon. "It's almost time for us to go."

As the sky lightened, Fletcher's anxiety grew. The farthest he had ever hiked was seventy miles over six days. Their journey was five times that long. He scanned the abandoned base and was unnerved at how quiet it was. No jeeps. No Hueys. No voices.

Just them, alone in the enemy's garden. Forsaken.

THE first four days were mercifully uneventful. With the war over, there were few active patrols left in the area. They had encountered Charlie only once, and even then, he appeared more concerned about being snared in one of his own traps than anything else—a concern Fletcher shared. Twice Jack had sniffed out trip wires he had missed. On both occasions, it had been late in the day. Fletcher found that his concentration began to waver after about nine hours. Jack, however, seemed never to tire.

They had been walking most of the afternoon when Fletcher noticed an old wooden sign ahead of them. Part of its message had been weathered away, but the core had survived: LAOS.

Sometime during the day, they had crossed over the border. By his calculations, they had already covered more than sixty miles. He was overjoyed at how quickly they had progressed, but during the last few hours, Jack had developed a slight limp. After checking Jack's paw to ensure he hadn't picked up a thorn, Fletcher decided the injury must relate back to the shooting and worried what condition the Labrador would be in a week from now.

Stopping for a moment, Fletcher lay Jack down and stretched out his back legs. He pressed his hand down gently on the scar above his hip, and Jack yipped in pain.

"All right, Jack, all right. We'll slow down."

Checking the area, he found a well-covered spot near the base of a tree where they could spend the night. As always, he climbed the tree to get a better look at their surroundings. Satisfied, he opened the knapsack and took out their food for the evening. Three dog biscuits each and a packet of soup to share. The soup would've tasted a good deal more appetizing had they been able to heat it, but they couldn't afford the attention a fire would bring.

"I'll never take any food for granted again. Get some sleep, Jack; we've got a long way to go. We're barely down the driveway."

BY DAY seven, Jack's limp had deteriorated from a slight hobble to the point where his back right paw only touched the ground every third or fourth stride. As concerning as it was, it didn't slow him much—not yet, at least.

Over the past two days, however, Fletcher's legs had started to cramp. His calves locked up every few hours. Each attack would force them to stop so that he could massage out the spasm. The whole process delayed them for around ten minutes at a time. A worrying sign was that the intervals between the cramps were getting smaller, their grip lasting longer.

On the positive side, they had managed to safely cross the Ho Chi Minh Trail. Fletcher wished the trail led to Thailand. That way, they might've been able to stow away on the back of a truck. But bisecting the path meant that they had covered a hundred miles. It was an important milestone. But still two thirds of their journey lay ahead of them.

Nightfall brought with it welcome rain. Fletcher positioned their canteens under some leaves, and the water funneled down until they were full. Making the most of the situation, they both drank until their stomachs were bloated. The water was delicious.

Using a thin ground sheet to shelter them from the downpour, Fletcher watched as the water pooled at their feet. He had been truly grateful for the shower, but now his thoughts turned to where they would hole up for the night. The prospect of sleeping in the mud was becoming more and more likely by the minute.

Whether it was the driving rain or just a lapse in concentration, Fletcher didn't see the animal until it was right on top of them.

He stared straight into its eyes, less than ten feet away, but still couldn't believe what he was seeing.

The animal was stalking them. Hunting them.

It seemed impossible. Was he hallucinating? he wondered.

The predator's striking orange stripes lit up the gloom.

Fletcher slowly withdrew his sidearm, mindful of making any sudden movements. The tiger crouched down, the muscles in his shoulders writhing like snakes coiling under a silk sheet. His variegated coat appeared almost fluorescent in the pouring rain. The last thing Fletcher wanted to do was shoot him. Tigers were not known to hunt humans, but this one was clearly hungry. Jack let out a low, threatening growl. Fletcher quickly grabbed his collar.

The tiger, almost as big as a small car, took a half step forward. He was now within striking range.

Fletcher cocked his gun. "Find something else, friend," he said in a deep, steady voice.

The animal took a step back. Fletcher waved the pistol in a slow circle. "That's it. . . . Move away." The tiger slowly backtracked through the trees. Then, just as suddenly as he had appeared, he vanished.

"Did I imagine that?" Fletcher asked, easing his grip on Jack's collar. The Lab's hackles were raised like angry licks of flame.

"I think he's gone. I hope so."

But for how long? he wondered. Would he return later while they slept? They would have to find somewhere safe to rest. This meant a tree. But most of the trees in the area were too thin. Soon it would be too dark to continue their search and they would be forced to spend the night awake.

"Come on, give us a break," Fletcher pleaded, scanning the trees.

Dejected, he took a deep breath, and as he did, something flickered in his vision. Was it metal? Glass?

At first, he thought his eyes were deceiving him, but as he moved closer, his doubts evaporated. A small truck, stripped of its wheels and engine, was wedged between two trees.

"How the hell did this get here?" He laughed. He stepped up to the driver's door and was about to open it when he realized it might be booby-trapped. After satisfying himself that it wasn't wired to anything, he carefully clicked it open.

He felt like crying. The windows were intact, and the front seat bench was big enough for both of them. "It's like the Ritz!" he cheered. "C'mon, Jack. Get in."

Once inside, Fletcher stripped off his wet clothes and used a small towel to dry Jack's coat. Within minutes, all the windows had misted up. The harder it rained, the less likely it was that they would be found. They were dry and warm and safe.

DAY fifteen. Fletcher removed his socks and wrung out the sweat that was now tinged red with blood. The coppery stench made him feel nauseous. He looked down in dismay at his feet. They were covered in thin cuts and blisters. He had lost two toenails, and his right heel was cracked.

Jack wasn't faring any better. His back right leg was now a useless appendage. He was reduced to dragging it behind him, no longer able to hold it up. The hair on top of his paw had been worn away and replaced by a thin, wet scab.

Infection had already set in; Fletcher could smell it. He decided to administer two vials of their precious penicillin to Jack. After he was done, he strapped up the paw with a torn section of his shirt. "There, Jack. That should help."

They were both in some pain, but of more immediate concern was their food reserves, which had dwindled faster than Fletcher had calculated. They were down to just three soups and fifty-seven biscuits.

Not nearly enough, given the energy they were expending.

Fletcher forced his shoes back on and winced as he tightened the laces. Standing up was always the worst. The pain brought on a wave of nausea that he had to contain at all costs. If he vomited, he would lose the little food he had just eaten.

Jack waited until Fletcher started moving again before trotting up to point, searching and sniffing for danger.

The more they walked, the better Fletcher felt. Each step was closer to Thailand—closer to home.

The pain seemed to numb after an hour, until all that was left was a sense of heaviness at the bottom of his legs. That, and the sensation of sweat and blood squelching between his toes.

By nightfall, Fletcher calculated they would have covered over two hundred and fifty miles.

Only a hundred miles to go. He was starting to believe.

～ TEN

DAY twenty brought another impossibly dark night in Laos. Fletcher had become used to functioning without light and was no longer perturbed by the insects that occasionally wandered over his body. For the most part, they were harmless. Even snakes barely factored on his list of things that were likely to harm them.

What was of growing concern, however, was a painful and disturbing throbbing that had gnawed its way into the lower half of his legs. His feet had become so swollen that to take off his shoes, he had to remove his shoelaces.

Jack was in worse shape.

Using the canvas sheet to conceal the light, Fletcher shined his flashlight onto Jack's bandaged paw. He needed to change the dressing. As he unfurled the dirty rag, the smell that emerged made his eyes water. The wound was covered in a thick, murky layer of pus and blood. The skin around the area was tight and swollen. Fletcher unscrewed the lid from one of the canteens and poured water over the wound. As he gently prodded the area, he could feel there was a buildup of fluid under the skin. He unpacked his knife and a box of matches and began to burn the tip of the blade. After a few seconds he tightened his grip around the top of Jack's leg.

"This will hurt, but I promise you'll feel better afterward."

He pushed the knife into the middle of his paw, and a thick wave of pus splashed up onto the blade.

Jack whined and tried to withdraw his leg.

"I know it hurts boy, but we have to do this."

IN THE MORNING, FLETCHER was relieved to see that the swelling in Jack's paw had come down. Fletcher mixed a bowl of soup and gave it all to Jack. He needed the energy to fight off the infection.

"C'mon, Jack. Another week we'll be in Thailand. From there—*somehow*—I'll find us a way home."

Jack rose slowly and wagged his tail. He stepped forward and managed to touch the ground with his injured paw. He quickly lifted it up, but it was a sign of improvement.

As the day went on, Fletcher felt increasingly detached from their situation. His head felt light and dizzy. He had also begun to lose sensation in his legs. But that wasn't the worst of it.

Paranoia, like a silent cancer, was starting to creep under his skin. Suddenly Charlie was everywhere—hiding in the grass, waiting behind bushes, stalking him from behind. Twice he almost shot at trees that he was convinced soldiers were hiding behind.

The lines between reality and delirium were starting to blur. And then the dead started showing up.

He saw the two officers he had assassinated in the tunnel complex sitting in a tree, fresh blood seeping from their wounds. Then the first man he had killed in Vietnam—a young, barefoot soldier—appeared through the jungle ahead of him.

He couldn't take it anymore. He stopped walking and dropped to his knees. His tongue was thick and swollen. He was barely able to swallow. He opened one of the canteens and took a sip. He poured the remaining contents into Jack's bowl. As he listened to him drink, he lay down.

"I have to rest, Jack," he whispered. "I'm just so . . . tired."

He was exhausted. He just needed to stop for a while.

To close his eyes. Just for a minute.

A KICK.

Fletcher tried to open his eyes, but the late-afternoon sun was blinding. There were several dark figures crowded around him.

Was he still hallucinating?

He tried to talk, but one of the figures rammed something into his face. This was no dream; the pain was excruciating. As he struggled to his feet, voices shouted at him.

Another strike to his head. Then one against his back.

The onslaught took his breath away. He tried to raise his arms to defend himself, but the back of his hand was violently swatted down by the butt of a rifle. He felt, and then heard, the bones crack.

As his vision narrowed, he heard Jack attack one of the men. From the sound of the man's cries, he was being torn to pieces.

"Please leave my dog. *Please* . . ." Fletcher shouted, collapsing to the ground. "Jack . . . ruush . . . ruush. . . . Get out of here!"

Fletcher felt his world begin to recede. But just before its blackness was drawn over him, he was afforded one final sight. It would break him in every way that a man could be broken.

A soldier smashed the butt of his rifle into Jack's face, spun it around, and as an early twilight carried Fletcher away, two shots were fired.

THREE days later Fletcher woke up with a start.

"Easy, mate," a voice issued from behind him. "You're pretty banged up. Been out for a few days."

He was lying on a hard mud floor. His head was wrapped in a strip of green material, and he was sweating profusely.

"You're bloody lucky to be alive."

"Where am I?" he managed.

"The end of the line, I suppose."

Fletcher absorbed his surroundings. The prison was no bigger than six or seven square yards and made entirely from thick bamboo struts bound together by wire. Through the space between the bars, he could see five or six bungalows in the distance. There was a lookout tower some eighty yards away, on top of which two guards were sharing a cigarette.

"What's your name, friend?" The voice belonged to a tall bearded man with a mane of curly blond hair. His accent was unmistakably Australian.

"Fletcher," he replied. "Where are we?"

"We're in a prison camp."

"Still in Laos?"

"Yeah."

"How far from—"

"Thailand? About fifty-five miles west, I reckon," he said, then laughed. "But we may as well be on another planet."

Fletcher thought of Jack. He recalled seeing the Labrador hit in the face and hearing two shots. The image scalded him like a branding iron. Had Jack been killed?

"Tell me," Fletcher said, clearing his throat. "When they brought me in, did you see if they were carrying a dog?"

"A dog? What . . . yours?"

"Yes."

"Why would they bring your dog back with you?"

Fletcher's reply was barely more than a whisper. "For food. Please, do you remember seeing anything?"

The man frowned. "I saw them bring you in, and I'm pretty sure they weren't carrying a dog."

A vague hope lifted Fletcher. If Jack had been killed, the soldiers probably would've brought his body back to camp.

"Look, I know it's none of my business," the Australian continued, "but the war ended weeks ago. You only just arrived. Where have you been?"

Fletcher looked down and noticed that his legs were tied to one of the thick bamboo struts. "We were on our way home."

IN THE days following his capture, Fletcher forged a comfortable bond with the Australian, Matthew Summers. They debated different ways of escaping but did not come up with a plausible solution. Fletcher learned that there had been another soldier in the cage, but shortly before his arrival, the man had been dragged down to the river and shot in the head.

Fletcher spent much of his time replaying the moment of his capture over in his mind. Was it possible that Jack was still alive? Had he maybe been shot but escaped? Was he lying in the jungle somewhere, slowly bleeding to death? As these dark thoughts continued to plague him, a soldier in his early twenties approached their cage carrying two tin cups. The young man had been surprisingly kind to them. He had given them extra food and warm soup.

The soldier carefully pushed the cups inside the cage and backed away. "Drink tea. Get better. You see. *You see!*" It was the same four sentences from the day before. "War over. Soon you go home!"

"No," Matthew replied, pressing his finger against his temple. "Soon we go dead."

The young soldier shook his head. "No . . . war finish. . . . No more dead! Home soon for everyone!"

"Thanks, mate, but they're going to kill us. Trust me."

The soldier knelt down and tried to get Fletcher's attention. "You feel better? Is tea help?"

Fletcher nodded. "Tea help. Thank you."

A smile dawned on the man's face. He was overjoyed to finally draw out a reaction from Fletcher.

"More food?"

The soldier's keenness to help was a mystery.

"More food is good," Matthew replied eagerly.

The soldier quickly stood up and ran off. Within minutes, he returned with a large wooden bowl brimming with rice.

It was more food than Fletcher had seen in days.

As Matthew accepted the bowl and began scooping handfuls into his mouth, Fletcher reached out through the bars and gently grabbed the young man's arm. "What's your name?"

The man regarded Fletcher warily. "My name Lee. Lee Tao."

"I'm Fletcher, and this is Matthew. Why are you helping us?"

The soldier leaned in closer to the cage. "You not remember?"

"Remember what?"

"Small village near Suang. You save us!"

For a moment, Fletcher had no idea what he was talking about, but then a memory—flimsy and distant—darted across his mind. During one of their assignments, they had come across a small village that Charlie was tormenting. The Vietcong forcibly recruited able-bodied young men into their army. Those that refused were killed and their wives and children beaten and raped. As it happened, the Fat Lady waited for a particular band of soldiers who were due back to recruit more men. As Charlie marched into the village, intent on more bloodletting, the Fat Lady was ready. The firefight lasted less than a minute. It was the only time Fletcher had ever extracted any joy in taking other men's lives.

"More men returned and made you join them, didn't they?"

"They very angry. My wife, they were going kill her."

"I'm sorry. How long have you been here?"

"Five months," Lee replied. "Please . . . Is my wife still alive?"

"I don't know. I'm sorry."

Lee's expression darkened. "Eat, Mr. Fletcher. I see you tomorrow." With that, he stood up and ran toward the bungalows.

THE next morning, Fletcher woke up with a fever and a debilitating headache that bordered on a migraine. He had a nasty dose of flu. Rubbing his eyes, he tried to swallow and discovered that he could add a raging throat infection to his list of ailments.

"You've been out since early last night," said Matthew. "I was beginning to think you'd never wake up."

"I've been conserving my energy. I was thinking of crawling to your side of the cage today."

Matthew smiled. "And why would you want to do that?"

"Change of scenery. Maybe I'll have better luck on your side."

"I thought you said you were a writer, not a comedian."

Fletcher managed a smirk. "Any idea what time it is?"

"Must be around eight. I wonder what's keeping our friend this morning. He's late."

"He might be in trouble for yesterday."

Matthew carved his initials in the sand with a small stick, then the Australian flag. "I hope you're wrong."

"Yeah, me, too."

"It's a good thing you helped out his village. These things all happen for a reason, you know."

"Lucky coincidence, that's all."

"You think so? I think it's karma. You defended him and his wife, and now you're being repaid."

In the distance, a group of soldiers headed toward them. Their rifles gleamed. Matthew strained his eyes. "This doesn't look good."

They were all highly animated. As they came closer, yelling and gesturing with their hands, the man in front raised his rifle and pointed it at Matthew.

"Wait. Wait! You can't d-do this," Matthew began, backing into the corner. "Your government has signed a treaty. This is not—"

But his words were cut short by a single bullet that tore through his face and blew a hole out the back of his head. A thick, wet blood cloud filled the cage.

Fletcher closed his eyes and waited for his bullet. His final thoughts were no different to the ones that kept him from his sleep.

His girls and Jack.

THE shot never came. In its place was callous laughter.

By the time Fletcher wiped the blood from his face, the soldiers had already opened the cage and were removing Matthew's body. One of the men made a comment, and the others laughed. Fletcher felt like lunging at them and clawing out their throats but had little strength to draw on.

The shooter tapped the barrel of his rifle and blew a kiss at Fletcher. Then, one by one, the soldiers filed away, dragging Matthew's bloodied body behind them.

Although they had only known each other a short while, Fletcher had grown fond of Matthew. He was a kind and warm man with a son back home in Perth.

That yet another father was forever lost to his child was profoundly sad. What greater tragedy in life is there than not watching your child grow up? Fletcher wondered. The answer, he knew only too well, was none.

As the morning progressed, Matthew Summers quickly assumed his position in Fletcher's psyche as the latest inhabitant to pry at his sanity. It was becoming a crowded space. Fletcher stared out through the bars and noticed Lee Tao approaching him. He was carrying something in his arms, but it was hidden under a dark green cloth. Fletcher was relieved the young man was still alive.

As Lee approached the cage, he bowed his head as a mark of respect at Matthew's death. "I sorry about your friend, Mr. Fletcher," he offered in a whisper. "You no hurt?"

"I'm all right."

"I bring soup and special food."

He removed the cloth and presented a bowl of rice and soup.

"Lee, they'll kill you if they find out what you're doing."

"I don't care. I hate this life. I rather . . . be dead." His optimism from the previous day had all but evaporated.

"Listen to me," Fletcher said, shifting closer toward him. "The war is over. You could return to your village now. They wouldn't come after you. You can find your wife and start over."

"No more village left. My wife gone. I saw in your eyes."

"You saw *nothing* in my eyes. I really don't know about the village. It could still be there. Your wife might still be alive."

Lee ignored him. "Must eat, Fletcher, please."

"Why are you doing this? They're going to kill me anyway!"

Lee shook his head. "No. I help you. To . . . go away."

Fletcher marveled at how this relative stranger was willing to risk so much for him. "No escape, Lee. This is the end."

"No. You still have far to live."

"It's all right, Lee. I should've died a long time ago."

"No, you must live."

"Why? What makes you say that?"

"I was part of patrol when we find you sleeping. I watched. You must escape. He need you. He hurt badly but is still alive."

Fletcher felt his face go numb.

"Yellow dog. I saw him last night at river."

Fletcher couldn't believe it. Was Jack really still alive? "Are you sure, Lee? How do you know it was my dog?"

"Yellow," Lee replied. "It's your dog."

"But he was shot!"

"No. Soldier tried to shoot but missed. Your dog run away. His legs hurt, but he still able to walk. He walks for you, Mr. Fletcher."

Suddenly a voice called out from the distance, and Lee leaped to his feet. A brief but intense look washed over his face. "I wish I live in your country. In America, you are free."

Fletcher didn't know how to respond.

"No hope here, just death," Lee continued. "Please . . . must eat. Food save you."

And then he was gone, running toward the voice that had summoned him, every inch a prisoner himself.

Fletcher's hands were trembling. His skin tingled with energy. Jack was alive. It was a miracle.

When he had calmed down sufficiently, he looked down at the food. He grabbed handfuls of rice and forced it into his mouth. He was nearing the bottom of the bowl when he felt something cold and hard. He quickly fished out the foreign object.

He stared at it disbelievingly and then slowly heard himself laugh. Was he losing his mind? Was it all a dream?

Food save you. . . .

It was a long, thin strip of metal. He was holding a blade.

~ ELEVEN

THAT night, Fletcher used the blade to saw through a dozen of the bamboo bars. He was tempted to try and escape right there and then but felt it was too risky. It would soon be daylight. He would wait until the following evening to break out.

He was massaging his hand to relieve a cramp, when he heard movement at the back of the cage. It was Lee, his face etched with concern. "You must go now, Mr. Fletcher!" he whispered.

Fletcher scrambled toward him. "Lee, what's going on?"

"They going to shoot you! I heard. Did you use knife?"

Fletcher nodded.

"Hurry . . . *Hurry.*"

"All right, Lee. But first answer one question. Do you want to leave this place? Do you really want a life in America?"

Lee's eyes widened, and a glimmer of hope flickered across his face. "Must . . . hurry."

Fletcher had his answer. "I'll come back for you, Lee. I'll take you to America. You have my word. Stay alive, and I'll find you."

Lee pulled a sack from under his shirt. "Food. Now go!"

Fletcher crawled across to the far side of the cage where he had sawed through the bamboo struts, and he kicked them out. He squeezed through the gap and replaced the bars behind him. If he was lucky, they wouldn't come for him for another hour or so.

As he turned around, Lee was standing in front of him. Instinctively, Fletcher embraced the young man.

"Your dog is under trees over there," Lee said, pointing to an area across the river. "He waiting for you."

Fletcher turned, ran a few steps, then stopped. "I'll come for you, Lee. I swear it."

Running hard, Fletcher hunched over as he approached the trees. "Jack . . . Jack . . . Jack," he whispered loudly. There was no sign of him. Fletcher scrambled from tree to tree. *"Jack!"*

Had he died during the night? A feeling of dread gnawed at him. He called out again, louder this time.

A faint whimpering issued from somewhere behind him.

He spun around. "Jack! Where are you?" he pleaded.

The Labrador emerged from between two trees. His back legs were buckled uselessly under his body, and he was using his front legs to drag himself into a patch of moonlight.

Fletcher dropped down next to him and scooped him up in his arms. He buried his face into the fur around his neck, partly to muffle his own crying and partly because he needed to feel Jack, to make sure he was real. "I thought I'd lost you!"

After holding him for a few moments, he pulled out of the embrace. Beyond Jack's pain, he could see the happiness in his eyes. "You tracked me, boy. I'm so proud of you! Well done."

Jack lifted his head and licked the side of Fletcher's neck.

"What's wrong with your legs?" he asked.

Jack's back paw, still bandaged, had swollen up like a baseball, but his other hind leg looked all right. Why wasn't he able to walk? Fletcher wondered. As his eyes followed the curve of Jack's legs, he realized what the problem was. His right hip had dislocated. Fletcher had no choice. He took hold of Jack's leg and gritted his teeth. "This is going to hurt, Jack, but it'll be over in a moment."

He made sure of his grip before twisting the leg and forcing it into the joint. Jack bucked at the sudden explosion of pain and then collapsed onto his side.

"Sorry, boy! It's over. I think it's back in. Just rest for a minute," he said, gently stroking Jack's head.

As he allowed Jack some time to recover, he weighed their options. The night sky was beginning to peel away from the horizon. They had the little bit of food Lee had given them but still had fifty miles to reach Thailand. They had no map, no medicine, and would soon be hunted by their captors. That, and Jack couldn't walk.

Fletcher knew they would have to run. He stood up and lifted Jack in his arms. Taking a breath, he looked at the sky. "You've taken everything from me. Just help me this once—please."

BY THE time the sun had risen above the mountains, Fletcher had made six or even seven miles. Jack had felt light initially but now weighed heavily in his arms. The worst headache of his life wasn't making matters any easier. On a positive note, his feet had healed over the past few days. All that remained was a distant ache as his boots fought for purchase on the slippery ground. His immediate concern was water. He was desperately thirsty. The sky overhead was clear, and they had not yet encountered a single water source.

By running, he knew he was taking a risk of crossing a wire or falling into a trap, but prudence was not an option anymore. He had to put as much distance between himself and his captors as possible. To further compound matters, the infection in Jack's paw had clearly spread to the rest of his body. He needed medical help if he was to survive.

Fletcher had to stop to rest. His back was aching, and his throat was burning. He still felt feverish. He lay Jack down and took a moment to catch his breath. He untied the knot of the food sack Lee had packed.

Inside were two loaves of bread, a jar of rice, and a canister of water. Unscrewing the lid off the canister, he carefully funneled the water into Jack's mouth. "That's it, Jack. Drink."

Then Fletcher took two long sips of his own and replaced the lid. He wished they could have more, but he knew they could afford only to drink enough to stay alive. It was all about survival now.

FLETCHER put one foot ahead of the other and tried to remain upright. His arms had become ungainly leaden weights, and his back ached as if his spine were a column of burning lava. He kept peering over his shoulder expecting to see soldiers behind him, but each time, there was nothing in his wake.

As the sun dipped over the trees ahead of him, he began to search for a place to spend the night. He needed time to rest.

He noticed a slight vale under some heavy foliage some fifty yards to his left. It looked perfect.

He carefully stepped down, parting the branches ahead of him. The hollow was just wide enough for both of them. He lowered Jack down gently onto his side and stretched out his arms.

Looking down at Jack, he could see he was hurting from all the jarring. Fresh blood seeped through the bandage on his paw. Fletcher sat down, took out the sack, and fished out one of the loaves of bread. He broke off a piece for Jack and gave him some water. Fletcher took a few sips himself and then quickly ate half the loaf. He was relying on the carbohydrates to give him the energy he needed for tomorrow—for one final push. He tried to get Jack to eat more, but he was not interested.

As the jungle's nightlife began to stir, Jack fell into a deep sleep. As if joined by an invisible tether, Fletcher followed after him.

AN INTENSE cramp in his shoulder plucked Fletcher from his sleep. At first, he thought something was trying to grab him and he instinctively swung out. Then he realized what was happening. He reached for the inflamed joint and massaged away the cramp.

Jack slept through the entire incident. Normally the slightest sound would wake him. *Something was wrong.* Fletcher pressed his hand against Jack's chest and felt for a heartbeat.

"Jack. Wake up, boy." *Nothing.* "Jack. . . . *Hey.*" He grabbed the skin around the Labrador's neck and pulled. Jack swallowed heavily, but his eyes remained closed. "Jack! Stay with me. Do you hear me?"

Fletcher quickly sat him up and tried to feed him. He got down two pieces of bread and a sip of water. When he was done, he rested the Labrador's head on his thigh. He put one hand on his chest and the other two inches in front of his nose.

Jack's condition was deteriorating by the minute. For the rest of the night, by sheer will alone, Fletcher was going to make sure Jack kept breathing. "Don't give up, Jack. Our journey's almost over."

THE morning took forever to arrive. When it finally did, Fletcher carefully lifted Jack up and climbed out of the hole. Jack had slept peacefully enough, but his condition was dire. In the hours before sunrise, he had picked up a worrying tremor and his breathing had become labored.

All that mattered now was moving quickly. Fletcher estimated they had twenty miles to the Thailand border. From there, however, there was no telling how much farther they would have to hike to find help.

Despite protests from his arms and shoulders, Fletcher began a slow jog. As he trundled forward, he realized his mind no longer seemed capable of complex thought. Time, distance, food, water, and Jack's condition were the only items of priority.

There was, however, one exception.

Like a continuous movie reel, images of his wife and daughter played in the background. Favorite memories would be broadcast over and over again. The day he met Abigail, the red dress she was wearing. Their wedding day. Kelly's birth. Her first day at school. As the memories drifted inexorably toward the crash, Fletcher tried to suppress them. But in the end, he was always left with the shell of a burning plane and the tortured screams of its victims.

By midday, Fletcher was carrying Jack over his shoulder. His arms could no longer take the weight. For Jack, it meant a more painful ride. Each jarring stride was transferred through Fletcher's shoulder and into the Labrador's rib cage. Thin rivulets of blood from Jack's wound ran down Fletcher's chest.

He kept searching for signs that they were no longer in Laos. Several times he stopped, believing he could hear activity from a nearby village, but each time, he was mistaken. Once he thought he had heard a child's voice, but it was only a bird.

His mind was starting to play tricks on him.

THEY had been heading west all day, and still there was no sign that they were in Thailand. Fletcher felt as though the jungle had become a giant treadmill and they had been marching around in circles. He half expected to turn a corner only to discover the Strip ahead of them. Had he finally become insane? Were they even heading west? Was he still locked up in his bamboo keep?

He had large welts and blisters on his shoulders and arms from carrying Jack. His left knee had locked up, and his right ankle had swelled to double its size. The infection in his throat had become so severe that he was beginning to taste blood.

But this was all background noise. Jack was dying.

What little life he had left was fading. In Fletcher's mind, Jack's remaining hours had become like sand slipping through his fingers. Soon it would be gone.

Fletcher was becoming frantic. Like a drunk trying to convince himself of his sobriety, he was trying to deny his growing sense of disorientation. He had blacked out twice, and his sense of paranoia was growing. He became convinced that a helicopter was doing sweeps over the area. It would swoop down low and hover above him. It *had* to be looking for them. Each time he heard the swish of its blades, he would scramble for cover, but the chopper seemed determined to hunt him down.

Was it real? As the thought infected his mind, he suddenly stopped walking. Through the trees, a bright orange glow reflected on the leaves. He rubbed his eyes, then slowly moved toward the light. Carefully he parted the branches ahead of him.

What he saw was madness. *His own.* His wife and daughter were walking through the jungle ahead of him.

Their bodies were engulfed in flames.

"Abby . . . Kelly!" Fletcher cried out in an almost primordial wail. Their clothes, their skin, their hair—everything was ablaze. He could smell their burning flesh. He screamed out their names, but his throat was so parched he could not get their attention. The harder he chased after them, the farther they moved away. "Abigail! Kelly! *Stop,* it's me!"

But they kept gliding away from him. They headed down a steep slope, thick with trees and bushes, but somehow it didn't impede them at all. Fletcher, clutching on to Jack, plunged down the embankment after them. Branches clawed at his face. He was running as fast as he could but still couldn't catch them. They reached the bottom of the slope, then quickly ascended another hill.

"Why are you running away? Please . . . stop!" he pleaded.

They suddenly drew to a halt. Abigail was holding Kelly's hand, but still their backs were turned to him. Fletcher scrambled up behind them. "Yes! Yes . . . Abby! Kelly!" He got within ten feet of them, close enough to feel the heat from the scalding flames, when they suddenly vanished.

"No!" he screamed, collapsing on the spot where they had stood. The earth was cool under his hands. He stared down at Jack. The Labrador blinked wearily, then closed his eyes.

"I'm sorry. We're lost, and I'm falling apart. There's no . . ."

But his words trailed off as something ahead of him caught his attention. In the distance was a cluster of huts. Next to them were three old buildings. On the roof of one building was a flagpole.

The colors of Thailand flapped gently in the warm breeze.

Fletcher stared at the scene. Twice he turned away, praying that when he looked again, the village would still be there.

It was.

This wasn't in his imagination. The Thai flag beckoned.

Summoning the last of his reserves, he cradled Jack in his arms and started to run. Tears were streaming down his face. He began to scream. His throat was burning with each word. Covering Jack's face with his free arm, he charged headfirst into the branches of a row of trees that separated them from salvation.

The Thai people heard his strained screams and stopped what they were doing. It was a typical village scene. There were people manning food stalls, carrying baskets, riding bicycles. Children were playing. As one, they waited and listened.

Suddenly Fletcher burst into view. He took a few steps, then slumped onto his knees. What strength remained in his arms drained away, and Jack rolled gently onto the ground. The villagers watched as Fletcher shouted, "Please help me. My dog is dying!"

The villagers, stunned, remained unmoved. All except one.

A young girl let go of her mother's hand and ran toward him. Lying on his side now, through half-closed eyes, Fletcher watched as she approached. She was beautiful. Her long black hair framed big brown eyes. Her smile warmed his heart. She knelt down beside him and placed her hand on Jack. Fletcher tried to speak to her but could feel himself slipping away. His body was shutting down.

The sound of a man's angry screams punctuated the air. Fletcher saw two Vietcong soldiers pushing through the crowd. As they reached him, they raised their rifles and shouted for the child to move. The mother scooped her up and disappeared into the crowd.

The soldier closest to Fletcher pressed the butt of his AK-47 into his shoulder and widened his stance.

Fletcher tried to lift himself up but couldn't. He felt paralyzed, empty. He had nothing left.

But Jack did. He lifted up on his front legs and dragged himself toward the soldiers.

"No!" Fletcher whispered. He stretched out his arm to try and stop him, but Jack was already beyond his reach.

The soldier curled his finger around the trigger and took aim.

Jack snarled and tried to lunge at the man but fell short, collapsing onto his chest.

Tears burned Fletcher's eyes. *"Jack!"* he screamed. *"Jaaack!"*

A helicopter, flying fast and low, suddenly roared over the treetops. The two soldiers immediately swung their rifles up at the chopper as it churned up a tumultuous cloud of dust and grass. As the Huey hovered above them, its blades cutting up the late-afternoon sun, a loud voice issued from the chopper's broadcast system.

Fletcher recognized the message. It was in Vietnamese. It meant "Put down your weapons or die." He knew what it meant, because they had often used the phrase during their missions. He felt himself laugh and then begin to sob like a small child.

How it could be? Was it possible? The voice belonged to a man from another world, another time. It was unmistakable.

It was Rogan.

TWELVE

By THE time Fletcher regained consciousness, three days had passed. He found himself lying on a mattress on the floor of a small hut. The thatch roof was draped in a ghostly veil of spiderwebs.

"I leave them up there to keep out evil spirits," a woman's voice offered. "They don't bother me, and I don't bother them."

Fletcher rubbed his eyes. "Excuse me?"

"The spiderwebs. They insulate the room against unwanted spirits. At least, that's what the locals believe."

"I'm sorry, but who are you?"

"A friend of a friend." She smiled. She was an attractive woman, probably in her early thirties, and she appeared to have some Asian blood in her, although her accent was distinctly American. She was thin, with long black hair and a kind face.

"My dog," Fletcher said. "Do you know what happened to him?"

"I think your friends should rather speak to you about that."

Fletcher felt his stomach tighten. "I want to know if he made it."

The woman knelt down beside him. "Everyone's very happy that *you* made it." Then she stood up and walked away.

"Please, I need to know—" Fletcher began, but stopped when he saw shadows on the wall alongside the doorway.

Will Peterson entered the room, with Mitchell Lord and Rogan Brock following behind. They carried Jack on a stretcher.

Fletcher's breath caught in his throat. "Mitch . . . Will . . ."

Will smiled. "We thought you might want to see this flea bag."

"He made it? He's alive?"

"He seems determined to hang around."

As they lowered him down, Fletcher couldn't help but cry. "Jack," he uttered, barely able to speak. "It's over. We made it."

The Labrador opened his eyes, saw Fletcher, and barked loudly.

Fletcher pulled himself to the edge of the mattress and threw his arms around his friend. Jack licked away his tears until Fletcher was able to reign in his emotions. Looking up at his three friends, he asked, "How did you know where to find us?"

"Later," Rogan replied. "Right now you need to rest. We'll talk through everything tomorrow."

EARLY the following morning, Fletcher staggered out onto the wooden deck that surrounded the hut. All three men were sitting on rickety cane chairs waiting for him.

"Some coffee?" Will offered, handing Fletcher a mug.

"Sure thing. Thank you."

The mug felt heavy in his hand, but its contents tasted heavenly. After a few sips, he looked up and noticed they were in a small clearing in the middle of a jungle.

"I didn't dream the last few months, did I? There was a war in Vietnam?" Fletcher asked quietly.

"I've heard of it," Mitchell replied.

"And we took part in it?"

"Against our better judgment."

"All right, that's a start," he whispered, bringing the mug back up to his lips. "So Jack and I really did hike out?"

"Close to three hundred and eighty miles," Will replied. "You made it to a village called Moyan in southeast Thailand."

"Where are we now?"

"Officially?" Rogan replied. "Nowhere. Lost. Missing in action."

A smirk skimmed across Will's face. "We're twenty-five miles north of Moyan. How much of your ordeal do you remember?"

"Flashes, mostly—pieces of a puzzle that don't fit together."

"Well then, let's at least tell you what we know," Rogan replied, pulling out a chair. "Get comfortable. This might take a while."

For the next hour, Fletcher listened intently as the story unfolded. He learned that after the incident on the Strip, Rogan had been arrested, but after pressure from various quarters, he was released. He found out about an American soldier captured in Laos and his subsequent escape. Suspecting it was Fletcher, Rogan managed to get hold of an out-of-service Huey that he had repaired and set up for flight. When Mitchell and Will caught wind of what he was planning, they insisted on being involved. And so it began.

Without authorization, they started brief flights between Thailand and Laos, searching around Laos's western border. Rogan was convinced that Fletcher would head for Thailand. It was the only logical move. After ten days, their breakthrough finally arrived.

"It was blind luck in the end. We were on our way back from a sweep when Mitchell saw you carrying Jack, running toward the village. By the time we turned the chopper around, two soldiers already had their rifles trained on you, but we distracted them before they could do any damage," Will explained.

"I remember hearing Rogan's voice being broadcast from the helicopter before I passed out, but what happened afterward?"

"We picked you two up and brought you back here. The lady you met yesterday is Shayna Sykes. She's in the Red Cross here in Thailand. She also happens to be a doctor. She operated on Jack and treated the infection in his leg." Will paused, reluctant to break the bad news. "But Fletch, she doesn't believe he'll ever be able to walk properly again. We'll have to wait and see how he recovers."

"I can live with that," Fletcher nodded, just grateful that Jack was alive. "How'd you find out about Shayna? Why'd she help?"

"Let's just say our commander had a hand in things," Mitchell replied. "He spent some time in Thailand several years ago."

"Wilson helped us? He knows about all this?"

"Officially, no."

"Wilson had something of an attack of conscience when he heard about what you did," Rogan explained. "That's when he suggested his daughter might be able to help."

"His daughter?" Fletcher whispered, rising to his feet and shuffling to the edge of the deck. "I have a memory of a helicopter doing sweeps over the Laos jungle. I spent hours hiding from it."

"You realize that was us," Will said.

Fletcher nodded. "If only I had known it then." He turned and folded his arms. "Why'd you guys do it?"

"Personally, I couldn't get enough of Vietnam," Rogan replied.

"Please, be serious. I need to understand."

Rogan stood up and walked over to Fletcher. "What you did for Jack was incredible. How could we turn our backs on that?"

Fletcher took a deep breath. "Jack and I owe our lives to you."

Rogan shook his head. "We've all kept each other alive. The point is, it's over now. I've made arrangements to fly us back home, Jack included. Three days from now this will all be a memory."

Fletcher turned away and gazed out into the jungle. "I'm sorry, but . . . I can't leave yet. There's something I still have to do."

"WHAT the hell are you talking about?" Rogan demanded.

"Look, I'm sorry, but I made a promise to someone."

"What promise? What could possibly keep you here?"

"When I was captured, a man helped me escape. I gave him my word that I would return for him and bring him to America."

"Are you out of your mind? You can't be serious," Rogan said.

"We didn't risk our lives so you could throw yours away based on some ridiculous pact you made with one of your captors!"

"Who is this man?" Mitchell intervened.

"His name is Lee Tao. He was forcibly recruited from that small village in the south we helped defend about five months ago. That's why he helped me—he remembered me from then. He gave me a blade, which I used to escape. Without it, I would've died. I can't just walk away. I couldn't live with myself if I didn't help him."

Rogan paced across the deck. "How far into Laos is this camp?"

"Fifty-five, maybe sixty miles."

"What's the protection like?"

"Pretty lightweight. No perimeter fencing. Three guard towers."

"Soldiers?" Mitchell asked.

"Maybe forty, but there could be more. Why?"

"Well, you better be sure. We'll need to know before we go."

"Before *we* go?"

"Gentlemen." Rogan sighed, looking to Mitchell and Will. "How do you feel about one last dance in our little slice of hell?"

Will thought for a moment. "We've come this far. I'll fly you wherever you need to go."

"One final whirl on the dance floor? Thought you'd never ask," Mitchell replied, bowing.

"No, forget it. I'm doing this alone. I won't endanger—"

"Carson, you keep thinking we need your permission for everything. We make our own choices here. And the decision's made. We're playing this out together. But before we take this any further, is there anything else we should know? Is there an orphanage in Saigon you'd like us to rescue?"

Fletcher looked up at the sky. "Actually, there is something. Lee has a wife in that same village we helped protect. We don't know if she's still alive, but if she is, we need to get her out as well."

THE REMAINDER OF THE WEEK was spent planning the rescue.

Mitchell got his hands on an aerial shot of the camp, which showed the three guard towers. Apart from the river, which guarded its western perimeter, its remaining boundaries appeared exposed.

Rogan said, "It's too easy. What kind of camp doesn't raise a proper perimeter? There must be mines. How'd you get out?"

"I crossed the river. Jack was waiting for me under the trees."

"Then that's how we'll go in. No one leaves their front door open like that, even if the war's over. We'll infiltrate at around two in the morning. That should give us enough time to make it back."

Fletcher stroked Jack, who was sleeping on the stretcher alongside them. He was concerned that the Labrador hadn't yet stood up. The prospect of him never being able to walk again filled Fletcher with dread. But Jack had recovered before.

"How close can you drop us?"

"Probably about three or four miles out," Will replied.

"Let's keep it at five to be safe," Rogan said, studying the photograph. "I'm confident we can fly in undetected."

Fletcher nodded. "When do you think Mitchell will be back?"

"I don't know, but if the woman's alive, Lord will find her."

They had woken up two days earlier to discover that Mitchell had disappeared. He'd left a note: "Gone for the wife." He made no indication of what his plan was or when he'd be back.

"I hope he makes it," Fletcher said.

Will clapped his hands and rubbed them together. "All right, then, everything's set. When do we dance?"

"Tomorrow night," Rogan replied. "Let's finish this."

THE water was bitingly cold. They waded halfway across the river and waited by a patch of reeds. The camp was quiet. A lone soldier sat on the guard tower closest to them, but he appeared to be sleeping. In fifteen minutes, they hadn't seen any signs of a ground patrol; the area separating the bungalows appeared deserted.

"You ready?" Rogan asked, scanning the camp with binoculars.

Together Rogan and Fletcher crawled up the embankment and

ran across to a large tree less than twenty yards away from the first bungalow. There were still no signs of activity.

"What makes you think he's in this one?"

"I saw him come in here at least twice a day."

Pressing the butt of his rifle into his shoulder, Rogan ran toward the front of the bungalow. Fletcher shadowed behind him. They stepped quietly up onto the wooden deck and listened. Only the sound of water, dripping at their feet, detracted from the silence.

"The door," Rogan whispered.

Fletcher stepped forward and quietly turned the handle.

The door opened with a slight creak.

Rogan moved through the doorway swinging his M-16 in a wide arc. He was able to make out two rows of soldiers sleeping soundly on the floor.

Fletcher immediately began to look for Lee. Using a flashlight that he had specially taped up with black cloth to diffuse the light, he quickly searched the first row and was halfway through the second when he found him.

Rogan knelt down beside him. "On three."

Fletcher raised his thumb. "One . . . two . . . *three.*"

They both threw themselves on top of Lee. Fletcher cupped his hand tightly over his mouth while Rogan held down his legs.

Lee immediately tried to fight his way free.

"Lee . . . *Lee,*" Fletcher whispered. "It's me. Look."

Lee's eyes locked onto Fletcher, and the fight immediately drained out of him. Fletcher slowly removed his hand.

"Mr. Fletcher . . . How . . . What you doing here?"

"We've come for you. To get you out of here."

"But . . . but—"

"I told you I'd come back for you."

Lee sat up and threw his arms around Fletcher as if they were old friends who hadn't seen each other in years.

"All right, you two," Rogan interjected. "Let's get out of here."

They quickly stood up and moved toward the door.

Back out on the deck, they surveyed the area for signs of danger.

There was still no patrol. But Rogan noticed a change on top of the guard tower. The soldier was now having a smoke. "We have to wait this out. Hopefully he'll finish and go back to sleep."

Sitting with their backs against the bungalow, they watched the guard. The man finished the cigarette and flicked the burning stub over the side of the tower. Then, without warning, he turned on his search lamp and ran it across the bungalow. The light washed over them before they had a chance to react. The guard hastily reached over to raise the alarm.

"We have to go—now!" Rogan said, scrambling to his feet.

As they ran, the guard opened fire. They threw themselves into the river and swam for the embankment. Fletcher glanced over his shoulder and watched as soldiers streamed out of their bungalows.

"They're coming! Move!" Rogan whispered loudly as he reached the bank. Together they sprinted into the bowels of the jungle.

"Where we going?"

"There's a helicopter waiting for us," Fletcher gasped, already out of breath. "About five miles from here."

"We never make it. These soldiers very fast."

AK-47 fire ripped through the branches above them.

"Just run!" Rogan called back.

ROGAN realized the soldiers were gaining on them. "Those trees," he gestured, pointing ahead. "Get up them."

With the soldiers only a hundred or so yards behind, they each scrambled up a tree. As Fletcher hurried to get into a shooting position, his M-16 slipped from his hand and fell to the ground.

Lee jumped down and hurried toward it. Just as he reached down, the first soldier rounded the corner. The man lifted his AK-47 and pointed it at Lee. But before he could pull the trigger, Rogan shot him twice in the chest.

Lee grabbed the rifle and threw it up to Fletcher.

"Down, Lee!" Fletcher shouted as the other soldiers appeared.

The second man tripped over his dead compatriot, bunching up the group. They never stood a chance.

From their elevated position, Rogan and Fletcher cut down the entire group within seconds. Their automatic fire obliterated them.

As the smoke filtered up through the trees, Lee stood up and walked over to the pile of bodies.

"Lee, wait. It's not safe. Come back."

Fletcher rushed down to him.

"War," said Lee. "Terrible war."

"This is the end," Fletcher said. "It's all over now."

"In America, there is no war."

"Not like this."

"We leave this place?"

"Yes, we most certainly do."

THE flight back to Thailand was an edgy affair. As long as they were over Laos, they were still at risk of being shot down. But as the first signs of morning lifted the gloom, they crossed over into Thailand and put down in a small open area. They jumped out and hauled a green-and-brown camouflaged tarpaulin over the Huey.

"Over here," Shayna called out. She was parked in an old jeep under a nearby tree.

"Where we going?" Lee asked.

"Somewhere safe," Fletcher replied.

After a short drive, they pulled up in front of Shayna's hut. A tall, dark figure was standing in the doorway waiting for them.

It was Mitchell.

"Mitch! You made it!" Fletcher called out.

"Of course. I see you did, too."

Rogan swung his rifle over his shoulder and climbed out of the jeep. "What took you so long, Lord?"

"Stopped to admire the bullet shells on the side of the road."

As they approached the stairs, Mitchell looked toward Lee and nodded as a mark of respect. "I've heard about you. Welcome."

"Thank you." He smiled. "I very happy to be here."

"Fletcher tells us you're to blame for saving his life."

Lee missed the joke. "Only after you all save my village. I very grateful for your help."

As they congregated together, Lee turned to Fletcher. "Thank you for coming for me. You sacrifice much to help, but . . ."

"What is it, Lee?"

"I sorry. I can't come away with you," Lee replied. "Not until I know for myself. Maybe my wife still alive. She mean everything to me. I cannot leave without knowing what happened to her."

Mitchell leaned forward and placed his hand on Lee's shoulder. "We thought you might feel that way." He stepped away from the door, and a petite young woman appeared behind him.

Lee's eyes widened in surprise, and he threw his hands over his mouth. "Tay?" he uttered.

"Lee," the woman replied in a whisper.

"Tay . . . Tay!" he repeated, and ran toward her. They embraced and collapsed to the floor, crying. "I thought you were dead!" he said, making no attempt to hold back his tears.

She replied in Vietnamese, and they embraced again. Fletcher, taken by the moment, glanced across at Shayna, who was fluent in several languages. "What did she say?"

Shayna dabbed her eyes with her shirtsleeve. "What we all dream our partners would say of us: 'I never stopped believing in you.'"

After Lee and Tay ended their embrace, Mitchell explained how he had tracked down her village and paid an old Vietnamese informant to get her out. After a day of walking and two days of driving, the man delivered her to a village on the outskirts of Saigon.

Mitchell looked up at Fletcher and smiled. "There's also some good news for you." He pursed his lips and whistled loudly.

Jack emerged in the open doorway, his tail wagging.

"Jack, you're walking!"

As if to prove it, he slowly weaved his way toward him.

Shayna shook her head as the Labrador brushed past her. "This is impossible. He shouldn't be able to stand, let alone walk. The bone density in his leg should not be able to support his weight."

"Jack has remarkable powers of recovery," Will replied.

"No, you don't understand. Recovery is one thing; this animal shouldn't be mobile. I knew he would never walk again; I just didn't have the heart to tell any of you."

"When it comes to Jack, anything's possible," Mitchell replied. "If you knew his past, you wouldn't be surprised. He's a survivor."

"Where did he come from?"

Fletcher looked up at Shayna and smiled warmly. "You wouldn't believe me if I told you."

Mitchell bent over to pat Jack as he passed. "What do you mean, Fletch? Did you find out which unit he was attached to?"

"No. He was never part of any unit in Vietnam. Although I've no way of proving it and you're probably going to think I've lost my mind, I know it's true. Jack didn't come from Vietnam. He came from somewhere . . . else."

Will frowned. "You've lost us."

Fletcher knelt down as Jack reached him. He rested his forehead against the side of the Labrador's neck. "Travis was right. He said Jack never belonged here—something about the look in his eyes. I believe I now understand why. My daughter, Kelly, died in a plane crash three days before turning seven. She kept begging my wife and me for this one special birthday present. She was adamant about it. She wanted a Labrador, whom she would name Jack."

Fletcher lifted up and opened his eyes. "I've never been more certain of anything in my life. My daughter sent Jack to save me."

EPILOGUE

Chicago
Ten years later

MORE than a decade had slipped by since Fletcher first passed through Hampton Lane's front gates. But still the cemetery appeared the same.

As their cavalcade wound toward the back of the cemetery, Fletcher cast his mind back to the war and their last days in Thailand. He recalled how they had all agreed to keep in touch, but despite everything they had endured, he always knew their friendships could not be sustained on the outside. Their bonds had been forged in another world.

Stepping out of his car, Fletcher made his way up the grassy embankment toward the large maple tree that still regularly haunted his dreams. As always, he knelt down and gently placed a white rose across each of his girls' graves.

Every visit still hurt him deeply; the wounds had never quite healed. He knew they never would. They were now just a part of his life. As he waited for the rest of the group to join him, he tried not to look at the newly dug grave alongside him. If he did, it would drain away what little courage he had summoned for the burial.

"You all right?" Marvin asked, joining him at his side.

"No, but thanks for coming. I really appreciate it."

"Nothing could've kept me away."

Marvin had been a loyal friend to him over the years, both before the crash and in the wreckage after it. Following his return to America, Marvin persuaded him to return to journalism. He got him to freelance for the newspaper and, after a while, to compose letters to his girls. It was almost impossible in the beginning, but after a few weeks, the words came a little easier. Eventually, Fletcher was able to write freely. He told them about the horror of Vietnam, but also how hope can exist in the darkest of places and of how much he missed them. He wrote about his attempted suicide and confessed that for a long time after the crash, thoughts of taking his own life never strayed far from his mind. But that had slowly changed. A year after returning from the war, Shayna Sykes arrived on his doorstep. In the months that followed, they became friends and, eventually, lovers. He had found a safe space in his heart where he could love Shayna without tarnishing Abigail's memory. He slowly began to understand that it was okay to give himself to another woman. Just as she had brought him back from the brink of death in Thailand, Shayna gradually taught him how to live again. She would even accompany him to the graves of his girls sometimes but decided not to join him on this occasion. This was their day.

Lee and Tay were next to reach the gravesite.

For them, their first taste of America had been difficult. There weren't many people prepared to welcome Asians into their neighborhoods after the war. But like everything, things improved with time. Prejudices softened; hatred dissipated. When the time was right, Fletcher helped them open a small art gallery in Miami, which was now turning over a tidy profit. The free life Lee had always dreamed of was now a reality. If that wasn't enough, they were blessed with two wonderful children.

Fletcher looked back and watched as Mitchell, Will, and Rogan made their way up the hill. It occurred to him that Mitchell was still walking in front, ever the point man. He still had his long black hair and the same look of madness lurking deep within his eyes. After the war, he joined a government agency. He was not permitted to talk about his job, and Fletcher had no desire to ask.

Will Peterson followed with a slight limp—a keepsake from his time as a hostage in Vietnam. He ran a successful charter airline with over a dozen aircraft under his control. At night, he drank. More than he ought to. He married twice, but both unions failed. Vietnam, it appeared, continued to cast its dark shadow over him.

Walking slowly at the back was Rogan. Fletcher had never quite come to terms with what his lieutenant had done for him—the enormity of his sacrifice. He was saddened to learn that in the outside world, Rogan lived alone in a small apartment in Detroit working as a night-shift security guard at a chemical factory. He wondered what kind of dark thoughts plagued his mind in the small hours of the morning. He had been a patriot, believing wholeheartedly in what they were fighting for. The hostile reception he received upon returning from Vietnam was too much for him to bear. It was a betrayal. It stripped away his spirit.

Yet another casualty of Vietnam.

Fletcher stepped forward and took a breath. As he looked at the people around him, he struggled to contain his emotions.

"Before we left Thailand all those years ago, we made a pact that regardless of where we were, we would all come together one last time. It means a great deal to me that you've each kept your word and made it here today. After Vietnam, I flew to Miami, initially to honor a promise I made to Travis, but have remained there ever since. The city has not only become my home, but it is also home to Lee and Tay, who have become close friends."

Fletcher continued, taking a moment to compose himself. "When we made this pact, I always prayed that today would be a great many years away. As it turned out, I was given ten full years. But you always want more. Each morning, Jack and I would go down to the beach. Jack loved to swim and run after seagulls. His exuberance never waned. In his last few months, when his hips began to fail, I would carry him to the beach and we'd stare out over the ocean together." He paused, his voice faltering. "It was a beautiful warm morning when he died. Just as I had carried him halfway across Southeast Asia, so he slipped away in my arms. I must've sat on that beach holding him for hours, stroking his face. It was Lee who eventually found us. He pried Jack from my arms, and Tay helped me to her car. I can't tell you where we drove that day, just that I cried all the way. I take great comfort in the last years of Jack's life. I know that he loved each and every day we shared—God knows I did. But," he said, no longer able to restrain his grief, "it doesn't make his passing any easier. I . . . I guess I just miss my friend."

The group crowded around Fletcher, and Rogan placed his hand on his shoulder. Fletcher rested his own hand on top of his lieutenant's but kept his head bowed. For a while, they were quiet as Jack's coffin was moved into position.

Mitchell walked across to a basket that was filled with a dozen white roses. He chose one, kissed it, and gently placed it on top of Jack's coffin. Marvin, Lee, and Rogan each followed suit. Fletcher could hardly see anymore. His tears had blurred his vision. He wanted to say more, but he knew the words would fail him. He stumbled up to the grave and placed Jack's leash on top of his coffin. "I wish we could spend just one more day together," he managed. "Just to watch you run, Jack."

Tay ran up behind Fletcher and wrapped her arms around him. Together they watched as Jack was lowered down. When he had come to a stop, each of the men shoveled a measure of sand into the grave until there was nothing of his coffin left to see.

Fletcher felt exhausted and drained. His head was reeling. He felt as if he were about to pass out. As Lee and Tay led him away, he looked back and saw that both Rogan and Mitchell were kneeling next to Jack's cross.

They were reading his epitaph.

Fletcher closed his eyes and read along with them.

Jack

I now know that Vietnam could never claim you.

Some souls burn too bright to be lost to the darkness.

Yet, as we part, know that our journey is not yet at an end.

Just as you found me, I will seek you out again.

You have my word.

Run to her, Jack; she's waiting for you.

I'll be along in a while.

Fletcher

Getting to Know
Gareth Crocker

Vital Stats

BORN: Johannesburg, South
  Africa, 1974
FAMILY: Married, two children
FORMER CAREERS: Journalist,
  copywriter, public relations
  manager
PETS: Three dogs, three cats
FAVE MOVIES: *Rocky, Braveheart,
  The Shawshank Redemption*
WEBSITE:
  www.GarethCrocker.com

SOUTH African author Gareth Crocker has been writing since he was nine years old. His initial literary creations were love poems that he sold to love-struck boys on the playground, who in turn would present them to the girl of their dreams. Crocker jokes that it was one of the more lucrative periods of his writing life.

His adult writing career began after college, when he spent several years as a young reporter for a community newspaper. However, he soon realized the miniscule pay was a problem should he ever want to support a family, so he turned to the corporate world.

In 1997 he joined a top South African public relations firm, where he says he learned that " 'PR' and 'fake' should sit smugly beside each other in the dictionary." After a few years he was responsible for hundreds of annual reports and company magazines. Eventually, though, he tired of the PR world.

Crocker began writing fiction, and armed with numerous manuscripts, he headed to London to find an agent. He spent eight days going door to door, dropping off copies of manuscripts with all the agents he could find.

Although he quickly realized finding an agent was much harder than he had naively imagined, luck was with him. He had dropped off a manuscript on the patio of an agent who happened to have locked herself out of her home that day. While she waited for the locksmith, she began reading *Leaving Jack* and liked it. She called Crocker and invited him to her office the next day. The author realized how lucky he was when he arrived at her office and saw mountains of unread manuscripts piled up—and she explained that it was only a month's worth.

After securing an agent, the next hurdle was finding a publisher, which took years. The problem, says Crocker, was that his story was something of a hybrid—a war story that was really more of a love story between a man and his dog. Therefore, publishers felt it did not fit into any specific market. Finally, though, they found a pub-

Dogs of War

The fictional canine hero of *Leaving Jack* is based on reality—military working dogs have been used by the United States since World War II. Originally a variety of breeds were utilized, but German Shepherds and Labradors soon emerged as the dogs of choice.

During the Vietnam War, dogs served in three main capacities. Scout dogs, usually German Shepherds, would walk "point" (out front) looking for trip wires and booby traps. Combat tracker dogs, generally Labradors, tracked missing personnel by following body odors and blood trails. Sentry dogs were used by military police to help protect bases, ammunition depots, and many other vital areas.

It is estimated that these Vietnam War dogs and their handlers saved over 10,000 lives.

lisher in the UK for *Leaving Jack*.

One reason Crocker wrote *Leaving Jack* was as a tribute to the real Vietnam War dogs who worked with American soldiers. Approximately 4,000 dogs served, but the U.S. government refused to bring them home at war's end. Only 200 made it back to America. The rest were abandoned. ∎

ACKNOWLEDGMENTS

Page 169: Sigrid Estrada. Pages 5, 170, 319, and 575: iStockphoto.com. Page 171: © Christian Liewig/Liewig Media Sports/Corbis. Page 317: Blake Little. Page 464: Brandy Allen. Pages 5 and 465: Clipart.com. Page 574: Kerry-Anne Crocker.

The volumes in this series are issued every two to three months.
The typical volume contains four outstanding books in condensed form.
None of the selections in any volume has appeared in *Reader's Digest* itself.
Any reader may receive this service by writing
The Reader's Digest Association, Inc., Pleasantville, NY 10570
or by calling 1-800-481-1454.
In Canada write to:
The Reader's Digest Association (Canada) Ltd.,
1125 Stanley Street, Montreal, Quebec H3B 5H5
or call 1-800-465-0780.

Some of the titles in this volume are also available in a large-print format.
For information about Select Editions Large Type call 1-800-877-5293.

Visit us on the Web at:
rd.com
readersdigest.ca (in Canada)